Anonymous

Springtime

Anonymous

Springtime

ISBN/EAN: 9783337372545

Printed in Europe, USA, Canada, Australia, Japan

Cover: Foto ©Andreas Hilbeck / pixelio.de

More available books at **www.hansebooks.com**

SPRINGTIME:

A Magazine for our

YOUNG MEN AND MAIDENS.

VOLUME VI.

London:

PUBLISHED BY JAMES B. KNAPP,

6, Sutton Street, Commercial Road, E.

1891.

SPRINGTIME:

A Magazine for Our Young Men and Maidens.

Vol. VI. No. 1.]　　　JANUARY, 1891.　　　[Price Twopence.

A Bad Calculation.

By ROBERT HIND,

*Author of ' Crosby Dalton: Local Preacher
and Village Demagogue,' ' The Ruby
Pendant,' &c.*

CHAPTER I.

THE DAYS OF YORE.

'The old lost life comes back to me
With starry gleams of memory!
　　　　　　　ROBERT BUCHANAN.

IT is just five-and-twenty
years since Joseph
Benson emigrated to
Australia,' Mr. Stuart
Harland said to his
wife after reading
aloud a letter he held
in his hand. ' You
remember him. He and I had been friends
from childhood. Both of us were rather poor
in those days, and lived with our parents in
two-roomed tenements. We should not be
able to accommodate ourselves to the circumstances now, I dare say, and yet at that time
we were happy enough.'

' And took a delight in making other people
unhappy,' Mrs. Harland replied in a tone of
reproach, which the merry twinkle of her eye
and the smile that suffused all her kindly face
belied.

' We were the pests of the neighbourhood,
I verily believe, and unconscionable tyrants to
the girls of our own age when we were boys.
But we meant nothing wrong, and I believe
none of you were much frightened of us,
although you pretended to be.'

' Not a bit.'

' It was hard for me to let Joe go out to the
colonies alone. It looked like going against
Providence to allow ourselves to drift apart
for ever in early manhood, after we had been
partners in a hundred escapades in our childhood and youth. But another fate held me
at home,' and Stuart Harland glanced lovingly
at his wife, who blushed as though she had
been a girl of twenty.

' He had no such tyrant to rein in his
ambitions. And Joe was more than ambitious,
he was decidedly romantic. I remember how
at a regatta before he was twenty he used to
hang about the outside of the circles of the
aristocracy, and open his great blue eyes in
wonder as he listened to their conversation,
which he declared he did not half understand,
although the words were simple enough ; and
then he would stand away at a favourable
distance to admire their refinements of face
and dress. I used to tease him about it and
declare he had missed his way in being born a
plebeian.'

' That accounts for his marriage, then,' Mrs.
Harland remarked.

' Probably, at least in part ; for you know,
dear, my opinion on that subject is that
marriages cannot be accounted for. But Joe
went out, very soon became a rising man, but
when still poor married an aristocratic Irish
lady. And from the very few letters I have
had I have reason to conclude the marriage
has been a success. Nobody who knows Joe
can help liking him, he is so manly, so self-

reliant and independent, so quiet and gentle-manly, and I should say his provincial accent will only give a finer flavour to his otherwise charming manner of speech. And he no doubt feels he has won a prize in the lady of his choice that he does not deserve, and accordingly treasures her all the more. The conditions have been eminently favourable for happiness.'

' And I suppose he has succeeded otherwise,' observed Mrs. Harland, with a woman's appreciation of the practical.

' Quite marvellously. I shouldn't wonder were he to sell out, if he did not find himself something approaching a millionaire.'

' Oh, dear! what shall we do?' Mrs. Harland exclaimed, looking round the room in a flutter of agitation.

' Why, what is the matter?' Mr. Harland inquired in evident ignorance of the cause of his wife's excitement.

' They should have sent their son to Oxford or Cambridge. What can we do in this place with the son of a millionaire whose mother is a " born lady?" '

' I commend their wisdom for sending him to a better place than either Oxford or Cambridge,' Mr. Harland bluntly replied. ' And if he is less than thankful for what he finds at " The Mount," he can go to Oxford or any other place it may be his pleasure to choose,' and as he spoke Stuart Harland's eye followed that of his wife round the room.

It was one of those rooms that nobody would ever think of calling an apartment, or of giving a name that had the remotest suggestion of lodgings. A ' home ' air was in every nook and corner of it. It was not large; indeed, but for the fine bay window, it might have seemed small. Not that it would have been really small even without the bay window. But the furniture was massive and substantial, and occupied a good deal of space. It was all of oak, neither very old nor very new. The walls were covered with pictures of a rare and valuable kind. One striking oil nearly filled a whole side of the room, and was a weird representation of some old world ceremony among the ruins of an abbey. Another, somewhat smaller, was a night scene

in Venice, with a fine stretch of water from the foreground to the background, constituting a remarkable bit of perspective, and mansions on either side, the one on the right-hand fore-gound being lighted for a festive occasion.

Stuart Harland had been a successful railway contractor, and had retired from business whilst still in the prime of life. ' The Mount' was not a large mansion, indeed it was small, but in its own way it was quite perfect. It had been built under its owner's supervision, and he knew there was not a bad stone or faulty piece of timber in it. He had a taste for pictures, and prided himself somewhat on his collection. ' There aren't many,' he was accustomed to say, ' but there isn't a " daub" about the place.'

When he had satisfied himself with his glance round, Mr. Harland again turned to his wife.

' I can easily account for everything I find in this letter, save one,' he said. ' It is just like Joe Benson, who, with all his romance, was as simple and unaffected as a child, to want his only son to know and learn to love this old place where he was born, and which I doubt not he still thinks of as his home, despite the grandeur of his Australian house and the success of his career. I never wander down ' the banks ' without thinking of him, and I never can have known Joe if he does not think oftener than I do of the old city of Rockingham. But Joe was a strong Nonconformist, despite his admiration of the refined ways of the aristocracy, and I should not have expected him to send his son to an English University to be educated for a clergyman.'

' Does he mean him to be a clergyman?'

' He doesn't say so, but he says Jack is to be a divinity student. That looks rather like it.'

'Perhaps Mrs. Benson's influence has altered her husband's views.'

' Possibly. But I understood Mrs. Benson belonged to the Society of Friends.'

' And when the Friends leave their own community they generally go into the Church of England,' Mrs. Harland said with some bitterness, for like her husband she was a

Dissenter of strong convictions, and a Methodist ; and in the little city of Rockingham, with its seven parish churches, its big wealthy cathedral, its university, most of whose professors were dignitaries of the church, its church charities and sisterhoods, there was little room for Nonconformity, and it was with difficulty it kept its roots in the place. What there was of it, however, was of a hardy type.

'We had better not come to conclusions till the young man arrives. One thing is certain, he will get as good an education here as he could at Oxford. I am told the professors are at least equal to those of the larger universities. Indeed, only last year Professor Fairfax declined the chair at Oxford, preferring to stay here. As Jack Benson is to be unattached too, excepting during the term in which he will try for his degree, when he will live in the Castle, he will have a better home than any of the attached students, and a mother who will look after him as well as his own.'

'It is a mercy Rye is as good as engaged,' Mrs. Harland said, 'or we might have been in danger of losing her too.'

'There you are! I declare it matters not what subject of conversation is started, a woman always ends it in the same manner. Why should Jack Benson and Rye Harland ever think of each other excepting as friends?'

'Of course not. Why should any young people ever think of each other as anything save friends,' Mrs. Harland said, with a little mock asperity, and feeling she had the better of the argument.

Mr. Harland felt this too, and smiled.

'I should say,' continued the lady, following up her advantage, 'he might go further afield and fare worse. I don't suppose he has ever seen in his Australian home such a wholesome looking girl as our Rye.'

At that moment the door opened and the young lady herself came in with her music portfolio, looking the picture of a healthy English girl. Her arrival, of course, made it necessary to give the conversation another turn.

CHAPTER II.

A DAUGHTER OF MUSIC.

'Sing of the weak man's tears,
Of the strong man's agony;
The passions, the hopes, the fears,
The heaped-up pain of the years,
The human mystery.'

ROBERT BUCHANAN.

RYE HARLAND was nineteen, and had a mind as simple and guileless as that of a child of ten. In this lay her chief charm. For, despite the outspoken opinion of her mother about her worth, and the equally strong though veiled conviction of her father on the same subject, there was nothing in her appearance to arrest, at first sight, the attention of an impartial person. Rye was of medium height and powerfully, some would say for a girl too powerfully, built. She had the strength of a young man. Her head was large and well-developed in the moral regions, and was crowned with an immense quantity of brown hair. Her face was round and plump, and her cheeks wore no delicate tints, but were red with overflowing health and vigour. For the rest, she had a shapely figure, with plenty of breadth of shoulder and fulness of chest, and carried herself with a somewhat boyish gait. Indeed, she was reckoned among her friends a 'Tom-boy,'—an opinion she never resented, but was proud of rather than otherwise.

Rye Harland loved outdoor exercise. To live in the fresh air was a joy to her infinitely greater than the wearing of fine dresses or attending evening parties. Not that she despised these. She was always well-dressed— after a fashion. It is necessary to say ' after a fashion,' for she was never seen out of doors excepting in thick-soled laced boots, with low heels, which were an outrage upon the tastes of her more æsthetic friends. And for evening parties there were none among all her circle of acquaintances so much in request as she. As a pianist she had no equal in all Rockingham, and her vocal powers were an object of envy to almost all who had been privileged to hear her sing. In addition to this, without being a humorist, she had such a power of making everybody feel comfortable and pleasant, that all who wished to have a very successful evening placed her name among the first of those to be invited.

Still, much as she actually did enjoy these indoor entertainments, they never affected her like a walk in the country. She knew the names of all the wild flowers of the district and of all the wild birds in it too. Better still, she knew the habits of these winged songsters, where their nests were to be found, and at what part of the day it was most interesting to watch them. This information was not the result of reading, but largely of her own observation. In the fields every summer she had a pet thrush or lark whose song she could imitate, and by that means entice it to her. So that she was really a far more interesting girl than a stranger meeting her for the first time would imagine.

Probably her mother gave the most correct estimate of her when she called her a wholesome girl. Her charms were not those of an Italian or Spanish lady. She had not the dark skin, black hair and eyes, and intensity of expression characteristic of a Southron beauty. Nor were her features finely cut. They were comely enough, and she just looked what she was—a healthy, unsophisticated English girl.

One mark of feature her pure soul and strong mind had put upon her outward appearance. Her eyes were a wonder to behold. They were a very dark shade of blue, lustrous, and withal full of tenderness. What feelings of pleasure, of kindness, of thoughtfulness shone out of those eyes! And what capability of love and loyalty might be read in them! In repose they conveyed the idea of sweet tenderness; under the influence of excitement they revealed a capacity for emotion that would put a pair of Italian eyes to shame.

'Here is a letter from Australia I should like you to read, Rye,' Mr. Harland said as his daughter came into the room.

The girl stood leaning against her father's chair as she read the letter. Its contents evidently pleased her.

'And how long shall we have to wait for him to come?'

'Do you think we can do with him at "The Mount," little mistress?' her father asked.

'I should think so. Why he *must* come, of course. You could not say he cannot live with us, and his father and you such dear friends!'

'Surely the fact that we were friends a quarter of a century since does not make it necessary for me to provide a home for his son now.'

'Oh well, but I think it does, father. Supposing you were sending me out to Australia I should expect Mr. Benson to provide me a home and look after me in every way. And I should be right too, should I not, mother?'

'Perhaps, but you are a girl. A young man can look after himself better. Besides, "The Mount" is not such a home as he will have been accustomed to. The Bensons, you know, are very wealthy.'

The young lady's eyes fell a little as she replied, 'If he is proud and stuck-up I hope he won't stay here. But surely you could not let him go to some of the lodgings of the unattached students where he would have to live in stuffy rooms and be neglected, instead of waited upon by a poor old woman.'

'Well, well, as the young mistress wills, so must it be; but remember when Jack Benson usurps your place as the tyrant of the household, and instead of you domineering over us, you find him domineering over you, no one will be to blame for having the intruder here but yourself.'

'I am strong enough to bear all the blame without special injury to my constitution,' she laughed.

'You must promise to be very attentive to him,' Mrs. Harland said. 'I dare say he will find a difference between being a student in a university, where the young men will think the "freshman" from the colonies a specially good object for playing pranks upon, and the only son and heir of a wealthy house, petted by everybody.'

'I hope he is not a spoiled boy,' her daughter said with some energy.

'A boy! He is twenty, and will not thank you for calling him a boy.'

' If he cannot take care of himself among the 'Varsity men, what else can I call him?'

' Ah well, we know nothing of him' yet. Still there is one thing we are certain about. He has left his father and mother and home for the first time in his life, and will feel very lonely, and sometimes sad. So we must all try to make things pleasant for him.'

This appeal was not in vain. It touched the right chord in the true and tender Rye, and she and her mother at once entered into a discussion about the arrangement of Jack Benson's rooms—the rooms he was to occupy at 'The Mount,' while he was there.

Having settled this important matter, and decided to commence active preparations the following day, Rye opened the piano, and for an hour or more flooded the house with magnificent harmonies,—harmonies which in a concert-room would have been greeted with round upon round of applause. For she was no mechanical performer, who had learned simply to hammer away at her instrument, and manage somehow to strike the right keys. There was a perfect understanding between her and her instrument, and the music that burst from it was simply the response and echo of the harmonies she felt in her own soul, which vibrated along the fibres of her being, and seemed, after stirring her from head to foot, to concentrate themselves in her fingers, drop upon the keys, and then burst upon the ears of the listener. It was a sight to observe her strong frame quivering as though under the tension of some intense feeling, and watch the lights and shades flit across her face. Her head shook, and her lips moved as though she were singing, but no sound escaped from them. She was intoxicated with her own melodies, that was all. What a variety of effects she produced! Often she would start with some of those dreadful productions of *Beethoven*, which remind one of the clatter of horses' hoofs, the beating of a thousand drums, the roar of cannon, and the crack of musketry, and the roll of the thunder-peal across the sky. It is all a conflict of sound. Then she would choose some sweet, melancholy piece from *Mendelssohn*, in which the sounds seem to die away in a sigh. Next, with an impatient gesture, she

would burst forth in some rollicking measures, as of a young heart determined to fling dull care to the winds. Then would come a pause, for the heart tires the most quickly of music that is wholly joyous, and once more the melancholy sighs would break forth for a little time, and then, with a few heavy strokes, she would fill the room with cries of utter agony, as of a human being in distress.

On this occasion all these variations fell upon the ears of her two listeners, and then the last stroke sent forth the sound of a crash —a thousand discords rolled into one—and the performer stopped, and for some minutes sat perfectly still, looking straight before her. She then rubbed her hands across her eyes, looked round on the real world, which, for a little while, she had forgotten, and returned to her place beside her father.

He had been moved by that tumult of melody, though he had not felt anything of the mingled joy and pain it had produced in the soul of his daughter. It was all a wonder to him—a mystery he could not fathom, and which he was at a loss how well to attempt to understand. Sometimes, too, he felt his daughter was a wonder to him, even more than her musical performances, and at these times he asked himself what her future would be. He trusted a happy one, but—

That ' but ' came up in his mind at this moment, causing a shade of anxiety to pass across his honest, kindly English face.

' Do you expect Arthur to-night, little one?' he asked tenderly.

Rye smiled and answered simply—' Yes, father.'

(To be continued.)

Evil Thoughts.

' WE shall not be hanged for our thoughts,' cries one. I wish that such idle talkers would remember that they will be damned for their thoughts; and that instead of evil thoughts being less sinful than evil acts, it may sometimes happen that in the thought the man may be worse than in the deed. He may not be able to carry out all the mischief that lurks within his designs, and yet in forming the design he may incur all the guilt.

Thoughts are the eggs of words and action, and within the thought lie compacted and condensed all the villainy of actual transgressions. If men did but more carefully watch their thoughts, they would not so readily fall into evil habits; but men first indulge the thought of evil, and then the imagination of evil. Nor does the process stay there. Picturing it before their mind's eye, they excite their own desires after it; these grow into a thirst and kindle into a passion. Then the deed is speedily forthcoming; it was long in the hatching, but in a moment it comes forth to curse a whole lifetime.

Instead of fancying that evil thoughts are mere trifles, let us regard them as the root of bitterness, the still in which the poisonous spirit is manufactured. Our Saviour puts evil thoughts first in the catalogue of evil things; and He knew well their true nature. If we would be lost we have only to indulge these: If we would be saved we must conquer these. Let us make a conscience of our thoughts: he that doth not do so will not long make a conscience of his words or deeds.

Rev. C. H. Spurgeon.

———◆◇◆———

The Supreme Test.

THAT is clear to every one who will see, and as easy to apply under all circumstances as it is plain. Can I do this and at the same time honour and please my God? Here is the touchstone to which we should gladly bring our whole life. It is strange, indeed, that the Christian world has not yet accepted this test universally and literally. How much needless agitation and questioning would be avoided were all to delight in this supreme test?

'There is,' says a modern writer, 'an old legend of an enchanted cup filled with poison and put treacherously into a king's hand. He signed the sign of the Cross, and named the name of God over it, and it shivered in his grasp. Do you take this name of the Lord as a test? Name Him over many a cup which you are eager to drink of, and the glittering fragments will lie at your feet, and the poison be spilled on the ground. What you cannot lift before His pure eyes and think of Him while you enjoy, is not for you. Friendship, schemes, plans, ambitions, amusements, speculations, studies, loves, business—can you call on the name of the Lord while you put these cups to your lips? If not, fling them behind you, for they are full of poison, which, for all its sugared sweetness, at the last will bite like a serpent and sting like an adder.

Dear Lord, in all our loneliest pains
Thou hast the largest share,
And that which is unbearable,
'Tis Thine, not ours to bear.

Beware of making your moral staple consist of the negative virtues. It is good to abstain, and teach others to abstain, from all that is sinful or hurtful; but making a business of it leads to emaciation of character, unless one feeds largely also on the more nutritious diet of active sympathetic benevolence.

Oliver Wendell Holmes.

———◆◇◆———

Mirage.

WE'LL read that book, we'll sing that song,
    But when? Oh when the days are long,
When thoughts are free, and voices clear,
Some happy time within the year:
The days troop by with noiseless tread,
The song unsung, the book unread.

We'll see that friend, and make him feel
The weight of friendship true as steel;
Some flower of sympathy bestow,
But time sweeps on with steady flow,
Until, with quick reproachful tear,
We lay our flowers upon his bier.

And still we walk the desert sands,
And still with trifles fill our hands,
While ever, just beyond our reach,
A fairer purpose shows to each.
The deeds we have not done, but willed,
Remain to haunt us—unfulfilled.

The Boyhood of Great Men.

JOHN WESLEY.

'IRE! FIRE!' That was the terrible cry that one wintry night rang through the village of Epworth, in Lincolnshire. It was close upon midnight, on February 9, in the year 1709. By some mischance or other the rectory had caught fire, and its roof of homely thatch and its walls of wood and plaster were grand prey for the flames. Clearly the house was doomed, but what about the inmates? The rector was the first to awake and give the alarm. In his excitement he put on one stocking and forgot all about the other, and, rushing from his own room, he discovered that only a door intervened between him and the deadliest peril. There was no time to be lost. He roused the nurse and the children that slept with her. He seized the children that were in another room, and hurried them, as they were, into the garden behind the house. The time was too short to dress or to save anything but themselves. His wife and others of the children escaped by the front of the house, and the rector, in his ignorance, thought they had perished. When the two shivering groups were united and heads were counted, it was found that all the children had been saved but one boy. He had been sleeping with the nurse, and in the hurry of escape she had overlooked him. The father would have dashed into the burning mass after him, but to get up the stairs was now out of the question. He could do nothing but commend his child to God. And yet they could hear his plaintive cries for help; they saw him climb to the top of a chest and stand by an open window. 'Fetch a ladder!' shouted someone. 'There is no time for that,' said

another, who, quick as thought, stood on the ground beneath that window, whilst a man of lighter build mounted on his shoulders, and the little boy jumped from the burning house into his arms and was saved. A moment later and he must have perished, for, even as he jumped, the roof fell with a crash, and laid the rectory of Epworth in ruins.

That boy, 'plucked from the burning,' was John Wesley, the founder of the 'people called Methodists.' One cannot help wondering what turn history would have taken if he had perished in those flames. But God wanted that boy. And when God wants a man or a boy He can always find him, and can keep him 'immortal till his work is done.' John Wesley was only six years old at the time of his rescue, having been born on June 17, 1703, in the same house that so nearly proved his grave. Oliver Wendell Holmes rather humorously suggests that the first thing a man ought to do is, several months before he is born, to look out for a good father and mother. Wesley was fortunate in his parentage. His father, Samuel Wesley, had been a Dissenter in his youth. But the Church of England cast its spell over him, and, long as he lived, it had no truer servant. He was a pious man, which is more than can be said of all his fellow-clergymen of that time; a man devoted to his parish, his wife, and his children. He possessed a mind too of no mean order, and wrote largely both in prose and verse. The good man had but one failing —he could not keep out of debt. The living of Epworth was not a rich one, and the mouths at the rectory kept increasing at such an alarming rate, that the rector was always in difficulties. A little while before John was born, he was actually imprisoned for debt, and during the greater part of his life his accounts balanced on the wrong side. And yet it is remarkable how cheerful he was through it all. Even when clothing, books, and everything had perished in the fire, he looked on the bright side of things. 'Come, neighbours,' he said, 'let us kneel down; let us give thanks to God. He has given me all my children. Let the house go. I am rich enough.' And indeed, if children could have enriched him, he was rich enough. He had three sons and seven daughters that reached maturity, and he had almost as many that died in infancy. And so John Wesley was not a spoilt child—he had too many sisters for that. And, had there been no sisters to tease and humble him, spoiling was no part of Mrs. Wesley's *régime*. She herself was her father's youngest child, and there were twenty-four brothers and sisters that had preceded her. Possibly she was spoilt, as the youngest child frequently is, but she never spoiled her own children. Her shrewd common sense had full exercise in the management of her household. A home with so many romping lads and lasses in it needed a strong will at its head. The first lesson she taught her children was that of obedience. At the marriage altar she had promised to obey her husband, and she kept that promise well; but among her children her will was supreme. Her children knew that. When she said 'No!' she meant it. It was one of her rules never to give her children anything that they cried for. She strictly limited them, unless they were sick, to three meals a day. Perhaps the lightness of her purse dictated that rule as well as regard for her children's health. For the same reason their fare would be none of the daintiest, but they were none the worse for that. What romps they would have in the garden, when their mother gave permission! Without that they dared not venture near it. What races they ran, what pranks they played in those country lanes! Their merry laughter would chase away dull care, and, if the fare at home was poor, the fresh breezes that blew into their faces from off the Lincolnshire Wolds would give them appetites ready for anything. At eight o'clock each night the patter of their feet was hushed on floor and stairs, and every head was laid on the pillow. Possibly most of them closed their eyelids at once, but, whether they did or not, Mrs. Wesley never allowed anyone to sit with them, until the long-sought rest had come. They knew from their earliest days that they had been sent to bed to sleep, and sleep they did.

It is said that we inherit our brains from our mothers. Certainly this might have been true of John Wesley. His mother possessed remarkable intelligence, and a mind that was masculine in its strength. Altogether she was *the* figure in that Lincolnshire home. The good rector's purse was often very empty, but he had a very proud wish that his children should be well-instructed. And so for twenty years his wife conducted single-handed the education of her children. The first school that John Wesley attended was in his own home, and the hand that held the spelling-book or administered the rod was that of his mother. No doubt he respected the rod, but he learnt to respect her more; and when he grew to manhood, and was puzzling out theology at Oxford, it was to his mother that he turned for help. Possibly her husband knew more about justification and predestination than she, but the student remembered the strong mind that had impressed him when a boy. It may be that one reason of her success with her children was that she never woke their minds up too soon. They all learnt the Lord's Prayer as soon as they could talk, but beyond that their minds lay fallow till they were five years old. But when she did begin her children knew it. She celebrated their fifth birthday by teaching them the alphabet, and before the first day of their education was over, they had mastered their letters. The work thus begun was kept up day after day for years. Could we have peeped into that rectory one morning we should have found Mr. Wesley in his study, thinking, perhaps, of next Sunday's sermon, or racking his brains for rhyme and reason to commit to paper, whereby he might earn £20 to keep that wolf—his creditor—from the door. You would hardly think, as you watch him quietly at work, that there are other human beings—a good round dozen, in fact—in the house besides. Don't the bairns cry, sometimes? Very likely they do, but you would not hear them, for one of the articles of their mother's creed has been that, if they cry at all they must cry very softly. If we look into another room, we shall see Mrs. Wesley with some of her children about her. Possibly with Bible in hand she is giving John a lesson in reading. Reading-books were scarce in those days, and money was scarcer still; and so the first chapter of Genesis served John Wesley as his primer for spelling and reading. Or else we might see them all seated round the table, doing some task she has set them, whilst she employs her few moments of leisure in adding the church accounts, or pondering the ways and means of the household. When we think of her six hours every day in the schoolroom, of the darning and patching that had to be done when those merry youngsters were in bed, of the care of the parish and the care of home, one wonders how she did all that she had to do. The secret of her success was that she did one thing at a time. Everything went as if by clockwork in her home. She had a time for everything, and managed others so well, because she managed herself.

'Her children rise up and call her blessed.' I have said so much about Mrs. Wesley, because her son's boyhood was so largely under her influence. She educated him for six years, and did it so well that, when he was eleven years old, he was fit to be entered as a scholar at the Charterhouse. Her mode of education was no 'cram.' She taught John Wesley to reflect as well as to remember. As a boy he betrayed a thoughtful mind. He did nothing without reflection. Even if pressed at dinner to have more from a certain dish, his invariable reply was, 'Thank you! I will think of it.' Moreover, his mother was deeply religious, and she made her son the same. Indeed, so remarkable was the piety that he displayed, that at eight years of age he was allowed by his father to share in the sacrament. And it was from the shelter of this poor but pious home, and from the care of a devoted and gifted mother, that he was sent to the large school of the Charterhouse. How homesick the little fellow must have been at first! What longings he must have had for one glimpse of that homely rectory and those Epworth lanes! We know how well he kept the injunction that his father had given him at parting, 'to run every morning three times round the garden' of the school. He wanted to ensure for his son the health that comes by sitting exercise. And indeed John needed something to keep him robust and strong, for,

as regards food, the Charterhouse was only Epworth over again. The bigger boys of the school preyed like greedy harpies on the younger, and took their share of meat as well as their own. During the five years that he spent there, bread was almost the only solid food that John Wesley had. Still he had already served a good apprenticeship to privation, and he bore his ills with cheerful fortitude. His books were his delight. He applied himself diligently to his studies, and had acquired ere he left a high position in the school. There is a story told about his latter days there in which we seem to see a foreshadowing of the popular preacher of the future. He was in the habit of gathering the boys of the lower classes about him, and entertaining them with outbursts of youthful eloquence. One of his harangues was cut short one day by the advent of the master, who requested that schoolboys' dread — a private interview. Wesley followed to the master's 'den,' and, when asked how it was that he sought the company of the boys beneath him, and was so rarely seen with the boys who were his equals, he gave the quick retort, 'Better to rule in hell than serve in heaven.'

In one respect Charterhouse injured him. We have already noticed Wesley's bent to religion when at home. Such piety so early may have been somewhat unnatural and precocious, but, had he remained under the Epworth roof, it might have become manly and healthy. But the Charterhouse killed it. To leave such a religious atmosphere as that rectory was, in any case, perilous to a boy only eleven years old. The temptations common to the life of a public school proved too much for him; negligence of religion grew into indifference. It is true he still read his Bible, and prayed morning and evening. Externally he was as religious as ever, but he was conscious of an inward collapse, which was not repaired for years. John Wesley left the Charterhouse at the age of sixteen far less religious than when he entered it. And here we must leave him. Our eyes follow him wistfully as we see the gates of Christ Church, Oxford, close behind him. But the boy on this side the college

✻

gates becomes a man on the other, and, as I have already trespassed unduly on the editor's space and on my readers' patience, I must leave them to learn for themselves how the man regained the religion that the boy had lost, and how God ordained John Wesley to begin the great Methodist movement—the mightiest revival of religion that the world has ever seen.   A. LEWIS HUMPHRIES, B.A.

The Migration of Birds.

VERY one knows or has heard Tennyson's beautiful song, of which the following are snatches:

'O swallow, swallow flying, flying south,
Fly to her, and fall upon her gilded eaves,
And tell her, tell her what I tell to thee.
 *   *   *   *   *   *   *
O swallow! flying from the golden woods,
Fly to her, and pipe and woo her, and make her mine;
And tell her, tell her that I follow thee.'

It is this 'flying south' of the birds, and their return, that our talk is to be about just now. Let us take the swallow as our first example. This graceful and familiar bird (see Fig. 1) is absent from our shores during the greater part of the year. Its departure is the sign that winter is not far away, and its return is hailed as the harbinger and promise of summer. It is the type of all migratory birds. As one has beautifully said, 'God sends us the swallow in the first days of summer to relieve us of the insects which the summer suns are calling into life. The home of the swallow is all the habitable earth; it knows nothing of winter or winter's cold; its whole life is a continued festivity, and its song an eternal hymn in praise of summer and liberty.' The earliest swallows reach this country about the middle of April, and are followed by others at varying intervals until the end of May. They have a marvellous instinct for returning regularly to their nests of the previous year, which are most abundant in places where winged insects are numerous and where water is to be found. Here they lay their eggs, and rear their broods. Then

as autumn approaches they begin to prepare to leave. They may be seen assembling in large flocks, especially towards evening, being much more sociable at this season than earlier in the year. In October they take their departure in a body. Before migration was understood it used to be thought that the swallows never left the country, but spent the cold season hibernating in hollow trees, holes of rocks, and the banks of pools and rivers. It is believed that individual swallows sometimes remain, for stragglers have been seen flying about late on in winter. Mr. Johns says: 'I was walking through a limestone quarry at Saltram on the bank of the Plym in Devonshire many years ago on the 24th of December, when I saw a swallow—whether a chimney swallow or martin I cannot positively affirm—wheeling about and evidently hawking for gnats near the face of the cliff. The season was a mild one, the air still, and the sun shining brightly against the limestone rocks, from which much heat was reflected. That the bird had been kept in captivity until the migratory season had passed, and then released, is certainly possible, but not probable. On any other supposition it must have remained either of its own free will, which is not likely, or from incapacity to accompany its congeners. Left alone, it probably found a sheltered retreat in the face of the cliff, and sallied forth whenever the weather was inviting, making the most of the short days, and, on the finest, contenting itself with a scanty meal. . . . But as "one swallow does not make a spring," so neither is one sufficient to upset a theory. There remains, therefore, the rule, with the one exception to prove it, that swallows do migrate.'

The common black swift is also an interesting example of migration. It is the strongest and swiftest of the swallow tribe, and, indeed, of all birds. It may often be seen in summer wheeling around church spires and other tall buildings. Leaving Northern Africa in March or April, it journeys leisurely northwards, numbers settling on the islands or along the northern shores of the Mediterranean; while the main body spreads over central Europe, or goes northward as far as the Orkney and

FIG. 1.—SWALLOWS MIGRATING.

the end of May the and then, as Mr. Adams inning of July the broods a few weeks spent in , as if training for the uddenly vanish. A week y be seen circling around nt Thebes, the walls of minarets of Morocco.'

Swifts appear to leave early for the reason that they are specially susceptible to cold. Mr. F. Smith, of the British Museum, tells that at Deal on July 8th, 1856, it became in the evening disagreeably cold. The poor swifts were terribly fluttered. 'Whilst observing these occurrences,' he says, 'a girl came to the door to ask me if I wanted to buy a bat. She had heard, she told me, that I bought all kinds of birds, and her mother thought I might want a bat. On her producing it, I was astonished to find it was a poor benumbed swift. The girl told me they were dropping down in the streets, and the boys were killing all the bats; the church, she said, was covered with them. Off I started to witness this strange sight and slaughter. True enough; the children were charging them everywhere, and on arriving at the church in Lower Street, I was

residence in Central Africa. It is virtually without feet, so that it really never perches on the ground, and is always on the wing. After its prodigious flight it seems to stand in no need of rest, but will start off at once in pursuit of food. For speed of flight the passenger pigeon of North America (see Fig. 2) comes nearest to the swift's record. It is believed to travel at the rate of one thousand miles a day.

The cuckoo is another well-known migrator

Fig. 2.—Passenger Pigeons.

astonished to see the poor birds hanging in clusters from the eaves and cornices. Some clusters were at least two feet in length, and at intervals benumbed individuals dropped from the outside of the clusters. Many hundreds of the poor birds fell victims to the ruthless ignorance of the children.'

The speed of the swift in migration is astonishing. Sober observers have computed that it can cover a distance of 250 miles in an hour, so that in seven or eight hours it can pass from its summer home in England to its winter

(Fig. 3), though it also used to be supposed to become torpid during winter. It arrives in this country about the middle of April (if the season be genial), and its 'wandering voice' is quickly heard. But,

     'Towards the end of June
      It alters its tune,'

which becomes less musical, and then ceases altogether. The old birds leave in July, first the males and then the females, while the young birds remain till October. The cuckoo's early departure seems due to the failure of the particular animal food on which its subsists. As Mr. Adams says, ' Considering its short stay and its extraordinary behaviour during its sojourn in Europe, one is lost in wonder to understand why it takes the trouble to come all the way to the bleak north in order to deposit its eggs in other birds' nests, and depart immediately afterwards. Altogether the British visit does not extend over three months, so that if the cuckoo built a nest and reared its young, there would be little time to spare.'

The migration of the common quail recalls the story in the Book of Numbers. All the showered on them from heaven, picking and cleaning them, *salting them* ("They spread them all abroad for themselves."—Numbers xii. 32), and packing them away in casks for transportation to the principal markets of the Levant ; that is to say, the migration of quails is to this part of Greece what the migration of herrings is to Scotland and Holland. "The Quail" says the French naturalist from whom we quote these facts, ' arrives in France early in May, and takes its departure towards the end of August.'

Why do birds migrate? Migration from our own climate southwards in the autumn

Fig. 2.—The Cuckoo.

incidents there related are true to the life. The birds came in the spring, they came also in the night; they came from the sea; they came in overwhelming numbers; and they flew low, or fell, as if exhausted by their long flight. To give an illustration of the immense flocks in which they travel, the Bishop of Capri, an islet at the entrance of the Bay of Naples, used to clear an income of £1,000 per year by his quails. He was hence humorously dubbed ' The Bishop of Quails.' ' In certain islands of the Archipelago and the coasts of Greece the inhabitants, men and women, have no other occupation during two months of the year than that of collecting the quails which are is of course accounted for by ' the failure of the food supplies here,' but that will not explain the return journey. For instance, when the swifts and swallows leave the warm climate of Northern Africa in the spring, insect life is even more abundant than it has been in the months preceding. The instinct of migration seems somehow constitutional—what we call innate, and Mr. Adams leans to the opinion that it is a habit inherited from the inconceivably far back times before the Glacial Epoch, when ' the climate of Central and Northern Europe, even far into the Arctic regions, was so mild and genial that animals and plants of equatorial latitudes flourished on land and sea.

At' that period, what are now the summer retreats of the birds, were their permanent homes. But the gradual invasion of the Glacial Epoch, drove them southward to their present limits ; and then as the cold declined they periodically returned, flitting back and forward between north and south ' through unreckoned ages,' until the habit and the instinct became fixed. It is an odd thought, and yet, no doubt, a true one, that the swallow whom we see flying south and then north again year by year, is the witness of wonderful changes which took place on our earth's surface millions of years ago.

St. Paul and Manners.

I SAW not long ago a peculiar seal-ring, one that a mother had had made as a birthday present for her son, who was away at school. It was a bloodstone, carved with the device of two mailed hands, one reaching to the other a cup, and around this an inscription, which was Greek to me.

'What does it mean ?' I asked, after a little study. 'Is it the "cup of water in the name of a disciple ? " '

The mother laughed.

' Not exactly,' she said. 'But it is a cup of water –the cup that Sir Philip Sidney gave to the dying soldier on the battle-field. You remember the legend. The motto you will find in the twelfth chapter of Romans, tenth verse—' In honour preferring one another.' I had it engraved in original Greek, so that every one couldn't read it, for this is between my boy and me. St. Paul has always been my teacher of good manners, and I thought this ring would please Tom, and at the same time remind him of some of the things that I cannot say to him now.'

' Will you tell me what you mean about St. Paul and good manners ? ' I asked.

She smiled a little and said, ' Why, I wanted above all things, as I suppose every mother does, that my boys should be well-bred, courteous, polite--in a word, gentlemen. But I soon found out that the continual teaching them to do, or not to do, each particular act was never going to make them what I wanted. It must be deeper than that ; and after a while I came back and rested on the Bible, and especially on St. Paul. Did you ever read this twelfth chapter of Romans with reference to manners ? No guide to etiquette, or rules for deportment, could do as much for one as that. My boys and I finally took the one broad rule :—' Be kindly affectioned one to another with brotherly love ; in honour preferring one another.' That, in its broadest sense, includes everything. The talking to disagreeable people, the being cordial and hospitable, the trying to entertain others, and give them pleasure with any talent we have, are all, I think, being kindly affectioned. And 'in honour preferring one another ' may mean everything, from the offering one's chair to the giving up of one's life.

' I think I learned this,' she went on, ' once when it was my lot to live for a time in a little Western village, with what you would call very common people. Uncultivated they certainly all were, but I saw there what a perfect substitute true Christianity is for good manners, as society calls them. There were some people there who never offended. Quaint and amusing they might be in their ways and expressions, but never rude, never curious or prying or conceited. They were always considerate and thoughtful, always full of some kind-hearted plan for other people's pleasure. They were kindly affectionate, and preferred one another. I remembered all this when I came to the training of my own boys, and so far St. Paul has been my authority on manners. I do not say that through him I can teach my boys to use the right fork for oysters, or to make a faultless bow, but I do say that I can teach them to be so manly, so gentle, so thoughtful of others, and unassuming about themselves, that, even if they blundered in every small social matter, they would still be undeniably gentlemen. The small matters of etiquette are mostly mechanical ; they can be easily learned outside, even if they are not in one's own home ; but it is with the great underlying principle, ' in honour preferring one another,' that the true training must begin.

—The Congregationalist.

Significance of Words.

THE ancients called the River Volga the Rha. Upon its banks grew a plant which the Greeks called the strange Rha—Rhabarron. We, to-day, eat it as rhubarb.

The island of Cyprus was named Kupros. A certain metal being discovered there, it was named Kupros, or copper.

The word *tandem* is a Latin adverb of time. By an amusing occurrence it came to have a different meaning for us. Long ago, some students hired a team to take a drive. But, being heavily loaded with that which inebriates, they were incapable of hitching the horses to the carriage. Finally, one bright genius suggested that they hitch one in front of the other. They did so. Driving merrily away, one of the company remarked, between his hiccoughs, that they were driving 'tandem, at length.'

Not long since, one of the great dailies, in reporting a public meeting, stated that a certain prominent man 'was the cynosure of all eyes.' Now, it did not mean to call this man a dog's tail, but it did mean to say, in an elegant way, that the gentleman was the centre of attraction; that all eyes were turned towards him. But in ancient times the mariners were able to direct their course only by watching the north star. Now this star, they said, was in the tail of the constellation of the dog. As the *cynosura* (dog's tail) was the one object of the heavens most observed, therefore anything the special object of attraction was called a cynosure, or dog's tail.

Two thousand years ago the common people of Rome had one officer specially to represent them. His authority was such that no law could be enacted without his consent. When a law of which he disapproved was passed by the Senate, the tribune standing in the open door of the senate chamber shouted out one word which has become familiar, ' Veto !'—I forbid.

The word 'calendar' records the fact that the Roman priests, having observed the new moon in the Assembly, publicly announced the new month, Kalendæ.

January, March, May, and June are named for the gods to whom these months were sacred. After he had reformed the calendar, Cæsar gave his own name, Julius, to the month which still bears it. His ambitious nephew, Augustus, took the next month for himself. December means tenth and November ninth, instead of being the twelfth and eleventh months, as with us ; for the Roman year began where our March is. The days of the week bear testimony to the now almost forgotten gods of our Saxon ancestors. Wooden, Tiw, Thor, and Fria cannot be entirely forgotten so long as we have Tuesday, Wednesday, Thursday, and Friday.

When we speak of 'pecuniary affairs,' it recalls the time when no such thing as money was known. At that time the standard of the value and measure of fortune was the *pecus* or *herd*. Then, money being invented, was stamped with the figure of an ox. The figure is gone from our coins, but the word 'pecuniary' still remains to remind us of other times and customs.

Though we may be able to write our autographs, we still speak of 'signing' letters and papers. This word 'signing' recalls the old times of ignorance, when the great body of the people could not write, but were obliged to make their mark or sign.

The word 'volume' means a roll. We would not speak of the books of our libraries as ' volumes ' but for the fact that the books of the ancients were rolls of parchment. We have applied the old name to the new form.

In ancient time philosophers believed in the animation of matter, and sought by alchemy to discover the spirits of material substances. This fact of history might have escaped us, had it not been recorded in such names as spirits of camphor and spirits of turpentine.

The familiar words of daily use, which point us back to other times, and relate for our information or amusement strange stories of the past, are innumerable.

New York and Its Environs.

HE social life of New York in the earlier days was characterized by the simplicity and frugality which marked the early settlers. But as the place grew in wealth and population a change gradually came over the habits of the people. The successful commercial men who came to New York from all parts of the country, became the real local magnates, and business prosperity became the chief sign and cause of social distinction. This state of things still exists. There is no other city in the United States in which money gives a man or woman so much social weight, and in which it exercises so much influence on the manners and amusements, and meets so little competition from literary, artistic, and other eminence. Here, if anywhere, the 'almighty dollar' holds the field. The luxury of domestic life is carried to a degree unequalled in any other city. The entertainments are numerous and costly, and the restaurants have achieved a world-wide fame. The number of horses and equipages has greatly increased within the last twenty years, under the stimulus given by the opening of the Central Park, the drives of which on fine afternoons in April and May and the early part of June present a scene of great brilliancy. The city is, however, almost completely deserted during the summer months by the wealthy, who go to country houses along the coast, from New Jersey as far up as the province of New Brunswick, or to the mineral springs of Saratoga, or to the Continent of Europe. Some years ago fine country houses sprang up along the Hudson River, the scenery of which possesses great grandeur, but of late its banks have been infested by malaria, and for this and other reasons the tide of fashion has been turned to the seaside, where beautiful villas have been reared. For people of small means, New York is not so well provided with summer entertainments, except such as are afforded by the beauty of the suburbs, and the water-side resorts which are within easy reach. The chief of these are Coney Island, which is really a continuation of the sandy beach that extends along the south side of Long Island. Its western extremity is distant from the Battery about eight miles, in a straight line, and its extreme length is about five miles. Since 1874, when capitalists suddenly woke up to the capabilities of the spot, a number of favourite resorts have sprung up upon the island, with monster hotels, in one of which as many as four thousand people can dine at once, with conveniences for surf-bathing, and a great variety of amusements. The Island is reached by steam and horsecars, by steamboats, and by carriages. The Germans have beer gardens on a grand scale, both on Manhattan Island and elsewhere, which they frequent in vast numbers. The Irish organize picnics to groves and woods along the Hudson and East Rivers, which are let for that purpose, and excursions by water down the harbour are very numerous. Indeed, for this kind of amusement there are few cities in the world so well situated.

New York has about thirty places of amusement of a theatrical character. Of these the Metropolitan Opera House is much the largest. Its stage is 96 feet wide, 76 feet long, and 120 feet high. It has seventeen entrances, six of which are 10 feet wide, and the whole structure is fireproof. It is capable of seating three thousand persons. Besides the theatres there are two fine concert and lecture halls, known as the Steinway and Chickering Halls. There are also numerous clubs of a social and political character, some of which have a very large membership. The Manhattan Club, which belongs to the Democratic party, has about six hundred members. The Union League Club, which was founded in 1863, in order to give to the Government during the war the organized support of wealthy and influential men in the city, has been ever since the Republican social organization. The Century Club represents literature, art, and the learned professions, and owns a valuable collection of pictures and a well-selected library.

The city is well supplied with parks and public gardens. There are in all thirty of these, including small open squares. The principal of these are the City Hall Park, containing six acres; the Washington Square, containing eight; Mount Morris Square, containing twenty. The Battery, which contains twenty-one acres, is situated at the southern extremity

is that known as the Central Park. It is situated near the centre of the island, and extends from 59th Street on the south to 110th Street on the north, with 8th Avenue for its western, and 5th Avenue for its eastern borders. It is one of the largest and finest parks in the world. Its length is $2\frac{1}{2}$ miles, and its breadth a little more than half a mile, and it encloses an area of 843 acres. It was originally an unpromising stretch of rocky

STAR BRIDGE, CENTRAL PARK, NEW YORK.

of the island, where the eastern and western rivers have their confluence and mingle their waters with those of the sea. It is an open grassy plot planted with trees, and laid out in gravel walks. Projecting beyond this is a castellated edifice built on a ledge of rocks, and now called Castle Gardens, from its containing within its limits the public gardens and promenade. It is a place that is much frequented, and fireworks are often exhibited in it for the gratification of visitors. But the chief park

ledges and stagnant swamps, but by engineering skill the very defects that once seemed fatal have been converted into its most attractive features; so that now it is one of the most beautiful pleasure grounds with which any city in the world is adorned. It is laid out with great taste, and planted with the choicest flowers and shrubs and trees, and competent judges consider it a masterpiece of landscape gardening. A large portion of it is occupied by the two Croton reservoirs: the smaller one comprises 35 acres and the larger one 107. There are also five lakes, which unitedly enclose an area of 43½ acres. The Park has eighteen entrances, four at each end and five on each side, and four streets cross it, to afford opportunity for traffic passing under the walks and drives. It has 10 miles of carriage roads, 6 miles of bridle path, and 30 miles of foot paths. It also has several most beautiful bridges, including the Star Bridge and the Rustic Bridge. Boating is practised on the lakes, and numerous swans, ducks, and other birds may be seen floating

tered by the Legislature in 1870. It is managed by a board of officers, including the Comptroller of the city, the President of Public Parks Department, the President of the National Academy of Design, and certain private citizens who are members of its corporation. The museum building, opened in 1880, was erected by the Park Department at a cost of one hundred thousand pounds. It measures 218 feet by 95, and is built of red brick, with sandstone trimmings. Among its valuable possessions are the Blodget collection of pictures, the Cesnola collection of articles

LAKE, CENTRAL PARK, NEW YORK.

about, and adding to the beauty of the scene. There is also a dairy connected with the park, a view of which is given in one of the accompanying engravings. It is a neat, artistic building, and is picturesquely situated, being surrounded by shrubs, flowers, and evergreens. In the park grounds there are several monuments and statues. Among the former is the celebrated obelisk which was brought from Alexandria in 1880, and among the latter are busts of the world's worthies, including one of Joseph Mazzini. The Metropolitan Museum of Art finds a place in the park immediately behind the obelisk. This museum was char-

taken from the Cypriote cities and tombs, two paintings by Rubens, two by Van Dyck, and many other works of eminent masters. It is open free to the public on four days of the week, and on the other days an admission fee is charged.

The National Academy of Design is situated at 4th Avenue. It has a frontage of 80 feet by 98. The outside is Venetian, the material used being grey and white marble, and blue stone. The first and second storeys contain offices, lecture-rooms, and rooms for art schools. On the third storey are large exhibition rooms, which are lighted from above.

Every year one exhibition of oil paintings and one of water colours are given, and in later years supplementary exhibitions have been added. The art schools are free, and are open to both sexes.

The American Museum of Natural History was incorporated by the Legislature in 1869, but its present building was not opened until 1877. It is situated in Manhattan Square, and is built of red brick with yellow sandstone facings. It has four storeys, and each of its halls measures one hundred and seventy feet in length, by sixty feet in width. It is

noble work. Among these was the Free School Society, membership of which was open to all citizens offering contributions to its funds. In 1826 it underwent a reorganization, and became the Public School Society, which continued to have charge of popular education in the city until 1853. It was supported in part by voluntary contributions, in part by subscriptions from those who desired to share in its management, and in a smaller degree by contributions from the school fund of the state. For fifty years it may be said to have done all that was done for popular education in New

DAIRY, CENTRAL PARK, NEW YORK.

governed by a board of twenty-five trustees, and is free to the public. It was erected by the Park Department, which has charge of it and the surrounding grounds. Among its treasures are fine collections of Natural History specimens, birds of North America, shells, geological specimens of New York State, and of Denmark, collections of stone implements from France, the Mississippi valley, and the museum of Prince Maximilian. The education of New York was for a number of years carried on by the enterprise of private individuals. They formed Associations for the purpose, and were the means of doing a

York city. During its existence six million children passed through its schools, and it expended every year a large and increasing revenue, and when dissolved it turned over one hundred and twenty thousand pounds to the city. After its dissolution educational matters were in the hands of a municipal board, composed of representatives elected by the different wards, but in 1864 the city was divided into school districts. The power of appointing the twenty-one commissioners and three inspectors for each of the eight school districts has since been given to the Mayor, and to the commissioners the power of appointing five trustees for each ward. The commissioners and inspectors hold office for three years, and the trustees for five. As an outgrowth of the common school system there is a normal college for the education of teachers, with a model school connected with it, and also the college of the city of New York, which began in 1848 as a Free Academy for the advanced pupils who had left the common schools. Six years later it was empowered to grant degrees, and in 1866 it was formally converted into a University.

The total number of scholars attending the City schools is about three hundred thousand, and the number of professors and teachers about three thousand. An Act providing for compulsory education was passed by the Legislature in 1874, and came into operation in the city in 1875. It compels every person in the control or charge of any children between the ages of eight and fourteen to cause them to attend some public or private school at least fourteen weeks in each year, eight of which are to be consecutive, or the pupils are to be instructed regularly at home, at least fourteen weeks in each year, in spelling, reading, writing, grammar, and arithmetic. The law is enforced in the city by the city superintendent, who has twelve assistants.

The schools, colleges, and other institutions not connected officially with the government are numerous. They include Columbia College, which was founded in 1754, and which is now the oldest university in the State, and the richest in the country. It has well equipped law, medical, and mining schools. Besides its academic department, it has a library of 20,000 volumes, and a rapidly growing income from the advance of its property in the city.

There are also several denominational colleges, including theological seminaries, together with medical colleges, and a large number of private schools which are frequented by the children of the wealthier classes.

M. JOHNSON.

It is not until we have passed through the furnace that we are made to know how much dross was in our composition.

Brindley, The Schemer.

JAMES BRINDLEY was born in the year 1716 at Tunsted, an obscure hamlet in the High Peak of Derbyshire. His father was a cottager, and was not over steady during the early part of his married life. His mother was an excellent woman, who was exceedingly anxious for the moral and intellectual training of her children. James was her first-born, and at an early age was engaged as a field-labourer. Early in his teens he manifested his engineering skill by making models of mills with his pen-knife, and fixing them to artificial streams, which were the outcome of his own contrivance. At seventeen years of age he bound himself for a seven years' apprenticeship to Abraham Bennett, a mill-wright in the village of Sutton, near Macclesfield. During his first two years he was slow and clumsy, and exhausted the patience of the foreman, who declined to teach the ' bungling apprentice.' He was thus thrown upon his own resources, which was providential, for it developed his own thought, and helped him to cultivate a spirit of self-reliance. At the expiration of two years Bennett was engaged to repair a mill at Macclesfield which had partially been destroyed by fire. Brindley was one of the working party, and the manager was impressed with one of his casual remarks, and accordingly requested him to undertake an important piece of work, to the great chagrin of Bennett and his foreman. Contrary to their anticipations of failure, the work was admirably accomplished, and Brindley secured his first triumph. At once his employer recognised his extraordinary abilities, and he was allotted the work of an ordinary workman, and the Cheshire millers began to make special requests for Bennett to send the young man Brindley.

Bennett was engaged to fit up a paper mill, on the principle that had been adopted by the Smedley paper mills, Manchester. He inspected the Manchester mills, but was unable to cope with the difficulties. Bennett was unwilling to give up the contract and to pronounce his efforts a failure. The whole affair became complicated, and Brindley was ridiculed by the engineers of the neighbourhood, who denounced his doings as a farce. Brindley, however, without telling his employer, walked from Macclesfield to Manchester, had an interview with the proprietor of the mills, and was permitted to inspect them. He stored his retentive memory with everything that he had seen, and then returned. His absence had been a source of anxious alarm to Bennett, who, in his despair, forthwith transferred the whole of the undertaking to his apprentice. Bennett revised the whole of the plans, and added new improvements of his own design, and satisfactorily completed the arrangements within the time allotted by the contract. Bennett was so pleased with the once unpromising apprentice that he made him foreman, and upon the death of his master Brindley removed to Leek, in Staffordshire, where he commenced business for himself. At first his progress was slow, but when the millers and mill-owners began to know him, they entrusted him with their work, and facetiously gave him the name of 'The Schemer.'

One of his earliest mechanical achievements secured him lasting fame. The Clifton coal mines were flooded with water, and the men were unable to reach the workings. Mr. Heathcote, the proprietor, having heard of the great ingenuity of Brindley, sent for him. He explained the circumstances to Brindley, who for a long time was buried in thought, when at length his eyes sparkled and his face brightened, for he had conceived a plan, which was to tunnel the solid rock, and thus to connect the collieries with the Irwell, which bounded the estate; and by pumping the water into the river the miners were enabled to resume work where previously the coal had been 'drowned.'

His name and fame are principally connected with the construction of canals or internal water highways. The Duke of Bridgwater having decided to connect his collieries at Worsley with Manchester, engaged Brindley as engineer. The Duke's plans were to descend from the collieries at Worsley by a series of locks into the Irwell. Brindley was opposed to the scheme because it would be costly and, in the end, unworkable. Brindley having surveyed the route, discovered that the natural difficulties were formidable and numerous. He had a bold idea, which at that time was completely new. His plan was to carry the canal on an aqueduct right over the river, and then by embankments across the lower lands on the northern boundary of the Irwell. When his recommendations were made known, he was laughed at by his fellow-engineers and publicly ridiculed. 'The Schemer' was not a man to be silenced by laughter, and he tenaciously, in spite of all opposition, clung to his plans. The Duke became anxious, and he consulted another engineer, who denounced the proposed aqueduct and embankment as being the climax of human recklessness and folly, and said, 'I have often heard of castles in the air, but never saw before where any of them were to be erected.' The Duke, notwithstanding the adverse criticism, continued his confidence in Brindley; consequently, the aqueduct was built and the embankment made, and in course of time the collieries by water communication were connected with Manchester. For years the Barton aqueduct was regarded as the masterpiece of engineering skill; and although in recent times Telford, Rennie, and others have worked greater wonders, yet Brindley's aqueduct was the 'mother' of them all. Subsequently, the Bridgwater Canal connected the two Lancashire towns—Manchester and Liverpool; and in these days of quick transit, when you can travel from one city to the other by railway in less than an hour, it is impossible to conceive what a benefit Brindley conferred upon the inhabitants of these two centres of industry. The first stage coach ran from Manchester in 1757, and although harnessed with six or eight horses, it required a day to reach Liverpool. Provisions, goods, and fuel were conveyed upon the backs of packhorses, and in winter the roads were impassable, consequently these commodities were at famine prices. Brindley's canal reduced, by one-half, the price of coal, and brought food at reasonable prices to the homes of the famishing.

Brindley's success in Lancashire caused him to commence 'The Grand Trunk Navigation Canal,' which united the Trent with the Mersey. Dying before its completion, the work was satisfactorily finished by his brother-in-law, Mr. Henshaw, and this was linked to the Severn by a branch canal from Staffordshire. So wrapt up was he in his schemes of inland navigation, that he is said to have answered a question that was humorously put to him on his examination before the House of Commons, ' For what purpose did he consider rivers to have been constructed ?' by at once facetiously replying, ' Undoubtedly, to feed navigable canals.' His inventions were the outcome of his own fertile resources, and were accomplished by simple means; seldom did he use any model or drawing. When difficulties presented themselves, he generally retired to bed, and he has been known to seclude himself for days together, until he had solved the problem.

His intense application shortened his days. On the 30th of September, 1772, he breathed his last at Turnhurst Hall, on the outskirts of Tunstall—the 'Mother' Circuit of Primitive Methodism—and a few days later was buried in the quiet churchyard of New Chapel, which is situated beneath the shadow of Mow Hill.

ALBERT A. BIRCHENOUGH.

The Magnet.

ITS PROPERTIES AND LAWS.

AGNETS are substances which have the property of attracting iron; this property was known to the ancients; it exists to a high degree in an iron ore, known to mineralogists as 'magnetite,' and having the chemical composition of Fe_3O_4. This ore is found in quantities in Sweden, Norway, Spain, Elba, and other parts of the world; it furnishes the best of iron. It was first discovered at Magnesia in Asia Minor; the name magnet is derived from this circumstance. It was known to the Greeks as 'Magnes.' In the 10th or 12th century this stone was discovered to possess the remarkable property of pointing north and south, when freely suspended. This proved a very important discovery; henceforth the magnet became of the greatest service to man, for by means of it he learned to trace his course through the pathless deep to every region of the globe ; from that time it was known as the ' lodestone ' or 'leading stone.' Another characteristic of the magnet is, that it communicates its properties to steel by rubbing or simple contact. If a piece of iron, or better a piece of steel, be rubbed with a lodestone, or natural magnet, it becomes magnetic, and is termed an artificial magnet. Of artificial magnets there are two kinds, temporary and permanent. Temporary magnets are such as are easily magnetised, but which lose their magnetism as soon as separated from the inducing magnet ; if we take a piece of iron and place it on the end of a magnet, it will at once become ' magnetic,' and may be made to attract iron filings ; if, however, it is taken from the magnet it loses its magnetism, and the filings fall off.

Permanent magnets are those which do not lose their magnetism when separated from the inducing magnet. Steel and cobalt are examples.

Iron can only be magnetised permanently by hammering it at the time it is connected with a magnet, the hammering develops ' coercive force,' or the power of resisting magnetisation or demagnetisation. Thus it is harder to get the magnetism into steel than iron, and harder to get the magnetism out of steel than out of iron; for the steel retains the magnetism once put into it, or has a deal of ' coercive force,' while the iron has none.

Until 1600, when Dr. Gilbert published his work ' De Magnete,' little was known of the magnet beyond the facts that it would attract iron, and when freely suspended, takes a north and south position. He observed the ' distribution of force ' in the magnet, *i.e.*, that the attractive force is greatest at the two opposite points, which are called poles, and that from the poles the force gradually gets less, until at a point, midway between the poles, there is no force at all; this point is named the 'magnetic equator.'

Suppose we now take a knitting needle, and, having magnetised it by stroking it from end to end with the pole of a permanent magnet, we suspend it by a thread, we find it takes up a definite position, or, as we should say, sets itself in the 'magnetic meridian.' The pole which lies towards the north is termed the north pole, or more correctly, the north seeking pole, and the pole pointing towards the south, the south seeking pole. The former pole is usually marked 'N,' and is distinguished as the 'marked' pole. If we bring a piece of soft iron to the respective poles, we find both poles equally attract it; but if we take a magnet in our hand, and present the two poles of it successively to the north pole of the needle, we shall see that one pole of the magnet attracts it, while the other repels it.

Repeating the experiment on the south pole of the needle, we shall find that it is repelled by one pole and attracted by the other, and that the same pole which attracts the north pole of the needle, repels the south pole, and *vice versâ*. Hence the first law of magnetism —'unlike poles attract, and like poles repel.' This double action of attraction and repulsion is termed 'magnetic polarity.'

A distinction was made by Gilbert between magnets and magnetic bodies. A magnet attracts only at its poles, and they possess opposite properties. But a magnetic body will attract either pole of the magnet; it has no 'magnetic polarity.' Repulsion is the test of magnetism.

The two kinds of magnetism are inseparable. It is impossible to obtain a magnet with one pole only. If a magnetised bar of steel be broken the magnetism is not lost; on the contrary, each piece acts as a perfect magnet, so that if we break it into forty pieces we should not destroy its magnetism, but have forty small magnets instead of one large one. If we again put them together, all the unlike poles being near each other the whole forty would act as one magnet, and have only two poles as before it was broken.

Magnetism may be communicated to a piece of iron without it touching the magnet. Place an unmagnetised bar of iron near some iron filings, the filings are not affected. Now bring a magnet near to the bar of iron, the filings are attracted, the presence of the magnet has 'induced' magnetism in the bar of iron. This is called magnetic induction, and may take place through unmagnetic bodies. For example, a magnet will attract iron filings, although a sheet of paper or thin piece of wood interpose. A magnet sealed up in a glass tube will act as a magnet. Gilbert surrounded a magnet by a ring of flames, and found it still affected by a magnet outside the flames. Across water, vacuum, and all known substances, the magnetic forces will act; with this exception, the magnetic force will not act across a screen of iron, or other magnetic material. A small magnet suspended inside a hollow iron ball will not be affected by an outside magnet. Thus a hollow shell of iron will screen the space inside it from magnetic influences.

A number of bodies are repelled from the poles of a magnet. Brugmans, of Leyden, in 1778 noticed that a lump of bismuth repelled either pole of a magnetic needle.

In 1845, Faraday examined a large number of substances, and found that whilst a great many are, like iron, attracted to a magnet others are feebly repelled. Such bodies are called 'Diamagnetic bodies.' Bismuth, Phosphorus, Zinc, Mercury, Lead, Silver, Copper, Gold, are 'Diamagnetic bodies.'

THE first thing you need after life is food: 'My meat is to do the will of Him that sent Me.' The next thing you need after food is society: He that doeth the will of My Father in Heaven, the same is My brother, and sister, and mother.' You want education: 'Teach me to do Thy will, O God.' You want pleasure: 'I delight to do Thy will, O God.' A whole life can be built up on that one vertebral column, and then, when all is over: 'He that doeth the will of God abideth for ever.'—*Professor Drummond.*

A Prison Incident.

A BOY'S FIRST DRINK.

Rs. Emma Molloy relates the following incident in one of her speeches, referring to the relation of temperance to crime.

In a recent visit to the Leavenworth, Kan., prison, during my address on Sabbath morning, I observed a boy, not more than seventeen or eighteen years of age, on the front seat intently eyeing me. The look he gave me was so full of earnest longing, it spoke volumes to me.

At the close of the service I asked the warden for an interview with him, which was readily granted. As he approached me his face grew deathly pale, and, as he grasped my hand, he could not restrain the fast falling tears. Choking with emotion, he said:

'I have been in this prison two years, and you are the first person that has called for me — the first woman who has spoken to me.'

'How is this, my child? Have you no friends that love you? Where is your mother?'

The great brown eyes, swimming with tears, were slowly uplifted to mine, and he replied:

'My friends are all in Texas. My mother is an invalid, and fearing that the knowledge of the terrible fall would kill her, I have kept my whereabouts a profound secret. For two years I have borne my awful homesickness in silence for her sake.'

As he buried his face in his hands, and heartsick sobs burst from his trembling frame, it seemed to me I could see a panorama of the days and nights, the long weeks of homesick longing, which had dragged their weary length out over two years.

So I ventured to ask: 'How much longer have you to stay?'

'Three years,' was the reply, as the fair young head dropped lower, and the frail little hand trembled with suppressed emotion.

'Five years at your age!' I exclaimed. 'How did it happen?'

'Well,' he replied, 'it's a long story, but I'll make it short. I started out from home to try to do something for myself. Coming to Leavenworth, I found a cheap boarding-house, and one night accepted an invitation from one of the young men to go into a drinking saloon.

'For the first time in my life I drank a glass of liquor. It fired my brain. There is a confused remembrance of the quarrel. Somebody was stabbed. The bloody knife was found in my hand. I was indicted for assault with intent to kill.'

Five years for the thoughtless acceptance of a glass of liquor is surely illustrating the Scripture truth that the 'way of the transgressor is hard!'

I was holding the cold, trembling hand that had crept into mine. He earnestly tightened his grasp as, imploring, he said: 'Oh, Mrs. Molloy, I want to ask a favour of you.'

At once I expected he was going to ask me to obtain a pardon, and in an instant I measured the weight of public reproach that rests upon the victims of this legalized drink traffic.

It is all right to legalize a man to craze the brains of our boys, but not by any means to ask that the State pardon its victims.

Interpreting my thought, he said: 'I am not going to ask you to get me a pardon, but I want you to write to my mother and get a letter from her and send it to me. Don't for the world tell her where I am. Better not tell her anything about me. Just get a line from her, so I can look upon it! Oh! I am so homesick for my mother!'

The head of the boy dropped down into my lap, with a wailing sob; I laid my hand upon his head. I thought of my own boy, and for a few moments was silent, and let the outburst of sorrow have vent.

Presently I said: 'Murray, if I were your mother, and the odour of a thousand prisons was upon you, still you would be my boy. I should like to know where you were.

'Is it right to keep that mother in suspense? Do you suppose that there ever has been a day or night that she has not prayed for her wandering boy? No, Murray, I will only consent to write to your mother on condition that you will permit me to write the whole truth, just as one mother can write to another.'

After some argument his consent was finally obtained, and a letter was hastily penned and sent on its way. A week or so elapsed, when the following letter was received from Texas:

'*Dear Sister in Christ:* Your letter was this day received, and I hasten to thank you for your words of tender sympathy and for tidings of my boy—the first we have had in two years. When Murray left home we thought it would not be long. As the months rolled on the family had given him up for dead, but I felt sure God would give me back my boy.

'As I write from the couch of an invalid, my husband is in W——, nursing another son, who is lying at the gates of death with typhoid fever; I could not wait his return to write to Murray. I wrote and told him. If I could, how quickly I would go and pillow his head upon my breast, just as I did when he was a little child.

'My poor, dear boy—so generous, kind, and loving. What could he have done to deserve this punishment? You did not mention his crime, but say it was committed while under the influence of drink.

'I did not know he had ever tasted liquor. We raised six boys, and never knew one of them to be under the influence of drink. Oh! is there any place in this nation that is safe when our boys have left the home fold?

'O God! my sorrow is greater than I can bear. I cannot go to him, but, sister, I pray you to talk to him, and comfort him as you would have some mother talk to your boy were he in his place.

'Tell him that when he is released, his place in the old home-nest and his mother's heart is awaiting him.'

Then followed the loving mother's words for Murray, in addition to those written. As I wept bitter tears over the words so full of heart-break, I asked myself the question: 'How long will the nation continue to sanction the liquor traffic, covenant with death, and league with hell, to rob us of our boys?'

Lovers of God and humanity, will you not work for the passage of laws that will save the boys and the agony of mothers like this? Similar cases are among us all the time.

—*The Pacific.*

The Blind Boy.

A LITTLE boy was standing in the way;
   His head bent forward, listening
     eagerly.
I touched him on the shoulder as I said,
'Come with me, I will see you safe across
This noisy bustling street.' But he replied,
'Oh no, I thank you very much, but I
Am waiting for my father.' 'You can trust
Your father then?' I asked. As if surprised,
He answered, 'Yes, indeed I can, for he
Will take me by the hand, and gently lead
Me on; and when I feel his hand in mine
I fear no harm; I know that I am safe.'
'Why do you feel so safe?' He raised his eyes,
All sightless as they were, and with an air
Of perfect trust his features lighted up,
With smile so sweet, replied, 'Though I am
   blind
My father knows the way, for he can see,
And he is sure to guide me safely home.'
Desponding Christian, brooding o'er the way,
Which seems so dark, doth not this poor
   blind child
Teach thee a lesson? If his faith was strong
When led by earthly hand, can'st thou not trust
Thy heavenly Father? who hath promised all
Who lean on Him, to guide them safely
   through
Life's paths, however rough, to endless bliss.
What though the way be dark, and thorns
   at times
May pierce thy tender skin; we have a sure
And certain hope of everlasting bliss,
When, in His own good time, He thinks it
   right
To take us to His home,—our home in
heaven.   JOHN RYLEY ROBINSON.

The Library.

T is no new book which we have to present to our readers for the New Year, but for all that a valuable and interesting one. And it has the additional recommendation of being supplied by our own Book Room. We mention it here because we fear it has passed out of the ken of many modern readers (for we live fast in these days), and it certainly deserves a better fate. It is entitled *Strange Footsteps, or Thoughts on the Providence of God*, illustrated by incidents new and old. The book is one of joint authorship, and bears on its title-page the honoured names of the Revs. C. and H. Kendall. Eight chapters, with introduction and conclusion, make up the volume. The general and special providence of God are illustrated under such headings as Recompense, Retribution, Little Things, The Poor, Answers to Prayer, Mental Impressions and Dreams; and some very wonderful incidents are brought together, well authenticated and pleasingly told. And yet, as the authors say, they have brought to market only a single brick of the building. The aim of the writers is popular and practical. They do not claim to be exhaustive or scientific. Let us take an illustration or two, first of all, from the chapter on Retribution. We think it a pity that the authors should have pressed their case so far as to find in the 'forty years'' wandering of the children of Israel in the wilderness a punishment graduated arithmetically to the number of the days (forty) during which the spies were absent, who brought such an evil and false report of the land. Two or three instances of this kind are somewhat fanciful, but the following story by John Ashworth is vouched for by himself: 'One cold winter day, a young man was seen going from Rochdale towards Marsland workhouse with an old man on his back; the young

man's strength being exhausted, he set down the old man in a sitting posture on the milk-stone (a large stone table on which the farmers disposed of their milk). While both were resting, the old man began to weep most bitterly. 'You may cry as hard as you like,' said the young man, 'but to the workhouse you shall go if my legs can carry you; for I will not be burdened with you any longer.' 'I am not weeping because thou art taking me to the workhouse, my son, but because of my own cruelty to thy grandfather. Twenty-five years since, this very day, I was carrying him on my back to the workhouse, and rested with him on this very stone. He wept, and begged that I would let him live with me the few days he had to live, promising to rock and nurse the little children, and do anything that he could; but I mocked his sorrow, turned a deaf ear to his cries and tears, and took him to the workhouse. It is the thought of such cruel conduct to my poor old dead father that makes me weep.' The son was amazed, and said, 'Get on to my back, father, and I will take you home again, for, if that be the way, my turn will come next; it seems it is weight for weight. Get on to my back, and you shall have your old corner, and rock the little children.' The reader will, perhaps, recall in connection with this Aristotle's anecdote of the man who, when his son dragged him by his hair to the door, exclaimed—'Enough, enough, my son; I did not drag *my* father beyond this.' Of the late Rev. Moses Lupton, a curious story is told by himself in the chapter entitled 'Dreams.' By the district meeting of 1833 he was stationed for Malton, but during the sitting of the Conference, and some days before he received news of his destination, he had a dream, and next morning said to his wife, 'We shall not go to Malton.' And then he proceeded to describe very minutely to her the town, the house, and the chapel, or hall, with its vestry, to which they would go. 'In that vestry,' he said, 'there will be three men accustomed to meet that will cause us much trouble; but I shall know them as soon as I see them, and we shall ultimately overcome them and do well.' Everything happened precisely as he had dreamed.

Glasgow was the city to which they were sent. The house reached they found it precisely as Mr. Lupton had seen it in his dream. Stairs, closed bed, a box in the corner, a grass plot outside, answered precisely. The hall for preaching was as he had seen it—entrance, pulpit, circular table, gallery, door covered with green baize and brass nails, exactly as he had dreamed. The three men of his vision were all there, too. 'They soon got into loose, dissipated habits; and, intriguing for some months, caused us very much trouble. But by God's help their schemes were frustrated, and I left the station in a healthy and prosperous state.' After these samples of its contents, we need scarcely urge our readers to procure this book without delay.

Sinai not Extinct.

SOME people imagine that Sinai is extinct. Certain pulpits seem to be pitched so far from the sublime mountain that its august peak is no longer visible, and its righteous thunders against sin are no longer audible. With this class of rose-water ministers the theology of law is voted obsolete and barbarous; the world is to be tamed and sanctified entirely by a theology of · love. They preach a one-sided God—all mercy and no justice—with one-half of His glorious attributes put under eclipse.

Even sinners are not to be warned, with tears and entreaties, to flee from the wrath to come. They are to be coaxed into holiness by a magical process which makes nothing of repentance, and simply requires a 'faith' which costs no more labour than the snap of a finger. This shallow system may produce long rolls of 'converts,' but it does not produce solid, sub-soil Christians.

Sinai is not an extinct mountain in Bible theology. Not one jot of its holy law has been lowered or repealed. In one very vital sense no Christian is 'free from the law.' It would not be a 'happy condition' for him if he were so, any more than it would be a happy condition for New York or Chicago to disband their police, and to let loose their criminals into the street.

So far from being a kindness, it would ·be eventual cruelty to any man, or any community, to place them beyond the reach of the just penalties of divine law. This is especially an unfortunate time in which to preach a limber-backed theology, which has no stiffening of the word 'ought' in its fibre, and which seldom disturbs men's consciences with the retributions of sin. Society will not be regenerated with Cologne-water.

We need more of the sacred authority of law in our homes, more enforcement of law in the commonwealth, more reverence of God's law in our hearts, more law preaching in our pulpits, and more 'law-work' in the conversion of souls which are to represent Christ by keeping His commandments.

REV. T. L. CUYLER.

Christ's Words.

WHEN some beloved voice that was to you
Both sound and sweetness, faileth suddenly,
And silence against which you dare not cry,
Aches round you like a strong disease and new—
What hope? what help? what music will undo
That silence to your sense? Not friend-ship's sigh,
Nor reason's subtle count. Not melody
Of viols, nor of pipes that Faunus blew.
Not songs of poets, nor of nightingales,
Whose hearts leap upward through the cypress trees
To the clear moon; nor yet the spheric laws
Self-chanted—nor the angels' sweet All hails
Met in the smile of God. Nay, none of these.
Speak *Thou*, availing Christ—and fill this pause.

ELIZABETH BARRETT BROWNING.

"NEVER ALONE."

"I will never leave thee nor forsake thee."—Heb. xiii. 5.

Copyright.—By permission.   Words and Adaptation to Music by WILLIAM PROCTOR.

When this world's winds are blowing,
  Temptations sharp and keen,
I feel a peace in knowing
  My Saviour stands between—
Stands to shield me from danger,
  When earthly friends are gone,
For He promised never to leave me—
  Never to leave me alone.
          No, never alone, &c.

When in affliction's dark valley,
  Treading the footpath of care,
The Saviour helps me to carry
  My cross when heavy to bear;
When my feet are entangled in briars
  Of sin, to tumble me down,
My Saviour then whispers His promise—
  Never to leave me alone.
          No, never alone, &c.

Adversity's clouds may gather,
  In poverty break o'er my head,
I then return to my Saviour,
  His table is already spread ;
Affection's ring on my finger,
  My head with blessings He'll crown,
For He promised never to leave me—
  Never to leave me alone.
          No, never alone, &c.

For me He died on the mountain,
  For me they pierced His side,
For me He opened that fountain,
  The crimson blood, sin-cleansing tide ;
For me He's waiting in glory,
  "Seated upon His bright throne,"
And He promised never to leave me—
  Never to leave me alone.
          No, never alone, &c.

"NEVER ALONE."

" I will never leave thee nor forsake thee."—Heb. xiii. 5.

Copyright.—By permission.   Words and Adaptation to Music by WILLIAM PROCTOR.

KEY D.

```
1. I've |seen  the lightnings|flash-ing,      And|heard  the  thun-ders|roll ;          I've
   :s |s :- :s | l :- :t |d' :s :- | - :- :s | s :fe :s | l :s :m | r :- :- | - :- :r
2. When|this world's winds are|blow-ing,      Temp-|ta - tions sharp and|keen,          I
   :m |m :- :m | f :- :f |m :m :- | - :- :m | m :r :m | f :m :d | t,:- :- | - :- :t,
3. When|in  affliction's dark|val-ley,       Tread-|ing  the footpath of|care,         The
   :d' |d' :- :d' | d' :- :s |s :d' :- | - :- :d' | d' :- :d' | d' :- :s | s :- :- | - :- :s
4. Ad- |ver-sity's clouds may|ga-ther,       In |po-ver-ty break o'er my|head,          I
   :d |d :- :d | f :- :r |d :d :- | - :- :d | d :- :d | d :- :d | s,:- :- | - :- :s,
5. For |me  He died on the|mountain,       For |me  they pierced His|side,         For
```

```
 |felt sin's break - ers |dashing,        |Trying to  conquer my |soul.          I
 |m :- :m | f :m :f |s :d' :- | - :- :- d' |t :d' :t | l :t :l |s :- :- | - :- :s
 |feel a  peace  in|knowing          |My Saviour stands be-|tween.   Stands
 |d :- :d ' t, :- :t, | d :m :- | - :- :- m |r :r :r | d :r :d |t, :- :- | - :- :s
 |Sa - viour helps me to|carry          |My cross when heavy to|bear ;   When
 |s :- :s  s :- :s |s :s :- | - :- :- s |s :s :s | fe :fe :fe |s :- :- | - :- :s
 |then re - turn to my|Saviour,        His |table is  al-read-y|spread ;   Af-
 |d :- :d ' r :- :r |m :d :- | - :- :- d |r :r :r | r :r :r |s,:- :- | - :- :s,
 |me  He opened that|fountain,        The |crimson blood, sin-cleansing|tide ;   For
```

```
 |heard the voice of my 'Sa  -  viour |Telling me still to fight|on,        And He
 |t :- :d' ' r' :t :s  d' :- :- | s :- :- |t :t :d' | r' :t :s |d' :- :- | - :- :s . s
 |to  shield  me from  dan  -  ger,  |When earthly friends are|gone,        For He
 |f :- :f | f :f :f |m :- :- |m :- :- |f :f :f | f :f :f |m :- :- | - :- :m . m
 |my feet are entangled in       briars |Of sin, to  tum-ble me|down,        My Sa-
 |r' :- :d' ' t :r' :t  d' :- :- |d' :- :- |r' :r' :d' | t :r' :t |d' :- :- | - :- :d'. d'
 |fec-tion's ring on my |lin  -  ger,  |My head with blessings He'll|crown,        For He
 |s :- :s |s :s :s |s :- :- |s :- :- |s :s :s | s :s :s |d :- :- | - :- :d . d
 |me  He's wait-ing in |glo  -  ry,  |" Seated upon His bright|throne,"        And He
```

```
 |promised nev-er  to |leave      me—      |Never to leave me a-|lone.
 |s :- :s | l :t :d' |s :- :- | m :- :- |s :l :s | f :s :f |m :- :- | - :- :-
 |promised nev-er  to |leave      me—      |Never to leave me a-|lone.
 |m :- :m | f :f :f |m :- :- | d :- :- |m :f :m | r :m :r |d :- :- | - :- :-
 |viour then whispers His pro  -  mise—    |Never to leave me a-|lone.
 |d' :- :d' | d' :s :l |d' :- :- | s :- :- |s :s :s | s :s :s |s :- :- | - :- :-
 |promised nev-er  to |leave    me—        |Never to leave me a-|lone.
 |d :- :d | f :r :d |d :- :- | d :- :- |s :s :s | s, :s, :s, |d :- :- | - :- :-
 |promised nev-er  to |leave      me—      |Never to leave me a-|lone.
```

CHORUS.

```
 |s :- :- | s :l :s |f :- :- | - :- :- |f :- :- | f :s :f |m :- :- | - :- :m
 |m :- :- | m :f :m |r :- :- | - :- :- |r :- :- | r :m :r |d :- :- | - :- :d
 |No,    never a -|lone;       |no,    never a-|lone;   He
 |d' :- :- | d' :d' :d' |t :- :- | - :- :- |t :- :- | t :t :s |s :- :- | : :- :s
 |                                       |s :- :- | s :s :s |
 |d :- :- | d :d :d |s :- :- | - :- :- |s :- :- | s :s :s |d :- :- | : :- :d
```

```
 |s :- :s | s :l :t |d' :- :- | s :- :- |t :- :- | t :l :t |d' :- :- | - :- :-
 |m :- :m | f :f :f |s :- :- | m :- :- |f :- :- | f :f :f |m :- :- | - :- :-
 |promised never to |leave      me—      |no,    never a -|lone.
 |d' :- :d' | t :l :s |s :- :- | d' :- :- |r' :- :- | r' :d' :r' |d' :- :- | - :- :-
 |                                       |s :s :s |
 |d :- :d | r :r :r |m :- :- | d :- :- |s :- :- | s, :s, :s, |d :- :- | - :- :-
```

Current Topics.

CHEERING SIGNS.

WHEN the ice begins to crack and break up you know that a freshet is setting in, and you expect soon to see the river break loose from its barriers and leap forward with resistless force. A similar process has often been observed in human affairs. They, too, sometimes become hardened and stationary. But never for long. The men who governed France before the Revolution of 1789, attempted to dam back the stream of progress; but as far back as 1753 Lord Chesterfield saw that their methods would only result in a larger and more destructive flood. Happier signs are observable at the present day. The old barriers are undoubtedly giving way, but the liberated stream is likely to carry blessings wherever it flows. What brought about the Revolution of 1789 was the surging rage of an indignant people; but the obstacles to present progress are melting away before the genial influence of enlarged ideas and broader sympathies.

Changes are coming, however, and the year 1891 is likely to witness their rapid development. All the signs betoken it. The new light that is breaking in upon us is enabling us to see that we are not quite so perfect as we had supposed. This is an unpleasant discovery, no doubt, but it is needful to save us from stagnation. It is easy to persuade ourselves that our conduct is all that the circumstances of our life demand, but when this comfortable conclusion is reached then our progress comes to an end. A sense of deficiency is necessary to force us to effort, and this sense of deficiency is just now becoming painfully real.

These new ideas are likely to produce important changes in the religious world. ' Have you ever noticed how much of Christ's life was spent in doing kind things—in *merely* doing kind things?' asks Professor Drummond in that beautiful little book of his, *The Greatest Thing in the World.* If our salvation does not make us like Christ, what is the use of it? Christians are beginning to feel the truth of this, and hence they have less to say about the comforts of religion and more about its duties. We are beginning to feel that it is not sufficient to be assured of our personal salvation. We are, in fact, becoming doubtful of the reality of any salvation that does not prompt a man to seek the salvation of others. There is, of course, nothing new in all this. The Apostle James told the Church of his time that ' Pure religion and undefiled before God and the Father is this, to visit the fatherless and widows in their affliction, and to keep himself unspotted from the world.' But the Churches of to-day are awaking to the fact that they have too much overlooked the practical side of Christianity.

It is the prevalence of this idea that has given such a wide acceptance to General Booth's scheme for the reclamation of the 'submerged tenth' of our population. A very few years ago such a scheme would have been scouted as a Utopian dream; but now it is eagerly hailed as a means of delivering us from disgraceful failure. The condition of the lapsed masses has touched the conscience of Christendom. Their wretchedness rises before us in grim mockery of all our professions. How little has been done to remedy it, and yet ' if the alchemy of science can extract beautiful colours from coal-tar, cannot Divine alchemy enable us to evolve gladness and brightness out of the agonized hearts, and dark, dreary, loveless lives of these doomed myriads?' If not, then Christianity must be pronounced a partial failure. But General Booth not only says the change can be effected, but he offers to lead the way. In the present state of public feeling such an offer could not be refused.

Mr. Booth's plan, as the readers of this magazine will know, requires £100,000 to start it, and £30,000 a year to carry it on. This represents a capital of a million of money, but no one considers that the desired result would be dear at the price. The money is flowing in from all quarters, and by the time these words see the light the required sum will very likely have been guaranteed. Some indeed doubt the expediency of intrusting so large an undertaking to the discretion of one man, but the public is always inclined to trust a man who believes in himself. And we will all watch the result of this experiment, in the hope that God intends by this man to lead His people forward to a larger enterprise and a grander success. Let one caution be added. The glamour of this splendid scheme should not be allowed to blind our eyes to the importance of maintaining the agencies already at work.

This revived Christian activity has taken another direction. The day that has seen the rise of this new interest in the suffering poor of our large cities, has also witnessed a magnificent outburst of zeal for the cause of missions in foreign lands. In regard to this branch of Christian service, too, the churches are realising a deeper sense of responsibility. The African Continent has been partitioned amongst the nations of Europe, but these nations must not be allowed to forget their duty. It is not enough to colour the map; something must be done to civilise the people. There is reason to hope that English Christianity will rise to the occasion. The Church Missionary Society has resolved to send out during the next five years one thousand missionaries to Africa and other parts of the world. Other societies are bestirring themselves as well, and the readers of these columns are well aware of the gallant attempt of Mr. Buckenham and his party to penetrate to the heart of that great region. They have had a laborious, but, so far as is known, a remarkably successful journey, and it is believed that by this time they have reached their destination. Primitive Methodists will anxiously wait for tidings of their welfare, and all true patriots will sympathise with their work.

Present appearances portend important changes in another direction. The year 1891 is likely to be a notable one in the political history of our country. At the time I write we are in the heat of the struggle about the Parnell leadership of the Irish party. Never within recent years has the political world been so convulsed. A party that was on the high road to victory has received a sudden check, and a nation that was on the point of tasting the sweets of self-government has had the cup dashed from its lips by the misconduct of one man. How these exciting circumstances may affect the policies of parties, or the future of the Irish people, it is at present impossible to say, but one thing has already been made perfectly plain. It will be henceforth impossible for a man whose life is known to be immoral to retain the confidence of the people of this country. The old idea that a man's private character had nothing to do with his public labours is exploded for ever. The present agitation shows that the public conscience will no longer tolerate this. However much the party politician may regret this fact, there can be little doubt that it is an immense gain to the cause of morality; and whatever helps to purify the public morals, helps to promote the public progress. It is still true that 'righteousness exalteth a nation, but sin is a reproach to any people.'

These are stirring times. The ice is giving way, and the river is flowing with increasing volume. New ideas are agitating the minds of men, and new purposes are inspiring their conduct. It is such influences as these that make you feel the 'wild pulsation' of which Tennyson sings. How shall we bear a worthy part amongst them? This is a proper question for the new year. The one thing we all need is the truth of God. ' God's seed will come to God's harvest,' wrote Samuel Rutherford to Marion MacNaught, the wife of the provost of Kirkcudbright, on sending back her little daughter, who had been spending her holidays with him. The letter forms the subject of one of Dr. Alex. Whyte's week-night addresses now being published in the *British Weekly* newspaper. The preacher gives a charming picture of the life in that Kirkcudbright home, and of the effect of Mr. Rutherford's letters, not only upon the daughter Grizel, but upon the whole family.

———————

'Mother,' said Grizel one day after her marriage, 'you have been very kind to me; you have given me half the house away with me; yet there is one thing I would like you to give me, I would like the letter Mr. Rutherford sent home with me when I was a little girl.' 'Oh, do not ask that, the provost would never consent to that, it is the only thing that takes him away from his Bible. In a quiet moment you might get him to give it you, or to leave it to you in his will, but I do not think he would part with it. Do you remember the day you were engaged, Grizel? 'Oh, yes, mother, I am not likely to forget that.' 'Well, your father wakened me that night to read me a bit of Mr. Rutherford's letter: "I am in good hopes that the seed of God is in her, and God's seed will come to God's harvest."' Happy are the young men and women who enter upon life's journey with the seed of God in their hearts. This is the one thing which, amidst every outward change, is sure to yield a rich harvest of blessing.

M. P. D.

The Power of Song.

AN actress in one of the provincial towns, while passing along the street, had her attention arrested by singing in a cottage. Curiosity prompted her to look in at the open door, when she saw a few poor people sitting together, one of whom was giving out the hymn—

> 'Depth of mercy, can there be
> Mercy still reserved for me!'

which they all joined in singing. The tune was sweet and simple, but she heeded it not. The words had riveted her attention, and she stood motionless until she was invited to enter. She remained during a prayer, which was offered up by one of the little company, and which, though uncouth in language, carried with it the conviction of sincerity.

She quitted the cottage, but the words of the hymn followed her, and she resolved to procure a copy of the book containing it. The hymn-book secured, she read and re-read this hymn. Her convictions deepened, she attended the ministry of the Gospel, and sought and found that pardon which alone could give her peace. Having given her heart to God, she resolved henceforth to give her life to Him also, and for a time excused herself from attending on the stage. The manager of the theatre called upon her one morning and urged her to sustain the principal character in a new play.

This character she had sustained in other towns with admiration, but now she gave her reasons for refusing to comply with the request. At first the manager ridiculed her scruples, but this was unavailing. He then represented the loss which her refusal would be to him, and promised, if she would act on this occasion, it would be the last request of the kind he would make. Unable to resist his solicitations, she promised to appear at the theatre. The character which she assumed, required her, on her entrance, to sing a song, and as the curtain rose the orchestra began the accompaniment. She stood like one lost in thought. The music ceased, but she did not sing, and supposing she was embarrassed, the band again commenced, and they paused again for her to begin, but she opened not her lips. A third time the air was played, and then, with clasped hands and eyes suffused with tears, she sang, not the song of the play, but—

> 'Depth of mercy, can there be
> Mercy still reserved for me!
> Can my God His wrath forbear?
> Me the chief of sinners spare?'

The performance suddenly ended. Many ridiculed, though some were induced from that memorable night to consider their ways—to reflect on the power of that religion which could influence the heart and change the life of one hitherto so vain. The change in the life of the actress was as permanent as it was singular, and after some years of a consistent walk, she at length became the wife of a minister of the Gospel of Christ.—*From 'English Hymns,' by the Rev. S. W. Duffield, D.D.*

SPRINGTIME :

A Magazine for Our Young Men and Maidens.

Vol. VI. No. 2.]   FEBRUARY, 1891.   [Price Twopence.

A Bad Calculation.

By ROBERT HIND.

*Author of 'Crosby Dalton : Local Preacher
and Village Demagogue,' 'The Ruby
Pendant, &c.*

CHAPTER III.

A CLOUD ON THE HORIZON.

> 'And all day
> He fevered in the hot sun-ray
> Behind her footprints. Ne'ertheless
> His thirst was turned to bitterness,
> His love to, pain.'—ROBERT BUCHANAN.

NOT long after her father had asked Rye Harland if she expected a visitor that evening, the servant announced Mr. Arthur Brixton. The young man himself did not wait to be invited in, but followed immediately on the heels of the maid who had opened the door for him.

Mrs. Harland met him most graciously, and Rye placed a chair in an inviting place near the window. Mr. Harland shook hands with the new comer, but was less frank in his manner than might have been expected in one of his rather blunt and straightforward temper.

'I was wondering if you would not enjoy a walk, Rye. "The banks" are at their best just now, and after a day in our stuffy office I can assure you a breath of fresh air would prove delightful,' and as he spoke he stood with one hand on the back of the chair that had been offered him.

'If father and mother can spare me ?' the young lady replied.

'Oh, of course,' the mother assented at once. 'There are two hours of daylight yet, and "the banks" must be beautiful.'

'Very well then ; a minute to put on my hat and gloves, and we will sally forth,' Rye said quite briskly, for there was nothing she liked much better than a roam by the riverside on a summer evening.

When the two young people had departed, Mr. and Mrs. Harland sat for some time in silence. The lady was perfectly happy in her mind, and was just thinking what a nice comfortable world this is, and how wise and beneficent was the overruling Providence. She had been a poor girl, the daughter of a common labourer, and her husband the son of a working mason. In their childhood both of them had known the pinch of poverty, but even in those days of privation, at least as she remembered them, there had been a good deal of merriment and sunshine in their lives. And now, before they had grown old and incapable of extracting any pleasure from their life, they were in circumstances of comfort. Their only child, Rye, was as good and simple and pure as an angel; and her friend, Arthur Brixton, a nice, promising lad, who would make her a good, kind husband by-and-by, and she did most sincerely hope that the by-and-by would be a long time in coming. It was true he was only poor, but he was good and respectable, and Rye would have plenty of money for both of them

Whilst Mrs. Harland was contemplating with so much satisfaction the prospects of her only child, a different class of thoughts possessed the mind of her husband.

'I should feel better pleased if young Brixton were ten thousand miles away,' he exclaimed in a tone more emphatic than even he, plain-spoken as he generally was, was accustomed to use.

'Why, what is the matter now?' his wife inquired, opening her eyes in astonishment.

'Nothing that is new. But I don't care for the young man's ways.'

'Well, now, that is inconsistent, Stuart. All Rockingham knows that Arthur Brixton is your *protégé*. It was you who took him by the hand when he was a lad and got him into the solicitor's office, and you have sought to befriend him at every turn.'

'That is true enough, more's the pity. But I could not tell that he would be spoiled. Indeed, I won't believe I have spoiled him. It is what is in us, and not what happens to us, that makes us good or bad. I liked his father and mother—honest, hard-working people, who always were respectable though poor, and always pleasant. They have been among the best and most consistent members of our Methodist society for the last twenty years. None of the blandishments of the parsons' wives or the small ways of the curates had a chance of enticing them from our chapel. I have often wished to do something for them, and was glad of the chance when I could befriend their son.'

'And you have not repented, I hope.'

'Indeed I have. It is no use hiding the fact either.'

Poor Mrs. Harland by this time was thoroughly in earnest to know the grounds of her husband's complaints. To her it was all a mystery.

'What has Arthur done?'

'Not much. But it is easy to see he is not happy. I have noticed it for some time. And I think I know the reason. There is a spirit of discontentment in him that is no good for so young a man—a mere boy indeed he is. He cannot take any interest in what is happening about him, or in the conversation of the company among whom he finds himself. His brow is clouded as though he had met with a great disappointment. And yet he knows nothing about disappointment. It is discontentment.'

'But surely,' Mrs. Harland said, 'he has no reason to be discontented.'

'None whatever.'

'Are you not a little unjust to him, Stuart?'

'I wish with all my heart that I may be mistaken.'

'What do you think is the reason of his dissatisfaction, if indeed it is as you say?'

'I can't tell, I'm sure. Perhaps an unhealthy ambition. I suppose there are people in the world who are never pleased with the state in which Providence has placed them, and are not prepared to wait till their industry and ability have improved their circumstances. They are full of envy of people who are a little better off than themselves, and these are the people who often go wrong in life and who nearly always make those about them unhappy. I should not mind much but for this last. It makes me angry, and anxious too, when I think of Rye's future.'

'You think Rye likes him?'

'That is a certainty. You know it quite well. And yet he hardly appreciates her. She will do her best to entertain him with accounts of her rambles in the fields and woods, and he will barely hide his indifference. And yet I imagine any one with a mind worth the name would be enchanted with what she has to tell. The organist at the cathedral, Dr. Armes, will listen to her performances on the piano with positive rapture, and yet young Arthur Brixton, who has some musical talent, and therefore ought to be able to appreciate her playing, will sit and scowl almost, hardly heeding what is happening.'

'Really, Stuart,' Mrs. Harland said, 'you frighten me.'

'And I am frightened myself. If only Rye did not care for him I should close the door in his face.'

Mrs. Harland sat for some time regarding her husband. Neither was in an enviable frame of mind, and anxiety and trouble were visible on the faces of both. Stuart Harland was a shrewd man, and his wife, knowing this perfectly well, could not dismiss his words from her mind, or persuade herself that his with the young man during his visits, and recently this feeling had been growing more intense. But she had never tried to account for it, and when he was gone

THE SERVANT ANNOUNCES A VISITOR.

complaints were groundless. She had never entertained the slightest suspicion of coming evil. And yet, just now, as she reflected on Rye's relations with Arthur Brixton, it did occur to her that she had often felt irritated kindly thoughts had invariably come back. She believed now, from her husband's words, she might explain her irritation.

Still, Mrs. Harland was a sanguine woman, and, with her very prosperous life, not at all inclined to take a despondent view of the future.

'There are more dangerous qualities in a young man than what you have called in Arthur's case discontentment,' she said after a while. 'It is only ambition, and it is one of your pet principles that no youth is worth anything who is not ambitious.'

'I do not discard any of my pet principles,' Mr. Harland said in a firm tone of voice. 'And I do not ignore them either in forming my estimate of this young man. If his only fault were ambition, my mind would be easier.'

'You say he is discontented,' Mrs. Harland continued, anxious if she might to be able to see matters in such a form as would leave her mind comfortable. 'Is it any wonder? He is clever. Everybody says so. And he comes here a great deal, and sees what comforts and luxuries money will buy, and then he goes home to their own little cottage to brood over its poorness.'

'There you have hit the mark exactly, Mrs. Harland. I should say he does brood. And this is just the dangerous thing in him. Why doesn't he go home, look into the pleasant faces of his father and mother, and thank God that people who are poor can be both good and happy?'

And for once Mrs. Harland felt unable to give her husband an answer to his question.

CHAPTER IV.

TWO MINDS: A CONTRAST.

'Such happy hearts are wandering, crystal clear,
　In the great world where men and women dwell;
Earth's mighty shows they neither love nor fear,
　They are content to be, while I rebel,
Out of their own delight dispensing cheer,
　And ever softly whispering, "All is well."'
ROBERT BUCHANAN.

IN all England it would be difficult to find a more desirable place of residence than Rockingham. Its situation is the most picturesque, and its associations, historical and other, are decidedly interesting and romantic. Being a small town of something less than fifteen thousand inhabitants, it retains its unity of life, and has not, like the large unwieldy commercial towns of the country, so far lost its personal identity that the individual members of the community know nothing and care nothing about the life and conditions of all the rest of the body politic. Nothing happens in Rockingham with which everybody does not become acquainted, and whilst this state of things has its disadvantages, there are many advantages connected with it also.

Although so small, a stranger, looking down upon its red-tiled houses from one of the surrounding hills, would conclude that it is a much larger and more populous place. It is not quite so regular in outline as a star-fish—indeed, regularity is a quality not to be found in it at all—but it has at least one striking point of resemblance to that denizen of the ocean—it is all arms and legs. This want of compactness, no doubt, makes it appear more extensive than it is, one of its thoroughfares being a mile in length, an unusual phenomenon in a town of its size.

Rockingham, like Rome and some other notable cities, stands on seven hills. The most majestic of the seven is in the very heart of the city, and is crowned with two imposing piles of masonry, one of them, the cathedral, being the most massive ecclesiastical structure in the country; and the other, an old feudal castle, in splendid preservation, being at present used as one of the colleges of Rockingham University. This hill is almost an island, the river Walmer flowing round its base between precipitous and finely wooded banks in the shape of a horse-shoe.

The curving glen formed by the course of the river round this hill is known to the people of Rockingham by the simple name of 'the banks,' and here on any fine morning members of the families of the cathedral and university dignitaries, and sometimes a representative of the household of some of the county nabobs residing in the neighbourhood, may be seen taking a gentle 'constitutional.' In the evening 'the banks' present a more lively appearance, excepting on Saturdays, when business and shopping interfere, for the tradesmen and their families, with some of the workpeople, take advantage of the beautiful grounds placed at their disposal by the Dean and Chapter.

Rockingham is proud of 'the banks,' and well it may be. It is a rustic retreat in the very heart of the city. There are places where the high banks shut the outside world from the view altogether, and nothing is to be seen save the wooded curving glen, a short reach of the river, all the more picturesque because of its limitations, and the grand old Prebend's bridge. At other points it is the same, save that the towers and minarets of the cathedral appear above the fringe of the tree tops. Yet again the beauty of the scene is enhanced and its seclusion undisturbed where an opening affords a glimpse of some old gable or roof of the city.

Rye Harland and Arthur Brixton were standing on the Prebend's bridge at the time that Mr. Harland was speaking his mind to his wife about his daughter's friend and companion. What they saw might have been a picture from dreamland. Behind them was a rather long view of the river with another bridge and a few houses in the distance, but they never looked in that direction. Before them the glen curved very sharply, so that only a small part of 'the banks' and of the river could be seen. But it was the loveliest bit of all. The water, dark brown in colour, was very still and noiseless. But it was almost crowded with pleasure-boats and canoes. The occupants of the boats for the most part wore cardinal colours, the brightest reds and blues, with here and there a lady in white. On the walks on either bank the people were quite as gaily attired ; and as they wandered leisurely to and fro, and the boats sailed in and out of sight, now in full view, and now lost behind the deep green of the foliage, they gave the finishing touch to a picture of exquisite beauty.

'What a fairy scene!' Rye exclaimed, when the two had been gazing for some time in silence.

Arthur was in no hurry to reply, and when his answer was spoken it had in it none of the ardour indicated by the tone of his companion.

'Yes, it is beautiful. "The Banks" are known to all the county to be charming,' he said, in a slow and listless manner.

Rye felt disappointed, as recently had often happened on account of her companion's mood. But she was patient and gentle, and although she felt she must try to rouse Arthur out of his all too reflective mental attitude, her reproof was of the mildest possible description.

'I was not thinking about what might be the opinion of the county, or even of our neighbours in the city. I felt intoxicated with pleasure by what is here—by what my own eyes behold, Arthur. Don't you?' she inquired.

Thus interrogated, the young man felt himself compelled to bring his mind to bear on his immediate surroundings.

'You will pardon me, Rye' (they had always addressed each other by their Christian names), 'but I am afraid I hardly saw this fine picture which has so much enraptured you.'

'That is strange, Arthur, and almost unpardonable. I have been here often, but I never saw "the banks" in so glorious a mood as they are this evening. It must be the light I think, for the effect of all these prettily dressed girls upon my eyes cannot be because they are really in finer robes than usual. I have read of Venice, and of scenes on Italian rivers, but they could not be more exquisite than this. These people in the boats, when I leave my imagination to have full play, appear to be something else than human beings. It makes me think of some lines in the greatest work of my favourite author. Shall I repeat them?'

'Do ; for you know I like your selections, even though I do not always show a proper interest in everything.'

'You won't call me a pedant, then ?'

'Certainly not.'

'Well, here they are—

"As a bright-kaleidoscope
Is shaken in the hand, and with no will
Trembles, dissolves, in ever-wondrous change,
The scenes upon that mighty stage did fade,
While the deep, voices of the unseen choir
Were rising, falling, all within my dream."

Tell me, Arthur, if it is not an apt description of what is now happening under your very eyes ?'

Even as she spoke, a brass band, hid in some bower at a distance, sent sweet strains of music on the air, and she, quick to speak before he answered her, added—

'There, even, are the "deep voices of the unseen choir."'

'A very noble description,' the young man was fain to confess, 'and how clever you are to think of the lines in this connection.'

Rye's brow clouded, and something of the softness died out of her eyes as she said,

'Why will you speak to me like that ?'

'I apologize most humbly,' Arthur said, evidently sorry for his fault.

The girl at once forgot her injury and turned again to the picture she had been admiring. The glen by this time was filled with a red glow, for though it was still early in July, [the hour was late and the sun was westering. She was greedily drinking in all the beauty her eyes beheld. And no patch of the picture was overlooked, no change of effect was unnoticed. The music that reached her ears was to her like the strains of some heavenly choir, and the spot on which she stood a veritable garden of Eden.

Other thoughts coursed through the mind of the young man. He was not quite out of his teens, and yet he could hardly remember ever once experiencing an hour of true repose and satisfaction. His mental movement was not like the quiet, steady flow of the great river, above which he and his companion were standing, but resembled rather the leaping, dashing fountain, ever seeking for unattainable altitudes, and ever feeling itself falling below its desires and expectations.

Only those who knew Arthur Brixton intimately, and who at the same time could see beneath the surface of his behaviour, had the least idea of the mental disturbance from which he suffered. For he was a young man of great self-control and reserve. To many, this appeared at first to be an innate gentlemanliness, but the observant were not long in wondering whether he might not ultimately develop into a misanthrope.

This tendency had certainly not gone quite

so far yet, and the rather gloomy expression of his countenance gave to the otherwise handsome youth a decidedly interesting aspect. For he was handsome, after a manner wholly different from Rye Harland. He had none of her ruddy glow of complexion or massiveness of frame. But he was exceedingly well-knit, and had 'endurance' almost written on every curve of his body. His features were finely shaped, his hair and eyes very dark, indeed, almost black, and his mouth firm, as of one who would not be easily turned aside from his purpose.

A critic might have said his mouth and jaws indicated obstinacy, and that the flash of his black eyes and the occasional cloud that crossed his face were ominous; but none would have denied to Arthur Brixton the claim to be regarded as more than ordinarily handsome. And his friends too might have argued that but for his obstinacy he would never have reached his present position, and that the cloud on his face was simply the result of the fierce battle in which he had been engaged to raise himself somewhat in the social scale.

He had succeeded, and to-day, despite long hours at the desk, was something of a scholar. But he still lived with his father and mother, honest, hard-working people, in a three-roomed cottage : and every day fretted and fumed because he was not equal to the most aristocratic of the Rockingham families. To be ignored by them was to him a personal insult, and yet when by some accident any of them were called to recognize him, he felt their patronizing air to be more stinging than absolute neglect would have been.

Living in the company of thoughts like these, Arthur Brixton could not possibly be happy.

'I am so thankful that I was born in Rockingham, and not in any other place in all the world,' Rye remarked after some little time.

'But every place has its own advantages, and there are drawbacks even to life in your favourite city,' he replied.

'But that does not matter so long as one is entirely unconscious of the drawbacks, does it ?'

' Very likely not. But it matters a great deal if one happens to be keenly alive to them.'

Rye opened her eyes wide and looked at him steadily as she inquired—

' And are you in that state of mind ? '

' I am afraid I must say " Yes." '

' Why ? '

' I scarcely know. It must be my constitution, I suppose ! '

' And pray under what special disadvantages do you labour ? I remember when first you began to be a visitor at " The Mount," you were pleased with mere trifles. Now you don't seem to be with us exactly, even when you come. You are always in a brown study. Are you pondering over your disadvantages ? You must be, and I should really like to know what they are.'

There was kindness in her voice as well as the grand ring of sincerity and earnestness. It was the tone of an honest heart, anxious if possible to render help where it might be needed.

' I could not tell you exactly, Rye. But although I am often displeased with myself, especially after I have been at " The Mount," and been shown so much kindness by you all, I chafe because we are poor and belonging to the humbler orders. I dream about the bishop and the canons of the cathedral, about the people who live in the old houses where their ancestors have lived for generations, and in the end get quite discontented with my lot. And then I resolve I will go away, try to become a millionaire, and come back to look down on all these fine people of Rockingham.'

' Oh, Arthur ! ' .

' Do you think me very wicked ? '

' I don't know ; but I am quite sorry to hear about this.'

' Why ? '

' It is not, it cannot be right to think such things. I am sorry your father is not rich, although he appears happy. But I think if I were very poor, I should not feel as you do. I should have father and mother, and with them would be more than content, and Rockingham would be the same delightful spot this lovely July evening, and the fairy picture on the river would be just as full of poetry to me.'

' You think so, doubtless. But you have never been poor like me.'

She took his hand, looked into his face, and with her great eyes full of sympathetic feeling said—

' Promise me, Arthur, that you will not brood over these things any more.'

The tone, the look, the whole attitude were irresistible, and although he was not quite sure he would succeed in the attempt, he said quite readily, for he was by this time in a happier mood—

' I will try to do as you ask.'

(*To be continued.*)

The Boyhood of Great Men.

THE RIGHT HONOURABLE WILLIAM E. GLADSTONE.

N the 29th December, 1890, Mr. Gladstone attained the ripe age of eighty-one years, so that in turning our attention to his boyhood we have to make two ends meet.

The position Mr. Gladstone holds is absolutely unique. He has attained the highest position to which any subject in these realms can aspire in the State. Three times he has been Prime Minister, and in attaining that position he has occupied nearly all the subordinate offices in the Government. As a financier he has not had his superior, scarcely his equal, during the present century ; and he stands to-day the greatest constitutional statesman of the age.

Mr. Gladstone is remarkable as an authority in every department of literature, while his Biblical studies have led him to publish a book on ' the impregnable rock of Holy Scripture ' within the last few weeks.

For all his eighty-one years he is remarkable for his youthful vivacity. Professor Stuart, a few days ago, said, ' We all get old in time, but where the pins of Mr. Gladstone's tabernacle are giving way, I have not yet been able to find out.'

The last public appearance he made was on the last anniversary of his birthday, at the unveiling of a fountain erected by the inhabitants of Hawarden village to commemorate the golden wedding of Mr. and Mrs. Gladstone. Thousands had come from all parts of the surrounding country, and there, with bared head, Mr. Gladstone ended one of his finest speeches with these noble words : ' There is something anomalous almost in offering to a person who has now touched the age of eighty-one the expression of a hope that he may have *many* happy returns of the day. What I do hope and trust, and what I am sure your prayers will support me in is, that whether these returns be very few, or not quite so few, for *many* they cannot be, they may find me engaged in my best efforts, however feeble, with the performance of duty.'

When called upon to look at such a man as this, at such an age and in such a position, his very exaltation might induce some to think that he had come through an experience different from that of ordinary mortals. But here the fact remains, this great man was once a child, a boy, and had to pass through the usual experience of human nature. It is quite true he was favoured in many respects in his start in life. He had behind him an ancestry he could trace back for generations, and of which he was justly proud. ' If Scotland is not ashamed of her sons,' he said, on one occasion, ' her sons are not ashamed of Scotland ; and the memory of the parents to whom I owe my being combines, with various other considerations, to make me glad and thankful to remember that the blood that runs in my veins is exclusively Scotch. His father, Sir John Gladstone, was a truly remarkable man, and his mother ' a lady of very great accomplishments, of fascinating manners, of commanding presence, and high intellect ; one to grace any home, and endear any heart.' Mr. Gladstone, their fourth son, was born on December 29, 1809, at Liverpool. From his birth he was surrounded by wealth and all the advantages that wealth could command. Amongst other advantages was that of a private tutor. The Rev. William Rawson, afterwards the first vicar of Seaforth, was his earliest preceptor, and a man of solid acquirements and upright character. For him Mr. Gladstone always had the most profound respect, and visited him on his death-bed.[*] Another tutor was Rev. Mr. Jones (afterwards Archdeacon Jones). It is said, in later years, that the Venerable Archdeacon found a perpetual theme for merriment in the reflection that the great financier and Chancellor of the Exchequer was hopelessly incompetent to master the early rules of arithmetic.[†] At the early age of three years Mr. Gladstone says he well remembers being carried on the back of a friend to see the famous election stir at Liverpool in 1812, when Canning contested that constituency in the Tory interest, and several lives were lost in the riot. From this time the family became Tory in its politics, and Canning exerted a most powerful influence upon every member of it. As soon as the boy could understand anything about public men and events Canning began to exercise that strange fascination of the mind of William Ewart Gladstone which has never wholly passed away. Mr. Gladstone, senior, discovered, at an early date, the acute and powerful intellect he had to deal with in his fourth son ; and like a wise father began to train and direct it in the best possible way. At the age of twelve years the father ' would discuss with him the public questions of the day, teaching him to think for himself, and to examine well the basis of opinions which he might have formed upon political and other subjects.'

Sir F. H. Doyle says : ' Shortly after taking my degree I spent some time with Mr. Gladstone at his father's house in Kincardineshire, a large, comfortable house, in a picturesque part of the country. While there I was struck with the remarkable acuteness and great natural power of Mr. Gladstone, the father. Under his influence, apparently, nothing was ever taken for granted between him and his sons. A succession of arguments on great topics and small topics alike, arguments conducted with perfect good humour, but also with the most implacable logic, formed

---

[*] See Smith's ' Life of Gladstone ' (Cassell).
[†] ' Anecdotes of Gladstone ' (P.M. Book Room).

the staple of the family conversation. Hence it is easy to see from what foundations Mr. Gladstone's skill as a debater has been built up.' At a very early age he put aside the juvenile literature and pursuits which please so many boys, and engaged in the pursuit of literature and learning which at once surprised and delighted all who came into contact with him. He was precocious, but it was not the precocity of genius, which flamed up and burned itself out for lack of fuel, neither did it degenerate into mediocrity as manhood approached. On the contrary, behind it, and accounting for it, there were not only mental power and capacity, but physical stamina and vital force.

In September, 1821, Mr. Gladstone was sent to Eton, one of the most famous and aristocratic schools in the kingdom, to follow up the studies which should fit him for his life work. And perhaps this was the best place to send a boy of his peculiar capabilities. Certainly he never needed pressure to compel him to learn, and pressure was not one of the faults at Eton. The only subjects taught were the Greek and Latin languages, the Greek Testament, Tomline on the Thirty-Nine Articles, and a little ancient and modern geography. The hours of tuition were not long. They had every week a whole holiday and a half, with a light day on Saturdays. On each of the other three days there were four school times, three of which lasted three-quarters of an hour each, and the fourth a quarter of an hour, making in all about eleven hours a week. Fagging and flogging were the most objectionable features; the former enabled the big boys to make slaves of the little ones, and the latter was sometimes carried out in the most brutal manner—even upon young men of twenty. Moral discipline there was hardly any, nor could there be much amongst from 500 to 600 pupils. But Eton was a splendid place for the culture of the physical frame, and for the introduction it gave to the highest circles of society. Mr. Gladstone, however, joined a band of distinguished boys, few in number, who applied themselves to learning out of school hours, and distinguished themselves for the depth

and solidity of their attainments. Towards the close of his Eton days in 1827, Mr. Gladstone was mainly instrumental in launching the *Eton Miscellany.* Two volumes appeared, to the first of which he contributed thirteen articles, and even more to the last. In fact, his devotion to literature at this time must have left him little time for the ordinary sports of Eton boys. At seventeen these remarkable words were penned by him : 'At present it is hope that buoys me up ; for more substantial support I must depend upon my own exertions, well knowing that in this land of literature merit never wants its reward. That such merit is mine I dare not presume to think ; but still there is something within me that bids me hope that I may be able to glide prosperously down the stream of public estimation."

Leaving Eton at the age of eighteen, Mr. Gladstone became the private pupil of Dr. Turner, afterwards Bishop of Calcutta, and two years later he went to Christ Church, Oxford, the most aristocratic of the colleges. Here he had a splendid choice of society, and found the pursuits and habits of study congenial to his taste. He found the Oxford University laid greater stress upon the knowledge of the Bible and of the Evidences of Christianity than upon classical literature, while some proficiency was required in mathematics and the science of reasoning. It was here Mr. Gladstone meditated seriously upon the vital matter of religion, and threw in his lot with High Churchmen. His debating powers were strengthened and matured by the debating society called the 'Oxford Union,' of which he was by turn the secretary and the president. He did not escape the atmosphere of Oxford without some injury. 'I trace,' he said in 1878, 'in the education of Oxford of my own time, one great defect. Perhaps it was my own fault ; but I must say that I did not learn when at Oxford that which I have learned since, the imperishable and the inestimable principles of human liberty.' In 1831 he went up for his examination, and completed his academical education by attaining the highest honours of the University, graduating double first class.

After spending some time in foreign travel

he entered Parliament in 1832 as member for Newark, and thus embarked upon that career of success and power so well known to all English-speaking people, during which he has conferred the most substantial blessings upon his people, and remains to-day the greatest constitutional statesman of the age.

JOHN GAIR.

Anecdotes About Hymns.

From the German.

No. I.—THE JEW, AND THE HYMN SUNG IN THE STORM.

ABOUT a hundred and sixty years ago there was living in Eastern Germany, apparently in the part then belonging to Poland, a Jewish family, of which the elder son had gone to settle in the western part of the country, not far from the banks of the Rhine. One day, the news was brought to the parents, who were both of them bigoted Jews, that this elder son, their hope and stay, was about to renounce the religion of his forefathers, and to be baptized as a Christian.

One needs to know with what horror an orthodox Jew views such a proceeding on the part of a member of his family to understand the dire pang which these tidings brought to the hearts of the father and mother. Whenever a member of such a family renounces the law of Moses, he is mourned over in sackcloth and ashes as if he were dead. So was it in this case. At once they despatched their younger son to the banks of the Rhine, that he might tell his brother of the sorrow their parents were feeling about him, and by exhortations, entreaties, and threats of his father's curse coming upon him, might induce him to renounce what they considered the deadly error of the religion of Christ. The son willingly undertook the commission, and set out on his long journey, for he was as bigoted as his parents. But on the way (he was travelling on foot) he arrived at a village in Brunswick, and was there overtaken by a storm. There was nothing to be done but for him to take refuge in the village inn, in the public room of which he found a number of persons assembled, driven there like himself by stress of weather. But what was his surprise to see that they had all hymn-books in their hands, and to hear them singing out of them, as was customary in Germany at that period, during a tempest. But what struck him most was the fervour and devotion with which they sang, and the whole scene made the greatest impression upon the mind of the young Jew.

'How?' he thought within himself. 'Are these then the Christians, of whose ungodliness and idolatry I have heard so much? From whence then comes this fervent devotion, which is evidently quite sincere? Surely those who sing and pray thus, and even in such a place as an inn, cannot be heathen or ungodly men. Their piety, then, must have some close connection with Christianity.'

The impression thus made upon his mind was no transitory one. It followed him on his journey—that journey which he was taking on purpose to draw his brother away from the Christians. Himself wavering in his mind between Judaism and Christianity, he was all the more susceptible to the entreaties of his brother to join with him in confessing Jesus Christ to be the true Messiah. He studied the subject earnestly and deeply, and received with his brother the holy ordinance of baptism.

A certain indescribable feeling of affection towards the place where his first favourable impressions of the Christian religion had been received, seems to have led him to settle in the part of Germany where he had been driven by the storm to the village inn. He ultimately determined upon studying theology, became a pastor, and was finally made superintendent (a sort of bishop in the German Lutheran churches) at Tchöningen, on the Elm. His descendants, a much respected family of the name of Pauli, are still to be met with in the Duchy of Brunswick.

A modern poet has said :—

'Where thou hear'st singing, there rest without fear,
From the lips of the evil no songs we hear.'

The Heirs of All the Ages.

PAPERS ON THE HERITAGE AND RESPONSIBILITIES OF OUR YOUNG PEOPLE.

THE title at the head of these papers may bulk out as large, especially before the minds of young men and maidens. So far-reaching is its stretch and so full its range, that some may regard it as overshadowing rather than attractive. And certainly, within our limited space, we cannot be expected to deal in any detailed manner with a subject so extensive. However, let us remember that large ideals help to make large minds, and it is better that a subject be suggestive than exhaustive. And in the realities of life we go to big things, like the mountains, the seashore, and the great city, not that we may fathom or exhaust them by our explorations, but because we feel we need them. We need to get the fresh air, the invigoration, or the freedom and enlargement of life which they can give us. May we not approach a big subject of thought with similar feelings? And can we approach such a subject with a better purpose than to come back from it with the mind somehow freshened, enlarged, elevated, quickened to feel, and strengthened to face life's duties and demands? And if we aim to be true men and women—men and women of such a sort, as will in some measure fulfil the hopes of our dearest friends, of the Church, and, let us add, the hope of Jesus Christ Himself, then we cannot make up our minds too soon to the fact that life's real enjoyments cannot be divorced from its burdens, its battle and service—that joys come most to the man who does not seek them; that he who serves most, lives most; and the largest and holiest

life is that which lives least in itself and most in God and men.

With regard to those vast and silent ages which lie behind us, filled with the " congregation of the dead," and the results of whose lives descend to us as an unspeakable heritage, there are two things which bring home to us our obligation here, which show us our duty to the past on the one hand, and our responsibility to the future on the other. These two things are the *unity* of mankind, and their *development* and *progress* in the past, with all the service which these involve. In the great material universe around us, within which science finds its province of research, nothing has been made clearer to the present generation than the oneness and unity which run through the whole. So closely related, and so inter-dependent is one sphere on another, and one part to the whole, that things, apparently the opposite of each other, cannot exist without each other. The snowflakes, for instance, which fill the wintry air, and lock the activities of the earth in glistening ice, and which so rapidly dissolve with warmth, could not come to us without the heat of the sun. And that exhaustless life-force, which grows, and builds up so profusely vegetable and animal forms drawing the chemical elements which compose them out of the atmosphere and out of the ground, is the very force which dissolves again by the process of decay the identical forms it has created. It used to be thought that when plants and animals died their compound forms fell to pieces of themselves, under the action of the air to which they were exposed. But this idea is now proved to be entirely erroneous. If left to the action of non-living forces alone, dead matter would never dissolve, but would remain entire, like forms we have read of being preserved by the cold in glacial or polar ice. And as a consequence, the accumulation of waste material would soon become a great inconvenience to men, and by-and-by it would ' choke up the whole living world.' Then how is such waste removed? Well, as life built it up, so life dissolves it again into its original gases and chemical elements. Fire will do it, but the natural scavengers of the earth arc living things. What is known as putrefaction and decay, is the work of growing fungi, and myriads of active forms called bacteria—bacteria, so extremely minute that only the highest powers of the microscope can make them observable. The big and little therefore, about and beyond us everywhere, have relations and binding bonds. Nothing is isolated, nothing stands alone in God's creation. Individuality there is plenty, but independence none. Just as the earth is dependent upon the distant sun, so the mightiest forest pine is dependent upon the tiny moss which touches with soft beauty the surface of the savage rock, for that moss has helped to make the soil in which the pine grows. This great unity now, in nature—this something, joining apparently opposite things together, making them serve one another and welding a oneness everywhere, reflects itself in human nature. It is possible it may be the other way, that the unity of man reflects itself in nature, instead of the unity of nature reflecting itself in man. However, whichever way is the true one, the fact is there, that just as there is oneness in nature, so is mankind one upon the earth. And what the Bible asserts on this question—that God has 'made of one every nation of men for to dwell on all the face of the earth,' man's knowledge of man confirms. The basis of human oneness God has laid like a foundation, deep and permanent in man's constitution, but it can only be consummated in his spiritual character. And as the latter work is individual, or, as it depends upon the true enlightenment of the mind, the conquest of, and right use of the personal will and heart, obedience to God, and the right appreciation of our duties to our fellows—the responsibility of carrying out and completing what is evidently God's idea of the unity and brotherhood of our race, lies in the hands of men themselves. Every young man and woman then, with life before them, shares that responsibility in part. We are drops in the stream, however humble, individuals in the marching throng. We are linked to the men of the past by our very nature, that nature God has given us, and therein lies the ground of claim upon us by those who shall follow us. The unity of man-

kind impressed itself deeply upon the owner of Tennyson's 'Locksley Hall,' when he said :—

'Here about the beach I wander'd, nourishing a youth sublime,
With the fairy tales of science, and the long results of time ;
When the centuries behind me like a fruitful land reposed ;
When I clung to all the present for the promise that it closed ;
When I dipt into the future far as human eye could see ;
Saw the vision of the world, and all the wonder that would be.'

Allied with, and running concurrent with the unity of mankind, is that other fact of the development or outgrowth and progress of the race. The former of these facts must necessarily influence the latter. For as men draw closer together, or in other words, as they come to realize more the true oneness among them, their feelings towards each other must grow kinder, their help towards each other readier, and their general progress, as a consequence, more rapid. This has been so, for men never understood each other better than they do now, and the benefits of civilization were never greater or more wide-spread. 'Man,' says Emmerson, 'is the noble endogenous plant which grows like the palm from within, outward.' So he has grown individually and socially from the low condition in which the evidences of the long past ages of the earth reveal him. Man's history is now proved from the earth itself to reach far further back than six thousand years. Whether he has been evolved from some lower animal form or not is a matter entirely distinct from his antiquity. And, as the account of his creation in the book of Genesis fixes no time when the wondrous event took place, there is nothing there inconsistent with a longer human existence upon the earth than the 'unreliable' and usually received 'chronologies.' Human remains have been found in conjunction with those of extinct animals. These, with many evidences of his rude handiwork, his habits of life, as well as of his distribution over wide areas, point not only to man's great antiquity, but also go to show that he has risen up to his present high position of culture and civilization from a state of barbarism. In gravel accumulations and rocky caves, estimated to date back to what is called the Glacial or Great Ice age, many of the implements which man used have been found, and they are all of the simplest kind, made first of flint, stone, bone, or other unmanufactured material. In after ages they appear made of bronze and then of iron. Relics of his habitations and dwelling-places, as well as the structure of human languages, furnish proofs that man existed long before the historic period. It would be very interesting to enter into the condition of mankind, as shown by the remains of the race, which have been found at various times, and to trace his progress onward, as we might be able; but this is what we cannot attempt here; we can only suggest it—as we may do some other matters—as a subject for separate inquiry. But the fact of man's outgrowth and progress from such distant ages is a mighty thing, and has issued in wondrous results in modern times. Man ancient and man modern would show a mighty contrast if we could place them side by side. The one would be a savage, dressed in skins, perhaps a cannibal, or living on what he could catch, rather than what he could cultivate—a cave dweller, or erecting his hut upon piles over the waters of a lake to protect himself from his enemies. The other is a man highly developed and cultured, with a delicacy of sentiment, as in practical power, religion, liberty, sense of honour, and taste. He lives surrounded by the comforts and productions of his enlarged capacity of intellect and mechanical skill. He has discovered truths, and applied knowledge to the arts and industries of life. More or less he has conquered the forces of nature and turned them to serve him in a thousand ways. 'He hitches his wagon to a star,' and his messages to the lightning. He has about him a stored wealth of thought, beauty, skill, and treasure. And under a beneficent Providence, he possesses a religion which comforts him here in life's sorrows, and gives him hope of immortality in death.

All this and more is man's civilization to-day. And civilization, while it may differ among different peoples, as between the Chinese and Englishmen, yet is only the measure of man's progress under the Divine blessing.

Now, these two chains of connection with the past, these two lines of facts reaching back to the beginning of men, and then down to us, converging upon us, centreing in us, like two roads coming out of distant and unknown lands and converging upon the city; these two bonds—our unity with men, and the service they in the past have rendered us—create for us both obligation and responsibility. Our oneness with men gives us our duty, and the blessing of their service and sacrifice which we enjoy and share weights us with responsibility. The former constitutes our heirship, the latter our inheritance. And we who live in the present day have from our ancestors a splendid inheritance indeed. The more prominent features of this heritage it will be our purpose in succeeding papers to point out, and then to say something about the use we should endeavour to make of it. F. L. S.

The Rationalistic Chicken.
THE FIRST PROBLEM.

The Soliloquy of a Rationalistic Chicken.

Most strange!
   Most queer,—although most excellent a change!
   Shades of the prison house, ye disappear!
My fettered thoughts have won a wider range,
   And, like my legs, are free;
No longer huddled up so pitiably:
Free now to pry and probe, to peep and peer,
   And make the mysteries out.
Shall a free-thinking chicken live in doubt?
For now in doubt undoubtedly I am:
   This problem's very heavy on my mind,
And I'm not one to either shirk or sham:
   I won't be blinded, and I won't be blind.

   Now, let me see:
First, I would know how did I get in *there?*
   Then, where was I of yore?
Besides, why didn't I get out before?

Dear me !
Here are three puzzles (out of plenty more),
Enough to give me pip upon the brain !
    But let me think again.
How do I know I ever *was* inside ?

Now I reflect, it is, I do maintain,
Less than my reason, and beneath my pride,
    To think that I could dwell
In such a paltry, miserable cell
    As that old shell.
Of course I couldn't ! How could *I* have
    lain,
Body and beak and feathers, legs and
    wings,
And my deep heart's sublime imaginings,
    In there ?

I meet the notion with profound disdain ;
It's quite incredible ; since I declare
(And I'm a chicken that you can't deceive),
What I can't understand I won't believe.

Where *did* I come from, then ? Ah ! where,
    indeed ?
This is a riddle monstrous hard to read.
    I have it ! Why, of course,
All things are moulded by some plastic
    force
Out of some atoms somewhere up in space,
Fortuitously concurrent anyhow :—
    There, now !
That's plain as is the beak upon my face.

    What's that I hear ?
My mother cackling at me ! Just her way,
So prejudiced and ignorant, *I* say ;
So far behind the wisdom of the day.

    What's old I can't revere.
Hark at her : ' You're a silly chick, my
    dear ;
    That's quite as plain, alack !
As is the piece of shell upon your back ! '
How bigoted ! Upon my back, indeed !
    I don't believe it's there.
For I can't *see* it ; and I do declare,
    For all her fond deceivin',
What I can't see I never will believe in !
      REV. S. J. STONE, M. A.

Washington.

Our last paper was devoted to an account of the two Houses of Legislature which meet in the Capitol of Washington. In the present sketch we intend to give a description of the President's house, together with some of the remaining objects of interest in this beautiful city.

The residence of the President of the United States is called the White House—next in importance to the Capitol. It is situated about a mile and a-half from the latter building, at the western extremity of Pennsylvania Avenue. It is of about the size and character of many of the country seats of our middle-class gentry, such as baronets, squires, and wealthy commoners, who live in a comfortable but unostentatious style. It is a plain Ionic freestone edifice, painted white. The front of it measures 176 feet, and the breadth 86 feet. It has a good portico, a sweeping carriage drive up to the front, and a small lawn railed in before it ; while behind it there is a semi-circular projection and portico which look out on the River Potomac and the opposite shore of Virginia. Its erection was commenced in 1818, but it was not finished till 1829. Standing in its own grounds, adorned with fountains and shrubbery, it presents a very pleasing appearance. The rooms connected with it vary in size. Those which are used for receptions and for the President's personal use are comparatively small, and simple in decoration. The largest apartment in the whole building is that called the East Room, of which a view is given in the accompanying illustrations. It is 80 feet in length, 40 feet in breadth, and 22 feet in height, and as it is used for the general promenade of visitors on public occasions, it is not at all too spacious for the purpose.

The receptions of the American Presidents differ considerably from those which are given by Her Majesty Queen Victoria. The pomps and vanities, the empty forms and meaningless ceremonies of the latter are entirely absent from the former. In this, as in some other respects, the Americans can show us a more excellent way. The President receives his visitors standing in the centre of a small oval room, the entrance to which is directly in front of the hall on the ground floor. The introductions are made by the State marshal, who announces the names of the parties, and each person, after shaking hands with the President, and exchanging a few words of courtesy, passes into the adjoining rooms, to make way for others. There being no distinctions in rank, there are, of course, no vexed questions of precedence to disturb and irritate the company. Each one acts as though he feels himself to be on a perfect footing of equality with among the whole party, whether in the small 'receiving' room around the person of the president, or in the larger room of promenade, where as many as five hundred persons sometimes may be seen walking in groups, or in the small adjoining rooms to which parties retire for rest and conversation, nothing of a supercilious character is seen. The humbler classes —for of these there are some present at each reception, as the only qualification is that of being a citizen of the United States,—comport themselves with the greatest propriety, and though the pressure is sometimes excessive, for there are sometimes nearly 3,000 persons present in the different apartments, yet the

Tʜᴇ Wʜɪᴛᴇ Hᴏᴜsᴇ.

every other person, and if claims of preference are ever thought of at all, they are tested only by the standard of personal service or personal merit. And who shall say that that is not the true test of social greatness? As the world grows wiser less and less respect will be paid to rank, and place, and circumstance, and greater consideration given to the question of what the man is in himself. The words of the great poet, to whom Scotland and the world at large owe so much, will then find unqualified acceptance,—

> ' The rank is but the guinea stamp,
> The man's the gowd and a' that.'

The consequence is that at these receptions greatest harmony and goodwill characterize the proceedings.

The public offices of the Government are situated in the immediate neighbourhood of the White House. They include the Department of State, War Offices, Treasury, and similar establishments. They are spacious, neat, and well-built edifices, suitably adapted to their respective uses, but without anything superfluous about them. As each building occupies the centre of an open piece of ground with a lawn in front railed off on all sides, they have a commanding appearance from the ample space and area by which they are surrounded. In the State Department there are many valuable objects carefully preserved. One of these, which is contained in a glass case with folding doors, is the original Declaration of Independence, with all the autograph signatures; and above it is the first commission of General Washington as Commander-in-Chief of the American forces, signed by John Hancock. In the same room are the original treaties bearing the autograph signatures of George III. and George IV. of England; Louis XIV. and Napoleon of France; Prince Charles John of Sweden, Ferdinand of Spain, Alexander of Russia, and one in Arabic of the Sultan of Turkey. There is also a litho-

Indian chiefs who have visited Washington at the head of deputations. This building, which is employed by the State, War, and Navy Departments, is a massive granite structure, with a splendid roof. It is 567 feet long, 467 broad, and 128 high, and cost £2,000,000.

The Treasury building is mainly built of granite, in the Ionic style, and measures 468 feet by 264, with a court in the interior. It contains 500 rooms, and cost £1,200,000. The Interior Department building is situated on F. Street North, about midway between the Capitol and the Treasury. It occupies two squares of the city, being 453 feet by

WHITE HOUSE—SOUTH FRONT.

graphic facsimile of the Magna Charta of King John, taken from the original in the British Museum. Here are also kept the various presents made by foreign courts and potentates to American Ministers of State or other public officers, who are not allowed to retain them as personal gifts, so as to prevent bribery and corruption, but are bound to forward them to the Department of State, where they are preserved as national property. Among these are Damascus-blade swords, cashmere shawls, a diamond snuff-box, and a host of other valuable things. In the War Department there is a large collection of the portraits of

331, with an inner court. It is simple in its proportion, and in the Doric style. It is built in part of freestone, in part of marble, while the interior is of granite. It cost £540,000. Other important public buildings are the Agricultural Department, situated on beautiful grounds ten acres in extent; the Naval Observatory, with an electric time-signal and great equatorial telescope, the object glass, one of the largest in the world, being twenty-six inches; and the Army Medical Museum, containing valuable archives and a library of 40,000 volumes.

There are numerous scholastic and benevolent institutions, one of the chief of which is the Smithsonian Institute. It derives its name from its founder, and was established for the 'increase and diffusion of knowledge among men.' It was built in 1846, out of funds left for the purpose by James Lewis Macie Smithson, a distinguished English chemist, a natural son of the third Duke of Northumberland. The institution derived altogether about laneous character. It has established a system of exchanges of publications with 2,200 foreign scientific societies, and its library of 75,000 volumes is now amalmagated with the Congress Library. The building is in the Romanesque style of architecture, and is one of the finest in the United States. It was partially destroyed by fire in 1865, but has been entirely restored. Besides a lecture-hall,

EAST ROOM, WHITE HOUSE.

£103,275 from his bequest. By its constitution, the President of the United States is *ex officio* the presiding officer, and it is governed by a board of thirteen regents under him. It is in no sense a university or teaching institution, but confines itself to the encouragement of scientific research and the diffusion of its results. Besides an annual report, it has published several volumes of ' Contributions to Knowledge,' together with others of a miscellaneous character.

theatre, &c., it contains several scientific collections, among them the National Museum.

There are numerous churches in Washington, but they are inferior in architecture to the hotels and boarding-houses which are scattered throughout the city.

The water supply of the town comes from the Potomac. It is taken out of the river at the head of a cataract known as Great Falls, about sixteen miles above the city. It is brought to the distributing reservoir just above Georgetown, in an aqueduct passing through a receiving reservoir on the way, and is thence brought to Washington through iron mains. No pumping is done except to supply the suburbs on the bluffs. The water is excellent, and the supply ample. In order to give a stronger head in certain sections of the city, a tunnel has been constructed to conduct a part of the supply from the distributing reservoir to a third reservoir north of the middle of the city. Three bridges connect the city with the opposite shore of Virginia, the Potomac at this place being only a mile wide. Three railroads also afford the means of communication to its inhabitants, viz., the Baltimore and Ohio, and the Pennsylvania, which are connected with the north and west, and the Richmond and West Point Terminal, which extends southward. In addition to its railway connections, regular lines of steamers ply to northern and southern ports during most of the year. There is little trade and less manufacture, but as a political focus the city is maintained in prosperity by a constant influx of visitors, many of whom are attracted by the genial climate and the gay social life. The population of the district by the last census, taken in 1885, was 203,459, the white and coloured races being in the proportion of two to one, and the death-rate is very low, being under eighteen per thousand among the white population.

The position of Washington is unique, so far as the management of its local affairs is concerned. It is governed by three commissioners, appointed by the President of the United States. They perform the executive duties, the various departments of the civic government being apportioned among them. Legislation for the city district is enacted by Congress. The city has courts of its own, but the judges are appointed by the President. The people have no voice in the management of affairs. Thus in the capital of a great republic, we behold the remarkable spectacle of government by an absolute monarchy! And what is of more importance still, is the fact that Washington is the best governed municipality in the United States.

M. Johnson.

How to Weigh the Earth.

HAT an absurd idea!' I think I hear some reader exclaim. And on the face of it such a proposal does seem absurdly ambitious. When the old Hebrew prophet would convey to the people of his time the sense of the contrast between God and man, and of God's power to help them in their distresses, he asks, ' Who hath measured the waters in the hollow of his hand, and meted out heaven with the span, and gathered up the dust of the earth in a measure, and weighed the mountains in scales and the hills in a balance?' But some there are who are persuaded that if the prophet had lived in our day he would have found some other illustration of his point; for the march

Fig. 1.

of mind has enabled man to perform the feat which Isaiah in the above quotation ascribes exclusively to God.

But how is this wonderful work achieved? Let us begin by an illustration. The chapel where I worship bears on its front gable two large stone balls. Suppose the problem is to find the weight of one of these balls without detaching it from the place where it rests. First of all we will get a ladder, and mounting to one of these balls we will carefully examine its structure, and then measure the circumference of this stone globe. On descending to the ground once more we set somebody to calculate the number of cubic inches in our ball, while we, on our part, go off to seek the quarry from which we know the stone for the ball has been dug. Securing a small piece of it, we grind it down to the dimensions of a cubic inch, and then weighing this cubic inch of stone, it is easy, by a process of simple multiplication, to calculate the weight of the large stone ball.

And now let us apply this process to the question in hand. First of all we must ascertain the circumference of the earth. To anyone knowing anything of the properties of the circle this is easy if we know the distance between certain given points on this circle. From the arc we can calculate the whole circumference. And this was actually done 2,000 years ago by a philosopher named Eratosthenes. We give in Fig 1 an illustration of how he accomplished it. *a* stands for Alexandria, and *b* for Syene (called now Assouan).

Eratosthenes first sought to ascertain the number of degrees of the circle contained

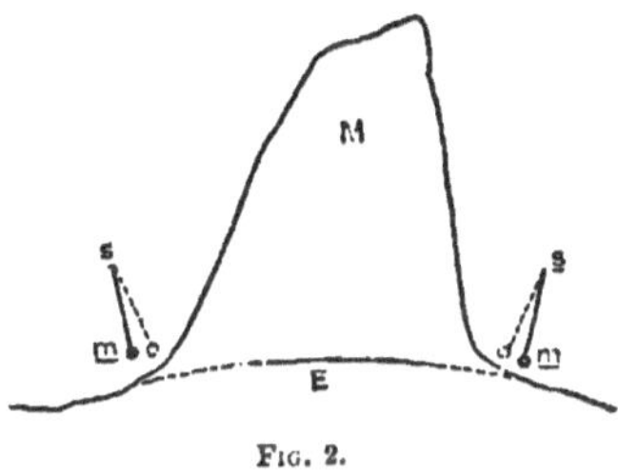

FIG. 2.

between *a* and *b*. He found that this represented about one-fiftieth part of the circumference, and knowing the distance between Alexandria and Syene, he was quickly able to arrive at the total length of the circumference of our globe. Dividing the circumference by about 3¼ we get the diameter, and from the diameter (speaking roughly 7,910 miles) astronomers calculate the solid content of the globe to be 259,370 millions of cubic miles.

But here a great difficulty arises. In the case of our stone ball we know it to be of the same material throughout, but the earth is composed of rocks of every degree of density. On the surface, these rocks are from two to three times heavier than an equal bulk of water, but the rocks nearer the centre of the earth must be much heavier on account of the

great pressure above them. What we want then is to be able to strike some average which shall fairly represent the mean density of our globe. This has been attempted in various ways which we will now try to describe.

We presume that our readers will readily understand what is meant by the attraction or *pull* of gravity by which a heavier body universally draws towards it a lighter. As Mr. Ackroyd says, ' The sun pulls at all the planets around it; the planets pull at the sun, and at each other, and every particle of matter in the universe pulls at every other particle.' In the accompanying illustration (Fig. 2),

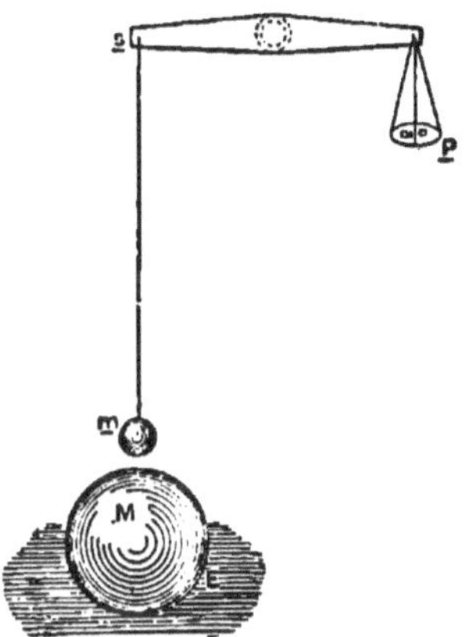

FIG. 3.

let M represent a mountain standing on the surface of the earth, E, *m* is a small weight suspended from *s*, which, apart from the mountain, would hang directly downwards to the centre of the earth. But the mountain M has something to say to this little weight, and pulls it out of the straight line towards its own mass as shown in the engraving. Of course, the measurement of this deviation is a very delicate affair, and can only be done by the proper instruments. Chimborazo in South America caused a deviation of eleven seconds. A mountain named Schiehallien in Perthshire, Scotland, caused a deflection of between four and five seconds, while Arthur's Seat, near Edinburgh, produced a deviation of between two and three seconds. From these observations it was deduced that the mean density of the earth was about five times that of water. A second method of determining the pull of the earth is represented in Fig. 3. There is depicted here a chemical balance of very great sensitiveness to which a small weight m is attached, and then balanced with great exactness. A heavy mass of metal, M, is now brought directly under m, so that its pull is added to that of the earth, E. Mr. Poynting, of Owens College, Manchester, calculated from the increase of weight in m, in this experiment, that the mean density of the earth was $5\frac{3}{4}$.

Perhaps the exactest method is that which is associated with the name of the Hon. Henry

under $5\frac{1}{2}$. Experiments o the same kind carried out by Reich in 1837, and by Baily in 1840, gave substantially the same result.

Another method is that of the pendulum. It is known that a pendulum makes 86,535 vibrations during a period of twenty-four hours in London, while in the same time at the equator it will make only 86,400, because the pull of the earth at the equator is so much less than its pull at the latitude of London. It occurred to someone to ask whether this might not be used to determine the differing density of our globe as we proceed towards its centre. In 1854 the Astronomer-Royal, Sir George Airy, fixed at the bottom of the shaft of Harton Colliery near South Shields, a pen-

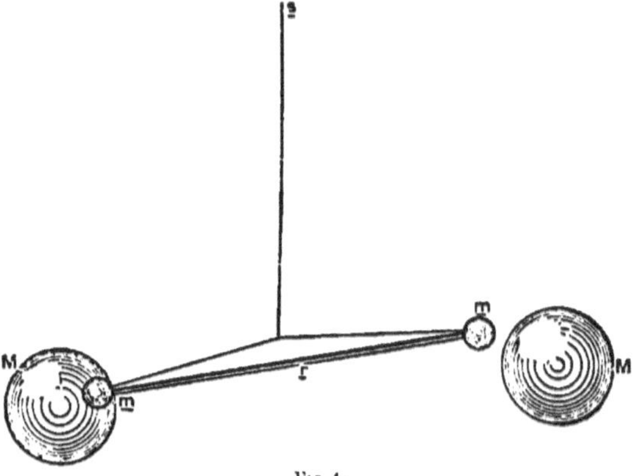

Fig 4.

Cavendish. He suspended (see Fig. 4) two small balls at the extremities of the rod r, and then carefully observed their position by means of a telescope and a graduated arc. He now brought near to these small balls two much larger ones made of lead, and having taken every precaution to protect the balls from currents of air he measured the deviation of the small balls towards the large ones with the utmost exactness. He then calculated what would be the pull of his large leaden balls, supposing they were as big as the earth, and, knowing the mean density of lead and also the attractive force of our globe, he was able by comparison and calculation to arrive at the result that the earth's mean density is just

dulum, which lost $2\frac{1}{4}$ seconds per day as compared with a similar one fixed at the top. The distance between the two pendulums was 1,200 feet, and by a series of calculations, which we cannot here explain, Sir George Airy arrived at the conclusion that the mean density of the earth is about $6\frac{1}{2}$. But similar experiments with the pendulum made on Mount Cenis gave the density as slightly under 5, and if the balance be struck between these two, it will be found to be just a little above the average of $5\frac{1}{2}$ yielded by the other methods.

As Mr. Ackroyd says, 'In all these experiments,' the influence of a known mass on a lesser mass is compared with the earth's influence or pull on it, and then by many and various calculations the earth's density is arrived at. It will give,' he continues, 'some idea of the labour expended in getting to know the influence of our known mass M when we mention that Schiehallien had to be accurately modelled and surveyed, and that the densities of its various mineral constituents had to be ascertained, while in the case of the Harton Colliery experiments the surrounding country had to be extensively surveyed, the strata had to be studied, and their specific gravities taken.'

What, then, is the final result of all our experiments and calculations? Roughly speaking, a cubic mile of water weighs 410 million tons. If this be multiplied by $5\frac{1}{2}$ (the mean density of the earth), and the result by 259,373,000, the number of cubic miles contained in our globe, we shall find that the weight of the earth is somewhere near 5,840,000,000,000,000,000,000,000, or, expressed in words, five thousand eight hundred and forty trillions of tons. But how can we conceive such a sum? After all the old Hebrew prophet is right. We may succeed in weighing the earth, but the figures we obtain are so vast that our limited intellects are not able to form any clear or definite conception of them. We have got into a deep, where all definite human thought is drowned, and indefiniteness of such dimensions is to us, practically, infinity —for as Carlyle well says, ' What a man sees but cannot see over is to him as good as infinite.'

Wholesome Fiction.

OME of you may have wondered why your elders have generally taken so much care in directing the course of your lighter reading, and have counselled you, with admonition and warning in their tones, with respect to novels.

Possibly you have thought their strictures too severe, too puritanic ; and while you have given your friends credit for the best intentions you have set it all down to an antiquated way of thinking and a narrow pietism of their own.

Before, however, you come to such a conclusion you had perhaps better make a pause. I am free to admit that there has been, and still is a fear of novels, wholly morbid and unwarranted— the mere result of ignorance, and a narrow outlook on life, the fruit even of a kind of religious squeamishness. But that there is need for caution, great caution, and wise discrimination, both as to the quantity and quality of the fiction we read, no right-thinking person will for a moment dispute. Hence the qualifying term in the title of our paper ' Wholesome Fiction.' This means that unwholesome fiction is abroad, and that it behoves you to give it a wide berth, if you would keep a sweet taste in your mouth, and realise in yourselves the true, the beautiful, the good.

Prose-fiction has been described as of two kinds ; (1) the romance, which is the legend of heroic ; (2) the novel, which is the news of common life. For general purposes we may take this division as satisfactory. Romance, with its giants and enchanters, its ghouls and fairies, its weird exaggerations and impossible adventures, belongs to a remote and unenlightened period, but was not without its broad lessons in valour and in virtue. The novel is the growth of modern life, and forms nearly the sole literary nourishment of a large class of the population. Without being prosaic on the one hand or unduly extravagant on the other, it deals in a natural way with men and things in daily life. It seeks or ought to seek to amend the foibles and vanities of actual men and women, to commend virtue and condemn vice, to illustrate that Providence ' which shapes our ends,' to depict in living colours the working of great principles or great passions, and over all so to cast the glamour of imagination, humour, pathos, and fancy, that our attention shall be awakened and secured with a distinct combination of pleasure, with instruction as the result.

It may be quite true that fiction is not fact, and that the embellishment which is ' the illuminated alphabet of larger children ' carries us a considerable distance from bare truth and minute accuracy ; but we readily allow ourselves to become the victims of the pleasant delusion, for it is useful. It helps to keep the spirits up, 'even the pack-horse goes better with his bells'—it gives a fillip to healthy aspirations, it makes truth concrete and gives an actualness to the ideal, it refines as well as regales the fancy, it serves to show the possibilities of life, and under the enticing guise of humour or of pathos it points the moral which we had been slow to recognise. Fiction, wholesome fiction, may be regarded as the 'fine art' in literature, and we are not sorry that under proper limitations it should have with us much of the influence which in other countries belongs to the stage. The stage, we fear, will never be purified from the vices and perils which seem to be its natural accompaniments, but between the backs of a pure novel you have a good substitute, aye, and something better. Imagination has its wholesome pleasure, while reflection also has its chance in the quiet pondering of the printed page.

Dr. Johnson, writing to Mrs. Thrale about the education of her daughter, said :—' She will go back to her arithmetic again, a science suited to Sophy's cast of mind ; for you told me in the last winter that she loved metaphysics more than romances. Her choice is certainly laudable, as it is uncommon ; but I would have her like *what is good in both.*' Hannah More traced her earliest impressions of virtue to works of fiction ; and Adam Clarke gives a list of tales that won his boyish admiration. Books of entertainment led him to believe in a spiritual world, and helped to keep him from being a coward. He declared that he had learned more of his duty to God, his neighbour, and himself, from *Robinson Crusoe,* than from all the books—except the Bible—that were known to his youth.

It will be our object in a few brief papers to point out some of the marks of wholesome fiction, and to refer you to some of the chief writers of it. Before doing so let me offer one or two precautionary hints.

Be careful to make the Bible the test and touchstone of all your reading. Let your mind be seasoned with the spirit of its teaching, and as you know it to be the Book of God, give it its rightful place as the god of books. Your moral taste will then be healthy and pure, and you will readily reject whatever seems to savour not of virtue, righteousness, and truth. It is remarkable to how large an extent the best writers of this or any age or land have been indebted to the Bible for their noblest ideals, their best inspiration, and how supreme and regulative the influence it wields in the entire field of literature. At twelve noon of every day at Greenwich Observatory there drops an electric ball in sight of the ships going out to sea, and of the business men and clerks on the wharves. At that instant you may see the captains and merchants and clerks taking out their watches and regulating their time accordingly. ' It is Greenwich time,' they say, and that observatory is the chronometer for the world, from its meridian we reckon to or from all longitudes. The Bible is God's chronometer for right thought, right feeling, right conduct. To be guided by its principles is to be saved from many hidden perils that lurk in books, and that beneath the flowers of romance and poetry conceal the death's-head of moral evil. You will of course understand that I do not mean you should reject every piece of fiction which does not directly teach morals and religion. The novel writer is not a mere homilist or catechist. But all the same, if he be a true writer will he (not less effectually, because he does not seem to do), impress you with healthy moral truth. And you, on your part, if you be a true reader, that is, if your mind is well toned by Bible teaching, will be able to make the very best use of the imaginative page as it gleams beneath your eye. Keep your Bible then ever to the front.

Remember, also, *you cannot claim excuse for soiling your mind with unwholesome literature on the ground that wholesome fiction is so scarce.* Never were its stores so abundant or so choice. Ask any respectable bookseller to show you his list, or better still, inquire of your minister, who will show you our own book-room catalogue, and you will be astonished at the supply so rich, so varied, so cheap. If you follow your minister's advice you will avoid serious peril. There are, alas! a great many who devour bushels of trash in the shape of merely foolish stories, which give them all sorts of mawkish and mistaken impressions of life. As it has been pithily said, ' They are as much possessed with the ideas introduced to their minds as a child in a nursery is by the images and incidents of a fairy tale. They grow to believe that life around them is full of those glittering possibilities which may elevate them to the same social level as romance heroines. They go to the dress circle at the play with the word "Kismet" trembling on their lips, and they are anxiously expecting to see their "fate" at a half-crown concert.' Now there can be no excuse for you, should you enter this enchanted ground, this fool's paradise, on the plea that bad fiction crowded out the good, and so led you astray by the imposing array of temptation. It is, I contend, rather the other way on. And it is bound to be increasingly so year by year. There can be no excuse for reading trash, simply because there is so much that is really good within our easy reach. Sir Walter Scott's works will always keep a large popularity by their power of description and their dramatic force, their historical colouring, and wonderful, truthful creative power. Thackeray's amaz-ing productions of life, true to nature as a Flemish painting, will always hold a command-ing place. Charlotte Brontë's 'Jane Eyres,' &c., with their mysterious insight into inmost thoughts, and power of putting these thoughts into words, are miracles of moral anatomy and studies of style. Dickens, with his wondrous humour, graphic touch, and abounding vitality, offers you an inexhaust-ible fund of enjoyment to lighten the tedium of life. Anthony Trollope's fictions are photo-graphs of nineteenth century life in pen and ink. Wilkie Collins and Charles Reade share between them very high honours as masters of English realistic romance. In the works of the latter especially, whatever of stirring or sensational incident they may have, is introduced quite as much to point the moral as to adorn the tale. 'Such works as "Hard Cash," "It is never too late to mend," and "Put yourself in his place," have served to enlighten public opinion on subjects so im-portant as lunacy-laws, criminal procedure, the regulation of prisons and trades-unions.' Colonel Lockhart, James Payne, George

Meredith, Justin McCarthy, Walter Besant, George Macdonald, Hardy, Black, Blackmore, Buchanan, Mrs. Oliphant, Mrs. Lynn Linton, Mrs. Cashel Hoey, Mrs. Alexander, Mrs. Edwards, Mrs. Riddell, Mrs. Henry Wood, Miss Braddon, Miss Broughton, Annie Swann, and many others, have catered well to healthy tastes, and laid us under lasting obligations to their genius. But I must call a halt to my pen, and leave for another occasion some remarks on a few of these authors.

I will close by reminding you that even *wholesome fiction should not occupy a supreme place in your library.* It must be kept in its true place, as a relish, not as our daily bread. It may refine, amuse, indoctrinate in a light, superficial way, give us wise thoughts and keen observation, but it cannot supplant serious study, or give comprehensive know-ledge, or plant the highest inspirations within you. Your home training, your Sunday-school days, your hours of devotion, let us fondly hope, have done, or are doing this for you: thus laying a well-compacted foundation on which you may raise a fair superstructure adorned and embellished with graces and gifts alike moral and literary, sober and serene. H. Y.

The Hand of God.

LOOSE not Thy hold, O hand of God!
  Or utterly we faint and fall.
  The way is rough, the way is blind,
    And buffeted with stormy wind;
Thick darkness veils above, below,
From whence we come to whence we go;
  Feebly we grope o'er rock and sand,
But still go on, confiding all,
  Lord, to Thy hand!

In that strong hold salvation is;
Its touch is comfort in distress,
Cure for all sickness, balm for ill,
And energy for heart and will.
Securely held unfaltering,
The soul can walk at ease and sing,
  And fearless tread each unknown strand,
Leaving each large thing, and each less,
  Lord, in Thy hand!

The Attitude of the Church to the Gambling Spirit of the Age.

HE cause of gambling is the selfishness of men. It has its origin in the greed of the human heart and the insatiable hunger for riches. Men are in haste to be rich, and gamble to get money. They are not content with the daily round of plodding industry, but must at one great swoop become suddenly rich. The greed of gain masters them, and leads them captive as a galley-slave. The lust of gold is one of the vilest of passions, and leads to the worst of evils. It drinks up the life-blood of men and leaves them with a shrivelled manhood. It cannot be doubted, however, that men at times are led to gamble for exhilarating excitement, as well as for the love of gain. They are anxious to feel the thrill of a new sensation, to have their energies roused, and the depths of their being moved. Excitement, within certain limits, is both healthful and necessary. Sluggish men specially need the stimulus of gentle excitement to play well their part in life. But it is carried to fearful extremes. The motley crowd that formerly gathered to witness the tragic scene of a public execution were drawn together by a morbid excitement. It was the same spirit that animated the vast crowds that witnessed the gladiatorial scenes of ancient Rome. The sailor who has been cradled on the mighty deep prefers the perils of the sea to the quietness of home life. The storms at sea, the grandeur of the scenery, and the strangeness of foreign lands excite and sustain him in his perilous occupation. Men resort to intoxicating drinks to excite their passions. Various games of skill and strength are resorted to, which produce pleasure, and

lead to healthy recreation. But when the spirit of betting absorbs men they become frantic with excitement. They become subject to a species of madness, and are ready for every evil work. Tacitus narrates that the ancient Germans would stake their property, their wives, their children, and themselves. And it is sadly too common in this country for men to gamble away the money and the property upon which their families are dependent for sustenance. Whatever the pleasures of this betting excitement, it is of a grovelling and degrading kind, appealing to the baser principles and passions of men. Deceit and fraud, lying and treachery are skilfully handled by the betting fraternity. They take advantage of the ignorance and weakness of man, and resort to any expedient to accomplish their direful purposes. But the root principle of gambling is the selfishness of men. It is the cursed love of gold that impels men. The spirit of Mammon masters them and leads them on.

' Mammon the least erected spirit that fell
  From heaven; for e'en in heaven his looks and
    thoughts
  Were always downward bent, admiring more
  The riches of heaven's pavement trodden gold
  Than ought divine, or holy else enjoyed.'

It cannot be morally right to obtain that for which we do not give an adequate equivalent. If a man receives wages it is for work done. The skilled artizan is remunerated according to the quality and quantity of his labour. The lawyer and the doctor are rewarded for their professional services. The tradesman supplies goods to his customers at reasonable prices. He has a fair return for his capital and labour, and the customer has value in goods for his money. There should be a just and honourable relation between all classes of society. No exorbitancy on the part of the seller, nor craving for deduction on the part of the purchaser, should be practised. But there is such selfishness in human nature, and a want of scrupulousness in all classes, that the one endeavours to take advantage of the other. This is strikingly brought out in the ancient record, ' It is naught, it is naught, saith the buyer; but when he is gone his way then he boasteth ' (Prov. xx. 14). Such tricks in trade if not actionable are certainly dishonest; and to make them a subject of boast is to proclaim that a man is an artful knave who has met with another simple enough to be cheated. There are thought-readers in the world who can wonderfully reveal a man's inner self; but none surpass the mountebank, who assured the company he would show them what was in every man's heart; nor did he find it difficult to fulfil his pledge, for standing up in the midst of them he simply said, ' You all wish to buy cheap, and to sell dear.' He was applauded, for everyone felt it to be a description of his own heart, and was satisfied that all others were similar. People say they must live, but it is surely possible to live honestly. Every man may rightly claim what he legitimately makes by honest industry, but under no circumstances can it be right to deceive and oppress the ignorant and the weak in order to make money. It is a bad omen when men begin to think of taking short cuts to wealth, instead of making it by force of intellect and dint of labour. The keen competition of the business world has led to sad adulteration and fearful tricks in trade. No man should think of making money except by honest labour, either of body or mind. But the evil of betting stealthily creeps upon men. It often commences in playing at cards for small sums of money. The odds at stake give keenness and zest to the game. Sometimes this is done in the quietness of the parlour or the seclusion of the drawing-room; but working-men frequently play in groups in some secluded spot in the open air. The Lord's-day is sadly profaned by gamblers, who waste its precious hours in shuffling cards or playing at pitch-and-toss. The spirit of betting permeates all the ramifications of society. Both rich and poor, high and low, are infected with this gambling mania. Wherever there is a contingency in notable things and events there is betting. A great trial, a Parliamentary election, and even the collection at a school anniversary, have been the subject of bets. Anything will do that involves hazard or risk, and offers money. Betting has contaminated nearly all our indoor games and public sports. Card-playing,

bagatelle, billiards, football, and cricket, are all tainted with this gambling spirit. No man can form an adequate idea of the enormous evil of betting. Fifty sporting papers are published in or near London. Every morning journal has its column devoted to the latest London betting. There are offices in our cities and towns for the sweepstakes of the Derby and the University Boat Race, and bookmakers ply their nefarious arts in public places and about our public works to catch the industrious artizan. Not long ago the writer conducted an open-air service during the dinner hour at the entrance to one of our public works, and while he and others were holding a religious service on one side of the road, the bookmaker was carrying on his ruinous business on the other. Nor does this excite our surprise, for under the shadow of the Cross they gambled for the garment of the innocent and holy Jesus! Every true patriot should set his face like a flint against this monstrous evil of betting. It is sapping the foundations of our national character, destroying confidence, and paralysing industry. It is at the bottom of nearly all our trade depression and financial disaster. The human wreckages that have split on this gambling rock are fearful to contemplate. If it be said that there are risks on both sides, and that they stand on equal ground, we respectfully submit that the winner, in many cases, has superior information to the loser. There is a way of getting authentic information as to winning horses which only the initiated are aware of. A person regularly corresponds with the different training stables of the country, and receives correct information as to certain horses, how they are succeeding in training, and which are likely to run, and win in certain races. This information is privately published, and the paper sent to subscribers for a yearly subscription; while information is given as to any particular horse on the receipt of a fee. So that hundreds of letters come to this gentleman week after week, by which he is rising to wealth and affluence. Racing and betting are not the haphazard businesses some people imagine them to be, but a systematic course is regularly pursued by the fully initiated. When we consider the whole system of horse-racing we cannot but condemn it. We have wondered that distinguished statesmen and even members of the royal family should patronise it, and that the sittings of the House of Commons should be suspended for the Derby Day. To put the noble horse to such cruel torture we cannot but regard as wicked, for, let any person gaze upon it after the race, and he will find it sweating at every pore and trembling in every limb; its sides bleeding with the vigorous spurring and its back blistered with repeated whipping. This is a proper subject for the Society for Prevention of Cruelty to Animals, and we are only sorry the Society has no jurisdiction on the racecourse. But from the aristocrats of our country down to the middle and lower classes the spirit of betting has filtered through every grade of society. Working-men and women, clerks, shopmen, working-boys, and even schoolboys, are sadly addicted to gambling. Englishmen have long frowned on Monte Carlo, the gambling hell of the Continent, where many a fortune has been lost, and suicide has followed as the consequence; but, as horse-racing is the national sport of Englishmen, we look upon the racecourses of our country as so many gambling hells, that blight, wither, and destroy multitudes of souls from year to year, so that to our mind they are

> 'Black as night;
> Fierce as ten furies, terrible as hell.'
>
> JOHN WORSNOP.

(To be continued.)

The Library.

FOR creating and fostering a taste for history in young readers we know of nothing better than the stories in which great writers, like Sir Walter Scott, have attempted to reproduce for us the essential features of life and character in the far back times of the past. Who does not know more of James the First by reading 'The Fortunes of Nigel,' or of Louis XI. from 'Quentin Durward,' than

by the ordinary methods of history alone? You come back to the study of the histories proper with a new relish and a deeper insight; and while getting your mistakes of fact corrected can see much more clearly than was at all possible by the older method what sorts of forces and persons were at work in the period you have sat down to study. In reading history the total impression, the instinct of the whole, so to speak, is much more important than pedantic exactness of detail. We have to mention this month an author who is, of course, not to be compared with Sir Walter Scott for power and genius, but who, nevertheless, has a very considerable faculty for reproducing the life of bygone days. The story now lying before us is entitled 'Micah Clarke,' and is written by A. Conan Doyle. It is a story dealing with Monmouth's rebellion in 1685. The hero is the son of an old Puritan who had fought on Cromwell's side in the Civil War; and in his turn is found arrayed against the royal cause. The principal historical characters in the book are Monmouth himself, the Duke of Beaufort, and Judge Jeffreys. The 'infamous judge' is thus described. ' He was wrapped in a cloak of crimson plush with a heavy white periwig upon his head, which was so long that it dropped down over his shoulders. They say that he wore scarlet in order to strike terror into the hearts of the people; and that his courts were for the same reason draped in the colour of blood. . . He was a man who in his younger days must have been remarkable for his extreme beauty. He was not, it is true, very old, as years go, when I saw him, but debauchery and low living had left their traces upon his countenance; without, however, entirely destroying the regularity and beauty of his features. He was dark, more like a Spaniard than an Englishman, with black eyes and olive complexion. His expression was lofty and noble, but his temper was so easily aflame that the slightest cross or annoyance would set him raving like a madman, with blazing eyes and foaming mouth. I have seen him myself with froth upon his lips, and his whole face twitching with passion, like one who hath the falling sickness. . . . . It must indeed have been an evil government where so vile and foul-mouthed a wretch was chosen out to hold the scales of justice.' Monmouth is thus depicted. He 'was at that time in his thirty-sixth year, and was remarkable for those superficial graces which pleased the multitude and fit a man to lead in a popular cause. He was young, well-spoken, witty, and skilled in all martial and manly exercises. . . His nature was vain and prodigal, but he excelled in that showy magnificence and careless generosity which wins the hearts of the people. . . He was reckoned well-favoured, but I cannot say that I found him so. His face was, I thought, too long and white for comeliness, yet his features were high and noble, with well-marked nose and clear, searching eyes. In his mouth might perchance be noticed some trace of that weakness which marred his character, though the expression was sweet and amiable.' In the course of the story the hero has some wonderful adventures. He is pursued by bloodhounds, snared by a rope stretched across the road, being mistaken for some other man, is thrown into prison as a feint by the Duke of Beaufort, and sentenced to death, the Duke himself, however, showing him a secret way out of the dungeon at dead of night. After the affair near Keynsham Bridge he captures a certain Major Ogilvie, whom he treats so well that when Micah is in danger of being hung the Major's influence procures his safety. These items will give some little idea of a story which to historical exactness and vividness, adds the glowing colours of personal experience. In it we get close to the actors in those stirring days, and find ourselves pleasantly making acquaintance with persons who have hitherto been to us little more than mere names. The book belongs to the 'Silver Library' of Messrs. Longman, and is worth possessing and reading by old and young.

When Work is Done.

It is as if the world were glad !
Whether in light or darkness clad.
The hour is never dull or sad
　　When work is done.

SPECIAL NOTICE.

WE are pleased to inform readers of *Springtime* that the Book Committee has decided to set apart, each month, a portion of space for replies to the questions of correspondents. We submit an outline of the arrangements.

1. The name shall be ' The Young People's Page.'

2. Information may be sought through this medium on social, moral, philosophical, theological, and spiritual questions by any reader of *Springtime*.

3. All communications for this department of the magazine must be sent, post paid, to the Editor, 35, Freegrove-road, Holloway, London, N.

4. Writers may attach to their communications either their full names, their initials, or such other marks as they may deem best.

5. Correspondents will oblige by making their queries, &c., as brief as they can, consistent with clearness of statement.

EDITOR.

To be beaten but not broken ; to be victorious but not vainglorious ; to strive and contend for the prize, and to win it honestly or lose it cheerfully ; to use every power in the race, and yet never to wrest an undue advantage or win an unlawful mastery ; verily in all this there is training and testing of character which searches it to the very roots, and this is a result which is worth all that it costs us. BISHOP POTTER.

God holds the key of all unknown,
　　And I am glad ;
If other hands should hold the key,
Or if he trusted it to me
　　I might be sad.

What if to-morrow's cares were here
　　Without its rest ?
Better that He unlock the day,
And as the doors swing open say,
　　' My will is best.'
REV. JOHN PARKER.

FREE GRACE.

S. J. VAIL.

2 O escape to yonder mountain !
  Now begin to watch and pray ;
Christ invites you to the fountain,
  Come, and wash your sins away.

3 Grace is flowing like a river ;
  Millions there have been supplied ;
Still it flows as fresh as ever
  From the Saviour's wounded side.

4 Christ alone shall be our portion ;
  Soon we hope to meet above—
Then we'll bathe in the full ocean
  Of the great Redeemer's love.

FREE GRACE.

Key F.   S. J. Vail.

|d :— :m |s :— :m |m :— :r |r :d : |f :— :f |m :— :m |
1. Hark! the gos - pel news is sound-ing: Christ hath suf - fered
|d :— :d |m :— :d |d :— :t, |t, :d : |d :— :d |d :— :d |
2. O es - cape to yon - der moun-tain! Now be - gin to
|m :— :s |s :— :s |s :— :f |f :m : |l :— :l |s :— :s |
3. Grace is flow - ing like a riv - er; Mil - lions there have
|d :— :d |d :— :d |s, :— :s, |d :d : |d :— :d |d :— :d |
4. Christ a - lone shall be our por-tion; Soon we hope to

|r :— :d |r :— :— |d :— :m |s :— :m |m :— :r |r :d : |
on the tree; Streams of mer - cy are a - bound-ing;
|s, :— :d |t, :— :— |d :— :d |m :— :d |d :— :t, |t, :d : |
watch and pray; Christ in - vites you to the foun-tain,
|s :— :fe |s :— :— |m :— :s |s :— :s |s :— :f |f :m : |
been sup-plied; Still it flows as fresh as ev - er
|t, :— :l, |s, :— :— |d :— :d |d :— :d |s, :— :s, |d :d : |
meet a - bove— Then we'll bathe in the full o - cean

Chorus. ff

|f :— :f |m :— :d |m :— :r |d :— :— |l :— :l |s :— :m |s :— :s |m :—:— |
Grace for all is rich and free. Oh, be saved, His grace is free!
|d :— :d |d :— :d |d :— :t, |d :— :— |d :— :d |d :— :d |t, :— :t, |d :—:— |
Come, and wash your sins a - way. Oh, be saved, His grace is free!
|l :— :l |s :— :m |s :— :f |m :— :— |f :— :f |m :— :m |r :— :s |s :—:— |
From the Sa - viour's woun - ded side. Oh, be saved, His grace is free!
|f, :— :f, |s, :— :s, |s, :— :s, |d :— :— |f, :— :f, |d :— :d |s, :— :s, |d :—:— |
Of the great Re- deem - er's love.

rit.

|f :— :f |m :— :m |r :— :fe |s :— :— |d :— :m |s :— :m |m :— :r |d :—:— |
Oh, be saved, He died for thee! Oh, be saved, He died for Thee!
|r :— :r |d :— :d |t, :— :l, d, t, :— :— |d :— :d |m :— :d |d :— :t, |d :—:— |
Oh, be saved, He died for thee! Oh, be saved, He died for Thee!
|s :— :s |s :— :s |s :— :r |r :— :— |m :— :s |s :— :s |s :— :f |m :—:— |
Oh, be saved, He died for thee! Oh, be saved, He died for Thee!
|t, :— :t, |d :— :d |r :— :r |s, :— :— |d :— :d |d :— :d |s, :— :s, |d :—:— |

Current Topics.

THE DRINK TRAFFIC IN NORWAY—AN EXAMPLE.

N a speech delivered at Taunton in 1831, Sidney Smith related the following anecdote :—' In the winter of 1824,' he said, 'there set in a great flood upon the town of Sidmouth ; the tide rose to an incredible height, the waves rushed in upon the houses, and everything was threatened with destruction. In the midst of this sublime storm, Dame Partington, who lived upon the beach, was seen at the door of her house, with mop and pattens, trundling her mop and squeezing out the sea-water, and vigorously pushing away the Atlantic Ocean. The Atlantic was roused, Mrs. Partington's spirit was up. But I need not tell you that the contest was unequal. The Atlantic Ocean beat Mrs. Partington. She was excellent at a slop or a puddle, but she should not have meddled with a tempest.' Mr. Smith was illustrating the folly of the attempts the House of Lords was then making to stop the progress of reform, but his anecdote gives an even better illustration of the futility of many an attempt to deal with the evils of the traffic in drink.

Ever since the reign of Henry VII. this country has been attempting to cope with the evils of this diabolical trade. Whenever these evils have become a little more manifest than usual, some Mrs. Partington was sure to appear with her mop and begin to vigorously push away this Atlantic Ocean of drink, but in spite of all such efforts the traffic still continues, and its evils still increase. It would not be fair to compare General Booth to another Mrs. Partington, for he does not present his scheme as a mop to push back the tide of evil, but rather as a boat to rescue the helpless multitudes who are going down beneath its flood. In this work he deserves all encouragement, but we must not expect too much from it.

When a town is inundated by a flood, boats must be got out to rescue the inhabitants, but when it can be done the floods should be prevented. This is what ought to be done with the liquor traffic. General Booth admits that the drink is the prime cause of the mischief he seeks to undo. Everybody admits this. Then why not deal with the cause? You may spend any number of millions in attempting to rescue the victims of vice and poverty, but what progress will you make if you do not deal with the influences that have brought them where they are? By all means let General Booth and others like him have the boats to save the drowning multitudes, but do not let us think our duty done until we have stopped the flood.

But again comes the question, How is this to be done? Dr. Spence Watson, of Newcastle-on-Tyne, has been telling the readers of the *Speaker* newspaper how they manage the liquor traffic in Norway, and the account he gives is well worth considering in these days of expensive experiments. Unlike the elaborate schemes sometimes suggested for dealing with the matter in this country, the plan they follow in Norway is remarkably simple. But simple as it is, it has reduced the consumption of spirits from, 2,612,520 gallons in 1876 to 1,189,440 in 1887. What this means for the social life of the nation may well be imagined.

The plan was established in 1871 by an Act of Parliament which directed that ' societies which bind themselves to apply the possible profit of their trading in aid of objects of general public benefit and utility, and whose articles of incorporation are confirmed by a resolution of the magistrates and Municipal Council, and are sanctioned under the royal seal, may hold one, several, or all the licences to retail ardent spirits to be issued in the locality.' Seeing that in all Norwegian towns the Municipal Council, either alone or in association with the magistracy, is the licensing authority, when such a society is formed by their sanction, there is nothing to hinder it obtaining as many of the existing licences as it requires. Consequently, these societies have been formed in fifty-one out of the fifty-seven towns in Norway which have a licensing authority. In five towns no licences whatever are granted, and in only three small places, with an aggregate population of 1,280, are spirit licences still in private hands.

In order to show us how the plan works, Dr. Watson looks to the town of Bergen. The Society here began its operations on January 1, 1877, with a capital amounting to about £4,500 in our money, held by sixty-nine shareholders. It took over fourteen places of business, each of which was placed under the care of a person whose character was approved by the Municipal Council. The bars are generally placed in conspicuous situations, so that every one going in or out may be plainly seen. The bar-keepers have each a fixed salary, and have no interest in the amount of sales. Every precaution, indeed, is taken against any inducement to drink being held out. The bars are clean, and the attendants, all males dressed in special uniform, are courteous and attentive, but there are no seats, no snugs, no loitering. Quietness and decorum are strictly enforced. Children are not allowed to enter the premises, and no drink must be supplied to any person who shows signs of having already consumed as much as he can take without being unsteady.

These rules would no doubt be very unpleasant to the English toper, but what would he think of the time regulations observed in these Bergen spirit bars? They do not open until eight o'clock in the morning. They are closed from noon till half-past one, and at eight o'clock business ceases for the day. On Saturdays they close at five o'clock, and also on the days preceding holy festivals. They do not open at all on such festivals or on Sundays. The spirit drinker has evidently little encouragement at Bergen.

The society, however, has not yet control over the wine and ale trade. The licence to deal in these liquors is more easily obtained than is the spirit licence; and many of them have been granted by the Crown, and some of them are perpetual. The object of the society, however, is to obtain full control of the whole traffic, and to this end it has already purchased four of the perpetual licences, and is forming a fund for the purchase of the remainder. This is felt to be a necessity, for the severe restrictions they have placed upon the spirit trade has tended to increase the trade in wine and ale.

The net results, however, are very encouraging. Bergen, it must be remembered, is a flourishing seaport town, with a population which has grown from about 40,000 in 1877 to about 50,000 in 1889. But whilst the population has increased, the consumption of spirits has diminished. In 1889 the sale of spirits was less by 15,000 quarts than it was in 1877, though the population was 10,000 more. Then the apprehensions and summonses for drunkenness and similar offences, which were 1,186 in 1876, were last year only 729. This does not appear to be a great decrease, but you have to remember the great increase of population, and the fact that beer and wine had not been put under the same regulations as spirits. But besides this, the society had employed two detectives and two special policemen to look after such cases. Fewer drunkards would therefore escape detection in 1889 than in the year before the society began its operations. It is worth notice, too, that the applications for spirits from persons of tender age, or from persons in an inebriated condition, fell from 12,812 in a single quarter in 1877 to 12,610 in the whole year of 1889.

But what has been the effect of these changes upon the social life of the town? Partial as they have been, it is scarcely too much to say that they have solved the problem of 'Darkest Bergen.' Dr. Watson says you cannot walk through the streets without being struck by the rarity of extreme destitution to be met with, and people who knew the place twenty years ago pronounce the improvement to be most remarkable. Bergen of course is a small place, but what is said of it in this respect is more or less true of the whole country. In the face of such testimony as this, why should we in this country be so anxious for the trial of elaborate and expensive experiments in social amelioration? If the restriction of the drink trade has done so much good in Norway, might we not expect that it would effect a similar change here? No one can really dispute this. But then we have come to regard the drink-flood as a necessity in this country, and hence we are fain to seek relief in 'boats,' and other life-saving appliances.

Though the societies that have the control of the spirit trade in Norway are chiefly intent upon lessening the sale, they, nevertheless, make a profit at the business. Now what has the Bergen Society done with its profits during the thirteen years of its existence? By their articles of association the shareholders are to receive five per cent. per annum upon their paid-up capital, and in this way £3,140 have been appropriated; Excise duties, rates and taxes have absorbed £30,305; the reserve fund has taken £4,445; and purchase of premises, &c., £10,365. But besides all this, the sum of £64,155 has, according to law, been devoted to 'objects of general public benefit and utility.' A Dublin brewer has just been made a lord in recognition of his beneficence in giving half a million of money for the erection of better dwellings for the poor of London and Dublin, but the inhabitants of Bergen are not dependent upon the spasmodic charity of wealthy liquor dealers. They disburse the profits themselves.

Dr. Watson gives a long list of the institutions that have benefited by this £64,155, and it is enough to make the English philanthropist blue with envy. There is, for instance, a society for beautifying and planting the hills round about the town, and it has been helped to the amount of £4,770, the museum has got £4,890, and the Nygaard park has got £5,085. Then the sum of £3,070 has been given to the Bergen Labourers' Waiting Rooms, where good and cheap food can be obtained; £500 to the School Board Commissioners towards the cost of sending diligent but delicate children into the country, and boarding them during their holidays; £775 to the society for providing children's playgrounds; £835 to the aged handicraftsmen's home, and so the list goes on.

But a considerable part of these profits for the sale of drink has been devoted to the temperance cause. What will our temperance reformers say to the following figures? The Bergen Temperance Society has received £210, the New Total Abstinence Society £770, the National Total Abstinence Society £665, the Bergen Society of Abstainers from Alcoholic Drinks £390, the United Order of Good Templars £555, the Heimdal Inebriates' Home £535, the 'Fremoad' Total Abstainers' Society £45, the Blue Ribbon Total Abstainers' Society £20, and the 'Olaf Kyrre' Good Templars' Lodge £55. Why, all this reads like a dream, and yet it is the actual state of affairs at Bergen, which indeed seems to be the earthly paradise of the temperance cause.

It should be explained that the drink regulations in Norway are somewhat similar to what is known as the Gothenburg system in vogue in Sweden. There is, however, an important difference. Whilst the surplus profits in Sweden are devoted to the relief of the rates, which is to some a powerful temptation to encourage the trade, in Norway no institution supported by the rates can receive any benefit whatever from this source. Though by no means free from defects, the barrier which the Norwegians have erected against an inundation of drink is proving itself to be no 'mop' of Mrs. Partington's handling. And it would be more successful than it is were it not for the selfishness of travellers who congregate in the large hotels in the tourist season. In Christiania, indeed, it has been found necessary to grant special licences to one or two of the great hotels where English people mostly gather. This is really too bad. But to the average drinker, it seems, appetite is supreme. This is the secret of our difficulty at home. But when the sense of patriotism fails to restrain the passions of men, the nation must protect itself by the strong hand of the law.   M. P. D.

SPRINGTIME :

A Magazine for Our Young Men and Maidens.

Vol. VI. No. 3.]   MARCH, 1891.   [Price Twopence.

A Bad Calculation.

By ROBERT HIND,

Author of ' Crosby Dalton : Local Preacher and Village Demagogue,' ' The Ruby Pendant,' &c.

CHAPTER V.

FROM THE COLONIES.

'Full of strength and motion stately,
Were thy face and form unto her;
And thy blue eyes pleased her greatly,
And thy clear voice trembled thro' her.'
ROBERT BUCHANAN.

HAT a disappointment it will be to all of us if by some accident he cannot come in this train!'

The speaker was Rye Harland, who, with her father, was pacing up and down the platform of Rockingham railway station, awaiting the arrival of the four o'clock express from London. Her remark concluded with a ripple of laughter, indulged in mainly at her own expense, for she was conscious that her heart was in a flutter of excitement. From the day that she had read the letter from her father's Australian friend, naturally she had thought a great deal about the young man from the colonies who would be a member of their household for the next three or four years. This coming event was of a nature too unusual to allow her to forget it. Besides, the changes that had taken place in the arrangements at ' The Mount ' in anticipation of the new arrival, kept reminding her of what was about to take place.

Decidedly romantic in mental tendency, she had thought much about what he would be able to tell her of Australia—its native population, the colonists who live in the bush, and of society in the large towns. More than in these things she felt she would be interested in an account of the flowers, the trees, the wild birds, and the domestic animals of that southern land. And of course she wondered what Jack Benson would be like. His name was what all names should be, homely and pleasant in sound. But that was not a guarantee of the excellence of the young man himself ; she hoped he would have two qualities at least. First, that he would be sensible, and not empty and frivolous ; and secondly, that he would be a gentleman at heart. Rye had somewhat pronounced opinions on this latter point. She had a contempt for the young men who gave more attention to their collars and cuffs, than to the improvement of their minds. At the same time she knew a gentleman would dress well without affecting the ' loudness ' that attracts attention ; hitting the happy medium which shows on the one hand self-respect, and on the other hand modesty. But her ideal gentleman must have the essential quality, kindness of heart, which would manifest itself in good manners and gentleness of conduct to all.

Her reflections, it will be observed, had been of a very general kind. Never had she so far descended to particulars as to attempt to picture to herself whether Jack Benson would be tall, or dark, strong or delicate, active or phlegmatic. But during the last day or two she had been conscious that her excitement had been steadily growing, and as she was too simple-minded to affect to hide it, her elders had been not a little interested in observing her movements.

'I wonder who will feel the disappointment most?' Mr. Harland inquired, looking steadily into her eyes.

Rye's laughter again rippled among her words as she said—

'Why, I will, beyond a doubt. I declare,' she added, reprovingly, 'one might suppose that we had a friend dropping in from Australia every week, judging by the cool way in which my father has regarded this event.' And as she spoke she half-pretended to be vexed with her natural guardian.

'What do you expect to come from over the seas?' Mr. Harland asked.

'I scarcely understand what you mean,' was Rye's answer.

'Well, let me explain, then. I expect Joe Benson's son. And I don't suppose he will differ a great deal from the young men we know. He will probably not be a paragon, but will have some of the faults generally characteristic of inexperienced young men. I fully expect he will not be without some of their excellences either. In fact I am not looking for anything remarkable, but just such a young man as you may meet with any day in any part of England.'

Rye was not at all satisfied with this speech. It did not harmonize with her reflections about their expected visitor, but she had no opportunity then of expressing her own opinions. The train was dashing into the station as her father was speaking, and the next minute they were eagerly scanning the passengers who had stepped down on the platform.

"That must be our friend," Mr. Harland said, as they followed a young man towards the luggage van.

Mr. Harland admitted to himself that his picture of their visitor was not true to the reality. He had told his daughter that a young man was coming who would be simply the essence of commonplace; and now as he

watched this stranger giving his directions to the porter, he was convinced that there were qualities in him which even to one who saw him for the first time were impressive, and which would always serve to distinguish him in a crowd.

Above the medium height, broad-shouldered, deep-chested, and heavy-limbed, Jack Benson looked the embodiment of physical health and power. Until his face was scanned, it might have been thought he must be five-and-twenty or thirty years of age, for there was none of the looseness of build that is sometimes observable in a young man barely out of his teens. Every muscle and joint was well-knit, and he carried himself, not with the dexterity and lightness of tread characteristic of the dandy, but with the swing of a giant, which nevertheless, on account of a suggestion in it of conscious power, was exceedingly picturesque.

'All addressed "Benson, passenger to Rockingham,"' he said to the porter attending to him, in a tone as direct as the words themselves. But he did not stand by whilst the porter piled up his luggage, but surprised that worthy son of toil by the ease and dispatch with which he dragged out the heaviest of the articles himself.

The two who had come to meet him stood aside whilst this was being done, and Rye, always delighted to gain a little triumph over her father, said—

'Your opinion is changed by this time I presume, sir?'

'In what?' Mr. Harland inquired.

'Could you meet with such a young man as that in any part of England any day of the year?'

Mr. Harland only shook his head, smiled, and instead of giving her a reply to her question, muttered something about a 'naughty girl.'

Rye Harland felt that Jack Benson was a young man very much to her taste. She loved naturalness, and had a strong aversion to the merely conventional and unreal. And she knew that their visitor in this respect at least must be a kindred spirit. It was a positive pleasure to see him doing the porter's work with twice the porter's quickness, and she wondered if his manner was wholly due to the influence of colonial life, and not partly to the unusual quality of his own nature. If the former, then his stay in England might take this charm from him; if not, then he would prove a delightful companion indeed.

'Welcome to Rockingham,' Mr. Harland said, extending his hand, whilst a smile, full of kindness, suffused his face.

Rye was a close observer, and little things did not escape her quick eyes. She wondered why Jack Benson did not smile. His face, which looked younger than his body, was not handsome. The brown complexion was taking enough, his eyes were a deep blue, the shade of a sapphire stone, and his black hair curled like that of a negro, but his features were not of a perfect contour.

All this she noticed, and in it there was nothing save what was pleasing. But still she wondered that the young man gave back no answering smile to her father's open look of welcome. For the face she was watching was not stolid. It was sensitive, and despite Jack Benson's directness of speech, and free, unconventional manners, she thought she detected in him a nature so finely strung, that like a sensitive stringed instrument it would feel and respond to the slightest movement in the atmosphere around it.

'I wonder if he is shy and feels awkward, and if all that hurry and work about his luggage meant so much effort to keep down his excitement and confusion?' she asked herself.

Anyhow she was glad her father was there, for without a third person old enough to be devoid of all self-consciousness, she felt she might have caught the contagion, and become shy and awkward too. Under his protection, however, she felt quite at ease, and was able to make the ordinary inquiries about the tediousness of the long journey in the train, and to express the hope that he would like Rockingham.

The trio walked from the railway station to the Mount, the distance not being great. The castle and the cathedral were in view, and the red tiles and quaint gables of the city.

'I have read of towns like this,' he said; 'but although my father often talks about it,

I had not expected that such an ancient-looking place existed now, even in old England.'

'And you have never seen anything like it?' Mr. Harland asked.

'Certainly not.'

'We who live in Rockingham think it is the most picturesque old town in the country.'

'It is delightful,' Jack said, with some fervour. 'What an irregular landscape, and what an irregular group of housetops! How beautifully the trees and river mix themselves in and out among the houses! And then the cathedral towers and that old feudal castle! I wish father and mother were here to see it all.'

The last words were spoken in a lower tone, and Rye, who had been both listening and looking, caught a perceptible twitch in his face as he concluded. The wish was expressed, not in the whining tone of a spoiled child, but with the manly feeling of an honest heart—a heart true to his parents, and unable to enjoy a pleasure without desiring those he loved best to participate in it.

Mr. Harland's opinion of the new comer may be gathered from his mental ejaculation—

'Thank God for a young man who does not call his father "the governor" and his mother "the old dame."'

CHAPTER VI.

TWO YOUNG MEN.

'Then, unaware, to notice I began
That he was trim and stout and like a man,
That there were tender tones upon his tongue,
And that his voice was sweet whene'er he sung.'
ROBERT BUCHANAN.

'You don't intend to forsake your old friends altogether, Arthur?'

The words were spoken in no serious manner; indeed, Rye Harland, who had addressed them to Arthur Brixton in a playful mood, had never thought that such an event would really happen. Her remark was intended more for the purpose of eliciting a reason for his absence from the Mount than anything else.

They had met by the riverside just under the cathedral. It was late in the afternoon, and both of them were on their way home—

Arthur from the office, and Rye from a call she had been making.

Arthur's look of unrest had deepened in the past week or two, and he was not quite at his ease when he felt himself under the clear, honest gaze of Rye Harland. Forcing up the ghost of a smile, which, however, extended no further than the corners of his mouth, he said—

'You have missed me then?'

'What do you mean, Arthur?' Rye asked. As she did so the playful smile died from her face. 'Of course we have missed you; surely you have not thought otherwise?'

'Well, not exactly. But you have Mr. Benson with you, and your minds for many a week have been fully occupied with him; and now that he is here I do not care to intrude.'

Rye Harland was not without some pride of her own, and this speech from her old friend wounded her deeply. She did not reply immediately, and when she did speak her words came slowly, and were barely audible.

'I won't say you are jealous, Arthur, because there is nothing to be jealous about; but you should not imagine wrong things, nor always be putting others into competition with yourself. I am sure father and mother will always be glad to see you at the Mount, as they have been in the past.'

Saying which she left him to his own thoughts. They were not likely to yield him much satisfaction, for, argue as he would, he could not persuade himself that the part he had acted was either judicious or reasonable. The Harlands had talked a great deal in his presence about Jack Benson, the son of Mr. Harland's friend. He had learned from what had been said that this young man was like himself in one respect—an only child, and in another vastly different, for his father was immensely rich and a member of the New South Wales Parliament. He had noted what preparations had been made for his coming, and all he had seen and heard, instead of awakening a feeling of generous interest in his own mind respecting the young man from the colonies, had gone to feed the spirit of discontentment and jealousy which was every day growing stronger in him.

Rye's rebuke produced one result, which, although temporary, was good whilst it lasted. It opened his eyes to the silliness of his behaviour, and made him feel a little contempt for himself. The sting of the rebuke lay in the fact that she had not said anything about how his presence at the Mount would affect her. Had she found Jack Benson's company so delightful then, that she could do without his altogether?

Arthur Brixton was no coward, and when this possibility dawned upon him he felt it like a challenge to conflict, and resolved that the challenge should not remain unheeded; for, if the truth may be told, he had indulged in day-dreams, and in them all Rye Harland had played a considerable part. What else was to be expected. She was the only friend he had, and from the time of his boyhood they had been much together. Besides, Arthur Brixton would have been of a strange temper indeed if he had never been charmed by so amiable a girl as the daughter of his patron.

Why, long ere this, had not the grand step been taken, and the whole matter settled? Considering the difference in the social position and prospects of the two young people, it might have been thought that Arthur would have been afraid of having his suit rejected. Had he been naturally inclined to underrate himself, the generous conduct of his friends would have more than counterbalanced this tendency. But Arthur Brixton was not the victim of a weakness of that kind. Although he did not admit it to himself, the cause of the present state of affairs was simply that his ruling passion was an inordinate ambition; and if the truth must be told of him, he had felt inclined to wait for years and years, and at the time that he believed he could do best for himself arrange his matrimonial affairs. If Rye Harland was then inclined to favour his suit, she might or might not have her chance.

Arthur had never said this much even to his own heart, and yet there is no doubt that half unconsciously he had taken up this position. The dissatisfaction he had cherished regarding his humble position, and his envy of those who were rich and well-connected, had led

RYE AND HARLAND.

him into the habit of calculating in what way anything that happened or was likely to happen, could help him to attain the object of his ambition. And even the most sacred feelings of the heart did not escape the worldly contamination.

Jack Benson's appearance on the scene, however, had created a complication. Arthur did not wish to be second in the regard of Rye Harland ; and his courage and love of conflict with difficulties, caused him to long to break a lance, metaphorically speaking, with the new comer.

Little more than an hour had passed till

Arthur was ushered into the comfortable dining-room at the Mount. All the members of the family, including Jack Benson, were present; and when the two young men were introduced, it was interesting to note the difference between them. They both had a dark complexion, but there the likeness ended. The Australian was the more powerful of the two, but Arthur Brixton's movements were more graceful. Arthur had indeed all the quiet self-control of one 'to the manner born.

Notwithstanding his apparently careless demeanour, his powers of observation were on the alert from the moment he entered the room, and he keenly sought to measure the other, whom already he regarded as a combatant regards his foe. Jack, on the other hand, although he did not return the smile with which he was greeted, was perfectly frank, and met Arthur with the picturesque swinging movement that was natural to him.

Presently they settled down to music. Arthur took a violin, which he played splendidly, and Rye took her place at the piano.

'What shall it be?' the young lady asked.

'We might try a selection from Beethoven's symphonies, if Mr. Benson cares for our favourite composer. And if he plays the violin, I shall be glad to turn over the leaves,' Arthur said.

Rye thought her old friend was in one of his finest moods, and was correspondingly glad, for she liked Arthur, and wished her cousin, as she had begun to call Jack, to think well of him too.

'I must pray to be excused. Beethoven is beyond me,' Jack Benson said, and the glitter of Arthur's deep-set eyes brightened with satisfaction.

From Beethoven they passed to Jensen, and then to Schumann, whose 'Dreams' suited Rye's talents almost as well as Beethoven.

Arthur, for an amateur, was a really good violinist, and this evening he excelled himself. With what tenderness—a tenderness so firm that the sound never sunk into mere weakness —he drew the bow, and how true and sad were the tones of his violin as they blended with,

whilst remaining distinct from, the louder notes of the piano. There was an infinite yearning in the music he made, and in so far it was a correct interpretation of his own feelings; and if the notes were sometimes too piercing and clear, and lacking in weirdness, this defect was in a large measure covered by the piano accompaniment.

Jack Benson was strangely affected, for he had never heard such a performance before In Arthur Brixton there was something of triumph when he laid down his instrument.

'I hope,' he said, 'Mr. Benson will give us the pleasure of hearing him.'

'I wish I could,' Jack answered; 'but I only play simple airs, not this classical music.'

'But you like it—you like Beethoven, I am sure?' Rye asked; and her manner betrayed that she was not quite sure, but would be greatly disappointed if he did not. 'We are quite of the opinion of those critics who say that Beethoven is the Shakespeare of music.'

'I like it, certainly. I could not tell you how much your playing has affected me; I felt I wanted to touch those keys, to have a violin in my hand—anything, in fact, to help you in producing these glorious harmonies, and yet I cannot.'

'But you can sing?'

Jack shook his head.

'You should not tease, Rye.'

'I have heard you, sir, humming a tune.'

'It must always have been the same.'

'So you admit it, then; and you have a favourite, too. We will have it in this very hour,' she asserted with emphasis.

'Don't, please; you will inflict a torture on yourselves and make me feel ashamed.'

'Not at all. I know the tune—a favourite everywhere, too; sad, pathetic. "Tired" it is.'

There was a little scorn in Arthur Brixton's eyes when he heard this, and he concluded he had 'measured his man' as far as music was concerned.

Rye turned up her music, and quickly found the copy. With a firm, steady touch she brought out the first notes. Jack turned to the copy and commenced.

He began badly, like a man seeking for something of whose whereabouts he is not quite certain. The first two or three notes were not by any means true, but when he had passed these his voice became steadier. There was no dash in his style, and no evidences of training in his voice, but his rendering of the simple song was pleasing and pathetic. As he sung there was more than complaint in the words—they became the utterance of a heart satisfied to be weary, because of the sweetness and joy of rest which weariness brings.

Rye turned and looked at his powerful frame, and understood why, in the consciousness of his strength, he had succeeded, without knowing it, in giving the song what to her was a new rendering. It had in it its usual pathos, without any touch of childishness. The notes were not the groans of exhaustion and weakness, but the tragic cries of a dying hero.

'Thank you very, very much,' Rye said.

'I cannot apologize,' Jack answered, 'for what was not my fault, although I know I made some positive mistakes, in addition to showing the general faults of one who has not had a musical education. But you should not have pressed me to sing.'

'You did not hit the mark quite just at first,' Rye admitted, with her usual simplicity, 'but you sung the piece beautifully nevertheless. That was because you felt it; and I am so pleased that I purpose to take your musical education into my hands.'

Jack Benson still did not smile, but he was pleased, and bowed low as he might have done to a princess.

'It is my mother's favourite song,' he remarked.

When Arthur Brixton left the Mount that night he was not quite sure that his musical talents had made so good an impression as the much inferior gifts of Jack Benson.

To Jack himself the question of what impression had been produced had never occurred. He had sung to please the company, and having succeeded in that, felt fully rewarded.

(To be continued.)

The Traveller's Tree.

A EUROPEAN traveller, on his way from the coast of Madagascar to the capital, Tananarivo, in the interior, had emptied his water-flask, and was suffering from thirst. He asked one of the natives of his party when he should be able to obtain water.

'Any time you like,' said the native, smiling.

The European saw no signs of springs of water; but the natives conducted him to a group of tall, palm-like trees, standing in a cluster on the edge of the forest, with straight trunks and bright green broad leaves growing from the opposite sides of the stalk, and making the tree appear like a great fan. The white man gazed admiringly at the tree.

'You think it is a fine tree,' said the native, 'but I will show you what it is good for.'

He pierced the root of one of the leaf-stems, at the point where it joined the tree, with his spear, whereupon a stream of clear water spurted out, which the European caught in his water-can, and found cool, fresh, and excellent to drink.

The party having satisfied their thirst and taken a supply, the native who had spoken went on—

'This tree, which is good for us in more ways than one, we call the traveller's tree.'

'But where does the water come from that the tree contains?' asked the white man. 'Is it taken up from the soil?'

'Oh, no,' said the native. 'The leaves drink in the rain that falls on them, and when it has passed all through them it becomes very pure and sweet.'

'And are there many of these trees on the island?'

'There are so many that sometimes one sees no other trees for a mile; and very often we take no provision of water when we travel, because we know that we shall find the traveller's tree.' ·

'And you say there are other things that they are good for?'

The native answered by asking another question.

'Do you remember,' he said, 'the village that we passed through this morning, with its wooden huts roofed over with leaves? Those huts were made of nothing but the traveller's tree. The wood splits easily, but makes rough planks for floors, and the walls of the houses are made of the bark. With the branches we make the rafters, and the leaves cover the roof. But this is not all that the good tree does. We are coming soon to a village whose people I know, and I will show you more.'

The native was eager in his haste to show to the traveller what the tree still had in store for him, and the European, for his part, felt no little curiosity. They arrived soon at the village, and the guide conducted the traveller to the hut of a friend, who received them very hospitably, and soon spread a meal for them.

First he placed upon a sort of table a spread made of some vegetable substance, very light and pretty; then he set before his guests two drinking vessels of a material which the white man did not recognize, and then he gave them two utensils, which, although rude in shape, served in the stead of knife and fork.

In the midst of the table he placed a large bowl, filled with cream of very appetizing appearance. In another vessel there was a quantity of oil, with almonds floating upon it.

'Before we begin,' said the guide, 'I must tell you what I promised. Everything that there is upon this table comes from the traveller's tree. You see this table-cloth? It is made of the fibres of the leaves of the tree. These drinking-cups, these plates, these knives, are made of the wood or the bark of the tree. What you take to be cream is a dish made of the seeds of the tree, pounded up with meal, and mixed with a kind of milk drawn from the trunk of the tree. What you think are almonds are little cakes made of these seeds, and oil is pressed from the skin or shuck

of the seed. As for the water you are about to drink, you know that already. And we get not only these things, but some of the people of Madagascar have made a kind of cloth that they wear out of the fibre of the wood.'

Terrestrial Magnetism.

 HE earth itself is a great magnet. This discovery was made by Dr. Gilbert, and is regarded his greatest. But how is the earth's magnetism made evident? First, by its action on a freely suspended magnet-needle. Second, by its inductive action on iron or steel. With regard to the first, what is its action on a freely suspended magnetic needle? The earth's action on a magnetic needle is directive only; this may be seen by a simple experiment. If a magnetic needle is floated on water it rotates until it is in the magnetic meridian, when it points north or south, but there is no progressive motion in any direction. Thus the compass needle points north and south, or, to be precise, to the magnetic north and south poles. These poles do not correspond with the geographical poles of the earth. The magnetic north pole of the earth is more than 1,000 miles from the actual pole. In 1831 it was found by Sir J. C. Ross to be situated in Boothia Felix, just within the Arctic circle. The south magnetic pole of the earth has never been reached. We may note that the magnetic poles coincide very nearly with the regions of greatest cold. At most places on the earth's surface, the compass needle does not then point truly north and south. In 1881, the needle in London, pointed at an angle of 18° 33' west of the true north. The direction in which the needle points is called the magnetic meridian, and the angle which the magnetic meridian makes with the geographical meridian, is called the angle of declination or variation. The existence of 'declination' was discovered by Columbus in 1492, although the Chinese are said to have had a previous knowledge of it.

In 1576 an instrument maker, Mr. R.

Norman, discovered that a magnetic needle balanced on a horizontal axis, tends to dip downwards towards the north. Such needles are called dipping needles, and the angle they form with the horizontal is called the ' dip ' or inclination of the needle. The earth's action on the dipping needle may be easily understood if the reader provides himself with a good bar magnet and a common knitting needle. Let the needle be magnetized and freely suspended over the bar magnet, and as it is moved along the magnet, from one pole to the other, it passes through every variation of dip. Placed at one pole of the magnet, say, the north, the needle becomes vertical with the south end downwards, and as it is moved towards the other pole the dip becomes less and less, until at the equator of the magnet the needle is horizontal; beyond this the north end begins to dip, and its inclination increases, until the needle is again vertical with its north pole downwards over the south pole of the magnet. The needle in being drawn along the magnet continually enters into new lines of force, and the variation or dip is caused by the needle successively placing itself in these lines of force. The earth, like smaller magnets, has its lines of force, and the dipping needle places itself parallel to them. Thus at the poles it is vertical, and at the equator—half way between the poles—it is horizontal. The dip in London is nearly 70°.

Magnetic maps and charts are drawn for the convenience of navigators and others. Such maps may be made by finding out those places at which the declination is the same and joining them by a line. In 1888 the declination at Torquay, Stafford, Leeds, Hartlepool, and at Bristol was the same. Thus on a magnetic map these towns would be joined by a line, and that line called an ' Isogonic ' line, or line of equal declination. In the same way we might make a magnetic map, with lines joining the places at which the angle of dip was equal. Such lines are called ' Isoclinic ' lines; they run round the world like the parallels of latitude, but are irregular in form.

Let us now turn to the second evidence of the earth's magnetism—viz., the earth's mag-

netism is made evident by its inductive action on iron or steel.

Any piece of iron or steel which remains long in one position becomes more or less magnetized. Thus, if fire-irons, which have usually stood in a nearly vertical position, be examined by their influence on a needle, they will be found to have acquired some magnetism, the lower end being the north-seeking pole. The induced magnetism is stronger when the bar of iron or steel is placed in the magnetic meridian, *i.e.*, parallel to the lines of the earth's magnetic force.

By way of experiment, take a bar of soft iron and hold it in the position referred to, namely, at an angle of 70° with the horizon, pointing north and south in direction of magnetic needle, and it becomes a magnet and will attract iron filings or a needle, or cause the magnetic needle to deflect; the end which is downward is the north-seeking pole. If the position of the bar is reversed the poles are reversed. Move it out of the magnetic meridian and its magnetism disappears, unless, indeed, you have made it a permanent magnet by striking it with a hammer when in the above position, and thus developed coercive force. Steel bars may be feebly magnetized in the same way.

Both the declination and the inclination are subject to changes ; some of these changes take place slowly, others yearly, and others again every day. The daily variations are very slight. In Europe the north pole moves towards the west from sunrise until about an hour after noon, when it returns towards the east until about 10 p.m. ; after this it remains quiet. These delicate variations appear to be connected with the course of the sun. The action of the sun and moon in raising tides in the atmosphere may also account for them.

The annual variations correspond with the movement of the earth around the sun. In London the total force is greatest in June, and least in February, but in the southern hemisphere the reverse is the case. The angle of dip is less during the four summer months than the rest of the year. There are other changes which require many years to run their course.

In 1580 the compass at London pointed 11°
east of true north. In 1657 the compass
pointed true north; it then gradually moved
westward, until, in 1816, it attained a maximum of 24°; from that time it has gradually
diminished to its present position of 18°; in
England it diminishes at the rate of about 7'
per year. Probably about 1976 it will point
true north again. In all parts of the earth
both declination and inclination are changing
similarly.

The Legend of the Robin.

HE old British monks, in their fanciful
musings, in which, however, they
sought to convey and maintain
religious truth, devised this
able:—

As our Saviour was bearing His cross to
Calvary, His head being then crowned with
thorns, which pierced His brow, a robin flew,
and, perching on that wreath, plucked out
therefrom a thorn. The gory drops fell off
and crimsoned the robin's breast with the
Saviour's blood. And since that proud hour
the robin race have borne this red sign of
God's favour. I copy a part of the English
lyric:—

'Bearing His cross, while Christ passed forth forlorn
His God-like forehead by the mock crown torn,
A little bird took from that crown one thorn.
To soothe the dear Redeemer's throbbing head,
The bird did what she could; His blood, 'tis said,
Down dropping, dyed her tender bosom red.
Since then, no wanton boy disturbs her nest;
Weasel nor wild cat will her young molest;
All sacred deem the bird of ruddy breast.'

This, of course, is a conceit that has no
foundation in fact. Yet what a sacred, and
even sacramental, fancy is it; thus to affix to
a bird, so common as the robin redbreast, the
signet of that hour when, mocked with a
crown of thorns, when pierced by our sorrows,
and wounded for our transgressions, our
Saviour staggered on to the crucifixion!
Well may this 'bird of ruddy breast,' when
he stands proudly erect, with full bosom all
crimsoned over, remind us of this devout
conceit.

'Sweet robin, would that I might be
Bathed in my Saviour's blood like thee;
Bear in my breast, whate'er the loss,
The bleeding blazon of the Cross;
Live ever, with thy loving mind,
In fellowship with human kind;
And take my pattern still from thee,
In gentleness and constancy.'

BISHOP DOANE.

We may derive another thought from this
religious fancy. Many are they who wear a
circlet of thorns, whose sharp points sting and
poison. Cares, trials, disappointments, bereavement, and secret sorrows compose those thorns.
The beholder sees the brow of beauty decked
with diamonds. That may not be the real
crown. It is only a mockery. For an invisible
circlet of thorns pierces that head until it aches
with anguish. But the birds of sacred song
often pull out a thorn, or ease the throbbing
wound. Hence, God has given us not only
the comforting thoughts of sacred poetry, but
He has imparted to gifted persons the talent
of musical composition, whereby they have
attuned these poetic thoughts with the charming cadences of melodious sound. And thus
we have sacred song. How much fit music
enhances the soothing power of helpful words?
Many an aching heart has found a spiritual
anodyne, in the tender melody of 'Jesu, Lover
of my soul.' Often has a hesitating Christian
girded up the loins of resolution by the inspiring notes of 'Stand up! stand up for Jesus.'
Oh, how many sufferers, languishing on beds
of sickness, are comforted every day by the
singing of one of the old hymns! The Psalmist
declares of the saints, '*Let them sing aloud on
their beds.*' Paul and Silas, cramped as they
were, with their feet fast in the stocks, faint
from want of food and from the horrible
scourging, sang praises unto God in the dead
of the night, even as the nightingale disburdens
her whole soul upon a dark sky. Many a
vexation would pass out of our minds if we
would sing over it. He who has a holy song
in his heart is stronger, both to suffer and
to labour, than the one who has a hymnless
soul.

REV. GEO. S. MOTT, D.D.

The Attitude of the Church to the Gambling Spirit of the Age.

Part II.

UT what is the attitude of the Church towards the gambling spirit of the age? It is one of decided hostility. While true to her character and mission she can have no fellowship with the works of darkness. But her first duty is to set her house in order before she commences with the world. It is well to look to ourselves before we begin to reform other people. It seems a peculiar anomaly to attempt to put other men right when you are sadly wrong yourself. It exposes one to the cutting rejoinder, 'Physician, heal thyself.' There are even now human beings to whom religion is nothing but disguised selfishness. And the Church has too frequently fostered this spirit of selfish greed. Its lotteries and raffles have sadly disgraced it, and one thinks if Jesus Christ were to come back again He would make a whip of small cords, and drive them out of His sanctuary. It is vain to say it is for the good of the cause, as this is the Jesuistical principle that the end justifies the means, or doing evil that good may come, and Paul would say the damnation of such persons. is just. The Church itself must be cleansed from this gambling spirit, and become pure and disinterested, noble and good. She must rise above all selfishness, and recognize the just rights of every man. The learned must never take advantage of the ignorant, but seek to instruct them, and show them a more excellent way. The wise must teach the simple, the strong help the weak, and the rich assist the poor, recognizing the equality of the race and the brotherhood of men in Christ Jesus.

There should also be a loftier morality in the Church, and the manifestation of the Christly spirit. This is a marvellous age for preaching, but a moderate one for good living. Christ is everywhere preached in these days, and in every variety of method, from the blare of trumpets, the beating of drums, and the planting of banners of the Salvation Army, to the stately services of the venerable cathedral. It seems to us as if the world were almost sick of preaching. And what is specially needed is not so much the preaching of Christ as the living of Christ, the manifestation of the Christly spirit in the everyday life of man, in the family circle, the workshop, the mine, the place of business, and the marts of commerce. If Paul rejoiced in the preaching of Christ he would have rejoiced far more in the living of Christ, or the exemplification of the spirit of Christ in the lives of men. A man may be moral without being Christian, but he cannot be Christian without being moral. Morality can never be divorced from Christianity. But we have been shocked with the morality of some professedly Christian men; and both the Church and the world have been stunned with their dishonesty. So that we have been tempted to think with Hamlet,

> ' To be honest, as this world goes,
> Is to be one man picked out of ten thousand.'

But if the Christian religion be anything it is righteousness and goodness. And these must be manifested in the every-day life of religious professors. It will then be seen that

> ' A Christian is the highest style of man.

The pulpit also should give no uncertain sound, but speak out forcibly on this growing evil of betting. It must never lose touch with the masses of the people, but seek to purify and ennoble them. Shall society become dishonest and corrupt, and the pulpit be a dumb oracle? Should it not be the leader of everything that is virtuous and good? It is to be feared that we preachers do not give sufficient prominence to the ethics of life, but dilate on popular themes. In some cases we have been so much taken up with the evangelistic propaganda as to overlook the moralities of life. We have need to come down from our stately eminence to the commonalities of every-day life. Society should be reminded of the first principles of morality, honesty, truthfulness, justice, and uprightness in all the relations and connections of life. We require an ampler illustration and enforcement of the golden rule—'All things whatsoever ye would that men should do to you, do ye even so to them : for this is the law and the prophets' (Matt. vii. 12). And the practical development of this rule in the every-day life of man would put a new face on society at large. There should also be personal efforts to save these gamblers from their ruinous course of conduct. If we can gain access to them we may reason with them, and show them a more excellent way. Kind words have always been influential and powerful, and if we can let them see and feel that we are interested in them and seek their highest good, our efforts may be successful. Sympathetic intercourse with gamblers will have far more influence over them than strong denunciation of their conduct. But, if need be, we should not hesitate to put the law in force against incorrigible offenders who fatten on the simple and credulous of society. Any one gaming or betting in an open or public place may be treated as a vagrant, and vagrants are punishable with one month's imprisonment, or with being sent to the House of Correction ; but we would not have recourse to law unless moral means had failed, and we have faith in the ultimate triumph of righteousness.

But special care should be taken to save our young people from betting. The proverb is, ' Prevention is better than cure,' and every effort should be made to save them from being entangled in the net of the betting fraternity. The danger is of them getting into the whirlpool of this gambling excitement and destroying themselves. As so many indulge in betting, they are specially exposed to temptation. These subtle gamesters will entice them by suggesting that they may make a little money; they need not speculate much, but only venture a little ; but the beginnings of

evil should be avoided. Principles of thorough honesty should be instilled into our young people. They should scorn to receive money unless they legally inherit it, or honestly earn it. If a person puts a shilling into a lottery, and wins a piano that is worth twenty pounds, he has no moral claim to it, because he has not given an adequate equivalent for it. Chance has given him the advantage over others who were as foolish as himself. Value for value is the only righteous principle in all the transactions of life. This must be engraven on the hearts of our young people. When an American wit proposed a toast on one occasion, he said the youth of his country reminded him of the three degrees of comparison—First they tried to get on, then they tried to get honour, and then they tried to get honest. We would reverse this order, and admonish our young people to determine at all cost to be honest ; and if it please God to give them honour, their moral honesty will be the safest foundation of their future eminence. An unhappy princess once wrote the inscription, ' Oh, keep me innocent, make others great.' And if our young people keep innocence, and do the thing which is right, they will have peace and happiness, and these are superior to wealth and honour. But a great deal of the betting of the world is mixed with the sports of men. Sport is largely something to bet on ; and what shall we say to these things? We cannot do away with the amusements and recreations for our young people ; these are as necessary to the healthy development of their nature as their daily bread. Suppose we were to do away with cricket and football and other games. If these could be banished from the world while the old gambling spirit remained it would create other objects upon which to bet. But a wise expediency will avoid those games which lend themselves too easily to it. Shakespeare cries—

' O opportunity! thy guilt is great.

It would be sad for us to appoint the season that they may sin the more conveniently. But let the eternal principles of truth and righteousness be instilled into their hearts, and these will be the best safeguard against the assaults of evil.

'Take then no thought for aught save truth and right.
Content, if such thy fate, to die obscure.
Wealth palls and honours; fame may not endure,
And noble hearts soon weary at the light.
Keep innocence, be all the true man ought;
Let neither pleasure tempt, nor pain appal.
Who hath this, he hath all things, having nought;
Who hath it not, hath nothing, having all.'
JOHN WORSNOP.

The Cat.

THE cat is perhaps the most domestic of all our home pets. It comes nearest to you, takes possession of you, now appropriating your shoulder, now your knee, and even your couch, clinging to your house more than you do yourself, using liberty, not for roaming or escape, but to return and rest more securely in a shelter tried and proved. The cat belongs to what is called the *Fëudæ* species, in which the teeth and claws are at the maximum of development, the instinct and appetite having correspondent aptitude to consume and gloat over a victim caught. The cat falls upon its prey with its front paws, which are armed with five strong, hooked, compressed claws. With these paws it can strike a sharp and effective blow, the muscular development of the paw being especially strong, and contrived for the purpose of attack and defence. The cat has remarkably good hearing, equally good is its power of smell, and its sight is also very accurate, especially in the dark. With its senses so acute, its tread remarkably soft, and excellent power of spring, its action in conflict with rats or mice is often most deadly and sure. It is thought that our present domestic cat is a descendant from the wild European cat, but this is doubted by some eminent authorities. Our common house cat does not seem to have been known to the ancient Britons. The sculptures, paintings, and embalmed mummies of the ancient Egyptians show to us that such a domestic animal was known in the homes of Egypt. The wild cat was once known in Britain, and it may still be sometimes met with in the north of Scotland and some parts of Ireland. It abounds in greater abundance in the wooded countries of Russia, Germany, and Hungary. Suppose we saw a wild cat approach us, we should be as much afraid of it as of a fox; a domestic cat would be excused for its intrusions, because its liberty with strangers is often taken as a sign of the love and confidence with which it is treated. Some seem to think that it is a sign of weakness to make a pet of a cat—a weakness to be met with most often in old maids, or with those who are eccentric, who must expend their affections in a strange way. But history tells us of stranger pets than the cat, even associated with some of the greatest men. Goethe made a pet of a snake; Tiberius, the Roman emperor, of a serpent; Honorius, Roman emperor, of a hen. Louis II. when ill could only find interest in an exhibition of dancing pigs, and of Cowper, the poet, it is said he was at no time more happy than when feeding his tame hare. Amongst those who made a pet of the cat was Canon Liddon; some of the most gracious and kindly things have been said by this great preacher. 'Those,' he says, 'who declare that cats care only for places and not for persons, should go to the *Cat Show* at the Crystal Palace, where they will see recognition between cat and owner that will cure them of such an opinion. Their exhibition is a humiliation for some cats, which it will take them days to get over. A row of distinguished cats were sitting each on his cushion with their backs turned to the sightseers, whilst their faces, when from time to time visible, were expressive of the deepest gloom and disgust. Presently two little girls passed through the crowd to the cage of one of the largest cats crying, "There's Dick!" Instantly the great cat turned round, his face transfigured with joy, purred loudly, and endeavoured to scratch open the front of the cage that he might rejoin his little friends who were with difficulty persuaded to leave him at the show.' M. Champfleury, an eminent authority on cats, says, in speaking of their language, there are sixty-three different *myows*. 'But,' he adds, 'no one has completed the notation of these different cries.' It is not singular that such a docile, interesting animal should win our confidence and love, when we find in it such clear indications of preference and affection. If the cat has its sympathies, it has also its antipathies, and these antipathies are often manifest in a very marked way. I knew a ministerial friend who had a horror of cats. On entering a strange house he would inquire if such a creature was in the house ; if so, he would request the people to put it out. He lived next door to us. We had a fine grey cat which sometimes played in his garden, and we were obliged to part with it on this account. One day I asked him the reason of his dislike. He said he believed that all cats were enemies to him. He had proved this, because whenever he had tried to be kind with a cat, it had resented him by scratching him. He gave me one or two instances that seemed a striking confirmation of what he said. In showing much indulgence and kindness to the cat we are in danger of spoiling it, by permitting too much companionship and familiarity. This is done when we allow it to come to the table at meals, to sleep in the bed with children, to lie on the curtains or cushions, for in so doing it often marks them or tears them with its paws by stretching its legs when it awakes from sleep. On the other hand, a great injustice is done to a cat by giving it to a young child to tease and play with. It is also a great injury to a child, who should be taught true respect for the life of animals in the very beginning. As to the ailments of cats, they do not seem to be very common or pronounced. Puss generally knows how to take care of herself, and she seems to prefer her own remedies when anything ails her. Let us counsel then those who have cats to treat them with kindness mingled with firmness. Let the treatment be uniform, and especially insisted upon when they would make free with strangers. Then they will know your will, and the rule of the house. It will seem to be a piece of the discipline of the house, and no dishonour to those who may find it a home. If advancing in years do not part with it. It may be there by your hearthstone when others are gone who used to caress it—the remaining inmate of your house when death has emptied the home of loves and friendships you can never replace.

European Rulers.

THE EMPEROR OF RUSSIA.

ALEXANDER ALEXANDROWITCH succeeded to the throne by a painful accident of his own creation. His elder brother, Prince Nicolai, was Crown Prince. He was a man of finer mould, of broader political conception, and freer from prejudice and superstition. By an accidental blow the present emperor caused his death. This was recognized as unintentional by its victim, who in dying commended his empire and bride to him ; the latter he married eighteen months after, the former he assumed the Crown of on March 15, 1881.

The present emperor was born at St. Petersburg on March 10, 1845. He soon fell into collision with the immoral conditions of the Russian court, and during his youth was estranged from it and his parents. He is a man of rigid honesty, of pure and unstained life, of simple and frugal habits ; hence the *morale* of his father's times he fiercely detested. His education was seriously neglected. He has none of the accomplishments of contemporary sovereigns, having received only the ordinary education of an officer of the guards.

He is conscientious in the performance of his State duties. He has reformed the court all round, dismissing the mercenary parasites and political speculators who reduced his father to insolvency and made him so unpopular. He has purged its whole life, so that the moral sensitiveness of the most chaste is unoffended. People act and speak there in a new atmosphere ; the incredible extravagance of his father's reign has been supplanted by regulations economic almost to parsimoniousness. He is upright, has a peculiar horror of a lie, believes he holds the throne as a trust from God, and seeks to rise to the measure of its responsibility. Men may quarrel with his ideas and methods, but his motives stand unimpugned.

He, like his race, is very superstitious. At the coronation services it rained. This was a presage of bad times. As the emperor, however, crossed the Kemblin-square, the sun emerged from behind the cloud. This was a prophecy of good. A species of pigeon held sacred by the Russians flew through the hall and alighted on the imperial dais. This was esteemed a propitious omen. The emperor shares, fully and strangely, the superstitious susceptibilities of his race.

He is narrow in his conceptions, believes in his commands as monarch being absolute, and when once he has uttered a decision, whatever changes occur to suggest reconsideration, it is irrevocable. He has a sensitive heart, but the grievances of his subjects never reach him. He is not in touch with the life of his people, and is inaccessible to them. He receives all reports and acts through ministers, whose instrument he unconsciously is, and who make everything they touch reflect their own opinion.

The Russians are an intensely loyal race. This is accentuated by their ecclesiastical relations to the emperor. He is the head of their church, the keeper of their faith and conscience. Despite all this there is growing a national sentiment which the censorship of the Press, the vigilant supervision by government officials of all schools, public meetings, and societies, the severity of penal laws against political sins, will not suppress or defeat. Modern ideas are creeping in, and political aspiration is being excited. From this emperor, with his peculiar mental bias, his present advisers, and his avowed principles and intentions, no great reforms are expected. He has already partly undone the grandest act of his father's life—the liberation of the serfs. Russia has had no great revolution, but it is feared the conditions of one are being slowly formed. Will no master of statescraft rise to save it?

The emperor has two individuals by his side who 'rule the rule.' One is the empress. She does not interfere in political or governmental affairs, but is ever active in philanthropic and benevolent movements. She has become a typical Russian, leading its society with taste and tact, and is the foster-mother of every patriotic aspiration and effort. She is universally popular.

The other is M. de Giers, who directs the Russian foreign policy. In him the emperor has complete confidence. He is recognized as a wise and safe statesman, and does much to moderate the emperor's racial prejudices which, if unrestrained, might provoke serious continental strife.

I. LOCKHART.

Philadelphia.

PHILADELPHIA is the principal city of Pennsylvania, and takes rank as the second city in the United States, New York standing first. It lies about eighty-five miles to the south-west of the latter place, and is situated on the west bank of the Delaware River. Its area is larger than that of any other American city, being about 129 miles. It is twenty-two miles in length at its longest point, and its breadth varies from five to ten miles. The Schuylkill River runs through the city, an divides it into two portions, which are nearly equal in size, and which are connected by eight bridges situated at different points. The length of river frontage on the Delaware is nearly twenty miles, and there are five miles of wharves. Schuylkill has sixteen miles of frontage, with four miles of wharves. It will thus be seen that the city affords extraordinary accommodation for shipping. The very heaviest vessel can navigate the Delaware at all seasons of the year, and the harbour connected with it is one of the best protected in the country.

The history of Philadelphia down to the period of the War of Independence is virtually the history of Pennsylvania. The patent granted to William Penn for the territory embraced within the present Commonwealth of Pennsylvania was signed by Charles II. on the 24th of March, 1681 ; and in the autumn of that year Penn appointed three commissioners to proceed to the new province, and lay out a great city. His instructions were to select a site on the Delaware, 'where it is most navigable, high, dry, and healthy—that is, where most ships can best ride, of deepest draught of water, if possible to load or unload at the bank or quayside without boating or lightering of it.' The site of the city was soon determined on, and the laying out of the city was proceeded with according to the modified instructions of Penn. What was then projected now constitutes the old part of the present city, and covers about 1,300 acres. The seat of government was fixed in this town by the meeting of the governor and council on the 10th of March, 1683, and the General Assembly met two days after. For 117 years the city continued the capital of Pennsylvania, and was the most important town, commercially, politically, and socially, in the colonies during the whole of this period. The man, next to Penn, whose influence was most deeply impressed on the town and colony was Benjamin Franklin, whose power was felt almost on his first landing in 1723, and its impress is visible to-day. He originated the present university, the American Philosophical Society, the Library Company, founded the Hospital, and organized the first fire-engine brigade in the city. During the struggle for independence Philadelphia was the virtual capital of the colonies, and the scene of all the stormy events of those troublous times. The first Congress of the new nation met in its Carpenters' Hall, and it continued the seat of the United States Government until the city of Washington was specially projected for that purpose.

The old city was somewhat contracted in area for years, but in close proximity to it numerous other towns sprang up, and the district became a very populous one. But in 1854 a Consolidation Act was passed by the Legislature of the State, and the old limits were extended so as to embrace all the territory then known as the county of Philadelphia. This arrangement abolished all the other distinct districts, and transferred all their franchises and property to the consolidated city under one municipal government.

The greater part of the present city is laid out in the form of a figure called a parallelogram, with streets at right angles to each other. Each of these plots contains about four acres divided by one or more small tho-

roughfares. The main streets running north and south are numbered from First to Sixty-third Streets, and those running east and west are generally named after trees and shrubs. Thus, while the main street is called Market Street, others are called Chestnut, Walnut, Pine, Spruce, &c. With few exceptions the principal streets are fifty feet wide, but Fourteenth Street is 113 feet, and Market Street 100 feet wide. The streets are paved chiefly with bricks, but some of them have flagstone sidewalks. The wholesale business houses are situated principally in Chestnut and Market Streets; the retail shops in the upper part of Chestnut Street and Eighth Street, while Walnut Street in the southern part of the city, and Spring Garden and Broad Street in the northern part, are the chief streets for large and handsome private houses. Nearly all the streets have lines of tramways, and the tramcar system has done a great deal to increase building, until the city has become famous for its homes. There are 160,000 dwelling-houses, and at least two-thirds of them are owned by their occupants. There are several parks and squares in the city. Four of the former, named Washington, Franklin, Rittenhouse, and Logan, have a combined area of twenty-nine acres. Six of the squares have a united area of eighteen acres. But besides these, the spacious Fairmount Park has an area of 2,791 acres, including 373 acres of the surface water of the River Schuylkill. This park lies in the north-west section of the city, and the river just named, together with the Wissahickon Creek wind through the greater part of it. The great Centennial Exhibition was held in the park in 1876, and the Horticultural Hall and Memorial Hall are allowed to remain in it as mementoes of so interesting an event. On the outskirts of the park is situated the garden of the Zoological Society, which covers 33 acres.

Among the buildings of Philadelphia that occupy a position of prominence, either for their architecture or historical associations, is the State House, also called Independance Hall. It was commenced in 1731, and was opened four years later. It is 100 feet long by 44 broad, and just before the Centennial celebration its external and internal appearance was restored as nearly as possible to its original condition. It was the scene of almost all the great civil events during the War of Independence. The Pennsylvania Hospital, Carpenters' Hall, and the old brick Swede's church, were all erected between the years 1700 and 1770. Another building of special character is the Post Office, which was completed in 1884, and which cost £1,600,000. It is of the Romanesque style of architecture, and was ten years in building. It is 425 feet long, 175 broad, and 164 high. The new City Hall is a remarkable building. It was commenced in 1871, and is the largest single building in America. It covers an area, including courtyards, of about four and a half acres, being 486 feet by 470. It contains 520 rooms, and the topmost point of the dome, on the tower, is 537 feet above the court-yard. It has cost about £2,600,000.

Philadelphia occupies an honourable place for the number and magnitude of its educational and philanthropic institutions. One of the chief of these is the Girard College. It was called after Stephen Girard, its founder. He began life as a poor boy, but by industry, tact, and business ability he succeeded in amassing a large fortune. While living, he was remarkable for his munificence to deserving institutions, and he left in his will the noble sum of £400,000 for the establishment of the college which bears his name. It is intended for the benefit of orphan children, but children who have lost their father only are also admitted. Preference is given to

PHILADELPHIA.

applicants born in the city of Philadelphia; next in order stand those born in any other part of Pennsylvania; then come those who have been born in New York; and lastly those born in the city of New Orleans. Applicants must not be under six nor over ten years of age. Five male and seven female teachers conduct classes, which commence with the alphabet, and include the higher branches of an excellent commercial education. The college buildings stand in a spacious enclosed park, and are six in number. The main building resembles in design a Greek temple of Corinthian architecture. It has eight columns at each end and eleven on each side, and these, like the building itself, are of native marble. Four other buildings, two on each side of the main edifice, are also of marble, but without columns; and the sixth building, which is of more recent erection, is of ordinary stone. These buildings are used as dormitories, class-rooms, dining-rooms, rooms for officers and teachers, infirmary, and wash-houses. The front of the college has a statue of Stephen Girard, the founder, and behind this statue there is a marble sarcophagus, or stone coffin, which contains his remains. Three hundred children receive an excellent education in this establishment, and at fourteen or eighteen years of age are apprenticed to some trade. Since the opening, about 1,300 children have found a home within its walls. The House of Refuge for juvenile delinquents has done a noble work. It has two divisions—one for boys, the other for girls. In its chapel the girls sit upstairs and the boys below. The two classes can see the minister, but not each other. Each inmate of the House has a little room exclusively his or her own, with a bed, chair, and table. Outside the boys' division there are workshops, where they engage in making cane chairs and other useful articles of furniture. There are two other divisions, A and B, into which all the inmates are divided according to their personal behaviour. The institution is partly supported by voluntary contributions and partly by the State.

Philadelphia has several good libraries, and is the head-quarters of a number of learned societies. It has 622 places of worship, of which the largest number belongs to the Methodist denominations; and the population, which is rapidly increasing, is about 900,000. The city is supplied with water by the Fairmount Waterworks, which are said to be of a very complete character, and which occupy a picturesque position. From the bank of the Schuylkill River there rises a perpendicular cliff, some seventy or eighty feet. On a little plateau between its base and the river the grounds are prettily laid out with paved walks and ornamented with statues, and trees spring from the crevices of the rocks. The great reservoir, which is formed on the summit of the natural mound, is reached by about ninety steps, and the walks along their margin afford magnificent views of the river and city. The pumps are worked by water supplied by the first dam of the river. The fall is not great, and to make up for it the water-wheels are made extra long. The works were designed and executed by Mr. Graff, to whose memory a monument has been erected in the grounds.

M. JOHNSON.

A Song in the Night.

'Rest in the Lord, and wait patiently for Him'
(Psalm xxxvii. 7).

REST thou in Him—no need for fear—
　Thou knowest not His plan for
　　　thee,
　　But well thou know'st that He
is near;
Then rest in Him, rest quietly.
Not much seems left of earthly joy—
　But O thy Father knoweth best!
Let this blest word thy thought employ—
　And rest.

Wait thou for Him—take what He sends,
　Sure that His every thought for thee
In naught but love begins and ends;
　Then wait for Him, 'wait patiently.'
For thee may rise—thou canst not tell—
　New joys, e'en this side heaven's gate;
If not—He always chooseth well—
　Just wait.

AMY J. PARKINSON.

Sapphires and Rubies.

'It cannot be valued with the gold of Ophir, with the precious onyx, or the *sapphire*. No mention shall be made of coral, or of pearls; for the price of wisdom is above *rubies*.'

HUS does the poet of the 'Book of Job' sing the praises of wisdom. We shall not stay to inquire whether the Bible names of the precious stones above mentioned correspond to the stones *we* know by these terms. The point of the quotation from the Bible bard is truth. Clay is a silicate of aluminium; the gems are an oxide.

Corundum is the name given by mineralogists to all varieties of crystallized alumina, some of which are green, some yellow, and some almost grey. It is the red and blue varieties to which we give the respective names of rubies and sapphires. The green corundum is known as an Oriental emerald, the yellow as the Oriental topaz.

The secret, then, of the value of these gems does not lie so much in their mere chemical composition. The base or chief ingredient of them is extremely common. It is rather in the form which that element assumes in rubies and sapphires that the preciousness consists. They are first of all beautifully crystalline, clear, translucent. The vision of

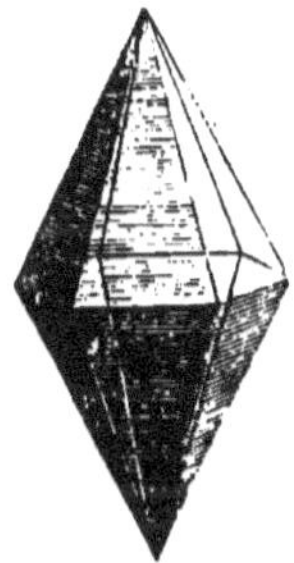

FIG. 1.—CRYSTALLIZED ALUMINA.

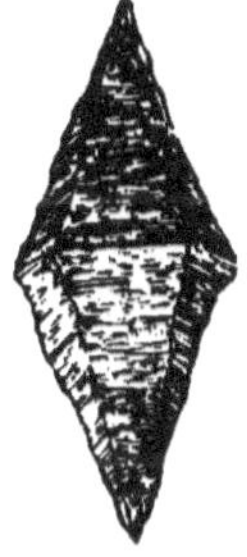

FIG. 2—A ROLLED CRYSTAL OF SAPPHIRE.

the preciousness of these gems, and we shall try to discover what gives their value to the stones whose names head this paper. Does the secret lie in their chemical composition? Chemistry is a great leveller. It teaches us that the charming tints of the autumn leaves are but due to mineral constituents, like iron, which the plants or trees have absorbed from the soil, and the colours of which come to preponderate in the leaf when the chlorophyll or *green* vegetable colouring matter dies. So chemistry tells us that rubies and sapphires, for all their dazzling beauty, are but *alumina*. Alumina is the oxide of the metal aluminium, which is one of the chief ingredients of common clay; and though it is not at all exact to describe rubies and sapphires as 'crystallized clay,' the expression contains much *poetic*

God which Moses and his companions is said by the writer of 'Exodus' to have had is thus described: 'And they saw the God of Israel: and there was under His feet *as it were a paved work of a sapphire stone, and as it were the body of heaven in His clearness.*' In Fig. 1 we give a drawing of a characteristic form of crystallized alumina, and in Fig. 2 what is called a rolled crystal of sapphire, because the crystals, 'instead of being sharply cut (as in the first illustration), so as to present faces which are quite flat and edges which are quite straight, are frequently more or less rounded, as though they had been rolled and rubbed among pebbles in the bed of a stream.' Hence the worn appearance. Occasionally sapphire is colourless, and is then sometimes sold as diamond, but in its best state it is, when properly cut and polished, a most exquisite translucent blue. A piece of sapphire which was dug out of the alluvial soil within a few miles of Ratnapoor in 1853 was valued at upwards of £4,000. Sacred to Jupiter among the ancient Greeks, the sapphire was one of the stones in the breastplate of the Jewish high priest. In ' Q.'s' wonderful story of ' Dead Man's Rock,' which tells of ' the quest and finding of the Great Ruby of Ceylon,' that priceless gem is thus described: ' Colliver lifted the smaller lid. Instantly a full rich flood of crimson light welled up, serene and glorious, with luminous shafts of splendour that, as we

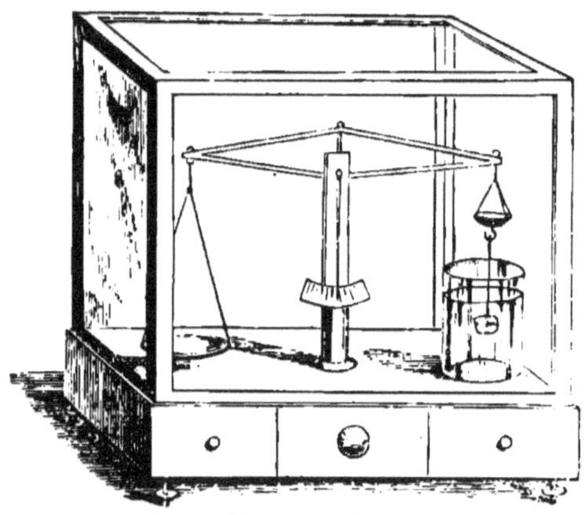

Fig. 3.—Hydrostatic Balance.

looked, met and concentred in one glowing heart of flame—met in one translucent, ineffable depth of purple red. Calm and radiant it lay there, as though no curse lay in its deep hollows, no passion had ever fed its flames with blood: stronger than the centuries, imperishably and triumphantly cruel—the Great Ruby of Ceylon!'

But these precious stones are not only noted for their colour and brilliance, but also for their hardness. Taking the diamond's hardness as 10—according to the scale of the Austrian mineralogist Mohs,—the ruby, the sapphire, and other varieties of corundum may be represented by the figure 9—the sapphire being perhaps slightly harder than

the ruby. These can scratch every other stone, except the diamond, and are themselves to be scratched by the diamond only. This test of hardness serves often to distinguish an Oriental emerald, or green corundum from an ordinary emerald ; and a true ruby from a spinel ruby or a garnet. The well-known substance used in polishing called emery-powder is a very impure form of alumina, and is related in hardness to the coarser varieties of corundum.

Still another feature distinguishes these precious stones, and contributes to their value, namely, their specific weight or density. The specific gravity of a body, as we have before explained, is its weight as compared with that of an equal bulk of water ; and there is no surer or safer test known to the mineralogist than this. Our illustration in Fig. 3 shows how it is managed. First of all the stone is weighed in air in the ordinary way; and then, suspended in water by the aid of a piece of horse-hair, it is weighed again. If the weight of the stone in air be divided by the loss of weight it undergoes when weighed in water, the quotient will represent the specific gravity. Thus, suppose a ruby weighs eighty grains in air and only sixty in water ; the difference of weight is therefore twenty grains. Divide the original weight eighty by the difference, twenty, and the result is four, which is the specific gravity of the ruby. But how is this? you ask. Thereby hangs an old and interesting story.

Hiero, the king of Syracuse, about 230 B.C. had committed to a jeweller a certain quantity of pure gold, of which to make a crown for him. When the crown was delivered, the king, suspected somehow that the goldsmith had kept back part of the gold. The weight was right, but the colour did not seem quite the thing. He applied to his friend, the philosopher Archimedes, to investigate the matter. The crown was not to be injured in any way during the process, and Archimedes was for a long time at a loss how to perform his task. One day, while intent upon the problem, he went, as was his custom, to the bath, and observed that, the bath being about full when he stepped into it, a portion of the water overflowed. It instantly occurred to him that that water must be equal in bulk to his own body, and instantly the means of satisfying Hiero's doubts suggested itself to him. It is said that overjoyed at his discovery he leapt from the bath, and ran naked through the streets of the city, crying "*Eureka! Eureka!*" "*I have found it! I have found it.*" He procured two masses, one of gold and the other of silver, each equal in weight to the crown. Filling a vessel very accurately with water, he ascertained exactly what weight of water was displaced—first by the gold mass and next by the silver mass. Making the same trial with the crown he found that it displaced more water than the gold and less than the silver. He was then able to inform the king that the crown was an alloy of gold with some other metal—most probably silver or copper. His discovery may be thus stated : the loss of weight which any body heavier than water sustains by being weighed in water is precisely equal to the weight of a quantity of water occupying the same bulk as the body in question. This law, and the story of the way in which it was ascertained, will explain the process used in finding the specific gravities of precious stones. When we say that rubies and sapphires have a specific gravity of four, we mean that they are four times as heavy as an equal bulk of pure water.

India, Ceylon, and Burmah are the sources of our supply of these precious stones. In Burmah all stones above a certain weight are claimed by the king ; and the finder of a large stone consequently contrives, before showing it, to break it up into fragments. One old traveller states that the throne of the Great Mogul was adorned with 108 rubies, of from 100 to 200 carats each. Q.'s 'Great Ruby of Ceylon' may perhaps be that said to have been possessed by the king of Ceylon, of which Marco Polo tells us that it was a span long, as thick as a man's arm, and without a flaw. A city was offered for it by Kubla Khan, but the Ceylonese king refused to part with it. It is not known what has become of it.

The Boyhood of Great Men.

ADAM CLARKE.

IRELAND claims Adam Clarke as one of her sons. His eyes first opened to the light in the little village of Moybeg, in the county of Londonderry. The date of his birth is uncertain, for the parish register, which chronicled each new arrival, was so badly kept at the time that Adam appeared that no record of his birth is to be found. But, record or no record, he *was* born, and, as nearly as we can tell, that important event happened some time between the years 1760 and 1762. He resembled many others who have acquired fame in that he was born into a home of poverty. Ireland was then, as now, a land of meagre resources. No doubt in the hall of the squire and in the home of the vicar the fire burnt with a merry glow, and the table was laden with plenty, but it was otherwise in the dwelling of James Clarke—the village schoolmaster and father of Adam. Like an impulsive Irishman, he had married in haste and ere his position in life had become assured. Poverty and hardship were the natural consequences. A little while before Adam was born the Irish home was broken up, and the schoolmaster, in search of happier fortunes, had embarked on board a ship bound for America ; but the project was relinquished at the last moment, and the repentant runaway settled once again in Ireland. But he found that it was easier to break up a home than to re-establish it ; and so, when Adam came to swell the domestic circle, fortune's tide was running very low, and the family exchequer was nearly empty. But nature, with kindly foresight, had well equipped him for his lot. He was a sturdy little fellow, able to run about when only nine months old, and, for a child, unusually hardy and strong. There is a story told of his strange fondness for snow. He called it his brother, and when it lay thick upon the ground, he would steal out almost naked in the early morning, and, digging in it what in his childish speech he called rooms, he would crown his work by sitting down, half naked as he was, in his chilly habitation.

When he was old enough to leave his mother, his grandparents took charge of him. It was their intention to rear him, and so reduce the drain on the schoolmaster's purse; but their benevolent purpose was thwarted by the perversity of Adam. He was always getting into mischief. A girl once told her younger sister to 'go to the nursery and see what baby is doing, and tell him he mustn't.' Adam must have closely resembled that baby. He overflowed with youthful spirits, and, instead of keeping close by the side of his grandmother, he roamed down the lanes, or climbed over walls, or, with a perverse liking for doing that which was forbidden, would be found leaning over the mouth of a draw-well, and peering with venturesome curiosity into its watery depths. His freaks and frolics made the life of his grandparents anything but a bed of roses, and it was without a reluctant pang that they restored the little urchin to his own home.

There the tide of fortune turned a little as time went on. A removal was made to another village, and Mr. Clarke became the licensed schoolmaster for that countryside. How many scholars he had we cannot tell, but we know that he was their sole teacher, and that his curriculum embraced the whole range of education from reading and writing, for which his pupils paid $1\frac{1}{2}$d. and 2d. per week, up to the ancient classics, instruction in which was assessed at 7s. a quarter. Those were high fees for the place and time, but they were well deserved. The hour of eight each morning saw the master at his desk, and the boys on the benches before him, and, with the exception of a break of one hour for dinner, the daily work went on continuously till four o'clock in winter and eight o'clock in summer. The holidays for the whole year, when put together, did not cover more than three weeks. Before and after school hours Mr. Clarke the teacher became Mr. Clarke the small farmer, and a little addition was made in that way to the domestic resources. But it was a life of chronic poverty and struggle, more acutely felt by his parents than by the merry Irish boy who was their son. Adam thrived on his rough nurture. His days were spent in dame Nature's school, in sight of hills and meadows. His nights were occupied in reading by his father's fireside, or in the enjoyment of the simple recreations of Irish village life. He attended the village singing class—a necessary institution in those days, for in the parish church there was no choir to usurp the singing, but every member of the congregation was expected to take part in the service of praise. And so Adam spent his nights in learning to sing, or else he went with others to the house of some neighbour, and there, while the men wove linen, and the women turned the spinning wheel, and the children either filled the bobbins or held aloft the flaming piece of fir that did duty for a candle, some aged crone would tell tales of other and more warlike times, and the evening hours, as if endowed with wings, would speed quickly away.

Possibly with some of my readers their thoughts of Adam Clarke are bound up with the solemn-looking volumes of his Commentary on the Bible resting on their father's bookshelves. And we naturally infer that he, who could create such a monument of learning as a man, must have been unusually clever as a boy. But the reverse was the case. At school Adam was dull and even stupid. The alphabet was for a long time a terrible difficulty, a veritable 'asses' bridge.' In reading he made such slow progress, that at eight years of age, when a strange teacher called at the school and put the scholars through an examination, Adam went forward, and passed the ordeal in such a halting manner, that his own teacher felt called upon, for his own credit's sake, to remark that 'that lad was a grievous dunce.' 'Never fear,' said the examiner, patting Adam on the head, 'this lad will make a good scholar yet.' How far he believed his own prophecy is doubtful, but that encouragement was much better for the poor boy than the terms 'stupid!' 'dunce!' which his own master flung at his head, and the chastisement with which his failures were emphasised. He had no sooner learnt to read English with any aptitude than he was put to Latin, and again he was baffled. He spent two days in trying to commit to memory two lines. The master's patience was exhausted. ' If you do not speedily get that lesson,' said he, ' I shall pull your ears as long as Jowler's.' Jowler was a boy belonging to the school, and that threat, combined with the scorn of his schoolfellows, roused Adam to a supreme effort. He mastered that lesson, and though his after studies taxed him severely, he. never found the same difficulty again. His dulness was not due to lack of brains. He learnt slowly, partly because the text-books in that villageschool were wretched productions, and partly because his teachers lacked sympathy and patience. Adam's mind refused to be crammed. When the reason of a thing was explained to him he could remember the thing itself. He made rapid progress when he found a congenial subject. He revelled in history, and turned his knowledge of Greek mythology to good account in a smart satire in verse that he composed on one of his school-fellows. It is no mean production for a boy only nine years of age. The love of reading grew upon him. Books for children were scarce on his father's shelves. Their neighbours were even more scantily furnished, and the lending library was unknown. The only way of getting them was to buy them, and so the pence that Adam and his brother earned for good behaviour went into a common fund, and, instead of passing over some old dame's counter for toys or sweets, were duly exchanged for some penny or even sixpenny book that caught their fancy. But the books that they bought showed that, with all their love of reading, they were real children. They spent happy hours over ' the famous and delightful history of Tom Thumb,' or ' the Adventures of Jack the Giant Killer.' ' Robinson Crusoe' and the ' Arabian Nights' were well thumbed. And the time spent in their perusal was not altogether thrown away, for it was the weird fascination of the ' Arabian Nights' that first kindled in Adam that taste for Oriental history which was so useful in his study of the Bible. One thing that the reading of these romances did for him was to inspire his childish mind with a strong faith in a supernatural world.

If that faith tended towards superstition, we must remember that the boy lived in the land of hobgoblins and ghosts. The story is told of his attempt to secure a copy of a work on magic called ' the occult philosophy of Cornelius Agrippa.' He heard that a schoolmaster eight miles away had a copy. He got a letter from his father asking for the loan of it, and, though he knew not the road, boldly set off. His mother sought to deter him by telling him that he would be lost. ' Never fear, mother,' said he, ' I shall find the way well enough.' ' But you will be so weary by the time you get there.' ' Never fear,' answered Adam, ' if I reach there and get the book, I hope to get as much out of it as will bring me home without touching the ground.' Some say he expected to return home on the back of an angel. However, the loan of the book was refused, and the little fellow had to trudge back just as he came.

It may seem strange that such superstition could exist in an intelligent and Christian home. But Mr. and Mrs. Clarke were neither better nor worse than most people about them. Adam's mother was a Presbyterian, whilst her husband was a Churchman. She had a wonderful knowledge of the Bible, and could frequently frighten her son into obedience by some apt quotation from its pages, but her harsh Calvinism had no attraction for him. Beyond the daily repetition of prayers taught him by his mother, and the rigid observance of Sunday, he gave no evidence of religion. He was never outwardly wicked, and, with the exception of a passion for dancing, acquired at the village singing-class, he ran into no moral danger. When a full-grown lad he had two narrow escapes from death. In one case he fell from a horse, as he was bringing a sack of grain from a neighbouring village. The other adventure, which was far more serious, happened when he was living by the sea-side. He rode his father's horse into the sea and, rashly venturing beyond the breakers, was caught by a heavy wave and swept under. The boy remembered no more until he found himself stranded on the shore, whilst the horse was slowly walking homewards about half a mile away. Such narrow escapes from death no doubt inspired sober reflection, but no abiding impression was made on him until the Methodists came to the village. At first Adam went to the meetings expecting to see some fun, then his mother went, and, finding among the Methodists a religious life which was missing at either the village church or chapel, she joined them, and opened her home for the Methodist preachers. Little did she think that her son Adam would be one of the foremost men in the ranks of that ministry. But God purposed that, and by slow degrees was preparing the worker for his work. Silently the good seed was ripening. So great was his eagerness to hear the preachers, when they were in the neighbourhood, that more than once after eight o'clock at night, when his day's work was done, Adam hurried several miles away to hear a sermon. He read good books in search of light. He went carefully through the New Testament, earnestly searching to see ' whether these things were so.' It was some time before the change came. His mind had long been the scene of conflict, but one morning, as he knelt in the field where he was at work, he was enabled to trust Christ as his Saviour. The conflict was past, the light had come, and he had the inward assurance that God had indeed forgiven him. And so commenced the religious life of the boy, who as a man nobly served his generation, and in the host of Methodist worthies still remains ' a burning and a shining light.'

A. Lewis Humphries, B.A.

Witness of the Spirit.

THE Apostle John says, ' He that believeth on the Son of God hath the witness in himself.' And that is one comment upon the prayer of our Lord, ' I thank Thee, Father, that Thou hast hid these things from the wise and prudent, and hast revealed them unto babes.' It is not by any demonstration of logic that a sinner recognizes himself to be such. There is not one in a thousand of those who persist in their rebellion against God but knows himself to be a sinner. And he knows it, not as the conclusion of a formula, but by the actual perception of his spirit. He does not read the judgment he pronounces against himself by any physical means, but by spiritual insight. The preacher may tell him a thousand times, and prove it by strongest arguments, that he has no strength in himself to extricate himself from his spiritual bondage, but he will not believe it until he has been inwardly convicted of sin and has made his own attempt to get rid of sin.

A man may cease to sin in some special direction or directions, as, for instance, he may cease to swear, to lie, to get drunk ; but that does not take away his sin or the burden of condemnation on account of sin ; and those greatly err and cause untold spiritual damage who tell us that reformation is conversion. The Spirit of God does not give Divine witness to corroborate the results of human endeavour through human strength. But that Spirit gives His witness to the work He has Himself accomplished.—*Christian Advocate.*

' Kiss Me—Farewell ! '

MORE than thirty years ago, one lovely Sabbath morning, eight young men, students in a law school, were walking along the banks of a stream that flows into the Potomac River, not far from the city of Washington. They were going to a grove, in a retired place, to spend the hours of that holy day in playing cards. Each of them had a flask of wine in his pocket. They were the sons of praying mothers. As they were walking along, amusing each other with idle jests, the bell of a church in a little village about two miles off began to ring. It sounded in the ears of those thoughtless young men as plainly as though it were only on the other side of that little stream alongside of which they were walking.

Presently one of their number, whose name was George, stopped, and said to his friend nearest to him that he would go no further, but would return to the village and go to church. His friend called to their companions, who were a little ahead of him—' Boys ! boys ! come back here. George is getting religious.

We must help him. Come on, and let us baptize him by immersion in the water.'

In a moment they formed a circle around him. They told him that the only way in which he could save himself from having a cold bath was by going with them. In a calm, quiet, but earnest way, he said :

'I know very well that you have power enough to put me in the water, and hold me there till I am drowned ; and if you choose you can do so, and I will make no resistance ; but listen to what I have to say, and then do as you think best.

' You all know that I am two hundred miles from home ; but you do not know that my mother is a helpless, bed-ridden invalid. I never remember seeing her out of bed. I am her youngest child. My father could not afford to pay for my schooling ; but our teacher is a warm friend of my father, and offered to take me without any charge. He was very anxious for me to come, but mother would not consent. The struggle almost cost her what little life was left to her. At length, after many prayers on the subject, she yielded, and said I might go. The preparations for my leaving home were soon made. My mother never said a word to me on the subject until the morning when I had to leave. After I had eaten my breakfast she sent for me, and asked if everything was ready. I told her all was ready, and I was only waiting for the stage. At her request I kneeled beside her bed. With her loving hands upon my head, she prayed for her youngest child. Many and many a night since then have I dreamed that whole scene over. It is the happiest recollection of my life. I believe that until the day of my death I shall be able to repeat every word of that prayer. Then she spoke to me thus :

' " My precious boy, you do not know, you never can know, the agony of a mother's heart in parting for the last time from her youngest child. When you leave home, you will have looked for the last time, this side of the grave, on the face of her who loves you as no other mortal does or can. Your father cannot afford the expense of your making us visits during the two years your studies will occupy.

I cannot possibly live so long as that. The sands in the hour-glass of my life have nearly run out. In the far-off, strange place to which you are going there will be no loving mother to give you counsel in time of trouble. Seek counsel and help from God every Sabbath morning from ten to eleven o'clock ; I will spend the hour in prayer for you. Wherever you may be during this sacred hour, when you hear the church bells ringing, let your thoughts come back to this chamber, where your dying mother will be agonizing in prayer for you. But I hear the stage coming. Kiss me—farewell ! "

' Boys, I never expect to see my mother again on earth. But, by the help of God, I mean to meet her in heaven.'

As George ceased speaking, the tears were streaming down his cheeks. He looked at his companions. Their eyes were all filled with tears.

In a moment the ring which they had formed about him was opened. He passed out and went to church. He had stood up for the right against great odds. They admired him for doing what they had not courage to do. They all followed him to church. On their way there each of them quietly threw away his cards and his wine flask. Never again did any of those young men play cards on the Sabbath.

From that day they all became changed men. Six of them died Christians, and are now in heaven. George is an able Christian lawyer in Iowa ; and his friend, the eighth of the party, who wrote this account, has been for many years an earnest, active member of the church. Here were eight men converted by the prayers of that good Christian woman. And if we only knew all the results of their examples and their labours, we should have a good illustration of the influence of a mother's prayers. *Bible Models.*

IF PRAYER speed not, we must be sure that the fault is not in God, but in ourselves. Were we but ripe for mercy, He is ready to extend it to us, and even waits for the purpose.—*Trapp.*

The Easter Lily.

IN a corner of the garden,
Wafting out a perfume rare,
Stood a lily tall and slender,
Nodding in the summer air.

Warmed by every fleck of sunshine,
Fanned by sweetest south wind's blow,
With no thought of a to-morrow,
The lily only lived to grow.

In the silent midnight watches,
When the gardener lay asleep,
No one seeing but the angels,
Only stars their vigils keep.

Then the lily's head was drooping
(Even flowers must have a rest),
And the lovely snow-white petals
Leaned against her swaying breast.

But the sun, in eastern splendour,
Raised the beauteous head once more,
(After sleep there comes a waking),
And she nodded as before.

But the winter frost has touched her,
Laid his fingers on her head,
Not in silent benediction,
But to lay her with the dead.

Dead? Ah! no, she is but sleeping,
In her heart the germ still lives;
Summer sun ere long will clothe her
With the beauty that God gives.

So in life, God's chosen garden,
We must sleep to wake and know,
In the sunshine, or at midnight
We should ne'er forgetful grow.

Brighter than the Easter lily,
Sorrows past, and no more sleeping,
On the resurrection morning—
After sorrow comes the reaping.

M. B. BELL.

The Library.

THE records of Arctic exploration have furnished material for some of the most interesting books ever written, and many a boy, fired by these recitals, has wished to sail away into the far frozen North, and brave the rigours of an Arctic winter. One depressing feature, however, marks the very great majority of these expeditions—they have commonly failed to attain their object, except when, as in the case of the Franklin search parties, the explorers confined themselves to comparatively low latitudes. A book lies before us just now, however, which tells in charming style the story of a quite successful expedition to find the North-East passage; and we would urge all our readers who do not know the book to make its acquaintance without delay. On June 22, 1878, a ship called the *Vega* left the naval port of Karlskrona in Sweden, for the purpose of circumnavigating Europe and Asia, passing through Behring's Straits, and returning home by the Pacific and Indian Oceans, the Suez Canal, and the Mediterranean. The object of the expedition was happily accomplished, though the ship and its crew had to spend a long Arctic winter of ten months within a very short distance of the Pacific Ocean. The chief commander of the *Vega* and director of the entire expedition was Professor Nordenskiöld, since created Baron for his exploit. He had become persuaded that the river water of the great Siberian rivers the Obi and Yenisei must form along the coast an open channel which would permit the passage of a vessel hugging the shore all the time as closely as the soundings would permit. The most careful preparations were made for the undertaking. The ship was strengthened and protected in every way that experience could suggest, iron tanks being so arranged as to be capable of offering powerful resistance in case of ice pressure. The scientific equipment for physical, astronomical, and geological researches was most complete; and the dietary was chosen with much care and pains. Preserved provisions, pemmican, fresh

ripe potatoes, cranberry juice (as a preventive of scurvy), were provided in plenty. The course was from Tromsoë, past North Cape, through the Kara Strait into the Kara Sea and so on to Cape Chelyuskin, the northernmost cape of the Old World, which was passed on August 18. Companion ships were despatched to explore the Obi and the Yenesei, and the *Vega* pressed on past Liakhof Island and the Bear Islands until, on September 28, progress was stopped near Kolyuchin Bay within a few miles of the open water at Behring's Straits, though whalers had on several occasions previously not left this region until the middle of October. ' It was an unexpected disappointment which it was more difficult to bear with equanimity, since it was evident that we would have avoided it if we had come some hours earlier to the eastern side of Kolyuchin Bay. There were numerous occasions during the preceding part of the voyage on which these hours might have been saved.' Perhaps the most interesting chapters, however, in this book are owing to this detention —those numbered eight, nine, and ten—which deal with the preparations for wintering, the actual experience of that season, and the history, physical characteristics, disposition, and manners of the curious Chuckchê people who inhabit North-Eastern Siberia. They are a people closely related to the Eskimo—hardy, but exceedingly indolent when want of food does not force them to exertion. They are very affectionate and fairly honest, but incorrigible beggars. They would not steal, but would not scruple to secrete any article once sold, and offer it again for purchase without compunction. The whole chapter treating of them specially is crammed with interesting facts. Here is a selection :—' The children are neither chastized nor scolded ; they are, however, the best behaved I have ever seen. Their behaviour in the tent is equal to that of the best brought-up European children in the drawing-room. They are not perhaps so wild as ours, but are addicted to games which closely resemble those common among us in the country. Playthings are also in use : for instance, dolls, bows, windmills with two sails, &c. If the parents get any delicacy they always give each of their children a bit, and there is never any quarrel as to the size of each child's portion. If a piece of sugar is given to one of the children in a crowd, it goes from mouth to mouth round the whole company. In the same way the child offers its father and mother a taste of the bit of sugar or piece of bread it has got. Even in childhood the Chuckchês are exceedingly patient. A girl who fell down from the ship's stair, head foremost, and thus got so violent a blow that she was almost deprived of hearing, scarcely uttered a cry. A boy who fell into a ditch cut in the ice on the ship's deck, and in consequence of his inconvenient dress could not get up, lay quietly until he was observed and helped up by one of the crew.' Behring's Straits were passed on July 20, 1879, and after a pleasant voyage the *Vega* reached Stockholm on April 24, 1880. No more charming volume of Arctic adventure was ever written. The translation is admirable, and the illustrations are clear and vigorous. Altogether there are nearly two hundred of them.

Anecdotes about Hymns.

II.—A BLESSING FROM A VERSE OF A HYMN.

A MARRIED couple of the artisan class lived for many years unhappily together, and never attended any place of worship. One evening, as the father, who had come home tired from work, was sitting wearily to rest himself beside the stove, his little boy began to repeat a verse of a hymn he had just been learning at school. We are not told what the hymn was, but it produced a strong impression upon the mind of the father. He could not rest for thinking of it, and at last said to his wife :

' My dear wife, just listen to *that*, and don't let us any longer live as unhappily together as we *have* done. The verse that boy has just been singing has thoroughly upset me. Next Sunday, if you have no objection, we will go together to the Lord's Table.'

She agreed, and surely if that sacred feast was ever a season of blessing to any soul, it was to those two, who always afterwards attended church regularly.

'WAIT A LITTLE WHILE.'

By permission.   Words and Adaptation to Music by WILLIAM PROCTOR.

He knew that I was weary
  And longed to reach my home,
He smiling kissed my forehead,
  Saying, 'Soon the time will come;
Thy crown is not completed,
  It yet shall brighter shine
With gems of rarest lustre
  Ere thy soul shall cross the line.'
    Dear pilgrim, don't grow weary, &c.

He knew how I had lingered
  Upon a bed of pain,
Unfit for active labour
  To win the souls of men.

Again He whispered sweetly,
  'Thy cross is hard to bear;
Soon in the realms of glory
  Thou a conqueror's crown shalt wear.'
    Dear pilgrim, don't grow weary, &c.

I told Him I loved singing,
  And how my comrades came
To sing beneath my window
  About His precious name.
Then Jesus whispered softly,
  'Thy time shall not be long,
For soon amongst the angels
  Thou shalt sing a glad new song.'
    Dear pilgrim, don't grow weary, &c.

These lines were composed on the following circumstance:—A good Christian who had been confined to his bed for about twelve months, awoke from his sleep, and calling his wife to the bedside, said, 'I have been walking with Jesus.' She replied, 'Bless the Lord.' He then said, 'I asked Him how long it would be before He called me home; Jesus answered, "Wait a little while."' He died the same evening. Friends, during his long illness, had been in the habit of assembling together to sing his favourite hymns beneath his bedroom window.

'WAIT A LITTLE WHILE.'

By permission.   Words and Adaptation to Music by WILLIAM PROCTOR.

KEY B♭.

:s₁ | s₁.,m :m :r | r.d :d :d | d :-.t₁ :d.l₁ | s₁ :— :s₁ | l₁ :-.t₁ :d.l₁
1.I've | had a walk with | Je - sus, | He led me by the | hand, And | bade me not grow

:m₁ | m₁.,s₁ :s₁ :f₁ | m₁ :m₁ :s₁ | l₁ :-.se₁ :l₁.f₁ | m₁ :— :m₁ | f₁ :-.s₁ :l₁.f₁
2.He | knew that I was | wea - ry And | longed to reach my | home, He | smiling kissed my

:d | d.,d :d :d | d :d :d | d :-.d :d.d | d :— :d | d :-.d :d.d
3.He | knew how I had | lin - gered, Up- | on a bed of | pain, Un - | fit for ac-tive

:d₁ | d₁.,d₁ :d₁ :d₁ | d₁ :d₁ :m₁ | f₁ :-.f₁ :f₁.f₁ | d₁ :— :d₁ | f₁ :-.'.f₁ :f₁.f₁
4.I | told Him I loved | sing - ing, And | how my comrades | came To | sing beneath my

---

s₁.d :d :r | m :-.f :f.m | r :— :s₁ | s₁.,m :m :r | r.d :d :d
wea - ry, For | soon the an-gel band | Would | leave their home in glo - ry, Un-

m₁ :m₁ :s₁ | s₁ :.s₁ :s₁.s₁ | s₁ :— :f₁ | m₁.,s₁ :s₁ :f₁ | f₁.m₁ :m₁ :s₁
fore-head, Saying, | 'Soon the time will | come; Thy | crown is not com- plet - ed, It

d :d :t₁ | d :.r :r.d | t₁ :— :t₁ | d.,d :d :t₁ | d :d :d
la - bour To | win the souls of | men. A - | gain He whispered sweet-ly, 'Thy

d₁ :d₁ :s₁ | d :-.t₁ :t₁.d | s₁ :— :s₁ | d₁.,d₁ :m₁ :s₁ | d₁ :d₁ :m₁
win - dow A- | bout His precious | name. Then | Je-sus whis-pered soft - ly, 'Thy

---

d' :-.t₁ :d.l₁ | s₁ :— :s₁ | l₁ :-.t₁ :d.l₁ | s₁.d :d :r.r | m :-.d :r.,t₁ | d :—
seen by mor-tal eye. And | bear my fainting | spi - rit To a | bright-er home on | high.

l₁ :-.se₁ :l₁.f₁ | m₁ :— :m₁ | f₁ :.s₁ :l₁.f₁ | m₁ :m₁ :fe₁.fe₁ | s₁ :.m₁ :f₁.,f₁ | m₁ :—
yet shall brighter shine With | gems of rarest | lus - tre Ere thy | soul shall cross the | line.'

d :-.d :d.d | d :— :d | d :-.d :d.d | d :d :d.d | d :.d :t₁.,d | d :
cross is hard to bear; Soon | in the realms of | glo - ry Thou a | onqueror's crown shall | wear.'

f₁ :-.f₁ :f₁.l₁ | d :— :d₁ | f₁ :-.f₁ :f₁.f₁ | d. :d₁ :l₁.l₁ | s₁ :.s₁ :s₁.,d₁ | d₁ :—
time shall not be long, For | soon amongst the angels Thou shalt | sing a glad new | song.'

CHORUS.

s₁ | s₁.,m :m :r | r.d :d : | d :-.t₁ :d.l₁ | s₁ :— :s₁ | l₁ :-.t₁ :d.l₁
m₁ | m₁.,s₁ :s₁ :f₁ | f₁.m₁ :m₁ : | l₁ :-.se₁ :l₁.f₁ | m₁ : :m₁ | f₁ :-.s₁ :l₁.f₁
| Dear pilgrim, don't grow wea - ry— | Wait a lit-tle while, I | know the way is
d | d.,d :d :d | d :d : | d :-.d :d.d | d :— :d | d :-.d :d.d
d₁ | d₁.,d₁ :d₁ :d₁ | d₁ :d₁ : | f₁ :-.f₁ :f₁.f₁ | d₁ :— :d₁ | f₁ :-.f₁ :f₁.f₁

---

s₁.d :d : | m :-.f :f.m | r :— :s₁ | s₁.,m :m :r | r.d :d :
m₁ :m₁ : | s₁ :-.s₁ :s₁.s₁ | s₁ :— :f₁ | m₁.,s₁ :s₁ :f₁ | f₁.m₁ :m₁ :
drea - ry— | Wait a lit-tle while. I | trod the path be - | fore Thee—
d :d : | d :-.r :r.d | t₁ :— :t₁ | d.,d :d :t₁ | d :d :
d₁ :d₁ : | d :-.t₁ :t₁.d | s₁ :— :s₁ | d₁.,d₁ :m₁ :s₁ | d₁ :d₁ :

---

d :-.t₁ :d.l₁ | s₁ :— :s₁.s₁ | l₁ :-.t₁ :d.l₁ | s₁.d :d :d.r | m :-.d :r.,t₁ | d :—
l₁ :-.se₁ :l₁.f₁ | m₁ :— :m₁.m₁ | f₁ :-.s₁ :l₁.f₁ | m₁ :m₁:fe₁.fe₁ | s₁ :-.s₁ :s₁.,s₁ | s₁ :—
Wait a lit-tle while.Thou shalt live with Me in glo - ry—On-ly wait a lit-tle while.
d :-.d :d.d | d :— :d.d | d :-.d :d.d | d :d:d.d | d :-.m :f.,r | m :—
f₁ :-.f₁ :f₁.f₁ | d :— :d₁.d₁ | f₁ :-.f₁ :f₁.f₁ | d₁ :d₁:l₁.l | s₁ :-.s₁ :s₁.,s₁ | d₁ :—

[See Note on opposite page.]

Current Topics.

THE WESLEY CENTENARY.

IT is exactly a hundred years ago, the second of this month of March, since John Wesley ended his earthly pilgrimage. His influence, however, still lives on, and the whole Methodist world is to unite in a centenary commemoration of his death. At the time we write the form this commemoration is to take has not been decided upon, but it is understood that the Presidents of all the Methodist Conferences in this country will take part in religious services at City-road Chapel, London. This is well. Much is sometimes made of the differences between Christians, but these differences are but superficial after all. We are gathered together in different groups and we work in different methods, but we. all acknowledge the same Head, and preach the same Gospel. And on such an occasion as this it seems fitting that the different branches of the Methodist family should unite in offering thanks to Almighty God for all the blessings He has conferred upon them through the instrumentality of the man whom they all acknowledge as the founder of their Church.

At a time like this, many associations gather round the 'small house beside the yard in front of City-road Chapel,' where the old warrior for Christ laid aside his armour, and in tones of wondrous triumph bid adieu to the scenes and friends of his earthly conflict. What a death-bed scene that was. He had reached his eighty-eighth year, yet only a few days before he had preached his last sermon. He only kept his room from the Sunday to Wednesday. During that time he dozed and wandered a good deal, but in his wanderings he was always preaching or meeting classes. Once, after a restless night, being

asked if he suffered pain, he answered 'No,' and began singing,

    'All glory to God in the sky,
      And peace upon earth be restored!
    O Jesus, exalted on high,
      Appear our omnipotent Lord.'

Finding speaking difficult, he asked for pen and ink, but he could not write. A friend offered to write for him. What did he want to say? 'Nothing,' he replied, 'but that God is with us. The best of all is, God is with us.' Then lifting up his dying arm in token of victory, and raising his feeble voice, he again repeated the heart-reviving words, 'The best of all is, God is with us.' After this he shook hands with his friends, who said they had come to rejoice with him, saying, 'Farewell—the best of all is, God is with us. He causeth His servants to lie down in peace. The clouds drop fatness.' Again and again he tried to sing the hymn 'I'll praise my Maker.' On the Wednesday morning, as Joseph Bradford was praying with him, he said 'Farewell,' and sweetly passed away.

The memory of such lives as that of Wesley cannot and should not be forgotten. It is through such men that God reveals Himself to the world, and the record of their lives is a testimony to the presence and power of a living Saviour. The lives of good men are the richest heritage we possess. If it be true that the labours of John Wesley were needed in the eighteenth century, it is also true that at the present time we need the guidance of his experience and the inspiration of his example. And if the present celebration only helps to encourage a re-study of the life of that grand old Christian hero, it will prove a great blessing to the religious life of our time.

What mighty influences the life of one man can set in motion. Look at Methodism. It was a great movement during Wesley's lifetime, but it has become far greater since. At the time of Wesley's death there were one hundred thousand members in connection with Methodism, but who would have thought then that in less than a hundred years, it would become the mightiest evangelical organization in the world, with a membership of 4,688,093, and a population of nearly 23,500,000 directly under its influence. These were the figures given at the great Ecumenical Conference held in London ten years ago, and since then great strides have been made. It is customary to ascribe the methods which have led to this marvellous success to the genius of Wesley for government; but in the employment of lay preachers, and in the establishment of the class meeting, he was scarcely his own master. The moulding forces of that great movement were Divine. John Wesley was merely the instrument through whom they operated. This was the secret of his greatness, and it is this that shows us that true greatness is within the reach of all.

But it is not alone in the vigour and strength of the Methodist Church that you see the result of the great evangelical revival of which Wesley was the acknowledged leader. When the Methodist preachers first began their work, the moral life of the English people had fallen into strange depths. In many of the rural and mining districts the people were in a state little better than that of barbarism, and in many of the towns, scenes of outrageous vice and profligacy might be witnessed too shocking to describe. Highwaymen infested the outskirts of London, and sometimes even members of the royal family were stopped and robbed by them. The clergy were said to be ' the idlest and most lifeless in the world,' and even the Nonconformist ministers had lost much of the zeal for which they had been distinguished at an earlier time. But the revival preachers had no sooner entered upon their mission than a change began to manifest itself. All the churches were quickened by a new enthusiasm, and open profligacy began to disappear. But ' the noblest result of the religious revival,' says Mr. Green, in his ' History of the English People,' 'was the steady attempt, which has never ceased from that day to this, to remedy the guilt, the ignorance, the physical suffering, the social degradation of the profligate and the poor. It was not until the Wesleyan movement had done its work, that the philanthropic movement began.'

But Wesley's success was not achieved without incessant toil. Few men have ever laboured so hard as he. It is said that he preached 42,400 sermons. Up to within a short time of his death he appears to have been in the enjoyment of a wonderful amount of vigour. ' My sight,' he writes in 1774, 'is considerably better now, and my nerves firmer than thirty years ago. I have none of the infirmities of old age, and have lost several I had in my youth. The grand cause is the good pleasure of God, who doeth whatsoever pleaseth Him. The chief means are—(1) My constant rising at four for about fifty years; (2) My generally preaching at five in the morning, one of the most healthy exercises in the world; (3) My never travelling less, by sea or land, than 4,500 miles in a year.' Travelling was then a very different thing from what it is now. His journeys were chiefly taken on horseback, and he frequenty employed himself with reading as he rode along. He had several narrow escapes of being put to death by infuriated mobs. He was also wonderfully preserved from accident. Just before he was eighty he relates how he fell backwards downstairs, head foremost, and yet he went on his way none the worse for it. It was not until about a year before his death that he acknowledged his growing infirmities. ' However, blessed be God,' he writes, ' I do not slack my labour.'

One is apt to think that a man so intensely earnest must have been somewhat morose and repellant. But this was far from being the case. His cheerful countenance, his winning smile, his long grey locks, and his blended dignity and gentleness, we are told, made him an object of special love and admiration to the young. The poet Southey once said to a Methodist preacher, ' I was in a house at Bristol where he was when a mere child. On running down stairs before him, with a beautiful little sister of my own, whose ringlets were floating over her shoulders, he overtook us on the landing, when he took my sister in his arms and kissed her. Placing her on her feet again, he then put his hand upon

my head, and blessed me; and I feel,' continued
Mr. Southey, highly impassioned—his eyes
glistening with tears, yet in a tone of grateful
and tender recollection—'I feel as though I
had the blessing of that good man upon me at
the present moment.'

Wesley, too, was a man by no means devoid
of humour. 'I remember,' says a lady, 'the
quiet waggery of his look one morning at my
aunt's. . He had slept at our house, and when
he came down in the morning, he said as he
sat down, "Sister Dale, your bed is like a true
Englishman." "What do you mean, Mr.
Wesley?" said my aunt. "Why," said he,
"it never flinches." Dear man, his bed had
been hard. I laughed, though I was sorry.
Ah! I love to think of him as he was that
morning, his wit so sweetly toned, his humour
in such innocent play with his goodness.'
Another lady tells us of the care he took of his
personal appearance. The washerwoman had
brought his linen, and was waiting for her
money, but Mr. Wesley was not pleased with his
ruffles. 'I really think,' said he, 'that these
ruffles are dirtier now than before they
were washed.' The woman answered saucily,
'Dirtier, ar' 'em! an' 'spose they are? they
are good enough for a canorum (Methodist).'
'The dear little man,' says the narrator, 'made
no reply, paid the woman, and then looked at
the ruffles again in a way which made me
think that dirty ruffles were a greater trial to
him than the washerwoman's abuse. He
smiled at my mother and said, "Sister Harris,
I must ask you to get these things made decent
for me. Dear, dear, they really are the worse
for the washing!" Dear little man, he was
so particular about his ruffles.'

In the hazy distance of the past the good
qualities of a hero are liable to become exaggerated, but such little touches of nature as are
revealed in these anecdotes make the man more
real to us and also more lovable. Mr. Wesley
was in every way a remarkable man, and we
make these few notes in the hope of inducing
our friends to read his life for themselves.

M. P. D.

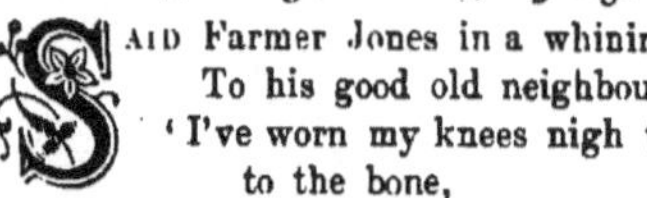

Hoeing and Praying.

Said Farmer Jones in a whining tone,
　　To his good old neighbour Gray,
'I've worn my knees nigh through
　　　to the bone,
But it ain't no use to pray.

'Your corn looks just twice as nice as mine
　　Though you don't pretend to be
A shinin' light in the church to shine,
　　An' tell salvation's free.

'I've prayed to the Lord a thousand times
　　For to make that 'ere corn grow;
An' why yourn beats it so, an' climbs,
　　I'd gin a deal to know.'

Said Farmer Gray to his neighbour Jones
　　In his easy, quiet way:
'When prayers get mixed with lazy bones,
　　They don't make farmin' pay.

'Your weeds, I notice, are good an' tall
　　In spite of all your prayers;
You may pray for corn till the heavens fall,
　　If you don't dig up the tares.

'I mix my prayers with a little toil,
　　Along in every row;
An' I work this mixture into the soil
　　Quite vig'rous with a hoe.

'An' I've discovered, though still in sin,
　　As sure as you are born,
This kind of compost well worked in
　　Makes pretty decent corn.

'So while I'm praying I use my hoe,
　　An' do my level best
To keep down the weeds along each row,
　　An' the Lord, He does the rest.

'It's well for to pray both night and morn,
　　As every farmer knows;
But the place to pray for thrifty corn
　　Is right between the rows.

'You must use your hands while praying,
　　If an answer you would get;　[though,
For prayer-worn knees an' a rusty hoe,
　　Never raised a big crop yet.

'An' so I believe, my good old friend,
　　If you mean to win the day,
From ploughing clean to the harvest's end,
　　You must hoe as well as pray."

Christian Leader.

SPRINGTIME:

A Magazine for Our Young Men and Maidens.

Vol. VI. No. 4.]   APRIL, 1891.   [Price Twopence.

A Bad Calculation.

By ROBERT HIND,

Author of ' Crosby Dalton: Local Preacher and Village Demagogue,' ' The Ruby Pendant,' &c.

CHAPTER VII.

OLD FRIENDS AND NEW.

'I cannot give a name to what I want,
I cannot tell you why I grow so sad.'
                    ROBERT BUCHANAN.

ELL me, cousin Jack, if you ever before saw a spot half as lovely as this.'

'There are so many lovely spots in and about Rockingham, that I hardly dare give the palm to any one of them. Take the old city itself, for instance, and some of the places in the Banks. I should say this is not quite equal to what you could find nearer home.'

'Ah, yes! that is true. But I was meaning out of Rockingham. Of course there is no place like the river scenery there. My mind was away in Australia, and I am afraid my main object was to persuade you to pronounce in favour of our English scenery, and against that of Australia.'

'Which was scarcely fair, Cousin Rye.'

'Perhaps not. But you see, like all little-minded people, I am jealous for my own. And I do think that Kepier Abbey is the grandest old ruin I have ever seen, and its situation, the sweetest retreat for which even a poet could wish.'

'There are fine places in Australia, but I am willing to confess we have no scenery that is so likely to induce an artist to commence mixing his colours, or a poet to sing of Paradise, as this.'

The two were standing on the bend of the Walmer, six miles below Rockingham. The high curving banks were thickly wooded with pines and the hardy mountain-ash, and the flow of the river was exceedingly rapid. Close by was Kepier Abbey, once the home of a rich brotherhood of monks, and tradition says, not unfrequently in dangerous times its vaults contained the gold plate and other treasures of Rockingham Cathedral, between which and the abbey was a subterranean passage. Several of the windows and gables had resisted successfully time's demolishing hand, and were standing there perfect in the matter of masonry, although, of course, they were totally without glass. The ruin was extensive, and had beyond doubt in its day been a place of some importance.

The situation had been well chosen alike for its beauty and its seclusion. Doubtless, the old monks who built the numerous structures of this class that flourished in the country during the middle ages showed no little taste in selecting the places where they built their homes. At the first, too, they were industrious, and carried out plans for adding to the natural beauty of the sites, which, in our modern life, would be regarded as extravagant. But after all their main aim was to ensure seclusion, partly for the sake of safety in war-times, and partly that they might give themselves up to meditation without fear of interruption. They could not well have hit on a more suitable place than the site of Kepier Abbey for all these purposes, for to this day, when the county may be regarded, as a whole, one of the busiest in England, the old abbey is still 'far from the madding crowd's ignoble strife.'

'Have you been here often?' Jack inquired, when they had stood some time in silence drinking in the loveliness of the scene.

'I could not tell you how often. Many times every summer.'

'But you haven't a picnic many times every summer, have you?'

'Oh no. I came alone.'

'Rather a long way for you, I should imagine, that is, if, as I presume, you walk.'

'It is a little too far, I grant, to walk both ways. But I take a long rest when I get here.'

'And you never tire of coming alone to a place with which you have grown familiar?'

'Tired! I should think not. I only wish as I come that there may be no one else here. I hope you don't think me selfish, but I do like to find the place wholly deserted, and myself the one person in possession.'

'Then to-day you are not having one of the most delightful of your experiences.'

Rye would have told him he was fishing for compliments, had she been less unsophisticated. But she never thought of looking for any unworthy meaning in the words of others.

'It is very enjoyable,' she said, 'quite as pleasant, though in a different way, as I have ever known. I think it must be because I am proud to show you—a stranger who has never seen it before—the abbey from all the points of vantage, which, of course, I know quite well.'

Rye Harland had other companions than Jack Benson. There were quite a dozen young people of both sexes with her. Arthur Brixton, of course, was there, and was at

that moment seeking to interest three of the company with an account of the abbey—its history, and the various styles of architecture that had been followed in its erection. These were matters of which he was as well able to speak as any one, save, perhaps, some few of the learned antiquarians of the neighbourhood; for Arthur loved reading, and knew a little about most things, and considering his small advantages, a good deal about some. He could speak well, too, so that to persons of ordinary intelligence, the story he was telling should have been full of interest.

Clearly, however, one of his little audience of three did not quite appreciate her privileges. Instead of listening to the speaker, and directing her eyes to the parts of the ruin he was pointing out, she kept her gaze steadily fixed on Rye Harland and Jack Benson, who were admiring the scenery at some distance. This careless listener might be eighteen years of age, though her face indicated that for one so young she had probably seen something of life, perhaps more than was good for her.

None would deny her claims to beauty— and to beauty of a striking and unusual kind. Her creamy complexion was unrelieved by the slightest suggestion of a blush. It was placid and pure simply; her eyes were large, black, and lustrous; her hair matched her eyes, and her figure, though slight and supple, was well rounded, and suggestive of much strength and endurance.

Isa Saunders had not lived long at Rockingham, and as this was the first time she had been to Kepier, it seemed strange she was not anxious to know a little of its history. In truth, it had been specially for her edification that Arthur had undertaken his task. He was quick-witted, and with some scorn and chagrin, took in the situation. His old friend Rye was paying what he thought a quite unnecessary amount of attention to Jack Benson, and evidently Miss Saunders, the beautiful girl who had lately come among them, envied Rye her place. He, Arthur Brixton, was nobody; this gentleman from Australia seemed destined to make him insignificant in the eyes both of old friends and new.

When he had finished his explanation he left the rest of the party, and struck into a thicket of firs, where he was sure no one would follow him. He felt it was necessary for him to be alone awhile. There was a battle to be fought, and a problem to be thought out. The conflict was forced upon him by the 'contrariness' of his circum-

any moral disease—he had a mind perfectly healthy, untroubled by a single envious thought. With Arthur it was different. The evil temper that had been more or less with him for years, had lately made a dangerous development, and, helped by the new circumstances created through the presence of Jack, made him incapable of seeing things in their normal condition.

He threw himself down in his shady bower

HE FELT IT WAS NECESSARY FOR HIM TO BE ALONE AWHILE.

stances he thought, whereas, in reality, it came to him through his own unhappy disposition. Jack Benson entertained no unfriendly feeling towards his 'cousin's' old companion. He was not even conscious of a cause of rivalry, and although in his innermost heart he had not been able to feel the enthusiastic regard for Arthur he desired to feel, he did not think otherwise than kindly about him. But Jack was not the victim of

and laughed. But the laugh was not pleasant to hear, and his face was not that of a happy young man. He thought of the two most interesting young ladies of the party, Rye Harland, innocent, pure-minded, and clever in quite unusual ways. This much he knew, despite the fact that he was unable to appreciate her worth or understand of what extraordinarily fine qualities she was possessed. He had always hoped, sometimes earnestly, sometimes in a spirit of indifference, that she would consent to be his bride some day, if he ever asked her; and he did not blame himself much for not being certain whether she would always be first in his estimation or not. But he did not want her to be in the possession of another until his own plans were settled; and yet with this young Australian on the ground, of whom every one was so fond, there was a danger that he might lose her completely.

Supposing he did, there was Isa Saunders, as beautiful—far more beautiful than Rye—for her black hair and eyes, and her whole appearance were suggestive of sunny Italy. Her people, too, were more inclined to give evidence of their wealth to the public than the Harlands; and although little was known about them, it was admitted that their style of living could only be justified by large means.

Yes, Isa Saunders was a girl that might satisfy even his ambitions. But would he satisfy hers? He thought of her indifference to his effort to please and entertain her, and of her evident desire to be in the company of Jack, and positively began to almost hate that unoffending young man.

Oh, the pain that comes from an evil passion! What misery it creates! What destruction it inflicts on all true joy and noble, generous feeling!

Sometimes, too, it paralyses the power to put forth effort, and transforms its victim into an indolent misanthrope. Arthur Brixton had not been quite so completely conquered by the evil spirit he was harbouring in him. He felt equal to some thought, and he was also resolved to act before all his chances were gone. Alas! for the motives that lie at the root of human action, and the feelings that may prompt men to the most serious steps of life! In no case should the question of marriage be considered excepting from motives of pure, high-souled affection. Otherwise it is playing false with the most sacred of relationships. But Arthur was in no frame of mind to take account of these higher considerations. His spirit was tossed, like a piece of wreckage, on the waves of his un-

healthy ambitions. The loveliness of the scene, its quiet and seclusion, failed to calm him, all because his first desire was not to be good and true and manly, but to be powerful, and a person of great social influence.

<h2 style="text-align:center">CHAPTER VIII.</h2>

TAKING THE TIDE AT THE FLOOD.

> ' And what if the world, moreover,
>   Should silently pass me by,
> Because at the dawn of the struggle
>   I labour some storeys high!
> Why there's comfort in waiting, working,
>   And feeling one's heart beat right.'
>
> ROBERT BUCHANAN.

It was just sundown ere the picnic party reached Rockingham. In the walk home Isa Saunders had had the wish gratified that had all the day been burning in her heart. She and Jack Benson had been together all the way, and when, that night, in the privacy of her own room she came to think of it, she felt perfectly satisfied with all she had said and done. For had she not been in her very best mood? and when she tried, was there any one who could be more entertaining?

Jack Benson had been pleased with his companion in an indifferent, superficial way, although, if the truth must be told, he had not been over-attentive to her brilliant conversation. His mind had been wandering elsewhere. Ever since his arrival at Rockingham, Rye Harland had compelled his admiration. This admiration had increased each day he had known her. Her naturalness, especially, had impressed him, and had been peculiarly grateful to his colonial mind. It had been all the more so because of the contrast it presented to much of the life of Rockingham, which was old-fashioned and conventional; and as their acquaintance ripened, and he began to learn how much his friend knew and loved all that was beautiful, above all, how pure was her mind, and how loyal her heart, his admiration had developed into a sentiment deeper and more sacred.

The new feeling, however, brought with it no joy. He saw quite clearly that Rye and

Arthur Brixton were meant for each other. If they were not actually engaged, the reason probably was because of their youth, and because Arthur was scarcely yet settled to a career.

The complication was exceedingly annoying. And yet Jack was sure his vexation was not wholly selfish. Arthur was not a favourite of his, and he did not believe that that young man was at all worthy of his Cousin Rye.

No wonder he had felt preoccupied as he had walked home by the side of Isa Saunders, and knew that the place which he would have chosen before all others in the world was at that moment occupied by Arthur Brixton.

'Why doesn't she hold herself free for some one else?' he thought. 'I could submit to the arrangement even though I liked her twice as much as I do, if only her lover were made of noble material.'

Jack would have been still more ruffled in temper could he have overheard the conversation between Rye and Arthur at that moment. Arthur had in reality asked Rye to enter into a formal matrimonial engagement with him. The young lady had heard his words without any surprise. At what time the first thought upon the subject had entered her mind it would have been impossible for her to say. He had always been such a special friend; they had been thrown together so much; he had been such a favourite at the Mount; everything had served to convey the impression to her mind that she had belonged to him, and he to her; and her temper was so decidedly uncritical and unquestioning that she did not think, now that a crisis had come, if their feeling towards each other was of a nature to warrant such a step as Arthur had proposed.

'What has led you to mention this to-day, Arthur?' Rye inquired, with her usual *naïveté.*

Had her lover been as frank as herself what a story of evil thought and feeling he would have had to tell in answer to her question. But frankness was not one of his virtues. He could, however, tell part of the story, and make it helpful to his suit.

'I have been, I am very unhappy. You know this, and I have felt very lonely besides. But for this I would have waited until my prospects were a little better. They will, they shall be better. But I could not bear to be alone in my struggle any longer, and although I have always hoped we should be all in all to each other, and for some reasons would rather have waited until my position was improved before saying this, to-day, as I thought of you, I felt I must tell you what was in my heart.'

Arthur's sentences were not in his usual easy style. They were short and laconic, and not in the least eloquent. But there was a strange 'catch' at his throat, and a bright fire in his eye. Intense feeling prompted what he was saying, and his words, if they did not kindle the grand passion in the bosom of his hearer, at least awakened a feeling very much akin to it. Rye felt moved to a great tenderness and pity. She asked herself no questions about the state of her own heart or of Arthur's. There was some sense of pride within her as she thought that he had chosen her to be his helper in his loneliness and trouble. One good effect was certainly produced upon her mind by the event. It awakened in her a new feeling of womanhood, and therefore marked a distinct stage in her experience and development.

When the newly plighted lovers arrived at the Mount, they found Mr. and Mrs. Harland alone in their comfortable dining-room. Rye went straight to her father, leaned against the back of his chair, and in a serious voice, in which, however, there was no quiver or hesitancy, said—

'Arthur has something to say to you;' and she looked at both her parents.

The old gentleman glanced up inquiringly, and the young man at once responded—

'I have told Rye that I love her, and have asked her to enter into an engagement.'

Mr. and Mrs. Harland, notwithstanding the closeness of the friendship that had existed between the two young people in the past, were both taken aback. Observing their astonishment, Arthur, who, for so young a man, was remarkably unabashed, continued—

'I am unable to provide your daughter a house like this at present, but I mean, somehow, to get on in the world. How, I hardly know; but I think I can. Rye is willing to wait awhile until my affairs look brighter, sir. I have never been indolent, or afraid of hard work, and if you will consent, I will do my best.'

Arthur could not have chosen a line of argument likely to be more effective with Mr. Harland than the one he had adopted. Mrs. Harland saw at once that the young man had won his suit as far as Rye's father was concerned. A month ago she would have been delighted with the turn of events, but to-day she had different thoughts.

'Why should you not both remain free to take your own course, Arthur?' she broke in before Mr. Harland had time to say a word; 'and then, when you are established in life, you could make the engagement should you continue in the same mind.'

'We should be happier if you could give your consent,' Arthur pleaded; and he looked at Rye to help him.

'Whatever father and mother deem best,' Rye said; 'but in my heart I shall always consider myself engaged after what has passed between us to-night.'

'In that case, then,' Mr. Harland said, 'neither of us will withhold our consent; and we hope you will be happy together.'

Not much more was said that night. Mr. Harland tried to persuade himself he was pleased, but in reality he was very depressed. The question occurred to him, 'Am I selfishly unwilling to allow another to have any share in the love of my darling, or is it that I am afraid that other will not care for her as she deserves?' But he could not answer his question satisfactorily.

Later Jack Benson came in. He had attended Isa Saunders to her home, and had stayed there half an hour. When he returned, Arthur was already gone, and Rye was in her own room. Mrs. Harland informed him of what had occurred. Strange to say, the news confounded him, although all along he had known that it must be so. He muttered some commonplace remark, expressing the hope that his cousin would be happy, and then went to the little side-table and began rummaging industriously among the books that were piled on it. Whether he had expected to find what he wanted there or not, it would be difficult for any one save himself to tell; but his quest was fruitless, and accordingly he went to his own room.

Poor Jack did not know what was the matter with him. And yet his ailment was one very common among young men of his age, as measles and whooping cough are among children. The symptoms were not unusual either, as the reader may learn from what occurred when he had shut the door of his room. First he sat down in a chair near the window. A writing desk was in front of him, and on this he put his head, and covered his face with his hands. He did not groan or weep, but no one could have seen him at that moment and said he was happy. In a few minutes he rose, threw himself into a large easy chair near the empty fireplace, kicked the unoffending hassock to the other side of the room, and generally behaved himself in a most unbecoming manner. He was not exactly pale — his nut-brown complexion hardly admitted of that interesting aspect of countenance—but his colour was not natural, and the lines about his mouth were drawn, and not pleasant to see.

'I am making an ass of myself,' he hissed between his set teeth; 'and yet how am I to help it?'

In time his drawn features relaxed, he rose from his feet, and for some minutes paced the floor.

Jack was fighting the first battle of his life, and he was winning.

When he had conquered himself he went downstairs and found Rye alone.

'I came,' he said, 'to wish that you and Arthur may be very, very happy, and I do it most sincerely.'

Rye thanked him, and then he went to bed. She could not help wondering, however, that his tone was so serious, his words so few, and that he had expressed his good wishes in so formal a manner.

(To be continued.)

The River Nile.

ITHOUT exception the river Nile is the most wonderful river on the globe. The ancient Egyptians used to hold it sacred, and considered it the home of their god Nilus. For upwards of fifteen hundred miles it has no tributary. 'Alone it opposes a burning sun; alone it flows and overflows, and brings each year the seed-time, and secures the harvest.' Its annual overflow is one of the greatest marvels in the world. For unknown centuries it has risen to nearly or quite the same height, and within a few hours of the same time. Its rise is measured by nilometers, the chief of which is at Rhoda. These nilometers are slender pillars of marble, upon which the measure is marked. So important is the height of the water that the amount of taxation was formerly regulated by it.

Pliny says that 'a rise of twelve cubits meant famine, thirteen starvation, fourteen cheerfulness, fifteen safety, and sixteen delight.' For this reason many of the statues of the Nile of the Roman period are represented with sixteen children playing around the god of the river. In our time this river rises to a much greater height than formerly. Now nineteen cubits is considered tolerable, twenty excellent, twenty-one adequate, twenty-two complete, and twenty-four ruinous.

When the overflow approaches Cairo, usually at or near the end of June, then the 'Nile criers" begin their work. They are men whose business it is to keep the people informed how much the Nile has risen during the last twenty-four hours. The day before the crier's duties begin he goes through the streets, accompanied by a boy, whose duty it is to respond at the proper moment, for the announcement is made in a sing-song tone, and this is what they sing:

'God has looked graciously upon our fields.'

Response: 'O day of glad tidings!'
'To-morrow begins the announcement.'
Response: 'May it be followed by success!'

Before the crier proceeds to give the information he, with the boy, gives a lengthy chant, in which he praises God, implores blessing on the prophet and on all believers; especially upon the master of the house before which he happens to stand, and all his children.

After all this has been gone through with, he tells how many inches the Nile has risen that day. Every day till September he goes through with this ceremony, when the river reaches its height. For his valuable services he claims his 'baksheesh,' sometimes humbly, and sometimes saucily.

VINNIE MANN.

'Look Up and not Down.'

OOK up, look up; if you look down,
    You see the earth so bare and
       brown,
    With faded leaves blown here
  and there,
In aimless motion, through the air.
You see the long and dusty roads,
Where mortals march with heavy loads,
And here and there, on every beach,
The shining wreckage out of reach.
Or up or down, or east or west,
There's endless weariness, and quest
For love or gold or lore unknown,
Or pleasures which have come and flown.

But lift your eyes. The heavens are bright
With changeful splendour day and night.
Give now your soul a chance to try
Its fluttering wings across the sky;
You blind and cripple it with fears,
You make it count the days and years,
This deathless thing of fearful power,
Whose worlds are widening hour by hour.
Beyond all hindering bands and bars,
Beyond the undiscovered stars,
It knows a pathway; let it roam
In search of God, and heaven, and home.

ELLEN M. H. GATES.

Our Domestic Pets.

THE CANARY.

IRDS are the choristers of the air, and in their music we find no songs of revelry; the man who whistles his ribald notes as he goes to work is rebuked by their pure and innocent minstrelsy. There are, however, silent members of this great choir, and there are those of whom you would imagine their great endeavour is to put the rest of their company out of tune. Those birds have much more to say to us than we care to hear; we have never fully understood their mission or their music. We have come to think of them very kindly, as they are ever hovering about our dwellings; and anxious to share the charms of their nature, we have invited them to our homes. In granting domicile, we show no particular favour to our own English birds; they are for the most part far too plain in feather, and poor in voice. We are kind to the foreigner of the canary kind, and to them we assign the favoured place among our domestic pets of the feathered sort. The canary is a bird of the island that bears its name, and in its own native home, where it enjoys its freedom, its voice is much more powerful than here. Buffon, the eminent naturalist, says, 'If the nightingale is the chorister of the woods, the canary is the musician of the chamber.' It may be said to be a born musician, and as such it has a good ear, a retentive memory, and a faculty of imitation; and as is often the case with this faculty of imitation, it may choose to imitate the lower instead of the higher. So we have heard of a canary whose cage was hung out at the door in fine weather; it learned the poor twitter of the sparrow, and lost in conse-

quence its own fine power of song. It is rare to find such degeneracy in the canary voice. We can generally depend upon its music. It sings in all seasons; its song is heard in the house of mourning, when all other music is put aside; it cheers us in the dullest weather; it inspires childhood, and is the delight of the recluse. There are two varieties of the canary, the plain and the variegated; all varieties spring from these two. The first consists in the plumage being of a deep yellow over every part of the body except the wing and tail. In the wing and tail are deep black feathers. The value of a bird is decided by the purity of its breed, and the even character of the marks which may be found on the eyes, wings, and tail. The German canary is the best songster; it is small, short, and thick, with a large throat. The canary can form particular attachments to those who wait upon it regularly, and is capable of gratitude. Habitual attention is necessary to secure its confidence. It will respond to the familiar voice, and will even come to the hand and shoulder. We had a canary that had its perfect liberty in the house. It slept on the top of the curtain pole, went into its cage when it liked for food, and came to our plates on the breakfast table or at tea. On one occasion it got away through an opening in the best room window, but came back again. We trusted it too much, and thought it was far too clever, and one day it escaped without returning again. At a public exhibition of birds, a canary had been taught to act the part of a deserter, and flew away, pursued by two others who appeared to apprehend him. A lighted candle being presented to one of them, he fired a small cannon, and the little deserter fell on one side as if killed with the shot. Another bird appeared with a small wheelbarrow for the purpose of taking away the dead; but as soon as the barrow came near, the little deserter started to his feet. In domesticating the canary it is desirable that there should be found companionship of the same kind of bird. In putting these birds in company, male and female, a cage from three or four feet long, two feet high and wide, affords ample convenience and comfort. A cage made of mahogany is best. If wire is preferred, then tin wire is better than brass, as the brass may corrode, and upon it may be found corrosive poison. The cage should be placed on a stand surrounded by plants in pots, at a south window. It should be covered up warmly in winter, and on sunny days the window should be opened so as not to be in draughts. Every cage should have water in glass fountains, the mouth of which should go into the cage. A bath should be provided of water not quite cold, and when used should be taken out. It is recommended that rape and hemp seed should be given, especially on cold days; maw or poppy seed in moulting; in building their nests, hard-boiled eggs mixed with stale bread crumbs. There should be given to them chickweed, garden cress, or lettuce three or four times a week. A little oatmeal or groats might be put in their cage every other day. A little apple or pear might be stuck in their cage now and then. They enjoy chickweed, plantation stalks, or millet in the ear. If they have got weak, a rusty nail in the water will be found beneficial. If they have used too much green meat, then a lump of chalk in the water will do good. No one should keep a bird in a cage without attending to its comfort and health; yet there are many who get birds in a cage without any knowledge of their habits, or of that treatment which is best suited for them. In such circumstances the owner of birds should get some good book that treats in a practical way upon bird life. If our readers do not know of a better guide we would recommend ' Bird-keeping : A Practical Guide to the Management of Singing and Cage Birds,' by C. E. Dysen, published by F. Warne & Co., Bedford-street, Strand, London. Let us remember that these feathered choristers were made for man, for his enjoyment and happiness. They sing not for themselves, but for man, who is the great listener of creation, and into whose senses God has poured a thousand delights. Amid our false finery they teach us lessons of true beauty in dress, and amid our home sadness they preach to us a lesson of joy, even in imprisonment. We may have such a love for birds that we may

have those of different kinds, and yet we learn to respect each after its own kind. ' No man,' says the Rev. T. Vincent Tymms, ' troubles himself to find out which is best entitled to be called the bird. They have all got backbones alike, all wings, all hearts alike, and all hatched from eggs, and having all these four things, so we know them all to be birds. Let us learn, then, to think of Christian men of different Churches as of one family, having one hope, one God, Father of us all, and one Mediator between God and man, the man Christ Jesus.

Possibilities.

By Mrs. A. Giddings Park.

WHAT does the bulb of the lily know,
    As it lies in the cold, dank mould,
Of its wavy petals as white as snow,
    And its wonderful heart of gold ?

What does the bud on the rose spray know,
    Close shut in its calyx green,
Of the marvel of beauty to burst and glow
    In the sunlight's golden sheen ?

What does the tiny acorn know,
    Hid deep in the dark hillside,
Of the grandeur that out of its germ may grow,
    The mighty forest's pride ?

Sweet as the lily, more fair and bright
    Than the rose in the desert wild,
More grand than the oak in its towering might
    Is the soul of a little child !

If from blackened roots and shapeless seeds
    Such beauty and grandeur spring,
What to the spirit that heaven leads
    Will Eternity's æons bring ?

Ah, how can the soul of man forecast
    Its glorious destiny,
Or out from the dead and buried past
    Gain a hint of what yet may be ?
              Sunday Magazine.

The Natives of North-West India, and their Temples.

MONG the natives of various parts of India there is a wide difference as to their social and religious observances. Those residing in one part are often most ignorant as to what are the leading characteristics of their brethren in various other parts.

The population of India is about 250,000,000. The aboriginal races, known by various names, such as Konds, Bheels, Santals, Koles, which are scattered all over the country, are supposed to number about one-tenth of the entire population. They are chiefly found in the forests, mountain districts, and the outskirts of towns. Three-fourths of the people of India are Hindus, and are divided into numerous castes. Among those belonging to the higher or aristocratic castes there is much gentleness and culture; but among the ryots or rural classes there is a vast amount of ignorance and superstition, only one man out of seventeen and one woman out of every five hundred being able to read and write.

In Northern India there are several important rivers and streams, many of which take their rise up among the Himalaya range of mountains. In addition to these there are canals and other methods of irrigation that materially help to preserve the north from the painful and disastrous famines that have frequently visited the south, and by means of which devastation and death have been witnessed to a terrible extent. It is much more level in the south than in the north, and the climate there is much warmer. In Southern India, too, the work of missions began at a much earlier date than they did in the north, and the successes there have always been greater than in the last-named part of the country.

The area of the North-West Provinces, which are situated between Bengal and the Punjab, is about 85,000 square miles, with a population somewhere about thirty millions. The people generally are of slight build, graceful, and well proportioned. They are vigorous and athletic, and are capable of accomplishing wonderful feats. In appearance they are oval-faced, with black hair, soft polished skin, and regular features. The complexion varies from a deep olive to a light transparent brown. Their garments are of fine cotton, and are ordinarily wrapped round the shoulders, and occasionally over the head. In many things the natives imitate the English, especially in relation to their houses, which are often adorned with verandahs and Corinthian pillars. But they cling to their own peculiar mode of dress, which, considering their habits and the country in which they dwell, is perhaps more suitable, at least to them, than even ours would be. Caste is one of the most powerful things in their social life. In a small town or village there are not infrequently thirty or more distinctions created in this way. Among the wealthier castes there is a strong liking for European society and customs. Carriages of the most handsome character are ordered direct from England. Few, however, go so far as to eat with the English. To do so in most cases would mean the breaking of their caste, and the ostracizing of themselves from persons occupying similar positions in society.

The chief food supplies in the north-west are a coarse kind of flour, called attah; rice, which is the staple food; flesh of fowls; fish, milk, vegetables, and fruits.

The houses in which the natives dwell have generally thick mud walls, and are of very mean appearance. The customs prevailing among them in their home life are altogether different from what they are in this country. At marriage the son takes his wife to his father's house, and not to one of his own. Here the will of his father is supreme, and on his death the eldest son takes the place of authority. There is but one purse kept, and all the earnings of the family are put into it, and all the expenses paid out of it. The head of the family has almost absolute control over

Natives of N.W. India.

all the members, and also over all business transactions. There is one advantage connected with this system. It renders it unnecessary to have any poor-laws or poor-houses, as each family supports those of its own members who are in old age or enfeebled health. The degradation of woman commences at her birth, and continues throughout life. When married and her husband is from home, as is frequently the case for long intervals, her position is often painful and humiliating. Should her husband prove unfaithful or unkind, she has no means of obtaining protection or divorce. Girls are often married, and sometimes to old men, before they are twelve years of age, and are seldom consulted in relation to their future husbands. After five years of married life, if no son be born, the wife may be superseded by another. The birth of sons is always accompanied by great rejoicing, but the advent of a daughter is accompanied by sorrowful manifestations. Among the higher castes the wife is not permitted to take her food along with her husband, but must attend to him as a servant does to her master in this country; the evening is the only time she is permitted to have any conversation with him. On the death of her husband she has to submit to the most humiliating things, and pass through the most painful ceremonies. Enforced widowhood is strictly upheld, even though the poor young girl may be under ten years of age when she becomes a widow. But in many parts of India a marked change is coming over the social life of the people. Many of their absurd practices have already become obsolete, and others are doomed to follow.

There is much superstition associated with their religious observances. In each family there is a priest to present their sacrifices and to conduct their worship. His presence is specially essential at the time of birth, marriage, and death, as on such occasions there are a number of religious observances to be gone through. Initiation into Hinduism begins at eight years of age. Every boy arriving at that age is told some word which he is not to communicate to any person, but which he is to repeat mentally over one hundred times every day. Strict adherence to this is a special sign of sanctity of character. Generally it is the name of some deity that has been selected for him. From their earliest years the children are taught to bring their offerings to, and bow before, the idols. There is no wonder that the system is perpetuated, for its customs and practices are instilled into the children in the most careful and assiduous manner. In their way the people are very religious. Even if their moral character be low, yet they will go through their religious duties in the most punctilious manner. Among the masses of the people it is a religious duty to bathe daily, and to raise their hands and bow towards the sun. The most common position for worshipping is to sit cross-legged upon the ground; although, in their religious books, there are hundreds of sitting and standing positions in which they may perform their

religious duties. Quite a number of animals are regarded as sacred by the natives, chief among these being the monkey, the snake, and the buffalo.

The temples are of various sizes; although, as a rule, they are very small, and will admit only a few persons at once. But even those that are admitted do not sit on seats as is done in English places of worship. They stand, or lie prostrate for a time before the deity they worship, and after performing a number of genuflections, and offering their gifts to the priests in charge, they quietly retire. In the temple the worship is really done by the priest, and there is no attempt at instruction or edification in relation to the people. In connection with many temples there is an outer court in the form of a quadrangle with verandahs round; in these pilgrims from a distance may reside for a day or two. A great number of temples have been built by individuals as a way of atoning for sin, or as an expression of gratitude for favours bestowed upon them. It is considered a specially meritorious thing to erect a temple, even if there be no necessity for it, or if it never be used. There are a few large temples in the North-West Provinces, but by far the largest number are of small size. They are frequently to be seen in gardens and groves, and though not large, they are often picturesque and costly.

The following description is given of the temples at Hurdwar, a town situated in the North-West Provinces, on the banks of the Ganges, near to the place where the sacred river emerges from the mountains:—'The temples,' says the writer, ' are very numerous. The walls are generally covered with paintings, both internally and externally. The principal temple is a massive brick building. I entered by a large doorway, and, ascending a flight of stone steps, found myself in a spacious court, in the outer walls of which were found numerous habitations for the Brahmin priests. In the centre of the court is a large cupola raised on pillars, under which is the gigantic figure of the Brahmin bull, Nundi, in solid white marble, well sculptured, and of chaste appearance. Carved wooden palisades sur-

INDIAN TEMPLE.

round the whole. Around the bull are a great number of lesser idols, all in marble, and two large elephants in plaster, with howdahs on their backs, containing the figures of rajahs coming to worship. Many other temples surround the court. There stands Siva, with ten arms. In one hand he holds a sword; in another a dagger; in another a cup filled with the blood of the slain; in another a wreath; and in another a man's head just severed from its body, with blood streaming down into a dog's mouth, which is open to receive it. There is Vishnu with his foot on Siva, and his sword raised to slay his prostrate foe. In another place we see Vishnu reposing on the body of Amanta, the many-headed or thousand-headed serpent. The serpent is coiled up on the bosom of the ocean, where it is floating, and its numerous heads are bent over the god in the form of a canopy, as if to shield him from danger while he takes his noontide nap. Lakshmi, the sea-born goddess of beauty (she is the consort of Vishnu) is seated by, with her hand raised as if she were imparting to her unconscious lord some bit of wholesome advice. Besides these, there are a host of others far too numerous to particularize.'

The English Church Mission has done much work in the North-West of India. There are at present about fifty native preachers, over seventy educational institutions, 4,500 pupils, and 3,500 converts in connection with the mission; and they are realizing pleasing success. The American Presbyterians and the American Episcopal Methodists have also succeeded in doing a splendid work between Bengal and the Punjab. The Presbyterians, from Allahabad westward, have numerous stations, and pay much attention to Zenana visitation. The American Episcopal Methodists have missions in Oude and Rohilkund. At Benares the Baptists and London Missionary Society struggle on amid many discouraging circumstances, but not without a measure of success. At Cawnpore, Lucknow, and Delhi, the Baptists and other Christian societies are seeking to lead the people from the errors and superstitions of their old faith to the Gospel of Jesus Christ. To many, not fully acquainted with the peculiar difficulties that beset missionary work in Northern India, the progress has not appeared commensurate with the efforts put forth, and the time and money spent. The consequence has been that reflections have been made respecting the methods that have been adopted. It is easy, however, to complain, but not so easy to point out methods that would be more successful. Much patience and a great deal of hard work will yet be necessary before a religion so deeply rooted in the national mind as Hinduism is, can be replaced even by the Christian faith.

R. S.

DEFINITIONS OF CHRISTIANS.—The Scripture gives four names to Christians, taken from the four cardinal graces so essential to man's salvation:—*Saints*, for their holiness; *believers*, for their faith; *brethren*, for their love; *disciples*, for their knowledge.—*Fuller*.

The Historic Incidents of Nain.

THE historic city of Nain derives its name from its 'beauty,' or 'pleasant' surroundings. It is picturesquely located on the beautiful plain of Esdraelon, some ten miles in extent, bounded on the east by the town of Scythopolis (Bethshan), and on the west by Mount Carmel. It is watered by the brook Kishon, which, after flowing in a serpentine-like manner, empties itself into the Mediterranean Sea. This plain is also called the Valley of Jezreel. In ancient times, on account of the fertility of the soil, the pleasant surroundings, and the refreshing and invigorating mountain breezes, one of the Samaritan kings resided in the vale. Adjoining the palace grounds was the vineyard of Naboth the Jezreelite, coveted by Ahab, and who refused to sell it, because of historic family associations, it having been the 'inheritance of his fathers.' Imperious Jezebel interposed, and caused Naboth to be cruelly murdered on the false charge of blasphemy. Jehovah avenged Himself of the dastardly outrage, for faithful Elijah, in unmistakable terms, foretold the tragic death of the haughty queen. 'The dogs shall eat Jezebel by the wall of Jezreel,' which punishment was fulfilled to the very letter when Jehu captured the town.

Overlooking Nain are the pointed peaks of Hermon, referred to by the Hebrew Psalmist: 'Tabor and Hermon shall rejoice in Thy name. As the dew of Hermon, and as the dew that descended upon the mountains of Zion.' Modern travellers have asserted that Hermon, and not Tabor, as formerly believed, was the scene of the Saviour's transfiguration.

Two miles westward from Nain is Mount Tabor, detached from surrounding mountain ranges. In its general outline it resembles a cone. Writers of antiquity have exaggerated its height, and represent it as gaining an altitude of four miles. Its probable height, however, is a little over a thousand feet. The calculations of Josephus stated the elevation of the mountain to be thirty furlongs, and the basal circumference twenty-six furlongs.

The summit presents the appearance of an egg-shaped plain of about a quarter of a mile in extent, covered with rich productive soil. At the dawn of summer mornings, the cap of the mountain is covered with cloud-wreaths of white mist, which disappear with the warmth of the sun. The view of Tabor from a distance is very fine. Pococke in rapturous strains describes it as one of the finest objects of nature that he had gazed upon. The rugged sides of the mountain are clothed with herbage and adorned with wooded groves, in which the rock goat and fallow deer roam, and the red partridges build their nests. On the top of the hill are the ruins of the walls built by Josephus, and also of grottos and churches of a more modern date. The insulated situation of Tabor caused it to be used in Old Testament times as a military stronghold. At one period of its history, the fortifications were so formidable that Antiochus could only capture it by strategy, and not by the tactics of war. The emperors of Rome gained possession by entering into a treaty of friendship with the defenders, which they never meant to keep, and was speedily violated in the most brutal manner. The Empress Helena, in her religious zeal to perpetuate the alleged scenes of sacred story, established two monasteries on Tabor in honour of the ancient prophets—Moses and Elijah. From the heights of Tabor may be seen one of the finest of natural panoramas, consisting of hills, dales, and rivers.

During the earliest period of the ministry of Jesus, and immediately following the delivery of the ever memorable sermon on the mount, He, along with His disciples, determined to visit the city of Nain. While climbing the steep ascent leading to one of the narrow gateways belonging to the encircling walls, Jesus met one of those familiar solemn funeral processions, which since the transgression and fall of Adam are to be found in all climes. The surroundings were all the sadder because the young man was cut off in the flower of his early manhood, and he was 'the only son of his mother, and she was a widow.' The heart of the 'Man of sorrows' was pierced by the mournful spectacle ; in gentle tones he said to the sonless and sorrow-stricken widow, 'Weep not.' Violating Jewish ceremonies, Jesus approached the bier, and, touching the young man in the presence of the wondering spectators, said, ' Young man, I say unto thee, Arise. And he that was dead sat up, and began to speak, and He delivered him to his mother.' The sympathetic crowd was stricken ' with great fear.' Being Bible readers, they remembered that at Shunem, on the slopes of the opposite side of the hill on which Nain was built, Elisha had raised from the bed of death the child of the woman who had so hospitably entertained him during his time of need. The beautiful plain of Jezreel, stretching from the foot of the hill, had witnessed some of the grandest scenes in the miracle-working life of Elijah, who also had reanimated the soulless body of the Sareptaian widow's child in the Phœnician village, on the distant northern coast. The admiration of seeing the widow of Nain's son raised to life found vent in the cry, ' A great prophet is risen up amongst us,' and ' that God has visited His people.'

While in Nain, and very probably the same day that Jesus raised the widow's son, a deputation came from the Baptist as he lay in the gloomy prison of Machærus, inquiring, ' Art Thou He that should come, or look we for another ? ' Much has been written on the subject of John's real or affected doubts concerning Him of whom he had pronounced on the banks of the Jordan to be God Almighty's Lamb ' that taketh away the sin of the world.' Some expositors have asserted that the question was merely asked to remove the doubtful impressions of John's crestfallen disciples, and others maintain that the question was a reminder that Jesus should at once assume regal honours, assert His kingly authority, and manifest His political power by freeing His great forerunner from ' the black castle ' fortress of Herod. It is evident that the imprisonment of John had enfeebled his constitution and dejected his spirit. His strong nature, like those of Moses and Elijah, had become unstrung while incarcerated in the foul dungeon, unvisited by friends, and pining beneath the rigid prison fare, real doubts concerning Christ's mission had asserted themselves. John was a man of great severity.

His language was forceful, for he had pictured
Jesus coming in volcanic destructive force,
with axe in hand, to cut down the impenitent
sons of men, and a fan in the other, wherewith
he should separate wheat from chaff, the
wheat to be gathered and garnered, and the
chaff to be burnt with unquenchable fire.
Christ's message of mercy and works of love
were a great surprise to the rigid prophet who
had mentally drawn the picture of a Messiah
whose language would be trumpet-toned and
whose work would be destructive. Jesus,
apparently, treated the messengers and question with indifference ; His reply being
delivered in measured tones. Pointing them
to His mighty works as being the credentials
that ' He was the sent of God,' He quoted
from Isaiah's prophecy, and said, ' Go and tell
John what things ye have seen and heard ;
how that the blind see, the lame walk, the
lepers are cleansed, the deaf hear, the dead
are raised, to the poor the Gospel is preached ; '
and then added for the special edification of
His hearers, ' And blessed is he whosoever
shall not be offended in Me.' After the withdrawal of the deputation, Jesus spoke in
eulogistic terms of His servant John, and
pronounced him to be the last of the prophets.
' And far more than a prophet. For this is
he of whom it is written, Behold, I send My
messenger before Thy face, who shall prepare
Thy way before Thee.' With calmness the
Saviour concluded by reminding them of their
special spiritual opportunities. ' But he that
is least in the kingdom of God is greater than
he,' which may be explained by one of our
proverbs as being ' The least of that which is
greatest, is greater than the greatest of that
which is least.'

Jesus, during his visit to Nain, accepted the
hospitality of Simon the Pharisee. The host
was a man of considerable social importance,
and in all probability was influenced by a
spirit of curiosity, or by complying with something that Jesus had said. As the Pharisees
were very particular in their objection to eating
with persons outside their own ranks, Simon
compromised the matter by making the invitation as formal as possible. All the customary
niceties of etiquette that the Pharisees showered

upon visitors were studiously withheld. No
kiss of welcome, no water to wash the weary
feet, and no perfume for the hair, would impress the visitor that Simon was trying to
confer great honour upon Him by allowing Him
to share the bounties of his well-spread table.
While seated in Oriental manner, a poor outcast woman pressed through the] throng of
spectators, and violating Jewish customs which
forbade the presence of women from their
feasts and suppers, proceeded, with feelings of
deepest humility, to wash the feet of Jesus
' with her tears, and did wipe them with the
hairs of her head, and kissed His feet and
anointed them with the ointment.' Simon was
horror-stricken at the woman's presence and
audacity ; and his passing thoughts were, ' If
this man were a prophet, he would have known
what kind of woman this is that toucheth Him,
for she is a sinner.' Jesus read the unspoken
thoughts of Simon, and then related the
parable of the creditor and his two debtors,
and asked Simon's interpretation thereof.
Jesus, with Nathan-like pointedness, applied
the teaching of the parable to Simon's viola-
tion of the laws of Jewish hospitality, and said
unto him, ' Seest thou this woman ? I entered
into thine house, thou gavest me no water for
my feet ; but she hath washed my feet with
tears and wiped them with the hairs of her
head. Thou gavest me no kiss ; but this
woman, since the time I came in, hath not
ceased to kiss my feet. My head with oil thou
didst not anoint ; but this woman hath
anointed my feet with ointment. Wherefore
I say unto thee, her sins, which are many, are
forgiven, for she loved much : but to whom
little is forgiven, the same loveth little.' The
incidents of this memorable interview are
pictured by one of our poets in lines of exquisite
beauty :

'She sat and wept beside His feet ; the weight
Of sin oppressed her heart ; for all the blame,
And the poor malice of the worldly shame.
To her were past, extinct, and out of date ;
Only the sin remained—the leprous *state*.
She would be melted by the heat of love,
By fires far fiercer than are blown to prove
And purge the silver ore adulterate.
She sat and wept, and with her untressed hair,
Still wiped the feet she was so blessed to touch ;
And He wiped off the soiling of despair
From her sweet soul, because she loved so much.'

NAIN.

History repeats itself, says the annalist; and as the outcast of Nain found acceptance with Jesus, so the despised outcasts still find a royal welcome in the loving heart of Jesus, for 'this Man' still 'receiveth sinners, and eateth with them!'

At the present time, Nain is reduced to an insignificant and deserted village, consisting of a few houses, inhabited by the fanatical followers of the Arabian prophet—Mahomet. The only antiquities extant are the numerous graves, hewn in the hill-sides, of former generations.

ALBERT A. BIRCHENOUGH.

Wholesome Fiction.

No. II.

SIR WALTER SCOTT.

ITH the main facts of Sir Walter Scott's life, you are doubtless for the most part familiar; and it does not come within the scope of this paper to dwell upon them. He was born in Edinburgh in 1771, became a member of the Scottish bar, a county sheriff, and was one of the chief clerks of the Scottish Court of Session. His literary gifts brought him great wealth, with which he built Abbotsford. His unfortunate business connections with a publishing firm occasioned him great loss, and we have the touching spectacle of the great man sitting down to write himself out of his money embarrassments—an honest task, and one which shortened his days.

From boyhood he had a marvellous gift of story-telling, and an imagination which peopled every old castle, ruined house, or muirland that came under his eye. He first became known to literature as a poet, and devoted his genius to border romance. His 'Lay of the Last Minstrel,' 'Marmion,' 'The Lady of the Lake,' the 'Lord of the Isles,' and other productions became exceedingly popular. Floddenfield and Bannockburn, Staffa and Loch Katrine, Norham and Lindisfarne, receive a graphic picturesqueness from his touch, and have given a freshness of interest to border legend and narrative, to Scottish history and scenery quite unequalled.

But it is as a novelist that Scott's genius and fame reach their highest point. John Ruskin, that prince of English prose, gives him a foremost position in a list of a hundred best writers, and says that every line of Scott is worth reading. He has also been described as the 'father of modern fiction.' For variety and richness of narrative, animation and sustained energy of action, realistic force, racy humour and tender pathos, ease and simplicity of style, his works have merited the highest eulogy. Probably his best novels are 'Waverley,' 'Guy Mannering,' 'The Antiquary,' 'Old Mortality,' 'Ivanhoe,' 'Rob Roy,' and the 'Heart of Midlothian.' But all of Scott is good. 'All is great in the Waverley Novels,' says Göthe, 'material, effect, characters, execution.' His novels and poems together give us 'the most brilliant and diversified spectacle of human life which we have had since Shakespeare.' 'Waverley,' his first venture, proved a conspicuous success. It gives us a very powerful delineation of the manners and feelings of the Highlanders, their attachment to the House of Stuart, and their ill-starred devotion to the person and the fortunes of 'bonnie Prince Charlie.' Scott's power of uniting history with fiction was one of the great sources of his strength. We get as correct (and a much more lively) idea of events as can be gathered from the grave and more detailed narrative of the historian. But beyond this, as in all his prose, we have a most varied delineation of character, a ripe, chaste humour, and a moving pathos, which constitute the lasting triumph of the author. His portraits of Prince Charlie, the noble baron of Bradwardine, the simple faithful clansman Evan Dhu, and the poor fool David Gellatley, with his snatches of song and gleams of sensibility, give proof of his description of character and his rich humour. So also does the foray which spoilt the baron's breakfast, and Evan's wrath at Waverley for regarding the plunderer as a common thief, when 'to take a tree from the forest, a salmon from the river, a deer from the hill, or a cow from a lowland strath is what no Highlander need ever think shame upon.' While for pathos nothing can surpass the agony of Flora at her interview with Waverley—her brother meanwhile awaiting his doom, and she accusing herself 'as if the strength of mind on which she prided herself had contributed to his ruin.'

'Guy Mannering, or the Astrologer,' by its weird incident and astrological whimsicalities is admirably suited for a winter's tale in Scotland, or indeed anywhere else. Nothing can add to the charm, the hilarity, and vitality of such portraits as that of Dandy Dinmont, or the shrewd and benevolent lawyer Pleydell (no unfitting counterpart of Scott himself), the weak, but amiable squire, as pleased as the 'king himself, honest gentleman,' at his commission of Justice of the Peace, 'the long-lost heir, with his chequered fortunes, the villainous smuggler Dirk Hatteraick,' 'the simple, uncouth devotion of that gentlest of pedants poor Dominie Sampson,' or the crazed and superstitious old gipsy, Meg Merrilies, whose loyalty to the House of Ellangowan so relieves and humanizes her savagery. It is of interest to know that many of the characters in this story were drawn from life, and a cave near Rueberry in which a Dutch skipper used to store his smuggled goods has ever since been known as Dick Hatteraick's cave.

'Old Mortality' has been regarded by many as the greatest of Scott's performances. The strange title was the name or rather nickname of a small farmer of Dumfriesshire, of the Cameronian sect. Neglecting his farm and his family, 'he devoted the latter years of his life to visiting the grave-yards of the different parishes in which those whom he regarded as martyrs for their religion had died from the hardships brought on by long imprisonment, or from injuries sustained in attempts to escape; the object of his visit being to keep in repair the monuments and gravestones designed to preserve the memory of their virtues and their fate.'

The story (says Lockhart) is formed with a deeper skill than any of the preceding novels. The characters are contrasted and projected with a power and felicity which neither he nor any other master ever surpassed. It may be allowed that Scott's Conservative leanings and border-gentry instincts and his 'man of the world' view of things have led him to exaggerate the foibles, and disparage the virtues of the Covenanters. Notwithstanding this, to Lockhart 'it is very doubtful whether the inspiration of chivalry ever prompted him to nobler emotions than he has lavished on the reanimation of their stern and solemn enthusiasm.' You must judge for yourselves by reading the work. Graham of Claverhouse is a striking figure. We have been accustomed to regard him as ruthless, bloodthirsty, and unsparing in his treatment of the Covenanters. Macaulay denounces him in the bitterest terms. If any single word could be said in extenuation of Claverhouse, that word is said by Scott; it is always well to hear both sides, and to view the conduct of men from other standpoints than our own predilections. We can promise you a treat in the perusal of 'Rob Roy,' 'Ivanhoe,' or 'the Bride of Lammermoor'—all widely different in scene, character, incident, and plot, but each revealing the author's highest qualities; and we must draw this sketchy paper to a close by mentioning the 'Heart of Midlothian,' which will amply repay a leisure hour. This novel, founded on fact, struck a deep human chord in the hearts of persons of all classes of society. It is a tale of sin and sorrow, a story of what had nearly been a painful tragedy — the execution of a girl for the murder of a child who was still alive. How thrilling is the touching record of the weakness and the peril of the disgraced Effie Deans, and the humble heroism and unswerving truthfulness of Jeanie her sister. How, indeed, like Burns, has Scott 'made rustic life and poverty grow beautiful beneath his touch,' and has sounded the depths of human feeling with a master's plummet. Jeanie's weary, but brave pilgrimage to London, and her intercessory interview with Queen Caroline will ever live in honest and kindly hearts. With what tearful, searching eloquence does Jeanie urge her cause. 'O Madam, if ever ye kend what it was to sorrow for and with a sinning and a suffering creature, whose mind is sae tossed that she can be neither ca'd fit to live or die, have some compassion on our misery! Save an honest house from dishonour, and an unhappy girl, not eighteen years of age, from an early and dreadful death. Alas! it is not when we sleep soft and wake merrily ourselves that we think on other people's sufferings. Our hearts are waxed light within us then, and we are for righting our ain wrongs, and fighting our ain battles. But when the hour of trouble comes to the mind or body—and seldom may it visit your leddyship, and when the hour of death comes, that comes to high and low—lang and late may it be yours! Oh, my leddy, then it isna what we hae dune for ourselves, but what we hae dune for others that we think on maist pleasantly. And the thoughts that ye hae intervened to spare the puir thing's life will be sweeter in that hour, come when it may, than if a word of your mouth could hang the haill Porteous' mob at the tail of ae tow.'

It is noticeable that Scott's heroes are generally inferior to his heroines. This we take to be a tribute to his genius. His must be a spirit 'touched to finest issues,' who can portray with truth and delicacy of feeling the noblest qualities in woman, and Scott has excelled in this. His meek yet high-souled Rebecca in 'Ivanhoe,' Diane Vernon, poor Amy Robsart, Lady Ashton, Margaret Ramsey, and the truly noble Jeanie Deans, with others, are the finest creations of his pen, not even surpassed by Shakespeare.

Scott was intensely and widely human, and therefore we never find anything fastidious, sentimental, or snobbish, about him. He lived and he wrote as a man among men. Accordingly, the poor have a large share in his sympathetic descriptions; while the rich and powerful are never allowed to escape censure where truth demands it simply because of their social superiority. Scott holds up the mirror to Nature, and lets her reveal all that honestly may be known. His catholic humanity of spirit leads him to show that there are bright streaks in the darkest characters, and that something may be said for a Dirk Hatteraick, a Bothwell, a Queen Mary, or a Meg Merrilies. For wholesome

and attractive presentation of moral truth, not with the set method of a preacher, but possibly as powerfully impressive in some respects, we commend to you the famous writings of this ' Wizard of the North.'

H. Y.

Song of the Water.

You may find me in the mountain,
    In the little gurgling rills;
I am gushing from the fountain,
    And coursing down the hills.
I am rolling in the billows,
    And on the breakers ride;
My home is with the mariner
    Out on the ocean wide.

You may find me in the dew-drop
    That is glistening on the flowers;
I come to drooping nature
    In cool, refreshing showers.
I am glancing in the sunbeams
    From my cloud-spangled house on high,
And I come in dewy sadness,
    With tears that never dry.

You may find me in the river,
    Rushing on with ceaseless roar,
Until it meets its comrade
    By some far off distant shore.
I am found in misty ether,
    Hanging, quivering o'er the earth,
And gathered up like pearl-drops
    Ere the clouds have given me birth.

And I come in fleecy whiteness,
    Drifting, drifting lightly down,
Covering hill and vale and meadow
    With a pure and spotless gown—
An emblem of the beauty
    And the purity above,
Where the angels shine in glory
    In yonder world of love.

I bring health, and joy, and gladness
    Where'er I am used aright;
I sometimes chase the shadows,
    And make all faces bright.
Then fill each costly goblet,
    As you gather round the board,
With pure and sparkling water
    Brought from nature's choicest hoard.

Heirs of All the Ages.

PAPERS ON THE HERITAGE AND RESPONSIBILITIES OF OUR YOUNG PEOPLE.

s expressive of the manner in which the past is with us in the present, and of how we enter into its grand inheritance, one of our poets has said:—

'Heir of all the ages, I—
   Heir of all that they have wrought,
All their store of empires high,
   All their wealth of precious thought.

Every golden deed of theirs
   Sheds its lustre on my way ;
All their labours, all their prayers
   Sanctify this present day.

Heir of all the good, and more,
   Bought by labour, heart, and brain,
All accumulated lore,
   Deep and high and wide domain.

Heir of all the faith sublime,
   On whose wings they soared to heaven,
Heir of every hope that time
   To earth's fainting sons hath given.

Heir am I, and now possess
   Earth and universe combine,
Past and future, all to bless,
   Lo! the infinite is mine.'

One of the primary and most prominent forms in which our ancestors have stored up for us what they had to give us is *Literature*. This term, in its wide sense, covers a large field, embracing all that has been written. And who could classify, if they had the chance, all the literary productions between the clay tablets of the ancient Chaldeans and the modern poem, or the latest book of travel? But literature is usually divided into several parts, as, for instance, the literature of the ancient world, the middle ages, and modern times. Literature is the stored thought of the ages or countries to which it belongs. It is knowledge garnered like grain in harvest. It is man's record of himself, of his inner and outer life, of what he has been and what he has done, also what he hopes for. It is by comparing the written thought and knowledge of one age with those of another, that we see how man has progressed, and how the ideas of one age and country have influenced another, and in some deep sense joined the ages or countries together. As compared with the other productions of mankind, the highest and best is literature. All else perishes, but thoughts live. They are seed-germs that never exhaust themselves, never die. Ideas govern the world. They are as fresh to one age and country as another, when they are true and good. Wheat is good seed and useful: sow it anywhere where it can grow, and it will give you a fruitful and profitable harvest. So it is with men's best thoughts in all ages. They are vital, 'spermatic,' not leaving the man who reads them what he was. They move him, transform him, and make him a richer man.

The vehicle of literature is books, and we live in the age of books. In the earlier part of the middle ages, in this country, books were so scarce that whole towns might be found not possessing one. Even some rich monasteries could not boast of anything more than a missal or prayer book, which constituted their entire stock of literature. But now, a necessary piece of furniture in the workman's cottage is its row of books. Sunday-school prizes now constitute the nucleus of a library in every scholar's home. The number of books which have been written no man can tell. But the greatest library in the world—that in the British Museum—contains, at present, upwards of 1,500,000 books and 100,000 manuscripts. Whether more than those exist or not, we need not trouble ourselves to inquire, but turn to face the certainty that, amongst books as amongst other things, there is rubbish. As there is no harvest all grain, so in books there is much straw, and here we need both to brush aside and winnow. 'I go to visit occasionally the Cambridge Library,' says one, ' and I seldom go there without renewing the conviction that the best of it all is already within the four walls of my study at home. The inspection of the catalogue brings me continually back to the few standard writers who are on every private shelf, and to these it can afford only the most slight and casual additions. The crowds and centuries of books are only commentary and elucidation, echoes and weakeners of these few great voices of Time.' In all solid reading —reading which is not merely for amusement but culture —that is true, there are a select number among the select writers whom you must go back to ; a small circle of master minds in whose books you find the substance of what others give you. So common is human nature, so much the same everywhere, and so thoroughly has it been studied and understood by the few leading minds, that it is difficult for those who come after them to improve upon what they have said. But to distribute their thoughts is something, and a writer who sometimes acts as interpreter to the mass frequently does a splendid service. Books, then, as the medium of thought and knowledge, as Longfellow remarks,

> 'Leave us heirs to ample heritages,
> Of all the best thoughts of the greatest sages,
> And giving tongues unto the silent dead.'

Individual taste and aim in life, as well as religious objects, should have something to do in guiding us to the books we should read. Books proper for one person may be less so for another, therefore, no one can select books for us separate and independent of ourselves. But our choice being made gradually as we require it, let us use books and make them the companions of our lives. Through the three-fold medium of literature, public libraries, and cheap books, it is now the privilege of the humblest minds to come into contact with the noblest. Whether far distant or long dead, it is our privilege to know those great men better than their neighbours knew them. By their books they take us into their confidence, we share their privacy, accompany them in their rambles, and know their deepest minds. The effect of their fellowship is to quicken our own minds, increase our thinking power, store us with facts which are knowledge, multiply our enjoyments, enlarge our life and make it altogether nobler, happier, and more useful. Literature has drawn nearer life and become more

practical in these modern times. It used to be the luxury of the rich and learned, and even limited to them. A poor man could not own books, and if he could they were of small value to him, because they were so abstract, learned, and unpractical. But literature now takes hold more of natural things. It is less speculative and more true. It is more in sympathy with the common people. Instead of seeking truth only through 'reason' and 'space,' and the pursuit of the 'infinite,' it now discovers to man sublime truths in common things—in things about him, in nature, and in the ever varying aspects of human life. Literature, at last, has come down from the empyrean ; it has 'stooped to conquer,' and begun to be of general use. Books are also truer and more correct generally. The errors of previous writers get corrected, their superstitions dispelled, and modern writers know very well that if they are not careful and true in their statements, they will soon be found out. By presenting the oldest truths in a more attractive manner, by enlarging man's application of them, also by opening up to him the wonders of nature as science, by blending amusement with instruction, and by gathering the wide world somehow near and around the reader with the many excitements of its forest, sea, and city life, which he otherwise could never hope to witness, literature is very much enlarging and benefiting man, and making the world a much more interesting place to him.

But let us not forget that as 'everything great springs from conscience,' literature debases itself and is the lowest when it panders to mere passion and selfish greed, either in youths or men and women ; and it is highest and grandest when it ministers to the conscience and stimulates men to the love of God and all that is God-like, as it does in the dear old Bible. And for this great and valid reason, however other books may interest us, let the Bible ever be to us the Book of books.

F. L. S.

It is the easiest thing in the world to discover all the defects in a man when we do not like him.

Birds Exterminated by Man.

THE coming of man upon the earth has created a reign of disorder and destruction throughout nature. Beasts and birds originally had to cope with enemies on an equal footing, but within the last few hundred years a most terrible enemy with which they are entirely unable to contend has appeared upon the scene. This destructive foe is man ; not in a primitive state, but armed and aided by the shot-gun, and a hundred other death-dealing instruments. As long as the human race depended upon the offensive and defensive powers furnished by Nature, the beasts of the field were able to hold their own, and even the use of the bow and arrow failed to make marked inroads upon these hosts of four-legged creatures. But art, and the onward rush of civilization, has added a new theme to the problem of life, and one that we will do well to stop for a moment and consider. In the hurry and tumult of the nineteenth century we are committing follies that our descendants in the twentieth century will deeply deplore. I repeat that we will do well to reflect upon our actions, and if possible modify them before it is too late. I doubt if there is one in a hundred of our people who realize to the full extent the vast changes that we are producing in the peaceful work of nature. Not only are our larger animals disappearing, but our forests are being destroyed, and the very ground we walk on is gradually melting away.

The last thirty years has seen two species of birds disappear from the American farms, and we of the present day are calmly witnessing the rapid extermination of one of our distinctive and largest American animals—the bison or buffalo of the West. The group of helpless or wingless birds has suffered most, and all of the larger animals have felt the power of destructive man. When the North-

men passed along our coast, they saw perched upon every rocky cliff of our north-eastern shore-line great awkward birds with a mere trace of a wing. This clumsy bird, the Great Auk, unable to fly away, fell an easy victim to the clubs of the sailors, and from that day till the early part of the present century the war of extermination went rapidly on, until not a single one was left. The chief factor in the extinction of this waterfowl was the fishermen who visited its otherwise secluded resorts. These people killed them in large numbers, using the young for bait. The last one seen was in 1844. For many years the disappearance of this bird had been predicted, but the other one, the " Pied duck," was never dreamt of as on the road towards extinction. This duck was a strong flier, not brilliantly plumaged nor particularly sought after for its flesh, and there is no other evident cause why the bird should become so suddenly extinct than that people visiting its resting-places ruthlessly destroyed the eggs. There are other birds following in the same path, and to my mind, nothing but the strictest game laws can prevent the total extermination of our turkey, once so common, and of our mallards and canvas-backs, and scores of other birds.

There is one small area of the earth, the island of Mauritius, that seems to have been a sort of a store-house for odd forms of birds, some that were left over from the geological ages of the past. The advent of civilized man upon this island has been marked by a series of exterminations. One of these birds was the dodo, a flightless bird, blackish grey in colour, and about the size of a large swan. There was a tuft of beautiful white plumes on the back. From all accounts the dodo laid only a single egg and never constructed a nest, simply depositing its treasure in some grassy spot in the forest. When the sea-faring Mascarenhas brought his Portuguese explorers to Mauritius in 1598, these birds were by no means uncommon, but in less than a century's time the fate of the dodo was sealed, and the last living one disappeared in that short period before the merciless advance of man, his domesticated animals, and all that follow in his train. It would be difficult to conceive of a being whose surrounding circumstances, added to its own feeble resources of defence, were better combined to insure its speedy and certain extirpation. It was unfortunate in living on an island, which it was unable to leave by flight or swimming in the sea; it was conspicuous for its size, was fairly good food, and it was awkward and stupid, for its very name is derived from a Portuguese word meaning simpleton. Its first experience with man was a fatal one. Mauritius has been peculiarly unfortunate in the loss of species by the aid of man, but this is simply a speedy accomplishment of what is just as certainly, though more slowly, taking place on every hand where man is at work. Several species of parrots, doves, an owl, a peculiar starling, all among the land birds, and several interesting waterbirds, have now completely vanished from one or the other of this group of islands.

On our own continent we have a still more remarkable illustration of this terrible power possessed by the forces of civilization. The Indian is the victim in their case. The white man has waged a war to the death with the red men until a once populous race has been reduced to a practical nonentity. In this war tribes have one after the other disappeared, until finally the remnants have been compelled to surrender as a conquered race. Many a tribe has become extinct in this struggle of life and death, and it is as yet uncertain whether the Indian as a type will not eventually be wiped out of existence. In the race of extermination the buffalo has kept pace with the Indian until within the last ten years. The introduction of railroads in the far West has been the death-blow of the bison. This animal, which a quarter of a century ago roamed about in vast herds over the western prairies, is now in the last stages of extermination. Prof. Baird recently sent out a party to ascertain the true state of things, and a few months ago they returned with the report that the few which are left are in small herds in poor feeding grounds, and likely in a very few years to become entirely extinct. Note the case of the beaver, the moose, and in fact all our large game, and you see the same

tendency toward total extirpation. Even the water is subject to the will of man, and every year we can trace the effects of sewers, mains, and dams upon the sea and river fishes. Strict laws and artificial aid alone can stem this onrushing tide, and it is high time we began thinking about it and attempting some check ere it is too late.   RALPH S. TARR.

Current Topics.

THE FRIENDS OF RUSSIAN FREEDOM.

HE struggles of the Russian people against the oppressions of an autocratic government have awakened the deepest interest throughout the civilized world. Vivid descriptions of their sufferings have been published, and English people have been led to marvel that such cruelties could be possible in the closing years of the nineteenth century. There, however, were the facts, vouched for by witnesses whose word could not be disputed. But strong as might be their indignation against the blind fury of the Russian Government, there seemed to most people to be no way of protecting its unfortunate victims. Some, however, thought differently. They believed that the mere expression of their sympathy would do something. In Russia itself the greatest care is taken to conceal the cruelties perpetrated upon political prisoners, and the Liberals have no means of explaining their views to the world. On the contrary, every effort is made to create prejudice against them as dangerous revolutionaries. It is easy to understand how greatly this must aggravate their sufferings. But it was thought that a paper might be published in England, which would not only give accurate accounts of their treatment, but which would give them an opportunity of putting themselves right with the world. The fact of such a paper being published by a committee of Englishmen, it was believed, would not only be a great encouragement to those who are struggling against the intolerable despotism of Russia,

but the fact that its doings were keenly watched might even have a deterring effect upon the Government itself.

With the object of starting such a movement, three noble-hearted men—Dr. Spence Watson, of Gateshead, Mr. T. Burt, M.P., of Morpeth, and Mr. W. P. Byles, of Bradford—issued a circular appealing for the co-operation of all who might think with them upon this matter. The result was the formation of the ' Society of Friends of Russian Freedom.' It is not yet a large organization, but it has obtained an influential committee, composed of members of all political parties in this country. It issues monthly a penny paper, called *Free Russia*, which is edited by a Russian political exile in London. Now and again an exile manages to escape from Siberia, and some of these men are employed in giving lectures throughout the country. The work has also been taken up with great heartiness in the United States, and the Society is now even prepared to assist the escape of political exiles.

But are not these men ' Nihilists ' ? it may be asked. Will' the good people who call themselves the ' Friends of Russian Freedom ' actually lend their help to men who are banded together for the purpose of universal destruction ? Well, not exactly. Certainly there is an extreme party amongst Russian Liberals, but the term ' Nihilist' is really a nickname applied by the Government to all who oppose its methods, whether they throw explosive bombs or merely ask leave to petition the Crown for redress of grievances. After the Crimean War the Government of Russia was driven to make some reforms. The serfs were liberated, the Press was partly freed, the courts were reformed, and some measure of local self-government was established. Those reforms were full of promise, but, alarmed by its own liberality, the Government almost immediately began to curtail them. This, of course, excited protests on the part of the people, and these again begat reprisals on the part of the Government. The condition of the liberated serfs became worse and worse. Given too little land to live upon, and compelled to pay

about 83 per cent. of the taxation of the State, they fell into debt. The money-lender became an institution in every Russian village, and, as he charged an average of 250 per cent., the condition into which the borrowing peasantry fell may well be imagined. Their sufferings added fuel to the flame of discontent. Revolutionary clubs, known as 'Circles of Self-improvement,' began to be formed in the towns, and about the same time a remarkable movement, known as 'going to the people,' broke out all over the country. Thousands of educated young men and women, fired by an ardent desire for their welfare, went out to live amongst the peasants in the villages, to share their toils and help them in their difficulties. The daughters of the Russian aristocracy, clad in coarse peasant dresses, would be found in the remotest, dreariest villages of the empire, acting as school teachers, nurses, or midwives, and sharing the hard, precarious lives of the common people. Such self-sacrificing devotion was surely worthy of all admiration, but in the eyes of the Government officials it was only indicative of sedition. They took their measures accordingly. The more active leaders were exiled to Siberia, and hundreds of arrests were made in the large towns. The harshness of these proceedings drove some of the finest spirits in Russia to desperation. An extreme party was formed, and they boldly avowed their adoption of a policy of ' terror,' which resulted in a long series of dreadful crimes, culminating in the assassination of the Emperor in the year 1881.

And yet, bad as were their methods, the objects of these men seem to us perfectly reasonable. When things were at the worst, they even promised to desist, if the Government would only show a disposition to do three things—first, remove the existing restrictions upon freedom of speech and of the Press ; second, guarantee personal rights against capricious, illegal, irresponsible action on the part of the executive authorities ; and third, allow the people to participate in some way in the national government. These, they said, were the things for which they were fighting, and, if satisfied that the Government would grant them, they, as a party, would refrain wholly from acts of violence and maintain an attitude of expectancy. This, however, was disregarded at the time, but a few years afterwards the Moderate Liberals made one more appeal to the Emperor. This time they were more successful, and he even signed a proclamation announcing his intention to summon a national assembly and to grant a constitutional form of government. His decision, however, had been taken too late. On the very next day, and before his intention was made public, he was assassinated.

After this fearful crime all thought of reform seems to have been abandoned. Repressive measures were applied with redoubled vigour, and the Government still appears to be becoming more and more reactionary. About a year ago, Madame Tzebrikova, a lady of literary distinction in Russia, addressed an appeal to the Czar on the present situation. Her letter was expressed in plain, but perfectly respectful terms. Believing that Russian emperors see and hear only what they are allowed to see and hear by the officials, who stand between them and the masses, she felt it her duty to inform the present ruler of the real state of affairs. 'The whole system,' she told him, 'is driving into the ranks of malcontents, into revolutionary propaganda, even those to whom blood and violence are hateful;' and she warned him that 'the measure of patience is overflowing; the future is terrible.' What was the reward of her candour? Her letter was looked upon as a personal affront to the Czar; she was immediately thrown into solitary confinement, and there she lies still, without any prospect of a legal trial or of regaining her liberty.

It is the brutal treatment of political offenders in Russian prisons which has most profoundly excited the indignation of the people. And the descriptions of this treatment are truly horrible. Whole batches of suspects, many of them boys and girls of fifteen and even fourteen years of age, are thrown into prison and kept in solitary confinement for months and years, whilst the police scour the empire in search of evidence against them.

Official papers prove that young men and women have often been kept from one to four years in solitary confinement, and then acquitted by the court or discharged without trial, because the police had been unable to find as much evidence as would have justified their detention over-night. Then what must this solitary confinement be to young people? Seized upon at dead of night, and shut up in a narrow cell, without books, with very little light, and with never a kindly face to look upon and never a friendly voice to cheer them, many become insane, and many sink into decline.

Here is a case which happened in 1886. A young girl, not yet twenty years of age, named Fedoteva, a student in one of the high schools for women in St. Petersburg, had been arrested upon some political charge, and after being kept for nearly a year in solitary confinement in the House of Preliminary Detention, her health gave way. She was removed, dangerously ill, to the hospital, where she died in the delirium of brain-fever. Upon being apprised of the death, the mother went to the Chief of Police and asked at what time her daughter would be buried. She was told that the funeral would leave the hospital at a certain hour on the following day. When she came at the appointed time to pay the last and only possible tribute of love to the lifeless body of her dead child by following it to the grave, she found that the funeral had taken place the night before. When she appealed to the Chief of Police to know where the body had been laid, the only reply she received was—'That is our business.' The authorities had taken this course to prevent any demonstration on the part of the girl's schoolfellows that might have drawn public attention to the fact that she had died in prison untried. It is only natural that such heartless conduct as this begets a deep desire for revenge.

We are indebted to Mr. George Kennan, an American traveller, for the fullest account of these barbarities. He travelled two years in Siberia, and he gives heartrending accounts of the sufferings of the poor exiles on their way thither. But startling as his descriptions are, they fail to give such a sense of horror as that awakened by recent accounts from that far-away region. In the autumn of 1889, some female convicts at Kara, failing to get any redress for their grievances, actually resolved upon a hunger strike. For seventeen or, according to another account, for twenty-two days they refused to taste their food. One woman showed symptoms of raving madness in consequence of starvation, and another resolved to sacrifice herself in order to put an end to the intolerable situation. Obtaining an interview with the chief official, she struck him in the face. Her idea was that after such an insult it would be impossible for the man to keep his post. She herself expected to be hanged, but the authorities resolved to apply the lash. This is felt by all educated Russians to be a mortal insult, and when the men convicts heard of it they threatened to poison themselves in a body. The woman, however, received a hundred blows, and two days afterwards she died. As soon as the news reached the men's prison, they carried out their threat, but only two died. Three of the women poisoned themselves outright. The administration was now horrified at the result of their own work, for it seems that nothing alarms them so much as the death of their victims. Such tragedies can scarcely be concealed, and they create a bad impression.

Such facts surely speak for themselves, and if they do not awaken the sympathies of Englishmen, then the spirit which inspired the people of this country to lend their aid to the Italian patriots in their struggle for freedom, and which in more recent times was so profoundly stirred by the 'Bulgarian atrocities,' must have died within us. We cannot believe that this is so. The English are really a generous people, and we cannot believe that they will turn a deaf ear to the cry for help that comes to them from the wilds of Siberia. The Russians only ask our sympathy. This surely is easily given, and it is by no means so feeble as might be supposed. 'The power of sympathy,' says Dr. Spence Watson, 'is boundless, and it acts with intense force upon those who are most in need of it.' And he tells us that already they have received letters from Siberia, expressing gratitude so intense as to make them feel ashamed that they had been able to do so little. M. P. D.

God is my Trust.

WHEN on my day of life the night
    is falling,
      And in the winds, from un-
        sunned spaces blown,
I hear far voices out of darkness calling
    My feet to paths unknown.

Thou who hast made my home of life so
    pleasant,
    Leave not its tenant when its walls decay;
O Love Divine, O Helper ever present,
    Be Thou my strength and stay.

Be near me, when all else is from me drift-
    ing—
    Earth, sky, home pictures, days of shade
      and shine,
And kindly faces, to my own uplifting
    The love which answers mine.

I have but Thee, my Father. Let Thy
    Spirit
Be with me then, to comfort and uphold;
No gate of pearl, no branch of palm I merit,
    Nor street of shining gold.

Suffice if—my good and ill unreckoned,
    And both forgiven through Thy abounding
      grace—
I find myself by hands familiar, beckoned
    Unto my fitting place.

Some humble door among Thy many man-
    sions,
    Some sheltering shade where sin and striv-
    ing cease,
And flows forever through heaven's green
    expansions,
    The river of Thy peace.

There, from the music round about me steal-
    ing,
I fain would learn the new and holy song,
And find at last, beneath Thy trees of healing,
    The life for which I long.

          JOHN G. WHITTIER.

CHILDREN'S PRAISES.

F. ELLIOTT.

From Olivet they followed,
  'Midst an exultant crowd,
Waving the victor palm branch,
  And shouting clear and loud;
Bright angels joined the chorus,
  Beyond the cloudless sky,—
'Hosanna in the highest,
  Glory to God on high!'

Fair leaves of silv'ry olive
  They strewed upon the ground,
Whilst Salem's circling mountains
  Echoed the joyful sound;
The Lord of men and angels
  Rode on in lowly state,
Nor scorned that little children
  Should on His bidding wait.

'Hosanna in the highest!'
  That ancient song we sing;
For Christ is our Redeemer,
  The Lord of heaven our King;
O may we ever praise Him,
  With heart, and life, and voice,
And in His blissful presence
  Eternally rejoice

CHILDREN'S PRAISES.

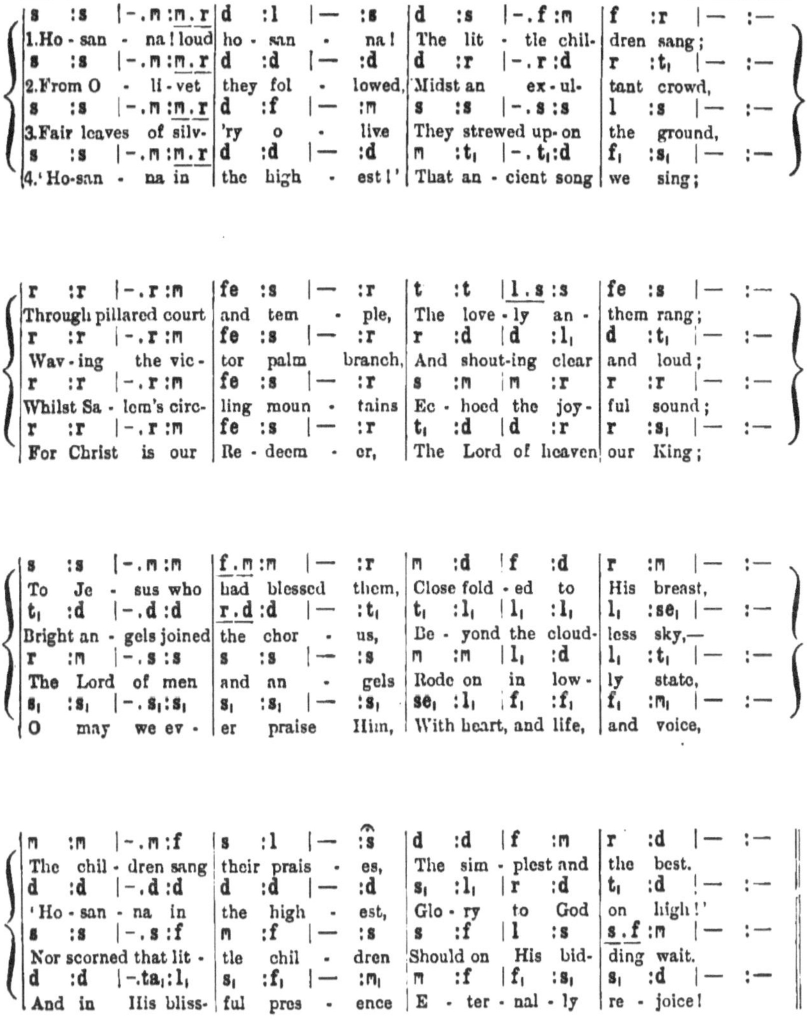

The Young People's Page.

Alpha desires to know (1) whether the tithes of the ancient Israelites were their acknowledgment for their farms and holdings; and (2) whether they were a legal exaction irrespective of their individual generosity, as pious persons, and that therefore the alleged duty of giving one-tenth of our income to God's cause does not apply to us, but (3) we are to give what we like or *can* according to conscience.—These questions can be answered only by an appeal to the Scriptures. Referring to these writings we find that tithes are a very ancient institution dating from a period long anterior to the existence of the Israelitish people. We are told that Abraham paid tithes to Melchizedek. (Genesis xiv. 20.) His grandson Jacob, following his example, solemnly vowed that he would give a tithe to the Lord, on his return to his father's house, of all the substance he might acquire in Mesopotamia. The payment of tithes both by Abraham and Jacob was a purely voluntary offering, and a grateful acknowledgment of the supremacy and providence of the Divine Being; and as these patriarchs held no farms, their tithes could have no relation to such holdings. The tithes paid by their descendants, the ancient Israelites, were paid on the same principle. Tithes were enacted by Moses for the maintenance of public worship and other pious purposes; but there is no intimation that they were other than voluntary offerings. No executive was appointed to enforce their payments; this is implied in the complaint and expostulation of the Lord, because of the people withholding the appointed tithe (Malachi iii: 8—12). So also in the New Testament, to contribute a tenth part, neither more nor less, of our income to the cause of God is not a matter of injunction. The rule is to give as the Lord has prospered us (1 Cor. xviii. 2). Our giving is to vary with our gettings; and to be square with our conscience it is imperative that we exercise both vigilance and prudence in relation to our temporal affairs; and such oversight will possibly remunerate us to an extent equal to our giving. But not only are we to give proportionately ourselves,—we are to do our best to get our children into remunerative occupations, that they also may have the means of doing good. (Titus iii. 14.)

A. E. S. asks: Can a member of our church be justified in attending secular concerts and high-class theatrical amusements?—A 'member of our church' cannot be justified in any action that contravenes its rules. Now one of our rules is this: 'No person must be admitted as a member, nor be allowed to remain one, who attends vain or worldly amusements.' Now a concert is for amusement, and secular music means worldly music as contradistinguished from sacred music. High-class theatricals come under the same category; they are secular. The habit, therefore, of attending such amusements is manifestly contrary to our connexional rules. But the question should be put on a higher level—not on a denominational but a Christian platform—or, in other words, on the basis of New Testament teaching. Now suppose that in a certain piece of secular music or theatrical amusement there is nothing, when it is considered *per se*, that is objectionable on the score of morality, the question would naturally arise, What good is there in it? The most favourable answer that could be given would indicate its relation to æsthetics, by affirming that a man of refined nervous susceptibility would experience a certain measure of gratification. All this may be admitted, and yet we should fail to discover in this any relation to spiritual life. Read Paul's prayer for the Ephesians (chap. iii. verses 16-19), and then endeavour to realize for yourself, if you can, how the most refined sensuous pleasures tend to impart any of the characteristic elements of spiritual life to the soul; but this you will fail to do. Again, is it not so that *attendance* at such amusements tends to create a morbid craving for repetition, and, yielding to this influence, our spiritual tone is reduced, and less interest is consequently taken in what tends to promote our own or others' greatest good? All things considered, our answer to the query of *A. E. S.* is a negative.

A. E. M. inquires: Are the rules written by John Wesley for the guidance of the people called Methodists recognized and adhered to by existing bodies of Methodists other than Wesleyan?—We believe that the rules written by J. Wesley for the guidance of Methodists are not in their entirety carried out by any section of the Methodist Church.

Curiosities of Sound and Vibration.

NOT many evenings ago, while a young lady was singing, the glass shade on a gas-burner broke, frightening the singer nearly out of her wits, and though the chandelier contained nine glass shades, the one immediately in front of where the lady stood was the only one broken. Her voice, which was loud and strong, had shattered the glass. This seems strange, but it is not less strange than true. I know a person who can break a small tumbler of thin glass by holding it before his mouth and making a peculiar trilling noise. While away up amid the Alpine solitudes of Switzerland a few years ago, I noticed the muleteers tied up the bells on their mules, and was told that the protracted combined tinkling would start an avalanche. A dog barking will make the strings of a pianoforte sound, and, after all, vibration of the strings is what makes all the music.

Vibration is simply a moving to and fro, as we see the pendulum of the clock do. All things have a certain vibration, though we cannot always see it. Some things have a number of vibrations in their different parts, and when two things vibrate in time with each other, and are near each other, though it is only air that connects them, the movement of one is affected by the other. The lady's voice broke the shade in the chandelier because the two vibrated in time with each

other, and the motion of the voice so increased the motion of the glass as to loosen its particles and allow them to fall apart. When two clocks whose pendulums have the same range of vibration are in the same room, and the clock doors are open, if the pendulum of one is set in motion the pendulum of the other will also move. This is the reason: every time the pendulum of the first clock vibrates it sends a puff of air in the direction of the pendulum of the second clock, and these puffs, continued regularly, set the pendulum of the second clock going. When two pianos are in the same room, if the strings of one are struck, not only will they vibrate, but also the corresponding strings of the other piano, providing that the forte pedal of the second piano has been depressed. If you whistle a note into a piano or violin, the string of the instrument in unison with that note will audibly take it up.

I noticed the boys carrying milk about the streets of London in pails which hang from a yoke on their shoulders, and are held off from their bodies by hoops just below their waists. If these boys kept up a regular step, the vibration of their bodies would increase the vibration of the milk until that was spilled. The little fellows may not quite understand the philosophy of the matter, but they know they must change their step from time to time to keep the milk in their pails.

A strong gust of wind will uproot a majestic tree when it comes just in time with the tree's own swing or vibration. Some years ago there was considerable trouble and annoyance in one of the mills in Massachusetts, because the walls and floors of the building were shaken on certain days by the machinery. At these times nearly all the water in the pails would slop out by the motion of the factory. It was finally discovered that on this particular day the machinery went at a rate in keeping with the vibration of the building, and the trouble was readily overcome by making the machinery work either slower or faster than had been the custom.

The first iron bridge ever built was that at Colebrooke Dale, in England. While it was building a fiddler came along and said, 'I can fiddle that bridge down.' The workmen, little alarmed, bade him fiddle away to his heart's content. Whereupon the musician tried one note after another upon his instrument, until he hit one in tune with the movement of the bridge, and the structure began to quiver so perceptibly that the labourers begged him to cease and let them alone, which he did; otherwise the structure would surely have fallen.

Anecdotes about Hymns.

FROM THE GERMAN.

III.—SONG LEADING TO REPENTANCE.

 SMITH, who was much addicted to drink, and of a violent and unfeeling disposition, had got to such lengths in evil-doing that he now spent the greater part of his time in the public-house, constantly beat his wife, and rendered the poor woman's life so miserable that she often felt tempted to put an end to it. But the smith had for a neighbour an earnest Christian man, and often did he hear from his house the sweet sound of hymns being sung.

'What song is that?' he one day asked, and in answer, he was told the name of the hymn, and the opportunity was taken of begging him to go to the chapel his friend attended. He went out of curiosity, and came again from time to time, but still continued his evil courses. One day, after having been at the public-house, he beat his wife, and went away again, without leaving her a farthing towards buying bread. But just at that moment, the effect of the holy words, which he had lately been in the habit of hearing, began to make itself felt within him— his conscience began to be pricked. Instead of returning to his boon companions, who were waiting for him, he felt as if he must of necessity be alone for awhile, and entering a little wood near the banks of the river Rhone, began to weep bitterly. 'Wretch that you are,' he said to himself, 'you have caused nothing but pain and sorrow to the best of women — you must repent.' And like the publican, he smote upon his breast. From that time forward he became a new man. His neighbours laughed at him, but he never gave them any other reply than, 'The Gospel is true, God has in me given a proof that it *is*, or words to that effect. He gave up his occupation of a smith, perhaps thinking it was one likely to tempt him back into his old habits, and gained his livelihood as a silk-weaver. He became as gentle as a lamb. His wife, who had formerly led such a miserable life, was now frequently in the habit of saying, 'I am so happy, I can hardly believe he is the same man.'

'Don't You Believe Him.'

THE Arabs tell a story to show how a mean man's philosophy overshoots itself. Under the reign of the first caliph there was a merchant in Bagdad equally rich and avaricious. One day he had bargained with a porter to carry home for him a basket of porcelain vases for ten *paras*. As they went along he said to the man, 'My friend, you are young and I am old; you can still earn plenty; strike off, I beseech you, a *para* of your hire.' 'Willingly,' said the porter. This request was repeated again and again until, when they had reached the house, the porter had only a single *para* to receive. As they went upstairs the merchant said, 'If you will resign the last *para*, I will give you three pieces of advice.' 'Be it so,' said the porter. 'Well, then,' said the merchant, 'if any one tells you that it is better to be fasting than feasting, do not believe him. If any one tells you that it is better to be poor than rich, do not believe him. If any one tells you that it is better to walk than to ride, do not believe him.' 'My dear sir,' replied the astonished porter, 'I knew those things before; but, if you will listen to me, I will give you such advice as you have never heard.' The merchant turned round, and the porter, throwing the basket down the staircase, said to him, 'If any one tells you that one of your vases is unbroken, do not believe him.' Before the merchant could reply the porter made his escape, thus punishing his employer for his miserly greediness.

SPRINGTIME:

A Magazine for Our Young Men and Maidens.

Vol. VI. No. 5.]   MAY, 1891.   [Price Twopence.

A Bad Calculation.

By ROBERT HIND,

*Author of ' Crosby Dalton : Local Preacher
and Village Demagogue,' ' The Ruby
Pendant,' &c.*

CHAPTER IX.

GENERALSHIP.

' Some cannot use their wings at all ;
Some try a feeble flight, and fall.'
ROBERT BUCHANAN.

HY are you always so
silent now, cousin
Jack ? When first I
knew you, you were,
so I thought at least,
the most entertaining
of companions ; now you
are one of the most un-
communicative ?' It was Rye Harland who
was speaking.

'I have changed, then, have I ?'

' Well, I think so, and I should have been
ever so much better pleased now, if, instead of
allowing my opinion to settle the matter, you
had entered into an argument to show you are
just the same. You seem not to care whether
you are changed or not, and quite indifferent
to what I may think about it.'

' On the last point I will claim not to be
indifferent ?'

' Are you unwell ? or homesick ? or out
of love with university life ?—which is it ?'

' None of your guesses has hit the mark.
You can see my health is good. I like the
university better far than I expected I would.
Indeed, I am beginning to acquire a warm
affection for everything about the place. The
wisdom and goodness and learning of the professors take hold of one's imagination and
heart, and though there are one or two that do
not command my esteem like the others, their
failings only amuse, and do not repel me.'

' But,' Rye said, when she had heard
this expression of his views about the university, ' I asked if you were homesick, and
you have carefully avoided that part of my
question. Forgive me,' she added, hurriedly,
as she glanced into his face ; ' and, please, we
will say nothing more about it.'

Rye had repented of having pressed her
question. Her quick observant eye had seen
a look of pain shoot across Jack Benson's
face.

' Yes, I will answer your question. I am not
homesick. How can I be when my friends at
the Mount make so much of me ? I told them
at home, in my very last letter, that I was
trying to be not more faulty than when I left
them, but was afraid when we met again they
would find me sadly spoiled, and all through
the too great kindness of my friends here.'

' That prediction, at least, won't be fulfilled,' Rye asserted, emphatically. ' But all
the same, you miss those you left in
Australia ?'

' Yes, I miss them. You cannot understand
what a clever woman my mother is. I never
did consciously try to deceive her. But, as
you are now learning, I am subject to my
" moods," and she always saw when they
had come on, and always knew, even better

than myself, the cause of them. I never told her of them, but often at these times she would seek me out when I was alone, enter into conversation with me, lead me right up to what was causing me pain, and make me heartily ashamed of my pettishness.'

Jack Benson said all this as simply and frankly as if he had been talking to a brother. There was no sense of shame in speaking about his mother, and the interest she had taken in him.

'I wish, oh, so much, she had been here,' Rye said. 'Instead of troubling you with questions, like me, she would have known what ailed you, and how to cure you into the bargain. I envy her her gifts.'

'This moody feeling must be driven away,' Jack said, shrugging his shoulders.

'You will put it away, won't you?' Rye asked, coaxingly. 'If you try, you can contribute as much as, and more than any one else, to the pleasure of the company to-night.'

'For the sake of cousin Rye, I shall do my best,' he said.

Rye would have been happier if there had been less significance in the tone of voice in which Jack made the last remark. To her it seemed as though there was no reason in himself, in the gathering they were about to join, in anything indeed in the wide universe, apart from her wish, to make him feel it worth his while to reveal what was best in him.

The two were on their way to the house of their friend Isa Saunders. Three days previously Isa had come to the Mount with an invitation for Rye and Jack. She had sent invitations to several young people, most of whom she did not know, but as they were near neighbours she hoped they would come.

'You see we are strangers, and don't know many people in Rockingham. But we have gone to St. Mary's church since we came here, and have seen all the people who live in Canongate, and we hope they will make us welcome to this dull old city of theirs. And I do want to know them.'

Rye thought her new friend had chosen to pursue a strange course in seeking to make friends with her neighbours, but as Isa had not extended her invitations beyond those

living close to her own home, excepting to people whom she knew, thought that probably her plans would not be resented.

These arrangements of course had been made under the direction of Mr. and Mrs. Saunders. Isa's father, indeed, had shown a very great desire to cultivate the acquaintance of his neighbours. He had deemed himself quite fortunate in finding a house in Canongate, for houses there were not often available. Fine old dwellings they were, built not for the pleasure and satisfaction of those who looked at them from the outside, but for the comfort of those who lived in them. The front and back doors, if such a distinction could be made, both opened out on the same thoroughfare, for the very good reason that there was no road on the other side of the houses. But there was plenty of garden ground, and a fine view of the river and banks.

These old dwellings, most of which had been built two or three hundred years ago, were now occupied by church dignitaries, university dons, members of that peculiar confraternity of mortals who can best be described as the fag-end of county families, together with one or two prosperous men of the legal profession.

The presence of Mr. Ralph Saunders there was an incongruity. When certain elderly maiden ladies in passing saw the showy modern furniture as it was being taken out of the van, they received quite a shock. Their astonishment could not have been greater if a band of half-naked savages had been erecting a wigwam at their door.

The first reports that reached their ears about these new arrivals did not help to reconcile them. True, they heard that Mr. Saunders was very rich, and that was in his favour. But then he was a man on 'Change, and that was sufficient to condemn him; for these people, who thought it was a sin not to have money, thought it even more sinful to earn money either by work, or trade, or speculation—and all these methods in their eyes were about equally wicked.

To do Mr. Saunders justice, he was astute enough to take in the situation, and had sufficient self-control to hide whatever chagrin he felt on account of this old-world pride. But he meant to have his way, nevertheless. Hitherto he had lived in the large commercial town where he still had his office, and had not previously met with specimens of human nature of the type that lived in Canongate. In that large town he had been a nonconformist. In Rockingham, however, he saw nonconformity would not do. The churches were crowded, the chapels half empty, and nonconformists were despised by the very set into which he was resolved to penetrate. Accordingly Mr. Saunders and his family had been conspicuously present twice every Sabbath at St. Mary's.

This step was a master-stroke, and he was not slow to see that it had visibly told; and when, after he had been in Rockingham only a month, he gave the largest subscription to the new church schools, he felt confident he had about won the game.

But he was mistaken. Canongate wanted to be mollified, for it respected Mr. Saunders' wealth; it was decently grateful, too, for his liberality to the church and its schools. In addition to this, it recognized and appreciated Isa's handsome face and figure. What more did Canongate want? If it still held back, surely its demands would be unreasonable.

Unreasonable or not, Canongate was not yet conquered. True, it was not quite so militant as before; but it had not yielded its ground by a single inch, and, probably, had Mr. Saunders heard himself discussed at afternoon tea by these good people, his self-control would have failed him.

'It is not his fault, I suppose, that he is not a gentleman,' one lady said.

As the lady in question was an authority on these matters, this remark was rightly regarded as an eternal ban upon the absent Mr. Saunders, as far as Canongate society was concerned. The Rev. John Wigham, the handsome young rector of St. Mary's, was present on that occasion, and showed considerable cleverness in avoiding the expression of an opinion on the subject. He was thankful for the subscription he had received for his schools, and had a conscience that told him it would be traitorous to join in the vixenish tirade against the stranger, to which, nevertheless, he was rather delighted to listen. For, truth to tell, he had no great esteem for his new parishioner. There had been too much self-consciousness in the manner in which the gift had been made, to please him; and he had noticed that although Mr. Saunders was under average height, he had remarkably long fingers, which twitched in a way that suggested they would do well for a rake. The crisp notes, too, seemed to stick to those long fingers as though they had been smirched with some gummy substance; and yet, when he examined them, he observed, with some amusement, they were clean and new. The interview, indeed, had left a bad taste in the clergyman's mouth, and made him wonder if Mr. Saunders was an honest man.

Of these views and discussions the subject of them was in happy ignorance. Believing, as he did, that he had already destroyed an unreasonable prejudice, he had suggested to his wife the propriety of having a few of the young people of the immediate neighbourhood for an evening. The plan was carefully discussed, and every detail provided for, and yet it was to be understood outside that the whole arrangements were informal, and merely intended to recognize the kindness of friends who had shown an interest in Isa, and to extend her acquaintance to two or three neighbours to whom she had not yet been introduced.

It was on their way to this gathering that Rye Harland and Jack Benson had the conversation above narrated.

CHAPTER X.

CHECKMATED.

'And I saw the faces,
    And some were glad,
And some were pensive,
    And some were mad;
But in all places,
    Hall, street, and lane,—
'Twas a frozen pleasure,
    A frozen pain.'

ROBERT BUCHANAN.

THE members of the Saunders family were not of the class of people who are put out of temper by disappointments. Their past experience had disciplined them to meet unpleasant emergencies with composure, and, if desirable, even a show of pleasantness. For life had been a battle with them all along, and the heads of the house, at least, many years ago had come to the conclusion that in warfare of all kinds, but especially in social warfare, strategy is the one thing needed more than every other to ensure success.

When Rye Harland and Jack Benson joined the party, no one could have told, by looking at Mrs. Saunders, that her heart was full of bitterness. And yet but for the fact that she was an absolutely obedient disciple to the social philosophy of the family, she would have either been manifesting all the signs of a rage, or hiding herself out of sight in her own room. For their little plan had utterly failed, and none of the people whom they had desired most to see had come. Instead they had sent little notes, marvellous alike for the severe neatness of the stationery and the scarcely veiled icy rebuffs therein contained. Some of them indeed were works of art, and revealed a dainty skilfulness in wounding the pride and checking the ambitions of those to whom they were addressed, that could only have come through inherited genius in the art combined with long experience, and which must have afforded a wicked pleasure to the good people who had written them.

Never before had the Saunderses received such a check. These letters were quite a new thing in literature to them, and the master and mistress of the house, having always an interest in what was new to them in social life, had made them a special study. They must be credited with understanding what was meant by these missives. Blunter intellects than theirs would have seen in them only the essence of politeness, and a sincere regret that their young people were unable to accept the invitation which Miss Saunders had been good enough to send. But Mr. and Mrs. Saunders knew better, and accordingly felt profoundly mortified.

'We have fixed on a most unfortunate time for Isa's homely gathering,' Mrs. Saunders said, as she welcomed Rye and Jack. And she said it so good-naturedly that her auditors

believed her only regret was for the young people. 'All the Canongate friends whom we expected had made previous engagements. Of course we might have altered our arrangements and fixed another afternoon, but we thought it better for you who could to come. And I do hope that, although it will be even quieter than we intended, you will all enjoy yourselves.'

A group of girls were talking beside the large window looking out upon the river banks, and Rye, leaving Jack, joined them at once.

'I am glad you have remembered Arthur Brixton, Mrs. Saunders,' Jack said, glancing across the room to where his friend was standing by himself, looking at some photographs of Scottish scenery.

'He was nearly forgotten, I must confess. We remembered him only yesterday afternoon.'

Mrs. Saunders did not add, as she might have done, that he had been invited only after several refusals had been sent in.

'That, I suppose,' Jack said, 'won't matter so long as he is here.'

'And why, may I ask, are you so glad? Are you so fond of each other that you are wretched when parted?'

'I was not thinking of myself at all,' Jack replied, frankly. 'But cousin Rye, I am sure, will enjoy the evening all the better when her lover is at hand.'

'You are very thoughtful and unselfish,— for a young man, quite unusually so,' Mrs. Saunders said; and there was a significant accent in her tone as she spoke.

The two seemed to have nothing further to say to each other, and presently Jack joined Arthur.

'You might tell me,' he said, 'who the young ladies are whom I don't know. I shall be getting an introduction to them when they have finished their initial gossip; I suppose girls must always have a little confidential talk together before settling down to business properly on these occasions—at least that is the case as far as my observation will allow me to judge. Anyhow, when the introductions come, I shall be glad to be sure of their names, for if I hear them for the first time then, I am too much occupied with their features to remember the names afterwards, and this sometimes proves awkward.'

'I shall be glad. The young lady talking to Rye, with the bright eyes, girlish face, and small figure, is Miss Cranston. Her father is a rich builder and member of the town council. They and their ancestors have lived in Rockingham for generations and are much respected. The tall, fair girl beside them, who never speaks, but, as you will see, is a good listener, is her cousin. They belong to the Congregational church. So do three of the four others talking to Miss Saunders.'

'But why,' Jack inquired, interrupting his friend, 'do you say they belong to the Congregational church?'

'You are not an absolute stranger in Rockingham still, and cannot surely be entirely ignorant of our modes of thought,' Arthur replied. .

'I hardly follow you, I must confess,' Jack answered.

'Well, there are two, perhaps I should say three, methods of differentiating people one from another in this ancient city—one is the religious test, the classes being divided into churchmen and nonconformists; the others being the tests of wealth and of old-standing social distinction. If three qualities are possessed by any one man—churchmanship, wealth, and proper social connections—that man is without blemish; if some of them are wanting, he is a person to be suspected; and if none of them exist, he is an outcast and a reprobate.'

Jack could not help noting the bitterness with which Arthur spoke.

'I suppose caste feeling exists everywhere. We have it even in Australia, although not in a form so highly developed. I have been surprised more than once with the evidences of it I have seen and heard since I came here, but your account goes beyond anything I could have believed. I hope it is an exaggeration.'

'It may be, but my conviction is that it is the truth moderately stated. Just see the evidences of it here. There is only one person present belonging to the Church of England—Miss Grenfell, the daughter of the canon, and the fourth of the group of whom I was speaking. But it is said he is considered too Bohemian by the other clergy of the town.'

Jack began to see Arthur's drift, and felt compelled, much against his will, to reconsider what had been said to him by Mrs. Saunders about the 'unfortunate' time.

Two or three more young men came in, and the conversation became animated. It was quite surprising to observe the ease with which Arthur Brixton accommodated himself to the company and surroundings. He might have been to the manner born, and yet he was the son of very poor parents, and born in a very little cottage.

Thoroughly at home as he seemed, he was the most observant person present, and noted the sumptuous appointments of the house not without curious feelings. But why did he not give more attention to Rye? After their first greeting he scarcely spoke to her the whole time. He found opportunities of engaging in conversation with most of those present, and it was surprising how often, if it was indeed by accident, he found himself by the side of Isa Saunders.

Rye was not quite happy. In other days, had she felt she had had as much ground to be offended she would have taken an early opportunity of saying so, for she did not like secrecy even about her feelings. But her new relationship had wrought some change in her. She felt shy about matters which, before, she would never have thought of keeping to herself.

Jack Benson, too, by his very sensitiveness felt that something was wrong, and thought he perceived in what direction the cause of Rye's unhappiness was to be found. Had he been less true and manly, he would have been tempted to feel elated, but he was only angry, and once or twice his fists unconsciously tightened, as though he would have been glad of a chance to test his strength with some one whom he was regarding at the moment as a personal enemy.

As for Isa, she, it must be confessed with regret, was not ignorant that possibly she was taking part in an affair which might prove, to one, at least, something of a tragedy. Isa was not flattered by Arthur's attentions. He would not have been there but for Rye's sake, and perhaps not even for that reason, had all her expectations been realized. For what was he? 'Nobody!' she thought, in answer to her own question. He was nobody in himself, but, of course, as Rye Harland's lover he was to be considered; and there was triumph in her eyes as she watched and took part in the drift of events.

(*To be continued.*)

The Sultan of Turkey.

BDUL HAMID II., as the supreme figure of the Sublime Porte, knows that a crown is not a pledge of security or peace. Remembering the fate of several of his predecessors, the conspiracies natural to an Oriental Court, the antagonism his enlightened policy has created, he feels a Damocles' sword is hanging over him. His uncle, Abdul Aziz, died a suspicious death—either suicide or assassination; his brother was deposed after a few months' rule; and hence his tenure of the throne is uncertain.

He was born in 1842, his mother being a Circassian. His education was entrusted to a wise and upright woman. He had no taste for languages, but scientific and literary pursuits he followed diligently. Being delicate in health, he lived a retired life and entered little into the physical recreations of his country. Until he had actually begun to assert the prerogatives of Sultan, he had not exhibited his present firmness and force of character. He was in this a surprise to the ministers who elected him.

In appearance he is of medium height, with a masculine physical frame capable of much endurance. His hair is dark, his beard cut to a point, and his features sharp and regular. There is a fixed expression in his face of uneasiness and anxiety, as of one who feels that beneath him there is a mine which may unexpectedly explode.

It was a crisis in the affairs of Turkey that demanded the deposition of his incapable brother and his assumption of the rule. Its army was disorganized and unpaid. As a country it was insolvent; it was overrun with a system of brigandage; and the court factions made permanent reform or rule impossible. With firmness and coolness he superseded the then existing form of government, established himself as absolute sovereign, and with his hand thus on the helm proceeded to an immediate readjustment. He repaired the above evils, established elementary schools, raised the position of woman, liberated and encouraged the press and literature generally, and stimulated the national commerce. He conceived and directed the execution of these reforms himself, his ministers being merely passive agents. He has proved himself a liberal-minded and benevolent ruler, and a new kind of Sultan to his people.

A year after he ascended the throne the war with Russia commenced, in which Ottoman bravery and patriotism were strikingly exhibited. This war, whilst somewhat improving Turkey's relations with other nations, certainly placed Abdul Hamid more securely on his own throne, and gave him personally complete control of all State affairs, which he has used wisely and well. From that date the whole political and social conditions of Turkey have been ameliorated.

His life is a very industrious one. Here is a typical programme for one day. He rises early, spending little time with his toilet. He first recites his prayers and drinks his coffee. After breakfast he attends to domestic affairs, for there is quite a little nation within the Court, with very conflicting interests. At ten o'clock, his secretary and ministers bring to him all State despatches and reports. After dismissing this business he reads home and foreign newspapers. He then lunches and takes two hours' physical recreation. He again returns to State affairs and governmental committees. At the dinner which follows, the diet is simple, and no spirituous liquor is drunk by the Sultan. His evenings are devoted to the reception of visitors, or he retires to his harem and enjoys the society of his family. His chief pleasure is listening to his daughters sing and play. He is a capable pianist and often acts as accompanist. He is personally very benevolent and kind. He has only once signed a death-warrant, and does not believe in capital punishment. He contributes large sums out of his private purse to relieve distress. He converted a great portion of his jewellery into cash to aid the Treasury when in need, and reduced his staff of servants to support a deserving charity. The atrocities and evils of his empire are not of his creation or direction. He, like all Oriental rulers, has to trust to ministers who intercept and defeat many of his wise and benevolent projects.

It is hoped his moderate and wise policy will consolidate his disjointed empire. No Sultan of recent times was so secure in his throne or so popular with his subjects. Turkey has confidence in Abdul Hamid, and his past policy and reforms have created hope and confidence in the Ottoman races. It is hoped he will live to restore Turkey to an honourable position amongst European nations.

JAMES LOCKHART.

Fearful of Consequences.

A CYNICAL person has said, foolishly, that the chief evil connected with wrong-doing is that of being found out; a statement which might come appropriately enough from the mouth of a savage, and which finds apt illustration in the following anecdote taken from the life of John G. Paton, missionary to the Island of Tanna, in the New Hebrides :—

One morning the Tannese, rushing toward me in great excitement, cried, 'Missi, missi, there is a God, or ship on fire, or something of fear, coming over the sea. We see no flames, but it smokes like a volcano. Is it a spirit?'

One party after another followed in quick succession, shouting the same questions, to which I replied, 'I cannot go at once. I must dress first in my best clothes. It is probably one of Queen Victoria's men-of-war, coming to ask me if your conduct is good or bad, if you are stealing my property, threatening my life, or how you are using me.'

They pleaded with me to go and see it, but I would not. The two principal chiefs came running up, and asked, 'Missi, will it be a ship of war?'

'I think it will, but I have no time to speak to you now; I must get on my best clothes.'

'Missi, only tell us, will he ask you if we have been stealing your things?'

'I expect he will.'

'And shall you tell him?'

'I must tell him the truth.'

'Oh, missi, tell him not! Everything shall be brought back to you at once, and no one will be allowed to steal from you again.'

'Be quick,' I said. 'Everything must be returned before he comes. Away, away, and let me get ready to meet the great chief of the man-of-war.'

Hitherto no thief could ever be found, and no chief had power to cause anything to be restored to me; but now, in an incredibly brief space of time, one came running to the Mission House with a pot, another with a pan, another with a blanket, others with knives, forks, plates, and all sorts of stolen property.

The chiefs called me to receive these things, but I replied, 'Lay them all down at the door; I have no time to speak with you.'

I delayed my toilet, enjoying mischievously the magical effect of that approaching vessel. At last the chiefs, running about in breathless haste, called out to me, 'Missi, missi, do tell us, is the stolen property all here?'

Of course I could not tell, but, running out, I looked on the promiscuous heap of my belongings, and said, 'I don't see the lid of my kettle!'

'No, missi,' said one chief, 'for it is on the other side of the island. But tell him not, for I have sent for it, and it will be here to-morrow.'

And the next day it appeared.

The Boyhood of Great Men.

GEORGE WASHINGTON.

ENERAL WASHINGTON was a great man, how great we can hardly imagine. It is in the United States of America that his greatness is fully realised, and his memory fondly cherished. We can, however, try to obtain some idea of this wonderful man by recounting a few of the main facts upon which his greatness rests.

General Washington was the founder and father of the United States of America, the greatest Republic the world has ever seen. He was the greatest General of the eighteenth century, and is crowned with the undying glory of having conquered the British Army in America. He was the first President of the vast Republic he had founded. By his wisdom and ability, to a large extent, the constitution of that republic was framed, and by his care and untiring zeal it was made to work successfully. There is no name so honoured, and no memory so cherished throughout the United States, as those of George Washington. Every schoolboy is taught his history and worth, and advised not only to aim at his greatness, but to closely copy his bright and beautiful example. George Washington was not only wise and great, but good and worthy. He was truthful and transparent as the light; honourable and upright in every relation of life; kind and courteous to all who came into contact with him; a godly, God-fearing man in private and public; a noble, benevolent Christian, decked with the meekness of humility which made him loved as well as feared at home and abroad.

This great man was once a boy, and had to fight his way through the dangers and troubles of his condition to the high place he ultimately attained. True it is that George Washington began life with some advantages anyone may be thankful for; but amongst them was neither the age nor the country in which his lot was cast. He was born on February 11, 1732, in the far-off region of Pope's Creek, about half a mile from the Potomac, in Westmoreland, Virginia, then a comparatively desolate region of America. The age was one of decided disadvantage when compared with the age we live in. The people lacked the comforts and conveniences of life that surround us abundantly. But George Washington had advantages for which he was thankful to the last hour of his life. He had a splendid father, and a wise, excellent mother. They were wealthy, as far as land and substance could make them. When five years old, George removed with his parents to the banks of the Rappahannock, where one vast, unbroken forest on either side met his view. Here they were exposed to the fierce onslaught of the wild Indian when on the war-path. These were the days of slavery, when every planter and proprietor worked his land with slaves, and in the midst of it George was brought up.

George's father was a good man, with a noble soul and a desire that his boy should become a good and useful, if not a great man. He taught him to be generous and unselfish. He showed him the works of God; he led him into a reverent worship of his Maker, and instilled into his young and tender mind a belief in God's all-giving and ruling providence. Mr. Washington could not bear a liar in his house, and always encouraged George to speak the truth. When asked who had ruined a cherry-tree with a hatchet, George confessed at once, and his father said, ' Come to my arms, my boy! You have paid for the cherry-tree a thousand times over. Such an act of heroism is worth more to me than a thousand trees.'

George's first taste for military glory was caught when his elder brother Lawrence entered the army, and fought in the cause of England against Spain in the West Indies; and when he came back after two years' service he told the story of sieges, and battles, and hair-breadth escapes under strange skies, until the boy's soul was all on fire, at the age of ten ; and from that time his play-ground became a camp, and his pastime the marshalling of mimic troops, and the fighting of sham battles.

These were not the days, nor that the country, for such schools as were required to train a boy of George Washington's capacity. And yet George was blessed with a wise if not a learned schoolmaster. Mr. Hobby was an old soldier who had lost a leg in battle. He had settled down as tenant under Mr. Washington, and combined the offices of gravedigger, church-keeper, and schoolmaster. His education was limited, but he had that kind benevolence that education could never supply; he was a Christian gentleman, and possessed the wisdom that enabled him to teach lessons to the boys which made them men in the best sense. His was not the rude rule of physical force, but the rule of love and emulation. Mrs. Washington's opinion was, 'Mr. Hobby will do the best he knows . . He is a good man, and looks after the morals of his scholars ; and that is a good deal in educating children.' George was diligent in his studies, and overcame difficulties, not because he had uncommon capacity, but because he had uncommon industry. George soon became the most important scholar in the school, and the leader of it in physical exercises as well as in learning. Mr. Hobby used to say, ' The boy that reads and spells well will be likely to do everything else well.'

It was while at this school that George suffered the first great loss of his life, in the death of his father. They thought ' a world of each other.' The father had taught, and led, and loved his little son with all the fervour of a great nature, and George had proved his love for his father by yielding the most implicit obedience to him ; and when his father died he said he would never be happy again.

But he had his mother left, a strong, tender woman, in every sense just fitted by nature, custom, education, and grace to govern and train a strong boy like George. She had George transferred to the school of Mr. Williams at Bridges Creek, the best school in Virginia, where he was taught land-surveying, another link in the chain that led him up to the high position he afterwards filled. When he had advanced far enough he laid aside the pastime of playing soldiers, and betook himself to the solid employment of surveying the surrounding region. He kept regular field-books and entered boundaries, and prepared diagrams with a completeness and neatness that astonished all who saw them. There was nothing of the careless or sloven about him. During the whole of his school-days he was so conspicuous for his honesty, truth, bravery, and justice that he was always the head boy of the school.

It was while busy with school work that the thought struck him that one day he would be a man, and that now was the time to prepare for it. With characteristic energy he started to put his idea into practice, by writing out into copy-books all manner of receipts, bills of exchange, notes of hand, wills, land-warrants, bonds, and many other things, as though he was preparing to run a lawyer's office. He called his book a ' Book of Forms.' Another book, still preserved and shown at Mount Vernon, contains arithmetical problems. Another, again, contains a series of drawings of boys and animals. Another contains odds and ends of prose and verse he had read and enjoyed. All these were an education in themselves, and gave him such marvellous skill, readiness, and exactness as he displayed when required to conduct business, draw legal documents, and manage delicate affairs of state in after-life. But perhaps the most remarkable manuscript is that containing one hundred and ten *Rules of Behaviour in Company and Conversation.* They have been recently published under the title of ' George Washington's Rules of Civility,' edited by Mr. Conway (Chatto & Windus, London), who has discovered the original of them in the British Museum, a book written in French nearly three hundred years old. Only a few can be given : ' Associate yourself with men of good quality if you esteem your reputation; for it is better to be alone than in bad company.' ' Wherein you reprove others, be unblameable yourself, for example is better than precept.' 'Labour to keep in your heart that little spark of celestial fire called conscience.' 'If you speak of God or His attributes, let it be seriously in reverence; and honour and obey your parents.' 'Let your recreations be manful, not sinful.' 'Speak not injurious words neither in jest nor earnest; scoff at none.' 'Seek not to lessen the merits of others.' 'Reprove not the imperfections of others; for that belongs to parents, masters, and superiors.' 'When another speaks be attentive yourself.' 'Speak not evil of the absent.' 'Show not yourself glad at the misfortunes of others.' 'Let your conversation be without malice or envy.' These rules he got off not by heart only but by practice, and they became part of himself. When he became great, before an admiring world he acted them out in private and in public.

But whatever advantage he derived from school and schoolmasters, from lessons taught and examples set away from home, it is to his home-life that he owed the greatest debt, and specially to his mother. The loss of his father was a terrible bereavement; but happy it was for him that his mother survived to hold the reins of government with a strong and unwavering hand, steadily to guide his young years. Mrs. Washington was a ruler of the old glorious type. Everybody obeyed her will, and she was wise and just in her commands. Her husband had the most perfect confidence in her capacity and prudence, and left her full power to manage his estates when he died. The first lesson she taught her son was the duty of obedience. He must learn to obey, or he would never be fit to command. She regularly gave him lessons from the Bible, and next to it she relied on Sir Matthew Hale's 'Contemplations, Moral and Divine.' Their library in those days was not extensive, but they made up for this by the thoroughness with which they mastered the few books they had. Sir Matthew Hale's instructions on wealth, honour, drinking, gambling, obedience, honesty, devotion, reputation, found a splendid soil in which to grow and produce a rich harvest.

Before he was sixteen George left school, and not long afterwards he had a place found him as midshipman on a British man-of-war. He donned the uniform, his box was placed on board, and he came to say good-bye to his mother. She burst into tears and said, 'I cannot let you go, George, it will break my heart.' 'Mother,' he said, 'I will stay at home; I cannot go to cause you so much grief.' And though his heart was set upon it, he relinquished the chance and stayed at home.

Instead of going to sea he went to live with his brother Lawrence, who was much older than himself, and here he received his lessons in the science and art of war, which were of immense service to him in after-life. From there he went to spend some time in the Fairfax family. One day Lord Fairfax said to him, 'How would you like to survey my land for me, George?' 'Nothing better,' said George; 'I like surveying.' And thus it came to pass that he went into the wilderness amongst the wilds of nature, and endured hardship and danger, which formed another essential part of his education. This led to his being appointed public surveyor, so thoroughly and accurately did he do his work.

But now George Washington is approaching manhood, and hence we shall have to leave him to work his way up to the high destiny that lies before him. But we cannot help saying that he had his first taste of actual war, his baptism of fire, when only nineteen years of age. He had grown a fine athletic young fellow, over six feet, could run with the fleetest, could wrestle with the strongest, and endure with the hardiest. He was grave and thoughtful beyond his years, so that many took him to be a grown man while yet but a youth. He was appointed to a military command in the district, and was engaged on the side of England to keep the French out of our territories and the Indians from ravaging the colonists.

It may not be open for every boy to become as great as General Washington became, but any boy may learn to be as honest, orderly, truthful, brave, thorough, benevolent, and noble, by obedience to parents, worship of God, and devotion to duty.　　Joĥn Garr.

Vesuvius.

ESUVIUS is regarded as the most famous volcano in the world. It is situated in the plain which lies along the shores of the Bay of Naples, in the south of Italy. It is nearly due east of the city of Naples, one of the most picturesque cities in the world. Vesuvius has occupied a large place in the thoughts of scientists, and has always possessed exceptional interest for geologists. From its operations information has been obtained as to the probable causes and general character of volcanic action. But there are still many mysteries associated with the subject.

The term volcanic action embraces all the phenomena connected with the expulsion of heated materials from the interior to the surface of the earth. The openings by which this heated material reaches the surface include volcanoes, hot springs, and gas springs. A volcano may be defined as a conical eminence which is composed wholly or mainly of material that has been thrown up from below, and which has accumulated at the surface round the vent of the eruption. As a rule, it presents at its summit a cup-shaped cavity called the crater, at the bottom of which is the funnel by which communication is maintained with the heated interior. Volcanoes depend upon the internal heat of the planet as their prime source of energy. But the precise mode whereby this internal heat manifests itself in volcanic action is a problem by no means easy of solution. There can be no doubt that one essential exciting cause of this action is the descent of water from the surface. Steam invariably plays a chief part in volcanic eruptions; it issues in vast clouds from the crater, and continues to rise copiously from the lava even after the molten rock has travelled for some miles and has assumed a solid surface.

The eruptions of Vesuvius are often preceded by a failure or diminution of the wells and springs of the district. But more frequently indications of an approaching outburst are conveyed by sympathetic movements of the ground beneath. Rumblings and groanings from a subterranean source are heard, slight tremors succeed, increasing in frequency and violence, till they become distinct earthquake-shocks. The vapours from the crater then rise more abundantly into the air. In the meantime the lava column of the volcano will be seen to be slowly ascending, forced upward and kept in perpetual agitation by the passage of the vapours through its mass. If a long previous interval of quiescence has elapsed there may be much solid lava towards the top of the vent which will tend to restrain the ascent of the molten portion underneath. A vast pressure is thus extended on the sides of the cone. Should these be too weak to resist, they will open in one or more rents, and the liquid lava will issue from the outer slope of the mountain, or the energies of the volcano will be directed towards clearing the obstruction in the chief throat until, with tremendous explosions, and the rise of a vast cloud of dust and fragments, the bottom and sides of the crater are finally blown out, and the top of the cone disappears. The lava may now escape from the lowest part of the lip of the crater, while at the same time an immense number of bombs, dross, and stones are shot up into the air, most of them falling back into the crater, but many descending upon the outer slopes of the cone, and some even upon the country beyond the base of the mountain. The lava rushes down at first like one or more rivers of melted iron, but as it cools its rate of motion lessens. Clouds of steam rise from its surface as well as from the central crater. Indeed, every successive convulsion of the mountain is marked even at a distance by the rise of huge ball-like wreaths or clouds of steam, mixed with dust and stones, forming a vast column which towers sometimes a couple of miles above the summit of the cone. By degrees these diminish in frequency and intensity; the lava ceases to flow, the showers of dust and stones dwindle down, and after a

ERUPTION OF VESUVIUS—AUGUST 27, 1872.

time, which may vary from hours to days or
months, the volcano becomes more tranquil.

A lava stream at its point of escape from
the side of a volcanic cone occupies a comparatively narrow breadth; but it usually
spreads out as it descends and moves more

slowly. The rate of movement is regulated by the fluidity of the lava, by its volume, and by the form and inclination of the ground. Hence, as a rule, a lava stream moves faster at first than afterwards, because it has not had time to stiffen, and its slope of descent is considerably steeper than further down the mountain. One of the most fluid and swiftly flowing lava-streams ever observed on Vesuvius was that erupted on August 12, 1805. It is said to have rushed down a space of nearly four miles in the first four minutes, but to have widened out and moved more slowly as it descended, yet finally to have reached a village situated on the shore of Naples in three hours. Long after a current has been deeply crusted over with slags and rough slabs of lava it continues to creep slowly forward for weeks or even months.

The height of Vesuvius varies from time to time to the extent of several hundred feet. The cause of these variations is to be found in the successive eruptions. Its usual altitude is about 4250 feet. Vesuvius really consists of two parts, the smaller and more northern portion being known as Monte Somma. The latter reaches a height of 3747 feet, and its cliff half encircles the present active cone, and descends in long slopes towards the plains below. This precipice is considered to have formed the walls of an ancient crater of vastly greater size than that of the present volcano. The continuation of the same wall round its southern half has been in great measure obliterated by the operations of the modern vent, which has built up a younger cone upon it, and is gradually filling up the hollow of the older crater.

At the beginning of the Christian era, and for many previous centuries, no eruption had been known to take place from the mountain, and the volcanic nature of the locality was perhaps not suspected by the inhabitants, who planted their vineyards along its fertile slopes, and built their numerous towns and villages around its base. The sagacious and observant geographer Strabo, however, detected the probable volcanic origin of the cone, and drew attention to its cindery and fire-eaten rocks. From his account and other references in classical authors, we gather that in the first century of the Christian era, and probably for hundreds of years before that time, the sides of the mountain were richly cultivated, but towards the top the upward growth of vegetation had not concealed the loose ashes which still remained as evidence of the volcanic nature of the place. On this barren summit lay a wide, flat depression surrounded with walls of rock which were festooned with wild vines. The present crater wall of Somma is doubtless a relic of that time. It was in this lofty rock-girt hollow that the gladiator Sparticus was besieged by the governor Claudius Pulcher, and from which he escaped by twisting ropes of vine branches and descending through an unguarded notch in the crater rim.

After remaining in a state of quiet for centuries, the volcanic energy began to manifest itself in a succession of earthquakes in A.D. 63, which spread alarm far and wide through the Campania. This preliminary earthquake phase of volcanic excitement was succeeded by a catastrophe which stands out prominently as one of the greatest calamities of human history. On the 24th of August, 79, the earthquakes which had been growing more violent culminated in a tremendous explosion of Vesuvius. A contemporary account of this event has been preserved in two letters of the younger Pliny addressed to Tacitus, the historian. From this narrative we can gather a tolerably clear conception of the general characteristics of the eruption. 'Abundant and increasingly violent earthquakes followed by an extraordinary commotion that accompanied the outburst of the volcano, when chariots would not remain still even on level ground, when houses were shaken so as to threaten destruction to their inhabitants, and when the unsteadiness of the land gave rise to great disturbance of the sea, which, in its agitation, retreated from the shores and left numerous marine animals uncovered, the well-known pine tree-shaped cloud of steam, dust, and stones towering above Vesuvius and spreading out far and wide over the surrounding country, the constant flashes of lightning marking the highly electrical condition of the column of erupted material, the showers of light cinders and ashes

that fell at a distance from the mountain, and the rain of hot pumice and pieces of block or glowing lava around the centre of eruption, the total darkness for three days produced by the diffusion of the finer volcanic dust through the atmosphere, the fiery glare that overspread the cloud canopy as each explosion uncovered the glowing surface of the lava column in the chimney of the volcano, and the wide covering of ashes, which, like a mantle of snow, was found to have been spread over the surrounding country when the darkness cleared and the catastrophe came to an end.'

Great destruction of life and property resulted from this explosion. Three towns, at least, are known to have been destroyed, viz., Herculaneum, at the west side of Vesuvius; Pompeii, on the south-east; and Stabiæ, still further south. Excavations within recent years have been carried on in an extensive manner in connection with Herculaneum and Pompeii, and those exhumed towns have thrown much light on the life and customs of the citizens of these Roman cities.

After this frightful outbreak, Vesuvius remained comparatively quiet and inactive for about 1500 years, and by the end of the seventeenth century the mountain had resumed much of the same general aspect that it presented in the days of Pliny. Its crater walls, which were about five miles in circumference, were covered with trees and brushwood, and at their base stretched a wide grassy plain on which cattle grazed and the wild boar lurked in the thickets. At length, after a series of earthquakes lasting for six months and increasing in violence, the volcano burst into renewed activity. Vast clouds of dust and stones, blown out of the crater and funnel of the volcano, were hurled into the air, and carried for hundreds of miles, the finer particles falling to the earth even in the Adriatic and at Constantinople. Though the inhabitants had been warned by the earlier convulsions of the mountain, so swiftly did destruction come upon them that 18,000 persons are said to have lost their lives.

Since this great convulsion which emptied the crater, Vesuvius has never again relapsed into a condition of total quiet and inactivity.

Every now and again it has broken out into eruption, sometimes emitting only steam, dust, and dross, but frequently also streams of lava. During the present century there has been no fewer than twelve eruptions more or less severe. One of these occurred in June, 1858, when the cone of the volcano sank 195 feet below its former elevation. In 1871 the mountain again began to show signs of a renewal of disturbance, and early in 1872 the eruption gradually increased in violence till April 26, when lava burst forth on all sides, one tremendous stream being 1,000 yards wide, and 20 feet deep, flowed to a distance of three miles in twelve minutes. A detailed account of this eruption was published by Palmieri, whose official connection with the mountain enabled him to give an authoritative and highly useful sketch of the scene. Since that time other eruptions have occurred, but fortunately unaccompanied by the horrors which characterized that of 1872.

A rich banker belonging to Naples formulated a scheme for the laying down of a railway from Naples to the margin of the crater. The scheme was carried into effect, and the railway was successfully opened in 1880. The waggons, which are capable of accommodating sixteen persons, are drawn up the incline by means of a wire-rope, and each waggon is provided with a patent brake, which is so powerful that immediately it is applied, it brings the vehicle to a standstill. In this way provision is made for the safety of the passengers should the rope at any time break. This railway ascends to within 150 yards of the mouth of the crater.

Many years ago on one of the ridges an observatory was established for the purpose of watching the progress of the volcano. It was erected by the Neapolitan Government, and is maintained as a national institution. It is situated at a height of 2,218 feet above the level of the sea, and is under the official charge of Palmieri. A continuous record of each phase in the volcanic changes has been taken, and some progress has been made in the study of the phenomena of Vesuvius, and in forecasting the occurrence and probable intensity of eruptions. M. JOHNSON.

Pass It On.

HAVE you had a kindness shown?
 Pass it on!
'Twas not given for you alone,
 Pass it on!
Let it travel down the years,
Let it wipe another's tears,
Till in heaven the deed appears—
 Pass it on!

Did you hear the loving word?
 Pass it on!
Like the singing of a bird?
 Pass it on!
Let its music live and grow,
Let it cheer another's woe;
You have reaped what others sow—
 Pass it on!

'Twas the sunshine of a smile—
 Pass it on!
Staying but a little while;
 Pass it on!
April beams the little thing,
Still it wakes the flowers of spring—
Makes the silent birds to sing—
 Pass it on!

Have you found the heavenly light?
 Pass it on!
Souls are groping in the night!
 Daylight gone!
Hold thy lighted lamp on high,
Be a star in some one's sky,
He may live who else would die—
 Pass it on!

Be not selfish in thy greed,
 Pass it on!
Look upon thy brother's need,
 Pass it on!
Live for self, you live in vain;
Live for Christ, you live again;
Live for Him, with Him you reign—
 Pass it on!

Rev. Henry Burton, M.A.

The Lake of Gennesareth.

IN ancient times the Lake of Gennesareth was designated the sea of Chinneth, from a city of that name skirting the shore, and belonging to the tribe of Naphtali. Gennesareth, it is thought, is a corruption of Chenneth. During the New Testament epoch, it was called—on account of its situation—the sea of Galilee. It was also termed the sea of Tiberias, in honour of the city built by Herod Antipas, which became the capital of Galilee, and the market-place for the European, Asiatic, and African races. Its modern name is Tabareeah, and the scattered people living upon its banks, like the generations of the past, pride themselves in calling it a sea. In the gospels three of the Evangelists always spoke of it as a sea, and Luke only speaks of it as being a lake.

This celebrated harp-shaped lake has all the appearance of an inland sea, being thirteen to fifteen miles in length, and from six to nine miles in width, being about the same length as our English Windermere, but exceeding it in breadth. It lies in a natural basin, encircled with steep and overhanging hills. On the eastern shore was a fringe of green, a quarter of a mile in breadth, beyond were the treeless masses of rock, indented with fissures made by the torrents of centuries. On the opposite shore, the mountains were more gently sloped. This amphitheatre was luxuriant and the products almost rivalled the tropics. It was a veritable paradise of natural beauties and products. The surface of the lake is five hundred feet below the water level of the Mediterranean. The transparent waters are a lovely blue, reflecting the shades of a cloudless sky. The lake abounded with fish, which found employment for thousands of fishermen. The scene was quite animated, hundreds of boats of all descriptions, and for pleasure, commerce, transport, and fishing purposes floated upon the lake. In some places the beach is shingly, and covered with a mosaic work of shells of exquisite beauty. On the western slopes are hot springs, and the waters are still used for medicinal purposes. The principal tributary of the lake is the famous river Jordan. Entering upon the northern shore, its course may be distinctly traced throughout the whole extent of the lake. The outlet is at the southern extremity where the Jordan flows onwards to the Dead Sea.

On the margin of the western coast was the historic vale of Gennesareth, embowered with gardens, orange and olive groves, that surpassed everything that was to be found throughout the whole region of Palestine, and verified its name of 'the Garden of Abundance.' The peculiarly sheltered situation of the valley, along with the amazing fertility of the soil, produced abundant harvests that ripened a month earlier than in other districts. The representatives of many nationalities dwelt in the neighbourhood of the lake, because it was 'the way of the sea.' The population was as dense as some parts of manufacturing Lancashire are to-day, the whole neighbourhood was a beehive of human industry. Josephus represents the cities and villages of Gennesareth as being exceedingly populous, the people being attracted thither on account of the fertility of the soil. He describes the smallest of the towns as containing a population of fifteen thousand inhabitants, who were so industrious that they cultivated every available acre of the land surface. Four important roads converged upon the boundaries of the lake which became the highway of nations, and along which passed the trading caravans from Egypt to Palestine, and from Phœnicia to the river Euphrates.

Immediately after Christ's expulsion from Nazareth, He resided in the sea-board city of Capernaum, which, for eighteen months, was the centre of His wonderful ministry.

His labours were confined within a small geographical area, and comprised the five sea-board towns of Capernaum, Magdala, Dalmanutha, Bethsaida, and Chorazin. Not a syllable is uttered respecting His preaching in the streets of fashionable Tiberias. His sermons

MAGDALA.

were delivered to the agriculturists and fishermen of the neighbourhood. The words of Jesus, spoken in the vicinity of the lake, will retain their preciousness when the sayings of Grecian philosophers are forgotten. Sacred memories are associated with the lake towns. In Capernaum He healed Peter's wife's mother, the paralytic, the centurion's servant, and raised the daughter of Jairus. In Capernaum He called Matthew the publican from the tax-gatherer's table to be His follower; and on an adjoining mountain He delivered the Beatitudes. His outflow of healing power was manifested on the opposite shore of the lake, where He 'cast out devils;' and on the north He manifested His compassion by feeding the multitudes from the unlimited resources of His own marvellous providence. During the period that He lived in the city, He was regarded as a resident, for the authorities demanded from Him the tribute-money that was paid by the ordinary citizens. Being penniless, Peter obtained the coin of payment from a strange purse—the mouth of a fish.

'His own city,' as Capernaum was termed, was coupled with Bethsaida and Chorazin as being one of the places where He had performed 'many mighty works,' which failed to convince the people of His Messiahship, and to bring them into fellowship with Himself. ' And thou, Capernaum, which art exalted unto heaven, shalt be brought down to hell: for if the mighty works which have been done in thee, had been done in Sodom, it would have remained until this day; but I say unto you, that it shall be more tolerable for the land of Sodom in the day of judgment than for thee.' The punishment overtook the inhabitants when it was destroyed by the Romans. A second Capernaum was hurriedly built upon the site of the former city. And this was completely destroyed by the Saracens. Nothing remains to distinguish the site but the ruins by the water's edge, in which the fox and jackal roam during the solemn hour of night.

A little south of Capernaum is Magdala— El Mejdel, as the moderns term it—consisting of a few miserable hovels, peopled by Mohammedan dwellers, who have so degenerated in the social scale, that unblushingly they allow their children to play in the public streets in a state of nudity. The famous orchards and groves of gospel times have completely disappeared, and instead there are a few solitary thorn-bushes. In the background of the village is a huge limestone rock honeycombed with caves. From a ravine flows a stream of water, meandering through the plain, the banks being covered with entangled thorn-bushes, willows, and oleanders. Magdala was the birth-place of Mary Magdalene, who held a foremost place amongst the Marys of gospel story. The sacred narrative is silent respecting the girlhood of the Magdalene. Both Mark and Luke speak of her demoniacal condition before she became a follower of Jesus, and they both represent her as one ' out of whom went seven devils.' The general impression that—previously to coming to Christ—she had been a woman of questionable virtue, is entirely without support. Her character has been greatly maligned by the founders of so-called Magdalen hospitals and other kindred institutions with which her name is associated. Even such an able writer and exegete as Archdeacon Farrar identifies her as the woman who anointed the feet of Jesus at the supper-table of Simon the Pharisee; the Archdeacon's data being based, not upon scriptural teaching, but the vagaries of Jewish legend. Geikie differs from Farrar, and says, ' A surprising interest attaches to Mary Magdalene, from the unfounded identification with the fallen penitent who did Jesus honour in the house of Simon the Pharisee. There is nothing whatever to connect her with that narrative, for it confounds what the New Testament distinguishes by the clearest language to think of her having led a sinful life, from the fact of her having suffered from demoniacal passion. Never, perhaps, has a figment so utterly baseless obtained so wide an acceptance as that which we connect with her name. But it is hopeless to try to explode it, for the word has passed into the vocabularies of Europe, as a synonym of penitent frailty. Legend, with a cruel injustice, has associated her name for ever with the spot now sacred to her, as the ' lost one reclaimed by

Jesus.' This noble woman of Magdala was devotedly attached to the Saviour and His cause. The love which He had manifested, awakened a practical response, for 'she ministered unto Him of her substance.' It fired her soul with heroism, she stood by His cross, and visited at grey dawn of morning His empty sepulchre. Mary Magdalene was privileged with the first glimpse of the Christ of the resurrection, who requested her to go and tell the disciples that 'I ascend unto My Father and your Father, and to My God and your God.' With promptness, she went and told the little band of disciples that 'she had seen the Lord;' thus being honoured as the first to announce the Saviour's resurrection— one of the foundation principles of Christianity.

The Gennesareth lake will be for ever associated with interesting incidents in the life of Jesus. On its waters Peter, James, and John were engaged as fishermen when they were called to the Apostolate. Their daily calling received a new and a spiritual meaning when Jesus said, 'Follow Me, and I will make you fishers of men.' At once they complied with His request, 'for they left their nets and followed Him.' Surrounded as the lake was with high hills, it was subject, at certain periods, to sudden squalls and tornado-like whirlwinds, which greatly endangered the lives of the crews. One of these scenes is pictured by the pen of the evangelists: 'And they launched forth, but as they sailed Jesus fell asleep, and there came down a storm of wind on the lake, and they were filled with water, and were in jeopardy; and they came to Him, and awoke Him, and said, Master, Master, we perish. And He arose, and rebuked the wind, and said unto the sea, Peace, be still. And the wind ceased, and there was a great calm. And they, filled with astonishment, exclaimed, What manner of man is this: for even the wind and the sea obey Him.' The lake was the scene of the second miraculous draught of fishes. After the Saviour's resurrection Peter said to the apostles, 'I go a fishing,' and his companions joined in chorus, 'We also go with thee.' After a night's fruitless toil, in the mists of early dawn there stood a figure upon the shore whom they failed to recognise, who asked if they had caught anything? They disconsolately replied No. 'Cast the net on the right side of the ship, and ye shall find.' They did as they were bidden, and their net was full of great fishes, numbering one hundred and fifty-three. The incident reminded them of a similar event that had transpired in those very waters. John whispered to Peter, 'It is the Lord.' Peter, fastening his fisher's tunic around him, with characteristic impulsiveness leaped over the side of the boat, and having swam to land, flung himself at the feet of Jesus. He was joined by the rest of the seven, with whom the Saviour dined. That incident is full of encouragement to disconsolate religious toilers.

> 'Full many a dreary anxious hour,
>   We watch our nets alone,—
> In drenching spray and driving shower,
>   And hear the night-bird moan.
> At morn we look and naught is there,
>   Sad dawn of cheerless day;
> Who then from pining and despair
>   The sickening heart can stay?'

Josephus, in his fascinating 'Wars of the Jews,' graphically describes a terrible sea fight that took place upon the waters of Gennesareth. The Jewish historian minutely describes the lake and its beautiful surroundings, as being 'the ambition of Nature where it forces those plants that are naturally enemies to one another to agree together; it is a happy contention of the seasons, as if every one of them laid claim to this country; for it not only nourishes different sorts of autumnal fruit beyond men's expectation, but preserves them a great while; it supplies men with grapes and figs during ten months in the year.' Within thirty years after the death of Christ, the Roman power invaded the peaceful shores of Gennesareth. The panic-stricken people fled in all directions. Some imprudently took to the lake as a place of refuge. A fierce contest took place, the number of the slain on the coasts, along with those that were massacred or drowned, amounted to over six thousand. Hundreds of Galileans were stabbed to death by the swords of the Roman soldiers. Those who tried to escape by diving and swimming were killed with darts, and others who sought protection from the crews of the Roman vessels had their hands or heads cut off. The historian, describing the scene after the battle, says: 'One might see the lake full of dead bodies, for not one of them escaped; as for the shores they were full of shipwrecks and of dead bodies all swelled; and as the dead bodies were inflamed with the sun and putrefied, they corrupted the air insomuch that the misery was not only an object of commiseration to the Jews, but even to those that hated them, and had been the authors of that misery.' Vespasian caused twelve hundred 'old and useless' prisoners to be cruelly slaughtered in the stadium; other six thousand were sent as serfs to join the workmen of Nero in digging through the isthmus of Athos, and over thirty thousand more were sold as slaves. Thus the terrible woes of prophecy were fulfilled.

ALBERT A. BIRCHENOUGH.

Chumming.

Go find an honest fellow.'

'And here's a hand my trusty friend,
And gie's a hand o' thine.'—BURNS.

THERE is a place in my theory of inspiration for that subtile something which is seldom defined with sufficient clearness, but which is known by the general name of suggestion. And as I have received such an inspiration from the gracious spirit presiding over the serial literature of the Connexion, like a faithful evangelist, I must write a gospel on chumming. A dispensation of this gospel is, with much grace, committed unto me. Having a feeling of responsibility, in common with that felt by the Apostle Paul, I may use his weighty words with reference to my obligation, ' Woe is me if I preach not the Gospel.'

It may be presumed, as social life is a strong characteristic of this age, that a gospel on chumming is greatly needed. It should be as 'glad tidings' to young men and maidens, and also to fathers and mothers, who are, generally speaking, as often offended as they are pleased with the chums whom their children choose, and to all those who are doing their utmost to keep pure and prosperous the path of human life. Its truths should sweetly break on willing ears, and gently drop into loving, trustful hearts. ' My doctrine shall drop as the rain, my speech shall distil as the dew, as the small rain upon the grass' (Deut. xxxii 2). A gospel on chumming may seem as an idle tale to the miserable misanthrope, whose heart has never warmed to a chum. Such a wretch of humanity is like a wooden post stuck up by itself in a clot of clay; he is destitute of social life, and joy, and friendly association.

'Living, he forfeits fair renown,
And, doubly dying, shall go down.
To the vile dust, from whence he sprung,
Unwept, unhonoured, and unsung.'

To some punctilious pharisees, whose faith is limited, such a gospel may seem a stumbling-block, and to those philosophers whose knowledge is particular, it may be foolishness; but to many of the young people in our church, and also to many who are not young, it may be the means of salvation from social danger and from moral degradation.

The word chum has come of late into such general use in free conversation, and also in popular literature, and that mode of life which is known as chumming has been, and is now, so common with all classes of society, that there is little or no need to define, or to give a description of them. To some ears the old words, comrade and comradeship, may sound more pleasant and polite than the words chum and chumming. The latter words sound harsher and more guttural than the former; they are less liquid and more slangy, but, by common consent, they are meant to convey the idea of a more familiar acquaintance, and a closer attachment. A chum is a chamber-fellow. Chumming is the art of reciprocal association, each fellow being closely and mutually related to the other. That other being is, in some measure, his other self, in whom he finds his complement, and with whom there is that fusion of soul which old Dryden, the poet, has so well described:—

> I had a friend that loved me;
> I was his soul—he lived not but in me,
> We were so closed within each other's breast,
> The rivets were not found that joined us first,
> That do not reach us yet: we were so mixed,
> As meeting streams; but to ourselves were lost.
> We were one mass; we could not give or take
> But from the same; for he was I, I he.
> Return my better half, and give me all myself,
> For thou art all.
> If I have any joy when thou art absent,
> I grudge it to myself; methinks I rob
> Thee of thy part.'

To chum with a kindred soul is a necessity of man's nature. He is gregarious, and naturally seeks to associate with his kind. To deny himself the company of his fellows is to suppress one-half of his nature, and to stunt and weaken the other half. Those who set at defiance the social instincts of their nature, by separating themselves from society, and habitually shunning company, ought to suspect the possession of a cynical disposition, and a strong flow of morbid feeling. The recluse is neither a healthy nor a happy man. He is ' apt to run to waste and self-neglect; to fancy himself lonely and abandoned, and his heart to fall to ruin like some deserted mansion, for want of an inhabitant.'

> ' Forsaken and friendless, my burden I bear,
> And the sweet voice o' pity ne'er sounds in my
> ear.'

Very few young people are without a number of chums, and no person need be without some. A youth who cultivates the habit of conversing with his fellows, and has a fair share of kindness and good-nature, will soon find himself the soul and centre of an admiring group of chums. He may be poor in worldly goods, but he will be rich in the favour of his fellows. It is one of the pleasures of old age to recall the memories of early associates, to cherish in the imagination the scenes of by-gone days, and to reflect, perhaps with a shade of sadness, on the departure from this life of many a youthful comrade and friend :—

> ' I've seen sae mony changefu' years,
> On earth I am a stranger grown;
> I wander in the ways of men,
> Alike unknowing and unknown:

> Unheard, unpitied, unrelieved,
> I bare alane my lade o' care,
> For silent, low on beds of dust,
> Lie a' that would my sorrow share.'

A word or two should be said on the selection of chums. A chum should be chosen with the greatest care. It is said that the law of affinity—like to like—determines the character of our chums. It is true that parties are drawn to each other by having something in common which makes them congenial to each other. And it is probable that the uniformity of this law of affinity, which seems to rule everywhere, has given strength and point to the numerous proverbs on this subject—such as, ' Birds of a feather flock together;' ' He who goes with wolves soon learns to howl;' ' Show me your company, and I will tell you what you are?' ' Walk with wise men, and thou shalt be wise; but the companion of fools shall smart for it' (Prov. xiii. 2, Revised Version). Wise and virtuous companions must prove a blessing, while foolish and wicked chums are sure to prove a curse. ' You may depend upon it,' said Lavater, ' he is a good man whose intimate friends are all good.' Companions mirror conditions. That which is within has its reflex in that which is without. A man's character is judged by the character of those with whom he associates, and his chumming will be a blessing or a curse to him according to the character of his chums. The Psalmist David, who had a profound knowledge of the nature of man, had sufficient reason for saying, ' Blessed is the man that walketh not in the counsel of the ungodly, nor standeth in the way of sinners, nor sitteth in the seat of the scornful' (Psalm i. 1). It is the merest truism to say that from the chums and companions of youth, the character of most men is moulded, and their course in life shaped; ' that as our bodies take in nourishment suitable to the meat on which we feed, so do our souls as insensibly take in virtue or vice by the example or conversation of good or bad company.' It is known in botany, that certain plants, placed beside other plants, begin at once to injure them. And it is, alas! too true, that certain parties have been injured in character and reputation from the first hour of their chumming with evil companions. The greatest care should be taken in the choice of chums. It would be well for those who have an almost fatal facility for making friends, to inquire whether those they are selecting are likely to help them to live 'a life of noblest breath,' or to make it more difficult for them to pursue their course of truth, and purity, and honour. Be careful in the choosing of your chums. Should you be deceived in some of them, and find them injurious to you, after all your attempts to improve them, you may, without affecting pride, or being rude, drop them from your list of intimate companions.

> 'Then judge yourself, and prove your man
> As circumspectly as you can;
> And, having made election,
> Beware no negligence of yours,
> Such a friend but ill endures,
> Enfeeble his affection.

It is a favourite maxim with moralists, that chums should be chosen from those more gifted and in higher position. Such a principle could not have any general application. It would preclude the more gifted and high from chumming with those less gifted and more lowly conditioned. There are some good examples of chumming, with mutual benefit, which do not conform to this rule. The highest of all is found in that of the Man of Nazareth. 'It is supposed that, in order that we may improve, we should have the companionship of those better informed ; but the association of an ignorant man, willing and desirous of learning, in calling forth the stores and resources of the mind, develops and calls into existence powers which, without the exercise, would never have been exhibited. The teacher, by the act of teaching, is taught. The preacher finds a spiritual enlargement as the result of his own sermon. A conversation with one of limited intelligence does not dwarf the resources of the mind ; it does not take from, if it does not add to, its power. In no sense shall we ever find that mental power, by its exercise, goes from us, as virtue and Divine life left the Master by the touch of faith. By exercise the mind and muscle are enlarged.'

The benefit of looking up to a chum is great and direct, and that of having a companion who delights in our society and looks up to us, if less direct, is nevertheless great and helpful. . There enters into the latter a little of the inspiration and luxury of doing good. 'Every friend,' says Richter, 'is to the other a sun, and a sun-flower also : he attracts and follows.' While the maxim of having nothing to do with a man unless you can get something out of him, savours too much of selfish utility, it may, as a general principle, be recommended to young people, who will find it an easier thing to choose an unwise chum than to cast him off when his foolishness has been discovered. A false and foolish chum is a constant danger—a living allurement to mischief and evil.

All the unwise associations formed by young men and women cannot be charged upon their parents ; but it is to be feared that sufficient care is not taken in the selection of those admitted into the family circle, and with whom the sons and daughters are brought approvingly into the closest contact. Circumspection of all strangers allowed within the family gates cannot be too strict. Nor should the gross and glaring faults of the 'fast young man,' and the 'good fellow' be partly condoned by that foolish saying, 'Oh, he is no man's enemy but his own,' as if he could be his own enemy, without being the enemy of every one with whom he associates. A man who is his own enemy is the enemy of the most of those virtues which make a perfect manhood. He is not true to his own nature, nor is he helping others to be good.

Blessed are those who have true and trusty chums.

Blessed are they who are not ashamed of their poor, but honest companions.

Blessed are those who, having failed in their attempts to reform their foolish chums, are not afraid to forsake them.

Blessed are they who can shun an evil chum, and not be pharisaical.

Blessed are they whose chums are the disciples of Christ, for then their chumming with each other shall help them to make life brighter and better. D. McKinley.

The Safety Lamp and its History.

E sit before our coal fires and enjoy their warmth without much thought of the dangers implied in winning the coal, or of the ingenuity and applied science by means of which these dangers have been minimized or overcome. Every now and again we are startled out of our complacency by some terrific colliery explosion, in which tens or it may be hundreds of lives are lost. Let us try to understand why these explosions occur, and how it has been sought to avoid them.

An explosion, strictly speaking, is the too rapid burning and expansion of a gas. The gas, which by its combustion causes the explosions in coal mines, can be easily studied without descending the pit. Let our readers place in a clean vessel under pure water a number of leaves and other parts of plants, cover up the vessel loosely, and expose its contents to the action of the air and sun. Decay will set in, and a miniature artificial stagnant pool will be produced. From this pool bubbles of gas will arise, which may be much increased in quantity if the mass at the bottom of the vessel be gently stirred. This gas is called marsh gas, and chemists will tell the experimenter that it is made up of a mixture in certain proportions of hydrogen and carbon, and is hence called a hydro-carbon. The hydrogen is derived from the water and the carbon from the plant-substance. And now let our experimenter leave his vessel and betake himself to the side of some pool of stagnant water that may lie near his home. Let him provide himself with an apparatus similar to that represented in our engraving. (Fig. 1.) A good-sized bottle is fitted with a sound cork in which a hole is bored large enough to allow to pass through it the stem of a funnel. As in the picture, let the inverted bottle with its funnel be held in one hand under the water,

while with the other, the operator, by means of a stick, stirs up the material at the bottom of the pool so as to liberate the imprisoned gas. Gradually the bottle will become filled with the gas, which will be found to exhibit the same properties as that produced at home. It has no particular taste or smell; but if a lighted match be applied to it it will catch fire and continue to burn until the gas is exhausted. It is called marsh gas because found in stagnant ponds and marshes as the result of decaying vegetable matter. It is not an active

FIG. 1.—COLLECTING MARSH GAS.

poison, though it cannot be breathed safely for any length of time. It kills by excluding oxygen rather than by its own properties.

But it has one deadly property which is the source of all the danger in coal-mines. With ordinary air it forms a highly explosive mixture. If a mixture be made of one part or volume of marsh gas with eight or ten of atmospheric air it will explode with tremendous violence on a light being applied to it. 'Other hydro-carbons besides marsh gas have this same power of forming explosive mixtures with air. This is particularly true of the hydro-carbon in petroleum, and the lamp explosions which we hear of altogether too frequently are due to the presence in the petroleum of certain volatile hydro-carbons, which should be removed in the process of refining. These are readily converted into gases, which, when mixed with air, give rise to the explosions.'

Now the gas of coal-mines is marsh gas which has been produced in much the same way as in the stagnant pool. None of our readers can be ignorant of the fact that the coal beds are the remains of vast primeval forests, which being gradually submerged by the subsidence of the land, underwent partial decay. This process of vegetable decay would inevitably give rise to marsh gas, part of which would, of course, escape into the free air above the water, but a great deal of it would necessarily be imprisoned by the layers of earth gradually covering up the decaying matter. There, collected in cavities, it would

FIG. 2.—FLAME EXTINGUISHED BY SPIRAL WIRE.

remain, until it forced its way out, or was set free by the miner in his research for fuel.

In the early part of this century much attention began to be directed to the frequent and disastrous explosions in coal mines, through the men working with naked lights in places where marsh gas had accumulated. In 1806 an explosion at West Moor killed ten miners. By another at the same pit in 1809, twelve lives were sacrificed. But one of the most fatal of these occurrences was that of 1812 in the Felling pit, near Gateshead, by which ninety men and boys perished. In the year following the same pit was the scene of a similar accident by which twenty-two persons lost their lives.

The problem was how to furnish sufficient light for the men to work by, without creating the risk of an explosion. The dim phosphorescent light from decayed fish skins was tried in vain. There was the ' steel mill,' furnished with a notched wheel, which being made to revolve against a flint struck out a succession of sparks. This apparatus was worked by a boy, in attendance on each miner. But the light so produced was as good as none at all, and the demand for coal on the part of the consumer, and for wages on the part of the men, caused much carelessness and loss of life.

Almost at the same time the minds of two men in very different positions in life were turned towards this problem. One was George Stephenson, colliery engineer at Killingworth, and the other was Sir Humphrey Davy, the brilliant natural philosopher and lecturer ; the idol and darling of the scientific world. The story of how they came practically to the same conclusion, and constructed lamps for miners based on the same great laws and principles, is one of the most romantic in the annals of scientific discovery and invention. Davy visited the collieries near Newcastle on the invitation of a committee, on August 24, 1815, and on the 9th of November following read his celebrated paper before the Royal Society and exhibited his proposed safety lamp. It was in the same month of August, 1815, that Stephenson, who had previously made many experiments on the inflammable gas in the Killingworth pit, requested his friend Nicholas Wood, the viewer, to prepare a drawing of a lamp which his fertile brain had already devised.

Let us try to understand the principles on which these respective inventions were founded. Every flame, let it be remembered, is a burning gas. A lamp burns because the oil in it is drawn up by the wick, heated, converted into gas, and then consumed. But, further, in order that a gas may burn, it must be heated to a certain point. Below that point it will not ignite; at and above it it will. Let us make one or two experiments. Take a spirit lamp like that drawn in Fig. 2, and after lighting it, bring down quickly over the flame a spiral of copper wire similar to that shown in the engraving. The flame will be almost instantly extinguished. Now such a spiral cannot act as an extinguisher does by excluding the air. The introduction of the copper spiral *cools down the flame*, or the burning gas, *beneath the point of ignition*, and so the flame dies out. Or hold above a gas flame (as shown in Fig. 3) a piece of wire gauze. No flame will appear above the gauze at first. But apply a lighted match to the upper part of the gauze, and a flame will immediately break out above as well as below. Or by holding the gauze about two inches above the burner before the gas is lighted, and then applying a light on the upper surface of the gauze the flame will appear there, but not below. The underside may then be lit likewise.

Now, how can these facts be explained? In precisely the same way as in the case

FIG. 3.—ACTION OF GAUZE UPON FLAME.

of the copper spiral. It is the cooling of the gases that cuts off the flame. The wire gauze placed in the flame conducts away a certain amount of heat. The gas which passes through it is cooled down slightly below its temperature of ignition and therefore cannot burn. These then were the principles which Davy discovered and afterwards applied in constructing his lamp, of which we give a drawing in Fig. 4. Protect your flame with wire gauze and see what happens on exposing it in a mixture of marsh gas and air, such as is found in mines. The explosive gas will pass readily through the gauze, and inside it there will occur a number of little explosions. But as the gauze conducts away some portion of the heat, the flame will not be sufficiently hot to ignite the mass of 'fire damp' outside, and

the miner is thus saved from any dangerous consequences. That bit of frail gauze is an effectual barrier against death. The processes of observation and reasoning, by which Davy reached this beautifully simple result, form one of the most delightful chapters in scientific research.

But, meanwhile, George Stephenson, working quite independently and in his own rude way, had solved the problem in practically the same fashion. His first idea was to construct a lamp with a current in its chimney so strong that it would prevent the inflammable air of

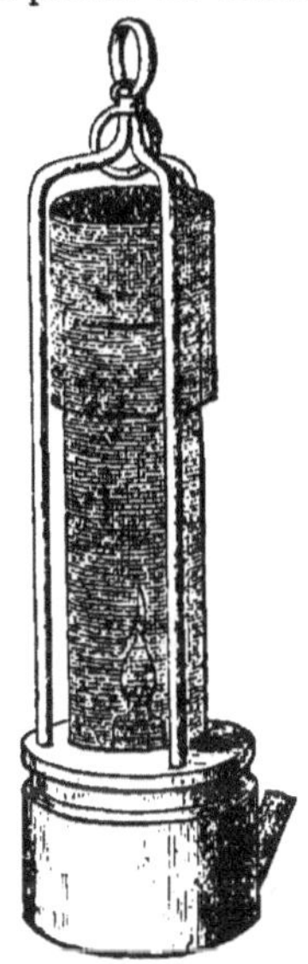

FIG. 4.—THE DAVY LAMP.

the pit from descending towards the flame; and this was, in fact, the principle of one of Davy's earliest experiments. This 'kind of lamp, however, was not very efficient, and Stephenson next turned his attention to passing flame through tubes of a small diameter, such as the barrels of several small keys. He now proposed to make a lamp by surrounding the oil vessel with a number of capillary tubes. 'It struck him,' as Dr. Smiles says, 'that if he cut off the middle of the tubes, or made holes in metal plates, placed at a distance from each other, equal to the length of the tubes, the air would get in better, and the effect in preventing explosion would be the same.' His experiments to this end proved entirely successful, and thus he and Davy, without knowing anything of each other's work, had hit upon precisely the same principle; for Davy's wire gauze is simply a multiplicity of tubes. Davy understood the philosophy of the matter, while Stephenson did not, but of the practical identity of their inventions there cannot be a doubt. When Sir Humphrey Davy's first model lamp was received and exhibited to the coal-miners at Newcastle, several gentlemen exclaimed, 'Why, it's the same as Stephenson's.' All honour, then, to the Killingworth engineman, whose ingenuity and perseverance enabled him to rival the work of the greatest scientist of the age.

Nicholas Wood, the viewer, said of the two inventions: 'Priority has been claimed for each of them. I believe the inventions to be parallel. By different roads they both arrived at the same result. Stephenson's is the superior lamp. Davy's is safe—Stephenson's is safer.' Later events have proved the substantial truth of this criticism. In an explosion at the Oaks Colliery, Barnsley, in 1857, the outburst of gas was so sudden that the Davy lamps were filled with fire and became red-hot, while the whole of the Stephenson lamps, over an area of five hundred yards, were almost instantaneously extinguished. Again, Mr. Galloway, an inspector of mines in England, has shown that explosions now occur mainly in connection with 'the firing of shot,' or blasting. The wave of air following the firing of the shot forces the flame through the apertures of the gauze of the Davy lamp. This cannot happen with the Stephenson lamp, in which the flame is surrounded with a glass cylinder.

Don't Hear Every Thing.

THE art of not hearing should be learned by all. There are so many things which it is painful to hear, very many of which, if heard, will disturb the temper, corrupt simplicity and modesty, detract from contentment and happiness. If a man fall into a violent passion, and call us all manner of names, at the first word we should shut our ears, and hear no more. If in a quiet voyage of life we find ourselves caught in one of those domestic whirlwinds of scolding, we should shut our ears as a sailor would furl his sails and, making all tight, scud before the gale. If a hot, restless man begins to inflame our feelings, we should consider what mischief the fiery sparks may do in our magazine below, where our temper is kept, and instantly close the door. If all the petty things said of one by heedless or ill-natured idlers were brought home to him, he would become a mere walking pin-cushion stuck full of sharp remarks. If we would be happy when among good men, we should open our ears; when among bad men, shut them. It is not worth while to hear what our neighbours say about our children, what our rivals say about our business, our dress, or our affairs.

The Library.

ONE of the best signs of the times in which we live is the increasingly intelligent attention which is being given to the study of the Old and New Testaments. They are no longer regarded as books handed direct out of heaven. Before Speke and Livingstone discovered the sources of the Nile, it was thought by Ethiopians and Egyptians to have its origin in the skies, and to flow straight from God. But now that we know whence it does come, it is invested for us and everybody with infinitely greater interest. Superstitious reverence has given place to rational understanding and appreciation. Just such is the case with the Bible. Some one has recently said that criticism has re-created the Old Testament. It used to be lamentably neglected as of no interest or utility, but now it is seen to be one of the most vital collections of books in existence. We have to introduce to our readers this month a little book which aims at doing, and succeeds in doing, the same service for the New Testament. It is a book which candidates for our ministry are expected to know; and we could wish that *all* our young men and maidens would purchase it, and so qualify themselves for taking a deeper interest in the public reading and exposition of the Scriptures than we fear is at present taken. The Bible is to too many a far-away book, to read which in public is regarded as the proper thing; but to how many its reading is of the nature of a charm or incantation, to be listened to with a dim sort of awe, as doing some mystical kind of good, but not at all to be realised or understood. But enough by way of preface. The book before us is entitled 'An Introduction to the New Testament,' by Dr. Marcus Dods; and we may mention, as some measure of its worth, that it is now in its sixth thousand. The name of the author is a guarantee of competence and solidity of treatment, while the style is so simple, and the arguments are so clear, that none need plead incapacity to grasp them. The broad divisions of the book are as follows:—The Gospels, The Acts, The Epistles (Pauline and Pastoral), Revelation. Under these heads Dr. Dods discusses, with great care, the dates and authorship of the several books or letters, the objections which have been taken to their reception, the doubts of their genuineness, their relation to the times to which they are said to belong, their general and special characteristics; and, indeed, every question which can emerge concerning them, as books that have actually a history, and were cogitated by human minds, and written by human hands. At the same time, that they are not merely human, but in a real sense inspired, Dr. Dods makes very plain. Of Matthew's Gospel he writes: 'It is fittingly placed next to the Old Testament, not because it was the earliest contribution to the New— for it was not that—but because it resumes and completes each strand of the former revelation. The long and chequered history related in the Old Testament finds its consummation and significance in the life of Jesus. . . . The motto of the life of Jesus, as read and rendered by Matthew, is 'I am come to fulfil' (v. 17). The stages in the history are marked with this design, 'that it might be fulfilled which was spoken by the prophet.' As to

Luke, Dr. Dods quotes and adopts Archdeacon Farrar's words : It is 'the Gospel of the Greek and of the future, of catholicity of mind : the Gospel of hymns and of prayers ; the Gospel of the Saviour ; the Gospel of the universality and gratuitousness of salvation; the Gospel of holy toleration ; the Gospel of those whom the religious world regards as heretics ; the Gospel of the publican and the outcast and the weeping Magdalene, and the crucified malefactor, and of the Good Samaritan, and of the Prodigal Son.' 'Renan,' says Dr. Dods, ' declares it to be the most beautiful book ever written, and exhausts his copious vocabulary in praise of its large-heartedness and sweetness.' Speaking of the Epistles in general, Dr. Dods writes: ' This species of literature, though it had not been common among the Greeks, was familiar to the Romans of the Empire, with its numberless foreign connections and ramified system of communication. To the early Church it became a necessity. There was no time to write books, and they would not have been much read or readily understood. Letters—direct, terse, brief—were the best and simplest means of communication. Of these letters Paul's are the earliest—nay, they, of all the literary relics of Christianity, are the first in point of time, if not of importance. As Dr. Dods well says : 'the order in which the Epistles of St. Paul now stand in the New Testament is meaningless, and has to all appearance been determined by the relative bulk of the letters, or by the comparative rank and importance of the Churches to which they were addressed.' Dr. Dods strongly urges the study of them in chronological order. He is specially interesting and instructive in writing of the Epistle to the Galatians (perhaps the most distinctively Pauline of all the Epistles), and we would advise our readers to take the letter in one hand, and Dr. Dods' *Introduction* in the other, and read the two together. If they don't rise from this fascinating bit of New Testament study with a kindled enthusiasm for the whole subject we shall be much surprised. But we cannot write further. Let our readers get this little book without delay. The publishers are Hodder & Stoughton, and the retail price is only half-a-crown.

A HUNDRED YEARS TO COME.

J. R. Osgood.

2. Who'll press for gold this crowded street,
   A hundred years to come?
Who'll tread yon church with willing feet,
   A hundred years to come?
Pale, trembling age, and fiery youth,
And childhood with its heart of truth,
The rich, the poor, on land and sea,
Where will the mighty millions be
   A hundred years to come?

3. We all within our graves shall sleep
   A hundred years to come;
No living soul for us will weep
   A hundred years to come;
But other men our lands will till,
And others then our streets will fill,
While other birds will sing as gay,
And bright the sun shine as to day,
   A hundred years to come.

A HUNDRED YEARS TO COME.

Key E-flat. J. R. OsGood.

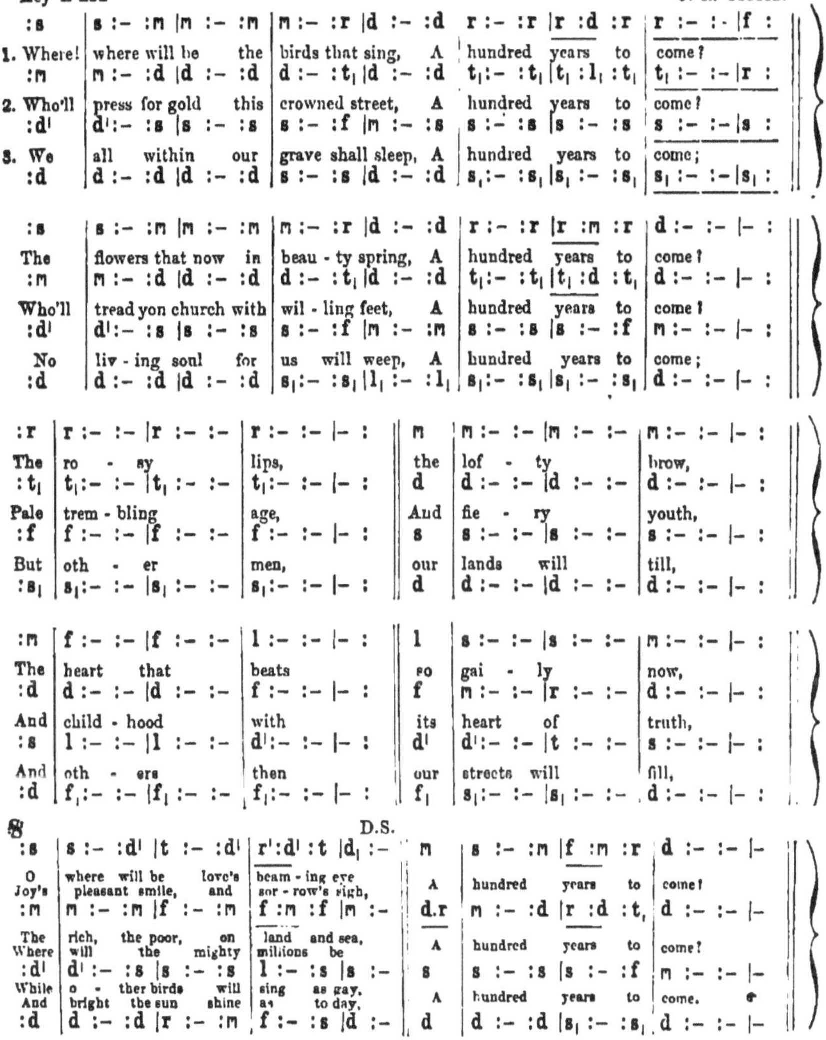

```
 :s   |s :- :m |m :- :m |m :- :r |d :- :d |r :- :r |r :d :r |r :- :- |f :   ||
1. Where! | where will be      the | birds that sing,  A | hundred years  to | come ?
 :m   |m :- :d |d :- :d |d :- :t, |d :- :d |t, :- :t, |t, :l, :t, |t, :- :- |r :   ||
2. Who'll | press for gold    this | crowned street,   A | hundred years  to | come ?
 :d'  |d' :- :s |s :- :s |s :- :f |m :- :s |s :- :s |s :- :s |s :- :- |s :   ||
3. We  | all  within   our | grave shall sleep, A | hundred years  to | come ;
 :d   |d :- :d |d :- :d |s :- :s |d :- :d |s, :- :s, |s, :- :s, |s, :- :- |s, :   ||

 :s   |s :- :m |m :- :m |m :- :r |d :- :d |r :- :r |r :m :r |d :- :- |- :   ||
 The  | flowers that now  in | beau - ty spring,  A | hundred years  to | come ?
 :m   |m :- :d |d :- :d |d :- :t, |d :- :d |t, :- :t, |t, :d :t, |d :- :- |- :   ||
 Who'll | tread yon church with | wil - ling feet,  A | hundred years  to | come ?
 :d'  |d' :- :s |s :- :s |s :- :f |m :- :m |s :- :s |s :- :f |m :- :- |- :   ||
 No   | liv - ing soul   for | us  will  weep,   A | hundred years  to | come ;
 :d   |d :- :d |d :- :d |s, :- :s, |l, :- :l, |s, :- :s, |s, :- :s, |d :- :- |- :   ||

 :r   |r :- :- |r :- :- |r :- :- |- :   ||   m  |m :- :- |m :- :- |m :- :- |- :   ||
 The  | ro - sy        | lips,           |     | the | lof - ty       | brow,
 :t,  |t, :- :- |t, :- :- |t, :- :- |- :   ||   d  |d :- :- |d :- :- |d :- :- |- :   ||
 Pale | trem - bling    | age,            |     | And | fie - ry       | youth,
 :f   |f :- :- |f :- :- |f :- :- |- :   ||   s  |s :- :- |s :- :- |s :- :- |- :   ||
 But  | oth - er        | men,            |     | our | lands will     | till,
 :s,  |s, :- :- |s, :- :- |s, :- :- |- :   ||   d  |d :- :- |d :- :- |d :- :- |- :   ||

 :m   |f :- :- |f :- :- |l :- :- |- :   ||   l  |s :- :- |s :- :- |m :- :- |- :   ||
 The  | heart  that     | beats           |     | so  | gai - ly       | now,
 :d   |d :- :- |d :- :- |f :- :- |- :   ||   f  |m :- :- |r :- :- |d :- :- |- :   ||
 And  | child - hood    | with            |     | its | heart  of      | truth,
 :s   |l :- :- |l :- :- |d' :- :- |- :   ||   d' |d' :- :- |t :- :- |s :- :- |- :   ||
 And  | oth - ers       | then            |     | our | streets will   | fill,
 :d   |f, :- :- |f, :- :- |f, :- :- |- :   ||   f, |s, :- :- |s, :- :- |d :- :- |- :   ||

 :s   |s :- :d' |t :- :d' |r':d' :t |d, :-   ||   m  |s :- :m |f :m :r |d :- :- |-
 O    | where will be     love's | beam - ing eye         |     | A   | hundred years  to | come!
 Joy's | pleasant smile,   and | sor - row's sigh,      |     |     |
 :m   |m :- :m |f :- :m |f :m :f |m :-   ||   d.r |m :- :d |r :d :t, |d :- :- |-
 The  | rich,  the poor,  on | land  and sea,         |     | A   | hundred years  to | come ?
 Where | will  the   mighty | millions  be           |
 :d'  |d' :- :s |s :- :s |l :- :s |s :-   ||   s  |s :- :s |s :- :f |m :- :- |-
 While | o - ther birds   will | sing  as gay,          |     | A   | hundred years  to | come.
 And  | bright the sun   shine | as    to day,          |
 :d   |d :- :d |r :- :m |f :- :s |d :-   ||   d  |d :- :d |s, :- :s, |d :- :- |-
```

D.S.

Current Topics.

THE GENTLE LIFE.

'And is this—Yarrow?—This the stream
Of which my fancy cherished,
So faithfully, a waking dream?
An image that hath perished.'

So Wordsworth expressed his disappointment when for the first time he looked upon the famous Border stream. This is a very common feeling. The real Yarrow is seldom equal to the picture of our fancy. This, however, has not been my experience with regard to a book which bears the title placed at the head of these notes. It consists of a series of 'Essays in Aid of the Formation of Character,' by Mr. J. Hain Friswell. It was published nearly thirty years ago, and a second volume was published soon afterwards. It is a good while since I first formed the desire to read these essays, but I am just now in the midst of them. And under their fascination I feel indisposed to talk about anything else. And the wish to share our pleasures with others is surely very natural. 'Whoever is delighted with solitude,' says Lord Bacon, 'is either a wild beast or a god.' Now, it is very delightful to wander over these genial pages, admiring the beautiful flowers that adorn them, tasting the delicious fruits that are to be found in such plenty, inhaling the exquisite literary aroma that pervades the whole; but these are things not to be enjoyed alone. You soon wish to express your gratification to others. 'We do not well,' said the lepers of Samaria, whilst they were glutting themselves with the spoils of the vanished Syrian host, 'we do not well; this day is a day of good tidings, and we hold our peace.' Like them, therefore, I hasten to invite my young readers to share the benefit and pleasure I have derived from the reading of Mr. Friswell's essays.

In his first essay he is careful to show the difference between leading the gentle life and being genteel. A true gentleman is well described in Chaucer's *Canterbury Tales :*—

'But who so is vertuous,
And in his port not outrageous,
When such one thou seest thee beforne,
Though he be not gentil borne,
Thou maiest well seine (this is in soth)
That he is gentil, because he dothe
As longeth to a gentil man.'

Gentility, on the other hand, is the counterfeit of the gentle life. It is difficult to define, for the word itself is a base diminutive. What 'gent' is to gentleman, so 'genteel' is to *gentilitas*. The gentle man is something, though hard to prove what; the genteel man is nothing, not even the shadow of a gentleman. A false idea of propriety becomes the idol to which the genteel man surrenders everything. It is not genteel, for instance, to work for your living, to speak your mind, to walk quickly in a busy street, to have an opinion, or ever to admire anything. On the other hand, to be idle, to be able to insinuate a falsehood, to saunter in the way of busy people, to follow the fashion, and to cultivate a dull, stupid, unenjoying stolidity, is to have attained the height of gentility. All this unreality is essentially base and vulgar, and must be unbearably dull. The gentle life is the very opposite of all this. 'To be humble-minded, meek in spirit, but bold in thought and action; to be truthful, sincere, generous; to be pitiful to the poor and needy, respectful to all men; to guide the young, defer to old age, to enjoy and be thankful for our own lot, and to envy none—this,' says Mr. Friswell, 'is indeed to be gentle, after the best model the world has ever seen, and is far better than being genteel.'

It must not be supposed, however, that we can afford to be indifferent to appearances. Far from it. 'Manners makyth man,' said William of Wykeham, and Mr. Friswell quite agrees with him. 'You had better,' wrote Lord Chesterfield to his son, 'return a dropped fan genteelly than give a thousand pounds awkwardly; and you had better refuse a favour gracefully than grant it clumsily. Manner is all in everything; it is by manner only that you can please, and consequently rise.' This is put so broadly as to be almost at variance with the argument of Mr. Friswell's first essay, but it really does nothing more than express the other side of the truth. Good manner, he tells us, is compounded of two things—self-respect, and a due observance of the feelings of others. Good manners consist in the polish put upon these, and are neither frivolous nor useless, as some religionists think. There is evidence enough and to spare, he says, not only that the Saviour was 'the first true gentleman that ever breathed,' but that His immediate disciples had studied manner as well as rhetoric. Whether we accept this latter statement or not, we must all agree that ' St. Paul, in his speeches and letters, is the very model of a gentleman ; as also are St. James, St. John, and others.' A perfect Christian, indeed, must be a perfect gentleman, for the spirit of Christianity, which expresses itself in kindness, forbearance, gentleness, conciliation, affection in manner and discourse, is of the essence of true politeness.

———

Mr. Friswell gives a good definition of education. Its object, he says, should be to fit a boy for after-life, expand his knowledge, brace up his mind, root out laziness, and give aim and direction to his intellect, as well as a general fitness for employment, and a wide knowledge of the rudiments of science and the causes of things. It is not at every school, however, that education of this kind can be had, and perhaps the private schools of the very rich are the most deficient. Many parents are induced to send their boys to such schools by the advertisement that the ' sons of noblemen and baronets ' are to be their companions. It is even said that in some cases the son of a poor baronet will be educated free at such a school, in order that the boy should act as a decoy-duck. And at the six o'clock dinner the poor lad is pestered by such questions as ' How is Sir Samuel ?' and ' How is my lady, your mother ? ' from the master or mistress, simply for the sake of pronouncing the title. This, of course, fosters every kind of snobbishness. But at a public school things

are different. There it is not rank, but pluck that wins. Bulwer Lytton used to tell a story of a proud little monkey walking into Eton schoolyard, and replying to the question, ' Who are you ? ' with ' Lord Dash, son of the Marquis of Dontknowwho.' ' Then,' said the cock of the school, a plain Bob Smith, ' there are three kicks : one for my lord, and two for the Marquis '; and the little recipient never forgot this lesson, the best he had in his life. The school is the ' landing-place, just before we begin to climb the stairs of life,' and what the boy has to learn is not to be vainer and weaker, but to be better and stronger.

———

We need to be constantly reminded that there is a great difference between success and greatness. ' Never catch at a falling knife or a falling friend,' says a Scotch proverb. This explains the secret of many a successful life ; but this policy never made a man great. To succeed, originally meaning to ' get under,' now means to ' get over ' any one. And this is virtually the doctrine taught in such books as Dr. Smiles' ' Self Help,' and by Benjamin Franklin in ' Poor Richard's Almanack.' Poor Richard urges constant exertion, constant labour, constant application. You are to rise early, and take advantage of the sluggard who lies in bed—' Plough deep whilst sluggards sleep.' You are to be the early bird, so as to get the worm ; you are to love money, for ' a penny saved is a penny gained,' and you are to do all with one aim—self. That this is the sure road to success no one will deny, but it is not success of the highest kind. A good man's conscience is sadly in the way of his worldly success ; but it is only in obedience to it he can obtain true greatness. And let no one make himself miserable if he do not make a mark in the world, for there is a profound truth in the poet's line—' The world knows nothing of its greatest men.' Young men aspire to shine, and there is no reason why they should not. But the way to gain moderate and honest success is to do just what a man can do—not attempting too much —and doing well whatever he does without a thought of fame.

Flirtation is severely condemned in these essays, but it seems that falling in love is by no means inconsistent with the gentle life. This latter practice is an old fashion, and Mr. Friswell is persuaded that it will 'yet endure.' Cobbett was of the same opinion. 'Between fifteen and twenty-two,' said he, 'all people will fall in love.' Shakespeare thought they were not out of danger until they had reached the age of forty-five ; whilst old Burton, the author of the 'Anatomy of Melancholy,' thought that the disease might attack a man at any age. 'There be old fools,' he said, 'as well as young fools.' The passion seems to be universal, and Mr. Friswell very finely says that this 'most enjoyable, freshest, and most beautiful portion of life should call forth the finest feelings.' So much happiness depends upon courtship, that it is really a serious matter, and there can be nothing more foolish than to suppose that it cannot be wisely directed. According to Cobbett, who had the knack of saying exactly what he meant, a man ought to look for eight qualities in choosing a wife. Those are — 1. Chastity. 2. Sobriety. 3. Industry. 4. Frugality. 5. Cleanliness. 6. Knowledge of domestic affairs. 7. Good temper ; and 8. Beauty. These qualities ought not to be difficult to find in this country. Of course the last one, which is perhaps not the least important, is entirely a matter of opinion. Plato had a theory that a beautiful soul always seeks a body equally beautiful to inhabit. But the real truth is that moral beauty will shed a glory over the plainest physical features. The lover's eye can see what none other is ever able to perceive, and if he be a true man he will cherish this faith. 'So as the sun rises in the morning, chasing away the darkness of the night, and tinting all the little clouds with a roseate hue, beautiful in its promise, noble in its strength, fit herald of a bright and pure day, even so should the true morning of life rise in each heart, and gild the coming day.'

There are some fine papers in this volume on Friendship and the Choice of Companions. Here, for instance, is a striking illustration of the danger of bad companions :—'Men and women, girls and boys, feel instinctively when they have fallen in with dangerous associates ; if they choose to remain amongst them they are lost. So in the high tide, vessels of light draught will float over Goodwin quicksands ; in summer, at low tide, the venturous boys and young people will play cricket thereon but neither can remain long in the neighbourhood. The time comes when the sands are covered with but a thin surface of water, and beneath is the shifting, loose, wet earth, more dangerous and treacherous than spring-tide ice ; and then it is that to touch is to be drawn in, and to be drawn in is death. So is it with bad company.'   M. P. D.

Anecdotes about Hymns.

FROM THE GERMAN.

IV.—THE HYMN BOOK.

 A MAN from another part of the country came one day into Pastor Weikes' church at Gohfeld in Westphalia, and when the hymn was given out, looked over the hymn-book of a member of the congregation, and joined in the singing. 'What a hymn book!' he said afterwards, 'what beautiful hymns! do let me look at it!' But what was his surprise to find that it was exactly the identical collection used in his own church. But here for the first time the external word had come to him as an inward voice—a voice speaking to his heart.

V.—THE POWER OF SONG.

A CONVERTED negress of the name of Deborah fell, with a child of three years old in her arms, into the fire and burnt her right arm to the bone. Mortification coming on, it was decided that the arm must be amputated. While the surgeon was busied with his preparations, Deborah begged a missionary, who was present, to sing with her 'a sweet psalm,' as she expressed it, which he did, following it with an earnest, heartfelt prayer. The amputation had to take place, but the negress declared that the singing had so strengthened her, as to make it quite easy for her to bear the pain. The operation proved perfectly successful.

SPRINGTIME:

A Magazine for Our Young Men and Maidens.

Vol. VI. No. 6.]   JUNE, 1891.   [Price Twopence.

A Bad Calculation.

By ROBERT HIND.

Author of 'Crosby Dalton: Local Preacher and Village Demagogue,' 'The Ruby Pendant,' &c.

CHAPTER XI.

SOCIAL AMBITIONS.

' It pained us sore to fancy he would learn
Enough to make him look with shame and scorn
On this old dwelling. 'Twas his manner, sir !
He seldom looked his father in the face,
And when he walked about the dwelling, seem'd
Like one superior.'

ROBERT BUCHANAN.

To a young lady of so frank a disposition as Rye Harland, reserve was likely to prove anything but comfortable. In the days of her childhood, like other specimens of human kind in miniature, she had at times been conscious of wrong-doing. Since those early days, however, she had never been troubled with any sense of guilt on account of actual sins. To the eyes of her father and mother alike all her doings had been open for inspection, and although neither of them quite understood her—a fact of which Mr. Harland at least was perfectly well aware—they knew that until she had given her hand to Arthur Brixton she had never sought to hide her true self from them.

Hers had been an innocent, healthy young life—a life as happy, too, as it had been pure. But now a change had come. She was the subject of thoughts and feelings of which she could not have told her elders. To keep them locked up in her heart made her unhappy—burdened her, indeed, with a feeling very much like guilt. She had many young lady friends, but none of them appeared to her mind quite the one to whom she could speak of matters so sacred and delicate.

Why was not Arthur available in this emergency of her inner life? If only she could have spoken to him on the subject, she sometimes thought, all might have been well, and her heart might have won back its old sense of contentment. But there were many reasons to prevent her from taking this course. First of all Arthur himself was her main cause of trouble. And then the quality in him that troubled her made it unlikely that he would do anything to relieve her.

Jack Benson still remained as a possible alternative. And in him she felt a confidence that grew stronger every day. He was kind always, but kindest of all when she was most troubled. By some method he appeared to penetrate through her reserve, and without any word from her guessed that her affairs were wrong. He was always considerate too, never bothering her with questions, but silently making her feel that she had in him a staunch friend and champion.

' If only Arthur were like him!' she thought, and then her sensitive conscience rebuked her for her unfaithfulness. But loyal as she was in heart, it was vain to put away the bold fact that Arthur's conduct since their engagement had not been that of a gallant lover. His old moody temper, which she had hoped and believed was merely a temporary habit of mind, had lately become more marked, and reflecting on what should have been their happy lovers' meetings, she could not remember one instance that had yielded her pleasure.

Arthur Brixton, the victim of a moral disease, had acquired an unenviable talent of robbing all who were about him of their peace of mind. A god had been set up in his heart that commanded his devotion, and to which he made daily sacrifice. A poor deity it was, to be sure, for written in plain Saxon its name was SELF.

Rye, in her reflections, had not yet arrived at the name of her lover's idol. The young man was not easy to read. No one would have said he was vain. Vanity, in the ordinary sense, was too poor and superficial a quality to account for the mental moods he revealed. The love of approbation was strong in him, but it lay too deep for ordinary observers to discover it. He was something of a mystery to all his friends, and all they seemed to know of him was that he was a young man of handsome appearance and remarkable talents, who nevertheless did not enjoy life himself, nor help others to enjoy it.

Something, Rye felt, must be done to relieve the tension on her mind, and though she felt it was not a satisfactory way of dealing with the difficulty, she resolved, when the next opportunity occurred to try to lead up to the subject of their relations. It cost her a struggle to determine on this course, but for weeks she had been sore in her heart, and on the night of Isa Saunders' gathering Arthur had wounded her deeply.

It was unfortunate, perhaps, that her first opportunity of carrying out her resolve occurred at a time when she should have been enjoying herself. The occasion was the University Regatta, the most popular of what may be called the public picnics of Rockingham. All the gentility of the old city turned out to see the young men use their strength and skill in rowing against each other. The river banks presented a most animated spectacle, and nothing could have been more delightful to the observer with a benevolent turn of mind than the harmony and high spirits of the respectable crowd who had assembled to witness the proceedings.

Rye and Arthur were there, and had wandered along the higher reaches of the river until a bend had hid the multitude out of their sight.

'It is well we are here, Rye,' the young man observed, frowning.

' Why ? '

' Perhaps the trees and running water will not remind us of what one is not allowed to forget among the "high and mighty," whose garments we have touched as we have watched the boats go past.'

' I did not observe that any one spoke unkindly to you, Arthur,' Rye said.

' No one did ; therein is one-half of my complaint. It is a curious crowd of men and women we have just left, and affords room for reflections of no ordinary kind. There are all the dignitaries of the church with their ladies, and representatives of all the old families of Rockingham. They bow to each other, gather in groups, and converse. But they never notice their grocer and his wife ; and yet the grocer is rich, and, for that matter, could not well be done without, even by them. He, poor man, is quite satisfied in being ignored, so long as he retains them for customers, and has his revenge by taking no notice of the man who started life with him and who was the companion of his youth, but who has committed the unpardonable sin of remaining a working man. Neither the grocer nor the working man suffers much perhaps, but I saw something that involved pain of no common kind to one person at least. In that crowd was a curate who had evidently married beneath him. He had brought with him his young wife and their baby, possibly thinking the outing would do them good. Her cheap, gaudy dress proclaimed her to be a mistake, and the consequence is that none of the other curates and none of those who knew him have felt it expedient to fraternize with him. The trio are there as much alone as though they had been in the heart of a desert, and though his wife knows nothing of it, his heart is bleeding at the cruelty of fashion.'

Rye's breath was taken away by this long tirade, and her answer was scarcely equal to the occasion.

'I did not observe. Perhaps,' she added, 'if they were very lonely, we might have made an excuse of some kind, and drawn them into conversation.'

'One case does not matter much. It is the fashion as a whole that hurts me.'

'There we differ,' Rye said, aroused a little into a spirit of opposition. 'What do I care about the general fashion? It is the particular cases—the cases of those who suffer—who appeal to my imagination. And I am sure I should not mind if nobody save my own special friends were to acknowledge me.'

Arthur knew this was true, and it compelled his admiration, whilst it condemned him for a total lack of the same spirit.

'There is something in the custom that embitters my mind, and makes me want to be other than I am.'

'And what, Arthur, would you be?' Rye asked, wishing in her heart he would try to be other than the misanthropic young man into which he had developed.

'Perhaps it would be difficult for me to tell you; and yet I have a distinct impression of what I would like to be. Could I choose my lot, no one in that crowd of fashionable people would pass me without recognizing in Arthur Brixton one who was their equal.'

Rye smiled at this, and deep in her heart there began to stir just the semblance of a feeling of contempt. Never before had she entertained such a sentiment towards her lover, and although it was too feeble for her to define it to herself, she gave a little shiver as it introduced itself into her consciousness.

'Your aim is not what I should be inclined to call a high one,' she remarked, with her customary frankness. 'I wish I could have said it was a worthy aim even. And yet,' she added musingly, as though she had ceased to speak to her companion, and was addressing her own heart, 'I have read of young men whose aims I should have re-

garded as more than worthy, as really noble and glorious.'

There was sadness in her voice and in the expression of her face. Arthur, ever quick to resent a lack of appreciation, looked angry and bit his lip.

Rye, however, who was the most kind-hearted of girls, and would have been one of the last to cause needless pain, hastened to console his *amour propre*.

'And this you have named is not one of your chief aims in life. You have wished to live well, to be good, and to serve others, I am sure.'

She looked longingly into his face, and waited for his confirmation of her words. At that moment he wished with all his heart that he could have responded to her appeal in the way she desired, with a clear conscience.

'If only I were as contented as you, I should have a hope of not failing altogether in being noble. If even you were always beside me, I think I might succeed.'

'That confession of weakness is not like you, and it does you injustice,' Rye interposed hurriedly.

'Perhaps; and yet every day, if I may be so frank with you, I grow more unhappy, and feel myself full of envy towards the great. I want to be rich, and yet I care nothing for the money in itself. Indeed, I have a contempt for those who are rich and nothing more. I must be dreadfully proud, and from this arises my inability to be content with my circumstances and prospects.'

Rye's mind was in a tumult whilst Arthur was speaking. She felt that this was the time when she must have a better understanding with her friend. He was an enigma to her, and she felt a little afraid of his moods.

And yet despite that she was goaded by her misery to attempt it, the task she was now undertaking filled her with a sense of shame such as she had never before experienced, and which she could hardly bear. For these reasons her eyes were downcast and her voice very low when she said—

'Perhaps, Arthur, you think you would have a better chance of altering your prospects if you felt yourself quite free—I mean

without any ties. I have surmised this sometimes lately ; and,' she continued, laying her
hand gently on his arm, ' I should be so glad
to see you realize all your wishes, and so sorry
to cast ever so little a difficulty in your way,
that I thought it best to name it to you.'

' You wish our engagement to be broken,
then, Rye ?' Arthur inquired.

' Do not misrepresent what I have said, and
do not let us speak of it otherwise than kindly,
Arthur. To name it has given me more pain
than you can know, and the circumstances
that have led me to speak to you about it,
have tried me sorely. I have not thought
about myself at all. But you are unhappy ;
and you are ambitious to do something great
or to become something great. I would do
anything I could to help you, and when I
name this it is because I want to help you.'

' And it is very good of you to show so much
interest in me ; but until you command me
to leave you, and tell me you are yourself
tired of me, I shall not listen to such a
proposal.'

Rye was silenced, but not satisfied. She
did not understand why, because, judging
others by her own frank disposition, it never
occurred to her that Arthur might not have
spoken all his mind. This much, however, she
felt conscious of, she would have been glad if
Arthur had resented her proposal more warmly,
and made some assertion of his devotion. For
this lack she accounted by the preoccupation
of his mind with his schemes for the future.

And still Rye Harland knew not the name
of the idol to which Arthur Brixton bowed his
knee, and on whose altar he daily laid the
sacrifice of his peace of mind.

CHAPTER XII.

PRINCIPLE AND EXPEDIENCY.

> ' And the pain,
> The agony, deepen'd, when the lover's face
> Came smiling to the dwelling, young and bright,
> With pitiless gladness.'
>
> ROBERT BUCHANAN.

' WHEN you have decided you will let me
know ?'

These were Rye Harland's last words to
Arthur on the night of the regatta, and he had
promised. They had been speaking about a
possible change of career from desk work in a
solicitor's office, and Arthur had hinted that
he would like to enter the university. This
was not surprising. The little time he could
spare had always been diligently employed in
mental improvement, and among the few completely happy hours he could remember were
those when, with a whole evening before him,
he had sat down to read at the large table in
his mother's kitchen. No wonder he sometimes envied the young men of the University,
as he had watched them in cap and gown go
past the office window where he was sitting
copying dry-as-dust legal documents. And
now he had resolved to be one of them. Before
arriving at this decision he had made a few
calculations, for three years in the University not only meant that he would cease to earn
money, but that he would have to spend a
great deal. Not so much, of course, as would
have been needed had he lived in one of the
colleges. He could be ' unattached,' and live
at home. He had saved a little money from
his allowance, and this store had been increased
by his earnings from night-work. It would be
a struggle, and he might require help ultimately, but he was not of those who are afraid
to risk something in order to carry out a large
purpose.

' And what profession do you mean to
adopt ?' Rye asked, when some days later he
had made her more fully acquainted with his
intentions.

' I think I shall be a clergyman.'

' You say a clergyman !' she remarked with
considerable astonishment. ' But you don't
mean a clergyman of the Church of England ?'

' Why not ? Or perhaps,' he added, ' I
should not ask the question, but tell you at
once that that is just what I do mean. You
are surprised, I see, and yet I should not have
taken you to be a bigot.'

' " Bigot " is a severe word,' Rye answered,
rather hotly, for she was a good deal aroused.

Arthur felt he had fallen into a mistake and
was quite willing to make amends.

' I withdraw the offensive word quite willingly. Still you object to me being a clergy-

man, and I suppose you would not complain if I were to become a Methodist minister, and I should like to know the difference?'

'If, in your opinion, there is no difference, you might please your friends, and be a Methodist minister.'

Arthur smiled, and inwardly commended the sharpness of his fair antagonist. But he did not look confused or give any indication of feeling himself beaten.

'I have not hid my ambitions from you, Rye,' he said, after a pause; 'and it seems hardly necessary for me to explain my reasons to you. You must know them. One of the principal objects I have in view in leaving the office and becoming a university student is to relieve me of the unhappiness I have always felt in meeting with people who would not recognize in me their equal. Caste feeling I know is stronger in Rockingham than in most other places, and I might live in some great commercial centre where the difference between Church and Dissent did not count for much. But the feeling has been growing upon me that I must, as far as I may be able, remove every barrier that prevents me from standing on equal ground with the most haughty of my neighbours. Dissent is one of those barriers, and it must, in my own life, be removed.'

Rye was staggered, not only by Arthur's words, but by the determined manner in which they were spoken. New feelings began to move within her towards Arthur, feelings that were wholly strange to her experience.

The young man did not receive his answer immediately, and the silence made him realize what before he had failed to do, that he was taking an important step in life, whose issues would stretch far away into the future.

'There *is* a difference between the Church and Dissent then, Arthur,' Rye at length remarked. 'As a churchman you will have access you think into society which, whilst you are a Dissenter, would not admit you. Is that the only difference? I think I can see others. In our little Methodist chapel I have heard so many good sermons, and during prayers have had so many good thoughts and desires awakened in me, that I should be afraid to leave it lest in

a new religious home I might find myself the subject of fewer good influences. Besides, I am a Nonconformist because I have been taught to believe that a State Church is wrong.'

'Are there no good Churchmen there?'

'Of course there are. Do not misrepresent me. The Church no doubt does good, but in so far as it is an *Established* Church it is wrong. And I do not think with my present convictions I could be anything but a Dissenter. I am not troubled about whether I am admitted into every circle of society in Rockingham or not. If I were, and could have that ambition gratified, I should likely not be content, but would want to move among the nobility, and after that I should probably be envious of royalty itself. And as I could not have all these ambitions met I should not improve my position much by moving up just one step. But I am glad to say these things do not trouble me.'

'You have never known the disadvantages of life in a cottage like me,' Arthur protested.

'Still, whether our home is a cottage or not we should all be conscientious, and have something different from small social ambitions to live for.'

Rye had not before spoken so strongly, and Arthur felt that some of her words were stinging. And yet for once he did not feel quite equal to the task of justifying himself.

'You think mine are small aims?' and as he spoke he turned pale.

But Rye was gaining light and knowledge as she talked, and was not at all inclined to modify her words.

'I am afraid I must say they are little aims, if all you are seeking for is the gratification of social ambition and pride. And they are worse than little if to realize them you are prepared to sever sacred ties, and forget obligations, and turn from all the friends of your life. I can hardly think you have considered what it all means, Arthur.'

'I have thought about it in many ways, but it is clear I had not comprehended the case fully,' he said rather angrily. 'That Dissent should have in Rye Harland such a stalwart champion is a point that had not occurred to my mind.'

'If my feelings on the subject are so strong, what will my father say?'

She addressed the question to herself rather than to her friend and did not expect him to reply. He perceived this and was glad to let the conversation drop. His own view was not altered in the slightest; and he was as certain his intention would be carried out in spite of all argument and all opposition as though it were already an accomplished fact. But it might be well, in view of the strong prejudices of Rye Harland and probably of her father, to keep his ultimate intentions to himself in the meantime. Accordingly he quickly determined in his own mind on a slight modification in his proposals in relation to his future; with which modification he hoped partially, at least, to satisfy his friends.

(To be continued.)

'I cannot get away from God.'

NOT many years since, a coachman was living in a gentleman's family near London. He had good wages, a kind master, and a comfortable place; but there was one thing which troubled and annoyed him; it was that his old mother lived in a village close by, and from her he had constant visits. You may wonder that this was such a trouble to him. But the reason was, that whenever she came she spoke to him about Christ and the salvation of his soul.

'Mother,' he at last said, 'I cannot stand this any longer. Unless you drop that subject altogether I shall give up my place and go out of your reach, where I shall hear no more of such cant.'

'My son,' said his mother, 'so long as I have a tongue I shall never cease to speak to you about the Lord, and to the Lord about you.'

The young coachman was as good as his word. He wrote to a friend in the Highlands of Scotland, and asked him to find him a place in that part of the world. He knew that his mother could not write and could not follow him; and though he was sorry to lose a good place, he said to himself—

'Anything for a quiet life.'

His friend soon got him a place in a gentleman's stable, and he did not hide from his mother that he was glad and thankful to get out of her way.

You may think it was a pity she thus drove him to a distance. Would it not have been wiser to say less, and thus not lose the opportunity of putting in a word in season? But she believed, in her simplicity, that she was to keep to the directions given her in the Word of God—that she was to be instant, not in season only, but out of season.

The coachman was ordered to drive out the carriage and pair the first day after he arrived in Scotland. His master did not get into the carriage with the rest of the party, but said he meant to go on the box instead of the footman.

'He wishes to see how I drive,' thought the coachman, who was quite prepared to give satisfaction. Scarcely had they driven from the door when the master spoke to the coachman for the first time. He said:—

'Tell me if you are saved?'

Had the Lord come to the coachman direct from heaven, it could scarcely have struck him with greater consternation. He simply felt terrified.

'God has followed me to Scotland,' he said to himself. 'I could get away from my mother, but I cannot get away from God!'

And at that moment he knew what Adam must have felt when he went to hide himself from the presence of God behind the trees of the garden. He could make no answer to his master, and scarcely could he drive the horses, for he trembled from head to foot.

His master went on to speak of Christ, and again he heard the old, old story so often told him by his mother. But this time it sounded new. It had become a real thing to him. It did not seem then to be glad tidings of great joy, but a message of terror and condemnation. He felt it was Christ, the Son of God, whom he had rejected and despised. He felt for the first time that he was a lost sinner.

By the time the drive was over, he was so ill from the terrible fear that had come upon him that he could do nothing else.

For some days he could not leave his bed; but they were blessed days to him. His master came to speak to him, to read the Word of God, and to pray; and soon the love and grace of the Saviour he had so persistently rejected became a reality to him, as the terror of the Lord had been at first.

He saw there was mercy for the scoffer and despiser, and he saw that the blood of Christ is the answer before God even for such sin as his had been; and he now felt in his soul the sweetness of those blessed words, 'We love Him because He first loved us!'

He saw that Christ had borne his punishment, and that he who had tried to harden his heart against God and against his own mother, was now without spot or stain in the sight of God who so loved him as to give for him His only Son. The first letter he wrote to his mother contained the joyful idings:—

'God has followed me to Scotland, and has saved my soul!'

'Whither shall I go from Thy Spirit? or whither shall I flee from Thy presence? If I ascend up to heaven, Thou art there; if I make my bed in hell, behold Thou art there. If I take the wings of the morning, and dwell in the uttermost parts of the sea, even there shall Thy hand lead me and Thy right hand hold me.'

—*The Watchword.*

The Golden Rule.

IN a cathedral, old and grey,
    The pride of an ancient city, six
      bishops met,
    And of the lesser clergy a vast
number, in solemn conference,
And discussed full learnedly the meaning of
    the Christian's golden rule—
'Whatsoever ye desire that men should do
    to you,
So do ye unto them;' and opinions differed,

And words waxed hot, and in the search for
    truth
Love was forgotten, and many minds were
    pained.

Outside, upon the granite steps,
Two ragged urchins sat, and as the shades
    of night came on
They nestled close against the carved pillars
    of the door,
And thus were partly sheltered from the
    wind and snow;

'Oh, Billy,' said the younger lad, 'I am so
    very cold,
And my head aches so,' and a shiver passed
    through his fragile frame;
'Here, Jimmy, I'll just fix ye,' said the
    older one,
And off he pulled his tattered coat, leaving
    his own arms bare,
And wrapped it round the child, saying,
'You ain't been well to-day, you need it
    more than me.'

The darkness deepened,
And the north wind drove the falling snow
Into a heap against the lads, till they were
    covered o'er
With a garment, beautiful, but cold as this
    world's charity.
The younger lad slept on till early morn;
    the elder,
Well, he sat and froze to death, his lean bare
    arms
Around his brother's neck, for whom he
    gave his life.

'Tis not in costly books,
Or conjugations of Greek verbs, that men
    will find
The deeper meaning of that glorious rule,
But they may read it in the frozen smile
    of that dead boy,
The city thought was not worth caring for,
A humble hero bravely facing death,
As he came with icy fingers on the north
    wind's blast,
A very Christ, who in the saving of another
Could not save himself.   S. H.

The Boyhood of Great Men.

Dr. CHALMERS.

EW cities in Great Britain are so rich in historic memories as Edinburgh. A volume could be written about the palace of Holyrood alone, and if only the stones of old Edinburgh could cry out, what a tale they could unfold of grim tragedy and heroic daring displayed in the streets of the ancient capital of Scotland! So recently as 1843 it was the scene of an immortal deed. The ministers of the Established Kirk had met in solemn assembly in St. Andrew's Church. Lord Bute, as the representative of the Queen, sat in the chair. For years there had been growing friction between the Church and the State. Many ministers resented the intrusion of the Civil Power in the management of the spiritual concerns of the Church. The question had long been debated on the platform and in the Press. Appeals had been made to the Queen and to Parliament, but in vain. At last the crisis had come, and the only course open to those who had protested was to sacrifice all that was involved in the Establishment, and withdraw from a Church which they felt they could no longer serve without disloyalty to truth and God. Accordingly they went forth, Dr. Welsh, their Moderator, leading the way. Behind him came the great thinkers and preachers, whose names were household words in the pious homes of Scotland, and they were followed by others who, if less great, were not less loyal to what they felt and knew. Out of the hall they trooped, numbering 470 strong, and leaving to Lord Bute a 'beggarly array

of empty seats. The crowd outside made way for that holy pilgrim band. Heads were uncovered as some venerable minister appeared. Blessings were muttered as they passed. Some cheered, others wept, whilst all felt as Judge Jeffrey did. No one had opposed the outgoing ministers more than he. He had spoken and written against them. He had poured scorn on their scruples, and had even predicted that when the crisis came they would yield. He was somewhat surprised when a friend burst into his presence that morning with the news that they were out. 'Who are out?' said Jeffrey. 'The Evangelicals,' was the reply. 'There they go, down High Street! Don't you hear the cheers of the crowd?' At once the Judge sprang to his feet, and swinging his hat in the air, gave a cheer that vied for strength with the loudest. 'Three cheers for old Scotland! Nowhere out of it could so grand a thing have happened.' The deed deserved that cheer, for it meant to those men the loss of church and income; it meant what was still harder to bear—the removal from the familiar home, bound to them by memories of the living and the dead. Turned out of their churches, many of them worshipped with their flocks, like the Covenanters before them, on the green hillside, or in the lonely glens, or on the seashore when the sobbing tide was low. But they had counted the cost, and went forth trusting in the promises of God, and in His name they laid, that self-same day, the foundation of a free and nobler Church.

The hero of that fight, and the man to whom fell by natural right the presidency of the disestablished assembly, was Thomas Chalmers. His days were then drawing near to the 'sere and yellow leaf,' for he was born on 17th of March, 1780. His birthplace was Anstruther, a small but busy seaport on the south coast of Fife. In the time when Scotland had a monarch of her own, her traders had looked with kindlier eyes on distant France than on their English neighbours across the Cheviots. Anstruther saw then its palmiest days, but its glory had not departed when Thomas Chalmers came to play upon its shore, and gaze upon its sea. His father was a prosperous shipowner and general merchant, with a purse sufficiently well lined to make fitting provision for the nine sons and five daughters that in course of time gathered round his table. It was well for them that their parents had such wealth, but better still that they were rich in the graces of God's Spirit. Thomas came of a good stock. The blood of a holy ancestry flowed in his veins. The type of religion in that home was perhaps somewhat severe, but the reverent observance of the day of rest, the daily reading of the Word of God, and his father's prayers at the family hearth, did much to shape the religious life of this great and gifted man.

From the shelter of that home he early went forth to seek the boon of knowledge. He was only three years of age when he entered the public school of Anstruther. It was not the thirst for knowledge that impelled him, but rather a desire to escape the tyranny of his nurse. His father was too much engrossed in business and his mother too cumbered with the cares of her enlarging household to pay much heed to its separate units. So his nurse treated the boy with a cruelty that burnt itself into his childish memory, and when the wrong was done, she, by false assurances of love, prevented him from seeking redress. We can hardly wonder if at that early age he showed but little taste for learning, though it was evident even then that he was a boy with brains. A story is told about him to the effect that, after prayers one morning, when the story of the revolt and defeat of David's favourite son had been read, the three year-old boy was found in the nursery, pacing excitedly up and down, and saying over and over again, ' O my son Absalom ! O Absalom my son, my son ! ' It was no ordinary child whose imagination could be touched in that way so early. At school no one could surpass him, when he had a mind to learn, but alas ! the mind was often lacking. From sheer laziness his lessons were frequently only half learnt or not learnt at all. Many were the times when the master consigned him to the coal-hole that he might learn there by constraint what he had neglected to do of his own free-will. Few scholars saw its black interior more frequently than he, but, to his credit be

it said, few more speedily purchased their release. Still we can judge how inapt he was as a student by the fact that at twelve years of age his spelling and composition were most defective. The blame must partly be laid at the door of his teachers. The head-master was nearly blind, and his temper had not grown sweeter with increasing years. He used to creep, cane in hand, behind a knot of boys, and listening till he heard something that merited chastisement, would suddenly dart the rod in the direction of the sound. But the boys grew too quick for him, and often he thrashed nothing but an unoffending desk. Thus whilst the one master was too severe, the other erred on the side of leniency, and both, as teachers, were sadly inefficient. And so young Chalmers cut but a sorry figure over his book and slate, but when these were dashed aside, and the merry throng rushed into the playground, he was ever to the fore. He was the soul of every game, the life of many a roguish prank ; for, wherever mischief was brewing, he was the arch-conspirator. Still his roguery was always 'innocent, and every bully in the school feared Chalmers's fist, and every oppressed youngster knew he had a friend in him. If ever, by mischance, the fun took a dangerous turn, and angry passions were roused, he was. ever prompt to cease the offence, and if that was not enough he fled before the rising storm. On one occasion he only just escaped a volley of mussel-shells, flung at him by his incensed companions, by flying into an old woman's cottage and seeking shelter at her fireside. ' I'm no for powder and ball,' said he—a saying which the old dame remembered, and that, as others thought, was sadly contradicted by the brave battles that he fought in the stormier days of his after life.

His education was not confined to what he learnt at school. He read at home, the book that apparently kindled his childish fancy being the ' Pilgrim's Progress.' He revelled in its pictures, whilst the stories of the Bible had for the boy a growing charm. He early decided that he would be a minister, that calling being probably suggested to his mind

*

by the frequent visits of divines to his father's home. His first sermon was preached to an audience of one—a schoolfellow, who sat listening with mock gravity whilst the future pulpit orator of Scotland held forth on the text, 'Let brotherly love continue.' He was still at the school in Anstruther when this took place. He remained there till 1791, when he became a member of the University of St. Andrews. The boy was almost too young to be subjected to the rough discipline of university life and thought, and perhaps it was well that Chalmers took his indolence with him, and for the first two years did little else but play. He entered with zest into such games as golf, football, and handball, and at St. Andrews he carried off the palm, as he had done before at Anstruther. But the third year of his college course witnessed a change. He commenced the study of mathematics, and forthwith his intellect sprang into life. For the first time he found a subject that enthralled him. His tutor was beyond all praise. With youthful ardour Chalmers gave himself up to his new-found love, and so intense was his enthusiasm for it, that even after he had in 1795 enrolled himself as a student of divinity, it was with difficulty that he weaned himself from his geometry to pay heed to disquisitions on predestination and free-will. Moreover, he was prejudiced against one of the lecturers, owing to a conviction which he had that this teacher enforced one doctrine in the class-room, but in his heart believed another. When reference was made in the presence of Chalmers to an able lecture by this man on some point in the Calvinistic creed, he surprised his companion by saying, 'I was not paying attention to it.' 'But why,' asked his friend, 'did you not attend to a lecture so able?' 'Because,' answered Chalmers, 'I question the sincerity of the lecturer.'

If that story gives us a glimpse of the man's soul in the making, we have also hints now and then of the future orator and preacher. By patient attention to composition, he soon remedied the defects of his training at Anstruther, and it was not until he had attained to correctness and conciseness of ex-

pression, that he gave reins to his splendid fancy. His voice was often heard in the college debating club, where, week by week, the knotty problems of theology were made the subject of searching discussion. With his alert mind and ready tongue he was ever to the front, either acting as the champion of debate himself, or delivering a speech in defence of one of the leading combatants. One event in his university career won him fame beyond the circle of the college walls. It was the custom for the students to meet together in the public hall for prayers both morning and evening. The devotions were conducted by the divinity students, and upon Chalmers in his turn fell the discharge of that duty. His first public prayer was simply an expansion of the Lord's Prayer, but it was so original and eloquent that it evoked universal admiration. His fame quickly spread. When Chalmers had to pray the hall, which was usually deserted by the public, was filled by a flocking crowd. Perhaps the most noticeable feature in his prayers was his description of the horrors of war, frequent mention being made of the conflict that we were then waging with France; but, apart from this, there was about his petitions a fiery, glowing eloquence, that must have made many of his hearers prophesy that the lad of sixteen who could pray so marvellously had a brilliant future before him.

And such a future in truth awaited him, but the summit was not to be scaled at one bound. And when he left St. Andrews in 1798, he sank for a while into the quiet drudgery of a private tutorship. A horse stood waiting at his father's door one day. Thomas Chalmers came outside, and, having taken leave of all the members of the home, he mounted, but did it so awkwardly, that, when he got astride the horse's back, he found himself facing its tail instead of its head. It was the work of a moment to put himself right; but it was not so easy to check his own mirth, or the ringing peals of laughter that pursued him, as his horse's hoofs bore him away from the Anstruther of his boyhood to the home where Thomas Chalmers was to begin the toil and conflict of the man.

A. Lewis Humphries, B.A.

Sketches of the British Isles.

SHETLANDS.

FACETIOUS writer has forcefully stated that many well-informed people in their ignorance of the origin, beauties, and history of the Northern Isles regard them as being 'The refuse of Creation—some of the rubbish for which no use could be found, and which was therefore tossed into the great lumber-room of the ocean, to be out of the way. A collection of rocks either uninhabitable, or inhabited by a race of men almost as untamed as the seals which play upon their shores. And with intellects very little developed.' The early settlers, however, of the Shetlands and Orkneys, being of Norse extraction, and living within a few hours' sail of the Baltic and the Elbe, the 'highway' of the European nations —were the pioneers of civilization and commercial activity in these remote northern isles.

The Shetlands are composed of about ninety islets, only twenty-five of which are sufficiently large enough to be inhabited, and the rest, by way of distinction, are called holms. Mainland is the largest and most important of the isles. And at least three-fourths of the surface area of the whole group belongs to it. On the south they are separated from the Orkneys by a channel fifty miles wide ; and they lie two hundred and ten miles west from Bergen, on the sea-board of Continental Europe. The whole area of the Shetlands is eight hundred and eighty square miles ; and they are united with the neighbouring isles of the Orkneys in constituting a Scotch county. Foula is the most northern of the group, and is rendered famous by the supposition of its having been the *Ultima Thule* of the ancient world. The coasts present a wild and rugged grandeur ; they are broken into numerous cliffs of fantastic pattern, some of them attaining the bewildering height of twelve hundred feet above the level of the sea. One characteristic geological feature of these northern coasts is the large number of deep, narrow caverns and expansive archways that have been hollowed by the ceaseless action of the restless waves. In some instances the sea front is supported with huge buttresses showing the intermediate strata. The sea-scouring pirates, who made the caverns their hiding-places, with their love of legend and superstition, gave the more striking coast features their fanciful names— such as ' The Giant's Leg,' from their supposed resemblances. A combination of natural agencies, such as rains, snows, frosts, and ice, on the upper surface—the springs and rills of waters within the rocks—together with the powerful waves from the Atlantic, have been the forces which have wasted the shores, and produced their grotesque appearance, as shown in the accompanying engravings. Specialists maintain that dismemberment begins at the top of the cliff by the influence of rain and frost, and the rent going down to the sea-level, is breached by the terrific force of the breakers, and the whole mass will fall into the foaming surge below, leaving chasms, pillars, and buttresses.

The general surface of the Shetlands is both rugged and unproductive. The highest summit of the interior mountain range is Rooness Hill, in the north of Mainland ; its highest peaks reaching an altitude of nearly fifteen hundred feet. There is a wild fascination attached to the western localities with their long stretches of treeless moorland, intersected with grey rocks, stagnant marshes, and weedy pools. The climate is exceedingly wet and tempestuous. For five or six months of the year, the sea swells and rages with such fury that the mariner has difficulty in reaching the harbours. The population is slightly over thirty thousand, who speak the English language ; but their Norwegian origin is manifested in their accent, words, and customs. The Shetlanders are below the average height, but are hardy and capable of great physical endurance. They are sanguine in temperament, and exceedingly hospitable. For ecclesiastical and other purposes the Shetlands

The Giant's Leg, Bressay.

are divided into twelve parishes. The people are natural lovers of education, and nearly all the parents, along with their children, are acquainted with the principles of the three R's —reading, writing, and arithmetic. The inhabitants are industrious, and make coarse cloth and linen for their own personal use. They also manufacture, for exportation, large

THE HOLM OF NORS.

quantities of knitted stockings and shawls, from Shetland wool. Some of the shawls are so fine in texture that they can be drawn through a wedding-ring; and they are almost as valuable as silk goods of the same size and pattern. The horses, cattle, and sheep belong to distinct varieties, that are peculiar to Shetland; and are specially characterised for their diminutive appearance and general hardihood. The horses or ponies of Shetland are full of animal spirit, and bear fatigue proportionately easier than larger animals. The cattle are shapely, and with the exception of the western Highland breed, are not surpassed by the herds of Great Britain. The cow yields excellent milk ; and the beef of the ox is of a superior class. The sheep is prized for its excellent wool. The birds of prey are numerous, and include eagles, hawks, and ravens. Large flocks of swans visit the lakes every year. Wild geese, ducks, and sea-fowl find a nestling-place upon the cliffs. Their shrill cries, blended with the discordant notes of the wind and the waves, produce a strange music that captivates the sentimental student of nature.

The Isle of Bressay is situated on the eastern coast of Shetland, and immediately opposite to Lerwick. Its greatest length is about six miles, and the width varies from one to three miles. The coastline is rocky and indented with several fantastic caverns. On the south are three noted headlands : the Ord being five hundred feet high, and inhabited by eagles ; the others, Bard and Hammer, are respectively about two hundred feet high. The interior of the island is hilly, but affords land suitable for cultivation, especially on the gentle slopes rising from the sea. There are a number of small lakes in the island which furnish excellent pastime for the disciples of Izaak Walton and the lovers of the line. The island is conspicuous for the absence of trees. Judging from the number of large tree-trunks of excellent preservation, found embedded in the peat moss, the island at a distant date must have been more favourable for the growth of trees than it is at the present. The remains of Pictish buildings are to be found in the island, and there are tumuli of the dead, in which human bones have been unearthed. There are several perpendicular, or ' standing-stones,' as they are called by the Shetlanders, one of which, on account of its conspicuousness, forms a landmark for the sailors upon steering their vessels into Bressay Sound. At the census of 1881, the population of Bressay was only eight hundred and forty-seven, who were chiefly employed in the cod and herring fisheries. To the ling fishing, or as it is locally termed 'far-fishing,' the port of Bressay sends into the teens of keel-boats, from eighteen to twenty feet long. Large quantities of kelp are manufactured in the island, as well as herring-nets, and Shetland hosiery. The fishermen of Bressay, in common with others of the same craft resident in Shetland, were formerly strong believers in legends concerning mermaids, krakens, sea-snakes, and other supposed fanciful creatures who lived in the waters of the North Seas. These extraordinary stories evidently had their origin, as Sir Walter Scott says, from ' the imperfect glance obtained of occasional objects, encouraging the timid or the fanciful to give way to imagination, and frequently to shape out a distinct story from some object half seen and imperfectly examined.' Years ago, some fishermen saw an extraordinary object in the Bay of Scalloway. Their fertile imagination and superstitious belief declared it to be a kraken. The frightened fishermen were afraid of approaching it, lest they should be wrecked by the suction of the sea monster. This supposed denizen of the sea turned out to be the hull of a ship that had been wrecked, and which had been overturned by the waves of the sea. A fisherman once declared that he had seen a huge sea-serpent a hundred feet long, which in all probability was a long Norway log.

Bressay Sound is situated between the shores of Bressay and Mainland. It is a well-known safe harbour of extraordinary dimensions ; its average breadth is over a mile, and at high water has a depth of fifteen fathoms. It has the reputation of being one of the finest natural harbours in the world. On the west centre is Lerwick with its tall lighthouse. Over two centuries back the sound presented a very animated appearance from the large number of foreign vessels that found shelter therein during the storms of the fishing season. It is still a much frequented resort, by numbers of English and Dutch ' busses,' and a rendezvous for outward bound whaling ships going to the fisheries of the Davis Straits, and the waters of Greenland. The southern entrance to the harbour is by far the safest.

The northern approach is narrow, and the current rapid. At low water may be seen an ill-fated sunken rock, called the *Unicorn*, because a war vessel of that name, sent in pursuit of the Earl of Bothwell, was unfortunately wrecked upon it.

On the eastern side of Bressay, and separated therefrom by a dangerous and narrow sound, is a rockwork islet called Nors, rising abruptly above the waters of the sea. Its perpendicular and rugged cliffs gain a height of nearly six hundred feet. The top is as flat as table-land, and has a circuit of about six miles in extent. On the south-east of Nors is a detached mass of rock or uninhabited holm, separated from Nors by a deep fissure sixty-five feet wide. The height of the Holm of Nors is one hundred and sixty feet. The sides are precipitous and rugged, and the surface is covered with grass, and in days gone by was used as a sheepwalk. The method of communication consisted of a cradle or chair, sufficiently large enough to hold a man and a sheep, that was attached to strong ropes, and thus swung across the yawning gulf, and the eddying waters of the fissure.

> ' Land of the whirlpool,—torrent,—foam,
>   Where oceans meet in maddening shock;
> The beetling cliff, the shelving holm,
>   The dark insidious rock.
> Land of the bleak—the treeless moor—
> The sterile mountain, sered and riven,—
> The shapeless cairn, the ruined tower,
>   Scathed by the bolts of heaven—
> The yawning gulf, the treacherous sand,
> I love thee still, my native land.
>
> Land of the dark—the Runic rhyme—
> The mystic ring, the cavern hoar—
> The Scandinavian seer sublime
>   In legendary lore.
> Land of a thousand sea-kings' graves—
> Those tameless spirits of the past,
> Fierce as their subject Arctic waves,
>   Or hyperborean blast.
> Though polar billows round thee foam,
> I love thee!—thou wert once my home.'
>
> ALBERT A. BIRCHENOUGH.

Ah! five-and-twenty years ago, had I but
  planted seeds of trees,
How now I should enjoy their shade, and
  see their fruit swing in the breeze.

—*Anon.*

Mary at Christ's Feet.

'And she (Martha) had a sister called Mary, which also sat at the feet of Jesus, and heard His word' (Luke x. 39).

THE Bethany family are mentioned by both Luke and John, whose narratives of different events connected therewith give us the same view of the respective characters and dispositions of the two sisters Martha and Mary. In the former we have an instance of active piety, in the latter of meditative devotion. Both women were excellent in their way, but the distinctive qualities of each require to be blended in one person to make a complete Christian.

Bethany was the place of their residence—a retired village, just outside Jerusalem, on the farther slope of Mount Olivet. To it Jesus and His disciples oft resorted, finding there quiet surroundings and hospitable entertainment, warm friendship and domestic enjoyment, in the home of Lazarus and his two sisters; homeless Himself, the Saviour hallowed and enjoyed the homes of His friends. ' Now Jesus loved Martha, and her sister, and Lazarus.' Luke gives us the picture of Mary sitting at the feet of Jesus—the usual posture of Jewish scholars in receiving instruction. Hence the expression came to signify discipleship, as when Saul says he was 'brought up at the feet of Gamaliel.' Christ was the Great Teacher sent from God, better than a thousand Gamaliels, however wise and learned. The attitude of Mary betokened her humility and eagerness to learn, as well as implying Christ's gracious condescension and willingness to teach. How many of the great preachers of our day would be willing to preach to one hearer, as Christ did at Bethany and at the well of Samaria, in the former instance in a house, in the latter in the open air, and in both to a woman? Both Jewish scribe and heathen philosopher would have scorned the idea of enlisting female disciples, but ' in Christ Jesus there is neither male nor female.' Men, women, and children are all invited to Christ, though it is perhaps true that women oftener than men, and the young rather than the aged, become His disciples and friends. Curiosity would like to know the unrecorded things spoken by Christ on public and private occasions, but piety rejoices to possess those which are actually recorded. He spake the word of God, not merely repeating what the prophets had previously uttered, but giving fuller revelations of the Father's character and of the purposes of redeeming love. 'The Spirit of the Lord God is upon Me, because He hath anointed Me to preach the gospel to the poor.' And as we read His conversations and discourses, we too may in spirit place ourselves at His feet, and listen to His voice. The devout soul feels—

> 'Oh that I could for ever sit
> With Mary at the Master's feet!'

Christ's discourse to Mary and her rapt attention were rudely disturbed by Martha's abrupt complaint: 'Lord, dost Thou not care that my sister hath left me to serve alone? Bid her therefore that she help me.' The burden of her self-imposed task was greater than she could bear, and it is easy, when oppressed with labour and anxiety, to become irritable and complaining. Brothers and sisters in the church and in the family are often tempted to complain of one another—the reason why Paul exhorts us to 'do all things without murmurings and without disputings.' If we do complain, it should be with just cause and in a Christian spirit. As for those who do not understand our Christianity, it is no wonder if they complain of our being 'righteous overmuch,' over-scrupulous, over-serious, or over-joyful. When David fasted his servants found fault with him, and when he danced before the ark it displeased Michal. But surely Christians have so much in common that they can afford to differ in a few things, including the kind and manner of service rendered to the common Master, who defends His one hearer from her sister's ill-natured fault-finding. Martha wished to entertain her honoured Guest in a worthy manner, as she thought, but there was too much elaboration about it to command His approval. Some-

thing simpler would suffice for Him. Mary, on the other hand, was longing for salvation, and listening to the words of His mouth. 'With Martha the pleasure of giving Him much is proeminent; Mary feels the necessity of receiving much. With Martha productivity, with Mary receptivity, stands in the foreground. Martha is the Peter, Mary the John, among the female disciples of Christ. Both have, therefore, their peculiar calling and special gift.' The perils and drawbacks of their respective dispositions are apparent. Martha's temper may degenerate into busy, bustling activity, without depth or reality of religious feeling; Mary's may become slothful case and passive quietism. 'Diligent in business, fervent in spirit, serving the Lord,' is the Divine precept for regulating our spirit and conduct; also the Saviour's warning: 'Seek ye first the kingdom of God, and His righteousness.'

But what is the meaning of the 'one thing needful' set in opposition to the 'many things' by which Martha was distracted. Adam Clarke and others contend that the meaning was that one dish or course for the meal was sufficient. This is reckoned by others a frigid or frivolous interpretation. They say that the contrast to Martha's 'many things' is Mary's 'good part,' and that good part the right reception of Christ. This is really the one thing needful for the life that now is, and for that which is to come. It is, in substance, the 'one thing desired of the Lord' by the Psalmist, 'that he might dwell in the house of the Lord for ever,' and the 'one thing done' by Paul when he 'pressed toward the mark for the prize of the high calling of God.' Rather, it is not so much the good in opposition to the bad, as the better in preference to the thing of lower excellence—' the more excellent way.'

Over-anxiety is contrary to perfect trust in God, and resignation to His will; it is injurious to ourselves both in soul and body, and to others; and it oft defeats its own end. Instead of care and cumber it is better to cultivate a calm and restful spirit. A combination of the meditative and active—of Mary's loving

MARY SITTING AT THE FEET OF CHRIST.

heart and Martha's busy hands—is the ideal of a perfect Christian.

There is a reason for choosing the good part; it shall not be taken away. Men cannot, and God will not take away that which 'maketh rich.' There are forms of service which will be superseded by higher and nobler. Martha soon lost the opportunity of ministering to the Lord by making Him a feast, but Mary 'kept His sayings and pondered them in her heart.' The Church is now occupied with kinds of activity which will not be needed by and by, but she will never cease to contemplate and to celebrate the character and the glories of her Lord. Till we stand before His throne in glory we must sit at His feet, and learn of Him, that we may find rest, and be fitted for work.

Christian thinkers and workers may learn by the difference, in form of service, as well as of temperament, between these two sisters, not only to tolerate but to esteem and assist each other. How often are we ready to say of others, already doing the work of God in their own way, 'Lord, bid them that they help *me*.' But why should we disparage another person's line of things, or wish to interfere with other servants of the great Master ? 'A church full of Maries,' says one, ' would perhaps be as great an evil as a church full of Marthas ; both are needed, each to be the complement of the other.'   H.

Wholesome Fiction.

No. III.

CHARLES DICKENS.

THE name of Charles Dickens is familiar to us all as a household word. Few authors, indeed, have achieved such a wide popularity in our own and other lands. He is one of the greatest writers of wholesome fiction which the century has produced, and without doubt is destined to have an enduring fame. His father was a clerk in the Navy Pay Office, Portsmouth, and was a good-natured, thriftless

sort of man. Charles, in his early boyhood, knew something of the pinch of adversity, and it is remarkable how keen were his sympathies with the poor all throughout his career as a writer. Family circumstances improving, he was placed in an attorney's office and practised as a reporter in the Law Courts ; afterwards making his way into the House of Commons where he distinguished himself as the best out of eighty or ninety reporters. Here, in his unemployed forenoons, he took up his time in studying and depicting the world of London he knew—its oddities, humours, streets, and houses, and thus laid the foundation of his future life-work. His ' Sketches by Boz ' and the ' Pickwick Papers ' introduced him rapidly to fame, and led him to trust henceforth to literature as a profession. The pictures he drew of middle and low life in London were irresistible, and quite a novelty in literature at the time. Caricatures they doubtless were, but they evinced such a broad, kindly humour, comicality of incident, variety of detail, felicity of phrase, reproducing the speech of the common people, and intimate acquaintance with human nature, as to place their author at once at the head of all his contemporaries.

'So much cant,' as one of his critics remarks, ' has been in fashion about the wisdom of our ancestors, the glorious constitution, the wise balance of King, Lords and Commons, and other such topics, which are embalmed in the " Noodle's Oration," that a large class of people were ready to hail with intense satisfaction the advent of a writer who naturally and without an effort bantered everything in the world, from elections and law courts, down to cockney sportsmen, the boots at an inn, cooks, and chambermaids.'

Dickens was a most prolific writer. We can only refer to a few of his more notable works. He had made his readers merry over ' Pickwick ;' he now thrills them with ' Oliver Twist.' This is a story with a purpose. It is a picture of ' dregs of life,' hitherto, as he believed, ' never exhibited by any novelist in their loathsome reality.' ' The submerged tenth,' as the phrase now goes, never had a more faithful or a more terrible delineation.

Poor Oliver, an orphan, brought up by the parish, is thrown among the most revolting and vicious scenes ; yet strangely, as we think, he does not sink to the same moral level. The atrocious ruffian Sykes, his murder of poor Nancy, whose devotion and heroism almost make us forget her shame, giving proof at the same time of the writers' ' unfailing power of sympathy, which was the mainspring of both his most affecting and his most humorous touches,' the irresistible and not quite inhuman Artful Dodger, Mr. Fang, the police-magistrate Bumble and Bumbledom, in which the working of the New Poor Law is humorously but keenly satirized, make up a picture full of intense and varied colour, lively, sad, pathetic, terrible.

His next work, ' Nicholas Nickleby,' was no less remarkable in its line. It served a public benefit in exposing the imposture, cupidity, and brutality connected with certain public schools. It held up to public odium the pedagogue Squeers and his prison-like school of Dotheboy's Hall. The delineations were true to fact. The originals were not far to seek, and richly merited every stroke of satirical invective. But the comic genius of Dickens is also here in full play. It is seen in the Squeers' family with their utter grotesqueness, in Smike their humblest victim, in the invertebrate chatter of Mrs. Nickleby, and in Mr. Vincent Crummles and his theatrical company, including the Phenomenon, 'establishing a jest, but a kindly one, for all times.'

The ' Old Curiosity Shop,' another of his masterly productions, abounds in grotesque and ludicrous scenes, but its pathos is its most prominent and pervading element. As it has been well pointed out, ' the effects of gambling are depicted with great force. There is something very striking in the conception of the helpless old gamester, tottering upon the verge of the grave, and at that period when most of our other passions are as much worn out as the frame which sustains them, still maddened with that terrible infatuation which seems to shoot up stronger and stronger as every other desire and energy dies away. Little Nell, the grandchild, is a beautiful creation of pure-mindedness and innocence,

yet with those habits of pensive reflection, and that firmness and energy of mind which misfortune will often graft on the otherwise buoyant and unthinking spirit of childhood; and the contrast between her and her grandfather, now dwindled in every respect but one into a second childhood, and comforted, directed, and sustained by her unshrinking firmness and love, is very finely managed.' We follow little Nell to the close, and amid the shadows that gather round the last hours, we have got the very poetry of pathos. We conclude with the author, that ' when Death strikes down the innocent and young, for every fragile form from which he lets the panting spirit free a hundred virtues arise, in shapes of mercy, charity, and love, to walk the world and bless it. Of every tear that sorrowing mortals shed on such green graves some good is borne, some gentler nature comes. In the destroyer's steps there spring up bright creations that defy his power, and his dark path becomes a way of light to heaven.' In proof of Dickens' versatility, how grotesque and how darkly hideous are some of the characters and scenes that appear in the body of the story. The virago Sally Brass, ' whose accomplishments were all of a masculine and strictly legal kind ; ' the demon-dwarf Quilp, whose weird and miserable end seems so fitting to his character ; the wretch whose whole life had been spent in watching, day and night, a furnace, till he thought it to be a living being, and its roaring the voice of the only friend he had ever known ; the despair, the recklessness, the destruction of the crowded poor in a large town—pass before us with startling vivacity, and with all their wildness are full of an instructive suggestiveness.

Dickens visited America, and in ' Martin Chuzzlewit,' which has been described as one of the masterpieces of Dickens' maturity as a writer, many of his American reminiscences are reproduced. The satire is, perhaps, too severe, and occasioned some resentment, but it was not altogether beside the mark. Throughout the story the evil and the folly of selfishness, by both a serious and comic handling, is powerfully rebuked. It is rebuked by Dickens' ridicule of young Chuzzlewit, whose sentiment, ' Do other men, for they will do you,' is applauded by the father, the head of the firm. It is also rebuked by a contrast of unselfishness—each of a different type—in Mark Tapley and Tom Pinch ; while the quackery and hypocrisy of Pecksniff, ' who never ceases to be laughable, and yet never ceases to be loathsome,' afford ample scope for the author's humour and quiet invective. Grotesqueness, too, reaches a high mark in numerous characters, notably so in the immortal Mrs. Gamp, the nurse, whose oddities of tongue are so side-splitting—' the glorified type of all the utterances heard to this day from charwomen, laundresses, and single gentlemen's housekeepers.' The ridiculous, but faithful portraiture, has, it is believed, done much to rid our hospital wards and sickrooms of Mrs. Gamp's successors.

Our limited space forbids us enlarging. We may just remark that in a subsequent novel, ' Dombey & Son,' Dickens deals as definitely as in Chuzzlewit with one of the chief vices of human nature, and seeks ' to show what pride cannot achieve, what it cannot conquer, what it cannot withstand.' Little Paul is a most wonderful creation—the deep pathos, the fine poetic haze that gathers round his death reveal the author at his best. After writing the chapter which relates the death of little Paul, Dickens, during the greater part of the night, wandered restlessly with a heavy heart about the Paris streets. His creations were thus warm and vital with his heart's blood.

We might also refer you to the series of his Christmas books, of which, perhaps, ' The Cricket on the Hearth ' is the most charming. His other works are numerous, and all of them, down to the last, ' The Mystery of Edwin Drood,' only half finished at his death, and which promised to be one of his best, reveal his characteristic high qualities. Do not, however, fail to read his ' David Copperfield.' In it he has introduced very much of his own life and experience, and we agree in the general view that it is, perhaps, the most perfect, natural, and agreeable of his novels. In Mr. Micawber, always expecting 'some-thing to turn up,' one of the most genial, humorous, and most real of all Dickens' portraitures, the author's own father is reproduced. The ways of seamen and fishermen are truthfully presented. Mrs. Micawber is a comical and kindly figure. Tommy Traddles and his happy-go-lucky youthful married state is to the life itself, and suggests the writer's memories of early days, as also do the little love idyll of Davy and Dora. The story of Little Emily and her kinsfolk reveals great art ; and the hypocrisy of the shuffling, slimy sycophant, Uriah Heep, gives occasion for what Dickens always displayed fierce strength in, his satire of sham and deceit. ' Of all my books,' he declares, ' I like this the best. . . . Like many found parents, I have in my heart of hearts a favourite child, and his name is David Copperfield.'

It will be seen that though Dickens in some respects resembled Scott, yet in others he differed from him. He was not, like Scott, ·a great historical romance writer, creating heroes of the lofty, magnanimous type charged with great causes, nor did he affect the sublime. His range of human character and life is perhaps more limited than that of Scott, and his heroines do not always excel after the same fashion. He is at home rather in scenes of private, domestic, and everyday life, as indeed no other writer before him had been. The humbler walks of life attracted his sympathy in an especial degree. Here he wields an enchanter's wand, and must always have the multitude for his audience. His distinguishing quality is his humour, or, as it has been put, his sensibility, ' that quality of which humour, in the more limited sense of the word, and pathos are twin products.' He is never stilted or affected. Everything is, as it were, absorbed into his nature by the quick sensibility and wide humanity with which he was endowed. He is comic and grotesque, tender and pathetic without strain or effort, and with an almost boundless variety of expression. His humour is not caustic and cynical, but kindly and broad ; perhaps less refined than on some occasions we could wish it to be, but never unhealthy and unreal. His large imaginative power and keen dramatic instinct give a reality to his descriptions quite unsurpassed. It has been said that his foible was his tendency to exaggerate, but this is the result of his vigour, and without it he could not have been creative as he was. We readily allow this licence to the novelist's brush, for by means of it, within certain understood limits, his characters are lifted out of the region of the insipid and commonplace. To Dickens nothing was opaque or wore a neutral tint. No man or woman was featureless; his creations are not mere stucco personages—lay figures lacking vitality or individuality—but genuine specimens of flesh and blood. But the word 'sensibility' does not convey all we mean as to the secret of Dickens' power. The sympathy of a generous human heart informs and inspires everything. His love of hearth and home is supreme and thoroughly English. A lady once exclaimed: 'Oh, do read to us about the baby; Dickens is capital at a baby.' And he sought to make men know themselves and their brother-men. Some have accused him of irreverence and want of piety, but, we think, without just cause. He was certainly an intense hater of shams and religious hypocrisy, and this, together with his sense of the grotesque, may, to some minds, lay him open to the charge of sneering at Christianity and its adherents. But a wider and deeper knowledge of his works will set this notion aside. A Mr. Charles McKenzie has just written a book entitled, 'The religious sentiments of Dickens, collected from his writings,' in which, not without good show of evidence, he refutes the accusation referred to. You will be able to judge for yourselves. I may, of course, suggest that in your reading of Dickens' references to chapel-going people, you will be none the worse for taking a little pinch of evangelical salt to correct or modify what may be unwittingly misstated or overdrawn.

H. Y.

A LITTLE girl was once questioned what it meant to be a Christian. She replied: 'It means to be just what Christ would be if He was a little girl and lived in my home.'

Frictional Electricity.

IN the year 1819 Professor Œrsted, of Copenhagen, discovered that a close relationship existed between magnetism and electricity. This discovery was of far-reaching importance; out of it grew the telegraph, telephone, and many other inventions of the greatest use to man. Professor Œrsted, for his discovery, is worthy of all honour as one of the great benefactors of the race. As the age of stone was superseded by that of iron, doubtless the age of steam will be superseded by that of electricity. In the meantime such restraints have been imposed upon the warlike, commerce so promoted, and the bonds of national brotherhood so strengthened, as to lead many to regard the electrical inventions of the age as important factors, under the providence of God, in the world's peace and prosperity. Before referring, particularly, to the close connection which exists between magnetism and electricity, we propose to speak of frictional electricity, and if opportunity permits, in a further paper, of current or dynamic electricity.

The name 'electricity' is derived from the Greek word 'ēlektron' (amber), in which substance its phenomena were first observed.

The knowledge the ancients possessed of electricity was almost limited to the fact that amber acquires the power of attracting light bodies to itself on being rubbed. Thales, of Miletus, mentioned this 600 B.C. Until nearly the seventeenth century amber and jet were the only two substances known to possess this property. That a large number of substances possessed it was first discovered by Dr. Gilbert, of Colchester. He called these substances 'electrics.' They are now spoken of as 'non-conductors,' because the electricity does not freely pass from them. Glass, sealing-wax, sulphur, resin, &c., are non-conductors.

A non-conductor is often called an 'insulator,' and a conductor supported by a non-conductor is said to be 'insulated.' Metals are the best conductors; hence, an iron building is the safest place in a thunderstorm.

The human body is also a good conductor. If a person standing on a stool with glass legs be struck or rubbed with a catskin, he becomes electrified to a very perceptible degree, and sparks may be drawn from any part of his body. Of course he is insulated by the glass legs of the stool. Air, when dry, is a good insulator. Dampness in the air is a great hindrance to electrical experiments.

There are two kinds of electricity produced by friction. These were formerly named after the substances to which they seemed peculiar, viz.: 'Vitreous,' or the electricity of glass, and 'Resinous,' or the electricity of resin. These terms are not now in use. Positive is used instead of vitreous (usually denoted by the plus sign $+$), and negative instead of resinous (denoted by the minus sign $-$). Neither kind of electricity is produced alone; there is always an equal quantity of both kinds produced; one kind appearing on the thing rubbed, and an equal amount of the other kind on the rubber. If we take a dry rod of glass and rub it with dry silk, positive electricity is excited on the glass, and negative on the silk. Rubbing a stick of sealing-wax with flannel, we excite negative electricity on the sealing-wax, and positive on the flannel. Let us now try a simple experiment. Suspend a pith ball by a thin linen or, better still, silk thread, to a glass support. Then touch the pith ball with a glass rod which has been rubbed with a dry silk rubber; thus electricity is communicated to the pith ball, and is unable to leave it, because the silk thread and glass support are non-conducters. The ball having been touched by the glass rod is no longer attracted to it, but, on the other hand, is repelled by it. Next, bring a stick of sealing wax, which has been rubbed with a piece of dry flannel, near to the pith ball, and it will be found that the pith ball, which was repelled by the excited glass, will be attracted to the sealing-wax. Thus a pith ball first touched by electrified glass will be afterwards repelled by the glass, but attracted to the sealing-wax. When we touched the pith ball with the excited glass rod, it became charged with the same electricity as the glass, and as it was afterwards repelled by the glass, we conclude that two positively electrified bodies

repel one another; or, in other words, bodies charged with the same kind of electricity repel one another. On the other hand, the ball charged with the electricity of the glass, *i.e.*, positive, is attracted to the sealing-wax, which is negatively charged; thus showing that bodies charged with opposite kinds of electricity attract one another. Symmer first discovered such phenomena as these, and they were independently discovered by Du Fay.

These are the most elementary facts; and from them some very important information has been obtained. Several theories have been advanced to account for these phenomena, but as they are all more or less unsatisfactory we will not particularise them. Suffice it to say, that while electricity resembles a fluid in that it apparently flows from one point to the other, it differs from every known fluid in almost every other respect. It possesses no weight; it repels itself.

Other effects than those already mentioned, viz., attraction and repulsion, testify to the production of electricity by friction. If a glass rod be rubbed briskly, it not only attracts light bodies, but a small electric spark may be taken from it by the knuckle. Such sparks are generally attended by a snapping sound, suggesting, on a very small scale, the thunder which accompanies the lightning flash.

To those of our readers acquainted with the previous article on 'Elementary Magnetism,' many of the terms now used are familiar. Remembering what was said of magnetic induction, they will easily understand electrical induction, or electrifying by influence.

We have already seen that a glass rod electrified by friction, when brought near to a pith ball, electrifies it. This is electrical induction. This action was discovered in 1753 by John Caton, and it will take place across a considerable distance, even across a large sheet of glass. Faraday discovered that the air between the electrified body and the conductor, has much to do with the inducing influence. Across some bodies the inductive influence passes more readily than across others; *e.g.*, paraffin oil, solid sulphur. Such are said to have great inductive capacity.

A simple instrument was devised by Volta,

in 1775, for the purpose of procuring, upon the principle of induction, an unlimited number of electrical charges from one single charge. This instrument is called the electrophorus. It consists of a tin mould filled with resin, or shellac (or perhaps better still, a mixture of resin, shellac, and Venice turpentine), and a movable tin cover, of rather smaller diameter than the mould (wood covered with tinfoil answers the same purpose), with an insulating handle. To use it, the resinous cake must be beaten or rubbed with a warm piece of woollen cloth, or with a cat's skin. By this means negative electricity is excited on its surface. When the cover is put on, its neutral electricities are separated by induction; the positive attracted to the under side, and the negative repelled to the upper side of the cover. This negative electricity is free—indeed, repelled electricity is always free, while attracted electricity is bound. If the cover be touched by the finger the negative escapes, and the cover, on being removed by the insulating handle, is found to be powerfully electrified with a positive charge; so much so as to yield a spark when the knuckle is brought near to it. The 'cover' may be replaced, touched, and once more removed, and will thus yield any number of sparks; the original charge on the resinous plate, meanwhile, remaining as strong as before. This is the simplest form of electrical machine. Space will not permit us to describe the cylinder, and plate machines; indeed, we must content ourselves with the statement of fundamental facts, hoping that such an interest has been created thereby as shall lead our readers to pursue the subject still further. Fortunately, there are many good and cheap books on the subject.

In conclusion, unless the Editor thinks we have already taken up too much valuable space, we will remind our readers that the charge of electricity resides only on the surface of conducting bodies. This important fact is proved in several ways. Terquem showed that a pair of gold leaves hung inside a wire cage could not be made to diverge when the cage was electrified. Faraday constructed a conical bag of linen-gauze, supported upon an insulating stand, and to which silk strings were attached,

by which it could be turned inside out. It was charged, and the charge proved to be on the outside of the bag. On turning it inside out the electricity was once more found outside.

Professor Clerk Maxwell proposed, in accordance with this fact, to protect buildings from lightning by covering them on the outside with a network of wires. Electrometers and other delicate instruments are screened from the influence of electrified bodies by enclosing them in a thin metal cover.

'He Careth for You.'

How strong and sweet my Father's care!
   The word, like music in the air,
   Comes answering to my whispered prayer,
      'He cares for thee.'

The thought great wonder with it brings,
My cares are all such little things;
But to the truth my glad faith clings,
      He cares for me.

Yet keep me ever in Thy love,
Dear Father, watching from above,
And let me still Thy mercy prove,
      And care for me.

Cast me not off for all my sin,
But make me pure and true within,
And teach me how Thy smile to win
      Who carest for me.

Oh, still in summer's golden glow,
Or wintry storms of wind and snow,
Love me, my Father; let me know
      Thy care for me.

And I will learn to cast the care
Which, like a heavy load, I bear,
Down at Thy feet in lowly prayer,
      And trust in Thee.

For naught can help me, shade or shine,
Nor evil thing touch me or mine,
Since Thou, with tenderness divine,
      Dost care for me.
      MARIANNE FARNINGHAM.

Anecdotes about Hymns.

FROM THE GERMAN

VI.—'Come to Me, saith Christ, Our Champion Strong.'

ONE Sunday afternoon a careless and ungodly man was passing St. Kilian's Church at Heilbroun, and thought he would go up to the door and read the names of the hymns to be sung at the service. Jestingly he said to his companion, 'Let us make haste and find out what they're going to sing.' He looked at the list, saw that one hymn given out was 'Come to Me, saith Christ, our Champion Strong (written by Schaffer, in 1688), was irresistibly attracted by the line, went in to hear it sung, was so greatly impressed by it that he stayed through the sermon, which impressed him still more, so that he became a changed man, and ever afterwards attended church regularly.

Our Domestic Pets.

THE DOG.

THIS noble animal is looked upon as the most sagacious of those creatures which man has given a place to in his own home, and which he has privileged by a place constantly near to him because of its companionship or service. In intelligence it may be said to rank next to man in the animal kingdom. It is capable of high training, and of following out a consecutive course, though that training must in all cases be in harmony with its instincts, and can never under any circumstances be what is called learned or elaborate. The intelligence of the dog seems to be in proportion to the cranial capacity and cerebral development which differ, dogs of the spaniel kind being superior to those of the bull or mastiff kind. Some have thought so highly of the dog as to credit it with rational intelligence like unto that which man possesses, but no matter how intelligent a dog may be found its life is almost wholly instinctive. By far the larger number of actions it performs are such as belong to a dog, and not to man. If it does anything different, it is the result of hard training, and what is done is soon forgotten when the training is suspended. The rational mind is capable of creativeness and inventiveness; it is liable to aberration and error. It is capable of idiocy, and hence there are idiotic men and women. But there are not idiotic dogs, and we never expect to meet with them, because their mental life is instinctive rather than rational, and instinct is never idiotic. Dogs domesticated are much more intelligent than those in a wild state. They can be humanized and made noble, and as a rule they reflect the culture and intelligence of the home in which they are brought up.

It is singular that naturalists are not able to trace the parent stock of this domestic animal. Some have thought it sprang from the wolf, and others from the jackal. The wolf has the largest number of points of identification, and yet there are such points of divergence that we cannot think they are one and the same. It seems that dogs of the greyhound kind, thin, and with erect ears, have the longest antiquity, the greyhound being traceable 3,000 years back. Alexander the Great is said to have introduced the mastiff to Europe; he was fond of large dogs, and in his travels dogs of large stature were secured for him. Dogs are of different kinds, but many of these kinds are mixed and modern; the pure types are few, and as to whether these may not have had a common origin, we would say this is not unlikely. In deciding the breed of dogs there are many marks to go by, but a general indication is the ear; as, for example, the ear of the greyhound is semi-erect and narrow; whilst that of the Newfoundland is large and pendant. Then other dogs are distinguished by the muzzle, the jaws, and the hair. Dogs are kept by man for use, to protect him, to watch his property, and many are kept for fancy or pleasure. Those dogs that are kept for pleasure exhibit the taste of the owner, and very strange and fantastical that taste often shows itself to be. Some prefer a large, monstrous dog, others the tiniest thing they can get hold of. Ladies in keeping dogs are in danger of making pets of them, and in the selection of these pets they are guided partly by fashions. A few years ago the poodle was the aristocratic pet-dog, of late years the collie has come into prominence. The farmer and butcher will tell you that they are obliged to keep dogs. 'They do not see what people want with dogs who have no use for them.' They who are almost daily indebted to the sheep dog, often seem to have the least gratitude for its services, and often speak of the dog generally in a manner that seems to us to be unworthy. In visiting the farm-house we have often thought the sheep dog received scant attention; if it could have sold its services it could certainly have secured more than it receives. There is true pathos and eloquence in these words of George Elliot, in one of her stories of clerical life. One of her characters is Amos Barton, a curious kind of compound, not loveable in appearance, yet having in him some excellent qualities that even more pretentious men do not possess. She compares him to an unattractive mongrel dog, and says : ' I have all my life had a sympathy for mongrel, ungainly dogs, who are nobody's pets, and I would rather surprise one of them with a pat and a pleasant morsel, than meet the condescending advances of the loveliest skye.' I do not see that it is wrong to keep a dog for pleasure or companionship if a person can afford it ; those who have proved the treachery of human companionship may well be driven to fall back upon the faithfulness of the brute creation, and those who are disposed to be treacherous themselves, will often be rebuked by the example of the faithful animal by their side. It is for service, however, that the dog should be employed, for that purpose it was made by the Great Creator, that it might be the friend and defender of man, and it is a degradation of a creature so capable, to think that it exists for a purpose below this. It is in this we find it has its chief merit, not in its

colour or marks or shape. It has proved by generations of long and faithful devotion that it can and will serve the interests of man.

' The dog,' says Buffon, ' is the only one whose fidelity is proof against temptation ; the only one which constantly knows its master and the friends of the family ; the only one which recognises its name, and the voices of the family.' Perhaps no animal has a more secure place in the affections of cultured people of Europe, and it is strange to find a different feeling towards the dog in many Eastern cities. It is singular that even the Jews at one time were led to speak of the dog with disdain. Perhaps the ancient Israelites had seen the superstition offered to the dog by their Egyptian taxmasters, and in their resentment of such foolish idolatry, had gone to the other extreme. They remembered, also, that its flesh for dietary purposes was reckoned amongst the unclean animals of Scripture. That spirit of ancient contempt for the dog in many places has continued till the present day. Dogs in Eastern lands are not harboured in the houses. They are compelled to live in the streets, and often present a poor and afflicted appearance. They divide the town in quarters, and guard the right of living where they are born. Europe is the paradise of dogs, and in no country are they better treated than in England. In proof of the exceptional position of the dog in England, let us give a description of the Prince of Wales' kennels, as supplied in the Christmas number of the Supplement to the *Stockkeeper*. The writer says, ' the Sandringham kennels are a fine row of buildings, and are far ahead of the dwellings of the people in East London ; the range contains fourteen kennels built of brick in a thoroughly substantial way, and are also ornamented. The yards are 10 feet by 11 feet, with well-bricked floors. Large metal watervessels are a notable feature in the yard, each of them placed under a tap always dripping. The kennels are heated by hot-water pipes, and ventilated. Each apartment contains a bedstead made of iron laths well provided with straw. Adjoined are a hospital, a distempered house, store rooms, and a commodious cooking kitchen.' Well, all this seems at first thought to be overdone, especially when we remember the poverty of hundreds and thousands of the people. Gentlemen of the aristocracy will give hundreds of pounds for a dog, whilst children of the poor cannot get bread. But let everything have its due. There are dogs whose deeds have been so heroic, whose services have been so valuable, that even kennels such as those of the Prince of Wales are not too good for them. But whilst the dog has its due, and the clever dog is honoured, let not the love of animals lead us to a neglect of the higher claims and relations of life.

The Library.

SOME few weeks ago we were asked to recommend to some friends desirous of making acquaintance with Browning's poetry some easily accessible volume or volumes which might serve as an easy introduction. We have lying before us at the present moment a little pocket volume of 'Selections,' which might serve the purpose pretty well, though there are poems in it we would not have included, and others much more representative of the poet are left out. However, recognizing the difficulty of selection for a small volume of slightly over three hundred pages, and to be published at the modest price of 1s., we ought to be fairly satisfied with what is here presented. For our young friends who want to know something of the great poet lately deceased, this little book will lead on to the larger volumes of 'Selections,' issued by the same publishers (Messrs. Smith & Elder), or, better still, to the great body of Browning's poetic work. We would warn our readers that they will not find Browning, at first, easy reading. He is not so simple as Longfellow, nor so musical as Tennyson, but to our mind he will repay reading much more even than the latter, to say nothing of the former. Browning is not a poet to be opened and dipped into at random in an hour of vacancy; he must be taken seriously or not at all. He has his own style and man-

nerisms, and the taste for him is like that for the tomato—largely acquired. But all who have learned to love the poet are just as enthusiastic as are those who worship the vegetable. We would not counsel our readers even to read straight on through the present little book. Will they allow us to advise them to take first and ponder well such poems as 'The Boy and the Angel,' 'The Pied Piper of Hamelin,' 'Holy Cross Day,' 'Hervé Riel,' 'Halbert and Hob,' 'Tray.' Then from these dramatic and stirring rhymes let them pass to the more inward and reflective poems, such as 'An Epistle—Karshish,' 'Cleon,' 'Pictor Ignotus,' 'Andrea del Sarto,' 'A Grammarian's Funeral,' 'The Statue and the Bust,' 'Abt Vogler,' and 'Rabbi Ben Ezra.' We shall be much surprised if, before they have reached the two latter—to our mind amongst Browning's finest work—they do not earnestly crave for more than the bounds of this little volume will afford. Suppose as a first taste we transfer to this page one of the songs from 'Pippa Passes' :—

> 'The year's at the spring,
> And day's at the morn;
> Morning's at seven;
> The hillside's dew-pearled;
> The lark's on the wing;
> The snail's on the thorn;
> God's in His heaven—
> All's right with the world!'

This is the song of a mill-girl in Italy, who, having only one day of holiday in the year, determines to spend it in wandering about her native village and its environs, singing her songs of simple pleasure. Her singing appeals to and brings out, unknown to herself, the best that is in all who hear her. The artist resolves to be true to his wife, the hesitating patriot is made brave, the bishop puts away the bribe. Or take these stanzas from 'Holy Cross Day.' This was the day on which the Jews were compelled to attend an annual Christian sermon in Rome, and Browning tries to put into verse what the Jews really said on thus being driven to church :—

> 'Thou! if Thou wast He, who at mid-watch came,
> By the starlight, naming a dubious name!
> And if, too heavy with sleep—too rash
> With fear—O Thou, if that martyr-gash
> Fell on Thee coming to take Thine own,
> And we gave the cross where we owed the throne.—

'Thou art the Judge. We are bruised thus.
  But the judgment over, join sides with us!
: Thine too is the cause; and not more Thine
  Than ours is the work of these dogs and swine,
  Whose life laughs through and spits at their creed!
  Who maintain Thee in word, and defy Thee in
    deed!'

Very fittingly the last words Browning ever wrote are included in this little volume. We will give them in full :—

'At the midnight in the silence of the sleep-time,
  When you set your fancies free,
Will they pass to where—by death, fools think, im-
    prisoned—
Low he lies who once so loved you, whom you loved so,
  Pity me?

'Oh, to love so, be so loved, yet so mistaken!
  What had I on earth to do
With the slothful, with the mawkish, the unmanly?
Like the aimless, helpless, hopeless, did I drivel—
  Being—who?

'One who never turned his back, but marched breast
    forward,
  Never doubted clouds would break,
Never dreamed, though right were worsted, wrong
    would triumph,
Held we fall to rise, are baffled to fight better,
  Sleep to wake.

'No, at noonday in the bustle of man's work-time
  Greet the unseen with a cheer!
Bid him forward, breast and back as either should be,
  "Strive and thrive!" cry "Speed,—fight on, fare ever
    There as here!"'

It is that splendid note of hope and cheer in all Browning's poetry which makes him so fit a companion for the days of budding manhood and womanhood.

By Actual Proof.

DR. B. W. RICHARDSON, the noted physician, says that he was once enabled to preach an effectual temperance lecture by means of a scientific experiment. An acquaintance was singing the praises of wine, and declared that he could not get through the day without it.

'Will you be good enough to feel my pulse as I stand here?' asked Dr. Richardson.

The man did so.

'Count it carefully. What does it say?'

'Seventy-four.'

The physician then went and laid down on a sofa, and asked the gentleman to count his pulse again.

'It has gone down to sixty-four,' he said in astonishment. 'What an extraordinary thing!'

'When you lie down at night,' said the physician, 'that is the way nature takes to give your heart rest. You may know nothing about it, but the organ is resting to that extent; and if you reckon the rate, it involves a good deal of rest, because, in lying down, the heart is doing ten strokes less a minute.

'Multiply that by sixty, and it is six hundred; multiply it by eight hours, and, within a fraction, there is a difference of five thousand strokes; and as the heart is throwing six ounces of blood at every stroke, it makes a difference of thirty thousand ounces of life during the night. When I lie down at night without any alcohol, that is the rest my heart gets.

'But when I take wine or grog, I do not allow that rest, for the influence of alcohol is to increase the number of strokes. Instead of getting repose, the man who uses alcohol puts on something like fifteen thousand extra strokes, and he rises quite unfit for the next day's work, until he has taken a little more of that "ruddy bumper," which he calls "the soul of the man below."'

Murmurs and Thanks.

SOME murmur when their sky is clear
  And wholly bright to view,
  If one small streak of dark appear
In their great heaven of blue.
And some with thankful love are filled
  If but one streak of light,
One ray of God's good mercy, gild
  The darkness of their night.

In palaces are hearts that ask,
  In discontent and pride,
Why life is such a weary task,
  And all good things denied.
And hearts in poorest huts admire
  How love has in their aid
(Love that not ever seems to tire),
  Such rich provision made.

               TRENCH.

YOU MAY FIND ME IN THE MOUNTAIN.

YOU MAY FIND ME IN THE MOUNTAIN. 189

KEY D. E. ELLIS, Stockport.

|s :— :l |s :— :— | — :— :l | t :- d':r'|d' :— :— | s :— :—
|m :— :f |m :— :— | — :— :f | r :- m :f |m :— :— | m :— :—
You may find me in the moun - tain,
|d' :— :d'|d' :— :— | — :— :f | s :— :s | s :— :— | d' :— :—
|d :— :d |d :— :— | — :— :d | d :— :d | d :— :— | d :— :—

|s :— :s |s :— :— | — :— :f | r :- m :f | m :— :— | s :— :—
|d :— :d |r :— :— :t, | :— :t,| t, :— :t,| d :— :— | m :— :—
In the lit - - - tle gurg - ling rills;
|d' :— :d'|t :— :— :s | :— :s | s :— :s | s :— :— | — :— :—
|m :— :m |r :— :— | — :— :r | s, :— :s,| d :— :— | — :— :—

gush - - ing
|d' :— :de'|r' :— :— | — :— :t | s :— :f | m :— :l | s :— :—
|m :— :m |fe :— :fe | fe :— :s | r :— :r | m :— :re | m :— :r
I am gush - ing, gush - ing from the foun - tain,
|l :— :l |l :— :l | l :— :s | s :— :s | s :— :fe | s :— :t
|l, :— :l,|r :— :— | r :— :— | t, :— :t,| d :— :— | d :— :s
gush - ing

|l :— :t |d' :— :— | — :t :l | s :— :r'| d' :— :— | — :— :—
|r :— :s |s :— :— | l :s :f | m :— :f | m :— :— | — :— :—
And cours - - - ing down the hills.
|d' :— :r'|d' :— :— | — :— :d'| d' :— :t | d' :— :— | — :— :—
|fe :— :f |m :— :— | f :— :f | s :— :s | d :— :— | — :— :—

|m :— :m |t :— :— | — :— :t | d' :- .t :l | t :— :— | m :— :—
|m :— :m |t :— :— | — :— :t | d' :- .t :l | t :— :— | m :— :—
I am roll - - - ing in the bil - lows,
|m :— :m |t :— :— | — :— :t | d' :- .t :l | t :— :— | m :— :—
|m :— :m |t :— :— | — :— :t | d' :- .t :l | t :— :— | m :— :—

| : :m |t :— :— | — :— :t | d' :- .t :l | t :— :— | m :— :—
| : :m |m :— :— | — :— :m | m :- .r :d | t, :— :— | — :— :—
And on the break - ers ride,
| : :m |se :— :— :l | :— :se| l :- .se:l | se :— :— | — :— :—
| : :m |m :— :r | d :— :t,| l, :— :l,| m :— :— | — :— :—

|m :— :— |m' :— :— | — :re':m'| f' :- m':re'|m' :— :r' | d' :— :—
|d :— :— |s :— :— | — :fe :s | l :- .s :fe| s :— :f | m :— :—
My home is with the ma - ri - ners
|s :— :— |d' :— :— :d'| :— :— d'| :— :d' d' :— :t | d' :— :—
|d' :— :— |d' :— :— :d'| :— :— d'| :— :d' d' :— :s | l :— :—

|l :— :— |s :— :— | — :fe :s | m' :— :r'| d' :— :— | — :— :—
|f :— :— |s :— :f | m :re :m | s :— :f | m :— :— | — :— :—
Out on the o - cean wide.
|d' :— :— |d' :— :t | d' :— :d'| d' :— :t | d' :— :— | — :— :—
|f :— :— |m :— :r | d :— :d | s :— :s,| d :— :— | — :— :—

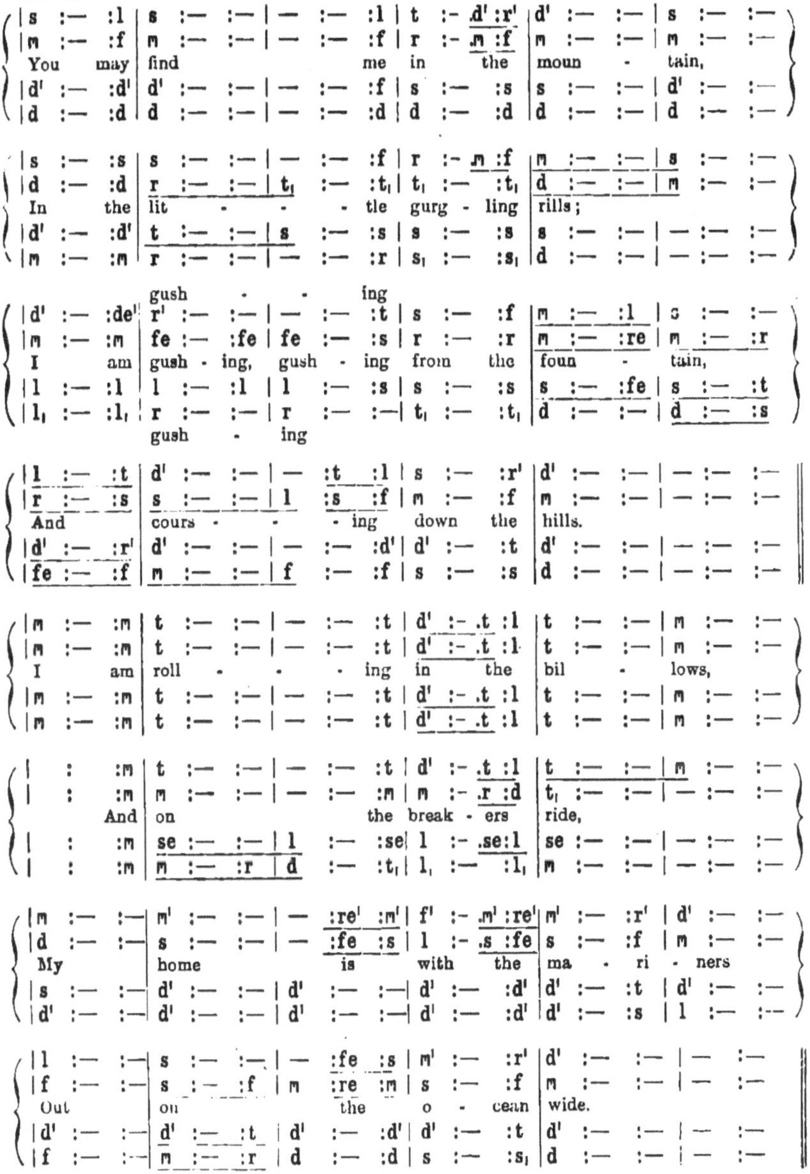

Current Topics.

OUR VILLAGES.

HERE is something delightful about the name—an English Village. It is full of poetic associations, and in the townsman's mind it conjures up all sorts of pleasant feelings. But when you get to the village itself the poetry very often flies away. The cottages may be very picturesque, but the hard and hopeless lives of many of the people are very distressing to behold. This state of things, however, cannot be allowed to continue. It is thought that a door of hope might be opened by giving the villagers self-government. Mr. C. T. Dyke Acland recently invited the House of Commons to affirm the need of this, but his motion was thrown out in favour of a proposal put forth on the part of the Government to establish district councils. Village councils, however, must come. The labourer has got the right to vote for a Member of Parliament, and he ought to have the right to share in the management of his parish. District councils will be all very well in their place, but until we get parish councils the administration of this country will never be satisfactory.

The state of many of our villages is an utter disgrace to a free country. They have not only lost all power of self-government, but one by one their privileges have been filched away. And now the Squire is in many cases more completely master of the situation than he even was in the days when the villagers were compelled to labour as his slaves. There are, no doubt, many country gentlemen who look well after the material welfare of their cottagers, but the present system puts a terrible power into the hands of unscrupulous men. And the scathing lines of the late Charles Kingsley are an only too true description of the consequences that have followed. These

are the words he puts into the mouth of a discontented villager :—

'You have sold the labouring man, Squire,
   Body and soul to shame,
To pay for your seat in the House, Squire,
   And to pay for the feed of your game.

'When packed in one reeking chamber,
   Man, maid, mother, and little ones lay;
While the rain pattered in on the rotting bride bed,
   And the walls let in the day;

'We quarrelled like brutes, and who wonders?
   What self-respect could we keep?
Worse housed than your hacks and your pointers,
   Worse fed than your hogs and your sheep.'

The sanitary inspector has undoubtedly done something to improve the condition of the villages, but the thing to be aimed at is to give the villagers the power to attend to such matters themselves. 'My great desire,' said Dr. Arnold, 'is to teach my boys to govern themselves; a much better thing than to govern them well myself.' To be governed by others is serfdom, to govern ourselves is liberty. It is this spirit of independence that needs to be awakened in the villagers of England. The people in the country districts of America enjoy self-government, and Professor Bryce tells us that 'no better schools of politics' — than their township meetings—'can be imagined, nor any better method of managing local affairs more certain to prevent jobbery and waste, to stimulate vigilance and promote contentment.' In Switzerland, too, the Communal meetings have produced a type of villagers who are a credit to the country, and why should this land of free institutions not afford its rural population an opportunity of acquiring the art of self-government?

It was so once. The primitive constitution of our old English forefathers was a true democracy. In that old time, more than a thousand years ago, it was the custom of the freemen of each little village community to meet together under the shade of some ancient tree, or on the village green, to regulate the various rights over the common lands, and to pass yearly bye-laws for the common good. Once a year, or oftener, they would take an oath of mutual fidelity, called the 'peace-pledge.' 'For the nourishing of brotherly love,' they swore, 'they would be good and true loving brothers to the fraternity, helping and counselling with all their power if any brother that hath done his duties well and truly come or fall to poverty, as God them help.' This was before the Norman Conquest, but such village meetings lingered on till later times, and it was the spirit fostered by them that rose up in defence of national liberty in the days of the Stuarts. Even so late as a generation or two ago, the parish vestry, composed of the ratepayers, with the rector in the chair, had the management of all local affairs, and there was no other governing body between it and the court of magistrates who administered the business of the county. This once important body has now sunk into a meeting for the yearly appointment of churchwardens and other officers connected with the parish church, and with which dissenters do not care to have anything to do. How the public business of the parish gets transacted very few seem to know.

The privilege of self-government must be given back to the villages, adapted, of course, to the changed condition of the people. It would not do, for instance, for the rector or vicar to be the *ex-officio* chairman of the council, or for the meetings to be held at a time when only the farmers or tradesmen could attend. It must be an assembly of all the householders in the parish; it must be held after work-hours in the evening, and to protect its members from undue influence, the voting must be under the protection of the ballot. Such a meeting would have plenty to do. It ought to have the management of all charities within the parish ; it ought to have some voice in the administration of poor relief, and allotments would naturally come under its supervision. Then there are the important questions of education, and the management or banishment of the liquor traffic. There are few villages which have the power at present of effecting any improvements at the public expense, and many a thickly populated parish has no engine or other means of extinguishing fires. These are a few of the matters that

would occupy the attention of the village parliament, and their consideration would call out the latent talent of the neighbourhood.

It has been said that two things are needed to retain our rural populations. To check the flow of country people to the towns, the life in our villages must be made more interesting and more profitable. The establishment of village councils would help to supply both those conditions. The power of self-government would at any rate make village life more interesting. Of that there can be no doubt. The affairs of a village may be well enough managed by a landlord or his agent, and yet its life may be dulness itself, whereas if its affairs be put into the hands of the people they will become objects of unfailing interest. Then the institution of such a governing body would give the first opportunity to many a village for the holding of public meetings and lectures upon subjects not sanctioned by the squire and the parson, and would also open the way for the establishment of other forms of public worship than that at present pursued in the parish church. In many cases,· no doubt, the Council would see its way to build a village hall, and support a village library; and who knows in how many ways the life of an English villager would be broadened and uplifted? To enjoy privileges like these he must now go to the towns, and if he be a man of independent spirit he very often does so. For, as Mr. Acland truly says, 'There are many self-respecting working men who will not live all their lives where there is no public building under public control available for their own organizations, and where the dwellings are to be held only on condition of keeping in the good books of the landlord's bailiff.'

But how will Councils increase the material prosperity of the villagers? At any rate, there can be little doubt that the lack of such popular control has resulted in their impoverishment. What has become of the common lands upon which the villagers used to graze their cows? They have been absorbed by the landlords, sometimes by means of private Acts of Parliament, and sometimes by direct usurpation. Between the passing of the first En-closure Act in 1709 and the year 1845 it has been calculated that more than seven million acres of land were enclosed. In some cases, no doubt, the poor man received a bit of land in lieu of his common rights; but the bit of land was soon sold, the money spent, and his children at any rate were none the better for the concession. It is doubtful whether such cases of robbery have altogether ceased even yet. Then, again, how have the charities in our country parishes been administered? Here is a case which took place a very few years ago. A charity yielding a large revenue, left for the free education of the children of a certain village, was actually diverted from its original purpose, and devoted to the establishment of a middle-class school in another county. The poor children of that village have now to pay school fees, in order to enable the sons of the gentry to have the advantage of attending a highly-endowed boarding-school. Such iniquities would have been impossible had there been a village council to guard the rights of the villagers themselves.

With much fear and trembling, Parliament now seems disposed to give the country labourers facilities for renting small allot-ments of land. It must not, however, be expected that there will at first be any great rush for these allotments. Where are the labourers to get the capital to work them? And if they have got the capital, many will not have the courage to speculate. The treatment to which he has been so long subjected has made the farm labourer in many cases somewhat cautious and suspicious. To allay these suspicions the allotment system must be placed under the management of the village councils. The High Church clergyman must not have the power of using the village allotments for the purpose of proselytizing the parents, as he now uses the village school for the purpose of proselytizing the children. It is not to be expected that any form of self-government will bring back to the villages the little industries which the factory system of the towns has swept away, but there are other ways in which

a country life may be made profitable. It is not too much to hope that the new municipal life of our villages may awaken a spirit of en-terprize, which in time may enable the English peasantry to successfully compete with their brethren in France and Denmark for the supply of fruit, butter, and eggs to the great produce markets of this country.

The son of an average agricultural labourer has at present no civil career before him. He may have developed fair abilities at school, but if he wishes a sphere for their exercise he must make for the towns. By means of a Methodist Church, he may, indeed, rise to a position of commanding influence amongst his fellows, and may receive a fine training for the management of public affairs, but all this simply intensifies his desire for a town life. He cannot take any part in the municipal life of his own village, and whilst he remains upon the farm he can seldom see any opportunity of increasing his slender income or even protect-ing himself from the uncertainties incident to his calling. What a change the establishment of village councils would make in the pros-pects of such a youth! The council would afford him a far more inviting sphere for the exercise of his administrative powers than anything he would be likely to find in a town, an allotment would supply him with per-manent and profitable employment in the craft in which he is most skilful, and the increased life and movement would attach him ten times more firmly to his native place.　　M. P. D.

A Sharp Answer.—When the late Rev. G. J. Wood, the eminent naturalist, began to preach, he often startled his congregation by his original ways of stating things. For in-stance, a certain platform orator had ques-tioned the existence of a soul, and Mr. Wood preached a sermon upon it. 'If,' said he, 'that man were to confront me, and ask whether or no I possessed a soul, I think I should astonish him not a little by my answer; for if that question were put to me, I should reply, 'No.' Every one present now strained their attention, wondering what such an answer meant, when the preacher went on, '*Man has no soul.* Man *has* a body; man *is* a soul.'

SPRINGTIME:

A Magazine for Our Young Men and Maidens.

VOL. VI. No. 7.]   JULY, 1891.   [PRICE TWOPENCE.

A Bad Calculation.

By ROBERT HIND.

Author of ' Crosby Dalton: Local Preacher and Village Demagogue,' ' The Ruby Pendant,' &c.

CHAPTER XIII.

CORNERED.

'But he was dumb, and with a pallid frown,
Switching his fingers quick, was looking down.'

ROBERT BUCHANAN.

ARTHUR BRIXTON was nothing if not prudent, and he was sure it would be better for Mr. Harland to hear of his intentions about the future from himself rather than that any unfavourable impression should be produced in the mind of that gentleman by reports in the town, or by conversation with Rye. For he had no wish to break with those who had been his best friends and who, he felt sure, were of greater real worth than most of the new friends he hoped to make when he should have gained a footing in that other world he was at present so anxious to enter.

When, a little while after his altercation with Rye, he found himself alone with Mr. Harland in the library at the Mount, he at once plunged into the subject uppermost in his mind.

' I am not unmindful, sir, of all the interest you have taken in me,' he said, ' and I hope you will approve of my intentions about the future. I have thought that I should succeed more quickly were I to enter the university.'

' You have come to that conclusion after thinking about it, have you ?' and there was a slight emphasis on the word ' thinking,' as though the speaker was a little sceptical on the point.

' Yes. In truth I have thought a great deal about it.'

' In my opinion, then, I must tell you, you are mistaken. Success in life, by way of the university, is in many cases success of a substantial kind ; but like most things that are substantial, it is not attained quickly. In reality it means that you are going back to school awhile before commencing real business. What will you do afterwards ?'

' I should like to be a divinity student.'

' And, then ?' Mr. Harland inquired, with blunt directness.

Arthur felt himself in a corner, and was in his heart glad he had not begun these negotiations with Mr. Harland till Rye had spoken her mind to him. The operation had been unpleasant, but it had put him on his guard, and prepared him the better to evade the objections of her father.

' I did think of the pulpit, sir.'

Perhaps Arthur thought this was well put, not committing him either to Dissent or to the Church of England. But he could not help noticing that Mr. Harland's face flushed somewhat, and that there was an angry light in his eyes. Arthur wondered why, and he was not allowed to remain long in doubt.

Mr. Harland was not ignorant of Methodist

doctrine and usage, and his convictions on religious matters, including those relating to the ministry, were very strong. To hear a young man say that he had been thinking of the pulpit, as he might have said he had been thinking of the colonies, or the legal profession, or a trade, sounded to him like the extravagance of frivolity. Arthur himself should have known better, and in truth did know, but the head is a poor guide to the conduct of any conversation, if not helped by the heart.

'Have you received a call to the ministry?' Mr. Harland asked in a rather stern tone.

This was a phase of the question he had not thought of, but the query made him realise how great a mistake he had made in naming so sacred a subject in such a commonplace manner.

'It has been borne in upon my mind, sir, that I ought to aim in that direction.'

Mr. Harland softened at once. He did not know what equivocation Arthur was guilty of. On the other hand, he was glad and proud that the young man, who would probably be his son-in-law, had been chosen by God to a calling so honourable, and that the call had not been resisted. Even so he interpreted Arthur's last remark.

'And you would like to enter the university to prepare for it?'

'Yes.'

'Young men who enter the Methodist ministry generally go to the Methodist Theological Colleges.'

'Let me fully explain, Mr. Harland. I told you I had thought a great deal about this subject. For some reason or other, the shape it has taken has been that I should be a Church clergyman. In conversation with Rye, I have been led to see there may be objections to that. And so I thought if I could enter the university without being bound, at the end of the course I could determine on whether to be a minister of the Methodist or of the established Church.'

'In which case a prophet will not be needed to predict the result,' Mr. Harland said, and there was no mistaking that he meant that Arthur would become a clergyman.

'Some of our ministers have been in the university,' Arthur said, 'and are considered loyal men. And surely you will not deny that there are advantages in university life not available elsewhere.'

'I do not deny what you say. I wish all our ministers were university men. And for that very reason I should be glad if the universities were truly national institutions, rather than what they are, Church of England seminaries. When you say that our own ministers who have been to the university are loyal, I agree also, but they were loyal when they went.'

'And I am not?' Arthur asked, flushing to the roots of his hair. Still although he resented the implied accusation, he knew quite well there were grounds for it. He remembered too that Rye knew there were grounds for it.

'Do you think,' Mr. Harland asked, 'that anyone of the present loyal Methodist ministers who have had a university training, went up as you intend to go up, leaving the question open as to whether they would be Churchmen or Nonconformists? If they had they would not have been Nonconformists to-day. They were true to the faith of their fathers, because it was their own faith, and their convictions were not of the kind that would allow them to leave the question open.'

Poor Arthur was having an uncomfortable time. Surprises seemed to be awaiting him at every turn, and all his forethought and acuteness availed him nothing in his difficulties.

'Mr. Benson is a divinity student,' he ejaculated.

The words slipped from him half unconsciously, and he was not certain after they had been spoken that they might not prove a mistake. Indeed in this conversation he was not sure of anything excepting that 'the unexpected would happen.' Still the suggestion was mean, and the method of getting out of his difficulty one that reflected no credit upon him.

One effect he perceived had been produced, which was that the thoughts of Mr. Harland had been turned from him to the young Australian.

'Jack Benson is a divinity student!' Mr. Harland repeated, as though addressing himself. He said nothing more for some time, and Arthur, seeing he had caused a diversion in his own favour, resolved to follow up the advantage.

'Yes, he is a divinity student, and I have not heard he means to be a Nonconformist minister. And yet I suppose his father is a Methodist.'

'We will say nothing further on the subject to-night, Arthur,' Mr. Harland remarked, making an effort to speak kindly. 'You have taken me by surprise, and I should not like to come to a hurried decision on a matter so vital. And I suppose you will see that, as Rye's father, I have some interest in your future. But we will talk about it again in a few days.'

When Mr. Harland was alone he wondered that he had made no inquiries about Jack Benson's intentions respecting a career. His astonishment at his lack of curiosity on this subject was not lessened by the remembrance that this was the very point in the letter from his old friend announcing that Jack was coming to England that had seemed mysterious to him.

Of course Jack could do without a career well enough, being the only child of a very rich man. But he thought that neither the young man himself nor his father would be in favour of such a life. Indolence and luxury, Joe Benson knew, often meant wickedness, and Jack himself, it was apparent, had convictions on the subject, and would not be content to live and do nothing.

Jack Benson had taken captive the hearts of Mr. and Mrs. Harland. They liked above all things the open manner in which he talked about his father and mother, and especially the naïveté with which he expressed his admiration of his mother. It was this, doubtless, which had prevented Mr. Harland from inquiring minutely into the cause of Jack's being a divinity student, and ascertaining if he intended to be a clergyman. The profound satisfaction he had felt in the young man himself had allayed all desire to ask questions about his career; confident of the character of his friend's son, he had no doubt that the manner of his life would be right.

CHAPTER XIV.

LOYALTY.

THE next day Mr. Harland found an opportunity of speaking directly to Jack Benson. He knew the young man would not resent his inquiries; and he thought he might be better able to solve the difficulty in which Arthur Brixton had placed him, if he was made acquainted with Jack's intentions.

'Your father is a Methodist still, I suppose?' Mr. Harland asked.

'Of course. And a very hearty one I can assure you. He thinks there are no Christians quite equal to the Methodists. I have heard him go through the argument that satisfies his own mind on the point a hundred times. Others are very good in their own personal character he says, but Methodists are the evangelists of Christianity, who prove by their work they believe it to be possible to get the world converted.'

'It is as I expected. And I am glad the cathedral services which, according to university regulations, you have to attend on Sabbath mornings, have not destroyed your own taste for our simpler worship at the chapel.'

'It would have been astonishing if I did not like Methodist worship, never having been accustomed to anything else till I came here. Besides, sir, I am a Methodist and a Nonconformist by conviction as well as training.'

Mr. Harland could have almost hugged the young man, so glad was he to hear these outspoken words.

They were in the dining-room at the time, the room most in use at the Mount, and which was the common property of all the family. Just at that moment Rye came in, and her father, impelled by the joyous feeling Jack had awakened in him, asked his daughter to come to his side. She stood leaning against him waiting for the pleasant information she was sure was about to be given.

' Have you ever asked Jack what he is going to be, Rye ? '

' No, father ; have you ? '

' No. And yet it does seem strange, and, indeed, in some ways unpardonable, that we should never have made one inquiry on the subject. We must have been so well satisfied with what he is that we cannot bring ourselves to think of what he may become afterwards.'

' What a pretty compliment, father ! ' Rye exclaimed, laughing and stroking his cheek. ' And all the prettier because you do not often attempt a compliment.'

' Do you think we might ask him now ? '

' I can answer readily. I should like to be a minister, and am aiming at that in my studies,' Jack said.

' Of what church ? ' Rye asked eagerly ; and was so very quick in putting the question that her father had no time to speak.

Arthur Brixton, and her altercation with him, had suddenly come before her, and caused all the laughter to die out of her heart. She could not help thinking how happy she might have been had Arthur been like Jack. Mr. Harland's thoughts were running in a similar groove, and he was wondering if his daughter, his one darling child, who deserved so well, had awaiting her in the immediate future some great trials and sorrows. He had not mentioned his interview with Arthur to her yet, and although she knew that Arthur had spoken to Mr. Harland on the subject, Mr. Harland believed that Rye was in ignorance of the whole affair. It followed, therefore, that he did not understand the reason of her eager inquiry.

' I could be minister only of one church,' he said.

' But you have not said which church, cousin Jack ? ' and the eagerness of her tone had increased rather than otherwise.

A shade passed over Jack's face, as of a keen disappointment. His eyes, too, wore a sorrowful look as he in low tones replied :

' My father's church. The church that has made him such a good man, and which he loves so well ; which even my mother, who knew little about it till she was married, has

learned to love even better than the Society of Friends, which took me into its Sunday school when I was a child, and which all my life has been putting Christian feelings into my heart. If I am to be a minister, I must be a Methodist. Always, of course, providing the Methodist church will have me.'

Big drops, clear as the dew, stood in the eyes of his questioner as the young man spoke, and Mr. Harland rose, stretched out his hand, and when he had steadied himself a little said :

' And the church that can inspire such feelings is worthy of the good fortune it enjoys in having such young men aspiring to be its ministers. At the same time we had once, before you arrived, a suspicion that you were to be a clergyman. It is not usual for Methodist ministers to have a university course, and as you were coming to be a divinity student, you will see we had some grounds for our suspicion. Knowing our own predilections you will understand how happy you have made us to-day.'

' Have you thought of the supposed social ban under which Nonconformists rest ? ' Rye asked, rather timidly.

' Not a great deal. My mind has been vaguely aware of it, but it has never appeared to me to be a matter of great importance.'

' You can never become a canon or a dean, to say nothing about a bishop, in the Methodist Church. And you will not be thought quite so good as a Churchman in many ways,' Rye said with a little toss of her head.

' Perhaps I shall survive. But what does it all mean ? I am completely puzzled with the distinctions that are observed in Rockingham.'

' I am afraid I cannot explain what it means. It has been here under my eyes ever since I was born, and it is a mystery to this day. What special value would be added to my person if I were to go to St. Mary's instead of the chapel on Sundays, I cannot tell. No doubt I am to blame for this, because I should very likely have understood the subject had I given it the attention it merits. But it has never, till lately, presented itself to my mind as an interesting and fruitful study, and hence at my time of life, with all

the special advantages of residence in Rockingham, I have to confess complete ignorance
upon a matter which to many of my neighbours is a primary question of life and
morals.'

' How scornful you have grown! quite all
of a sudden too!' Jack observed.

' I am afraid I have.   And it is wrong to be
scornful,' she said with regret. ' You will
forgive me and I will try to be better,' saying
which she bowed and left the room.

Mr. Harland's suspicions were awakened.
There must, he thought, be some reason for
this first outburst of bitterness from Rye, and
her remarks seemed so complete an explanation
of Arthur's position, that he began to think
they must have discussed the subject in no
very amiable mood.

This reflection made him rather glad. It told him that his daughter's heart was true. Not that he would have expected anything else. Her mind, at least, was healthy and free from the foolish morbid tendencies which Arthur had lately been revealing. Still, he reflected, where two young people are concerned it is not easy to guess what may happen, and he could not have blamed her very seriously if, when she found Arthur's mind set on the university, and inclined towards the episcopal pulpit, she had raised no objections, but favoured every one of his proposals.

A shiver passed over him as he thought what a bitterness that would have been to him. And yet with Arthur resolved on this course, and Rye seconding his arguments, he foresaw he would have been compelled to yield. That sorrow was to be spared him, because of the strong and righteous convictions of his daughter.

But what was the next step to take? He sought for Rye, and having taken her into the library said:

'Arthur has been speaking to me about leaving his present situation. He wants to enter the university.'

'Yes; he spoke to me about it, too.'

Mr. Harland was more convinced than before that this had already been a cause of trouble to Rye. Gladly would he have avoided giving her more pain, but he must know her feelings exactly before he could offer her counsel, and determine his own course.

'Do you know what he means to be in the end?'

'His mind does not seem fully made up, but I do not think he would object to become a clergyman.'

'And what would be your opinion on such a course, Rye?'

'I should not like it; it would make me very sorry.'

'I won't say more to-night; but I should like you to think out the case well, and we will talk about it two days hence. Everybody who knows me will admit that I don't hate the Church, that I should be glad to hear of its becoming far more useful than it is. But I am a Methodist, and I do not want my daughter to be anything but a Methodist, and if she feels as I do, and Arthur still persists, it may be best, perhaps, to alter the arrangements that exist between you. That will be painful, no doubt, but it may not be so bad as living in uncongenial conditions all your life, and I am certain it will not be so hard as going against your conscience.'

Two days of an ordinary everyday experience soon pass over, but to the inmates of the Mount these were not ordinary days. Rye was miserable, for the first time in her life utterly miserable. Her father was captious with everybody save his girl, to whom he showed more than his usual kindness, and for the most part moody and silent. Jack Benson was nervous and taciturn. Only Mrs. Harland seemed quite happy.

She knew the whole story, and said nothing to anybody. But at bottom she felt rather exultant. Women, in these matters, have a wider range of vision than men, and Mrs. Harland, in her heart, thought that the present complication of events might issue in a situation very much to her mind.

Old Time keeps an even, regular step, whether human hearts be happy or wretched, and so the two days came to an end. Mr. Harland again sought his daughter. She was very pale, but he observed that a new look of calm had appeared on her face.

'I have done as you asked me, father. And I cannot ever think of being a Churchwoman. I must remain a Methodist. And if Arthur can think of leaving the Methodist Church he is not what I have always thought him to be. We need not think hardly of him, but unless he can satisfy my mind on this point I shall have to ask him to give me back my promise.'

Mr. Harland held his daughter's hand as she spoke, and he felt it trembling in his. His own heart was in a flutter, too, but his face was lighted up with pride as he listened to her frank statement of her decision.

'Shall I explain your mind to him, darling?' he asked, as he kissed her cheek.

'I think I would rather do it myself, father,' she answered.

(To be continued.)

Believing in the Bible.

DURING Mr. Moody's meetings in New York City, a man brought a difficult passage to him with this question:—

'How do you explain that, Mr. Moody?'

'I don't explain it.'

'Well, how do you interpret it?'

'I don't interpret it.'

'How do you understand it?'

'I don't understand it.'

'Well, what do you do with it?'

'I don't do anything with it.'

'You don't believe it, do you?'

'Certainly I believe it. There are lots of things I believe that I don't understand. There are a good many things in astronomy, a good many things about my own system that I don't understand, yet I believe them. I am glad there are heights in that Book which I haven't been able to climb. I am glad there are depths I haven't been able to fathom. It is the best proof that the Book came from God.'

'But you don't believe in the Old Testament just as you do in the New Testament?'

'Yes, I do. We have one Bible, not two. The very things in the Old Testament that men cavil at the most to-day are the things the Son of man set His seal to when He was down here, and it isn't good policy for His servant to be above His master. The Master believed these things.'—*Young Men's Era.*

'Smoker's Heart.'

THIS is a disease said by physicians to be caused by excessive tobacco-smoking. Edwin Booth, the actor, who was recently reported to be struck with paralysis at Rochester, New York, is now believed to have been a victim to this disease. His case is by no means the first that has occurred in this country. While not generally so designated, it is believed by high medical authority that many of the supposed cases of death from paralysis or heart-disease are really caused by excessive smoking, which, it is alleged, affects the action of the heart and disturbs the circulation. 'The pulse will intermit—not with any regularity—sometimes one beat in four, sometimes one in ten, sometimes two or three at a time, and then comes trouble. The brain, missing its regular pulsations of blood, wavers, the heart flutters, and then follows a temporary collapse.' These are given as the symptoms of 'smoker's heart.'

A habit that tends to such results surely ought to be abandoned. We have known cases where physicians have advised the entire giving up of the tobacco-habit in order that such threatened results might be averted.

The use of tobacco is especially dangerous to the young, and it is gratifying that several of the state legislatures have recently passed laws prohibiting the sale of tobacco in any form to minors.

It is well known that tobacco contains nicotine, a deadly poison, and that only rare cases have been found in which its use has not been more or less injurious. To take it into the system is beyond all question an abuse of the body; and whether its use results in a premature death or not, it often weakens and always defiles the body, and is not infrequently a serious impediment to usefulness.

The tobacco habit, when once formed, becomes largely a heart-trouble. Though the reason pronounces it useless and dangerous, still it is continued. A certain cure for this kind of a bad heart is the total abandonment of the use of tobacco.

JOHN WESLEY'S father once had the curiosity to sit by and count while his wife repeated the same thing to one child more than twenty times. 'I wonder at your patience,' said he; 'you have told that child that same thing twenty times.' 'If I had satisfied myself by mentioning it only nineteen times,' she answered, 'I should have lost all my labour. It was the twentieth time that crowned it.'

Heirs of All the Ages.

PAPERS ON THE HERITAGE AND RESPONSIBILITIES OF OUR YOUNG PEOPLE.

EXT to literature, perhaps, the most valuable part of our inheritance from the past is

ART.

Most certainly art was one of man's first accomplishments; for after thought comes the expression of it, and idea, embodied to a certain object or end, is art. Art was, therefore, more or less necessary to the production of literature. So far as human productions of any kind can really be traced back, man is said to have been an 'excellent artist,' and must have been a close observer of life and things around him. His earliest known works show some degree of taste, a perception of the fitness of things, and a desire for the beautiful, as well as the useful. 'On many of his implements of bone, horn, and stone, there are scratched, evidently with some sharp-pointed instruments, pictures of many of the animals with which he came into contact. These likenesses are remarkably true to nature, and can be identified at once. Thus we have the reindeer repeatedly drawn and even shaded almost exactly as an artist would do it now. The cave bear is equally well represented. Their weapons, also, are often curiously carved into the forms of a deer, a horse, or other animals. We find figures of the ox, the Irish elk, the bison, and also such extinct species as the mammoth or woolly elephant! Such representations are the most ancient works of art known, and after those come the sculptures and paintings on the tombs and temples of Assyria and Egypt.

But we need more clearly and comprehensively to know what Art means, and what is embraced by the term. Art is the result of man's thought about, and observation of the world around him. It is the voluntary use and combination of the things and beauties by which he is surrounded to serve the ends he has in view. It has been described as 'an adjustment of *means* to accomplish a desired end.' According to the end man has in view, Art comes to be divided into two kinds, called the 'Useful Arts' and the 'Fine Arts.' This division seems to have begun early, for we may detect it in that stage of man's existence referred to in the fourth chapter of the Book of Genesis. The family of Lamech, in Cain's line, were a distinguished family, highly gifted, and whether conscious of it or not, they manifested originality, and those gifts of faculty and genius which, from their day, have wondrously enriched the world. Up to their time, men had been limited, in their movements and knowledge, by their fixed habitations. They dwelt in caves or under the shelter of the forest trees, and were tied to one spot. But Jabal conceived the idea of tent life, and began the nomadic life of the powerful early shepherd races, by carrying his home about with him. Jabal originated musical instruments and poetry, and his brother Tubal-Cain began to work in metals, and founded those arts which require hard tools for their culture.

The Useful Arts comprehend agriculture, building, weaving, mechanics, navigation, practical chemistry, and all those pursuits which adapt the knowledge of natural things and forces to the necessities and tastes of man. The Fine Arts embrace painting, sculpture, music, poetry, and architecture, all of which appeal to the senses, and are a medium both of expressing and giving the pleasure of the same.

Now, to dwell upon any one of those sections of art we have just named would more than fill the space allotted to us in these pages. We can only therefore indicate them, and leave our readers to follow them according to individual taste and calling in life.

Art is spoken of by some as distinct from nature. It is distinct only inasmuch as it is man's production. In all art, whether useful or otherwise, man is closely allied to nature; he is both guided and limited by her. Nature furnishes the model and suggests to him the object of his aim. Smeaton built the Eddystone Lighthouse on the model of an oak tree, as being the form in nature best designed to resist the forces of the sea. All optical instruments, from a pair of spectacles to the largest telescope, are formed on the principle of the eye they are made to assist. The pyramid is the sloping mountain imitated in stone, and that flower of Grecian architecture, the Corinthian capital, was suggested to the modeller of it by a piece of a pillar standing on a grave, with a flat tile laid on the top of it, and the acanthus leaf growing up and clustering round it under the flat top. The form and curving of the ship are regulated by the fluid she sails in. The roofs of our houses are shaped, not as we would, but to best meet and bear the wind, the snow, the rain. Music began in the whistling reeds by the wild marsh, or in some such sonorous sounds. As one has said, 'Art resides in the model, in the plan; for it is on that the genius of the artist is expended.' But while the model is necessary and art depends on nature, yet there is more in the artist than his art. The true artist exceeds nature not in truth, but in fulness and exactness. It is said, 'Turner was never satisfied merely to copy even the most glorious scenery. He moved and even suppressed mountains.' Just as the soul is superior to the body and all material things, so it conceives something beyond these, and that larger conception leaves its traces on all true art. Bacon says, 'The world being inferior to the soul, by reason whereof there is agreeable to the spirit of man a more ample greatness, a more exact goodness, and a more absolute variety than can be found in the nature of things.' Nature never makes a line as straight as man does. Why? Because the ideal of a line in the human mind is above the actual in nature; and in art, 'the ideal without the real lacks life, but the real without the ideal lacks pure beauty.'

The end of art, it has been said, is to 'please.' Art gives great pleasure, without doubt, but true art refines and profits through its pleasure. Mere pleasure is not its end. Fine art brings to us the true, the good, and the beautiful in things and men, and these are always an expression of the Divine, a manifestation of God. Beauty, then, everywhere is 'God's sacrament.' Let us drink it in wherever we see it, either from nature or from the human face divine. The heritage of art which we enjoy in very rich measure to-day is first in the use and interpretation of nature which it has given us. We never penetrated the world as we do now; we never enjoyed its productions and beheld and understood its beauties as we do to-day, and through the medium of the useful arts the most distant parts of the world are revealed to us. Then, in the second place, we are highly blessed at this day by the accumulated art treasures by which we are surrounded. It is utterly impossible to attempt to enumerate these. But we have them in the results of skilled workmanship, in the picture-galleries, the museums, and libraries. Nay, our very homes are made luxurious with the works and decorations of art. Art is breathing its spirit everywhere. It is a wondrous power in our civilization. It eases labour, improves our implements, embellishes our books, smooths the roughness everywhere. It multiplies the comforts and pleasures of life with its pictures and music. In fact, by what it enables us to do, it has become a mighty power for good in all our hands, if we will only learn how to use it. Our art-treasures are worth studying that we may be useful by them. We are told that Prometheus, of Greek mythology, once made a beautiful statue of Minerva, the goddess, with which she was so delighted 'that she offered to bring down anything from heaven which could add to its perfection. Prometheus, on this, prudently asked her to take him there so that he might choose for himself. This Minerva did, and Prometheus, finding that in heaven all things were animated by fire, brought back a spark with which he gave life to his work.' Just so, our music, our poetry, our skill in doing things, and all our culture, wants that spark from heaven, the love of Christ put into it, to perfect it; and so to influence us that we shall play, and sing, and work for the poor, the sick, the needy, and by our highest powers make life a blessed ministry of mercy and help. Let us remember the Gospel can use Art to save and perfect men. F. L. S.

Wonderful Workers.

'Summer isles of Eden, lying
In dark-purple by the sea.'

TENNYSON.

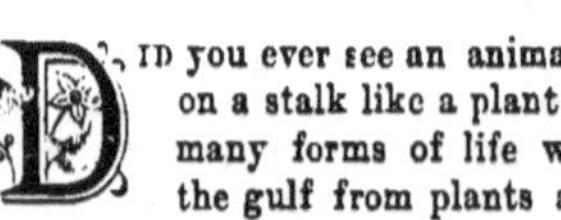

ID you ever see an animal that grew on a stalk like a plant? There are many forms of life which bridge the gulf from plants and animals, and partake of the nature of both.

The marvellously small insect called the coral-polyp is one of these forms. A mass of minute coral-polyps fasten themselves upon a rock in the sea, spread their tiny arms like a flower, and open their small mouths, and absorb the limestone from the passing water. Out of this limestone they build houses or shells about themselves. When you look at a piece of coral you notice that it is full of little pipes. In each one of these pipes there once lived a coral-polyp, and they were all fastened together by a thin skin.

From the rock upon which they fasten themselves they grow, and grow, and spread out like the branches of a tree, still clinging together as though they were one; yet each separate coral-polyp having a mouth and stomach of its own, and an independent life, new polyps are continually generated, and instantly begin to absorb limestone and build their limestone shells, thus adding to the great coral structure which is being formed. Old polyps are constantly dying, leaving their little pipes or shells to form part of the vast coral reef. Thus this mass spreads and grows and increases until reefs, miles upon miles long, and even islands are formed.

Very beautiful appears this coral reef, as you look down upon it through the clear sea water. The raging surf, which beats upon it so wildly, only strengthens and hardens it; for it hammers it with a wonderfully compressing force, while at the same time it bears to the hungry mouths of the tiny polyps new limestone from the bottom of the sea.

What mighty builders are these small polyps! On the north-east coast of Australia stretches a coral reef for nearly a thousand miles. Every island in the Pacific is fringed with coral. A ring-island, or atoll, as it is called, is a coral formation, the top of which appears upon the surface of the sea in the form of a circle of land. The atolls extend down many fathoms deep into the sea, like the great walls of a mountain.

These atolls were for a long time very puzzling to scientists. They observed that all coral reefs were formed in shallow water, the atolls being the only coral formation which extended deep into the sea. They had naturally supposed that the polyps of the atolls had begun their work in these deep waters and had built up to the surface. But what made their formation take a circular shape, like a huge round island with a lake in the middle? At last Mr. Charles Darwin told us why and how it was.

Long, long ago the sea bottom began to sink down lower and lower. Islands and continents were submerged into the great deep. The mountains and valleys, which now diversify the surface of the ocean's dark bottom, once stood out in sight of the blue sky; and many of the lofty peaks which we now see high above us were once hidden beneath the waters of the sea. These wonderful changes in the earth's surface were partly effected by earthquakes and partly by the subsidence of the land.

On the tops of the sunken mountains, the little polyps would start their work and build to the surface of the water, and so the atolls, or ring-islands, which now dot the whole surface of the Pacific Ocean are all built up from the tops of those submerged mountains. This accounts for their circular shape, and shows us also that they, too, like all other coral reefs, have been built in shallow water, and do not extend down into the depths of the ocean—no, not by the length of a high mountain.

Once there was a great continent joined to Australia and to New Guinea in the Pacific

Ocean, and now all that is left of it is a great number of atolls or islands marking the places where the mountain tops of the continent once stood.

Strange and unique life is found upon many of these atolls; creatures and plants whose formation is suited to the only subsistence possible upon a coral island.

One proof of the great age of the world is the gigantic construction of these minute coral polyps—so small that they are invisible to the natural eye.—*The Youth's World.*

Scenes in India.

THE RIVER INDUS.

THE Indus, which traverses the north-western side of India, is the great natural waterway in that part of the country. It takes its rise on the north side of the Himalaya mountains, 18,000 feet above sea level, and after travelling in a North-Westerly direction through Cashmere, its course is suddenly changed by the mountain ranges through which it has to pass. Taking a south-westerly direction it flows down through the Punjab, receiving in its course the waters from the 'five rivers' that give this part of the country its name. After leaving the Punjab behind, it skirts for hundreds of miles the edge of the great Indian desert, then on through the province of Sinde, and finally dividing itself into several branches it enters the Indian Ocean at different points. During its course it receives the waters of not less than ten principal streams that descend from the mountains.

Sometimes the Indus is spoken of as if it simply extended from the sea to Mooltan, but this is owing to the fact that near to the last-mentioned place it receives the waters of several tributaries, which bear different names. But apart from these tributaries it has a distinct course of its own right up to the Himalayas. For hundreds of miles after its rise it traverses a mountainous district which,

for more than six months each year, is covered with snow. After leaving the mountains it has a diversified character. In some places on its banks there is a good 'clayey' soil intermixed with sand, which is very fertile; but in many other parts its banks are covered with bushes or jungle-grass which, in some cases, grows to a great height.

In skirting the Indian desert, the footprints of various beasts of prey are everywhere to be seen on its eastern banks. This desert, which embraces 150,000 square miles, 'is not entirely sterile, but contains at intervals tracts of cultivable land; and the sandy portions are generally overgrown with coarse grass and jungle-shrubs after the rains. But this vegetation perishes completely in the hot months, and the true desert aspect is exhibited.'

The Indus is a longer river than the Ganges, but it has a less extensive basin. From Mooltan to the sea navigation is uninterrupted; but, beyond Mooltan, the river is in many places shallow and navigation is not so certain. Previous to the year 1844, great difficulties in respect to navigation existed, and exorbitant tolls were levied by the Ameers of Sinde on every passing trader; but since then these tolls have been removed, and the river has consequently recovered much of the importance of former times.

In ordinary circumstances, the Indus is in most places at least one mile in width, but in certain seasons it rises to a great height and increases its width to several miles. At such times it often changes its course, with the result that steamers occasionally run aground on some unsuspected sand bank. Near to the mouth of the river, the tides rise at full moon to the height of nine feet, and ebb and flow with much violence. Throughout the lower reaches especially, the river swarms with alligators, whose hard scales over their backs and sides seem to render them impervious to the musket shot. It also abounds with various species of fish.

On its banks, or in the neighbourhood where it flows, are the following towns:—Dera Ismael Khan and Dera Ghazé Khan, belonging to Afghanistan; Mittamcote, situated in the

BANKS OF THE INDUS.

Punjab; and Tatta, Kurrachee, Succer, Sehwin, Roree, and Hyderabad, in the province of Sinde. The two first-named towns acquire what little importance they possess through being on the caravan route from India to Candahar. Succer is a town of considerable importance, with an extensive fort garrisoned by European and native troops. 'Here the river is divided by a rocky island, on which there is an old Mohammedan mosque, called the Seven Sisters, after that number of princesses, who, it is said, are buried here beneath the seven cupolas which surmount the building.' Hyderabad, the capital of Sinde, is situated about four miles from the Indus, and has a population of 25,000. The swords, shields, spears, and matchlocks which are manufactured here have done much towards giving the town the fame that it possesses. Tatta is the ancient capital. It was a flourishing town in the time of Alexander the Great, who visited it as he descended the Indus with his army on

BANIAN TREES, INDIA.

his way to Greece. It was once noted for its fine silk, but nearly all its former greatness has disappeared, and it is now a poor-looking mud-built place. Some magnificent tombs, noted for their architectural beauty, are the only signs of its former importance.

The province of Sinde is greatly indebted to the Indus and its branches. In the neighbourhood of these streams the crops are abundant, but where their influence is not felt the country is barren and little better than desert.

BANIAN TREES.

There are many remarkably fine trees in India, especially along its southern shores. Whole forests of palmyra trees are to be seen in the neighbourhood of Tinnevelly and Madura, and some of them are an immense size, and are distinguished for great beauty and usefulness. 'This marvellous tree,' says the authoress of ' In Southern India,' ' which is the real staff of life to the people, covers many hundred square miles ; and though its lofty top is not so beautiful as the cocoa palm, with its crown of long graceful fronds, yet it is most picturesque and stately, and gives a thoroughly Oriental and varied aspect to the scene. The Shanars—worshippers of devils — who claim to be the original inhabitants of this part of the country, mount these branchless trees, sometimes to the height of eighty or ninety feet, to remove the sap or juice which has been drawn off in a small earthen pot at the top. This beverage is much used by the people, and is very refreshing, though it becomes intoxicating if left to ferment. This juice is called tadi ; hence probably the word toddy.' The cocoa-nut tree, which is exceedingly valuable to the natives, also abounds throughout India, and often grows to the height of sixty and even up to eighty feet. There is also the bamboo, the mimosa, and the tamarind, but the most unique and singular tree to be found in the country is the banian. Its branches send down shoots which take root and become additional stems to the parent tree. Milton thus describes it—

> 'Branching so broad and long, that in the ground
> The bending twigs take root, and daughters grow
> About the mother tree; a pillar'd shade
> High over arched and echoing walks between.'

Many of these trees are of immense size. Sometimes a single tree will cover three or four acres of ground, and will afford shelter for six or seven thousand persons. Unlike many other trees, the banian is not characterized by any great usefulness, except that of affording shelter from the burning rays of the sun. By many it is regarded as a sacred tree, and frequently Hindu temples are built under its spreading branches. In the neighbourhood of Broach there is a banian tree known by the name of Kuveer Bur, so called from a saint who is supposed to have planted it. It entirely covers a small island on the Herbudda river, and has been renowned for centuries, but it is not so large now as it was formerly.

Part of the soil on the island has been washed away, and with it has gone a portion of the immense tree, but it is still regarded as one of the noblest groves in the world. It has 350 chief trunks and more than 3,000 smaller stems. Its circumference round the principal stems alone is nearly 2,000 feet. Another banian tree not far from Barreah is said by Bishop Heber to be ' literally a grove rising from a single primary stem whose massive secondary trunks with their straightness, orderly arrangement, and evident connection with the parent stock, gives the general effect of a vast vegetable organ. The first impression which I felt on coming under its shade was, " What a noble place of worship ! " I was glad to find that it had not been debased, as I expected to find it by the symbols of idoltary, though some rude earthen figures of elephants were set up over a wicket leading to it, but at a little distance. I should exult in such a scene to collect a Christian congregation.' R. S.

Anecdotes About Hymns.

FROM THE GERMAN.

VII.—THE DYING MOTHER.

THE widow of the excellent Pastor Roller when upon her death-bed said, ' When I am in heaven I shall first look round to see my Saviour, through whose grace I am saved, then for my husband, then for my Lorchen (doubtless one of her children), then for my grandmother, for it was she who first brought me to God.' She fell asleep following with her lips a verse of the hymn 'Oh, God and Lord,' to which we alluded in a former anecdote. We give a free translation of the verse—

> Oh, Lord Jesus, I
> To the refuge fly '
> Of those wounds of Thine;
> Sin and death to nought
> Me I feel have brought,
> Yet that shelters mine.

Her son, who from 1811 to 1850 was pastor of a church near Dresden, said, on the occasion of this good mother's death, ' I thank you, good and loving mother, for all your love and kindness. Sleep sweetly, dear mother, and wake again on the resurrection morning. In Christ we shall meet again. Rest well, ye eyes that have so often wept, ye lips that gave so many loving kisses, ye hands that have so oft been raised to bless.' J. Y.

Sketches of the British Isles.

THE CHANNEL ISLANDS.

N the waters of the North Atlantic Ocean, and fringing the north-western coast of Europe, is the Archipelago known as the British Isles, consisting of four hundred and twenty inhabited islands, and over five thousand smaller interesting islets. The most northern point of the British Isles is Unst, in Shetland; and Jersey, in the Channel Islands, is the extreme southern point. The total land surface of the British Isles is over one hundred and twenty thousand square miles, being equal to one-thirteenth of the European continent. Geologists maintain that the British Isles, before the glacial period, were connected with the continent of Europe, their theory being supported by the identity of the plants and animals of the numerous islands of Great Britain with those of the Continent, oceanic islands having a distinct flora and fauna from those of continental isles. The charming islets of the Ecrehos, Bœuffetins, and Minquiers, located between Jersey and the shores of France, plainly indicate a former connection with the main-land, and thus confirm the supposition of a separation therefrom in, geologically-speaking, comparatively recent times. It is somewhat singular that while moles and toads are found in Jersey and Alderney, there are none of these, nor reptiles of any description, to be found in Guernsey, which lies nearer the ocean than the remainder of the Channel Islands.

The British Isles are situated in the centre of the land surface of the globe, which permits more outdoor labour to be performed throughout the days of the year than elsewhere in Europe. Emmerson remarks: 'The territory has a singular perfection. The climate is warmer by many degrees than it is entitled to by latitude. Neither hot nor cold, there is no hour in the whole year when one cannot work. Here we have a temperature which makes no exhaustive demand on human strength, but allows the attainment of the largest stature.' It was the boast of Charles II. that the British Isles 'invited men abroad more days in the year, and more hours in the day, than any other country.'

The Channel Islands are composed of a small group of islets lying off the north-west coast of France, the principal being Jersey, Guernsey, Alderney, and Sark. The others being the Casquets, Chausseys, Minquiers, Brecqhon, Burhon, Jethon, and Herm. The total land area is about seventy-five square miles. The total population of the Channel Islands in 1851 was over ninety thousand; it has gradually declined, for in 1881 it was only eighty-seven thousand.

The earlier history of the settlers is unwritten in book form, but it may be traced by the aid of the Cromlechs, Druidical remains, and other monuments of unhewn stone that are scattered throughout the islands. Probably the people who raised these rude temples belonged to the neolithic tribes of the Celtiberian race, who, becoming separated from the European continent during their sea wanderings by the combined action of tides, currents, and winds, were driven, and settled down upon the Channel Islands. Guernsey is referred to in the pages of the *Edda* --two distinct collections of Scandinavian literature, consisting, respectively, of prose and poetry. The 'Elder' *Edda* is a collection of lays that narrate the legends of Scandinavian gods and heroes, and was written in Iceland by Saemund Sigfusson during the years 1055-1132. The 'Younger,' or prose *Edda* is the production of an Icelander, Snorri Sturluson, who wrote about A.D. 1230. These ancient and interesting books had been lost for a considerable time, and were discovered in the years 1628 and 1643. These references to Guernsey in the *Edda*, together with the fact that implements and weapons of Viking character have been unearthed, are unmistakable proofs that the Channel Islands were, for a time at least, inhabited by the wandering and the pillaging Danish sea-rovers. It is more than probable that the islands were used by the Norsemen as depôts and places for reconnoitre during their attacks upon Neustra. For a brief period the islands were attached to Brittany. During the tenth century the Duchy of Normandy annexed the Cotentin—a peninsula on the north-west of Normandy, which became a stronghold of numerous barons and imposing wealthy abbeys. Many of the barons attended William in his conquest of England, and their services were rewarded by gifts of land. The names of some of the English aristocratic

treaty of St. Clair sur-Epte. The Normans however, did not introduce the feudal system in its completeness, as they did when they conquered England and made the parishes into manors, and allotted them to the powerful barons who settled therein.

In the Channel Islands, the barons, or seigneurs, generally, were absentee landlords, who received the rents from the allodial holders of the land. The resident, as in Norman-England, was not required to furnish soldiers for the king and country's protection. A

New Market, Interior (Channel Islands).

families are identical with the towns and villages of the Cotentin, notably such as Beaumont, Bruce, Carteret, Neville, and many others. The Channel Islands, along with the Cotentin, were seized and held by the powerful Dukes of Normandy, and were incorporated in that kingdom. The Normans introduced into the Channel Islands their own customs, institutions, and methods of government, which they had adopted from the legal system of the Franks, from which empire Normandy had been separated by the

system of parochial militia came into existence, that has been transmitted to the present time. When William of Normandy became King of England, these little islands, with their thinly populated communities, were added to . the English crown ; and although Normandy was eventually lost to the British empire, the Channel Islands have always remained a portion of the English realm.

The authenticated and written history of the Channel Islands commences during the twelfth century. When King John of England,

THE ECREHOW ISLETS—BETWEEN JERSEY AND FRANCE.

through his indifference and contempt for foreign rule, forfeited Normandy, Philip Augustus of France decreed the confiscation of the holdings of those Channel Islands seigneurs, who might adhere to the cause of John, and who, by their residence in Jersey, had become influential in moulding the opinions of local government. Gradually the seigneurs withdrew themselves from the sittings of the states, and the government was left to the mayors and rectors of the parishes, and the president of the councils was the lieutenant-governor, who was appointed by the crown. During the troublesome years that intervened between the reign of John and Henry VII., France made repeated efforts to conquer the islands. During the fourteenth century, the French for a few years held Guernsey, but, with help from Jersey, it was re-conquered by the English. Jersey, however, was taken by the French in 1461, and for about six years was subject to a French governor, who was ultimately driven therefrom by Sir R. Harleston.

During the reign of Henry VII. the privileges of the aristocracy and feudal jurisdictions were greatly curtailed, and the local militia was greatly improved. During the Stuart-Cromwellian period, Jersey took the side of Charles I., Guernsey, with the exception of Castle Cornet, which was with Charles, took the part of the Parliamentary leaders.

In 1651 the islands were conquered by Cromwell, who did not interfere with their ancient privileges, and specially excluded them from 'The Instrument of Government,' because they were governed by their own municipal councils.

In the year 1649, Charles II., then a young man, sought refuge in Jersey. After he came to the throne, France assumed a threatening attitude towards the Channel Islands, and the king reorganized and improved the local militia, and formed it into regiments. At that time the total population of the Channel Islands was about twenty-five thousand ; and the towns with their markets and institutions of various kinds began to increase in size and commercial importance.

Extensive covered markets have more recently been provided for the personal comfort of the buyers and sellers of the various branches of merchandise.

Early in the centuries, Christianity was introduced by missionaries from Brittany and Ireland, Dol becoming the centre of the Gallo-Roman hierarchy. About the twelfth century, when the islands were subject to Norman authority, the seat of ecclesiastical power was transferred from Dol to Contances, the ancient capital of the Cotentine. The exiled Huguenots fled in large numbers to the Channel Islands, and gave a considerable impetus to the doctrines of the Reformation, which were widely embraced by the native population. Considerable difficulty was experienced in the introduction of the ritual and practices of the Anglican Church. For a length of time the islands were subject to the spiritual authority of the Bishop of Contances, but in the year 1568 Queen Elizabeth was successful in attaching the islands to the diocese of Winchester, with which they have remained until the present time.

The Channel Islands afford a fine field of exploration to the geologist. Primary or granitic rocks are found in most of the islands. Alderney is composed of a mass of syenite, intermixed with hornblende, porphyry, and sandstone. On the north of Guernsey hard syenite is found, and on the south gneiss. Jersey contains a mixture of metamorphic rocks, conglomerates, and sandstones, accompanied with syenite and quartz, and large quantities of shale and blown sand. Sark is distinguished for its huge masses of very hard syenite with veins of greenstone and felspar. Granite is quarried in all the islands.

The Channel Islands are said to be 'a very costly appendage to the British crown.' Large sums of money have been spent in the erection of fortifications. In time of war their defence costs the home authorities fully £500,000 a year. The total amount of revenue collected in the islands, yearly, does not amount to £20,000.

ALBERT A. BIRCHENOUGH.

The Word 'Wife.'

HAT do you think the beautiful word 'wife' comes from ? It is the great word in which the English and Latin languages conquered the French and Greek. I hope the French will some day get a word for it instead of *femme.* But what do you think it comes from ? The great value of the Saxon words is that they mean something. Wife means 'weaver.' You must either be house-wives or house-moths ; remember that. In the deep sense, you must either weave men's fortunes, and embroider them, or feed upon and bring them to decay.

Wherever a true wife comes, home is always around her. The stars may be over her head, the glow-worm in the night's cold grass be the fire at her feet, but home is where she is, and for a noble woman it stretches far around her, better than houses ceiled with cedar or painted with vermilion—shedding the quiet light for those who else are homeless. This, I believe, is the woman's true place and power.

RUSKIN.

Cultivate Simplicity.

NE of the greatest charms of character is simplicity, but it is the charm which of all others appears to be most difficult of attainment or preservation. Simplicity is the note of real refinement, of thorough taste, and of genuine culture. The absence of it is the evidence of some form of immaturity, some kind of crudity of taste. The greatest things, the most beautiful things, and the most enduring things are always simple. Real elegance is a rare quality ; rare, apparently, because most people confuse it with some form of display or elaboration. There are countless houses where one finds every kind of comfort and luxury, but there are very few houses where one discovers real elegance, because in very few houses which represent large expenditures of money has the element of simplicity been preserved. Over-ornamentation, crowded rooms, and a general sense of oppressiveness are, as a rule, characteristics of most handsome homes. Simplicity is the exception : and yet simplicity is the infallible sign of genuine elegance. In mind and character, as the instruments of influence and of pleasure multiply, simplicity seems to slip away. There are few who can secure prosperity without parting with simplicity. First elaboration and then some false note of self-consciousness, inflation, or that kind of social pride which is only another name for vulgarity, are likely to manifest themselves. The man or woman who can preserve entire simplicity in a life which is constantly enlarging has a fine nature.

A Changeless Melody.

IME builds his arches one by one,
    A long, resounding nave,
        Which   echoes   clear   heaven's
            gospel tone
In rich, melodious wave :
    'God's love to man,
    Redemption's plan '—
This echo ne'er has found a grave.

Yet brain of busy man has tried,
    Adown the ages gone,
T'adjust the melody, ' Christ died,
    With harmonies His own.
        'To broaden thought'
        The purpose sought,
God's plan for man too narrow grown !

To-day the same attempted strain
    Makes discord. Futile aim !
'Twas nought before ; 'tis still in vain.
    Heaven's song is still the same—
        'Christ's blood is spilt
        To cleanse man's guilt,'
And life is only through His name.

ALICE ARMSTRONG.

The Origin of Volcanoes.

HE facts and descriptions contained in our last paper will have made it abundantly clear that volcanic eruptions are somehow connected with the action of heat, and with its passage from the interior of the earth to the surface. But the great question, which cannot as yet be said to be satisfactorily solved, is—Whence this heat? How is it produced?

For a long time the theory which held the field was that of the *interior fluidity of the earth.* This was part of the daring ' Nebular Hypothesis,' according to which the earth first existed as a vapour in the atmosphere of the sun. That atmosphere, it is supposed, once filled the whole space now included in our present planetary system. As the sun's atmosphere cooled it contracted, and threw off rings of vapour, which by the action of gravity and centrifugal force formed themselves into spheres or globes. These, cooling faster than the parent body, passed first into the liquid and then into the solid form, in which we now find our earth. The comparative volume of the earth in the solid and in the gaseous state is illustrated in Fig. 1. In Fig. 2 there is a fancy sketch of the earth circulating in space in the form of a gaseous star, while Fig. 3 gives the relative volumes of the solid crust and supposed fluid mass in the interior of our globe. The Nebular Hypothesis is strongly supported by the fact declared by Spectrum Analysis, that the chemical elements which compose the earth's crust exist also in a highly rarefied state in the atmosphere of the sun.

The considerations which are supposed to suggest central fluidity in the earth are as follows. 1. The increase of temperature as we descend into the bowels of the earth. The thermometer rises one degree Fahrenheit for every fifty or sixty feet we descend towards the interior, so that at some twenty or thirty miles below the surface the rocks ought to exist in a fluid or fused state. 2. Volcanoes, earthquakes, and hot springs prove, it is said, this immense central heat. These have not been local in their operation, but have appeared in every part of the world. 3. The shape of the earth is said to require some such supposition of fluidity. It is flattened at the poles and bulges slightly at the equator, which is just the form that would be taken by a fluid mass in rapid rotation. A solid sphere, being rigid, could not, it is contended, take this shape.

But against this conclusion several very strong objections have been urged. As to the increase of temperature as you descend from the surface, that is by no means uniform. But adopting, as Lyell says, the mean increase of one degree for every 65 feet of depth, ' we should reach the ordinary boiling point of water at rather more than two miles below the surface, and at the depth of about thirty-four miles should arrive at the melting point of iron,—a heat sufficient to fuse almost every known substance. At much greater depths and long before approaching the central nucleus, the heat would be so intense that we cannot conceive the external crust to resist fusion.' Lyell further asks, ' If the whole planet were composed of water covered with a spheroidal crust of ice fifty miles thick, and with an interior ocean having a central heat about two hundred times that of the melting point of ice : and if, between the surface and the centre there was every intermediate degree of temperature between that of melting ice and that of the central nucleus—could such a state of things last for a moment?' If we consider that the thickness of the earth's outer crust, supposed to cover the central sea of fire, bears the same proportion to the mass of the earth which a sheet of paper does to that of a fair-sized geographical globe, we shall find it difficult to imagine how such a frail barrier could resist such a mass of intensely heated fluid rock?

But, further, it has been cogently argued that the sun and moon ought to have a similar influence over the fluid ocean inside the earth, to that which these bodies exert over the ocean on our globe's surface—and all the more that the supposed central sea of fire is four thousand miles deep, and not simply four or five. How could a comparatively thin crust control the enormous force of such tides? Sir William Thomson, who has given very close attention to the matter, 'comes to the conclusion that it is perfectly impossible the crust of the earth can be so thin as hitherto supposed, and that to preserve its symmetry of

pressure at the centre of the earth. This will naturally tend to squeeze such bodies into solidity at the centre, although the actual temperature should be quite high enough to keep them fluid at the surface. It is a question of a contest between pressure and temperature—the former tending to solidify, and the latter to liquefy—and a contest in which pressure may, and no doubt does, gain the day.

On the whole, then, it seems more in harmony with all the facts and laws we know to

FIG. 1.—COMPARATIVE VOLUME OF THE EARTH IN THE SOLID (A) AND GASEOUS STATES (B).

shape, the earth on the whole must be as rigid as a globe of glass of equal size, and possibly as rigid as one of steel.'

Again, reason has been shown for believing that solidification would begin at the centre rather than at the surface. Water *expands* in the act of becoming solid; and so by pressure it can be kept liquid at nearly thirty degrees below its ordinary freezing point. But other bodies, like the rocks of which the earth is composed, *contract* in the act of becoming solid. Now take into account the enormous

say that the earth is probably more or less solid to its centre. If fluid, it is either like treacle or half-melted wax; or the thinner fluidity exists in parts—'enormous cavities filled with fluid rock which has hitherto escaped solidification from local causes, and exists at enormous pressure, bursting forth in weak places of the earth's crust, and giving rise to volcanic phenomena.'

There can be little question that steam is an active agency in volcanic eruptions. Sir John Herschell has pointed out that 'out of 225

volcanoes, which are known to have been in eruption within the last one hundred and fifty years, there is only a single instance of one more than 320 miles from the sea; and even that one, Mount Demawand in Persia, is on the edge of the Caspian, the largest of all the inland seas.' Mr. Dana, who has made most valuable and original observations on the volcanoes of the Sandwich Islands, speaks of the immense volume of atmospheric water which the porous lava must absorb. It is to this source alone that he attributes the production of the steam which propels melted volcanic matter to the summit of cones three miles high. The geysers of Iceland prove what a prominent part steam must play in volcanic eruptions generally. The expansive power of other gases, such as carbonic, sulphurous, and muriatic acid, must also be taken into account.

Sir Humphrey Davy referred volcanic effects to chemical action. He supposed that sea water penetrating to the metals stored in the earth in an unoxidized state, would cause sufficient heat to be evolved to melt the surrounding rocks, and would set free gaseous matters in volume large enough to cause an eruption. He observed that the fumes which escaped from the Vesuvian lava deposited common salt—but not finding hydrogen amongst the gases evolved from the crater, he was disposed to surrender his theory. But later investigations have shown that hydrogen *is* disengaged in large quantities. M. Abich says he clearly detected the flame of hydrogen in the eruption of Vesuvius in 1834. And as Dr. Danbeny suggests, the hydrogen arising from decomposed water would unite with sulphur to form sulphuretted hydrogen. This gas, meeting with sulphurous acid in the presence of steam, would again be decomposed, the hydrogen of the one, uniting with the oxygen of the other to form water, while the excess of sulphurous acid alone would escape into the atmosphere. This fully accounts for the comparative absence of both hydrogen and sulphurous acid, said to have been noted in many eruptions. By chemical interaction they have simply taken other forms.

It is clear that the subject yet needs much elucidation; and volcanic action seems to require many causes, and not any single one,

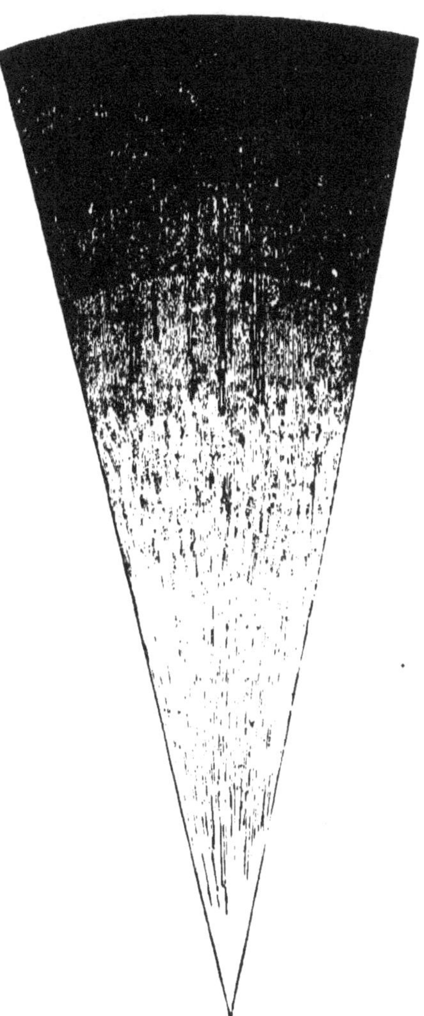

Fig. 3.—Relative Volumes of the Solid Crust and supposed Fluid Mass of the Earth.

for its full explanation. The era that is evidently opening for electrical science may yet add something from that side to the solution of the mystery of burning mountains, earthquakes, and boiling springs.

Current Topics.

THE ART OF PUBLIC SPEAKING.

N his rectorial address to the students of St. Andrew's University the other day, Lord Dufferin made some apt remarks upon oratory. This is always an interesting subject, and no one can deny that it is an important one. The art of saying what you think pleasantly and impressively is a desirable accomplishment anywhere and at all times. But in a country where speech is free, and the government is democratic, the man with the gift of oratory is sure to wield a great influence. Whether he be on the platform or in the pulpit, at the bar or on the floor of the House of Commons, the orator is the master of the situation. It is sometimes said that the power of oratory is not so great as it was. The newspaper editor, it is said, sways a greater influence than the public speaker, and the press is destroying the pulpit. This, however, is far from being the case. If any such change be taking place, it is only because the art of writing is more highly cultivated than the art of speaking. The man who wields a facile pen no doubt uses a mightier weapon than the sword, but the master of the human voice has at his command an instrument more potent and persuasive than either.

Oratory has never been very successfully cultivated in this country. And yet, as Lord Dufferin remarked, the English orator addresses the greatest audience in history. He employs a language which is already dominant in the world, and which is destined to cover the better part of three of its five continents. Is it not a pity that we don't learn to speak it more effectively? We have had a few great orators, certainly, but it is universally admitted that the average Englishman is a poor talker. In fact he rather prides himself on a blunt, brusque manner. Anything else would have an air of artificiality about it, which his soul abhors. And so, whilst it is quite right to labour assiduously for perfection in music and art, whilst the slightest literary fault cannot be overlooked in an essay, to pay any regard to the style of a spoken address is considered to be a manifestation of childish vanity. A book with a mistake here and there shows 'signs of haste,' but a speech expressed in stately language 'smells of the lamp.' The speech, in fact, is condemned because it manifests the care which the book is condemned for lacking. Thus it appears you are expected to study everything but your elocution. That will come naturally if at all.

Orators, like poets, are born, not made. Just so, but even the poet requires to put himself through a severe course of training before he can fully display the powers with which he has been endowed. Some people think that the orator can dispense with such training, but it is a mistake. If ever a man was a born orator that man surely was a Demosthenes, whose voice ruled Athens, and whose speeches are still regarded as the finest specimens of eloquence the world has ever seen. And yet when he began, he failed again and again. His carefully prepared harangues only gained him nicknames and ridicule. But for the advice of some friends, he would have retired in despondency. They, however, assured him that the causes of his failure might be surmounted, and he determined to make the effort. And he went to work in no half-hearted way. He stammered, he had a lisp, he was short of breath, and feeble in body. He strengthened his voice by speaking against the waves of the sea, he strengthened his wind by speaking as he walked up mountains, and he improved his utterance by articulating with pebbles in his mouth. He shut himself in a cave for weeks together, and shaved one side of his head to prevent him being tempted to go out, so that he might cultivate his art.

So, too, Curran, the Irishman whom Lord Byron declared to be the greatest orator of his time, only acquired his power by incessant toil. To overcome his stuttering speech and his provincial accent, he read aloud every day, imitating the tones of the most skilful speakers. His person was short and stunted, and he constantly recited before a glass, 'to acquire such gesticulation as was best adapted to his imperfect stature.' Another Irish orator of even wider fame, the noble Grattan, was so diligent in his early practice of the art that his landlady was filled with sad misgivings. 'What a sad thing,' she would say, 'to see the poor young gentleman all day talking to somebody called Mr. Speaker, and there is no Mr. Speaker in the house except himself.' The cases indeed are rare when such elocutionary drill is not required to prepare the speaker for his task. The easy flow of words, the distinct enunciation, and the graceful action which you so admire in the accomplished orator, are the result of downright hard work and severe discipline.

The best way of preparing a speech is much disputed. Some write every word and commit to memory (but they are careful not to let this be known) ; others write and commit portions of their speeches ; some trust only to a few notes, and others denounce the use of paper altogether. Elaborate preparation has somehow come to be regarded as a weakness. There are people who even think it sinful to prepare a religious address ; and a writer in the *Spectator* newspaper affirms that a speaker who spends time in polishing up the language of the speech he is about to deliver, is not a man whose judgment can be safely followed in public affairs. Such opinions are manifestly absurd. If ever a man obeyed the impulses of the Divine Spirit, that man was John Wesley, and yet his sermons betoken careful preparation. It is admitted by all that Demosthenes was one of the most sagacious and patriotic men of his time, and yet he would spend weeks in the preparation of a single address. Every sentence was carefully written out beforehand and committed to memory. This, too, was the plan of many of

the most distinguished of English orators. Curran went so far as to deny the possibility of anything worth hearing being produced without study. All his own striking passages—his ' white horses,' as he called them—were elaborately prepared. This, too, was the method pursued by some of the most distinguished orators of later times, as, for instance, by Dr. Punshon in the pulpit, and Mr. Joseph Cowen in the House of Commons.

This memoriter style has, however, its drawbacks. Lord Dufferin compares it to swimming on corks, and in case of a lapse of memory the breakdown would be instantaneous and complete. Sometimes, too, the prepared address is scarcely appropriate to the circumstances in which it is delivered. We have all heard of the preacher who was so indiscreet as to address the congregation as ' my *readers ;* ' and Lord Dufferin tells of a member of the French Chamber who, in the midst of the most profound silence, exclaimed, 'In vain does your clamour try to stifle my voice ; your rude howls do not intimidate me.' But this was not so bad as Quinctilian's orator, who was pleading against Cassius Severus. Suddenly stopping short, he cried out to his opponent, ' Why do you fix on me that angry scowl? ' ' I,' said Cassius, surprised, ' I was not even thinking of you ; but since you have written it, I am ready to oblige,' at the same time making a hideous grimace which threw the audience into fits of laughter. Such blunders, one thinks, might have easily been avoided by the greatest slave to the paper, but there are other dangers to be guarded against. The Lord Rector, who seems to have been in a playful mood, warned the St. Andrew's students to be careful, if they did write their speech, not to lose the manuscript. An unfortunate member of the House of Commons, he told them, o one occasion, came to his place primed with a great oration, but was so unhappy as to drop the manuscript. A mischievous colleague picked it up, and brought it to Sir Thomas Wyse, who had an extraordinary faculty of learning by heart. Some other business being on hand enabled this gentleman to retire to a committee room, and [duly prepare himself.

When the discussion came on, he watched his opportunity, and contrived to catch the Speaker's eye at the opportune moment. A great number of people had been let into the secret, and were watching the effect produced by the stolen thunder upon its rightful proprietor. At first he showed signs of being pleased with support from so unexpected a quarter; but when gradually he recognized his own well-polished periods flowing forth from alien lips, the look of surprise, indignation, and confusion which passed over his countenance was extremely comical.

The faculty of impromptu speech is what is evidently desired by the public men of the present day. The stately, ornate style of the Augustan age of English oratory has gone out of fashion, and the orator of to-day generally speaks in the style of an animated conversation. This is the style of speech most suitable for debate, and certainly it is the natural manner of a man who speaks on the spur of the moment. Mr. Gladstone is its greatest master, and when touched by something a previous speaker has said in debate, he often springs to his feet and delivers a speech of forty or fifty minutes' length, which, for felicity of language and beauty of arrangement, will compare favourably with the most laboured productions of other men. Such a power is a great endowment, but it is not to be acquired without previous study. 'The thought of a man who finds himself upon his legs, dilating upon a theme with which he is familiar, may be very far from being his first thought; it may be the cream of his meditations warmed by the glow of his heart.' This is the opinion of Mr. Spurgeon, who is almost as great a master of this style of speech in the pulpit as is Mr. Gladstone on the platform. He gives an amusing account of the way his powers were once put to the test. He was to preach in a certain chapel on one occasion, but having been detained on the railway, when he arrived, all breathless with running, he found the place crowded and another minister in the pulpit preaching. Seeing Mr. Spurgeon appear at the front door, however, the preacher stopped and asked him to come up and finish the sermon. Having ascertained what was the text, and how far it had been developed, he without hesitation took up the discourse at that point and finished its argument. But then, he explains, the 'minister was my grandfather, and in the second place the text was, " By grace are ye saved, through faith, and that not of yourselves, it is the gift of God." Any man,' he says, 'must have been a more foolish animal than that which Balaam rode, if at such a juncture he had not found a tongue.' His advice is therefore, 'Do not attempt to be impromptu unless you have well studied the theme—this paradox is a counsel of prudence.'

Mr. Beecher was an impromptu speaker. Some one once asked him if he never lost the thread of his discourse. 'Of course I do,' said Beecher. 'And what do you do then?' 'Oh,' said he, 'I simply stamp and holler till I find it again, and the newspapers say next morning, "At this point the reverend gentleman was uncommonly eloquent."' It is an easy thing to 'holler' for a man with a good flow of language; and such people are often tempted to think that preparation is unnecessary. Like Snug, the joiner, who acted the part of the lion, 'they can do it extempore, for it is nothing but roaring.' Successful impromptu speaking is really thinking aloud. Charles James Fox, one of the most brilliant debaters who ever lived, acquired the habit by constant practice. 'During five whole sessions,' he used to say, 'I spoke every night but one, and I regret only that I did not speak on that night too. Mr. Spurgeon gives some valuable hints on this point. The problem is to link thought with speech, and he thinks it would assist a man in i's solution if he endeavoured in his private musings to think aloud. 'So has this become habitual to me,' he says, 'that I find it very helpful to be able, in private devotion, to pray with my voice; reading aloud is more beneficial to me than the silent process, and when I am mentally working out a sermon, it is a relief to me to speak to myself as the thoughts flow forth.'

There can be no doubt that young speakers ought at first to carefully write out their addresses, whether they commit them to memory or not. Lord Dufferin recommended to his hearers a suggestion made to him by a privy councillor, who was a very powerful speaker, and who was able to hold the attention of the House of Commons for long periods of time. His plan was first to get thoroughly saturated with a knowledge of the subject, and then to write out his speech five or six times, each time destroying the sheets without looking at them. In this way he not only got into his head the articulated structure of his speech, but having clothed the same ideas over and over again with different forms of expression, when he went down to deliver himself at the House of Commons he had such a wealth of language at his disposal that he never had to hesitate for a word, or stumble over a single sentence. This would be a capital practice for a young man who desires to become a good extempore speaker. Let him first of all draft an outline of the argument he intends to pursue, and then clothe it over and over again with language. But let no man think he can speak well, whatever his powers of expression, upon any subject with which he has not made himself familiar.

After all is done and said, however, each one must choose the method that he finds most adapted to his own powers. And let us not forget the dictum of the old philosopher who held that a good orator must be a good man. If a speaker can impress his audience with the fact that he is a man of good principle, good sense, and goodwill towards the people he addresses, he will, says Quinctilian, persuade more powerfully than by the strongest arguments.   M. P. D.

The Tapestry Weavers.

LET us take to our hearts a lesson—
    no lesson can braver be—
From the ways of the tapestry
    weavers on the other side of
    the sea.
Above their heads the pattern hangs: they
    study it with care.
The while their fingers deftly work, their
    eyes are fastened there.

They tell this curious thing, besides, of the
    patient plodding weaver:
He works on the wrong side evermore, but
    works for the right side ever.
It is only when the weaving stops, and the
    web is loosed and turned,
That he sees his real handiwork—that his
    marvellous skill is learned.

Ah! the sight of its delicate beauty, how it
    pays him for all his cost!
No rarer, daintier work than his was ever
    done by the frost.
Then the master bringeth him golden hire,
    and giveth him praise as well;
And how happy the heart of the weaver is
    no tongue but his own can tell.

The years of man are the looms of God, let
    down from the place of the sun,
Where'n we are weaving always, till the
    mystic web is done—
Weaving blindly, but weaving surely, each
    for himself his fate.
We may not see how the right side looks:
    we can only weave and wait.

But, looking above for the pattern, no weaver
    need have fear.
Only let him look clear in'o heaven—the Per-
    fect Pattern is there.
If he keeps the face of our Saviour for ever
    and always in sight,
His toil shall be sweeter than honey, his
    weaving is sure to be right.

And when his task is ended, and the web
    is turned and shown,
He shall hear the voice of the Master. It
    shall say to him, ' Well done!'
And the white-winged angels of heaven, to
    bear him thence shall come down;
And God for his wage shall give him, not
    coin, but a golden crown.

IN taking revenge, a man is but his enemy's equal; in passing it by, he is his superior.

O TELL ME, STRANGERS!

2 SOLO—And if I take the narrow way
    O, will it lead to heaven,—
    Where every sorrow will be past,
    And every sin forgiven?
CHORUS—O yes! tho' darksome is the path,
    Bright joys are set before thee;
    But linger not, there's danger here,
    Poor wanderer, we implore thee.

3 SOLO—Then pilgrims I will go with you,
    Too long I've been a stranger,
    I'll choose the straight and narrow road,
    Nor linger here in danger.
CHORUS—Then welcome, welcome to our hearts,
    Poor weary, wand'ring brother!
    We'll tread awhile the stormy road,
    For who would choose the other.

O TELL ME, STRANGERS!

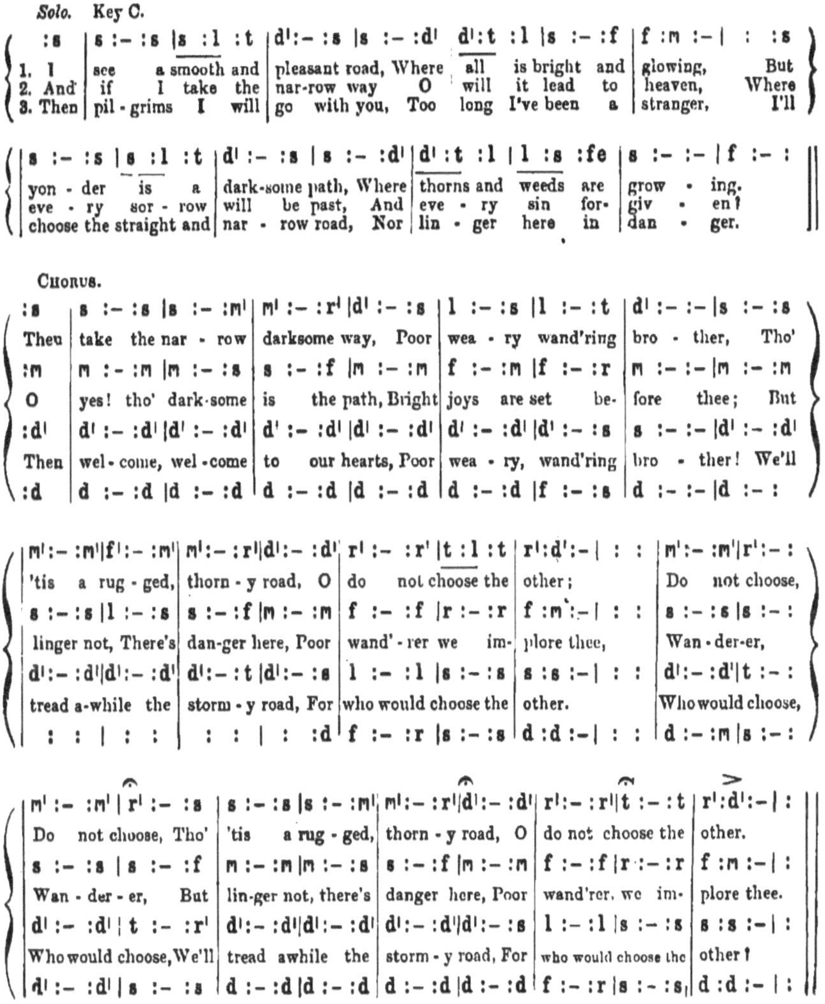

Solo. Key C.

```
:s | s :- :s |s :l :t | d':- :s |s :- :d' | d':t :l |s :- :f | f :m :- | : :s
```

1. I | see a smooth and | pleasant road, Where | all is bright and | glowing, But
2. And | if I take the | nar-row way O | will it lead to | heaven, Where
3. Then | pil - grims I will | go with you, Too | long I've been a | stranger, I'll

```
s :- :s |s :l :t | d' :- :s |s :- :d' | d':t :l |l :s :fe | s :- :- |f :- :
```

yon - der is a | dark-some path, Where | thorns and weeds are | grow - ing.
eve - ry sor - row | will be past, And | eve - ry sin for- | giv - en?
choose the straight and | nar - row road, Nor | lin - ger here in | dan - ger.

Chorus.

```
:s | s :- :s |s :- :m' | m':- :r' |d' :- :s | l :- :s |l :- :t | d' :- :- |s :- :s
:m | m :- :m |m :- :s | s :- :f |m :- :m | f :- :m |f :- :r | m :- :- |m :- :m
:d'| d' :- :d' |d' :- :d'| d' :- :d' |d' :- :d'| d' :- :d' |d' :- :s | s :- :- |d' :- :d'
:d | d :- :d |d :- :d | d :- :d |d :- :d | d :- :d |f :- :s | d :- :- |d :- :
```

Then | take the nar - row | darksome way, Poor | wea - ry wand'ring | bro - ther, Tho'
O | yes! tho' dark-some | is the path, Bright | joys are set be- | fore thee; But
Then | wel - come, wel -come | to our hearts, Poor | wea - ry, wand'ring | bro - ther! We'll

```
m':- :m'|f':- :m'| m':- :r'|d':- :d'| r' :- :r' |t :l :t | r':d':- | : : | m':- :m'|r':- :
s :- :s |l :- :s | s :- :f |m :- :m | f :- :f |r :- :r | f :m':- | : : | s :- :s |s :- :
d':- :d'|d':- :d'| d':- :t |d':- :s | l :- :l |s :- :s | s :s :- | : : | d':- :d'|t :- :
 : : | : : | : : | : :d | f :- :r |s :- :s | d :d :- | : : | d :- :m |s :- :
```

'tis a rug - ged, | thorn - y road, O | do not choose the | other; | Do not choose,
linger not, There's | dan-ger here, Poor | wand' - rer we im- | plore thee, | Wan - der-er,
tread a-while the | storm - y road, For | who would choose the | other. | Who would choose,

```
m' :- :m' | r' :- :s | s :- :s |s :- :m'| m':- :r'|d':- :d'| r':- :r'|t :- :t | r':d':- | :
s :- :s | s :- :f | m :- :m |m :- :s | s :- :f |m :- :m | f :- :f |r :- :r | f :m :- | :
d' :- :d' | t :- :r' | d':- :d'|d':- :d'| d':- :d'|d':- :s | l :- :l |s :- :s | s :s :- | :
d' :- :d' | s :- :s | d :- :d |d :- :d | d :- :d |d :- :d | f :- :r |s :- :s| d :d :- | :
```

Do not choose, Tho' | 'tis a rug - ged, | thorn - y road, O | do not choose the | other.
Wan - der - er, But | lin-ger not, there's | danger here, Poor | wand'rer, we im- | plore thee.
Who would choose, We'll | tread awhile the | storm - y road, For | who would choose the | other?

The Story of the Catacombs.

THE catacombs are numbered amongst the wonders of ancient Rome. The rocky soil beneath the city, being of volcanic origin, although too pliable for ordinary building material, possessed a sufficient consistency to admit of excavations, without the necessity of underground substructure, or artificial framework of any description. These honey-combed recesses consist of labyrinthal corridors, winding streets, and vaulted chambers, that intersect each other in every direction. If they were placed in continuous line, they would reach a distance of from eight to nine hundred miles. They were constructed without the mechanical appliances and rock-blasting explosives of the nineteenth century. During the early years of Christianity, from six to seven millions of Christians were buried herein. Jerome, writing in the fourth century, says: 'When I was a boy, being educated at Rome, I used every Sunday, in company with others of my own age and tastes, to visit the sepulchres of the apostles and martyrs, and go into the crypts dug into the heart of the earth. The walls on either side are lined with bodies of the dead, and so intense is the darkness as to seemingly fulfil the words of the prophet, "They go down alive to Hades." Here and there is light let in to mitigate the gloom. As we advance the words of the poet are brought to mind: " Horror on all sides, the very silence fills the soul with dread." '

Charles Dickens, during a continental tour, visited this remarkable city of the dead, and gives the following graphic word-picture of the scene and its teachings:—'A gaunt Franciscan Friar, with a wild, bright eye, was our only guide down into this profound and dreadful place. The narrow ways and openings hither and thither, coupled with the dead and heavy air, soon blotted out, in all of us, any recollection of the track by which we had come ; and I could not help thinking, good heaven ! if, in a sudden fit of madness, he should dash the torches out, or if he should be seized with a fit, what would become of us. On we wandered, among martyrs' graves ; passing great subterranean vaulted roads, diverging in all directions, and choked up with heaps of stones, that thieves and robbers may not take refuge there, and form a population under Rome, even worse than that which lies between it and the sun. Graves, graves, graves ; graves of men, of women, of little children, murdered with their parents ; graves with the palm of martyrdom roughly cut into their stone boundaries ; and little niches made to hold a vessel of the martyr's blood ; graves of some who lived down here for years together, ministering to the rest, and preaching truth, and hope, and comfort from the rude altars that bear witness to their fortitude at this hour ; more roomy graves, but far more terrible, where hundreds being surprised, were hemmed in and walled up ; buried before death, and killed by slow starvation. When I thought how Christian men have dealt with one another ; how, perverting our most merciful religion, they have hunted down and tortured, burnt, and beheaded, strangled, slaughtered, and oppressed each other, I pictured to myself an agony surpassing any that this dust had suffered, with that breath of life yet lingering in it; and how those great and constant hearts would have been shaken—how they would have quailed and drooped—if a foreknowledge of the deeds that professing Christians would commit in the great name for which they died, could have rent them with its own unutterable anguish on the cruel wheel, and the bitter cross, and in the fearful fire.'

A thrilling incident is related of a young artist, who had more zeal than prudence, who attempted to explore the catacombs, with only a torch-light and a thread for a guide. As he wandered through the underground passages, deciphering the inscriptions, and sketching the monuments, he became so absorbed, that, unconsciously, he slipped the ball of thread from his hands, and had proceeded a considerable distance before he discovered his loss. He retraced his steps, and had only travelled a few paces when his light went out. He was standing upon the brink of an open grave. His brain became confused at the thought of dying in such a place. He stumbled and fell, and providentially his hands struck the lost ball of thread : step by step he proceeded to the entrance, and with feelings of thankfulness gained the outside world of ceaseless activity.

The ordinary entrance to the catacombs consisted of a ladder, at the foot of which was a spacious street, with branching pathways leading to various sized chambers. On both sides of the main thoroughfares, the perpendicular walls were pierced with niches where coffins containing the dead were reverently stored away. The chambers were handsomely adorned with decorative art, and the walls were enscrolled with suitable quotations from the sacred Scriptures. In the centre of the main street was a capacious open square, used in the days of persecution by the Christians as a place for worship. The liberal use of ointments and perfumes in the anointing of the dead, destroyed all objectionable odours, and rendered the catacombs habitable. At the extreme ends of the corridors the roof was perforated with small apertures to let in the light. Where the refugees hid, the caverns were absolutely dark ; and by extinguishing their lights they were completely safe from the revenge of their enemies, who lost their way amongst the intricacies and winding paths of the vaulted chambers. The depth of these vaults was considerable, and, in some places, two and even three storeys were constructed above each other, thus presenting the appearance of an underground city. For months together, without a glimpse of day, the persecuted Christians lived in these gloomy recesses of the dead. The aged and poor were maintained by their friends, and also by the enterprising youth, who found employment in the city during the day, and returned with provisions during the shelter of the night.

Antiquarians have surprisingly asked, How could such extensive vaults be made in the days of severe persecution ? In answer thereto it must be remembered, by way of explanation, that the burial of the dead was considered a religious act, and the laws of imperial Rome protected the burial places of the dead, even those of slaves and criminals. Burial places could not be sold by their owners, nor alienated from their original purpose, and severe punishments were inflicted upon those who attempted any interference with them. The wealthy circles of Rome attached chambers to their burial places for the entertainment of relatives and friends who visited the resting-places of their dead. The Christians availed themselves of this custom and protection by extending the corridors of the catacombs, and holding therein their meetings of praise and thanksgiving. The government of Rome did not interfere in any way with the catacombs until the year 253, when Valerian issued a protest prohibiting the Christians 'to assemble in those places that they call cemeteries.' During the following year this law was repealed, and throughout the remainder of the century the Christians sought the retirement of the catacombs. About the year 300 Pope Sixtus II., along with his deacons, were cruelly murdered by the representatives of the Emperor, in the catacombs of Pretexatus, because he had disobeyed the laws of Valerian. At the termination of the persecution of Diocletian, the catacombs, along with other property, were transferred to the Bishop of Rome. During the fourth century the Christians buried their dead in the cemeteries above ground, and with the commencement of the fifth century they ceased burying their friends in the catacombs. The Emperor Constantine decorated the graves, and built monuments over the resting-places of the principal martyrs. Christian pilgrims flocked from all lands to inspect the catacombs, when wider and more convenient entrances were made for their convenience. When the Goths invaded Rome in the year 557, they ransacked the catacombs with the anticipation of finding hidden treasures therein. In 756 the Lombards wrought greater havoc. Paul I., lamenting the sacrilege of the spoilers, caused the bodies of the martyrs to be removed and reburied in the churches within the city walls, and for seven centuries the catacombs were practically forgotten.

In May, 1578, by the merest accident, the attention of Christendom was again concentrated upon the catacombs. Their re-discovery was occasioned by a landslip. Antonio Bosio, the 'Columbus of the subterranean world,' devoted a lifetime to the monumental and literary examination of the subject. There is an air of gallantry attached to the work of this *Old Mortality*, who, with hatchet in hand, forced his way through the . underground passages and crumbling graves, and recovered from forgetfulness the inscriptive memorials and monograms that had been traced fifteen centuries back by loving hands in memory of their dead.

'Inspired and sustained by a lofty enthusiasm, Bosio spent six-and-thirty years groping among these gloomy corridors, deciphering the half-effaced inscriptions, and making drawings of the remains of early Christian art. So habituated did he become to this troglodytic existence, that the Cimmerian gloom of the catacombs was more grateful to his eyes than the light of day, which dazzled and blinded him. His labours were prodigious, and often both severe and perilous. He had frequently to force a passage with his hands through the accumulated rubbish of centuries, and was constantly in danger, in the zeal of exploration, of being lost in the windings of the galleries, from which danger he had some narrow escapes. In his great work he describes himself as rushing along with breathless haste, the desire with which he burned adding wings to his weary feet. Again he is creeping serpent-wise through the low and crumbling passages, consoling himself for the difficulty and discomfort by the thought that this lowly attitude befitted the humble and reverent spirit in which a place consecrated by such memories ought to be approached. But he was rewarded for all his toil by the discovery of pictures bright with the colours of yesterday, and characters still sharp and angular from the primeval graving tool.'

D'Israeli, the elder, in speaking of the Her-

culean labours of Bosio, describes him as 'taking with him a hermit's meal for the week, this new Pliny often descended into the bowels of the earth by lamplight, clearing away the sand and ruins, till some tomb broke forth or some inscription became legible, tracing the mouldering sculpture, and catching the fading picture. Thrown back into the primitive ages of Christianity amidst the local impressions, the historian of the Christian catacombs collected the memorials of an age and of a race which were hidden beneath the earth.'

In the Oratorian Library in Rome are thousands of pages of manuscript, descriptive of the catacombs, written by the hand of Bosio, and still preserved as an illustration of his enthusiasm and genius. There is a tinge of sadness attached to his literary labours, for he was not permitted to see the printed book. While engaged in writing the last chapter, he was called to his reward. His book, however, appeared in 1632, and in less than forty years, eight editions were printed in the Italian, Latin, and German languages. Boldetti and Marangon were amongst Bosio's successors in exploring the catacombs. By a sad fatality their life-work was rendered useless, for their voluminous manuscripts were accidentally destroyed by fire.

During this century, De Rossi has devoted a longer period of his life to the study of the catacombs than any of his predecessors; having the advantage of the literary and archæological researches of more than two centuries, he was enabled to throw considerable new light upon the story of the catacombs. One of the special features being the fixture with 'chronological precision' of the exact periods of sculpture and decorative art that obtained in pre-Constantinian times.

ALBERT A. BIRCHENOUGH.

(To be continued.)

A GRAIN of corn, an infant's hand
May sow upon an inch of land,
Whence twenty stalks may rise and yield
Enough to plant a little field;
That field supply sufficient bread
Whereby an army may be fed.

SPRINGTIME :

A Magazine for Our Young Men and Maidens.

Vol. VI. No. 8.]   AUGUST, 1891.   [Price Twopence.

A Bad Calculation.

By ROBERT HIND,

Author of ' Crosby Dalton: Local Preacher and Village Demagogue,' ' The Ruby Pendant,' &c.

CHAPTER XV.

PARTED.

' They met and spoke and parted yet once more,
So calmly that the woman understood
Her hope indeed had gone away for good.'
ROBERT BUCHANAN.

URING the two days in which Rye Harland had been thinking out the first serious problem that had ever demanded her attention, Arthur Brixton had not been mentally inactive. His interview with Mr. Harland had given him to understand that his relations with his best friends were seriously endangered, and that they would not pardon him for leaving the Methodist church, even if by doing so he were to become the bishop of Rockingham.

What course was he to take ? The position was a very difficult one. For a little while he conscientiously attempted to reconcile himself to the thought of becoming a Methodist minister after he had finished his course at the university. He would work hard there, and he felt sure would distinguish himself. This would give him a certain advantage, and cause him to be very much in request, so that almost from the first he would take a leading position.

But, on the other hand, there were the limitations in the sphere of work and influence ; whilst lying completely outside his life, with its gates barred against him, would be the world of wealth and fashion and social power into which he longed to enter, and among whose people he wanted to play his part. And he felt he could not brook the idea.

He was too clever and calculating to imagine he had taken a full account of the situation when his thoughts had led him thus far. The Harlands were still to satisfy, and he could not afford just yet to do without them.

His reflections, taking this turn, made him uneasy. A time had been, and not far back either, when the realization of what was involved in his thoughts would have stricken his heart with a mortal dread of himself, and he would have sought earnestly for a worthier frame of mind. Even now he was not without a feeling of shame. But it was not to be denied that he had deteriorated morally, and allowed his unhealthy ambitions to make it possible for him to think out plans of action of which formerly he would have been incapable.

And so it came to pass that instead of allowing generous impulses to rule him, he was yielding himself up entirely to the consideration of questions of profit and loss. It was sad. Common gratitude should have prevented it. An ordinary sense of righteousness should have held him from it. He owed something to the man who had been his benefactor, and he owed more to the girl who had entrusted him with her all—with herself.

It was not pleasant to look in his face, when, in his little bedroom, he was examining his position on all its sides. 'There is nothing hid that shall not be revealed,' was once asserted by Him of Galilee, and the selfishness of Arthur Brixton revealed itself in the unpleasant expression of his face. And the face was so young, and withal so handsome.

Still he persevered with his task—the task of thinking out the situation. He would not, if he could avoid doing so, break with the Harlands, for in the enjoyment of their friendship he had more of what he longed for than he had gained in any other quarter. In the future he might be able to do without them, but not now. And after awhile he thought he had found out a way of meeting the emergency.

'You must allow me a little time, Rye,' he pleaded, when next they met, and the subject uppermost in the minds of both had been introduced. Those pleading tones had a strange effect upon her. They were not usual to Arthur, and, despite her natural tenderness and her pity for every kind of suffering, they did not improve him in her estimation.

'I hope I am not unreasonable, Arthur, but you have had some days to make up your mind. I am disappointed that it has not been easy for you to decide.'

'We do not appear to look at the matter in the same way. You think it should be easy to decide, whereas to me it involves so much either way that I have found it almost impossible to conclude which is right and which will be best.'

'How much more time will you want?'

'If you would only allow me to defer my decision till the end of my university course.'

'Why so long? It cannot surely take so much time for you to think out what will be right.'

'But I cannot tell what influence university life may have on me. It may give me a greater appreciation of Nonconformity; on the other hand, it may lead me to believe it would be wrong to be anything else than a Churchman.'

To Arthur, this reasoning was conclusive. He saw in it no sophistry, neither was there anything in the general position of which he thought he should be ashamed. It was to him an evidence of breadth of view and freedom from prejudice. But it did not satisfy his friend.

'We are coming to an understanding, Arthur,' Rye said in a quiet, firm tone of voice. 'Supposing in that coming time you were convinced it would be wrong for you to be anything but a Churchman, and I were quite as certain it would be wrong for me to leave Methodism, that would be a rather awkward situation.'

Arthur did not at once reply. He could not do so. When at last he spoke, his words were hardly to the point.

'How clever you are, Rye!'

She smiled faintly, but there was no feeling of pleasure in her heart.

'That is scarcely the question. You see my difficulty. Is there a way out of it? If there is, I should be glad to be informed.'

'You would not be very self-willed, would you?'

'We were speaking of right and wrong. The words were your own. You could not think of doing wrong yourself. I could not respect you if you were to go against your conscience. But surely you would never ask me to do what was wrong.'

Arthur had not reached the end of his arguments. He thought that man had the right to choose a career, that it was woman's duty to acquiesce, and that it would be wrong for her to object to this course. Such an argument he felt he could have used had Rye been his wife. She did not yet stand in that relation to him, however, and there was that in her attitude at this moment which showed she not only had the right to think for herself but was prepared to act upon it.

'Let me be candid,' she continued, and the hardness went out of her voice as she spoke, while her words were tremulous with suppressed feeling. 'I have no wish to dictate to you about your future, and I hope it may be good and happy, whatever you choose to become, but I have resolved that I cannot be anything save a Methodist. And I will not do anything that would seem to endanger my future in that respect. On the other hand, I do not wish to prevent you from carrying out your plans. I will give you back your promise to me, and you must give me back mine to you.'

Rye Harland's lips still moved when she had gone thus far as though she had more to say ; but no other words came, and although she did not weep, her strong frame trembled from head to foot.

Arthur was more than perplexed. Selfish as he was, he was not wholly bad. A strong sense of righteousness was active in him. It is true this quality did not penetrate into all the regions of his nature. It hardly touched him where his decisions had to do with complex problems. But he could not consciously act a hypocritical part in matters that were simple and easy of comprehension. And, although in his heart he had not acted righteously towards Rye since their engagement, but had allowed mean considerations to weigh with him when loyalty to her should have shut them out of his mind, he had done this because this sense of righteousness, strong in him where other matters had to be decided, hardly came into play in these more refined and difficult questions.

Not yet was he prepared to sacrifice his position as her lover. On the other hand, he could not pretend to put away all intention of severing himself from Nonconformity and gaining honours and influence in the Church of England.

'You cannot mean it,' he exclaimed.

'Yes, I mean it,' she continued when at last words came to her. 'I wish you to understand me fully, and yet I am afraid you hardly will. Even if you were to promise that you would be a Methodist minister, and in all sincerity renounce the thoughts you have lately been entertaining, to me it would not be satisfactory. My views of you have been altered by the fact that you have even had these thoughts. To you they may be perfectly right, and I do not judge your conduct absolutely, but only as far as you have been related to me. If ever I marry, my husband must be one who would no more think of leaving the

Methodist Church than he would think of breaking one of the commandments.'

'Is your decision final, then ?' Arthur asked.

'Yes, Arthur dear, it is final.'

And so they said good-bye.

'After all,' he said to himself, 'she gave me no choice, not even the alternative of yielding up my wishes and sacrificing my ambitions. My only course was to accept my dismissal. But even then he was not confident he had acted wisely, and his judgment told him that before the end came he might find that in his efforts to win a prize in life he had snatched at a shadow and allowed the substance to be lost to him for ever.

CHAPTER XVI.

DREAMLAND *versus* REALITY.

'Her love for him had ne'er been so intense
As it had seemed when he was far from thence;
And many a thing in him seemed little-hearted,
And mean and loveless.'

ROBERT BUCHANAN.

IT was early in the evening of a sultry September day when the interview that had freed Rye and Arthur from a position that had never yielded either of them much pleasure took place. The scene of the episode was the drawing-room, an apartment not much in use at the Mount. No third party was possible on such an occasion, but on the other side of the wall, that is, in the library, Mr. Harland sat, his face flushed with anxious excitement, and his eyes moistened with the strong feeling that would not be wholly suppressed. He would have been glad to save his daughter from the ordeal through which he knew she was at that moment passing, and his heart was stricken with pain because he could not undertake the task for her. But mingled with his pain was a strong feeling of joyful pride. In his daughter he was exceedingly confident, and was sure she would do both what was right and what was wise.

Despite this, however, he was glad when he heard the door of the drawing-room open, and footsteps going towards the outer door.

' The interview has been short to-night, and it is not difficult to guess what that means,' he said to himself.

THE SCENE OF THE EPISODE WAS THE DRAWING-ROOM.

Going to the door of the library he opened it gently and stepped into the hall. Arthur was already on his way to the gates, and Rye, with bent head, was coming from the front porch, whither she had accompanied him.

'Will my darling come into the library?' Mr. Harland inquired gently, taking her hand in his own as he spoke.

'We won't say much about it to-night,' he said considerately, for he was anxious, if he might, to spare her. Arthur has gone soon, and you could tell me the result of your talk with him. Only the result, mind.'

'Arthur and I have agreed to break the engagement, father.'

He stooped and kissed his daughter. She

stood a moment as one a little bewildered, then rubbed her hand across her eye-brows as was her wont sometimes when she had sat long at the piano and had been strongly moved by her music. Then she said 'good night,' and went away.

Calmly as she had borne herself through the past hour, no one save herself knew how much she had suffered. It was not that she felt she was making any sacrifice for conscience sake. In such a thought there would have been strengthening and comfort, and a resignation that would have upheld her, even as it has upheld all, martyrs and others, who have suffered for a Divine cause. She had been true to her conscience, but she perceived no element of sacrifice in her action.

That what had been done would prove to be for the best, she had not the slightest doubt. For she argued that her love for Arthur had lately been losing all its foundation of esteem, and the ideal halo which once in her eyes had shone round his head had disappeared.

. Had he changed very much? She did not know. Neither did she dream that it was her habit of mind to invest all whom she knew, and indeed everything she saw, with an ideal glory. To her poetic vision nothing in heaven above or in the earth beneath was commonplace, and no human being was made of poor clay. Like him of ancient story, afterwards as the chancellor of a great empire an exceedingly practical man, she was a dreamer, and saw men and things not so much as they were, but as they ought to be.

Perhaps it is inevitable that such dreamers, in a world like this, at times should be rudely awakened.

Arthur had much in him to fascinate an imaginative and poetic girlish mind. He was handsome. He was clever. He was better than his conditions of life. And even his fault of ambition, when not allowed to assert itself too much, had tended to make Rye think that if his environments were not those of a prince, in character he was decidedly kingly.

From their childhood they had been friends, and when he had bravely asked her for her heart and hand, it had seemed an arrangement so natural and fitting, that she had hardly asked herself a question about it.

The familiarity begotten of the new relationship had, however, effectually taken away some of her false ideas. Perhaps he had revealed himself more completely; perhaps her nearer point of view had enabled her to see through the halo her own imagination had thrown around his person. What was absolutely certain was that her regard for him had ever been waning, and his presence near her had never failed to make her unhappy.

In reality she had never loved him. But constituted as she was, the severance between them could not fail to wound her deeply. Sensitive far beyond what was usual even in a tender-hearted girl, and highly conscientious, with a large veneration for all the sacred ties of life, she felt she had been overtaken by a calamity in being compelled to act as she had done that night.

Slowly, and with a heavy footstep, she ascended the fine staircase of the Mount, and sought the quiet of her own pretty boudoir. It was immediately over the library, and Mr. Harland waited there awhile in the hope that he might hear her busying herself about the room, or begin to play the piano. But he waited in vain, for no sound reached his ears. After awhile he rose and joined his wife in the dining-room.

'Our darling has had a heavy trial tonight,' he remarked.

'It is over, then. Do you know what has come out of it?'

'They have broken their engagement, I suppose by mutual consent.'

'That is an end for which I am profoundly thankful.'

'But think of what it may cost her—think of what it has cost her already,' Mr. Harland expostulated.

'She will get over it all,' Mrs. Harland said with some assurance, 'and she had better suffer a little now, than a great deal afterwards.'

Remarks whose truth was so self-evident were not to be gainsaid, and Mr. Harland felt inclined to inwardly compliment his wife for her shrewdness and farsightedness, as he had done a hundred times before, when there occurred to his mind a thought that led him to doubt whether in this instance she was quite as meritorious as he had deemed her.

'Not long ago, my dear, you were very much in favour of this particular engagement, and now you seem glad it is ended, even at the cost of a world of grief to Rye.'

'But Mr. Harland,' the lady answered, her face beaming still with good-nature, despite the inclination of her spouse to be severe, 'even a woman may change her mind. A man is allowed that privilege, at least, and why should a woman be debarred from it?'

Mr. Harland did not attempt to pursue the subject further. Inwardly he meditated on the profound depths of a woman's mind, and the mysteries that might be locked up in it.

Presently strains of music broke on their ears. Rye had two pianos, one of which stood in the dining-room, and was regarded perhaps not so much her own, but rather the property of the whole house; the other was in her boudoir, and like all in that delightful and elegant retreat, was her especial property. The door of her room was ajar, and the harmonies at once arrested the attention of her father and mother. The former rose and opened the door of the room in which they were sitting.

'We must not miss this performance. It may not explain to us all she feels, but it would do so were our instincts as refined and spiritual as hers.'

A sound as of thunder rolling across the sky fell upon their ears, which, despite its general boldness and grandeur, had in it all through an undertone of pathos growing ever more passionate. For it was *Beethoven's Sonata Pathétique.* After awhile that war of passionate feeling came to an end and there was a pause. Then came the softer and more soothing *melody in F by Rubenstein,* whose effect is the same as a sail on the summer sea.

It was the calm of a bright evening after a day of thunder and rain, and it revealed exactly her recent experience. That experience had left her not unscarred. Not easily after this would she be able to remain long in an ideal state of mind. She had been accustomed to see the world of men and things from among the light and cloud of the skies in which she had soared, but now she had also touched the earth and seen them through no transfiguring medium, but as they really were.

Her new experience had hurt her, wounded her deeply indeed, but it had left no bitterness in her mind. She had fought her battle during the last two days very bravely; with equal courage had she gone through the sharp contest of that evening, and from all had emerged without taint of sin and without touch of bitterness. A little exhausted, a little pained, she still felt, but withal she was thankful, for she was conscious of her own integrity and of the favour of God.

Mr. and Mrs. Harland were not the only listeners to the strains of music coming from Rye's boudoir that evening. Jack Benson was standing in the doorway of his study when she began to play. At first as he listened there was a dark, angry scowl on his face, but when the performer had finished with *Beethoven* and commenced with the slow movements and quiet harmonies of *Rubenstein* his features relaxed.

Jack Benson, despite his apparently careless manners, was profoundly observant and deeply sensitive, and he thought he could see, enacted under his very eyes, a tragedy in real life. The spectacle moved him more than he cared to show, or even admit to his own heart.

(To be continued.)

THE UPWARD WAY. — When God intends to fill a soul, He first makes it empty; when He intends to enrich a soul, He first makes it poor; when He intends to exalt a soul, He first makes it humble; when He intends to save a soul, He first makes it sensible of its own miseries and nothingness.—FLAVEL.

TUMBLERS.—Glass drinking-cups have been found in Anglo-Saxon graves, and they are all round-bottomed. Such cups could not stand upright, and it has been supposed they were so designed in order to cause the drinker to empty them at once. This feature is said to have given rise to the word 'Tumbler,' which has been applied to our drinking vessels, though these do not possess the curious shape of the ancient cups.

The Story of the Catacombs.

(Concluded from page 224.)

THE monumental inscriptions and pictorial representations of the catacombs are of important interest, because they are interwoven with the history of early Christianity. It has been supposed that the origin of the Christian catacombs dates from the burial of the first Christian believer. Some of the catacombs were commenced by the wealthier Romans, who buried their dead in excavations made in their own gardens or vineyards, in resemblance of the burial of Christ in Joseph's tomb. Some of these graves were subsequently opened for the reception of the bodies of poor Christians, and thus the catacombs would be gradually extended until they reached their present dimensions.

The funeral ceremonies of the early Christians were very interesting. The corpse, having been washed, was anointed with fragrant gums and spices, wrapped in grave-clothes, and then carried in the arms of relatives, was lovingly laid in its last resting-place. A last, lingering look and a farewell prayer, and then the mason stepped forward, and with cement and tiles severed the dead from the gaze of the living.

The bodies differ in their state of preservation. In the graves of children nothing is found but dust, along with the playthings and trinkets that afforded them childish glee in ages gone. Among the toys that have been found are ivory dolls, fitted with wires which moved the lifeless limbs in a fantastic manner, and money-boxes with slits for the reception of coins. Occasionally toilet articles have been picked up, such as hair-pins adorned with pious mottoes, as *Romola, semper viras in Deo*—'Romola, may you ever live in God.' Where the body has been absolutely dry there remains the outlined form without the substance. In cases of dampness the body is in a state of partial preservation; while those which have been drenched with water have become petrified, and have the appearance and durability of images of stone. In some cases, when the in-rushing air penetrates the coffin, the apparently solid body dissolves like a spectre. When Campana was making excavations in his vineyard at Porta Latina, he found a columbarium containing a stone coffin some five feet long. Campana gave orders for the removal of the lid, and he gazed upon the face of a maiden who had died hundreds of years back. In the course of a few moments, the funeral robe, hands, face, and limbs began to fade and dissolve, and all that was left of the once lovely girl was a form-work of dust upon the floor of the coffin.

Historians differ in the probable number of the martyrs buried in the catacombs. At the lowest estimate the number must be very considerable. Eusebius, who was an eye-witness of the last of the persecutions, states: 'All these things were doings, not for a few days, but for a series of whole years. At one time, ten or more, then twenty, again thirty, or even sixty, and sometimes a hundred men with their wives and children, were slain in one day.' The Bishop of Cæsarea adds: 'We ourselves have seen crowds of persons, some beheaded, others burned alive in a single day, so that the murderous weapons were blunted and broken to pieces, and the executioners, wearied with slaughter, were obliged to give over the work of blood.' When Christianity was first introduced into Pagan Rome, the Emperors despised and ignored it, on account of its apparent insignificance. As it spread and made itself felt amongst the citizens, Nero became opposed to the new faith, and brutalized his character by being the first Emperor who persecuted the Church of Christ. Nero originated the brutal plan of clothing Christians in the skins of animals to be torn by ferocious dogs. Others were besmeared with pitch, and served the purpose of torches to light up the gardens of the palace. Public opinion regarded the Christians as being the enemies of Roman government, and were considered as exercising

evil influences. In the event of the Tiber out-
bursting its banks, or in case of pestilence,
famine, or earthquake, the cause was attri-
buted to Christian circles, and the cry was
both loud and revengeful, ' To the lions ! '
The mutilated bodies of the saints were picked
up, and reverently entombed in the catacombs.

The ' noble army of martyrs ' comprised
persons of all ranks and classes. Amongst
the most illustrious was Stephen I., Bishop
of the Church, who was greatly hated by the
Pagans. Driven from home, he sought the
refuge of the catacombs. The Roman soldiers
discovered his hiding-place, and found him
engaged in ministering in holy things ; allowing him to finish his religious rites, they
cruelly rushed upon him, and severed head
from body : his lifeless body was buried in
the underground sepulchre. One of his
attendants who shared his fate in death was
Hippolytus, respecting whom the voice of
tradition relates the following incident :—His
Pagan family resident in Rome, knowing of
his retreat, sent him daily supplies that were
brought by a little nephew and niece. Hippolytus became anxious about their conversion to the Christian faith. He consulted the
Bishop, who advised him to detain them the
next time they came, adding that their parents
in their anxiety for their little ones will be
sure to come and inquire for them. The
parents came, were baptized, and, along with
their children, so tradition states, were
cruelly murdered. The greatest interest is
attached to the catacomb of Callixtus, which
is approached from the celebrated Appian
Way. Along that road the Apostle Paul
travelled when he entered Rome ' an ambassador in bonds.' After dwelling for two
years ' in his own hired house,' he ' finished
his course ' at the block of martyrdom. ' By
the Appian Way,' says tradition, ' his body
was stealthily conveyed by night, and deposited
in an adjacent catacomb, and here wended
many a mourning procession, bearing to these
lowly crypts the remains of Rome's early
bishops, martyrs, and confessors.'

The names, epitaphs, and symbols recorded
upon the tombs, illustrate the faith that these
Gentile believers had in the unadulterated
doctrines of early Christianity. It is a significant fact that the ' voices of the stones ' have
no references to Mary, purgatory, or to the
worship of the saints. These heterodox principles were introduced into the Church at a
later date. When the primitive Christians
renounced Paganism, they adopted with the
new faith a new name, and these are chiselled
upon the tombs, such as, Anastasia, ' the
Resurrection ; ' Casta, ' Pure ; ' Constantia,
' Constancy ; ' Grata, ' Pleasing ; ' and Inno-
centia, ' Innocence.' Sometimes they adopted
a phrase as a proper name, as Acceptissima,
' very well pleasing ; ' and Deo Gratia, 'Thanks
to God.' Upon the graves of children, the pet
name of the family circle is recorded—
Agnella, ' Little Lamb ; ' Joamdilla, ' Merry
little thing ; ' Lepusculus, ' Little Hare ; '
and Rosula, ' Little Rose.'

The most numerous of the epitaphs is the
single word ' Dormit,' meaning that the
deceased sleeps. The saints regarded death as
sleep, hence they termed their burial-places
' Cœmeterium ' *i.e.* sleeping-places, and the
vault the ' Cubiculum,' the sleeping-chamber.
On a grave bearing date A.D. 329, is ' Lauren-
tius,' was born into eternity in the twentieth
year of his age. ' He sleeps in peace.' Others
read as ' Simplicia, who was also rightly so-
called.' ' Here lies Verus, who ever spoke
verity.' ' Aurelia, our very sweet daughter,
who retired from the world. Severus and
Quintinus being consuls. She lived fifteen
years and four months.' ' Sent for by Angels.'
' He went to God,' and ' everlasting rest of
happiness.' Some of the epitaphs are more
lengthy, and give an epitome of the spirit of
the times in which the martyr lived and died.
The following is a specimen : ' In Christ,
Alexander is not dead, but lives beyond the
stars, and his body rests in this tomb. He
lived under the Emperor Antonine, who, fore-
seeing that great benefit would result from
his services, returned evil for good. For
while on his knees, about to sacrifice to the
true God, he was led away to execution. O
sad times ! in which sacred rites and prayers,
even in caverns, afford no protection to us.
What can be more wretched than such a life ?
and what than such a death ? when they could

not be buried by their friends and relations. At length they sparkle in heaven. He has scarcely lived who has lived in Christian times.'

The pictorial representations of the walls and tombs are very numerous, and are of a thoroughly Biblical character. They comprise Noah in the ark; Moses striking the rock at Horeb; Daniel in the midst of the lions; the story of the fugitive Jonah; the three children in the fiery furnace; the adoration of the Magi; the resurrection of Lazarus; and Christ as the Good Shepherd, and the persecuted saints as the sheep of His fold. From the recurrence of this figure in the catacombs, it must have been a general favourite with the primitive Christians. The symbol is worked out in a variety of details. 'Sometimes the sheep appears to nestle with an expression of human tenderness and love on the Shepherd's shoulders; in other examples, it is more or less firmly held with one or both hands, as if to prevent its escape. In a few instances, the fold is seen in the background, which seems to complete the allegory. Frequently the Shepherd carries a staff or crook in His hand, on which He sometimes leans, as if weary beneath His burden. He is sometimes even represented as sitting on a mound, as if overcome by fatigue. Occasionally He is represented with a musical instrument, like the classical syrinx or Paris pipe, in His hand, as if to indicate the sweet persuasive influence of His word.' The oldest symbol is the fish, said to be derived from the initial letters of Christ's name and titles, which placed together in monogram form made up the word *fish*. The wreath and the palm-branch are found again and again, and point to the future world, where the countless throng appear in the presence of the throne, 'clothed with white robes, and *palms* in their hands.' The most common of the emblems is a bird with leaves in its mouth, and accompanied by the inscription '*In pace*.' The anchor represented the vigorous belief that they had in the life to come. 'There are but few instances of the symbol of the cross, and these are always found in the most remote and deepest labyrinths of the catacombs. The Christians, with

profound reverence for the passion of Christ, hid the symbol of His death from the gaze of the Pagans.

The persecutions imposed upon the Christian Church in Rome, during the period of the catacomb cruelties, did not crush it, but extended its influence and enlisted sympathizers. Then as ever 'the blood of the martyrs became the seed of the church.' For a season Christianity was the religion of the empire, and Christian senators sat in the national councils, Christian soldiers were numbered in the army, and Christian servants were to be found in the household of the palace. In the year 325 Constantine the Great succeeded his famous predecessors upon the Roman throne. He was the first Christian emperor, and is revered for his religious sincerity.   ALBERT A. BIRCHENOUGH.

Sketches of the British Isles.
JERSEY.

ERSEY is the largest, most populous, and by far the most important of the Channel group of islands. The rocky coast - board, balmy atmosphere, mild sea breezes, and quiet nooks of unrivalled beauty are special features of attraction to visitors and holiday-seekers. It is located about fourteen miles from the shores of historic Normandy, and ninety-five miles from Weymouth. The extent of the Island, from east to west, is eleven miles; and the greatest breadth is five and a half miles, and comprises a total area of forty-five square miles. In the year 1881, the population of Jersey was returned as 52,455, one half of whom were residents in the town of St. Heliers, and the remainder were scattered throughout the villages and hamlets of the island. The coast is specially indented with numerous expansive bays; the more important being St. Catherine, St. Brelade, St. Heliers, Grouville, and Boulay. The bay of St. Owen, from being exposed to the turbulent waters and terrific storms of the Atlantic Ocean, is considered unsafe for shipping purposes. The island is encircled with a natural defence-work of hard, rugged rocks, intersected with veins of greenstone and shale of a less endurable character, that have been eroded by the action of the waters of the sea, thus leaving numerous grotesque caverns and fantastic pillars of considerable extent and height. The land slopes to the south and west, and reaches its highest level on the north. The highest point of the island is Mount Mado, which gains an altitude of 473 feet above the sea. Geologists state that the hill is composed

St. Aubins, Jersey.

of porphyroid granite, which extends in a southerly direction, and terminates near the town of St. Peter's. On the north-east of the island are found masses of conglomerate; and the other part of Jersey is about equally divided between siliceous and schistose rocks.

Special attention has been paid by the British authorities, to guarding the island against the excursions of hostile foes, by the erection of fortifications and substantial defence-works. Fort Regent, adjoining the town of St. Heliers, overlooks the inner harbour, and a million of English money was spent on its construction. Elizabeth Castle is built on a small island in the Bay of St. Aubins, and defends the entrance to the harbour. Mount Orgueil Castle is erected on high ground, having command of the sea. Its oldest sections are Norman, and the stone-work of the imposing pile has become mellowed and grey with age. The most popular portions to visitors are the dungeons where the sturdy Puritan William Prynne was cruelly imprisoned, the Roman well, and St. George's chapel. An extensive view is obtained from the Castle. On a clear day may be seen the outline of the shores of Normandy and the tall spires of Coutances Cathedral. Special orders to visit the military and marine defences can be obtained at the local governmental offices. From six to seven hundred troops of soldiers are garrisoned on the island, and, in addition to the regulars, there are six well-disciplined regiments of local militia, with field batteries annexed to each regiment. There is a system of compulsory volunteer service in force, whereby one-tenth of the male population is enrolled in the militia or reserve forces. During the reign of William IV. the militia was specially recognized, and was styled ' Royal.' In the year 1849 the Queen of England favoured them with a special visit and inspection that was greatly appreciated.

The attempts of our French neighbours to capture and annex the island have been unsuccessful. During the year 1781, immediately after the French nation had allied itself with the revolted people in the British Colonies of America, a French adventurer, of the name of Macquart, who styled himself Baron de Rullecourt, landed in Jersey and marched to the market-place, or, as it is now called, the Royal Square of St. Heliers, where a short but severe battle was fought. The British forces were led by Major Pierson, of the 95th Regiment. Macquart and his followers were driven from the island. Pierson, unfortunately, was killed in the engagement. His heroic services have been acknowledged by Copley's famous picture of the battle, hung upon the walls of the National Gallery in Trafalgar Square, London.

St. Heliers, the chief town of the island, is picturesquely situated on the sunny slopes of the eastern coast, and overlooking the beautiful, deep blue waters of the Bay of St. Aubins. The view of Jersey obtained from the sea is unique and inviting. The extensive sea-board consists of red granite, with the pretty detached villas, enshrouded with masses of greenery, towering up to the crest of the tree-covered heights, presents a charming aspect.

highest grade. The Victoria College was erected in the year 1852; the curriculum includes classical, professional, and commercial training of the highest class, and the scholarships and exhibitions connected therewith are tenable at the English Universities. There are colleges and schools for girls, that have merited the highest reputation. The reading circles of the town have the privileges of a well-furnished public library, containing over seventeen thousand volumes of the various branches of scientific, historic, and popular literature. St. Heliers, being the capital, also contains the Government House, or 'Royal Court,' prison, lunatic asylum, and general

A few years back Jersey was simply an insignificant and unimportant village. Rapidly it has developed into an enterprising town, containing many streets, imposing private residences, and houses of business. It has completely surpassed St. Aubins, which was the original capital, and is built on the shores of the bay, immediately opposite to St. Heliers. St. Aubins has been described as 'one of the most beautiful spots in the world, having the temperature of the Riviera without its trying variations. The public buildings of St. Heliers comprise two Episcopalian churches, numerous chapels for Roman Catholics, and the various branches of Nonconformity. The town is well supplied with educational establishments of the

hospital. Shipping and stone quarrying provide employment for many artisans. The harbour, quays, and docks are extensive, and a large trade of considerable tonnage is conducted with the English and French nations. For residential, educational, or tourist purposes, St. Heliers presents many advantages. The leading and most frequented promenades of St. Heliers are La Coletta, which has become a pleasant resort, with superior bathing facilities; West Mount, where, from the hillside walks, extensive marine views are obtained; and the shady grounds belonging to the Albert Pier, and the Victoria College.

For ecclesiastical and civil purposes the

island is divided in twelve parishes, ten of them having the general term of 'Saint' applied to them, as St. Owen's, St. Brelade's, St. Lawrence's, St. Saviour's, &c., and the other two are Trinity and Grouville. The rectors and dean of Jersey are subject to the discipline and administration of the Bishop of Winchester. The antiquated parish churches, by their numerous restorations, have lost the ancient outlines of their original styles of

appointed by the English Crown, a High-Sheriff, and two Under-Sheriffs, the twelve Judges of the Royal Court, who are life-members, and are freely elected by the rate-payers, the twelve constables, who represent the parishes, elected triennially, and the twelve rectors. The Governor of Jersey is allowed a seat in the Council, but is only permitted to address the Assembly on Crown matters. No law passed at Westminster is binding without

ENTRANCE TO SEIGNEURIE PARK.

architecture. The livings are considered poor, and are the gift of the Governor of Jersey. The Channel Islands are the oldest appanage of the English realm, being originally a portion of the hereditary possessions of William the Norman, and yet Jersey, like Guernsey, has retained to a considerable extent its self-existent and independent form of government. The 'States of Jersey,' as the Legislative Assembly is termed, is composed of the Governor and High Bailiff, who are

the confirmation of the local parliament. Although the people generally speak English or Norman, all legislative and judicial business is conducted in French. The hall of Assembly is commodious, but is said to be a badly constructed building. The walls are adorned with numerous paintings, the most valuable being a full length portrait by Gainsborough of Marshal Conway. Practically, the people make their own laws, enjoy the privileges of home rule, and are exempt from the burdensome taxation of England. Crime of 'any magnitude is unknown; pauperism is greatly limited; and the people, by their industry and

beautiful scenery. Without a doubt, in no other area of the same extent can there be found such a combination of bays, sea-scapes,

A JERSEY COTTAGE.

economical way of living, have managed to deposit over £300,000 in the savings' banks.

In Jersey, there is an endless variety of

marine views, romantic wooded landscapes, flowing rivulets, verdant pastures, apple orchards, luxuriant gardens, and masses of fantastic rock, as there are in the adjoining islets. They may be numbered amongst the gems of creation, and are the pride of both residents and visitors. On the southern coast of Jersey are two miniature lines of railway, which terminate at St. Heliers. They branch eastward and westward, and afford splendid marine views. Other places of special attraction are the Waterworks' Valley, Bellozanne Valley, the entrancing beauties of Bonne Nuit, the waterfalls of Les Mouriers, the caverns, pillars, and fairy-like suspension bridge of Grève-de-Lecque, and the extensive romantic caverns adjoining Plemont Point. La Hogue Bie, or Prince's Tower, has become a noted view-point, from which long stretches of sky, land, and sea may be obtained. The genial climate has made Jersey popular as a health resort for English invalids and tired brain-workers. There is an annual average rainfall of thirty-five inches, but, owing to the soil being of a light and porous character, and evaporation rapid, the atmosphere is not too moist. The residents are favoured with an average of six hours sunshine during the days of the year. The hottest and most sultry weather is experienced in the month of August, and the coldest during February. The autumns are exceedingly beautiful; generally a second summer commences about the tenth of October that lasts until nearly Christmas, which is locally known as the *Petit Été de Saint Martin*, *i.e.*, 'Saint Martin's Little Summer.'

The people of Jersey are industrious, thrifty, and prosperous. The holdings are small, varying from five to twenty English acres, and the agricultural portion of the inhabitants are mainly yeoman proprietors, who work upon their own lands. The farm-houses and cottages of the peasantry are well-built, roomy, and clean, some of them being embowered with orchards, and fronted with well-kept flower-gardens are pictures of rustic beauty. The soil is light and very productive. Potatoes arrive at perfection very early in the season, and are exported to England in large quantities. They reach the London markets at least a fortnight earlier than those grown in the gardens of the West of England, and consequently fetch high prices. The exports of 'early' potatoes exceed sixty thousand tons annually, and are valued at £264,000. Wheat, hay, carrots, turnips, parsnips, and mangel wurzels are grown in large quantities. The people follow the French methods of cultivation, and the implements of husbandry that they use are of the most primitive description. At certain seasons of the year, sea-weed is gathered from the shores, and spread over the land for manuring purposes. Large quantities of sea-weed are also burned for the manufacture of kelp and iodine. The orchards and gardens are numerous. The cottagers pay special attention to the growing of fruit, which is of a superior flavour; large quantities of apples are used in the manufacture of cider, which is the common beverage of the peasantry; grapes, peaches, melons, strawberries, and chaumontel pears, which attain a large size, are grown in considerable quantities for the English markets. The peasantry live entirely upon the produce of the soil, or what they receive for it by way of exchange.　ALBERT A. BIRCHENOUGH.

American Views.

THE YELLOWSTONE PARK AND FALLS.

THE district which is the source of the Yellowstone River is one of the most remarkable, not only in the United States, but in any other country on the globe. It contains some of the most striking phenomena, and possesses scenery of the most beautiful and romantic character. Its weird, rugged, and natural grandeur invests the locality with peculiar charms. For centuries it remained practically a 'great unknown' country. Exploring parties had passed on all sides of it many a time, but it had never occurred to any of them to investigate its resources and phenomena. The consequence was that this strange region remained undiscovered until so late as the year 1870. This fact is the more remarkable when we remember that there was a regular settlement

RAINBOW FALLS.

within a comparatively short distance of it. Occasionally, reports had been circulated by hunters, that hot springs and geysers were to be met with, and wandering Indians had confirmed the statements. But it was not till the date above given that sufficient interest was taken in the rumours to warrant an investigation. Dr. Hayden, who was in charge of a Government survey party, turned his attention to the district, and the reports which he gave led Congress, in 1872, to reserve the region as a Grand National Park. Other exploring parties were set to work, and considerable headway was made in the knowledge of the locality. The result was that a very full map was prepared in 1885, which exhibited a detailed outline of the geographical and geological character of the entire district.

The area included in the Yellowstone Park is no less than 3,312 square miles. It is somewhat of the shape of a rectangle, and is sixty-one and four-fifth miles long and fifty-three and three-fifth miles broad. The greater part of it is situated in Wyoming, but some part of it is in Montana and Idaho. Its surface forms a large plateau which is about 8,000 feet above the level of the sea, and abounds with streams of various sizes, but the larger ones have cut deep channels for themselves. Rivers, mountains, ravines, gorges, forests, and geysers, make up this strange region. On the east side, there is quite a wild and rugged mountain-chain which is known as the Absaroka Range. It has several elevations, the highest of which is 11,000 feet. This range serves to separate the Yellowstone and Big Horn Rivers from each other, and it is considered to be unsurpassed in beauty and grandeur of scenery by any other locality in the United States. Another range, that of Gallatin, separates the Yellowstone and the Gallatin Rivers, and runs southward along the Park for twenty miles. Its highest point, which is just within the Park, is 11,050 feet. There is another group of mountains near the middle of the Park which are in the form of a horse-shoe, the highest of which is the Washburne, which is 10,346 feet. The Red Mountains are situated at the south, and Sheridan, 10,385 feet, is the highest. This part of the

Park is more elevated and broken, and just beyond its southern boundary rises into a confused haze of mountains.

The humidity of the locality is such that the rainfall gives rise to a large number of streams, which are somewhat characteristic in form and size. There are also numerous beautiful lakes and ponds. The Yellowstone and Madison Rivers both originate in the Park. The Yellowstone drains the eastern part, and flows into and through the Yellowstone Lake, which is a magnificent sheet of water, having an area of 150 miles. A few miles below the lake, the river, after a succession of rapids, leaps over a cliff, which makes the Upper Fall, which is 112 feet in depth. About half a mile further down, it makes another descent of of 300 feet, which is known as the Lower Fall. At this point, the river carries an average rate of water of 1,200 cubic feet per second. Both these falls and that of the Rainbow are exceedingly beautiful, though differing considerably in size and appearance. At the Lower Fall the river enters the Great Cañon, which for many scenic effects cannot be equalled. It is not so deep, comparatively speaking, but ranges from 600 feet at the head to 1,200 near the middle, and its length is about twenty-four miles. 'It is cut in a volcanic plateau, and its rugged, broken walls, which are inclined at very steep angles, are of a barbaric richness of colouring that almost defies description. Reds, yellows, and purples predominate, and are set off very effectively against the dark green of the forests upon the plateau and the white foam of the rushing river which fills the bottom of the chasm. Near the foot of the Great Cañon, Tower Creek, which drains the cavity of the horse-shoe, formed by the Washburne Mountains, enters the Yellowstone. Just above its mouth this stream makes a beautiful fall of 132 feet into the gorge in which it joins the river.' By-and-bye, the Yellowstone emerges at the mouth of the Gardiner River. The latter drains an area of elevated land by means of its three forks, and upon each of them occurs a very fine fall. The Madison rises in the western part of the park, and flows in a generally northward and westward course out

UPPER FALLS OF YELLOWSTONE.

of the park. Its waters are mainly collected from the rainfall upon the plateaus and from the hot springs and geysers, most of which are within its drainage area. There are several fine waterfalls upon this river and its affluents. Authorities consider that all the streams of this region show evidence in the character of their course of a recent change of level in the surface of the country.

The surface of the park is almost entirely covered with volcanic rocks, and in some parts of the mountain ranges the ancient volcanic fires which formerly extended far and wide, are still in existence, as is shown by the vast number of hot springs and geysers. There are said to be in this region no fewer than 3,000 of them, ranging from a few inches in diameter to that of several acres. Seventy-one of these are active, and some of them throw up streams of water to a height of 200 feet, and the temperature is such as to raise the water of the river several degrees.

‘In all these localities the water holds silica in solution in considerable quantities, so that as it cools and evaporates, it deposits siliceous matter, which has covered with a hard, white floor many square miles of these valleys, and has built up craters around the springs and geysers of considerable size, and of great beauty of form. Besides silica, the water of many of the springs contains sulphur, iron, alum, and other materials in solution, which in places has stained the pure white of the siliceous deposits with bright bands of colour. Upon Gardiner River, near the northern boundary of the park, there is a large group of springs known as the Mammoth hot springs, which differ from the others in holding carbonate of lime in solution. These springs have deposited so freely as to build up a hill 200 feet, from the top of which a spring boils out. The slopes of the mound have been built in the form of a succession of basins, rising one above another, growing gradually cooler as it descends. Upon the banks of the Yellowstone River, between the falls and the lake, there was, when the region was first explored, a geyser which at intervals of about four hours threw up a column of mud to the height of forty or fifty feet. In more recent times this geyser has ceased action.

These phenomena have been under observation since 1871, and while there have been changes in them, certain geysers having ceased and others having formed, no evidence of a diminution of power has been observed.’

As has been already intimated, the region abounds in forests. They are generally so dense that landmarks are invisible, and the traveller is forced to guide himself by the sun or by compass. The trees are mainly spruce and the yellow pine, and are not of much commercial value. Many kinds of game are plentiful. The Government exercises a sharp look-out in this respect. The game is protected by very stringent game laws. The consequence is that many animals find shelter here from the depredations of the sportsman. The elk, deer, antelope, mountain sheep, bear, and numerous others are abundant and tame. The only herd of wild bison left in the United States is to be seen in the park. The climate is peculiar in comparison with adjacent parts of the West. The temperature is semi-tropical. Frosts may occur in midsummer, and snow often begins to fall in September. We may add that this wild and romantic region is now rendered fairly easy of access by the Northern Pacific Railway, which has a branch line that approaches within a few miles of the northern boundary. From its terminus, stage coaches are regularly run to the park.

M. JOHNSON.

Deep Sea Wonders.

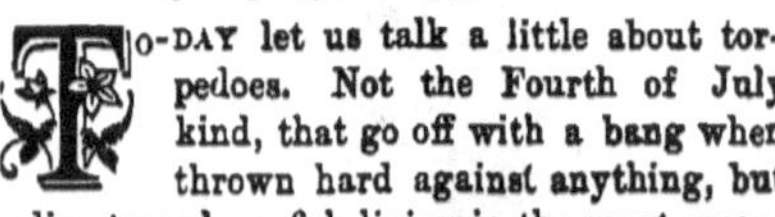

To-DAY let us talk a little about torpedoes. Not the Fourth of July kind, that go off with a bang when thrown hard against anything, but a live torpedo, a fish living in the great ocean. If you want to see what shape they are, just go into the kitchen and take a good look at the frying-pan, for they look about as much alike as anything I can think of. The body is round and flat just like the frying-pan, and the tail, being long and slim, would answer very well for a handle. However, if they were real frying-pans they would need pretty big stoves to use them on, for they have been known to weigh from eighty to a hundred pounds. Torpedoes are smooth and shiny, dressed either in plain brown, or in two shades of brown, spotted like marble. Some that want to look especially fine are said to wear a white vest, having a few black dots on it; but of course that shows only on the under side. They cannot see very far, for they have small eyes, but with their many sharp teeth crowded close together, they are able to give some pretty hard bites. They are lazy, sluggish fellows, being fond of deep water, where they lie at the bottom almost covered up by the mud.

On a cold night did you ever take pussy cat into a dark room and rub your hand over her fur quick and fast, so that the hair stood up on end, snapped, and even threw out sparks as you stroked it? If so, you must surely remember that when you asked about it mamma told you it was electricity that made it. To be sure, you did not know very much about electricity—only that it was the cause of the lightning, and sent the messages along the telegraph wires; but you were sure there must be a great deal of it, and that it was scattered about almost everywhere, for when mamma gave you a brush and let you brush her long hair, it stood out from her head and snapped, because electricity was there too. Now, the fish we are talking about, this torpedo, is what is called an electrical fish, because he has so much electricity about him. He carries it on both sides of his head between the eyes and first fins. He has so much of it that if you should touch him you would get some too. And you would not like it much either, for you would feel all over something as your foot does when it is what you call asleep; indeed, it would be worse than that, and you would have sharp pains and not be able to move for a while. This is what is called a shock. People in old times, thinking these were good for them when they had certain diseases, used to go to the fish, just as you go to the doctor, and take a shock instead of medicine. Other fish do not fancy the torpedo very much, for if he touches them they are likely to die from this electricity. Sometimes, even when they are in the water near

him, they tumble over without as much as touching him. He does not give out these shocks all the time, but only when he feels like it; and if he gives out too many right away, close together, he is likely to die.

There is another electrical fish living in the warm waters of the ocean, near the coral rocks. He is not a very large fish, but has such a long name that we should forget it very soon even if we tried to remember it; so instead of calling him by it we will let him go without any name at all. He is a beauty, all but his mouth; that sticks out too much to be at all pretty. Like all electric fish, he has neither scales nor spines, but is smooth and shiny; and oh, so many colours as he has! His back is brown, his belly sea-green, and his sides yellow, while he is spotted all over with red, green, and white spots. Then, too, his fins and tail are green, and his large eyes are red, tinged with yellow; so as he swims about in the water he makes quite a show.

There is a member of the eel family that can give these shocks too, and although he is found in fresh water, and we have really no right to talk about him now, still I am sure you want to hear a little about him as well as the others. He looks very much like any other eel, and you know they all are a good deal like fat snakes. He can give very strong shocks, so strong that when a man once put both feet on one he felt the pain from it all day long. These eels may be tamed, and then they will let themselves be picked up and played with just like any other pet, without doing a bit of mischief. But how do you suppose they go to work to catch them in the first place? Humboldt, a great traveller and naturalist, tells us one way of doing this. They are found in the rivers and pools of South America. Now, there are a great many wild horses in that country, so the natives, after getting around a drove of these, drive them into a pool where there are plenty of eels. As they rush in, the eels, disturbed and trampled on, give them shock after shock, not only on the legs, but on the body too. This hurts and frightens the horses so much that they try to escape, but as they hurry to get out of the water the men with shouts, clubs, and stones drive most of them back again, although some few do succeed in escaping and run off to the woods. Those in the water kick and stamp about and make a great time, but there are so many of the eels, and their shocks come so fast and are so powerful, that the poor horses can do but little, and often some of them fall down dead. After a time the men let them come out, when they either drop down on the bank worn out, or run off neighing with fright and pain.

But what about the eels? They do not feel very well either, for although they did not have quite as hard a time as the horses, they, too, are very tired; and as their electricity is all used up for a time, the men can pick up any number without being the least bit hurt by them. EMMA J. WOOD.

Wholesome Fiction.

THACKERAY.

ILLIAM MAKEPEACE THACKERAY was contemporary with Dickens, though somewhat later, as a novelist, and has achieved as remarkable and as deserving a fame. He takes rank with the first English fiction-writers of this century. His works are read by all classes and belong to what we may call the classics of wholesome fiction. He belonged to middle-class life, was called to the bar, but did not follow the legal profession. His first ventures as a writer and satirist were his 'Paris Sketch Book,' 'Irish Sketch Book,' the 'Chronicle of the Drum,' &c., and his welcome contributions to 'Fraser's Magazine' and that wittiest of periodicals, 'Punch.' But his great success began with his story of 'Vanity Fair—a novel without a Hero,' the illustrations for which were furnished by himself. Its severe delineation of character, wonderful knowledge of human nature, and keen satire of society's vanities and vices at once brought him to the front as the greatest satirist of his age. He is not the bright genial humorist, the lover of happy burlesque and comical caricature

that Dickens is, but his analysis of human character is keener, his plummet sounds a deeper depth, and his portrayal of the meanness, the snobbery, the hypocrisy and wrongdoing of society, especially in what we sometimes call its higher grades and walks, has a yet more caustic severity. To quote from Anthony Trollope, himself a writer of no mean repute, and one of Thackeray's friends and biographers: 'When the critics—the talking critics as well as the writing critics—began to discuss "Vanity Fair," there had already grown up a feeling as to Thackeray as an author, that he was one who had taken up the business of castigating the vices of the world. Scott had dealt with the heroics whether displayed in his "Flora MacIvors" or "Meg Merrilieses," in his "Ivanhoes" or "Ochiltrees." Miss Edgeworth had been moral; Miss Austen conventional; Bulwer had been poetical and sentimental; Maryat and Lever had been funny and pugnacious, always with a dash of gallantry, displaying funny naval and military life; and Dickens had already become great in painting the virtues of the lower orders. But by all these some kind of virtue had been sung, though it might be only the virtue of riding a horse or fighting a duel. With Thackeray it had been altogether different. Alas, alas! the meanness of human wishes; the poorness of human results! That had been his tone. There can be no doubt that the heroic had appeared contemptible to him, as being untrue.' So Thackeray became a satirist of real life. Heroines with celestial grace were not in his way. His Amelia does not reach that level by any means. Heroes of the grand type, full of resources, beautiful as brave, and never lacking in address or self-assertion, did not come readily to his pencil. He never saw them. Captain Dobbin is ungainly, shy and awkward, the son of a grocer, almost dull were it not for the true human worthiness that shines through as if in scorn of the gloss of the conventional or merely romantic.

In 'Vanity Fair' Becky Sharp and Rawdon Crawley are the heroine and hero of the story, but they are of the bad sort. Here our author parts company with other writers who had generally made or attempted to make their heroes virtuous and dignified. But Thackeray never condones vice, be it remembered. As it has been justly remarked—'He thought that more could be done by exposing the vices than extolling the virtues of mankind. No doubt he had a more thorough belief in the one than in the other. The Dobbins he did encounter seldom; the Rawdon Crawleys very often. He saw around him so much that was mean! He was hurt so often by the little vanities of people! It was thus that he was driven to that over-thoughtfulness about snobs and such like. It thus became natural to him to insist on the thing which he hated with unceasing assiduity, and only to break out now and again into a rapture of love for the true nobility that was dear to him, as he did with the character of Captain Dobbin.' We must allow Thackeray his cue if we would appreciate his excellencies. A double story runs through 'Vanity Fair,' and claims our interest to the end. Amelia Sedley and Captain Dobbin are the natural contrasts to Becky Sharp and Rawdon Crawley. We follow not without a degree of human sympathy the remarkable career of Becky—for she is the most striking personage in the book—as covetous, false, and unprincipled as she is witty, facetious, and clever, succeeding in everything for a time, but in the end left alone in her loveless lot. And we instinctively feel that while virtue is ever its own reward, wickedness is its own penalty. And this all the more that it is a *woman* who sits for this dark picture.

Amelia, on the other hand, is a gentle, honest, simple-hearted English girl, by no means heroic, but thoroughly feminine and true to nature. Between Becky and Amelia critics have drawn a sharp contrast by recognizing the one as the impersonation of intellect without virtue, and the other as that of virtue without intellect. Be that as it may, Amelia is not without sense, and may be taken as a good prototype for any of her age and sex. She is true as steel: marries her George Osborne, a weak, selfish fellow whom she adores, and who falls in action at Waterloo. Dobbin, the good hero of the story, is seen to advantage in the relation he sustains to the two lovers, and afterwards, when he seeks to win the widowed Amelia, whom he has long loved. In early days 'he has loved her—as one man may love another—solely with a view to the profit of his friend. He has known all along that George and Amelia have been engaged to each other as boy and girl. George would have neglected her, but Dobbin would not allow it. He had nothing to get for himself, but loving her as he did, it was the work of his life to get for her all that she wanted.' Fifteen years of widowhood follow the death of Osborne, during which, Dobbin, who becomes at length a colonel, woos in vain. But at the end she is won, and eighteen years of magnanimous though pining love—the love of a truly manly heart—gain for that noble, unselfish soul its prize. 'Vanity Fair' is a book of contrasts, full of deep, true human feeling and keen insight into character. Its moral anatomy is sometimes such as to startle us by its naked realism, but the lessons it conveys are always sound, searching, and good.

Thackeray's second great work was his 'History of Pendennis,' in which he aims at describing the gentlemen of the present age—'neither better nor worse than most educated men.' He protests that 'since the author of "Tom Jones" was buried, no writer of fiction among us has been permitted to depict to his utmost powers a *man*. We must drape him, and give him a certain conventional simper. Society will not tolerate the natural in our art.' In 'Pendennis,' however, we have no paragon of excellence. He is neither angel nor imp, but an average specimen of his class. Thackeray had to protest against our taking it for granted that '*our* boys from our public schools look us in the face and are manly; that our gentlemen tell the truth as a matter of course; and that our young ladies are refined and unselfish.' It is not so, and our author succeeds, and we think admirably, in unmasking the conventional guise and holding the unflattering mirror up to nature. We feel that Pen is very like the most of us; but then it is refreshing to find that there are better folks near us to rebuke kindly and to help faithfully; and so Warrington and Laura are his good angels—'angels so good as to make us wonder that a creature so weak should have had such angels about him,' for they are certainly among the finest characters he has given us.

Our limited space will not allow us to enlarge. The reader is referred to his other works, some of still greater power perhaps, as, for example, his 'Esmond,' 'The Newcomes,' 'The Virginians,' and others, not to speak of his burlesques and ballads. 'The Newcomes' naturally follows upon 'Pendennis' in the thread of its story; and 'Esmond' and 'The Virginians' should be associated together in our reading. Some think 'The Newcomes' was Thackeray's masterpiece. When, however, there is so much of the highest quality in his other productions, it is difficult to say which is best, and we must leave it to the taste of the reader. 'The Newcomes,' as it has been pointed out, is in the old vein—a transcript of real life. Its leading theme is the misery occasioned by that vice of the great and worldly—forced and ill-assorted marriages. It lays bare to view the cause of many a domestic sorrow—the skeleton in the closet, and denounces with unsparing severity and scathing satire the 'unhallowed traffic.' Lady Clara Newcome, a fair victim, touches us with her misfortune and her shame—the sad result of the evil against which our author inveighs. Colonel Newcome, the hero of the tale, impresses us with his courtesy, his kindliness and simplicity, his thorough gentlemanliness to the end. Ruined through the knavery of others, and dying as a poor brother in the Charterhouse, he carries himself nobly, with a delicacy of feeling and of demeanour that shows the true man undwarfed and undegraded by humblest surroundings and saddest lot. We almost wish for him a happier ending after the world's buffetings, but we are reminded of Scott's words: 'A character of a highly virtuous and lofty stamp is degraded rather than exalted by an attempt to reward virtue with worldly prosperity. Such is not the recompense which Providence has deemed worthy of suffering merit.' It is generally thought that Ethel Newcome is the best of Thackeray's female portraits. It is certainly

drawn with remarkable delicacy and truth. On the other hand, satire of the gentler sex is not withheld—as when he gives us a sight of a dozen silly London girls with their bare necks and shoulders sitting round Rummun Loll, the pretended Indian prince, and worshipping him as he reposes on his low settee.

Clive Newcome is a kind of better Pendennis, and the moral pointed in his case seems to be that the career of one who is idle and ambitious at the same time, is one equally of folly and of misery. The will to be, and to do something worth while, to make the most of what we are and have, to be industrious that we may excel, rather than to waste life in day-dreams is here forcibly taught us. Clive's unhappiness lasts to the close, and is sadly intensified by the abominations of his mother-in-law, Mrs. Mack the campaigner, a vividly drawn character, 'but a woman so odious that one is induced to doubt (so says Trollope) whether she should have been depicted.'

'Esmond' has been pronounced by one school of critics Thackeray's best creation. It has additional literary interest in its style which is an admirable copy of the Queen Anne period of which it writes, and in which its scenes are laid. Its hero is Colonel Henry Esmond a Cavalier and a Jacobite. The gay Chevalier is brought on the stage, and the great writers—Swift, Congreve, Addison, and Steele—figure with much interest. The story is also the most complete of any as a unity in itself, less free from wandering incident and detached memoirs of individuals, and cost Thackeray perhaps more thought than anything he ever wrote. Great carefulness is seen in handling the character of Esmond. He is made up of many virtues, and yet he maintains his character as a prig, for such Thackeray means him to be. That he does not turn out a wooden figure with his virtues so much stucco, and his whole make up inconsistent and absurd is the wonder, but that he is a real live person, so that the reader believes in him, is a tribute to the author's genius. Equal deftness and delicacy are shown in the portrayal of Lady Castlewood, one of the heroines, and in the turn of events which issues in Esmond's becoming her husband, though for years he had hopelessly wooed her daughter Beatrix. The romance of life is over when they marry — the lady is ten years her husband's senior, and there is a melancholy— too melancholy shall we say—picture of the decay of matrimonial love,,as if Thackeray can never get away from his text of ' Vanitas, Vanitatum.' But the most striking character is that of Beatrix. Her beauty is extraordinary, her charms and caprices carry all by storm. But she will not be *loved.* She lives to be *admired,* and she wishes to rise in the world and gain a proud summit of material ambition by the admiration she is able to evoke. With this, as ' with a sword. she must open her oyster.' Lover after lover is discarded, till a proud, cold duke offers his hand, and she already fancies herself the proud Duchess of Hamilton. The duke is killed in a duel ere he can fulfil his promise to marry her, and the gilded bubble bursts. Then the young Stuart prince, whom loyal hearts think they can make a king, comes on the scene. Beatrix is in hope again, but her ambition is foiled, and ' nothing but the disgrace of the wish remains.' So the melancholy tale proceeds. At length she condescends to be the wife of her brother's tutor, whom she gets by her intrigues made a bishop. Then we hear of her in the story of the Virginians, true to herself still. ' The bishop has been put to rest under a load of marble, and she has become a baroness, a rich old woman courted by all her relatives because of her wealth.' Of inner beauty there is none, the outer charms have flown, and what remains to her of material glory is but a tinselled emptiness. There is nothing strained here. All is true—terribly, and too sadly true.

Thackeray is more satirist than humorist, though of humour he had a rich vein when he chose to work it. He has been called a cynic —a dog that barks. Well, he barks to some purpose and not for barking's sake. He was in truth a great moralist. It may be truly said that the mere cynic gives himself up to satire, ' not because things are evil, but because he himself is evil.' Thackeray in this sense is clear of the charge. Trollope allows

that Thackeray permitted his intellect to be too thoroughly saturated with the aspect of the ill side of things, and that a sardonic melancholy was the characteristic most common to him. But never can it be averred that any ' girl has been taught to be immodest, or any man unmanly by what he has written.' His tone is more to denounce than to bless. His physic is always curative, never poisonous.

A good specimen of his satire of shams, of pampered selfishness, and of snug religious complacency is the following :—

' To be a good old country gentleman is to hold a position nearest the gods, and at the summit of earthly felicity. To have a large unencumbered rent-roll, and the rents paid regularly by adoring farmers, who bless their stars at having such a landlord as his honour, to have no tenant holding back with his money excepting just one perhaps, who does so just in order to give occasion to a good old country gentleman to show his sublime charity and universal benevolence of soul; to hunt three days a week, love the sport of all things, and have perfect good health and good appetite in consequence ; to have not only a good appetite but a good dinner ; to sit down in the church in the midst of a chorus of blessings from the villagers, the first man in the parish, the benefactor of the parish, with a consciousness of consummate desert, saying, '' Have mercy upon us, miserable sinners,'' to be sure, but only for form's sake, and to give other folks an example : a G.O.C.G. a miserable sinner ! So healthy, so wealthy, so jolly, and so much respected by the vicar, so much honoured by the tenants, so much beloved and admired by his family, amongst whom his story of grouse in the gun-room causes laughter from generation to generation ; this perfect being a miserable sinner ! *Allons donc !* Give any man good health and temper, five thousand a year, the adoration of his parish, and the love and worship of his family, and I'll defy you to make him so heartily dissatisfied with his spiritual condition as to set himself down a miserable anything. . . You might when racked with gout, in solitude, the fear of death before your eyes, the doctor having cut off your bottle of claret and ordered arrow-root and a litttle sherry—you might *then* be humiliated and acknowledge your short-comings and the vanity of things in general, but in high health, sunshine, spirits, that word "miserable" is only a form. You can't think in your heart that you are to be pitied much for the present. If *you* are to be miserable, what is Colin Ploughman with the ague, seven children, two pounds a year rent to pay for his cottage, and eight shillings a week? No, a healthy, rich, jolly country gentleman, if miserable, has a very support-able misery ; *if a sinner, has very few people to tell him so.'*　　　　　　　H.Y.

Current Topics.

HOLIDAY MAKING.

IF my readers have not yet had their summer holidays they are very likely preparing for them. They are to be envied. What is so pleasant as to look forward to a well-earned holiday? The anticipation, alas! is often far more enjoyable than the realization. But a holiday can always be made pleasant if we go the right way about it. Neither holidays nor anything else, however, can be satisfactory if we expect too much from them. And when we travel a long distance to reach some fashionable resort our expectation is liable to get rather high. Unless we be in search of information, it is not wise to go very far away. The pleasantest holidays are often those spent near home. 'Distant objects please,' Hazlitt tells us, 'because they imply an idea of space and magnitude, and because, not being obtruded too close upon the eye, we clothe them with the indistinct and airy colours of fancy.' If we are to be happy any-where we must carry the elements of happi-ness with us. There is much beauty all around us, if we only had eyes to see it. And if we cannot enjoy the beauty that is near us, we are almost sure to be disappointed with that we go a long way to see.

To enjoy a holiday thoroughly a good deal of philosophy is necessary. It is wonderful how miserable some people make themselves because they haven't learnt the art of taking things as they find them. Stepping on board the steamer at Inversnaid, near the head of Loch Lomond, one day, I found a young Highlander, in all the glory of his tartans, blowing away at his bagpipes. Without pre-tending to understand his music, you could not but feel how greatly it added to the interest of the scene. How often had those grand old hills listened to similar strains in very different circumstances! My equanimity, however, was a bit ruffled by a lady, who threw herself on to a seat near me with the audible wish that the fellow would 'stop that noise.' Now what did a lady like that want in the Highlands? Out of harmony with her surroundings, she would, I imagine, get neither benefit nor pleasure from her trip. Mark Twain and his friends in that wonderful tour of theirs through Europe made up their minds to admire nothing. They succeeded in puzzling the guide and in amusing other people, but 'The Innocents Abroad' is not an ideal guide-book. 'We live by admiration, hope, and love,' and if our holiday is to put new life into us, we must keep our eyes open for the beautiful and the true.

To thoroughly enjoy a holiday we must have earned it. Paul's dictum, 'If any would not work, neither should he eat,' ought to hold good with regard to holidays, and it does. Those who spend all their days in pleasure have a weary time of it. 'If all the year were playing, holidays to sport would be as tedious as to work.' But let the man who has been engaged the whole year in earnest and exhausting toil turn aside for a few weeks' recreation, and holiday will be to him a keen enjoyment. 'They speak of the luxury of doing good,' wrote Dr. George Wilson, of Edinburgh, when on a holiday, 'they speak of the luxury of doing good; but what is that to the luxury of doing nothing, especially when, as in my case, doing nothing is doing good? What did I do yesterday? Nothing. The day before? Nothing. What am I doing at present? Nothing.' Thus the days of his vacation passed over, and he gathered strength for future work.

———————

A holiday of this kind, however, would have small attractions for young folks. They find their pleasure in activity. And when away amongst the mountains they are sometimes in danger of over-exerting themselves. The exhilarating atmosphere of those regions works wonders upon young blood, and the holiday is often spoiled by too much being attempted. Nothing can be so foolish as the ambition to ' do' everything in a country. The Rev. W. J. Dawson tells us that the first time he was in Switzerland he met two youths who had gone on their tour with this determination. ' They refused on principle to sleep in bed whenever they could sleep in the train. As far as possible they did without sleep. I met them,' he says, ' three weeks later coming down from Monta Rosa. They were jaundiced, emaciated, cadaverous. Their lips looked black and cracked, and there were ominous dark rings under their eyes. They had seen everything, and they were physically exhausted. It was impossible that they could have had any real enjoyment, or that any particular impression they had received could be other than blurred and confused. They looked ready for their coffins. My friend, who was a physician, was brutal enough to tell them so ; whereat they snarled feebly, and remarked that " any way they had done Switzerland." It looked as though Switzerland had " done " them.'

———————

Pleasure ought not to be our only object even on a holiday. When the means are available it affords an opportunity of enlarging our knowledge that ought not to be neglected. The knowledge gained by travel is of great value. The stay-at-home is often narrow in his sympathies, and prejudiced in his judgments. A little travel is a wonderful corrective. This is especially true with regard to politics. We have an empire stretching into every quarter of the globe, and comprising almost every race of mankind. The government of such an empire is indeed a great task. How much better it would be performed if the English people travelled more. There, for instance, is Lord Randolph Churchill off to Africa for a holiday, and what does he find? He is sending home his impressions to the *Daily Graphic*, and he tells us that what he has seen has entirely changed his opinions of South African affairs.

———————

Upon no part of his career has Mr. Gladstone been more bitterly assailed by his opponents than upon his South African policy. When in 1880, after the Dutch Boers of the Transvaal had defeated the British troops, he entered into negotiations with them, and granted them the independence of their country, it was thought by large numbers of well-meaning people in England that he had miserably failed to maintain the national ' honour.' Lord Randolph Churchill was one who joined in this lament, but now that he has had an opportunity of looking into the matter on the spot he writes as follows, viz.:— ' The surrender of the Transvaal, and the peace concluded by Mr. Gladstone with the victors of Majuba Hill, were at the time, and still are, the object of sharp criticism and bitter denunciation from many politicians at home. Better and more precise information, combined with cool reflection, leads me to the conclusion that, had the British Government of that day taken advantage of its strong military position, and annihilated, as it could easily have done, the Boer forces, it would indeed have regained the Transvaal, but it would have lost Cape Colony. The Dutch sentiment in the colony had been so exasperated . . . that the final triumph of the British arms mainly by brute force would have permanently and hopelessly alienated it from Great Britain. . . . The actual magnanimity of the peace with the Boers concluded by Mr. Gladstone . . . atoned for much of past grievance, and demonstrated the total absence in the English mind of any hostility or unfriendliness to the Dutch race.' Truly we ought not to begrudge our legislators a little foreign travel. The breadth of view it would enable them to gain would add greatly to the interest and intelligence of our political discussions.

By all means have a companion with you on your holiday tour—that is to say, provided always that you can find the right kind of companion. There must be perfect confidence between you, and that kind of understanding which will permit you to be silent together without awkwardness. If you cannot find the right kind of companion you will certainly be better alone, but you must never neglect to secure the companionship of good books. You will want them on wet days, and you will find them a pleasant solace after a heavy tramp.   .

> 'Oh, for a booke and a shadie nooke,
> Eyther in doore or out;
> With the grene leaves whispering overhead
> Or the street cryes all about.
> Where I may reade all at my ease,
> Both of the newe and old;
> For a jolly goode booke whereon to looke
> Is better to me than golde.'

'He that loveth a book,' says Isaac Barrow, 'will never want a faithful friend, a wholesome counsellor, a cheerful companion, an effectual comforter. By study, by reading, by thinking, one may innocently divert and pleasantly entertain himself, as in all weathers, so in all fashions.'

Don't, then, forget to pack up a few good books in your portmanteau. And as we go in for a thorough change of scene on our holidays, why not seek a change of reading? Now is the time to take new excursions into literature or to revisit old scenes. This latter course is perhaps the most delightful of all, and it is often only at holiday time that one has the leisure to indulge in it. And this leads me to put in a plea for Sir Walter Scott. Somebody happily calls him 'the whole world's darling,' and he never grows stale. Happy is the man who has read him in his youth, and happy too is he who has the opportunity of re-reading him in after life. It may be safely said that in the whole range of recent literature, there is nothing at once so amusing and so elevating as Sir Walter Scott's novels. In an address to students many years ago, Dean Stanley spoke of 'the profound reverence, the lofty sense of Christian honour, purity, and justice that breathe through every volume of the romances of Walter Scott.' It is these characteristics that make them such fine reading for the young, but what makes them so grateful to the jaded palate of the modern novel reader is their genial humour. Modern fiction is so sad and often so muddy that a reading of Scott has all the tonic effect of a mountain breeze. He brims over with good spirits; and indeed he is the very *beau ideal* of a holiday companion.

If I were asked to name the finest of Scott's works, I should say 'Old Mortality' at once. This, however, is far from being the universal opinion. The fact, indeed, that no one seems able to determine which is the best, is a splendid testimony to their uniform excellence. There is scarcely a failure amongst them, and yet their variety of scene and character is truly remarkable. The reader is brought into the company of kings and queens, of beggars and clowns, of mercenary soldiers and chivalrous gentlemen, of eccentric wits and humorous pedants, of magistrates and lawyers, of servant girls and high-born ladies; and whether the plot is laid in the twelfth century, as in 'Ivanhoe,' or in the eighteenth as in 'Guy Mannering,' and the 'Antiquary,' there is the one touch of nature which makes you feel as if all the people were something more than creations of the imagination, and must have played their parts on the stage of life. Unlike some other works of genius the productions of Scott had the good fortune of being appreciated as soon as they appeared. Two thousand copies of 'Guy Mannering' were sold the day after publication at one guinea each. On the publisher asking Lord Holland's opinion of two of the stories which had just been published, he exclaimed, 'Opinion! we did not one of us get to bed last night—nothing slept but my gout.'

There is one curious failure in Sir Walter Scott's work. It is universally admitted that he never succeeded in depicting a genuine hero. But though he could not picture the life of a true hero, yet he could live it. Nothing that he ever wrote is more romantic and inspiring than his own life. He was a true man and he had an opportunity of proving his greatness both in prosperity and adversity. When fifty-four years of age the failure of his publisher, and of the printing house in which he was a partner, involved him in the enormous debt of £117,000. Refusing all offers of arrangement, he resolved to pay it off. He made a magnificent struggle, and in two years he cleared off nearly £40,000, and in three years more only about £54,000 remained, but his energies were exhausted. His last novel was written after more than one paralytic stroke had left its mark upon him. His was a beautiful death, and it was remarkable that when his memory for every other kind of literature had gone he seemed to have an intelligent grasp of the Bible. Desiring his son-in-law to read to him, he was asked to say from what book. 'Need you ask?' he replied, 'there is but one.' And when the fourteenth chapter of St. John's Gospel was read to him, he said, 'Well, this is a great comfort. I have followed you distinctly, and I feel as if I were yet to be myself again.' Truly he was a splendid fellow, and there have been few men who have done more than he to brighten and uplift the lives of common men. If any of my young friends have not yet made his acquaintance, there is a grand treat in store for them. And I repeat that nothing would be more likely to brighten up a holiday than two or three of his delightful stories.   M. P. D.

THE Christian's *heart* understands the atonement better than the Christian's *head*. It is a difficult doctrine for the brain, but a sweet and simple one to the affections.

Jonathan Edwards could not comprehend the atonement one whit more clearly nor intensely than the dairyman's daughter when she sang to herself:

> ' How glorious the grace,
>   When Christ sustained the stroke;
>   His life and blood the Shepherd pays,
>   A ransom for His flock.'   CUYLER.

Growing Old.

THEY call it 'going down the hill'
    when we are growing old,
    And speak with mournful accents
    when our tale is nearly told:
They sigh when talking of the past, the
    days that used to be,
As if the future were not bright with
    immortality.

But it is not going down; it is climbing
    high and higher,
Until we almost see the mountain that our
    souls desire.
For if the natural eye grows dim, it is but
    dim to earth,
While the eye of faith grows keener to discern the Saviour's worth.

Who would exchange for shooting blade the
    waving golden grain ?
Or, when the corn is fully ripe, would wish
    it green again ?
And who would wish the hoary head, found
    in the way of truth,
To be again encircled with the sunny locks
    of youth ?

For though, in truth, the outward man
    must perish and decay,
The inward man shall be renewed by grace
    from day to day ;
Those who are planted by the Lord, unshaken
    in the root,
Shall in their old age flourish, and bring
    forth their choicest fruit.

It is not years that make men old; the
    spirit may be young,
Though fully threescore-years-and-ten the
    wheels of life have run.   [of truth,
God has Himself recorded, in His blest Word
That they who wait upon the Lord they
    shall e'en renew their youth.

And when the eye, now dim, shall open to
    behold the King,
And ears now dull with age shall hear the
    harps of heaven ring,
And on the head now hoary shall be placed
    the crown of gold,
Then shall be known the lasting joy of
    never growing old.

SPRINGTIME.

O FOLLOW THE SAVIOUR.

CHILDREN'S DUET.

R. J. DRING.

3. 'Tis pleasant to walk in the steps that He trod When He was a stranger below: No friend is like Jesus; His staff and His rod Will strengthen and guide as you go.	4. O learn of Him now, for a glorious rest, And joys that will never decay, [fess'd, For us are preparing who His name have con- And learned His commands to obey.

O FOLLOW THE SAVIOUR.

CHILDREN'S DUET.

R. J. DRING.

KEY F. *Moderato.* (*For Accompaniment see opposite page.*)

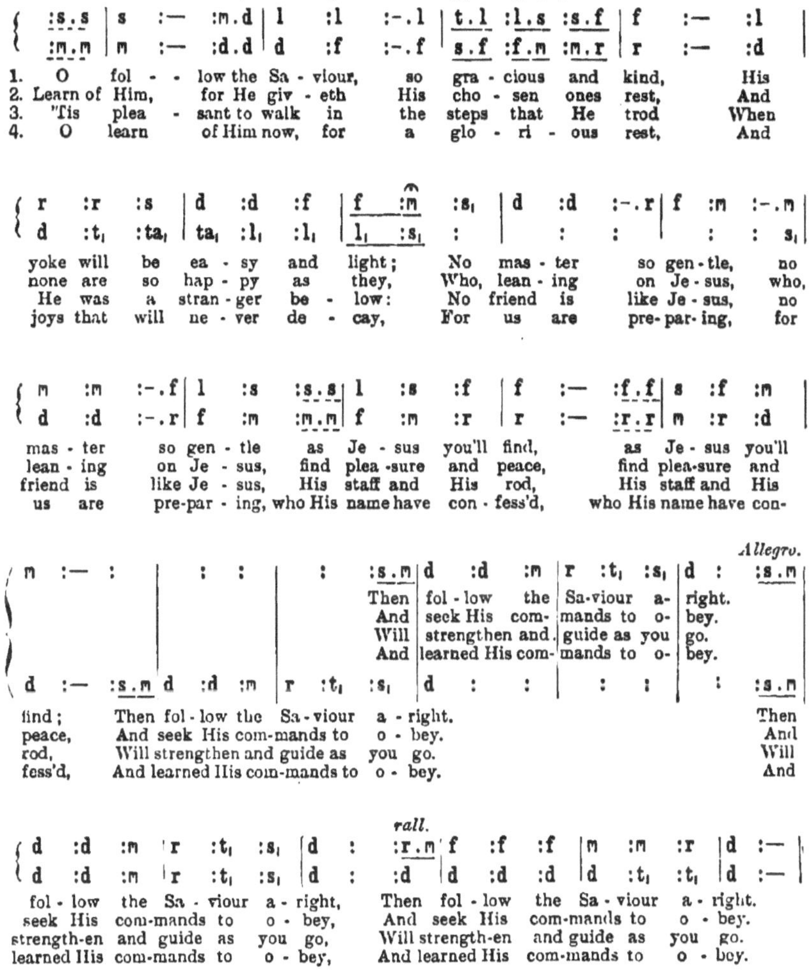

```
{ :s.s | s :— :m.d | l :l :-.l | t.l :l.s :s.f | f :— :l  |
{ :m.m | m :— :d.d | d :f :-.f | s.f :f.m :m.r | r :— :d  |
```

1. O fol - - low the Sa - viour, so gra - cious and kind, His
2. Learn of Him, for He giv - eth His cho - sen ones rest, And
3. 'Tis plea - sant to walk in the steps that He trod When
4. O learn of Him now, for a glo - ri - ous rest, And

```
{ r :r :s | d :d :f | f :m :s, | d :d :-.r | f :m :-.m |
{ d :t, :ta, | ta, :l, :l, | l, :s, : | : : | : : s, |
```

yoke will be ea - sy and light; No mas - ter so gen - tle, no
none are so hap - py as they, Who, lean - ing on Je - sus, who,
He was a stran - ger be - low: No friend is like Je - sus, no
joys that will ne - ver de - cay, For us are pre - par - ing, for

```
{ m :m :-.f | l :s :s.s | l :s :f | f :— :f.f | s :f :m |
{ d :d :-.r | f :m :m.m | f :m :r | r :— :r.r | m :r :d |
```

mas - ter so gen - tle as Je - sus you'll find, as Je - sus you'll
lean - ing on Je - sus, find plea -sure and peace, find plea-sure and
friend is like Je - sus, His staff and His rod, His staff and His
us are pre-par - ing, who His name have con - fess'd, who His name have con-

Allegro.

```
/ m :— : | : : | : :s.m | d :d :m | r :t, :s, | d : :s.m |
```

Then fol - low the Sa-viour a- right.
And seek His com- mands to o- bey.
Will strengthen and. guide as you go.
And learned His com- mands to o- bey.

```
\ d :— :s.m d :d :m | r :t, :s, | d : : | : : | : :s.m |
```

find; Then fol - low the Sa - viour a - right. Then
peace, And seek His com-mands to o - bey. And
rod, Will strengthen and guide as you go. Will
fess'd, And learned His com-mands to o - bey. And

rall.

```
{ d :d :m r :t, :s, | d : :r.m f :f :f | m :m :r | d :— |
{ d :d :m r :t, :s, | d : :d d :d :d | d :t, :t, | d :— |
```

fol - low the Sa - viour a - right, Then fol - low the Sa - viour a - right.
seek His com-mands to o - bey, And seek His com-mands to o - bey.
strength-en and guide as you go, Will strength-en and guide as you go.
learned His com-mands to o - bey, And learned His com-mands to o - bey.

The Library.

E received some little time ago from the Wesleyan Book Room a charming volume on Missionary Life in Ceylon, which we must lose no further time in bringing before our readers. It is entitled, *The Happy Valley; Our New Mission Garden in Uva, Ceylon,* and is from the pen of the Rev. Samuel Langdon. Before we are introduced to the story of missionary operations, there is an historical and descriptive sketch of the country. It is said that when Arabi Pasha was sent to perpetual exile in Ceylon he congratulated himself on being banished to Paradise. 'The first man Adam,' he is reported to have said, 'was exiled *from* the Garden of Eden. I am more fortunate in being exiled *to* it. For, you know, it is a tradition with Islam that the Island of Ceylon was the garden in which our first parents were placed, and from which they were expelled by Allah!' One of the highest mountains in Ceylon, and sacred to the Mohammedans, is called 'Adam's Peak.' After this preliminary description, the writer goes on to tell in chatty and charming style about his house and its surroundings. How he and his wife, or 'Nona,' selected their land, realized the need of a fence, and of more labourers got on good terms with the Tamil villagers, and laboured away among them with as much enthusiasm, and as much patience as they could command. They found that the scenery, though 'perfectly idyllic,' as the wife said, was the background of much sin, superstition, and suffering. The 'baby,' which 'Nona' took up in one of their visits, 'was exceedingly dirty, and after the first pause of astonishment screamed amazingly,' in spite of all the English lady's endearments. 'The women laughed good-humouredly at her failure, and the mother, taking the child and laying it on her lap, pounded its little head against her knees till peace was restored. We found that the house was a small village in itself, for numbers of men and women came out of the building into the yard to inspect the new arrivals. We were informed that several families were living together in this one house, with a result, physical and moral, such as a garret in the worst of London slums could not more than parallel. . . One or two of the children, who formed such a pleasant feature in the idyll, were suffering from loathsome skin diseases. Some of the elders exhibited on the unclothed parts of their bodies a combination of filth and disease, which, to an inexperienced visitor, was frightful to contemplate. The ignorance was lamentable. . . . The astrologer is the ruling priest here, and the horoscope is the village Bible. In that precious document the destiny of each individual is declared. . . . Added to all this there are devil ceremonies of the most horrible kind held when sickness prevails, and here you have the religion of the hamlet.' They devoted themselves largely, if not chiefly, to the women and children, and ere long were encouraged by substantial results. A girl's home was established, a missionary smithy, a carpenter's shop, a barley field and large vegetable garden. On Easter Sunday five big men stand before the 'extemporised baptismal font, decorated significantly, but not designedly, with Adam's apples,' and passion flowers. These men are converts from Buddhism, and each has been allowed to choose his own new name. The names of the Old Testament heroes are most in demand—Joshua, Moses, etc. They promise, God helping them, 'that they will for ever renounce idolatry, that they will take no part in Buddhist ceremonies or worship, that they will no longer serve the demon-gods and goddesses so universally worshipped in Ceylon, that they will forsake astrology, and will in future have nothing to do with superstitious heathen charms.' Nobody knows how these questions must search and try a candidate for baptism who has not lived in the Sinhalese villages, and see how the charms, astrology and demon-worship, renounced in the answers, are bound up with the daily life of the people. . . . .

The service is ended, and we walk up the hill to the Mission-house, thanking God for the increase, and for the promise of harvest that we see in the fields. There are several other villagers on probation. There is one man whose heart has been reached through bodily healing. There is another who has come to us from a village many miles away, a village which has only been visited once by the missionary. In passing through he gave tracts to the few who could read. One was given to an intelligent man who had been educated in a Buddhist monastery. He is impressed by it, and walks a journey of fifteen miles to get books, and to be taught the way of salvation. Other instances we call to mind, and we begin to speak with some pride about the success of our methods in our 'New Mission Garden.' ' Oh dear! ' says the ' Nona,' ' how much we talk about Paul's methods and Apollo's methods, old methods and new methods, and how often we forget that " it is God that giveth the increase! " ' Mr. Langdon is the author of other interesting little books on Ceylon, which are very fascinating, and should be associated with the present.

The Cork-Tree.

ORK comes from the bark of the cork-tree, or cork-oak, as it is called by the Spaniards. A species of oak, a native of the south of Europe and north of Africa, Spain, and Portugal, chiefly supplies the world with cork; and in these countries the tree is often planted expressly for the sake of the cork. It is said the cork-tree is not of great size, generally not more than twenty to forty feet high, much branched, with ovate oblong evergreen leaves, which are sometimes sharply serrated, as in the oak. The acorns are eatable and resemble chestnuts in taste.

The bark in tree and branches from three to five years old acquires a rough or fungous appearance, new layers of cellular tissue being formed as the outer parts crack from distension, until they are finally thrown off in large flakes, when a new formation of the same kind takes place. Cork, however, intended for the market must be stripped off a year or two before it would naturally come away, and the process is repeated at intervals of six or eight years. The bark of young trees and branches is either useless or very inferior in quality. It is only after the third peeling that really good cork is produced.

This barking of the tree does not injure it in the least, for it is not the removal of the whole bark but only of external layers of spongy cellular tissue, all or the greater part of which has ceased to have any true vitality, and has become an encumbrance to the tree, which, in time, as we have already said, it would throw off of itself; and therefore, instead of being injurious, when done with proper care it rather promotes the health of the tree, which continues to yield crops of cork for almost one hundred and fifty years.

In stripping off the cork incisions are made to the proper depth, and each piece is then cut away from the tree by a curved knife with two handles. The bark, after being cut into square pieces or sheets, is pressed to remove its natural curvature and flatten it. If it is found that simple pressing has not flattened it sufficiently it is soaked in boiling water for about two hours, or heated on the convex side, and the contraction thus produced strengthens it. It is then cut into slips, and these slips into squares, according to the required size of the cork. These are rounded by the cork-cutter by means of a broad, sharp knife ; the cork is held in the left hand and rested against a block of wood and the knife pushed forward, and at the same time its edge is made to describe a circular curve by a skilful turn of the wrist, when the cork stopper is ready for use.

The knife used requires constant sharpening ; the workman has a board before him on which the knife is rubbed on each side after every cut. Many attempts, it is said, have been made to cut cork by machinery, but not altogether successfully. A patent cork-cutting company was established a few years ago, but failed. The great difficulty in applying machines to this purpose arises from the necessity of continually sharpening the knife or cutters, for it is a curious fact that as soft a substance as cork blunts the tools used in cutting it far more rapidly than does the hardest and toughest metal. A cork-cutter's knife requires constant sharpening, while the tool that is used for planing, turning, or boring steel will work continuously for hours without sharpening.

In such machinery as can be used, the cork, after being cut into squares of the regular length, is made to revolve on grasping spindles and cutters of various forms, such as a revolving cutter-wheel, hollow cones with internal cutters, reciprocating blades, toothed cutters, etc., which are brought to bear upon the revolving cork.

We find it stated that some enterprising Americans have recently conceived the idea of raising cork-trees. They believe they can be successfully cultivated in the climate of California, and steps have been taken toward making the experiment. It is in such demand in America that the average annual importation of cork-wood to the port of New York alone is said to be 70,000 bales a year. A bale weighs 160 pounds, and is worth 20 dollars a pound, making a total value of the yearly importation 1,400,000 dollars. It enters, however, duty free, and is nearly all imported by one firm, which has a branch office in New York, the main office being in London and Lisbon. The firm owns vast forests of cork-wood in Portugal and Spain, and may be said to control the business.

With the exception of an inferior kind of cork-wood, grown in Algiers to a limited extent, all the cork-wood of commerce comes from the Spanish Peninsula, where the tree not only abounds in cultivated forests, but also grows wild on the mountains.

Besides the use of cork for stopping bottles, casks, etc., it is much used on account of its lightness for floats of nets, swimming-belts, or cork-jackets, etc.; and on account of its impermeability to water, and its being a low conductor of heat, the inner soles of shoes are sometimes made of it. All these uses are mentioned by Pliny; but the general employ-

ment of corks for glass bottles appears to date only from the fifteenth century.

One tree has been known to yield half a ton of cork-wood, and one pound of cork can be manufactured into 144 good-sized corks. The baled cork is sent to cork manufactories in the cities. The most extensive manufactory in America is at Pittsburg. Besides the ordinary demands for cork-wood a good supply of the buoyant material, after being burned, to make it still lighter than the original bark, is shipped to Canada and New England, where it is made into seine-corks.

Various other uses are made of this valuable bark, but we can now mention but one more. The Spanish-black used by painters is made by burning cork in close vessels, and the parings of corks are carefully kept by cork-cutters for the purpose.

J. K. BLOOMFIELD.

In Memoriam.

' SHE is not dead, but sleepeth.' Let your tears
  Be dried, your grief and sorrow pass away;
From this cold world's deep shadow she hath gone
To the full blaze of never-ending day.
Pain, weariness, and suffering, now have lost
All hold on her mortality; no more
Will sickness visit her; escaped from all
The ills of life, her joyous spirit now
Attunes her harp to loftiest songs of praise.
For ever past the toils and cares of earth,
Bliss, never-ending bliss, will evermore
Her portion be; with holy spirits joined
In fellowship of soul, waiting the time
When all her dearest, most belovèd friends
Shall meet her round the throne of God, and there,
Where parting is unknown, combine to praise
The Father, Son, and Holy Spirit, one
In Three, and Three in One, eternally.

JOHN RYLEY ROBINSON.

SPRINGTIME :

A Magazine for Our Young Men and Maidens.

Vol. VI. No. 9.] SEPTEMBER, 1891. [Price Twopence.

A Bad Calculation.

By ROBERT HIND,

*Author of ' Crosby Dalton : Local Preacher
and Villuge Demagogue,' ' The Ruby
Pendant,' &c.*

CHAPTER XVII.

DISAPPOINTMENTS.

' All women have a smile,
A happiness, a kind of second self,
Kept for fresh faces. Yet I saw full soon
The bield was homeless; little love was there.'
ROBERT BUCHANAN.

OU like your new life, Arthur ? '

The speaker was Isa Saunders, now one of Arthur Brixton's most familiar friends. They were in the handsome drawing room, whose windows looked down on the river-banks and commanded a fine view of cathedral and castle. He was often there, and was always made to feel he was welcome, although his friends would have felt more satisfied had he brought a few of his fellow-students with him occasionally.

' Yes; I like it very much.'

' And there are no drawbacks whatever; nothing you could desire different from what it is ? '

Isa Saunders spoke lightly, almost frivolously indeed, and yet, one with keen perceptions, might have thought her indifference was only assumed.

' That, Miss Saunders, would be to say a great deal, and for my part, I am not quite prepared to allow that life even at the 'Varsity is just the same as paradise.'

Isa was perfectly satisfied with this answer. She was seeking information, and wondering if some of her thoughts were right.

' But you have been there such a short time, and the change for one of your temperament must have been so congenial, that I concluded your eyes would be sufficiently glamoured to overlook anything that might not be quite perfectly agreeable,' she said, with the smartest emphasis on the redundant adverbs.

For Isa was nothing if not redundant. There was far too much emphasis in her style of speaking, her sentences were too wordy, and even her manners overdone with suavity.

' Oh yes; the change has been agreeable, and I should not like to go back to the office. And there are many pleasant things of which, as an outsider, I was totally ignorant, so that even the surprises, at least some of them, have given me satisfaction.'

' And some of them have been not quite satisfactory, then ? '

Arthur wondered whither his fair questioner was leading him. His self-will often rose within him on these occasions, and yet hardly ever to any purpose when he was talking with Isa Saunders. He had been able to close his heart against Rye Harland in the days which, although really quite recent, seemed now separated from him by whole years, and knew he had almost always been a mystery to her, but his obstinacy of spirit was ineffectual to resist Isa, even when he made a far greater effort to do so.

He wondered why. Sometimes he tried to. persuade himself it must be on account of Isa's superior strength of character; and sometimes he suggested to himself that if she was not stronger, at least she must have qualities that touched his soul more nearly.

But Arthur Brixton, self-deluded as he was in many things, had more than an average measure of mental perception, and was never quite satisfied with any solution of the question that presented itself to him; and it never occurred to his heart that Rye's natural dignity and refined feeling would not allow her even to think of using cunning in order to induce her friend to reveal himself; whilst, on the other hand, Isa had been accustomed to employ all kinds of little arts to carry out her purposes, and gain such information as she desired.

She laughed, and made no effort to hide her amusement, when he remained silent. So to act was really part of her plan.

'Never mind; don't tell me anything I ought not to know,' she said. 'Only you have no idea how much I am interested in that great seat of learning. I look out at this window by the hour and try to think of all that is going on within the castle walls. Even when I cannot see the caps and gowns, the picture of the professors stands out before me, surrounded with a lot of—I never know what to call them, for they are neither boys nor men, and these half-developed young gentlemen always look frightened, and the professors always look severe.'

It was Arthur's turn to laugh.

'A very interesting picture, truly, and not less interesting because it hardly agrees with facts.'

Isa managed to look half serious.

'I am disappointed,' she said; 'but how could it be otherwise when I have not been a student myself, and when the only one whom I have ever known intimately is so uncommunicative. And yet I do want to know what that mysterious place is like.'

'I can assure you the professors do not look severe in the least. They have quite gentle faces, are often exceedingly good-natured, and sometimes come down from their high places and condescend to be humorous. And, of course, in such circumstances, it is not in human nature, not even when it is half-developed and neither a boy nor a man, to look seriously frightened in such circumstances. There are times, I grant you, when these same professors wax eloquent, and pour out learning in floods. It astonishes the students a little on these occasions—at least, some of them. For there are those who are never astonished, and never serious but always comic. I believe they would try to be funny at a funeral?'

'How exceedingly interesting your true story is, much more so than my poor little fable. I should like to meet with some of those who are always comic.'

'I do not regard them as at all pleasant. They are the most aggravating creatures I know. In a little time their fun loses its witchery and palls upon you, and then they are both comic and irritating.'

'You have not cultivated the friendship of any of that class, then? Or have you had some of them among your friends and thrown them over because you are resolved to take life seriously?'

'I have had no special friends of that class.'

'Who are your special friends, might I ask?'

Arthur looked puzzled for a moment.

'I cannot say I have any.'

'What! no one friend with whom you walk, upon whom you can depend for a companion, and to whom you tell your secrets? I thought every one of you would have his own special chum?'

'Most of the students have, but not all. And I suppose I am one of the unfortunates.'

'That is a shame. But perhaps I should not say that. You may have chosen to live a solitary life. When I think of it, I always regarded you as something of a recluse. Very likely you mean to be clever some day, and astonish the world, and to be that you know you will have to pay the price. And so you are living among your books, and shunning the society of your flippant fellow-students. Have I rightly explained the situation ? '

Arthur was fairly in the meshes, and by this time had grown desperate and indifferent to consequences. In his normal mood his pride would have prevented him from revealing how keenly he had been wounded at times at the university. Even ther ehe found caste feeling very strong. One of the colleges was more aristocratic than the other. Besides, in the colleges themselves there were boundaries set up between different sections, and a great gulf fixed which prevented any from passing to the other side. Worst of all, Arthur was ' unattached ' and hardly recognized at all.

' Scarcely ; you see I am unattached, and have no chance of making friends. Those in the colleges ask each other to tea sometimes, and spend a pleasant evening together. I have no rooms to ask any of them to. And, of course, they don't ask me.'

' Jack Benson is " unattached ; " has he no special friends ? I should have thought you and he would have been inseparable.'

This conversation was every minute becoming more painful. Isa knew this, and she was glad. It was all a part of her plan. She wanted to know exactly how matters stood between Rye and Arthur. That their relations were not the same as formerly she knew quite well, but she was not yet fully acquainted with all that had happened, and was in absolute ignorance of the cause of the difference. But she flattered herself she would find out, and was resolved besides, if possible, to make the breach wider.

' But I have told you I have no special friends,' Arthur remonstrated with asperity.

It was Isa's policy to take no notice of this outburst of temper.

' He is unattached, too,' she continued, ' and will not be able to invite friends to his rooms, unless indeed he takes them to the Mount, which I should suppose would be a pleasant change for them. Is he very popular ? '

' I scarcely am able to tell you.'

Arthur was very near speaking an untruth, for he had noticed that Jack was something of

a favourite, and was treated with deference and respect by all.

' Never mind, you will have plenty of friends some day, when you beat them all at examination time.'

Arthur hardly knew whether to be pleased or angry with this remark. It was too much an expression of pity for him to be wholly thankful for it, and yet he thought there was kindness and appreciation in it too, and at this moment he felt he needed both.

He seldom went to the Mount. Only two or three times he had made a formal call since his engagement with Rye had been broken. They were always kind to him, and more attentive even than in the old days, but it was clear to him his footing there was changed, and it was always a relief when he found himself outside again.

The Harlands had a similar feeling. Their confidence in him was gone, and they had little respect for his character and still less for the manner in which he had chosen to act. But they wished him well, and had no thought of excluding him from their house and acquaintanceship. Whenever they thought of him the pain of disappointment rose in their minds, and they wondered if for the sake of the old days they might never have an opportunity of rendering him a service.

And still with all he had risked, and all he had sacrificed, Arthur himself was not happy. He seemed at present indeed almost worse off, as far as his chief ambition was concerned, than he had been before. In his desperation he went, he told himself, too often to the house in Canongate, and yet it was the only place where the conditions were congenial in which he now felt at home. And in his saner moments he could not help feeling some regret that they were not a little more like the friends at the Mount.

But still he had no thought of retreating. He would struggle with circumstance, fight his way through, and triumph in the end.

CHAPTER XVIII.

FRIENDSHIP UNMERITED.

'A never empty hand, a dim
　Dark eye for dews of ove to till,
A constant cup full to the brim,
　Hast thou, O fount upon the hill.'
　　　　　　　ROBERT BUCHANAN.

JACK BENSON was a puzzle to himself in those days. Often he was possessed by feelings he did not quite understand, and sometimes he was inclined to charge himself with folly.

'Cousin Rye is well able to take care of herself,' he would argue. 'And if she cannot, her father and mother, considering the length of time they have been in the world, cannot be without experience, and I do not see there is any reason for me to be greatly concerned. I don't like Arthur Brixton, I admit. And yet, were I questioned, I could hardly give a reason. Besides, what right have I to condemn him when those who have known him all his life are his friends ? '

He had soliloquized thus before the breach had taken place. But the state of his mind became far more mysterious when he knew their relations were strained. After the manner of muscular young men he felt he wanted to box Arthur's ears, or use measures even more violent, and this without knowing anything of the merits of the situation. The conversation that had taken place between Mr. Harland, Rye, and himself upon his prospects of a career gave him, upon reflection, some clue to the state of affairs. For he was exceedingly observant, and quick besides to draw an inference.

Always there had been in him a feeling rather akin to contempt for Arthur. Without exactly understanding how profound a hold the spirit of discontentment had taken upon that young man, he thought his silence and moodiness betokened that he was vain, and inclined to think himself not over well treated by destiny and circumstance. Such a mental attitude Jack could not tolerate. He regarded it as something akin to cowardice. A brave man, he thought, would have smiled at the situation, and gathered himself together to fight and conquer it.

No wonder, therefore, he felt rather glad at the prospect of a difference between his cousin and her lover. His admiration for Rye was almost boundless, and was mingled with a large element of veneration. For sometimes he regarded her as a superior being, and thought her purity of heart, and frankness of disposition, combined with the romantic way in which she looked at everything, constituted her almost more than human.

Unquestionably joy at the thought that she might break with one wholly unworthy of her was at the bottom of his heart. But his was not an unmingled joy. He saw she suffered. And on the evening when she had given back to Arthur his promise and claimed her own, as Jack listened to the wailing music she had made he was well-nigh beside himself with angry feeling.

Mrs. Harland the next day told him the result of that eventful interview. Had it been possible he would have spoken to Rye about it, but no opportunity seemed to come. Indeed without saying it he felt somehow that she was forbidding him to mention the subject. This, however, was only at the first. When a week or two had passed away, the look of disappointment and pain wore off, and though she scarcely appeared so trustful as of yore, she was more like her old self. And one day, quite voluntarily, she mentioned Arthur's name.

'Does wealth count for much among the 'Varsity men, cousin Jack ? ' she inquired.

'Another strange question, and one I have not thought of either. Still I should say it will have its influence on some minds.'

'And students who are rather poor will not be made so much of as those more fortunate ? '

'Possibly not. Still there are other things that count for more. If anyone makes the impression he is not a gentleman, he is in the worst plight of all, whether he be rich or poor.'

Jack wondered why she asked these questions. Shortly he was to be enlightened.

'I should be glad if you would befriend Arthur Brixton as far as you can. I can freely ask you to do so because he has been our friend so long, and although we are not as we once were, father and all of us would like

MRS. HARLAND THE NEXT DAY TOLD HIM THE RESULT OF THAT EVENTFUL INTERVIEW.

him to get on. And I have been afraid he might be at a disadvantage in some things.'

' I don't suppose I can help him much. He will get fair play, of course,—everybody does.'

Jack would have said more in the same careless, indefinite strain, but he perceived his words did not satisfy his cousin. After a minute's silence he added :

' We are hardly of kindred spirits, and he might think I was meddlesome were I to force my company upon him, or even attempt to be specially friendly.'

' Has he so many friends that he can afford to despise some of them ?'

' Well, I hardly know.'

' You have not fraternized much with him, then, indeed so little that you are in ignorance of his affairs altogether. For aught you know of him now, one might have thought you had never seen him outside the class-room.'

Rye did not mean it, and knew she had no reasonable grounds for doing so, and yet both the remarks themselves and her whole attitude showed she was inclined to blame Jack.

Anyone else doing so would have repented it. Jack knew it was unjust. He had a right to choose his friends, and, however anxious Arthur Brixton might have been to form one of that favoured circle, unless it was in accord with Jack's own wishes, it could hardly be expected that he could favour the advances which the other might make. Besides, he thought Arthur had never, as far as he had seen, made any advances.

There was reason for some resentment on his part, and anyone else speaking thus to him would not have been spared. But it was wholly different when the unreasonable person was his cousin Rye.

'I have not sought to fraternize with him. Indeed, I don't think we are particularly fond of each other, although there has not been an open difference between us, or anything approaching it. Only we hardly ever meet, and when we do, it happens that both of us have business requiring our attention. Why it should be, I don't know. It must be what they call incompatibility of temper. But if you desire it very much I will gladly sacrifice my own feelings,' he added with a smile, 'and his too, and see if there are no grounds existing upon which an acquaintanceship can be formed.'

'That is good of you, and I hope you will be repaid for your sacrifice.'

'I shall beyond doubt. Do I not enter into the engagement made because you desire it?'

For a little while Jack was quite glad at having an opportunity of doing a service which would cost him some effort for Rye's sake. But that feeling soon gave place to another. Why should Rye be so solicitous about Arthur's comfort? They were lovers no longer, and he had proved that she was not sufficiently dear to him to make it worth his while to sacrifice an ambition which was unworthy in itself, and therefore, altogether apart from her wishes, should never have been entertained. Most girls, almost any girl save Rye, he thought would have declined to have anything to do with him whatever, even as an acquaintance, after what had occurred. Could it be then that she loved him still, and was already hoping that events might take such a turn as would make them again what they had been to each other before?

Jack Benson had some penetration, but it was clear he did not comprehend his cousin. Good and kind he knew her to be, incapable of a selfish thought, and inspired by ideas so noble and so little likely to be realized in a world full of frail men and women, that it was difficult to understand how she had come by them. All this he knew, but he had not calculated how utterly free she was, from every taint of malice, and how actively generous her heart was towards all who had ever been her friends. She could be solicitous about Arthur's future as she had ever been, without any thought of his relations past or future with herself.

Jack, however, not comprehending her fully, thought she must have begun to regret the separation, and to long for a renewal of the old tie. If so, what was he to do?

'I will do as she wishes,' he thought. 'I will befriend Arthur if I may, but I do not think I will stand by and see her sacrifice herself to one so little worthy of her as I believe Arthur Brixton to be. I may be mistaken about him, but it seems to me that it would be better for an angel like her to die than to have her destiny linked with one of Arthur's poor moral calibre and grovelling disposition. Yes, she had better die than that should happen, and yet if she were to die, what would I do?'

Poor Jack had never before looked at this question. He had felt strangely in relation to all his cousin's affairs, but only half dreaming the truth, he had not cared to reason out the subject to an issue. And yet here he was confessing himself to be in love with one who only a short time ago was the accepted of another, and who he feared even now was wishing to renew that broken bond. Moreover, he had promised to be the friend of that fortunate rival of his, and help him to become popular and perhaps famous.

'It is the very irony of fate,' he muttered; 'but a promise is a promise, and I shall be true to my word.'

(To be continued.)

Heirs of All the Ages.

PAPERS ON THE HERITAGE AND RESPONSIBILITIES OF OUR YOUNG PEOPLE.

SCIENCE.

o say that prejudice against science had died out of men, would be to anticipate a condition of the human mind which still lies in the future. Science still, to some religious people, is unholy. The name to them carries a savour of irreligiousness and unbelief. Those same people are ready enough to share the daily benefits which science confers upon men, in the cheap comforts of life, the less suffering and the less manual labour; the increased and improved facilities of knowledge and entertainment, ease in travelling and in the swifter and more certain methods of communication with their friends in all parts of the world. Yet, against science they have a sort of moral recoil. It is so secular, so irreverent and undevotional that to study and practise it, is, they conceive, to waste time and not to be as good as one should be.

If such dear, good souls were not born before their time, they have either lived beyond it or seriously lacked something in their training; they are consequently out of sympathy with the enlarging life of the day, and they fail to see and participate in the increasing uses of the world and of themselves in it, which God is opening up to men through their own wisdom and effort. Those good souls that dread science never think that their ideas of religion may be at fault; they may be too mechanical and too limited. The radius of that which is holy may be wider than they thought. They also forget that the misuse of science is no proof that it is bad, that if science included in its ranks unbelievers

in the religious sense, this is not exceptional; that class of mortals are only too prevalent everywhere else. And science has now, and has had in the past, many devout and God-fearing men in her service. Think of Michael Faraday, of whom Sir Humphrey Davy said, 'the greatest discovery he ever made was Michael Faraday!' Think of Faraday going from his laboratory to take his turn as an elder in conducting the services of his church. Of Professor Clerk Maxwell cheering himself through his last illness by repeating George Herbert's and Richard Baxter's hymns. And of that fine enthusiast, Charles Kingsley, who, more than any other man, has shown us the holiness of science, how the knowledge of nature may help religion, and how scientific knowledge may help one the more successfully to fight disease and poverty as well as bow one's soul in presence of the sanctity of a fir-wood.

But what is science? Science simply means knowledge, but the knowledge embraced by science is real and exact, made such by experiment and proof. There are many suppositions and theories propounded in the name of science, but it is a mistake to accept these as science. True science accepts nothing it has not clearly demonstrated. And it only deals with what is demonstrable. The things perceived by the senses are the only guides we possess to a knowledge of the material world, and 'the inferences drawn from them by the faculties of the understanding are the legitimate conquests of physical science.' The moral laws of justice, truth, and charity, and that sublime conception of the supernatural which may be traced in nature, do not come to us through the senses; therefore they belong to a realm which science cannot explain. Science classifies knowledge into departments, and reduces the whole to system. Science, so far as the facts and phenomena of nature are concerned, may be said to be the discoverer and maker of knowledge; for it has not only *enlarged* the world to us, but it has *opened* it.

The heritage of science is comparatively modern. The true development, the unification and the application of the sciences to the service of man, may all be said to be embraced within the present century. But what an endowment has that brief period in human history given to the present and future generations? The mere detail of the discovery of scientific facts would be a marvellous and interesting record. The discoveries of science rival romance, and the patient toil, the sacrifices, and the martyrdoms which they involve, would immensely enhance our reverence for scientists and impress us with the sacredness of their cause. But it is in the bearing which those discoveries have on human character and destiny that their greatest interest arises. We are born into the same world as our fathers, but it is another world to us from what it was to them. Science has shown us that there is vastly more in it and vastly more to be got out of it, than they ever dreamt of. 'Fifty years ago,' says Sir J. Lubbock, 'the book of nature was like some richly illuminated missal, written in an unknown tongue; the graceful forms of the letters, the beauty of the colouring excited our wonder and admiration; but of the true meaning little was known to us; indeed, we scarcely realized that there was any meaning to decipher. Now, glimpses of the truth are gradually revealing themselves; we perceive that there is a reason—and in many cases we know what that reason is—for every difference in form, in size, and in colour; for every bone and every feather and almost for every hair. Moreover, every problem which is solved opens out vistas, as it were, of others more interesting.'

To summarize the benefits and results of scientific research would require volumes. But they begin in the vastly increased knowledge of nature we now have. And what sources of new pleasure does a knowledge of nature supply? It gives objects and attractions to country rambles that draw us away from baser things; it quickens the powers of observation and elevates the tastes of the mind. The study of nature is one of the best correctives for that ' indolence which is the vice of half-awakened minds,' and it is destined to take the place of low sports which men at present indulge in. While such sports are

mostly too physical and animal, the study of nature will provide health, recreation, and delight to the whole man. It has long been observed that insects visited flowers, but the reason why they did so has only been within recent years explained. Through the researches of Darwin, Müller, and others, it is now an established truth that insects fertilize flowers with pollen brought from other flowers. And to this beneficent though unconscious action of bees, butterflies, etc., we owe the beauty of our gardens and the sweetness of our fields. The shapes, the varied arrangements of flowers, their brilliant colours, their honey, and sweet scent, as well as their vigorous growth, are all due to the selection in their visits to them, exercised by insects.

The colour of insects and animals has long been observed. As children we knew that the lion was tawny, the tiger was striped, and the leopard had spots; but what the purpose of these colours and differences was, we never thought to ask, and if we had asked, no one could have told us. But science has shown us that colour in animals and insects is protective, and part of their power of self defence. The lion is sandy like the desert, the stripes of the tiger resemble the tall jungle-grasses where he lives, and the spots of the leopard are like spots of sunlight glancing through grasses and leaves.

One would hardly expect researches into the origin of life to result in changing men's ideas as to the nature of disease, also, in greatly improving surgery and lessening human suffering; but they have. The hunt after living germs in dead matter has proved the air around us to be laden with those organisms. Hence the germ theory of disease. It is well known that fevers, for instance, have a certain and definite course. 'The parasitic organisms are at first few, but gradually multiply at the expense of the patient, and then die out again.' Deadly, microscopic germs have, therefore, to be guarded against and resisted, and this fact has called forth sanitary science and taught society that by proper precaution it may save itself from the deadly epidemics of former times. The improvement in saving life may be judged from the fact that in the middle of last century the death-rate in London was one in every twenty-four, and now three in every hundred is considered excessive.

Science has marvellously improved education by better methods of teaching, and by books and newspapers. In 1814 the most improved printing press produced newspapers at the rate of 1,100 copies per hour. They are now turned out—larger papers, cut and folded—at the rate of 25,000 per hour. Industry and commerce have progressed by leaps and bounds—through improvements in machinery and through chemical discoveries and the appliances of steam and electricity.

Near the close of last century Lord Campbell did the journey from Edinburgh to London in three days and three nights. But his friends seriously warned him of the dangers of this enterprise, and told of several people who, in similar rash attempts, had died from the mere rapidity of the motion. What would such people say to-day if they found themselves actually transmitted across the country at the rate of seventy miles an hour? If it were not for our steamships and railways it would be utterly impossible at the present time to supply our country with food, and if so now, what will it be in the future, with a population increasing so rapidly as our own? Our choice is really between science and starvation.

Our space is more than gone; we must, therefore, conclude. ' In the achievements of science,' says Archdeacon Farrar, ' there is not only beauty and wonder, but also beneficence and power. It is not only that she has revealed to us infinite space crowded with unnumbered worlds; infinite time peopled by unnumbered existences; but also, that she has been, as a great Archangel of Mercy, devoting herself to the service of man. She has laboured not to increase the power of despots or add to the magnificence of courts, but to extend human happiness, to economise human effort, to extinguish human pain.' Science has made life easier and more tolerable for the humblest toiler. She has increased the safety of the sailor, and gone down into the mine to protect the miner. ' She points not to pyramids built during weary centuries by the sweat of miserable nations, but to the lighthouse and the steamship, to the railroad and the telegraph. She has restored eyes to the blind and hearing to the deaf. She has lengthened life, minimised danger, controlled madness, and trampled on disease. And on all these grounds, I think that none of our sons should grow up wholly ignorant of studies which at once train the reason and fire the imagination, which fashion as well as forge, which can feed as well as fill the mind.'

F. L. S.

'Lady Alice' over the Falls.

ow deep is the interest which is taken at the present time in all that concerns the great continent of Africa, whether considered geographically, politically, commercially, or spiritually! How deeply thrilling must be many of its scenes witnessed both by explorers and missionaries! How very exciting and yet suggestive is the scene represented by the accompanying illustration! Of this touching event Mr. Stanley furnishes the following graphic account: 'The commencement of the rapids was marked by a broad fall, and an interruption to the rapidly rushing river by a narrow ridgy islet of great rocks; strong cables were lashed to the bow and stern, and three men were detailed to each. A month's experience had made us skilful and bold; but the rapids were more powerful, the river more contracted, and the impediments greater than usual. On our right rose an upright wall of massive boulders, terminating in narrow terraces 300 feet high; behind the terraces at a little distance rose the rude hills to the height of 1,200 feet above the river. On our left rose a lengthy and stupendous cliff line, topped by a broad belt of forest, and at its base rose three rich islets, one below another, against which the river dashed itself. We had scarcely ventured near the top of the rapids when by a slackening of the stern cable a current swept the boat away into the angry, foaming, billowing stream, dragging one man into the maddening flood, who, despite the perilous position, was immediately rescued. "Oars, my boys, and be steady; Uledi to the helm," were all the instructions I was able to give; for now as we rode down furiously on the crest of the proud waves, the human voice was weak against the overwhelming thunder of the angry river. We were flying at a terrific speed past the series of boulders. Never did the rocks assume such solemn grimness! Never were they invested with such grandeur and yet such terrors, while we were the cruel sport of the waves which whirled us round like a spinning top, almost engulfing us in the reaching troughs, then hurled us on the white crests of others. Oh! with what feelings we regarded this awful power which the great river had now developed; how we cringed under its imperious and impelling force; how impotent we felt before it! What lightning retrospects we cast upon our past lives! One screamed, "We are lost, yea we are lost!" After two miles we were abreast of the bay at which we had hoped to encamp, but the strong river mocked our efforts to gain it; the flood seemed resolved that we should taste the bitterness of death. A sudden rumbling noise like the deadened sound of an earthquake caused us to look behind, and we saw the river heaved bodily upward as though a volcano was about to belch around us. Up to the summit of this watery mound we were impelled; then divining what was about to take place, I shouted, "Pull for your lives," a few frantic strokes brought us to the low side of the mound before it had finished subsiding, and before it had begun its fatal circling.'

After a few more dangerous experiences, which our want of space prevents us from enumerating, they landed on a sandy beach, and in about an hour they reached their friends at the camp. What a meeting! What congratulations and rejoicings, which may be more easily imagined than described!

We have already observed how rich in suggestiveness was this thrilling scene! How it reminds us of the storms and vicissitudes of human life! Now borne on the calm bosom of some majestic river; now precipitated over some perilous waterfall. Now walking through some flowery mead amid singing birds, springing flowers, and spicy breezes, and now lifted upon the crest of some tempestuous wave.

Does not the scene we are contemplating also remind us of that sweet re-union in heaven which the saints of the Most High will happily realize. Perhaps a dear father or mother, brother or sister, a dear minister, or member of the choir may be gone before. How will they be ready and waiting to bid us welcome on the eternal shore!

> ' There all the ship's company meet,
> 　Who sailed with the Saviour beneath;
> With rapture each other they greet,
> 　And triumph o'er sorrow and death.
> With songs let us follow their flight,
> 　And mount with their spirits above;
> Escaped to the mansions of light,
> 　And lodged in the Eden of love.'

How delightful to think of that great and glorious gathering around the throne of God and the Lamb! How important the question, ' Shall I be there?' Will all my readers be there? Shall we all, as the poet has it, ' Bear some humble part in that immortal song.' Let all our young men and maidens consecrate their youthful days to a constant preparation for that heavenly world.

There is another subject that this illustration cannot fail to bring to our recollection, namely, our great missionary enterprise in South Central Africa. It is a great joy to us all to hear that our missionaries to the Zambesi have reached their destination. They have crossed the majestic river, and entered the Berotse country. What a terrible wilderness they have crossed! What rivers and streams have they forded! What dense forests, deep ravines, and lofty mountains they have traversed! What hunger, thirst, hardships, and painful experiences have they known! But over them a gracious Providence has watched both night and day. We cannot but unite with them in gratitude to our heavenly Father for so markedly enabling them to overcome or endure the physical difficulties of their protracted journey; but now greater difficulties still await them—difficulties of a moral character. They have entered among myriads who sit in darkness, in the very ' region and shadow of death.' The inhabit-

ants of the Barotse country are confessedly in the most horrible depths of human depravity. No earthly power can raise them. Shall we not pray that the hands of our worthy missionaries may be clothed with omnipotent power, their minds filled with heavenly wisdom, and their lips touched with a live coal from the Divine altar. Never did our new mission party more truly need the fervent prayers of the whole Connexion than at the present moment. We imagine we hear their voice coming over the sea, crying, ' Brethren, pray, pray, pray for us.'

We all believe that there is a God in heaven, and also that prayer from every part of the world can reach Him, and further, that earnest prayer for the success of our missionaries is in strictest harmony with His holy will.

Are there not many ways in which our dear young people can aid the missionary cause? They can, as we have been suggesting, pray daily for a Divine blessing upon our worthy missionaries, both at home and abroad. Can they not also contribute or collect funds for the maintenance of these missionary operations? And, moreover, we may inquire— Are there not some among our Sunday School friends who are preparing to give, not only their prayers and tears, their contributions and labours as collectors, but also themselves to the missionary work? Hear we not the voice of the Lord, saying, ' Whom shall I send?' and who will go for us to the West Coast of Africa, to the banks of the Zambesi? Who says, ' Here am I; send me.' Oh for a speedy and hearty response. J. ASHWORTH.

The Boyhood of Great Men.

LORD NELSON.

Who has not heard of Lord Nelson? It is now almost ninety years ago since he received his fatal wound on the deck of the *Victory* in the great battle of Trafalgar, but his name is as familiar as if he had died but yesterday. He was not fifty years of age when he fell, but during his comparatively short life he had so won his way into the hearts of his countrymen as to become what Southey called him — ' the darling of England.' Honours of different kinds were paid to the national hero. There are few towns of any importance that do not contain some statue or monument standing as a permanent memorial of the splendid service which he rendered to our country, and if but few men have received such honours, none have more truly deserved them. He still wears the laurel wreath of fame, won nearly a century ago, and as we from this cold distance survey the man and his exploits, we can but endorse the enthusiastic judgment of the men of his own age.

Perhaps one reason of his popularity is that he was an Englishman to the core. It is a feather in the cap of East Anglia that that strip of England can claim to have given birth to the two greatest heroes of our country— Cromwell and Nelson. It was in the village of Burnham Thorpe, in Norfolk, that Horatio Nelson first saw the light on September 29, 1758. His father was the vicar of that parish—almost the only fact which we know about him. Beyond bequeathing to Horatio a weakly constitution, it is difficult for us to tell how far the father reproduced himself in his son. The mother of that home died when Nelson was only nine years of age, but brief as was the time they shared together, she left a lasting impress on her child. The influences of that quiet home and of his gentle mother sank into his heart, and though he was early called to face the temptations of a sailor's life, there was one habit, shaped in that Norfolk vicarage, which he never lost—the habit of prayer. And yet we should hardly have looked to that home as the birthplace of the greatest naval commander of his time. Burnham Thorpe was at some distance from the sea, far from the sight of the white-winged ships, and of everything that might foster the sailor spirit. But Nelson became an admiral because he was born one. His great-grandfather had in his day served in the navy of his country, and it seemed in this case as though by a freak, of which nature is sometimes guilty, his militant spirit, which had slumbered in the following generations, woke up again in his great-grandson. At all events Nelson early betrayed the bent of his fancy, and as we read of him at Downham engaging his leisure time in setting the market pump in action so that the gutters might be supplied with a stream along which he might sail his paper boats, we think that we can detect in that green-coated boy the promise of the man.

Perhaps Nelson's most striking characteristic was his absolute fearlessness. He could only have been a mere child when he wandered from his grandmother's house at Hillborough in quest of birds' nests. When dinner-time came and he was still absent, some feared that he had been stolen by gipsies. Search was made for him, and he was at last found sitting with the utmost calmness by the side of a stream that had proved too broad for his little feet to cross. And when his grandmother reproved the truant and said, 'I wonder, child, that hunger and fear did not drive you home,' his instant answer was, 'Fear never came near me, grandmamma.' The same dauntless spirit followed him into his school-life. That was not very long in duration, for Nelson was largely self-taught. But such education as he received from others was acquired first at a school at Norwich, and then at North Walsham. At the latter school, the master, who boasted the classic name of Jones, was remarkable for two things : for the merciless floggings which he gave to his pupils, and for some fine pears that grew in his orchard. The pears were a sore temptation to his scholars. How the'r mouths watered as they saw them! But thoughts of Mr. Jones' cane were enough to deter even the most daring from any attempt at appropriation. Nelson alone was bold enough to brave the danger. His comrades lowered him one night with sheets from the dormitory window, and very soon the pears were transferred to his pockets. But the boldness of the deed was all that he cared for. He refused to have any of the pears himself, but shared them all among his companions. 'I only took them,' said he, 'because every other boy was afraid.' And so popular was Nelson in the school, that, though Mr. Jones offered a reward of five guineas for the detection of the offender, no one was found willing to betray him.

Horatio's honesty does not show to advantage in that story, but there is another related of his boyhood which puts him in a better light. It must have happened whilst he was attending school at Norwich. Nelson and his elder brother William were in the habit of walking thither from home, but one morning, after a heavy fall of snow, they found the roads so difficult to traverse on foot that they turned back to the vicarage. Their father supplied them with a pony, and having seen them safely on its back, started them with the injunction that, if the road should prove impassable again, they were to give up the attempt to reach school that morning, 'but remember, boys,' said he, 'I leave it to your honour.' They found that, though locomotion was easier, the difficulties of the journey were by no means removed now that they were in the saddle, and William, who was not very eager for school, would readily have magnified their obstacles into a plausible excuse for turning back, but Horatio would not hear of it. 'We have no excuse,' said he ; 'remember, brother, it was left to our honour.' Thus early did Nelson evince that high sense of honour and that loyalty to duty which made him, on the morning of the battle of Trafalgar, signal from the masthead of his ship the memorable watchword, 'England expects every man to do his duty.'

It was the same feeling of honour that led to the early termination of his life at school. The living of Burnham Thorpe was only a poor one, and there were a goodly number of children at the vicarage. Nelson knew the rigid economy that was necessary to keep him at school, and at the same time make suitable provision for the other members of the family, and he speedily felt anxious to lighten his father's burdens by earning a living for himself. All honour to the noble boy for such an unselfish desire! He had an uncle, Captain Maurice Suckling, in the Navy, and in 1770, when only twelve years of age, Nelson got his brother William to write to his father, who was then at Bath, asking him to petition his uncle to find him a place on his vessel. The father respected his boy's wish and wrote, though with but faint hope of a favourable reply. The answer, when it did come, was sufficiently gruff. 'What has poor Horace done, who is so weak, that he, above all the rest, should be sent to rough it at sea ? But let him come, and the first time we go into action, a cannon-ball may knock off his head and provide for him at once.' So wrote Captain Suckling, but his bark was worse than his bite. Beneath a rough exterior he had a kind heart, and he interested himself in finding a place for his nephew. One dark morning, about four o'clock, Horatio, who had returned to school for a little while longer, was rudely wakened from his slumbers, and, after a hasty 'good-bye' to his brother, was bundled half-asleep into a trap that was ready to convey him first to his home, and then from the peaceful quiet of the vicarage into the troubled world beyond.

It was indeed a rough life that awaited him, and no one ever seemed less fitted for it than this delicate Norfolk boy. To serve on board a man-of-war in those days meant the endurance of hardship. That was the time of the press-gangs, when men were forced into the service, and in the event of resistance to their captors, had their skulls cracked into the bargain. Every neglect of duty, every disobedience to discipline was punished with the lash. It is no wonder that sailors became rough and brutal, and developed sensibilities as hard as the salt junk on which they largely subsisted. That was the world into which Nelson stepped in the spring of 1771. His father had accompanied him to London, but had left him to find his way to his ship at Chatham alone. It was a sharp, dull day in early spring. His uncle had not yet joined his vessel, and did not appear for several days after Nelson got there, and the little fellow wandered about the shore, simply bewildered by the novel spectacle of rollicking Jack-tars and the clustering ships, and feeling very home-sick and sad. A naval officer, who chanced to be a friend of Captain Suckling, pitied him and gave him some dinner, and then conducted him to the ship, where, until the arrival of his uncle, Nelson found himself without anyone who knew him or would speak to him the word of kindness he needed.

He did not stay long on board his first vessel. The war with Spain, for which the *Raissonable* had been put into commission, came to an abrupt conclusion, and Nelson was transferred with his uncle to a guardship in the Medway.

The quiet routine of his duties there were but little to his taste, and he was more suited by a voyage in a merchant vessel to the West Indies, from which he returned a thoroughly practical seaman, and with a strong dislike to the life of a man-of-war. However, his repugnance was overcome by his uncle, who gave him plenty of interesting work to do, and held out the promise of promotion. He had been home about a year when he secured a place on board a vessel that was about to sail to the polar regions, the object of the expedition being to discover whether there existed a north-west passage between the Atlantic and Pacific Oceans. The ships left the Thames on June 4, 1773, and arrived at Spitzbergen three weeks later. Here their perils began. The ice gathered round them and threatened to block them in, and at one time the idea of abandoning the ships to their fate was seriously entertained. It was while they were thus imprisoned in the ice that Nelson had his adventure with a bear. One night under the cover of a fog, he and another midshipman stole out of the ship. Nelson, armed with a rusty musket, in high spirits led the way over the ugly cracks in the ice. The adventurers were missed, and much alarm was felt, until, when the fog lifted about three o'clock in the morning, they were seen in the distance attacking a huge bear. They were summoned to return, but in vain Nelson's comrade urged him to obey. There was a wide gap in the ice between them and the bear, and to that they probably owed their lives, for the old musket had flashed in the pan, and their store of ammunition was spent. 'Never mind,' said Nelson, ' let me but get a blow at him with the butt-end of my musket and we shall have him.' His companion started for the ship, whilst the bear took to its heels, frightened by a shot that had been purposely fired from the vessel. Nelson had to return without the bear and in some fear as to the consequences of his daring. His officer admired the boy's courage, but sternly reprimanded him, and asked what motive he could have had for his conduct. 'Sir,' he said, pouting his lip as he was wont to do when reproved, 'I wished to kill the bear that I might carry its skin to my father.' Happily Nelson had no opportunity for a repetition of his adventure, for the ice speedily broke up, and released the ships from their peril, and the commander, deeming that the difficulties in the way of success were too great, turned his ships towards home, and that expedition ended as fruitlessly as the many that had preceded it.

It was a change from the cold of the Arctic Zone to the tropical heat of India, where Nelson was next stationed. It is not wonderful that a stay of eighteen months in that malarious clime was more than he could bear. He was smitten with a disease which reduced him to a mere bundle of bones and almost killed him. He was sent home to England, and the change saved him. But the voyage round the Cape was long and tedious. The future was so uncertain, and Nelson felt so friendless, that for days together he suffered from the deepest despondency. 'I felt impressed,' said he, 'that I should never rise in my profession. My mind was staggered with a view of the difficulties I had to surmount and the little interest I possessed. I could discover no means of reaching the object of my ambition. After a long and gloomy reverie, in which I almost wished myself overboard, a sudden flow of patriotism was kindled within me and presented my king and country as my patrons. My mind exulted in the idea; " Well, then," I exclaimed, " I will be a hero, and, confiding in Providence, I will brave every danger." ' The inspiration of that moment never left him. ' From that hour,' so he often used to say, ' there was suspended before his mind's eye a radiant orb that courted him onward to renown.' That was the tide in his affairs that led him on to fortune. From that time he rose step by step until to the Norfolk village lad was entrusted the defence of the watery frontiers of England, and until, by the splendour of his victories, Nelson had lifted the naval glory of his country to an eminence it had never attained before, and which it has never since lost.

A. Lewis Humphries, B.A.

Sketches of the British Isles.

BONCHURCH AND VENTNOR.

ONCHURCH is one of the oldest villages in the Isle of Wight. Monk's Bay, situated immediately below the village church, derived its name from being the supposed landing-place of the priests who came from the Abbey of Lire, in the year 755, to preach the Gospel to the rude islanders of those remote times. The Normans during the year 1070, four years after the landing of William the Conqueror, erected the present old church and dedicated it to St. Boniface, hence the origin of the name, St. Boniface's Church; which a later matter-of-fact generation has abbreviated into the present form of Bonchurch. The picturesque churchyard, embowered with trees, and within sound of the musical cadences of the sea, contains, amongst other graves of distinguished persons, the tomb of the Rev. W. Adams, author of ' The Shadow of the Cross,' and in reference to this book, a huge iron cross is attached to his tomb in such a manner that it casts a continual shadow over his resting-place. Bonchurch pond is an ornamental lake skirting the main road at the entrance to the village. Stately swans silently glide over the glassy surface of the waters, and several miniature islands decked with shrubs add to its general beauty. The lake is overhung with a light trellis work consisting of a green creeper, having the clinging properties of ivy, and a feathery flower resembling a ball of white sea-foam. The back-ground is formed of the sloping downs, covered with luxuriant foliage. This inland sheet of water, with its striking surroundings, without undue exaggeration may be regarded as one of the most exquisite scenes of beauty to be found in the entire range of the island.

The natural features of Bonchurch comprise a combination of steep rocks and sunny vales, pleasant woodlands and delightful waters, velvety slopes and flower gardens, and venetian skies and silvery seas. Probably no village has had so much said in its favour by its numerous admirers as Bonchurch, the queen of English villages. John Sterling, who spent his last days in the neighbourhood, and had dwelt in other lands, represents Bonchurch as being 'the best possible earthly fairyland, combining all the varied and fanciful beauty of enchantment with the highest degree of domestic comfortable reality.' Dr. Arnold, of Rugby School, who was a native of the island, described Bonchurch as being 'the most beautiful thing on the sea-coast on this side of Genoa.' A lady of considerable literary tastes, who spent some time there, has given the following word-picture of the village. Her general descriptive outline has the fascination of a prose-poem. Writing on a Christmas eve she says: ' Bonchurch is the perfection of beauty. Standing on an eminence the eye takes in, almost at a glance, a world of beauty. On one side is a vast extent of sea, often almost covered with vessels sailing to and from foreign lands; on the other side is a vast ridge of rocks and mountains called the Downs, covered with every variety and shade of green-bright, and fresh as in early autumn. Perched amid these jutting rocks, and peeping out of their bowers of everlasting green, are the dwellings of the aristocracy, and verily they remind you of the eagle's eyrie; upon one of these ledges of rock, far above the common herd of men, Lord Rivers has his seat. At every turn you are almost startled by a bird's-eye view of another and another of these lordly mansions, peeping out from amid the wild beauties of nature, and almost making you wonder whether mortals really are privileged to luxuriate amid so rich a profusion of natural grandeur. In Bonchurch there is a still more interesting object to me. Behind a jutting rock is a narrow pass, and your curiosity is awakened to know what lies beyond. There a commodious dwelling, hemmed in by rocks and waves, stands on the shore buried in foliage. It seems the very abode of the muses. Beauty and song are always around it. Care and sorrow would seem strange companions there. Last winter this fairy spot was the abode of Charles Dickens, and Brown, the famous caricature-sketcher for *Punch;* here for three months

they pursued their labours, and from this fairy spot, around which the waves are ever making music, emanated a thousand thoughts which have kindled as many varied emotions in ten times as many hearts.'

During the latter half of the seventeenth century a parish lad of the name of Hobson was apprenticed to the village tailor by the parochial authorities of Bonchurch. ' Tailoring,' says Hobson's biographer, ' was a species of employment ill suited to his enterprising spirit. He was one day sitting alone on the shop-board, with his needle—as it too often was, and Bonchurch went unclad in consequence—idle in his hand, and his gaze directed towards the sea, when round Dunnose, with its colours streaming and white canvas bellying over the blue sea came in sight a British squadron.' Quick as thought, and following his first impulse, he dropped his needle, sprang from the shop board, ran down the village street to the beach, jumped into the first boat he saw, and, plying the oars, speedily reached the admiral's ship, was received on board, and entered as a volunteer. The following morning the admiral's ship sighted a French squadron, and immediately a severe engagement took place. The runaway tailor's lad ' obeyed his orders with cheerfulness and alacrity.' After fighting for some hours, he inquired what was the object for which they were struggling, when he was told by the sailors that the action must continue until the white flag at the masthead of the enemy's ship was struck. ' Oh, if that's all,' Hobson exclaimed, ' I'll see what I can do.' At that precise moment the yardarms of the two vessels were interlaced, and the whole of the masts and rigging were enveloped in a dense cloud of smoke. Hobson, unperceived, sprang into the shrouds, walked the main-yard, gained the vessel of the French admiral, succeeded in reaching the masthead, and cut and carried away the French flag, and as quietly returned to his own ship. The English crew noticing the disappearance of the French colours, and supposing the flag to have been lowered in submission, shouted ' Victory!' and clambered on board the enemy's ship. The French were panic-stricken at the loss of their flag, and before the French admiral had time to rally his men, the ship was taken by the British sailors. Amid the wide-spread excitement, Hobson descended the ladders, and appeared on the main deck of his vessel, with the French flag wound round his arm, and lying in folds at his feet. The sailors were enraptured with the heroism and daring of the runaway lad, who, as a raw recruit, had so ably distinguished himself during his first engagement. Hobson rapidly obtained promotion, was knighted for his victory over the called the English Madeira. Mantell represents it as being 'completely sheltered on the north by the range of chalk cliffs, elevated above the influences of the mists and fogs of the sea-shore, possessing a soil composed of the detritus of chalk and sandstone, which rapidly absorbs and carries off superfluous moisture, yet supports a luxuriant vegetation; with an undulated and varied surface, enjoying throughout its whole extent a southern aspect, and fanned only by breezes which invigorate but do not chill.' The climate of

BONCHURCH POND, ISLE OF WIGHT.

fleets of Spain in Vigo Bay, and became an admiral of considerable distinction, or, as historians say, 'the pride of the British navy,' during the reign of Queen Anne.

From Bonchurch, westwards, is an irregular terrace, six miles long, and from a distance has the appearance of a huge fortification. This range of rocks is called the Undercliffe. It has been formed by a landslip, which originally was a portion of the overhanging downs, and which 'dipped' towards the shore. Most appropriately, this sheltered region has been the Undercliffe is mild, dry, and equable, which is proved by myrtles, geraniums, and other greenhouse plants and shrubs being kept in the open flower-beds during the months of winter. These unique climatic conditions are caused by the Undercliffe being flanked on the north by a mountainous wall, and on the south, being open to the life-giving influences of the sun, from his rising to his setting, during the limited hours, when sunshine is wanted most in northern latitudes

At the extreme boundary of this celebrated

range of rocks is Ventnor, 'The Metropolis of the Undercliffe.' Fifty years ago it was only a fisherman's village, and consisted of a few scattered houses on the shores of Mill Bay. Its obscurity was so great, that its existence was scarcely known in the northern portions of the island. The island railway extension, and the golden opinions of the medical fraternity respecting its genial climate, have contributed towards the prosperity and popularity of Ventnor. One authority says : 'Recent local meteorological observations have proved that the atmosphere is noteworthy for its absence of moisture, hours of sunshine, and also for the fact of its being cooler in summer, and warmer in winter than many places of a similar aspect.' Ventnor faces the south ; the handsome houses rise tier above tier on the gentle slopes, until they gain an altitude of three hundred feet above the shingly shore. In the suburbs is an imposing pile of buildings, with embattled turrets and towers, called Steephill Castle, which was occupied by the Empress of Austria during her stay at Ventnor in 1874. The town is governed by a Board of Health, who have paid special attention to the formation of roads and streets, water supply, drainage, sanitary, and other collateral improvements. The town is well supplied with churches and chapels. There are four churches belonging to the establishment, and numerous chapels for Wesleyans, Primitive Methodists, and other Nonconformist bodies. The London City Missionaries' Seaside Home was erected by the generosity of the late Captain Huish, and since his death the institution has been presented to the Society. The Royal National Home for the cure of consumption and diseases of the chest comprises two hospitals, chapel, and sixteen semi-detached villas ; it contains over a hundred beds, and is visited on the average by six hundred patients annually. The buildings are surrounded with twenty acres of pleasure and recreation grounds. In the business part of the town there are a number of superior shops, savings-banks, clubs, and other public institutions. The beach has an abundance of variegated shingle, and has a number of seaside attractions, which divert the mind and break the monotony of

life—'the long groove, in which we live and move.'

A lady visitor has forcefully stated that ' It is a splendid sight to stand on the Ventnor esplanade on a dark night, between the roar of the mighty world of waters and the town scattered in such wild beauty over the rocks, while from every window lights are glancing on the mountain and in the valley, and you gaze until you fancy they are suspended in the canopy of heaven and upheld only by the finger of Omnipotence.'

The prettiest part of the island is located between Ventnor and Niton, which includes the Undercliffe, and the inland stretches of St. Catherine's Down, its higher ridges being over seven hundred feet above sea-level. At a conspicuous point is an octagonal tower and other remains of a charity chapel, erected by Walter de Godyton as far back as the year 1323. He endowed it for the purpose of keeping a priest, whose twofold duties were to offer prayers for tempest-tossed sailors, and at the same time to keep a bright fire burning to give them warning of the dangerous rocks. During the last century a lighthouse was built, but owing to its flaming light being frequently hid by the clouds of white mists, it was replaced by one on a lower site, much nearer to the sea. A Russian merchant, out of the loyalty of his heart and purse, erected a column on the Down, as a memento of the visit in 1814 of the Emperor Alexander to England. Close by Niton is Blackgang Chine, formerly the most noted and wildest of the island coast ravines. It is much wider than Shanklin Chine. The tiny streamlet has laid bare the dark green clays and the intermediate layers of grey-brown sandstone which form the background of one of old Dame Nature's beautiful pictures. At this point the coast is extremely wild and romantic. Numerous ships and crews have been wrecked upon its sharp jutting rocks. The immediate locality is specially interesting to geologists.

Dr. Mantell says : ' Near this place, after recent slips of the cliffs, and the removal of the fallen *débris* by the waves, the uppermost of the wealden deposits, and the lowermost of the green sand, may be seen in juxtaposition ;

in other words, the line of demarcation between the accumulated sediment of a mighty river— some primœval Nile or Ganges, teeming with the spoil of the land and the exuviæ of extinct terrestrial and fluviatile animals and plants— and the bed of a vast ocean, loaded with the *débris* of marine organisms, of genera and species unknown in the present seas.'

About midway between Niton and Ventnor, and a little distance inland, is St. Lawrence, which formerly had the smallest church in England. Before the chancel was added thereto by the munificence of the first Earl of Yarborough, this unique religious edifice was only some twenty feet long and twelve feet wide; and the eaves, from the floor-line, were only six feet high. The emotions awakened in the heart of one of the visitors to the 'smallest church' of England have been described in the following pathetic lines:

' Peace reigns around thee. Oh! 'tis passing sweet,
From the world's din, and all its toils and strife,
To seek thy quiet shade ; to leave awhile
Life's round of cares, and still each passion's breath
By holy commune with the sacred dead.
How beautiful their rest where falls the shade
Of thy low walls, and ivy-mantled tower !
Where the unceasing murmur of the waves—
Making low music—as a requiem falls
Upon the pensive ear. And flowers are there,'
Man's bright companions in his hours of joy.
Nor less his friends when sorrow's adverse tide
With threatening front o'ertakes him. They are bright
And beautiful 'mid all, but brightest still—
Most beautifully fair—as watchers love,
By the still tomb.
                Entered the lowly fane,
We join the bending worshippers, with them
Pour forth to heaven our notes of grateful praise,
And, as they rise, the exulting voices
Of the uplifted waters swell the song,
Bearing from far-off lands and distant shores
One bursting hymn of universal praise.'

                ALBERT A. BIRCHENOUGH.

A Talk about the Moon.

THE moon is the earth's next-door neighbour. Not a very near neighbour, to be sure, for it is thousands and thousands and thousands of miles away ; but then it is a great deal nearer than any other heavenly body, and that makes it a next-door neighbour, does it not? And what a changeable person this neighbour is ! Sometimes she looks straight down upon us with her full round face: then she turns so far away that only a glimpse can be caught of her, and finally disappears entirely, and there is no use in hunting around for her among the stars, for she cannot be found anywhere.

Do you know what the moon is doing up there in the sky all the time? Well, she is enjoying herself taking a trip around the earth, for she is a great traveller, and no sooner does she get around once than she starts right off and tries it over again without resting a moment. Watch her for two or three nights, and you will see very plainly that she is moving. One night she shows herself even before the sun goes down ; then, as she grows larger, she will come later and later, till by and bye all the little folks will be in bed and asleep long before she peeps out from behind the hill.

Some nights the moon appears very bright —so bright that people say, 'Why, it is nearly as light as day,' giving the moon credit for the whole brightness, when really and truly it is not her light at all, but some that she has borrowed to send down to us. The moon does not give a bit of light by herself ; she is nothing but a dark world, something like this earth? Why, then, does she look so bright? Ah! you see, she wants to be beautiful as well as the stars; so when the sun shines on her surface, she catches up the light and reflects or throws it off again, and so we get what is called moonlight. This is the reason that she looks so different at different times. In her journeys around the earth, when she gets where the sun shines on the side turned this way, we have full moon, but as this bright side turns farther and farther away the moon grows smaller and smaller, till at last the moonlight is gone and the nights are dark. If you find this hard to understand, place a ball so that the lamplight will fall upon it, and then walk around it, and you will see how this is.

But the moon has dark spots upon its bright face, and astronomers tell us that these are caused by the deep valleys there. You know that often at evening time the hills will be all lighted up for some minutes after the sun has gone down, while the lowlands will be in shadow. Of course the sun shines on the moon in the same way, making bright the high mountains, but leaving the valleys as dark spots.

So much is known about the surface of the moon that maps of it have been made, and these are said to be more nearly correct than those of the earth. Get a map of the moon, and you will find that many of the mountains are called by those very names that you find out in your geographies at school. These wise men also tell us that the moon always keeps the same side turned this way, so that we really know nothing at all about the other side.

Could we take a trip to the moon, we should find a strange world, and one not very pleasant to look at.

There is no grass, there are no flowers, no trees, not a single green thing growing there, —and why? Because there is no water. True, in the map are names like the Sea of Rains, the Lake of Dreams, the Sea of Plenty, and many others; but this map was made years ago, before as much was known as now, and the old names have been left; but if you were there you would find dry seas, without a drop of water in them. Of course, without water and plants there can be no animals such as live on the earth. And then such high mountains and deep, deep valleys as are there! Many of these mountains seem to be hollow, so that if you want to cross one you must go up one side, then down into a hole, across that, and up its steep banks, and then down the other side of the mountain, before you are across; so it would take some time, you see. Sometimes there is a peak right in the centre of this hole, making the crossing still harder.

The very best time to visit the moon is during one of its nights. Do you know a night there is nearly half a month long, and the days are not a bit shorter? But then their nights are much pleasanter than ours. Do you ask why? Well, it is because this earth that looks so dark to us is all lighted up by the sun, till it appears bright and shining, and is their moon. And oh, what a great moon it is! Fourteen or fifteen times larger than the one that gives us light.

You know that an eclipse of the sun is caused by the moon's getting between that body and the earth; but there is nothing that can get between the earth and the moon, for everything is too far away; so what do you suppose makes that kind of an eclipse? Some evening notice a spot on the wall made bright by the lamplight. Next stand in such a way that your shadow will fall upon that very spot, and then see how bright it is. Now, if that bright spot were the moon and you were the earth, that would be a real eclipse, for it is the shadow of the earth falling upon the moon that makes one. It took people many years to find this out, but now they can tell a long time beforehand that an eclipse is coming.

Have you heard the story of Columbus? One time when in America with his men their food gave out, and they had to depend on the Indians. These people, not being very friendly to the whites, at last refused them any more, and there was danger of their starving. Columbus then told the Indians that the moon was angry, and would hide her face from them. Sure enough she did, for Columbus knew that an eclipse was coming, and the Indians, very much frightened, gave the hungry men the food they needed.

Emma J. Wood.

Vesuvius and Its Eruptions.

ESUVIUS is the principal vent in the volcanic district of Naples. This embraces not only the mainland which surrounds the Bay of Naples, but also the islands of Ischia, Procida, and Capri. It was anciently called the Burning Plains; and here, according to an old Greek fable, the shades of the dead walked abroad and met the living. The Styx and the Cocytus were also placed here, and the dreadful Lake Avernus was considered the entrance to the infernal regions. Concerning this lake, now a cheerful and salubrious spot, Lucretius tells us that birds could not fly over it without

being stifled. The mephitic, vapours often emitted by craters after eruptions undoubtedly produced these fatal results. Sir William Hamilton says that he several times picked up dead birds on Vesuvius during an eruption.

Before the Christian era Vesuvius had been so long quiescent that it was regarded as an extinct volcano. There were only dim traditions of destructive action, and Pliny did not include this mountain in his list of active craters. The beginning of what is called the Servile War in Roman History was associated with Vesuvius. In 73 B.C. some seventy gladiators sick of being exposed to be ' butchered to make a Roman holiday ' broke out into revolt. Their leader was Spartacus, a Thracian, a man of great ability and resource. He led his insurgent followers to the crater of the once-burning mountain, where they formed a camp; and soon their numbers increased to thousands. The Roman prætor with three thousand men surrounded the hill, hoping to starve out the rebels, but he was ignorant of the real character of this natural fortress. By means of scaling-ladders, woven out of the branches of the wild vines with which the sides of the crater were covered, they climbed the cliffs and attacked their enemies in the rear.

But Vesuvius was not dead—only asleep. In the year 63 A.D. she awoke from her prolonged repose, and shook the neighbourhood by an earthquake. Considerable portions of Pompeii and Herculaneum were thrown down, many statues were split, and six hundred sheep perished. Slight shocks were frequently felt in following years, until in 79 a terrific eruption took place. The elder Pliny lost his life through being suffocated by sulphurous vapours, in his endeavour to obtain a near view of the phenomena. The first sign of the eruption was, as the younger Pliny describes, ' a cloud which resembled a pine tree, first shot up to a great height in the form of a trunk, which extended itself at the top into something like branches. It appeared sometimes bright, and sometimes dark and spotted, as it was more or less impregnated with cinders.' Thick clouds of ashes, together with pumice stone and black pieces of burning rock, fell into the ship in which the elder Pliny had embarked ; and after finding shelter on shore in a house near the present Castellamare, he and his friends were obliged to abandon it, and set forth with pillows tied on their heads by means of napkins, to protect them from the tempest of falling stones. The falling ashes even caused a shoal in one part of the sea, the earth rocked, and the sea retreated from the shores, so that many marine animals were observed on the dry sand. Somewhat singularly the younger Pliny, though so circumstantial in his account of the eruption, makes no allusion to the overwhelming of the two cities. The first historian who alludes to them by name is Dion Cassius, who lived about one hundred and fifty

years after Pliny. And his account is full of fables. He tells us ' that during the eruption a multitude of men of superhuman stature, resembling giants, appeared sometimes on the mountain, and sometimes in the environs; that stones and smoke were thrown out, the sun was hidden, and then the giants seemed to rise again, while the sounds of trumpets were heard,' and so on. It was indeed supposed that the old race of giants whom the gods had long time held bound, had burst their chains, and had returned to earth to introduce chaos once more.

Dion Cassius also relates that the people of Pompeii and Herculaneum were "burned under showers of ashes while sitting in the theatre." Excavations, however, have since clearly shown that none of the people were destroyed in the theatre ; and there were very few indeed of the inhabitants who did not succeed in escaping somehow from both cities. Quite a small number of skeletons was discovered in either city. The skeletons of two soldiers chained to the stocks were found in the barracks of Pompeii and ' in the vaults of a country house in the suburbs were the skeletons of seventeen persons, who appear to have fled there to escape from the shower of ashes.' Near at hand was also discovered the perfect cast of a woman within a mould of volcanic paste with an infant in her arms. Her form was imprinted on the rock, but nothing but the bones remained. A chain of gold was suspended from her remains, and the fingers of the skeleton bore rings with jewels.

There appears to have been no lava discharged during the eruption of 79. The material under which Herculaneum is buried is a volcanic mud formed of the finer ashes mingled with water. Pompeii is interred beneath light loose ashes. The thinnest covering under which Herculaneum lies is seventy feet deep, while in places it is one hundred and twelve feet. It was nearer the volcano than Pompeii, which lies some twenty feet below the present surface.

Lava did not make its appearance in any eruption in the Christian era until the year 1036. A singular letter full of the superstitions of the time was written in 1060 to Pope

Nicholas II. by Cardinal Damiano. It tells how a servant of God dwelt alone, near Naples, on a lofty rock, hard by the highway. As this man was singing hymns by night, he opened the window of his cell to observe the hour, when, lo, he saw passing many men, black as Ethiopians. They were spirits of darkness, who said they waited first for Pandulphus, prince of Capua, who lay sick at that time, and then for John, the captain of the garrison of Naples, who as yet was alive and well. Then went that man of God to John and related faithfully what he had seen and heard. John, to prove the truth of the priest's story, sent a messenger to Capua, who found Pandulphus dead, and John himself did not live fifteen days. 'As often,' says the writer, ' as a reprobate rich man dies in those parts, the fire is seen to burst from Vesuvius, and such a mass of sulphurous resin flows from it as makes a torrent, which by its downward impulse descends even to the sea. And in verity, a former prince of Palermo once saw from a distance sulphurous pitchy flames burst out from Vesuvius, and said that surely some rich man was just about to die and go down to hell. Alas! for the blinded minds of evil men! That very night, as he lay regardless in bed, he breathed his last.'

From 1306 to 1631 Vesuvius was inactive, but the volcanic energies of the district did not slumber—for in 1538 appeared an entirely new mountain, hence called Monte Nuovo, near Lake Avernus. Summarising and seeking to reconcile the different accounts we have of this remarkable phenomenon, Sir Charles Lyell says:—' It seems clear that the ground first sank down fourteen feet on the site of the future volcano, and after having subsided it was again propelled upwards by the lava mingled with steam and gases, which were about to burst forth. Jets of red-hot lava, fragments of fractured rock, and occasionally mud composed of a mixture of pumice, tuff, and sea-water were hurled into the air. Some of the blocks of stone were very large, leading us to infer that the ground which sank and rose again was much shattered and torn to pieces by the elastic vapours. The whole hill was not formed at once, but by an intermitting action

extending over a week or more. A considerable part, however, of the hill was formed in less than twenty-four hours, and in the same manner as on a smaller scale the mud cones of air volcanoes are produced with a cavity in the middle.' The height of Monte Nuovo is 440 feet above the level of the adjacent bay.

Since 1306 the two most remarkable eruptions of Vesuvius have been those of 1631 and 1779. The former occurred on the morning of December 16th. Pliny's ' pine-tree' cloud was again seen, ' the volcano's black-flag,' as another calls it; showers of ashes, splashes of molten lava, and red-hot blocks fell thickly all around. Next day ' the whole mountain seemed to be melting.' As the people of Torre del Greco were leaving the town they were met by a torrent of molten lava from a side street. The part of the crowd which had already passed escaped, though with difficulty, but ' the rest found at once death and cremation beneath the fiery stream.' The effect of this eruption was to diminish the height of the cone of the mountain by some 540 feet, and to increase its circumference by an average of some ten thousand feet. The ashes from the monster's mouth lay thick thirty-six miles away, while stones of great size had been carried more than forty miles. About two thousand persons perished.

The series of eruptions about 1779 has been described at great length and most brilliantly by Sir William Hamilton and Dr. Clarke, but we have not space to give more than a few points. Jets of liquid lava, mixed with stones and scoriæ, were thrown up to the height of at least 10,000 feet, having the appearance of a column of fire. In 1793 millions of red-hot stones were shot into the air full half the height of the cone itself, and then bending, fell all round in a fine arch. The lava was in perfect fusion, and flowed with the translucency of honey, ' in regular channels cut finer than art can imitate, and glowing with all the splendour of the sun.' Sir William Hamilton writes : ' Dr. Clarke had conceived that no stones thrown upon a current of lava would make any impression. I was soon convinced of the contrary. Light bodies, indeed, of five, ten, and fifteen pounds weight, made little or no impression even at the source; but bodies of sixty, seventy, and eighty pounds were seen to form a kind of bed on the surface of the lava, and float away with it. A stone of 3 cwt., that had been thrown out by the crater, lay near the source of the current of lava. I raised it upon one end, and then let it fall upon the liquid lava, when it gradually sank beneath the surface and disappeared. If I wished to describe the manner in which it acted upon the lava, I should say that it was like a loaf of bread thrown into a bowl of very thick honey, which gradually involves itself in the heavy liquid, and then slowly sinks to the bottom.' We refer readers to a recent article in which we treated of the causes of volcanic eruptions.

Current Topics.

TONIC SOL-FA.

URING the month of July was celebrated the jubilee of the Tonic Sol-fa system of music. Fifty years ago, a conference of Sunday-school teachers was being held at Hull, and one of the subjects discussed was the difficulty felt by all in securing good and hearty singing in school and congregation. The conversation ended in a resolution charging Mr. Curwen, a young Congregational minister of Basingstoke, with the duty of finding out the simplest way of teaching music, and getting it into use. That was the event the jubilee of which has just been commemorated. Who will say after this that conferences are not a valuable means of helping on the progress of the world? Much fun is sometimes made of the 'resolutions' and 'motions' solemnly passed at such gatherings, and as surely disregarded after the assembly has dispersed. But the young minister who accepted the commission of that conference at Hull made it his life's work. And his son, who now tells the story of his labour, points with pardonable pride to results that have become world-wide in their beneficent action.

Mr. Curwen had already shown his aptitude for the work. Believing that music might be made a great help in his work as a minister, he had, two years before the conference, commenced to teach it in connection with his church at Basingstoke. He was no great musician, but he was a born instructor. He had a remarkable power of fascinating the young, and he soon gathered a class of 200 of them. Under his guidance they were not long in picking up a number of tunes, and their exercises seem to have had a pleasing effect upon their moral character. A husbandman assured Mr. Curwen that on their way home from school, instead of quarrelling and swearing as they had been used to do, they now sang hymns and pleasant songs. This was a very gratifying proof of the elevating power of music, and it increased Mr. Curwen's desire to make his work more permanent. Hitherto his pupils had learnt all the tunes they knew by the ear, but he was anxious to give them the power of reading the music for themselves. They would then be able to carry on their musical culture without the aid of a teacher. To this end he endeavoured to explain to them the mysteries of the staff notation, its clefs, rests, notes, and so forth, and he himself took private lessons in the art of sight singing, without, however, making much progress. But just about this period there was put into his hands a little book by Miss Glover, the daughter of a clergyman at Norwich. In this book a new system of notation was expounded, by following which he was able in less than a fortnight to sing at sight. He had at length found the idea by means of which he was to work the greatest musical revolution in modern times.

Mr. Curwen was himself the inventor of the Tonic Sol-fa system as we now know it. For though he got the original idea from Miss Glover, the developments were his own. Miss Glover, it seems, did not approve of all these developments, but the relations between these two musical innovators were of the most cordial kind. Mr. Curwen acknowledged his obligations to Miss Glover in the most handsome manner. He even sent her the proceeds of his first book, though he had invested all his savings in bringing it out; but she, with a generosity no less admirable, returned them with a friendly letter. She also declined to republish her own book, which had been long out of print, though Mr. Curwen wished her to do so in order that the public might know the original upon which he had built. It is pleasing to know that their kindly relations continued until the last. Two months before she died, Miss Glover assured her friend that he not only did her justice, but, she added, ' you try to make me famous.'

It was not to be expected that a movement like that, promoted by Mr. Curwen, would escape opposition. It was viewed very suspiciously by the publishers, and several printers actually refused to print Mr. Curwen's books. For twenty years the profits upon his sales did little more than cover the expense of publication. And when, at length, the demand for Tonic Sol-fa books became large, Mr. Curwen found that the publishers entered into competition with him. He, in his desire to spread the system, had given permission to any one to print music in the Tonic Sol-fa notation, but he was left to bear the cost until the system became popular, and then he found that outside competition deprived him of a considerable part of the return he had fairly earned. This, however, was a small trouble to one whose main purpose was the public well-being. In promoting this he had a far deeper satisfaction than the mere acquisition of wealth can ever bestow.

During the last fifty years there has been a remarkable extension of musical training amongst the masses of the people. The movement seems to have been contemporaneous with Mr. Curwen's career. About the time when he first turned his attention to the subject, Mr. John Hullah produced a great stir by the introduction of his system of popular musical study. For a time his success was remarkable. His system was adopted in the Government schools. The class he conducted in Exeter Hall, numbering 2,000 pupils, became one of the sights of London, and he was encouraged by the patronage of

the wealthy and the great. Mr. Curwen, on the other hand, worked chiefly among the masses, and it was not until after the long trial of thirty years that the Government condescended to notice his system. Long before this, however, its obvious merits had secured its adoption in many of the schools, but no grant was allowed for it until 1869, when the Government agreed to accept the Sol-fa system on the same terms as would from time to time be applicable to the staff notation.

Since its official recognition by the Education Department, the Tonic Sol-fa has far outstripped all other systems of musical training in the schools. In 1880, indeed, an attempt was made to drive it out of Government schools, but hundreds of the leading musicians of the country rose up in its defence; and though the attack was renewed in 1882, the system seems to flourish more vigorously than ever. The last educational returns show that out of the 2,886,651 children who are being taught to sing by note in the schools of the United Kingdom, 2,509,567 are being taught the Tonic Sol-fa system, whilst the remaining 377,084 are being taught other notations. The progress that has been made may be judged from the fact that whilst in 1883 the number of scholars who gained the grant for Tonic Sol-fa was 591,979, in 1890 the number was nearly four times as many. This proves that the system has, at any rate, gained the confidence of the teachers of elementary schools.

Dr. Barnardo has found the Tonic Sol-fa system a wonderful help in dealing with the waifs and strays that find shelter in his hospitable homes. The system is followed in both vocal and instrumental music, and the results are most satisfactory. The doctor tells of a boy who was one of the roughest he ever had, whose boast was that he could fight (and often *lick*) his master, who was perpetually in hot water. It was found that he had a good ear for music, and he was in due course put into the band to play a side drum. From that moment it seemed the evil spirit left him. He threw his whole heart into learning to play his drum well, and learning the cornet. The self-restraint made him steady, orderly, and painstaking. Eventually he was apprenticed to the shoemaking, and is now prospering at his trade in one of the midland counties, though music still remains his hobby, and he leads a band which now occasionally plays in the village church. Lately he called to see Dr. Barnardo, who found him a fine, well-grown fellow, married, with two young children, and with music written all over his face. 'Ah, sir,' he said in the course of the interview, 'I gave you a lot of trouble when I was young, but it was the band that saved me.' Dr. Barnardo tells of another of his boys whose singing in a church choir in Canada attracted the attention of a leading Q.C. and Member of Parliament there. The result was that the boy was taken into the gentleman's service, and afterwards adopted as his son.

Mr. Spencer Curwen, to whose articles we are indebted for our information on this subject, gives some delightful instances of the benefit of the Tonic Sol-fa system in foreign mission work. It is taught in at least two of the great missionary training colleges, and the missionaries make extensive use of it with the best effects. In Madagascar, out of 1,100 schools, 85 per cent. teach the system, and Mr. Curwen tells the story of an old Admiral of the British Fleet stationed there who was so delighted with the singing of the native children that he used to go ashore each morning to hear the scholars in one of the schools sing a Tonic Sol-fa song, he beating time the while with his walking-stick. It is extensively used in Africa, and at one mission station it is even printed. At Freretown, the Rev. J. W. Handford was in great perplexity what to do with a number of boys and girls who had been rescued by British cruisers from Arab-slave dhows, and to which the mission had supplied a home. They spoke half-a-dozen different languages, but he found that they were all able to appreciate music. And long before they could repeat the alphabet they were singing simple tunes at sight by Sol-fa from the blackboard. In six months they could sing in four parts, the elder boys taking tenor and bass. After this they would gather in the long dark evenings in the verandah of Mr. Handford's house, and by the light of a lamp sing away for two hours at a stretch for sheer enjoyment.

Take another instance. This time from Basutoland. When the Colonial government and the Basutos were some time ago engaged in hostilities, some three hundred loyal Basutos took the Colonial side in the war, and were accordingly camped with the Colonial forces. One Sunday afternoon, a volunteer attached to the column strolled into the camp of the friendly Basutos. Much to his surprise he found some of their soldiers with Sol-fa copies of 'Sacred Songs and Solos,' singing to their hearts' delight. To test their powers he selected one piece they had not sung before, and asked them to render it. Nothing loth, they sang it through with a confidence that astonished their visitor—their tune, time, and expression being all well marked.

This country has generally been regarded as far behind its Continental neighbours in musical talent, but Mr. S. Curwen now declares, upon the authority of such good judges as Gounod, Dvoràk, and Dr. Otto Lessmann, that choral music of the highest type flourishes better in Britain than in any other country in the world. Mr. Curwen very fairly claims much of this advancement as the result of the spread of the Tonic Sol-fa system, but I wonder where we should have been musically, had it not been for the taste for hearty congregational singing that Methodism has promoted. Mr. Curwen says that a Roman Catholic organist of Dublin told him that in teaching the elements of singing he found Presbyterians much more promising musical material than Roman Catholics, and he considered that it was their congregational singing that made the difference. Knowing that congregational singing in many Presbyterian churches was of the rudest kind, whilst the Roman Catholic Church was distinguished for its gorgeous music, Mr. Curwen expressed his surprise at the statement. But, his friend replied, 'that does not count. Our people listen to music, but do not take part in it. You may set a fine breakfast before yourself, but until you eat it you do not begin to gain nourishment or strength.'

It is to be feared that Methodist congregations are scarcely maintaining the heartiness of their singing. We have become so afraid of making mistakes that singing in Methodist congregations now seldom attains the triumphant swell that used to characterize it. It might be well if a few more of our choirmasters were to try the Sol-fa system. Mr. Curwen claims that it makes singers 'certain of attack, and sure of intonation,' and these certainly are points on which many choirs are painfully deficient. It should be said that the movement is directed by the Tonic Sol-fa College, which is an incorporated body, managed by a council composed of sixty members, nearly half of whom are professional musicians, and 'the rest include musical amateurs whose callings are so diverse as those of a County Court Judge, a stockbroker, two commercial travellers, a bachelor of science, several clergymen and schoolmasters, clerks, a journeyman jeweller, cutler, plasterer, chairmaker, and compositor.' The college fixes the standards of examination, trains teachers, and every year it grants about 25,000 certificates of merit. A splendid fifty years of work has been done, and Mr. Spencer Curwen is to be congratulated upon the vigour and success with which he carries forward the labour of his father. M. P. D.

Anecdotes About Hymns.

From the German.

VIII.— A Good Prescription.

 HYPOCHONDRIAC invalid, who for a long while had used various medical remedies to remove his melancholy, and found them unavailing, resolved at last that he would give up all such treatment entirely. But being attacked by an unusually severe fit of his old malady, he begged his medical attendant, Dr. Fehre, with deep sighs and earnest entreaties for help, to try if there were no remedy that could avail for his relief. The doctor wrote no other prescription than the last line of the Christmas hymn beginning,

> 'From heaven came down the angels bright
> To shepherds keeping watch by night,
> "A tender Babe," so ran their cry,
> "In yon hard manger now doth lie." '

The line in question was as follows:

> 'Patient, rejoicing evermore.'

And Dr. Fehre, who knew his patient to be fond of music, likewise wrote the notes on a piece of paper. No sooner had he done this than the patient laughed aloud, rose from his bed full of joy, and was never more troubled with fits of melancholy.

'Never Mind.'

> HAT'S the use of always fretting,
>   At the trials we shall find
>   Ever strewn along our pathway?'
> Travel on, and 'Never Mind.'

Travel onward; working, hoping;
   Cast no lingering glance behind
At the trials once encountered,
   Look ahead, and 'Never Mind.'

What is past, is past forever;
   Let all fretting be resigned,
It will never help the matter,
   Do your best, and 'Never Mind.'

And if those who might befriend you,
   Whom the ties of nature bind,
Should refuse to do their duty,
   Look to heaven, and 'Never Mind.'

Friendly words are often spoken
   When the feelings are unkind;
Take them for their real value,
   Pass them by, and 'Never Mind.'

Fate may threaten, clouds may lower,
   Enemies may be combined;
If your trust in God is steadfast,
   He will help you, 'Never Mind.'
                    Mary E. M'Cleary.

SCATTER SMILES AS YOU GO.

W. B. BRADBURY.

2 Scatter smiles, bright smiles, 'tis but little they cost ;
But your heart may never know
What a joy they may carry to weary ones
Who are pale with want and woe.

3 Scatter smiles, bright smiles, o'er the grave of the past,
Where the orphan's treasure lies ;
In the tear-drop that glistens there light will shine,
As the rainbow paints the skies.

4 Scatter smiles, bright smiles, o'er the young who have strayed
From the path where once they trod !
You may lead to the fountain of truth again,
You may bring them home to God.

SCATTER SMILES AS YOU GO.

Key A.

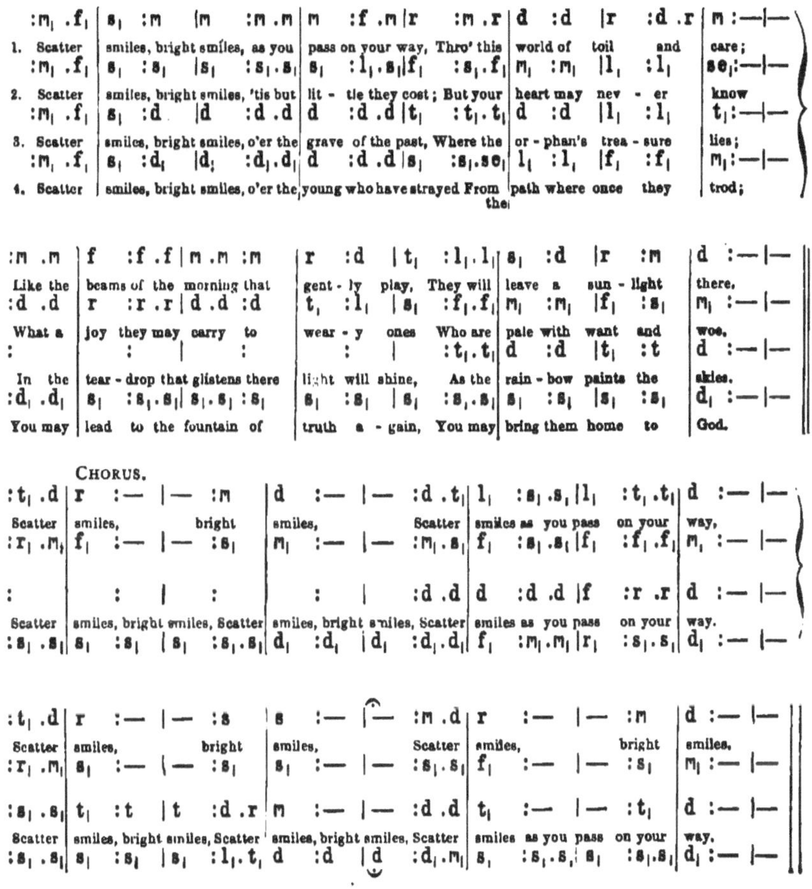

5 Scatter smiles, bright smiles, as you pass on your way
   Through this world of toil and care ;
   Like the beams of the morning that gently play,
   They will leave a sunlight there.

The Library.

E have before, in this section, strongly advised our readers in studying English History to put out of sight altogether the old landmarks (which were, in truth, no landmarks at all) supposed to be fixed by the accession or death of a king or queen; and also to forget all that they have learnt about the importance of most of the battles that have taken place. The true significance of English History lies in the growth of the nation, its liberties, its laws, and its political constitution. For the study of these aspects of English History no one has done more than Mr. Freeman, whose little book on *The Growth of the English Constitution from the Earliest Times* now lies before us. Some idea of its interest and value may be gleaned from the fact that the present is the third edition of the book. It is distinctly a popular work, the substance of which was originally delivered some fifteen years ago in Leeds and Bradford. Mr. Freeman frequently refers to the larger works of Hallam and Stubbs, and says, 'If I can send everyone who wishes to understand the early institutions of his country to the great work of Professor Stubbs—none the less great because it lies in an amazingly small compass—my own work will be effectually done.' The present little book comprises three chapters. The first treats of the origin of the English nation and its constitution; the second traces their gradual growth; while the third is mainly occupied in showing how the constitution in its growth has reverted to ancient principles. In the present day national assemblies of the Federal Commonwealths of Switzerland, Mr. Freeman finds the primitive model, 'the germs out of which every free constitution in the world has grown.' This primitive constitution was, he says, democratic in the best and broadest sense, namely, a government by the whole people, no class, whether high or low, being shut out. It contained, indeed, the three elements which we now possess—a monarchic, an aristocratic, and a so-called democratic. But the kings were freely chosen by all the people. It was 'a free commonwealth of warriors, in which each freeman has his place in the state, where the vote of the general assembly is the final authority on all matters, but where both hereditary descent and elective office are held in high honour.' Mr. Freeman knocks the bottom out of the theory that the word *king* means originally the *canning*, or *cunning* or able man. He roundly declares that the man who first said that had simply not learned his old English grammar. He derives it, and surely with strong reason, from the Greek *genos*, the Latin *genus*, the old English *cyn*, which are simply our words 'kind' and 'kin.' Mr. Freeman seems distantly to favour the derivation of *cyning* (the longer form of the word 'king') from the Sanscrit *ganaka*, which means 'father.' The dependence of the king upon the race or people is thus clearly set forth. It is easy to trace the growth of reverence for the king. As he came to reign over a larger and larger area he became less familiar to the mass of his people. He was more and more shrouded in a mysterious awe, and his subjects gradually became not only his subjects but his men, his personal servants; and here we have the beginnings of the feudal system in England as in other countries. But to check this tendency there happily always remained in England a National Assembly of some kind or other, in which at first every freeman had his place. But gradually the idea and practice of representation began to obtain—a few attending on behalf of the many—although the whole people always had an acknowledged right to attend the meetings. Mr. Freeman holds that the present House of Lords represents, or rather is, the ancient Witanagemot. He pays a very high tribute to Simon de Montfort, Earl of Leicester, who was practically the creator of our present House of Commons. After his defeat of Henry the Third, he called together, in the name of the king, not only the aristocratic knights from the counties, but also two citizens from every

city and two burgesses from every borough.
' It was in Earl Simon's parliament of 1265,
that the still abiding elements of the popular
chamber, the knights, citizens, and burgesses
first appeared side by side. Thus was formed
that newly-developed estate of the realm,
which was, step by step, to grow into the most
powerful of all, the Commons' House of
Parliament. Parliaments have of course
sometimes been instruments of tyranny. Thus
when the old nobility had been killed off by
the Wars of the Roses, and the new nobility
were the slaves of the king, who had given
them their honours, Parliament both in
Lords and Commons had become servile, and
it was not till the next century that the old
authority was reasserted.' We cannot stay
to summarize Mr. Freeman's third chapter,
wonderfully interesting though it is. He
shows how much we owe to an unwritten *Constitution* as distinguished from the written
Law, and how much we rest on precedent.
And so ' in a manner silent and indirect, the
Lower House of Parliament, as it is still deemed
in formal rank, has become the really ruling
power in the nation.' In modern form the
people have now got back all their ancient
liberties. ' The cycle has come round, the
days of foreign rule have been wiped out, and
England is England once again.' This is a
most fascinating book on a most fascinating
theme, and no young politician should be
without it.

Deep-Sea Wonders.

N some dark night have you
never sat by the window, and
seen a bright light suddenly
rush by, followed by other
smaller ones a little distance
apart? Yes, I mean the
engine with its head-light and the lights
from the lamps shining through the windows!
You would not expect to see an engine and
cars down several feet below the surface of the
ocean ; now would you ? and yet, a sight very
much like this may be seen down there. It is
a fish that carries a bright light on his head
that shines out just like the head-light on a
locomotive, and bright spots on his sides for
windows. May be you think that he ought to
be called the car-fish, but those who named
him did not seem to agree with you. His real
name is Scopelus, but he is called the brilliant
lamp-fish by some, because the lamp which he
carries on his head is such a very bright one.
These fish are a little related to the salmons,
and like all the lamp-fish of the ocean are
mostly found in tropical seas. They are caught
in nets, and are much sought after for making
pearls—not real ones that are found in oysters,
but make-believe ones, that men fix up. Each
Scopelus has somewhere about him a shiny,
scaly stuff, and the pearls are made out of
this.

Then there is the Bombay duck, whose name
does not suit the least bit, for instead of a
duck he happens to be a fish ; another of these
phosphorescent fish at that. Instead of carrying his light in spots, he scatters it all over
him, so his whole body glows as if on fire.
He is caught on the coasts of India, and after
being salted and dried is very good to eat. He
is a great eater himself, and every thing he
can get hold of seems to taste good to him. It
seems as if he ought to be able to catch nearly
any thing he wants to, for, although not a
large fish, he has big fins that carry him about
quickly. And then such a big mouth as he
has. Why, it opens 'way back of his ears,
and is filled full of long, slender teeth, hooked
at the points, so it must be hard work to get
away from him when he once gets a good hold.

Here is a long word. Get some one to say
it for you, so as to be sure to get it right. It
is Argyopelecus ; the name of another of these
lantern-fish living in the sea. The fish itself
is not as long as its name might make you
think. It is quite thick next to the head, but
tapers off suddenly to the tail, giving it a
queer shape. However, this little fellow
carries a good many lights—over a hundred
of them. These are scattered over his body,
not just as it happens, but each one in its own
place, so that all the fish of this kind are
alike. The wise men do not seem to agree
very well about these shiny spots. Some call
them eyes, and think they are to help see

with, as well as to give light; while others, not believing a word of this, say they are of no use at all, but are make-believe electrical organs.

There are many more of these fish having bright spots on them, hurrying through the ocean in different parts, and lighting up the darkness for themselves and for the rest of the sea people that live so far down that the sunshine can never reach them. One about a foot long has large teeth sticking out of his mouth like great tusks; while others, with large heads and long slim bodies, are able by their lights to hunt the smaller fish they like so well, while they in turn are chased, taken, and eaten, by larger fish that rush along almost as fast as rockets.

Next, let us talk about a family of mollusks. They seem to be quite fond of each other, for a large number of them always live together. Hundreds and hundreds of them, more than you could count, fasten themselves together in the shape of a hollow cylinder, closed at one end and open at the other. This cylinder may be only two or three inches in length, or it may be five feet. Most little sea animals take the water into their bodies through one opening, and after getting out of it the air, and whatever they can eat, throw it out another way. These little mollusks are so fixed that each one breathes the water in from the outside of the cylinder, and throws it out into the hollow tube, and the force with which this is done shoves it through the water with the closed end first. They look very pretty in the day-time, as they are brightly coloured, but when night comes on, then is the time to see them. And there is no need to hunt for them either; for they give such a bright light, and there are so many of them in all the warm seas, that one can scarcely help seeing them at almost any time. They give a changeable light that may be yellow, blue, red, or green.

One traveller writes of being on the ocean when there were so many of these light-givers that all on board could plainly see the fish swimming far down below the surface. Another tells of sailing through so many of these bright cylinders that the stars looked dim, and as the vessel turned up the water, great flashes of light would spring up by its side; and a naturalist took some of them into the cabin and made them give the light while he wrote down all he could find out about them.

Then there is the sea-pen. True, this does not give quite as bright a light as some of the others, but then it is pretty enough to look at, besides being worth noticing on account of its shape, which is like a pen—not the kind we have, but those pens made out of quills that grandpa used to write with when he went to school. Here is the quill part, also the feather part, which sometimes is open and spread out on the surface, and then is shut up close. If these were real pens, they would do to use in the dark, for they give out different lights, as they move through the water. May be they are some kin to the corals, for each pen, like the coral-branches, is made up of many little animals that take tight hold of each other, but, unlike them, they never fasten themselves to anything else.   EMMA J. WOOD.

The Nearest Task.

THE path that lies straight before us,
    And the duty that must be done,
    Is the path to be trod, the task to
      be wrought,
Ere the victor's crown be won.

Ever the task that lies nearest,
    And the path that lies plain in view,
Though that task and that path are the
      hardest, dear,
    That ever shall come to you.

The hardest tasks are the nearest ones,
    The every-day duties are those
Which seem not to count in the battle of
      life,
    But shall gain 'well done' at its close.

Then onward, with all thy strength, dear,
    For thy task is given in love;
And the toil and the task of every-day life
    Are but steps to the heaven above.

                EMMA S. THOMAS.

SPRINGTIME:

A Magazine for Our Young Men and Maidens.

Vol. VI. No. 10.]   OCTOBER, 1891.   [Price Twopence.

A Bad Calculation.

By ROBERT HIND,

Author of ' Crosby Dalton: Local Preacher and Village Demagogue,' ' The Ruby Pendant,' &c.

CHAPTER XIX.

TRUE TO HIS WORD.

> 'A spirit strong and true,
> Beauteous to human seeing.'
>
> ROBERT BUCHANAN.

ACK BENSON was in no danger of forgetting his promise to Rye, and being of an abnormally conscientious turn of mind, he was not likely to leave to circumstances the chief share in its fulfilment. The result was that occasionally he and Arthur were to be seen on an afternoon pulling a boat together up the river, or taking brisk walking exercise on the banks.

Arthur had not met Jack's first approaches in a friendly manner, but the latter, feeling he was under an obligation to succeed if it were possible, quietly persisted in his endeavours, and, in a little time, as he flattered himself was usual with anything about which he was desperately in earnest, he carried his point so far as to establish between them what in his own mind he called a ' comrade-ship of a sort.'

For their conversation lacked both freedom and frankness, and was altogether too formal to be the outcome of real friendship. In the circumstances perhaps nothing else could be expected. Arthur felt that Jack's kindness was scarcely spontaneous, and although he was in profound ignorance of its motive, he was sure there was one that had not appeared to him.

The time had been when he would have resented the action, and shut himself up more than ever; but since his talk with Ida Saunders, the fact of his loneliness had preyed upon his mind, and made him ask if he might not himself be partly to blame for his isolation. And he thought it best, as a consequence, to miss no chance of forming friendships with his fellow-students, however slender and even distasteful they might be.

And to have Jack Benson for a comrade was decidedly distasteful to him. Mainly because he felt himself in almost all respects inferior to him. It was galling for him as he went about the university to remember the evening at the Mount when he had played the violin and Rye the piano, and Jack had confessed himself to be without any musical gifts whatever. He had thought then that there were things which made him seem superior to the young gentleman from Australia, but he remembered that even then he had some doubts on the subject. And now he could not close his eyes to the fact that Jack was immensely popular with everybody. His company was sought by all the students; the professors and, Nonconformist as he was, the local clergymen invited him to spend an evening occasionally at their homes. He had not fully realized all this when he had talked with Ida Saunders about university life. But at that time he was just beginning his course, and even then he had an indistinct notion that Jack was well liked.

To one of Arthur's temperament it was not pleasant to be reminded by Jack's presence that he was not a social success, and the unpleasant feeling tended to make the conversation somewhat forced.

As for Jack, he had undertaken an impossible task. To those of a benevolent turn of mind it may not be supremely difficult to befriend one whom they cannot esteem, much less admire; but to befriend such an one and to be his friend are two different matters.

Nevertheless, with a dutiful devotion that deserved success, Jack waylaid Arthur at the class-room door, made engagements with him two or three times a week, and introduced him to other young men, with whom, considering his reserved and retiring habits, it is probable but for Jack he would never have exchanged words.

The term was drawing to a close, and the usual excitement was prevalent among both dons and students. The strain of the hard work necessary in the weeks just before the examination was making an impression on the faces of many, and on the spirits of some. Besides, there were other interests. The annual concert given just before the Christmas vacation was occupying the attention of some of those who were not wholly absorbed with graver studies.

Jack Benson had been asked to join the committee of arrangements, and had consented. Finding at the first meeting he attended that the committee was not complete, he suggested that Arthur Brixton's name be added.

'Who is Arthur Brixton, pray?' the honorary president inquired.

There was a smile in the eyes of some of those present. They were too well bred, however, to allow it to overspread their faces. They knew Arthur and they thought the president could not be wholly unconscious of the existence of that young man. Jack did not see the joke, however, and answered quite innocently:

'He is a friend of mine.'

'Oh!' the president replied; and silence followed. As no one else took up the matter, he at length continued,

'Strange I have not made his acquaintance. Does he belong to the Priory or Hatton Hall?' he asked, naming the two colleges of Rockingham University.

'Neither,' Jack answered. 'Like me, he is unattached.'

'Well, candidly, has he any special qualifications?'

Jack began to think that the president's questions arose from positive objections to Arthur rather than to ignorance of his existence. Had Arthur inspired him with a greater measure of esteem, he would have resented with some indignation the manner in which his suggestion had been received. He was, however, only doing all he could to fulfil his promise to Rye, and in the knowledge of his own feelings he could not be surprised that Arthur was not welcomed on the committee with open arms.

'He has very special musical qualifications, and I should say enough ability of other kinds to render good service on the committee.'

'All right, then, let us agree to it. Mr. Benson should know whether he is suitable or not, though I should never have thought of choosing any one who wanders about the place as though he were a perfect stranger, and had not a single friend in it.'

That evening at the Mount Jack remarked to Rye:

'We are making arrangements for the annual concert. There is plenty of musical talent among the students, and we hope it will surpass some of those given in recent years.'

'May your hopes be fully realized is my earnest wish. I am sure you deserve it.'

'I have grounds for thinking they will.'

'In what? Perhaps what in your estimation are reasonable grounds, to the minds of people less interested in the matter will seem rather trifling, not to say presumptuous. Young men are inclined to go that way,' she remarked.

'What a poor opinion you have of young men! Suppose I give you one other reason in addition to what I have named about the musical talent of several of the students ? '

' And then I shall be able to form an opinion for myself. Only I know if my opinion does not agree with yours you will conclude I lack judgment.'

This was not Rye's usual style, and Jack wondered what was ailing her. Looking into her kind beaming eyes, he could not think she was speaking in ill-nature, and he had misread her completely if she was capable of putting on a sarcastic mood.

' If your face did not belie your words, I should believe I had offended you somehow. And in that case I should be ready to apologise most humbly.'

Rye's face assumed a more tender expression than it was wont, and her eyes shone with a softer light than usual.

' Do you think I can guess what you are going to tell me ? Is not your other reason that Arthur is on the committee of arrangements ? '

Jack had intended to surprise as well as please her. He could not understand how she could have expected this, and more than half the pleasure he had anticipated for himself in giving the information was taken from him.

' You anticipated this ? ' he asked ; and in spite of all he could do, the disappointment he felt would not be kept altogether out of his voice.

' Not at all. Why should I ? I met Arthur to-day and he told me. Indeed, he showed me the letter he had received from the president asking him to become a member of the committee. The letter stated who had already accepted, and I observed your name in the list. I did not say so to Arthur, but I concluded you had procured that invitation for him. Arthur is clever in all respects, he has a fine musical taste, and is a splendid violinist, which are good grounds for thinking, as you have hinted, that he will render effective service on the committee. And as one who wishes the concert may be a success, I am glad. But I am glad for other reasons. I knew I could rely on your word when you promised me to be Arthur's friend, and do

all you could to save him from feeling isolated, but not every one would have thought his promise involved so much as you have.'

A reasonable young man, anxious to have the good-will of Rye Harland, would have thought he had scored a victory, and have felt correspondingly proud. No one could well be more anxious to enjoy the favour of that young lady than her cousin Jack, and those who knew him best would have been the most ready to acknowledge that he was sane and reasonable far beyond the average of the young men of his years. But Rye's words, flattering as they might seem, did not wholly please him.

They bound him more than ever to remember his promise—a promise which he must continue to honour, however disagreeable it might prove to him to do so. That was bad enough in itself, but there was another thought suggested by the state of affairs. It confirmed him more than ever in the impression that Arthur Brixton was still the possessor of Rye's affections. By this time, too, Jack Benson knew his own heart, and the thought of what he believed to be Rye's feelings was cruel as death. But he still did not think of doing other than befriend Arthur.

The time for trial by fire had come to him, and in his nature there was too much good metal for him to succumb in the midst of the ordeal.

CHAPTER XX.

QUICK RETRIBUTION.

' In secret ways and strong
God doth avenge man's wrong.'
ROBERT BUCHANAN.

NEITHER to Jack nor Arthur were the examinations at the end of this term of especial importance. And yet both of them passed with sufficient ease and credit to give promise of doing well when the time came for taking their degrees.

Arthur had worked hard for the concert ever since he had been asked to take an active part in the arrangements, and had shown rather more manliness and strength than he was often accustomed to display. He had indeed manifested an indifference to the opinions of others with regard to himself which was quite refreshing, and Jack was beginning to think that his comrade was improving.

For on more than one occasion he had perceived in the president's bearing towards Arthur cause for dissatisfaction. There were little slights practised, and a studied indifference shown that Jack would not have believed possible on the part of so polite and well-bred a young man as the president had he not seen it for himself.

At last even Arthur, who, conscious of his morbid sensitiveness, and resolved, if possible, to commend himself to the good opinion of those with whom he was acting by cultivating an attitude of self-forgetfulness, was reluctantly compelled to think that he was being unfairly treated.

'I shall not go to the committee again,' he said to Jack.

Jack had no difficulty in guessing what was the motive of this resolve, but he thought he had no right to assume this.

'You have a reason?'

'Yes, and you cannot be ignorant of it.'

'How should I know unless you inform me?' Jack inquired.

'Very well. My reason is that I am not wanted. The time has been when I would have flung up the appointment long ago, but I have tried to persuade myself I was mistaken once more by my over-sensitiveness. But even a person more thick-skinned than I would not have been impervious to the blows that have been aimed at me. You have noticed it?'

'I cannot deny it, and I am very sorry. The reason is beyond my comprehension.'

'Oh! the reason is plain. I am poor, and live in a little cottage with my father and mother, both of whom belong to the working-classes.'

'That cannot be the reason. I could have believed it of some of our men. But Everton is not a cad; on the contrary, he is one of the most manly, and generally one of the most amiable of comrades. I am bound to confess, however, that he is capable of making an exception to this.'

Arthur's eyebrows, which had been frowning at the commencement of their conversation, fell still lower as he said:

'We need not discuss the matter further, and you will perhaps be kind enough to ask the committee to relieve me of any further service.'

The committee met that evening, and one of them observed that Mr. Brixton was not present, and added, he believed it was the first time he had been absent. The president shrugged his shoulders and was proceeding to ask the secretary about the order of business when Jack Benson interposed:

'Mr. Brixton will not serve on the committee again. He asked me to say he wishes you to relieve him of any further work.'

Once more the president surprised Jack by the brevity, not to say brusqueness, of his method of dealing with Arthur. He asked for no reasons, but simply desired a show of hands of those who agreed to accede to Mr. Brixton's request, and thus the matter was disposed of.

At the end of the meeting, however, Jack walked across the Priory 'quad' with Everton, intending to give him a bit of his mind.

'You disposed of Brixton very easily to-night,' he said.

'By "you," you mean the committee?'

'Well, if you care to have it so: but the committee took its cue from the president's manner. I thought it strange that no reasons were asked, and even expected that an effort might have been made to retain him. Had it been so, possibly he might have been willing to continue to work with us.'

'I presume any one who desired him to remain was at liberty to say so, and use what influence he could to have his way,' the president replied, in the tone of a man to whom the subject is the opposite of interesting.

'You wish me to understand you had no such desire? At least, you have the virtue of absolute candour.'

Mr. Everton smiled, but did not reply. Jack, therefore, continued:

'As no one has deigned to ask for a reason, I will volunteer one. He thinks he has been treated with scant courtesy, and that the president of the committee has been the offending party. I am of the same opinion.'

Frank Everton flushed and looked for a moment quite confused; but he recovered himself quickly.

'He has found a valiant champion, at least; and as I may have seemed less than just, perhaps you, who have undertaken his cause so enthusiastically, should know whether I had reasons for acting so. Why you should be his friend I cannot understand, and, of course, have no claim to be told, but I am sure, when you have heard my story, you will do me the justice to admit that I had some grounds for feeling uncomfortable in having to act with him. I will tell you further, it was my regard for you that prevented me from asking him to retire from the committee.'

'My story,' he continued, 'is soon told. I knew hardly anything of him when you proposed his name to be added, although I had observed him as one of those solitary creatures who always remind me of the mediæval hermits, the men who thought themselves too good for any company save their own, and accordingly retired into the wilderness to live alone. At the first we did some work together, and I found he had some ideas, that, in my judgment, were both wise and original. I asked him up to my rooms, and we played together, he on the violin and I on the flute. I don't pretend that in that single fortnight we became friendly. He was too reserved by far for anything of the kind to happen. One day we were passing down Millgate together, and standing in the doorway of one of the houses there was a rather elderly man, wearing a rather greenish-black coat that was not originally made at a fashionable tailor's, who looked up, smiled, and nodded.

' "A friend of yours, Brixton?" I asked, and then remembering he belonged to Rockingham, I added, "but I suppose you know well-nigh every one in the old city."

' "Pretty nearly," he answered, and I noticed he looked confused and vexed. I wish you to know that my intention was to put him at ease about the old man, who looked decent enough, though rather withered and poor even for a working-man. So I said:

' " Rockingham is not well supplied with houses for poor people, I should imagine, judging from what I have seen of them from the outside. That was not exactly a model dwelling from which your friend was looking out." '

'The effect of all this was the opposite of what I had intended. Instead of putting him at his ease, he grew even more confused, so that I was fain to strike off at a tangent and begin to talk about music and the concert. But the circumstance made me curious—so curious that I made an inquiry or two at a little shop close by. I now know that that old man was Arthur Brixton's father, and that the house where he was standing was his home.'

Jack Benson, despite all he had formerly thought of Arthur, was a little astonished. But he would not condemn yet. His only reply to Frank Everton therefore was a monosyllable.

'Well!'

'You say "well." Cannot you see in my story some justification for my apparent lack of courtesy?'

'That is, Arthur Brixton is poor, and lives in a very poor home. Is that your reason?'

'You know quite well it is not. Come down to Breckeurig this "vac.," and I will show you my home. It is a little five-roomed farmhouse. The farm, though our own, is only small. My father works on it like any of his men, and my mother still manages the dairy. I will show you that I can plough myself, and do any other work connected with the place. I have heard your father is a millionaire and that you live in a big mansion. But I shan't pass my father and mother in their work-a-day clothes with a nod, nor feel ashamed of the little house that is my home, even when I am in the company of a millionaire's son, still less decline to acknowledge my relations to them. And from the time that I knew that Arthur Brixton was ashamed to own his, I was ashamed of him, and decline to have any correspondence with him beyond what is absolutely necessary. In my heart I am glad he is off the committee. Do you agree with me?'

'At least I cannot blame you.'

(To be continued.)

Going without a Religion.

I FEAR that when we indulge ourselves in the amusement of going without a religion we are not, perhaps, aware how much we are sustained at present by an enormous mass all about us of religious feeling and religious conviction, so that, whatever it may be safe for us to think—for us who have had great advantages and have been brought up in such a way that a certain moral direction has been given to our character,—I do not know what would become of the less favoured classes of mankind if they undertook to play the same game.

Whatever defects and imperfections may attach to a few points of the doctrinal system of Calvin—the bulk of which is simply what all Christians believe—it will be found that Calvinism, or any other ism which claims an open Bible, and proclaims a crucified and risen Christ, is infinitely preferable to any form of polite and polished scepticism which gathers as its votaries the degenerate sons of heroic ancestors, who, having been trained in a society and educated in schools, the foundations of which were laid by men of faith and piety, now turn and kick down the ladder by which they have climbed up, and persuade men to live without God and leave them to die without hope.

The worst kind of religion is no religion at all; and these men, living in ease and luxury, indulging themselves in the 'amusement of going without religion,' may be thankful that they live in lands where the Gospel they neglect has tamed the beastliness and ferocity of the men who, but for Christianity, might long ago have eaten their carcasses like the South Sea islanders, or cut off their heads and tanned their hides like the monsters of the French Revolution. When the microscopic search of scepticism, which had hunted the heavens and sounded the seas to disprove the existence of a Creator, has turned its attention to human society, and has found a place on this planet ten miles square where a decent man can live in decency, comfort, and security, supporting and educating his children unspoiled and unpolluted, a place where age is reverenced, infancy respected, manhood respected, womanhood honoured, and human life held in due regard —when sceptics can find such a place ten miles square on this globe where the Gospel of Christ has not gone and cleared the way and laid the foundations and made decency and security possible, it will then be in order for the sceptical *litterati* to move thither and then ventilate their views. But so long as these very men are dependent upon the religion which they discard for every privilege they enjoy, they may well hesitate a little before they seek to rob the Christian of his hope and humanity of its faith in that Saviour who alone has given to man that hope of life eternal which makes life tolerable and society possible, and robs death of its terrors and the grave of its gloom.

JAMES RUSSELL LOWELL.

Notwithstanding.

BRIEF are the days and few
  When the sky is utter blue,
  And the wind goes over the grass
Like the laugh of a Maying lass.
But our good is good to all,
And some perfect days befall,
  Notwithstanding.

We do what we can, and trust:
But our doing turns to dust,
And the night flows over the day
And washes its deeds away;
But whatso we truly try,
The world will not let it die,
  Notwithstanding.

Then courage, my brothers brave,
And the precious remnant save!
Our hopes are like lamps of fire,
Set high, to lead us higher.
No man has yet lived his dream,
But we climb by things that seem,
  Notwithstanding.

Bible Teaching on Religious Giving.

ow few people, comparatively, have read the Bible with a view to learn what it has to teach on the question of giving—giving of our substance to God's cause, and for God's sake! Too many of us seem to think, speak, and act, as if this subject were outside the scope of Scriptural teaching, or even serious personal responsibility; and that, if it is a duty at all, it is a duty which may be left to the fitful, uncertain, unreliable impulses of the hour. We recognize the duty of *holy living*, of practical and constant obedience to the divine law, of being doers of the work and not hearers only. We feel the necessity of *prayer*, to nurture our own spiritual life, to fortify against temptation, to spiritualize the mind and life, to ask for the daily supply of daily need, and to lift the whole nature into harmony and unity with God. We acknowledge that we are commanded to *work* in the Lord's vineyard; to prove the reality of our faith by its practical results in service for others; to consecrate whatever talents and time we possess to the glory of God in loving and cheerful efforts to bless our fellow-men. Living, working, praying, are all matters on which we acknowledge grave individual responsibility, and on which we look to the Scriptures for instruction and help. But may not ' giving' be properly classed with living, working, and praying, as a great spiritual privilege and duty? Are we not as like God when we give, as near God, as acceptable to God, as when we work or pray? What is more God-like than giving — giving from motives of love and gratitude to the great Giver of all, giving in recognition of the goodness we have received, giving from religious principle and conviction, and giving to mitigate the pain or minister to the happiness of those about us? What is a better test of character than this? What can afford better proof of the reality of our Christian profession? To pray may be easy; to give costs something. When is a believer more thoroughly in sympathy with his Master—' who gave Himself for us '—than when he gives of his substance to bless others? And especially when giving means sacrifice, self-denial, the surrender of some legitimate pleasure for Christ's sake.

It would be strange indeed if the Bible were silent on this great subject; if it gave no instruction on what is one of the main outlets of a spirit of benevolence; if it gave no precepts inculcating it, no rules regulating it, no examples illustrating it, and no warnings against the neglect of it, and against covetousness or indifference, the chief hindrances to its healthy exercise. It would be strange if so much were said—so many precepts and promises—about living, working, praying, and nothing about giving. The great institutions of religious worship and instruction can only be maintained by the labour and gifts of those who share their benefits; and has the responsibility for maintaining these institutions no place in Biblical teaching? Christianity is philanthropy. It means good-will to men. It teaches not only the Fatherhood of God, but the brotherhood of the race. It is the religion of benevolence. . And is it conceivable that the most beneficial religion the world has ever known, the one which cares most for the needy and helpless, and which most strongly inculcates sacrifices for the good of others, should have left its disciples and apostles without principles and precepts to guide their conduct on this great duty? They who imagine that Bible teaching on the question of giving is either indefinite or scanty have read the Bible to little purpose. We will inquire, devoutly, and with a purpose to practise what we learn, what the Bible has to say on this subject.

THE EXAMPLES IN PATRIARCHAL TIMES

will be interesting to us, as showing what was done in the early dawn of religious history. Two illustrative cases are given: Abram giving tithes to Melchisedek, and Jacob vowing to give to the Lord the tenth of all that the Lord's blessing should confer upon him. It is worthy of note that each of these distinguished men acts on the same rule—that of devoting a tenth to the Lord. Evidently this was an early and well-known rule of conduct on these matters. Whence did it come? Probably it was an express divine command handed down from earlier to later generations.

ABRAM GIVING TITHES TO MELCHISEDEK

is one of the striking scenes of ancient Scripture history. It possesses a special interest from the fact that it is the first notice contained in the Bible of ' the dedication of a distinct proportion of property to God.' There had been a war in the neighbourhood of Sodom, and the victors, as was the custom in those times, had seized the persons and property of the vanquished, and were proceeding with them to their own country. Among the captives was Lot, the nephew of Abram. Hearing of this, the heroic patriarch arms his dependents, pursues the retreating forces, overtakes them, defeats them, and recovers their captives and booty; and amongst them Lot and his goods. ' To God Abram owes his victory, and to God was due an acknowledgment of His aid. Accordingly, returning, he meets God's high priest, and to him he pays a tenth of all the spoils.'

Manifestly this was a religious act. Abram was fairly entitled to the spoils which his courageous dependents had rescued, but he declined everything for himself, save the tenth which was devoted to God. This patriarch is one of the noblest figures of Scripture history, devout, upright, magnanimous, a man of noble faith, of unflinching loyalty to duty, and withal courteous, considerate, sympathetic. Even in the New Testament he is held up as a model of faith, patience, and loyalty to God. His signal unselfishness in offering to Lot the choice of residence, when the land was unable to bear their united flocks and herds, was in complete harmony with all we know of his moral greatness. And it is not a little significant that the first lesson given to mankind, of which we have historic record, on definite and proportionate consecration of wealth to God, should

be by a man of such illustrious character and position.

JACOB'S VOW AT BETHEL

recalls a scene of singular pathos and suggestiveness. ' It is, indeed, a bright spot amid a dark world ; a green, smiling region within a surrounding desert; a transformation scene, which lights up the earth again with its former brightness, and points to the time when ·it shall be said of it with truth, "It is good to be here." ' Jacob is flying from the vengeance of his brother Esau, whom he has deeply wronged. He lies down at the close of the day to rest. So far as human companionships go, he is alone; but the eye which never sleeps watches over him, and the one hand ever ready to help employs this time of peril and friendlessness to display the freeness and fulness of its gifts. Fresh from his sin, God met the fugitive. During the night a vision reveals alike the presence and grace of God. The scene of the ladder, with angels ascending to heaven and descending to earth, is full of spiritual teaching and encouragement to this social outcast. God has not forgotten or forsaken him ; and though he has sinned, and sinned deeply, all the possibilities of life are not absolutely forfeited, pardon may be sought and found, and life made noble and beautiful after all. He awakes with a sobered spirit, and with a lofty purpose to serve God ; and one feature of the covenant into which he solemnly enters is ' of all that Thou shalt give me, I will surely give the tenth unto Thee.'

The fixing of one-tenth as the amount to be given to God lends countenance to the supposition already expressed, that this was a divine law well known and recognized, and that a dedication of property to God was regarded as a distinct and highly commendable act of worship. The scene, too, marks a wonderful change in the spirit of Jacob. Hitherto we have only known him as selfish and self-seeking ; as having a keen eye to the main chance, and as subordinating higher and nobler considerations to the solitary and sordid purpose of personal gain. Now he takes God into partnership in his earthly concerns, and religiously resolves to give Him one-tenth of his gains. When Esau came in famished from his hunting, instead of meeting his needs in a frank and brotherly fashion, Jacob used his extremity to drive a hard bargain and secure his brother's birthright; now the motive of loyalty to God so far prevails over the instincts of mere personal advantage as to prompt to a proportionate and systematic consecration of wealth to God.

It is remarkable, too, that no specific object is named as that to which the contribution is to be devoted. Abram gave tithes to Melchisedek, to an illustrious person representing God, and manifestly for a definite object. Jacob's vow brings out even more clearly the principle of giving a proportion to God, apart altogether from the specific object of religion or philanthropy to which it may be applied. If there were no ministry, such as that which Melchisedek may well represent, to support, God's claim and man's responsibility would still remain. What is to be done with the amount consecrated is another aspect of the subject, and must be left largely to the circumstances, conscience, and judgment of each individual contributor. The obligation to make the consecration, the principle of devoting one-tenth to God, apart from any particular set of circumstances in which it may occur, is what stands out clear and full in this incident.

It is, moreover, a vow for life. Whilst it is a single act of consecration, it covers in its fulfilment all Jacob's future. Abram's gift was a thankoffering for that *special* manifestation of God's favour in the success of his mission of rescue; Jacob's is a recognition of God's goodness in *ordinary* life.

The earlier gift celebrated victory—circumstances of exceptional divine interpositions on our behalf; the later acknowledged everyday obligations—the sunshine and rain which make harvests possible; the health, skill, and energy which bring prosperity; the comforts of home; and all in social and church life which ministers to peace, happiness, and usefulness. The lessons which these incidents of patriarchal times teach us are clear:—(1) That special manifestations of God's goodness and favour demand at our hands recognition in the form of gifts, proportionate to our condition, from grateful hearts to God and His cause; and (2) that the ordinary experience of the blessings of life—daily bread for daily needs—equally claims the same acknowledgment of divine goodness and faithfulness in the willing consecration of some portion—a tenth—of our income to His service and glory.

MOSES AND THE JEWISH TITHES.

We now come to another and fuller dispensation of divine truth, and one in which the principle of systematic consecration of wealth to God assumes the definiteness and fixity of direct legal enactments. The promise given to Abraham was in process of rapid fulfilment. God was making of Israel a great nation. The single families of Abraham and Jacob had now developed into a great community of, say, two millions of people, only needing the laws, institutions, and opportunities of national life to achieve a great destiny. What had existed previously as matter of mere personal obligation was now woven into the texture of their common national and religious life, and became matter of legal enactment, obligatory on all. The sacrifices, for example, had apparently up to this date been left to the impulse of each individual worshipper; they now became conspicuous features in a religious system, to the claims of which all must defer. And so with gifts to the cause of God. What had been previously determined by each man's judgment or conscience, or by obedience to some tradition, now became a national and religious duty, to compliance with which every sentiment alike of patriotism and devotion would prompt and impel. In the carrying out of this stupendous change, Moses, probably the greatest figure in Hebrew history, was the chief actor. To him belongs the distinguished honour of forming a great nation out of a horde of slaves; of formulating laws for the regulation and development of their corporate life; of fusing the national and spiritual features and functions of a great people in a manner perhaps unique in human history; and of laying all posterity under a debt—an unpayable debt—of obligation for his signal services to law, literature, and religion. Moses was God's selected and instructed agent in the carrying out of this greatest experiment of national education in spiritual truth which history has seen.

Now, in this remarkable collection of laws the obligation to devote a portion of each person's resources to God and His cause has a definite and prominent place.

(1) There was the tithe of the land, and of the fruit of the tree (Lev. xxvii. 30). This statute was explicit: not less than one-tenth was to be given. As revelation advanced, and religious light became clearer, and spiritual privileges greater, obligations did not shrink or diminish—they proportionately advanced. The purpose for which these tithes were given was clear—the maintenance of the ministry, the sustenance of the tribe of Levi, in whose hands the services of religion were placed (Numb. xviii. 27).

(2) There was the tithe for the maintenance of the various feasts and sacrifices. ' Thou shalt truly tithe all the increase of thy seed, that the field bringeth forth year by year . . . . . . the tithe of thy corn, of thy vine, and of thine oil, and the firstlings of thy herds and of thy flocks; that thou mayest learn to fear thy God always' (Deut. xiv. 22, 23).

(3) There was the tithe for the poor. ' At the end of three years thou shalt bring forth all the tithe of thine increase the same year, and shalt lay it up within thy gates. And the Levite (because he hath no part nor inheritance with thee), and the stranger, and the fatherless, and the widow, which are within thy gates, shall come, and shall eat and be satisfied; that the Lord thy God may bless thee in all the work of thine hand which thou doest.' It is uncertain whether this is a separate tithe from the two already mentioned, but, if not, it brings in new objects of sympathy and benevolence. Love and loyalty to God will produce their legitimate fruit of philanthropy and helpfulness to men. Supreme regard for the Creator can only elevate our conceptions of the worth of the creature, and draw out our sympathy in efforts to relieve want and distress, and promote human weal.

(4) There were, in addition, in this old Jewish law, ' offerings for special occasions' and ' freewill offerings' for times when exceptional instances of divine goodness and favour evoked from the grateful and sensitive heart some more than ordinarily generous expression of love and gratitude. What is the great purpose of these enactments?

There can be no question but that it is to counteract the selfishness of the human heart, and open within it fountains of generosity and benevolence. To secure this these claims were *universally obligatory*. No class was exempt from them. All shared, and hence all must acknowledge, the goodness of God. Even the Levite who received his tithe must in turn give tithes to Aaron and his sons (Numb. xviii. 26). The ministry is under just the same law as the people. The tithes, too, were *considerable in amount*. If a man now gives his tithe, or two shillings in the pound, of his income, ordinarily he fairly meets the responsibility of his position. Of course, where the income is larger or liabilities small, the proportion as well as the amount contributed should be increased. But it is calculated that a devout Jew often gave 4s., 5s., or even 6s. in the pound of his income to purposes of religion and philanthropy. Sometimes one-third of his income would be thus contributed. The tithes thus *intensified devotion*.

The donors were constantly impressed with the fact of their obligation to God. From Him came life, health, friends, and all earthly prosperity; to Him, therefore, must ever rise the accents of praise, the incense of fervent prayer, and the practical proofs of devotion in generous gifts. And, once more, the tithes *emphasised the claims of active philanthropy*. The poor must be remembered, the widow and the fatherless cared for, and the wants of the stranger supplied. God would link His people to Himself in the gracious bond of common ' good-will to men '; He would employ them in carrying out His own purposes of grace in being a ' Father to the fatherless, and a Judge of the widow in His holy habitation.' Regulations such as these were well calculated to foster and develop some of the rarest and best of human virtues; and whilst they secured the efficient maintenance of religious worship, and provision for the poor and needy, they conferred even richer benediction on the givers, for 'it is more blessed to give than to receive.'

T. MITCHELL.

Fruits.

'FRUIT' may be considered under three aspects. It may be looked at from the point of view of science, from the economical point of view as supplying the food-needs of men and animals, or from the æsthetic point of view suggested by the derivation of the word, as a means of enjoyment (Latin *fruor*, to enjoy). To the botanist a fruit is simply the matured pistil or ovary of the plant—that *pestle*-shaped organ which is seen in the centre of the flower. And what makes the fruit grateful and delightful to the epicure —the more or less sweet and juicy pulp—is disregarded by the botanist. To him a fruit may or may not be edible. Indeed he calls that 'fruit' which the other rejects. Thus the 'core' of an apple or pear is to him the true fruit, and similarly the tiny hard seed-like bodies embedded in the surface pulp of the strawberry are the fruit. The fleshy parts of the pear and apple are only enlargements of the calyx or cup of the flower, while the delicious strawberry is an enlargement of the top of the peduncle or foot-stalk. In Fig. 1 we give a drawing of a longitudinal section of a fig, showing the real fruits in the centre. The more prominent outer portion (or fruit from the economical or æsthetic point of view) is the enlarged and hollow top of the fruit-stalk. Generally speaking, there are in a fruit, popularly understood, three parts—the outer skin, the inner pulp, and the inmost seed. The skin has its stomata (or mouths) and its chlorophyll (or green colouring matter) precisely like the epidermis found on leaves. We have often admired a 'rosy-cheeked' apple, and may be interested to learn that this appearance is caused by the decay of the chlorophyll,

and the presence of mineral matters derived from the soil, just as in leaves which turn golden-yellow or russet-brown. The fleshy pulpy part of the fruit is formed by the action of light and warmth upon the cellular tissue of the pistil and ovary of the plant. It develops rapidly by the addition of cell to cell, until the mass becomes considerably enlarged. This cellular enlargement may readily be studied in the case of the orange (Fig. 2). Another change which takes place is, that the woody fibres of the plant become less and less prominent, and accordingly, as Dr. Robert Brown says, 'low-class pears are fre-

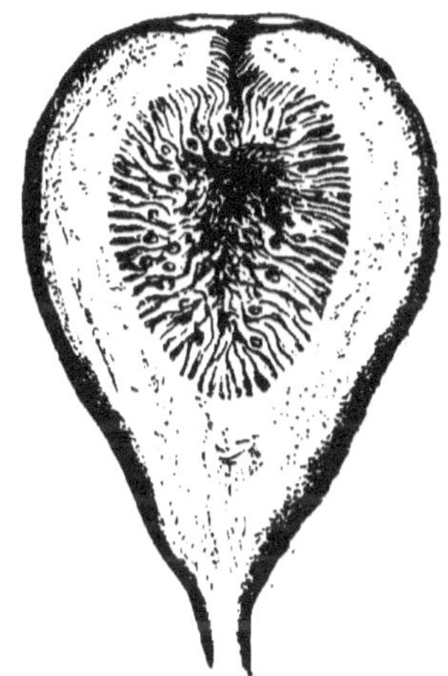

FIG. 1.—SEEDS OF FIG.

quently said to be woody, a term which needs no explanation. There is, indeed, always a tendency in nature to revert to the wild type. The aim of the gardener may be described as a desire to produce cellular tissue in preference to woody fibre, and the more of the one and the less of the other there is, the more succulent will be the pot-herb or the fruit. Yet in cutting across a pear the reader must often have felt the edge of the knife grate against some hard particles in the midst of the soft "flesh." These gritty specks were cells which had displayed a tendency to retrograde, by accumulating in their interior, not sugary sap and fragrant ethers, but "lignine," such as that which makes the once soft inner-layer of the ovary wall of the peach hard as stone.'

The chemistry of the fruit pulp is extremely interesting. 'Ripening' may roughly be described as the process of converting the starch and the vegetable acids of the plant into sugar. In their first stages fruits act like leaves, decomposing carbonic acid gas in the sunlight, absorbing the carbon, and giving back again the oxygen. But when ripe they reverse the process, and act like animals, giving out carbonic acid and taking in oxygen. At first they are sour, developing within their cells tartaric acid (as in grapes), citric acid (as in lemons, oranges, and cranberries), malic acid (as in apples and gooseberries). But as the ripening proceeds these acids and the accom-

Fig. 2.—Section of Orange.

panying tannin disappear, and sugar is formed in increasing quantity. It is not, however, the invariable rule for the acid to diminish. While in apricots and pears the malic acid decreases as the fruit ripens, in currants, cherries, plums, and peaches the same acid augments. Again, while in apricots and peaches the gummy matters increase, in currants, cherries, plums, and pears they diminish as the ripening process goes on.

The chemical substances produced in fruits vary immensely. In the corn-plants we have starch and gluten; in banana and bread-fruit, starchy matter of the pulpy sort; in nuts, fixed oils of various kinds; in many succulent fruits, sugar, gums, acids, and pectine. Coffee, cocoa, pepper, vanilla, and many other articles of commerce are from fruits. But at the same time, poisonous products are often found in parts of plants when other parts are harmless. Thus, the seeds of plums contain so much hydrocyanic acid that to eat many of them would be dangerous. Strychnia is obtained from the kernel of a fruit whose pulp is quite innocuous. On the other hand, the seed of the poppy is bland and nutritious, abounding in a wholesome fixed oil, while its capsule yields the poisonous opium.

Among well-known fruits the gooseberry, the apple, and the pear contain the largest proportion of water, and the grape, the cherry, and the peach the greatest amount of solid constituents. The grape and the cherry are richest in glucose and fruit sugar, while the gooseberry, the grape, and the apple contain the largest amounts of free acid. The peach is distinctly the richest in gummy matter, as might have been anticipated. It contains no less than 9 per cent., the pear coming next with 3 per cent. For the benefit of vegetarians it may be stated that fruits are not specially serviceable for tissue-forming, inasmuch as the proportion of albumen they contain is but small. Thus, Fresenius calculates that 'to obtain an amount of albuminous matter equivalent to the contents of one egg, we must eat more than a pound of cherries, nearly a pound and a-half of grapes, two pounds of strawberries, more than two pounds and a-half of apples, or four pounds of pears.' One of their chief uses is for respiratory or heat-giving foods, though they are better still for medicinal purposes, from the presence of vegetable salts. Their agreeable flavour (suggested by their name) is, of course, something thrown in extra. This flavour is found to be dependent upon several conditions: the proportion of acid to sugar, gum, &c., the delicacy of the aroma, and the proportion of soluble to insoluble matters. Gooseberries show, when ripe, in the yellow kinds, a proportion of six to one between sugar and acid, and in the red kinds four to one. Currants, on the contrary, show a ratio of only three to one. Strawberries vary with the season, the average being three or four of sugar to one of acid; but here the aroma is the chief feature, and the same may be said of raspberries.

It is an interesting circumstance that many fruits, like apples, pears, cherries, gooseberries, and currants, continue to live after being plucked. They exhale carbonic acid, and absorb oxygen and ripen. Hence it is a common practice to gather fruit when almost ripe, and keep it in drawers till needed, or in a fruit-room, with shelves allotted to the different kinds of fruits. Dry air, of a moderate and equable temperature, is needed, and careful ventilation must be kept up. We have known Victoria plums beautifully ripened by being wrapped in blankets and put away for a week or two in a drawer. By this means they were saved from the depredations of birds and small boys, who usually display a remarkable aptitude in selecting. for pillage the ripest specimens of fruit. Of all fruits apples keep best, and are therefore most gererally used. It is, however, one of the great advantages of our free trade system that oranges and apples can now be had, from some part or other of the world, about all the year round. In conclusion, we offer to our friends a practical recipe for preserving fruit—say cherries, plums, damsons, or gooseberries. Choose sound, almost ripe, fruit. Fill a wide-necked bottle, and cover the fruit with cold water. Then add as much salicylic acid as will cover a shilling, with as much fine sugar; cork tightly, shake well, and put away. By this means the writer has often had damson tart at Christmas.

Wholesome Fiction.

SOME LADY-WRITERS.

OMEN have not been behind their sterner compeers as writers of wholesome fiction. They hold in some respects a place quite their own. Their humour is not less genial although somewhat more subdued, and there is generally a touch of delicacy and a subtle grace of style that reveals the feminine hand. They have brought freshness and simplicity into the region of domestic fiction. Fertility and ingenuity in plot are by no means lacking, while the feminine imagination is also free from that coarseness in metaphor and illustration not seldom found in the masculine order. The intuitional faculty is keenly alive and informs much of their writing with a spirit of human and genial wisdom that readily comes home to the heart. Above all, a deep vein of religiousness, a healthy spirit of reverence for the true, the beautiful, the good, characterize the best of our female writers, and commend their productions to youthful readers. Here and there you may find a certain gossipy thinness and sketchiness that cannot be excused on the ground of relieving other parts of the writing, and which could be well done without; but, on the whole, the lady-writer fairly holds her own in the realm of wholesome fiction, as well as in other departments to which she has devoted her powers.

Nor has she been at all slow to make use of her pen. The list of lady-writers of fiction is an exceedingly long one, and their productions are legion. Nor does there seem to be any likelihood of a falling off, at least in the near future. We would fain believe that the growing mental and moral culture of the age will speedily and effectually veto the flippant, sensational, and fleshly novel; and that woman will be true to herself in this reform, we have no doubt, for her pen will be the last, we feel assured, to cater to any unwholesome taste.

A few names might be given, representative, more or less, of quite a host of good female-writers, and we shall be content to put you on the track of a healthy quest in the matter of fiction, without elaborating upon any one writer or work.

In speaking of lady-novelists, the name of 'George Eliot' (the pen name of Marian Evans) at once occurs to even an ordinary reader. Now, it is not our purpose to write an essay upon the genius of that gifted woman. A word of caution, however, may well accompany all our commendation of her. She has had and has still an incomparably wider influence than any author now or recently living. Perhaps too morbidly introspective, yet her words reveal fresh original power to a high degree, and faithful delineation of character, besides possessing a rare charm as regards style and manner. Without fully accepting the statement of one that George Eliot's novels are a complete system of moral philosophy, we may still allow that the position she takes up is that life is a tremendous series of human consequences, and that each one of us is under an appalling responsibility both to our fellows who are alive and to the posterity as yet unborn. And were all she wrote on the level and imbued with the spirit and teaching of 'Adam Bede,' we should not need to modify our meed of praise or the heartiness of our recommendation of her works. But her later novels show the school of negative religious thought to which she had become attached. Her theology is not all that we would desire; her strictures on evangelical religion, and her philosophy of Positivism, place her almost outside the class of pure fiction-writers, and give her a power which may be readily enough used, not for but against the principles and verities of our common Christian faith.

Other writers, of less genius and brilliancy, may be recommended to your suffrages, and especially to youthful readers, with more confidence and freedom.

Miss Muloch (afterwards Mrs. Craik), who died a year or two ago, was a prolific and most attractive writer. At the age of 23 she made a highly successful venture by her well-known fiction of 'The Ogilvies.' In 1850 she published 'Olive,' a romance; and shortly after, a picture of middle-class Scottish life, called 'The Head of the Family.' 'Agatha's Husband' succeeded, and many other books of similar merit. Her collection of short fictions and miscellaneous works, such as 'Avillion,' 'Nothing New,' 'A Woman's Thoughts about Women,' 'Domestic Stories,' 'Studies from Life,' 'Fair France,' 'Sermons out of Church,' 'A Legacy,' 'Plain Speaking,' &c. &c., bear testimony to her prolific genius, and are the fruit of a healthy mind. Her children's books, such as 'Rhoda's Lesson,' 'A Hero,' 'Bread upon the Waters,' 'Michael the Miner,' 'Adventures of a Brownie,' 'Twenty Years Ago,' 'My Mother and I,' 'The Little Lame Prince,' &c., are quite charming. But she is remembered chiefly as the author of 'John Halifax, Gentleman.' The work ran into eighteen editions, and is the greatest favourite of all her novels. It is charmingly written and a noble story of English domestic life. It shows the gifted authoress at her best. It has many beautiful pictures of home life—quite idyllic—and the one scene of the death of Muriel, the blind child, not to speak of others, is sufficient to place the writer among the immortals. Miss Muloch does not pose as the homilist, but insinuates moral instruction in a very natural and human way. Her mission, as a critic has put it, is to show 'how the trials, perplexities, joys, sorrows, labours, and successes of life deepen or wither the character according to its inward bent; how continued insincerity gradually darkens and corrupts the life-springs of the mind, and how every event, adverse or fortunate, tends to strengthen and expand a high mind, and to break the springs of a selfish or even merely weak and self-indulgent nature.' This mission she has carried out with eloquence, pathos, a subdued but genial humour, a happy delineation of character, and a spirit full of reverence for the sanctities of life and the sanctions of a high morality.

Reference might also be made to Mrs. Oliphant, whose tales illustrative of Scottish life are marked by a graceful simplicity and truth. One of the first is in the form of an autobiography, 'Passages in the Life of Mrs. Margaret Maitland,' and is full of quiet pathos and domestic incident. 'Harry Muir' is a powerful temperance tale—the hero, a good-natured pleasant youth, easily led into evil as well as good courses. 'Magdalen Hepburn' is a story of the Scottish Reformation, in which Knox and other characters of his age are introduced. The more recent works are 'Agnes, the Minister's Wife,' 'Chronicles of Carlingford,' 'John, a Love Story,' 'Squire Arden,' 'At His Gates,' 'Innocent,' 'For Love and Life,' 'The Curate-in-Charge,' and many others. Mrs. Oliphant has been described as the most versatile of our female novelists, 'sensational, domestic, and psychological by turns.' She has great knowledge of human nature and of 'society,' and extensive acquaintance with the modes and manners of foreign countries. 'The

Curate-in-Charge' is generally conceded to be one of her happiest efforts. It is a kind of ' exposé of the evils of patronage in the church; and though cynical, possesses scenes of true pathos, such as the death of the old curate, and the efforts of his daughters afterwards to support themselves.' Without further description of this gifted authoress and her works, we may say that she is one of those who recognise more fully than ordinarily the 'gravity of the daily issues of our life, the perpetual conflict of duties, the deeper motives of ordinary action, the ulterior tendencies of much that is petty and trivial, the irony which besets existence.'

Mrs. Henry Wood and Miss Braddon have sometimes been classed together as having points in common. Notably is this the case at least in their faculty of combining plot and melodrama with domesticity. The former, however, excels in the portrayal of character combined with wholesome moral teaching. She may not be a force of the highest kind in literature, but her circle of readers is a wide one. The average mind can profit from its perusal of such works as 'Danesbury House,' 'East Lynne,' 'Mrs. Halliburton's Troubles,' 'Verner's Pride,' 'Lady Adelaide's Oath,' &c. &c.; some of these have met with very great success.

Miss Braddon is very popular with the middle classes. She is not too highly complimented when described as ' an excellent writer of clear idiomatic English,' and latterly she has toned down her sensationalism without at all causing her story to suffer from flagging interest. She is ingenious and consistent in plot, and keeps up the interest less by delineation of character than by graphic and powerful descriptions of scene, and by startling surprises. ' Lady Audley's Secret ' (six editions of which were issued in as many weeks) and ' Aurora Floyd ' have been regarded as typical works, ' though dealing with repellent phases of life and character.'

A good word can be said for Miss Broughton, who, it is said, has many imitators, but few if any rivals. Her style is remarkably fresh and piquant, with little sentiment and conventionalism, but with a wholesome love of manliness. Her works are ' Nancy,' ' Good-bye, Sweetheart,' ' Red as a Rose is She,' ' Cometh up as a Flower,' &c. Not to mention others—as our space forbids—we may refer to Holme Lee (Harriet Parr), who has been mentioned by critics as one of the purest and brightest of the domestic school of novelists, and also a writer of some excellent essays. She excels in analysis of character rather than in plot. Other names possibly better known than some just quoted may serve the purposes of a future paper ere we close these brief and hurried sketches of authors and styles of wholesome fiction.   H. Y.

Nicotine.

I AM the Spirit Nicotine;
   'Tis I who glide the lips between;
   Through the lips I trace the brain;
   There I am a mighty pain.
I pursue my fatal track
Down the arched and marrowy back:
And the vertebræ grow slack.
Nought can hinder, nought can swerve,
I pervade each secret nerve;
Pick my meal with knife and dart
From the palpitating heart;
Quaff the leaping crimson flood
Of the rich and generous blood.
I the yellow bile diffuse,
Paint the face in ghastly hues.
Muscle and sinew
May not continue
To hold their wonted haughty pride,
The while I through the system glide.
Slowly I my purpose wreak,
Slowly fades the blooming cheek.
Gloomy fancies I suggest,
Fill with fears the hardy breast.
The limbs then fail,
The lamp burns dim,
Life hears death's hail,
And answers him.
Heart and liver, lungs and brain,
All their powers lose amain,
And yield to me;
And I! and I!
Laugh to see
My victim die.   *Jewish Messenger.*

Sketches of the British Isles.
LERWICK.

ERWICK, the capital of the Shetland Isles, is finely situated on the south-eastern shore of Mainland, and overlooking the expansive waters of the Bressay Sound. The plan of the town is irregular, and mainly consists of Pictish origin. The church has a beautiful Doric front, and is situated on the highest part of the town. A handsome town hall of imposing appearance and chaste design was built as recently as the year 1883. The spacious county buildings were erected in 1872. The population is a little over three thousand, who are employed in the fisheries and the making of straw plait. The bay possesses superior anchorage for vessels, and the ship-

LERWICK, THE CAPITAL OF THE SHETLAND ISLES.

one long street leading from the harbour ; on either side of the principal thoroughfare are a number of narrow lanes. The town was entirely demolished during the seventeenth century, and since then it has been rebuilt. The older houses are of poor construction ; the more recent ones are both substantial and roomy. On the margin of a lake are the ruins of an ancient castle, supposed to have been of ping trade has added considerably to the commercial prosperity of the town, the exports being fish, butter, hides, stockings, and rabbit skins. Lerwick has several chapels belonging to the United Presbyterians, Independents, Wesleyans, and others. During the year 1822, Samuel Dunn—who subsequently became famous with the Dunn, Everett, and Griffith controversy—was sent by the Wesleyan Conference as the first Methodist missionary to the Shetland Isles. Dunn made Lerwick his centre; he visited the people, and was successful in establishing societies, organizing Sabbath schools, training local preachers, and building chapels. Mr. Dunn's memory is still fragrant, and he has been fittingly styled 'The Apostle of the Shetland Isles.' Dr. Adam Clarke took a special interest in the moral welfare of the

understand every word he said." The Wesleyans have made considerable progress in the Isles, for they have four circuits and five ministers stationed therein.

On the western sea-board of Mainland and six miles distant from Lerwick is the ancient town of Scalloway, formerly the capital of the Shetlands. It contains a number of substantially built houses, a parish church, Indepen-

NEW TOWN HALL, LERWICK.

Shetlanders, and on more than one occasion favoured them with a visit. It was in Lerwick where the doctor, who was an encyclopædia of learning, was specially complimented. An aged woman, having heard of his celebrity, went to hear him preach at Lerwick. Upon her return from the service she said to her friends: 'They say that Dr. Clarke is a learned man, and I expected to find him such, but he is only like another man, for I could

dent chapel, and public schools. The inhabitants are entirely dependent upon fishing for a livelihood. East of the town is the embattled and turret-towered castle of Scalloway, situated on the harbour of Scalloway-Voe, that is studded with numerous rocks and islets.

Adjoining Lerwick, on the small islet of Mousa, is the famous broch, a fortified inclosure, or rude castle, which is the best known specimen of this class of building in existence.

These prehistoric circular-shaped castles are called 'duns' by the Gallic-speaking peoples, and are classified by antiquarians as 'Pictish towers.' These circular castles appear to have been far more numerous in the northern counties of Scotland and the northern and western isles than the more recent 'peels' found in the border valleys. In the three northern counties of Scotland alone there are at least the ruins of over two hundred brochs. They are peculiar to Scotland and are of ancient date, and evidently belong to the period before Britain was colonized by imperial Rome. They were used by the vikings of the north until the tenth century. Several thousand relics obtained from the brochs, and exhibited in the Scottish National Museum, furnish an interesting study. These ancient settlers cultivated the land, kept flocks and herds, fished in the seas, and hunted in the forests for their livelihood. The weapons and implements consisted of daggors, spears, and swords, and iron chisels, axes, and knives. Their bodily ornaments were brooches of silver and brass, bracelets, pins, and rings. They wore the manufacturers of these articles, for these have been found in the brochs, crucibles and moulds for casting purposes, and also metal in a rough state. The inhabitants appear to have been very ingenious, for out of the bones of animals they made their every-day requisites, such as buttons, combs, pins, needles, bodkins, and the miscellaneous articles needed for domestic use. Beads and bracelets were made of jet, and a superior class of beads were made of a coloured virtreous paste: the enamelled surface was highly decorated with spiral and other fantastic patterns. They used stone in the construction of hand-mills, mortars, pestles, hammers, cups, lamps, and general household utensils. Their pottery ware was of a superior class, shapely in design, and highly decorated. They were very industrious, as is evidenced by the numerous weaving-combs and spindle-whorls that have been found.

The brochs varied considerably in diameter, the largest extant being seventy feet, and the smallest forty feet in circumference. A great number of them possessed wells of water within the court or immediately contiguous, the outer well being protected by a covered approach-way of stone. The courts of the brochs were drained by channels ingeniously constructed under the outer wall. Special attention was paid to defence. In some instances they were built on lochs or islets, access being gained by stepping-stones placed at intervals in the water. Scott describes one near Lerwick, on ground in a lake which, at flood-tide, communicated with the sea. The approach being two or three inches under water, close to the broch, the causeway deviated by a sharp angle; the inhabitants were well acquainted with this fact, but strangers ignorant of the sudden curve, and thinking that the approach was perfectly straight, would find themselves suddenly plunged in seven feet of water. In every instance when the broch was built on a promontory, it was cut off by a deep ditch, and defended by ramparts and outworks. Clickemin Broch is defended with a gatehouse and guard chambers, situated at the terminus of the causeway.

The famous Broch of Mousa is in an excellent state of preservation, and without a doubt it is still in as good a condition as when it was first inhabited. It consists of a circular outer wall, fifteen feet thick, built of carefully-selected, endurable, time-weathering stones, piled securely together without the use of cement or mortar of any kind, and enclosing a circular area of about thirty feet in diameter. The exterior face-work of the wall has a slanting indentation becoming gradually narrower towards the top. The inner wall is perpendicular. The only opening consists of a doorway on the ground level, six feet in height, and about thirty inches in width. This tunnel-like entrance is fitted with stays for a door, and with bolt-holes in the sides of the walls for the insertion of a substantial bar of stout wood. On either side of the doorway are recesses for holding defenders. On the ground-floor are doorways leading to honey-combed recesses constructed in the thickness of the wall. About ten feet above the floor-level the wall is divided with an intervening space of about three feet across. At vertical intervals of from six to seven feet the intermediate spaces are covered with flag-stones bonded in both walls, and carried all round the building, thus furnishing a flooring for the chamber immediately above. The stair crosses all the galleries by gentle slopes in a spiral manner, and is without steps. The galleries are lighted from the inner area of the tower, which is roofless and open to the clouds.

Evidently the rude architect of those ancient times had not the science to construct an arch, or even a roof. The windows face the four points of the compass, and are formed in

grain and agricultural productions, and the stolen goods that these Norse sea-rovers brought thither from the more polished nations of Europe.

During the year 1155, when William the Lion was king of Scotland, Erland had captured a beautiful woman, the mother of Harold,—a Norwegian earl,—and had taken refuge in Mousa Broch. Harold attacked Mousa with a powerful army, but failed to capture it, because ' It was difficult to take by assault, and the besieged had made great preparations to enable them to hold out against Harold.'

SCALLOWAY CASTLE.

narrow, perpendicular rows, separated by the thickness of the flagstones, which perform double duty by being the top of one window, and the foot of the aperture above it. The outer wall was simply an enclosure around the council fire that was lit in the centre of the building. The original height of Mousa Broch cannot be determined; it is still forty feet high, and contains five encircling galleries. The evident purposes of the broch were to provide places of refuge, in the event of attempted murder and plunder by the hordes of hostile marauders; and also as storages of

The voice of tradition says that the inhabitants were prepared for a ten years' siege. The patience of Harold becoming exhausted, he consented to a treaty of accommodation, and his mother's honour was vindicated by her marriage with the captor.

Sir Walter Scott, in his ' Pirate,' has perpetuated the memory of Mousa Broch, by fancifully stating that one of his characters, Norna, built her rude dwelling-house near Lerwick with the stones carried from Mousa Broch.

ALBERT A. BIRCHENOUGH.

The Boyhood of Great Men.

SIR HENRY HAVELOCK.

NE dark day in November, over thirty years ago, there was despatched from India a sad piece of tidings which put all England into mourning. The Continental nations shared her grief, and, in the distant harbours of New York and Baltimore, all the ships for one whole day floated their flags at the half-mast as a tribute of respect to one whom America had never seen, but whose prowess and virtue she had learnt to admire. General Sir Henry Havelock was dead. It seemed as though it was but yesterday when men first heard his name. For years England had not known what a brave Christian she had in the ranks of her defenders. But the terrible Indian Mutiny broke out; smouldering discontent blazed into open revolt; and then came Havelock's chance, not to become great so much as to reveal the greatness that was his already. On the day of his death his name was on every lip. Men in wonderment still talked of the dashing generalship by which he had saved Northern India to the British Crown. With only a handful of troops behind him, and those ill-equipped and ill-provisioned, by desperate marches under a broiling sun, right in the teeth of treacherous Sepoys, who poured their murderous fire into his ranks, fighting four battles with them in twice as many days and winning them all, he pushed his way within the gates of Cawnpore. Alas! he was too late to achieve his purpose of mercy. The European women and children in captivity there were beyond any help of his; the perfidious Nana Sahib had butchered them all. The only traces of them was the room, ankle deep in blood, where they were hacked to death, and a well choked with their dead bodies. It was a sickening spectacle; and from it Havelock turned to attempt for Lucknow what he had been too late to achieve at Cawnpore. The former city still held out, though its English residents were in desperate straits. Havelock forthwith marched to its relief. Once he fell back to wait for reinforcements, but when these came, he and Sir James Outram pressed forward, and England held her breath, as, day by day, they cut their way, contesting every inch of it with a numerous and stealthy foe. Would Lucknow hold out until they came? Already they were much behind their time; wearily day after day the besieged had scanned the horizon to see the white glitter of their arms. Hope was deferred and hearts were sick, but one day there came, borne on the wind, the sound of the Scotch bagpipes and the steady tramp of men. It was Havelock with some Highlanders behind him. On they came, storming the enemy's post, silencing their guns, fighting hand to hand in desperate encounter, until, after much slaughter, the Sepoys were overpowered, and Lucknow and its garrison were saved. It was a historic sight when the three generals—Outram, Campbell, and Havelock—met within the walls of the English residency. Little did they think that their work was almost done, but so it was; and Havelock's was finished first. Even then the shadow of death was upon him. The privations of the march, which he had cheerfully shared with his men, proved too much for his iron frame. The life which, as though charmed, had escaped the hail of bullets, yielded to disease. He fell ill, and, though everything was done for him that could be, he gradually grew worse. It was soon evident that the brave soldier was fighting his last battle, but he had faced death too often before to have any fear now. 'I have for forty years,' said he to Sir James Outram, 'so ruled my life that, when death came, I might face it without fear.' On the morning of his death, calling to his side the son who had been his constant nurse, he said, 'Come and see how a Christian can die.' So, under an Indian sky, sustained by the faith which he had been taught in an English home, died Sir Henry Havelock.

He was then only a little over sixty years of age, having been born at Bishop Wearmouth on April 5, 1795. His father was interested in the shipping trade of Sunderland, having inherited a handsome business from his father before him. The family was not without enterprise, for to Havelock's grandfather belonged the honour of building the largest vessel that, up to his time, had ever been launched in the port. Out of the fortune amassed in his business, Henry's father purchased Ingress Park, near Dartford. Thither the family removed when the boy was but four years old, so that his early days were chiefly spent amid the rural beauties of Kent. Henry, with his elder brother William, was placed under the tuition of the Rev. J. Bradley, a curate who lived some distance away. From him he continued to receive his education till he was nine years old. It is wonderful how, even in those early days, the child was prophetic of the man. The blood of a Norse ancestry flowed in his veins, and it seemed as though, by his love of adventure and his insensibility to fear, Havelock thoroughly indicated his Danish descent. Like Nelson, he did not know what fear was. It is said of him that, one day, in climbing a tree to secure a bird's nest, the branch gave way and he fell. ' Were you not frightened ?' said his father to him, afterwards. ' No! ' answered the boy; ' I had too much to think of to feel afraid. I was thinking of the bird's nest I had lost.' On another occasion he appeared before his master with a black eye. It was a scar of honour nobly won and proudly worn. A big bully was ill-treating a little boy, and Havelock, in indignation, had stood forth in defence of the weak, and had given the bully the thrashing he deserved. Mr. Bradley inquired the cause of the discoloured eye, but could get no answer. To have explained would have meant involving others besides himself, and the boy's high sense of honour shrank from anything so mean, and made him endure a flogging rather than incriminate another.

He could only have been a child when he betrayed his interest in war. The Continent was then one armed camp, plunged into the thick of the struggle with Napoleon. The boy found him an interesting figure. With hungry eagerness he devoured the newspapers, tracked his movements, and was so interested in warfare as to cause his mother serious unrest. She had already decided that he should shine, not on the battle-field, but in the more bloodless arena of the law. Her hopes, brightened by a mother's fondness, pictured for her son the highest legal triumphs. ' My Henry,' she used to say, ' will one day sit on the woolsack.' But it was not in the choice of his calling that she was destined to influence her son. She did not make him a lawyer ; hers was the higher glory of making him a *man*. The distinctive note of Havelock's life was his religion. It is true that for a few years after he joined the army he lapsed, but his fault was not irreligion so much as indifference. With the exception of that brief period, he was an earnest Christian from his childhood to his grave; and how much that was due to his godly mother it is difficult to say. She gathered her children about her daily for prayer and reading of the Word of God, and in these daily devotions Henry took his part. Hence, when he left home to be a pupil at the Charterhouse, he carried with him not only the knowledge Mr. Bradley had given, but the seeds also of a manly Christian character that the loving hands of his mother had sown. At his new school he spent seven very happy years. The discipline was very severe, and there prevailed the odious system of fagging, with which the reading of ' Tom Brown's School Days' has made us familiar ; but these hardships were not enough to spoil his pleasure. He was taught to obey, and so learnt to command. Duty was his goddess, and at her shrine he worshipped. Whatever he took in hand he did thoroughly. In the boy there was that spirit which made him, when a man, say once to a young volunteer, ' Tell them in England that here we fight in earnest.' The same spirit was in him that made him, on the morning of his wedding-day, rush from the altar to attend a court of inquiry at Calcutta, though the marriage feast was thereby deferred until the evening. At the Charterhouse his motto was, ' Work first, play afterwards.' He denied himself all relaxation as long as anything remained to be done. This thoroughness in his work quickly converted him into a good scholar, and his advance in knowledge was attended by no weakening of his religious life. He practised private devotion, and, by thus feeding the inner life, he kept the outward pure and clean. Uniting with four of his school-fellows, he retired every day to one of the sleeping-rooms for prayer. It was a brave step to take. To be detected meant being dubbed 'Methodist' and 'hypocrite,' but none of these things moved him. When Havelock once felt a thing to be right, no amount of ridicule or opposition could turn him. He had in him a sturdy English backbone, and that always commands secret, if not avowed, respect. So Havelock found, and the farthest point to which his school-fellows ventured, was to give him the familiar name of 'Phlos,' a contraction for 'Philosopher'—a nickname that was at once a testimony to his sober, thoughtful habits, and to the respect in which they were held.

It was while he was at the Charterhouse that he was called to suffer the great sorrow of his life. Between Henry and his mother there existed a very tender attachment. It was, therefore, a great grief to the boy to find, on his return home one Christmas, that his mother was so ill as to be unable to take her share in the readings with which they were wont to while away the long winter evenings. She so far recovered as to be present at a merry family party early in January; but the excitement proved too much for her. Next morning, during family prayer, whilst Havelock was reading, she was seized with apoplexy, and suddenly exclaiming, 'I am very ill,' sank from her chair to the floor. It was the work of a moment to rush to her side and raise her up, and, whilst others hastened for medical aid, Havelock tenderly waited upon her. She rallied for a time, though the seizure interfered with her speech and rendered it unintelligible to all but Havelock. Love made him quick to interpret her broken words, and his patient only seemed happy when he was by her side. When the holidays came to an end, and it was time for him to return to school, the parting between the mother and

the son was a very painful one. He buoyed himself up with the hope that he should see her again, but she knew that they were saying a long 'good-bye.' When he was gone, it seemed as though the sunshine had left her, and her life, shrouded in deepest gloom, gradually faded away. When Henry was summoned home at the end of February, it was but to learn that she was dead. The tidings had been kept from him, and, on his arrival, his first request was to see her. The nurse drew back the curtains, and as she lay there, calm and peaceful, he bent to kiss her, thinking that she was only asleep. One touch of her cold lips, and the sad truth smote him that his mother was dead.

It was years before he recovered from the shock which that sudden discovery gave him. He went back to school, and sought to bury his grief in work. So diligent was he, that in the following April he was fourth in his class —among those who stood before him being a grandson of Sir Robert Walpole, and the scholarly Julius Hare. In the following year he was promoted to the head class in the school, and thereby came into closer touch with Dr. Raine, the head-master. To him Havelock was devotedly attached, and his death, in the course of the same year, was a great blow. From that moment there came a weakening of the links that bound him to the school, and when the new master came, and introduced innovations which, to Havelock, seemed at variance with the best traditions of the Charterhouse, it was not long ere he secured his father's permission to leave. Havelock was then in his sixteenth year, and had as yet no definite purpose before him. For a while he stayed at home, spending his time either in reading or in exploring the recesses of Ingress Park. But a cloud suddenly gathered over the family fortunes.

A hundred years before, one of Havelock's ancestors had lost heavily by the bursting of the South Sea Bubble, and it seemed as though the same ill-luck in speculation dogged the family still. Ingress Park had to be sold, and Havelock, being unable any longer to eat the bread of idleness, was forced to select a profession. He chose that of the law, and entered as a student at the Middle Temple. It seemed as though his mother's dreams might yet find fulfilment, and her son end his days as Lord Chancellor of England. But the future had another destiny in store for him. His porings over legal text-books and musty parchments were rudely cut short by an unhappy misunderstanding with his father. He could no longer draw upon the family purse, and so was forced to seek at once some calling in which he could maintain himself. Just at this juncture his brother William, now in the army, returned from the battle of Waterloo. His presence and the story of his adventures kindled in Henry the love of warfare that had slumbered since he was a child. The die was cast—he would be a soldier. He laid down the pen and took up the sword, and, within a month after Waterloo had been fought and won, Havelock had found a place in the English ranks. My readers must seek elsewhere if they would learn what a brave, true-hearted soldier he proved himself. For forty years he nobly served his country, nor was he less faithful to his God. Amid the thronging temptations of the camp and the battle-field, he kept his heart pure and his life untarnished ; and when he died, he left to his children the inheritance of a stainless ·name, and to his country the grief of having lost a great soldier and a still greater saint.

A. Lewis Humphries, B.A.

Anecdotes about Hymns.

From the German.

No. IX.—The Grain of Wheat.

 WORTHY man of the name of Jacob Haüser, who was in the habit of travelling about the country selling lace, happened one Sunday, in the course of a business journey, to find himself in a village, the pastor of which he knew by experience to be a somewhat uninteresting preacher. Haüser had not scrupled to bestow on this dull preacher the nickname of 'Master Strawfire.' On this particular Sunday morning it appeared to him that he might just

as well stay at the inn, or take a walk in the fresh air, as go to a church where he felt sure the preaching was so little likely to profit him. But in the meantime the villagers began to stream into church, and through the open door came the sound of voices singing a hymn which had always been an especial favourite with him, and which begins—

'Let God on high alone be praised.'

He began to hesitate, for the thought had occurred to him, ' Why should he not go also into the church, and be edified and quickened by joining the congregation in singing the hymns, if by nothing else ? '

Whilst he was hesitating in this manner, in his mind, he kept pacing up and down the pavement, till he chanced to glance at a hen walking about close by. But the creature went over the pavement on to the straw and rubbish lying in the middle of the road, and kept pecking at it, taking now one thing, now another out of it, and eating it up.

' Does that stupid creature eat straw and dirt ? ' he thought to himself—but looking nearer and more attentively, he perceived that she from time to time discovered a corn of wheat among the rubbish. Then, like a flash of lightning, the thought went through his mind of how foolish he was. ' You blind Hessian ! '* he said to himself. ·'Don't you think, that among the straw, which very likely has only just been threshed, there may be a good many grains of corn here and there which you'll just miss by staying away from church ?

' What if the sermons of that preacher *were* as worthless as straw; why might not some precious grains be found in them, or, at least, in some portion of the service ?

Accordingly, without more delay, he went in, and found the congregation singing a verse of a hymn, which we may thus freely translate.

' O Jesus Christ, our soul's salvation
God's own begotten Son, beloved,
Who workest reconciliation
For wanderers who afar had roved,
O God and Lord ! O Lamb most blest !
Accept the cry of souls distressed,
And on us all have mercy.'

---

* Jacob Haüser was a native of Hesse.

He listened with devout attention to the sermon, and eagerly gathered up the verses of Scripture quoted in it, found other grains of corn as well, took no notice of what was unprofitable, and frequently afterwards remarked that he had rarely felt more profited than he had on this Sunday from which he had expected so little.*

Current Topics.

MR. SPURGEON.

'THE REV. C. H. SPURGEON sleeps well at night. He has taken more nourishment, and gains strength but slowly.' This, at the time we write, is the latest bulletin regarding the condition of the pastor of the Metropolitan Tabernacle. For many weeks he has been in the clutches of a painful disease, and not only his fellow-countrymen, but people in almost every other country in the world have been watching the progress of the struggle with the keenest interest. Never before has the illness of a Dissenting minister evoked such widespread sympathy. Not only have the Nonconformist churches manifested a concern for the recovery of their brightest ornament, but the wife of the Archbishop of Canterbury has been one of the callers at Mr. Spurgeon's house, and even the chief Jewish Rabbi has sent a sympathetic letter. On July 12, the preacher in St. Paul's Cathedral not only expressed his personal sympathy with the sufferer, but asked his hearers to pray that 'he might be spared to be a light to the people.' The illness of this great evangelist has indeed revealed the essential unity of Christendom. We all claim him as a brother, and in the fear of losing him Christians of every name have laid aside their differences and united in earnest petitions for his restoration to health. Surely this is something to be thankful for. We differ in our views of truth, but we can all unite in our affection for a truth-loving man. Time was when Christians thought they honoured their Master by putting to death those who did not conform to their mode of serving Him. We have made great advancement since then, and if all the branches of the Christian Church can now unite in prayer for the preservation of a valued fellow-helper, may we not hope that the time will soon come when they will unite their forces, and be prepared to work in unison for the accomplishment of other objects?

Amongst the many letters received during his illness by Mr. Spurgeon, that from Mr. Gladstone had a special interest. He had himself just recovered from a severe affliction, and was at the time bowed down by the sudden loss of his eldest son. Addressing Mrs. Spurgeon, the aged statesman wrote as follows, viz. :—' Corton, Lowestoft, July 18. My dear Madam,—In my own darkened life at the present time, I have read with sad interest the daily account of Mr. Spurgeon's illness, and cannot help conveying to you the earnest assurance of our sympathy with you, and with him, and of my cordial admiration not only of his splendid power, but still more of his devoted and unfailing character. May I humbly commend you and him, in all contingencies, to the infinite store of Divine love and mercy, and subscribe myself, my dear madam, faithfully yours (signed), W. E. GLADSTONE.' To Mrs. Spurgeon's acknowledgment, the invalid added the following postscript—the first time he had been able to write since the commencement of his illness :— ' Yours is a word of love such as those only write who have been in the " King's country," and have seen much of His face. My heart's love to you.—C. H. SPURGEON.'

There can be no doubt that Mr. Spurgeon is one of the most remarkable men this country has ever produced. Few, however, excepting those who are associated with his work, have any idea of the kind of man he

---

* Those acquainted with the poetry of George Herbert may remember what that devout poet says respecting preachers—

' The worst say something good—if all lack sense,
God takes the text and preaches patience.'

really is, and no one can compute the immense influence he has exerted upon his time. He is not an old man, and yet few have done as much work. He entered upon his life's work whilst a mere boy, and before he was out of his teens he was called to take charge of an important Baptist church in London. By the time he was twenty-one he had become the most popular preacher in the country, and no building could be obtained large enough to accommodate the people who were anxious to hear him. After preaching in various halls, the Metropolitan Tabernacle was erected for his use. It has sitting accommodation for 5,500 persons, and though costing the sum of £31,332 4s. 10d., it was opened free of debt in 1861. The pastor was then only twenty-seven years of age, and yet his incessant toils were already beginning to tell upon his constitution. In spite of much pain, however, and many intervals in which work was impossible, he has, up to the present, kept together a congregation which has, Sunday after Sunday, filled the vast auditorium, and the membership of the church has grown from 313 at the close of 1854, shortly after Mr. Spurgeon took charge of it, to over 6,000 at the present time. Such success has been granted to no other man of our time, but it forms but a part of the wonderful achievements that have crowned the labours of Mr. Spurgeon. He has been an extensive author, and his works have circulated in hundreds of thousands. A church dignitary once remarked that the Metropolitan Tabernacle was simply a preaching room, and that when the gas was turned out and the door locked on Sunday night, it was no more thought of until next Sunday. He was much mistaken, for the Tabernacle is really one of the most important educational and philanthropic centres in London. In connection with it there are the Pastor's College, the Stockwell Orphanage, the alms-houses and schools, besides the Colportage Association, and many other agencies for the promotion of religious and philanthropic work. As all these institutions are supported by voluntary contributions, some idea may be formed of the energy required to carry them on.

Mr. Spurgeon belongs to a race of preachers. His grandfather was for fifty years minister at Stambourne, and his father is still a valued pastor amongst the Independents. Whilst quite a child the future orator began to reveal the possession of extraordinary powers. A minister who met young Spurgeon at his grandfather's was much impressed by his intelligence. One day, after calling the family together, this minister took the boy, who was then ten years of age, on his knee, and addressing the others said, ' I do not know how it is, but I feel a solemn presentiment that this child will preach the Gospel to thousands, and God will bless him to many souls. So sure am I of this, that when my little man preaches in Rowland Hill's Chapel, as he will do one day, I should like him to promise me that he will give out the hymn commencing,

> " God moves in a mysterious way,
> His wonders to perform.'''

This promise was, of course, made, and in after years it was carried out to the letter.

It was not, however, until he was sixteen years of age that Mr. Spurgeon was converted. Previous to that he was in danger of falling into infidelity, and for months was in a very distressed state of mind. The relief came very unexpectedly in a way which is best described in Mr. Spurgeon's own words : ' At last,' he says, ' one snowy day—it snowed so much, I could not go to the place I had determined to go to, and I was obliged to stop on the road, and it was a blessed stop to me. I found rather an obscure street, and turned down a court, and there was a little chapel. I wanted to go somewhere, but I did not know this place. It was the Primitive Methodists' Chapel. I had heard of those people from many, and how they sang so loudly that they made people's heads ache. But that did not matter. I wanted to know how I might be saved, and if they made my head ache ever so much I did not care. So, sitting down, the service went on, but no minister came. At last, a thin-looking man came into the pulpit, and opened his Bible and read these words : " Look unto

Me, and be ye saved, all the ends of the earth."
Just setting his eyes upon me, as if he knew
me all by heart, he said, "Young man, you
are in trouble." Well, I was, sure enough.
Says he, "You will never get out of it, unless
you look to Christ." And then, lifting up his
hands, he cried out, as only, I think, a Primitive Methodist could do, "Look, look, look!
It is only Look," said he. I saw at once the
way of salvation. O how I did leap for joy at
that moment! . . . I looked until I could
have looked my eyes away, and in heaven I
will look on still in my joy unutterable.'

That happy experience took place in the
Primitive Methodist Chapel at Colchester.
The chapel still stands, but the pulpit from
which that remarkable sermon was preached
has been removed, and it is now kept as a relic
in the Stockwell Orphanage. Fourteen years
after his conversion, Mr. Spurgeon preached a
sermon on the occasion of the anniversary of
this chapel, taking, most appropriately, for his
text, Isaiah xlv. 22. 'That,' said the preacher,
'I heard preached from in this chapel, when
the Lord converted me.' And pointing to a
seat on the left hand, under the gallery, he
said, 'I was sitting in that pew when I was
converted.' On account of this, Mr. Spurgeon
seems to have claimed to be somewhat of a
Primitive Methodist himself, for at one of the
meetings in connection with the opening of
the Tabernacle, at which representatives of
different denominations delivered addresses on
Christian union, the pastor himself spoke for
that body. Surely, the Primitive Methodists
had reason to be proud of their representative
on that occasion, and though he has not been
outwardly united with us, he has in many
ways shown his continued attachment to the
church that had the happiness of bringing him
to Christ.

An amusing account is given of Mr.
Spurgeon's first sermon. He had, shortly
after his conversion, been asked to walk out
from Cambridge to the village of Faversham,
about four miles away, to accompany a young
man whom he supposed to be the preacher for
the evening. On the way they talked of good
things, and then he expressed the hope that his
friend would be blessed in his labours. 'Oh
dear!' replied the other, 'I never preached
in my life. I never thought of doing such
a thing. I was asked to walk with you,
and I sincerely hope God will bless *you*
in *your* preaching.' 'Nay,' said Mr. Spurgeon,
'but I never preached, and I don't know that
I could do anything of the sort.' However,
his friend would take no excuse, and being
fairly committed to it, he relates how, praying
for Divine help, he resolved to make the
attempt. He fixed upon the words, 'Unto
you, therefore, which believe He is precious,'
for a text; and, having reached the meeting-
place, he says, 'We entered the low-pitched
room of the thatched cottage, where a few
simple-minded farm labourers and their wives
were gathered together. We sang and prayed
and read the Scriptures, and then came our
first sermon. How long or how short it was
we cannot now remember. . . . To our
own delight we had not broken down, nor
stopped short in the middle, nor been destitute
of ideas, and the desired haven was in view.
We made a finish, and took up the book, but
to our astonishment an aged voice cried out,—
"Bless your dear heart, how old are you?" Our
very solemn reply was, "You must wait till the
service is over before making any such inquiries.
Let us now sing." We did sing, and the young
preacher pronounced the benediction, and then
began a dialogue which enlarged into a warm
friendly talk, in which everybody appeared to
take part. "How old are you?" was the leading question. "I am under sixty," was the
reply. "Yes, and under sixteen," was the old
lady's rejoinder. "Never mind my age; think
of the Lord Jesus and His preciousness," was
all that I could say, after promising to come
again.' Having made a beginning, he did
not neglect the gift that was in him. At this
period he was acting as a school teacher in
Cambridge, and in the evenings and on
Sundays he preached in the villages around.
It is said that in this way he preached in one
year as many as three hundred and sixty-four
sermons.

It was at the close of the year 1854, shortly after he entered upon his work in London, that Mr. Joseph Passmore, the publisher, proposed to the pastor that he should issue a sermon weekly. Since then the sermons have appeared week by week without a break, and their number is now not far short of two thousand. For many years past these sermons have maintained a sale of about twenty-five thousand weekly, but some of the sermons have attained a circulation of hundreds of thousands. Perhaps the most remarkable of them was that on the subject of Baptismal Regeneration, of which three hundred thousand copies were sold. The sermons have been translated into many different languages, and truly wonderful accounts are given of the good they have achieved in various parts of the world. Writing to the pastor from Warschaw in 1882, Mr. F. H. Newton, of the German Baptist Mission, thus refers to his adventures: ' I have during the past few weeks been visiting a number of our Baptist churches in Silesia and Russian Poland, and I think you will be interested to hear of their activity and Christian faith. In almost every town and village one of the first inquiries put to me was, " And how is Brother Spurgeon ?" In many of the outlying stations, where no stated missionary can be sustained, your printed sermons are regularly made use of, and I am sure you will be thankful to our one Master to learn that here in Poland, and elsewhere, many of the church members attribute their first religious awakening to hearing some of those sermons read.' Here, too, is an interesting circumstance. Dr. Blaikie, while preparing his ' Life of Livingstone,' came across one of the sermons in the journal of the traveller. and thus wrote to Mr. Spurgeon of the discovery: ' I had in my hands the other day one of your sermons, *very yellow ;* it lay embedded in one of his journals—had probably been all over Africa—and had, in Livingstone's neat hand, the simple words, " Very good! " Would you like it ? '

The causes of Mr. Spurgeon's success have been much discussed. His magnificent voice, his wonderful command of language, and his lively fancy have all helped him in his work, but a far more important element in his power is his thorough genuineness. He is a whole-hearted believer in his Saviour. He has had a blessed experience of the truth he preaches, and out of the fulness of his heart he speaks forth the Word that is able to make men wise unto salvation. About the power of this Word he has no doubt whatever, and, aroused by an almost heart-breaking pity for poor perishing men, he puts into his message a fervid sympathy that, under God's blessing, has arrested the attention and opened the hearts of many thousands of men and women. Having to preach in the Crystal Palace on the day appointed for humiliation and prayer in connection with the Indian Mutiny, he went down to the building a few days beforehand to arrange where the platform should be placed. In trying the different positions, he cried aloud, ' Behold the Lamb of God, which taketh away the sin of the world.' Even this effort was not in vain. The words so strangely spoken went with power to the heart of a man who was at work in the Palace, convinced him of sin, and led him to the sin-atoning Lamb, in whom he found forgiveness and peace. This voice is now only able to whisper in a sick-room, but the churches have not yet lost the hope of once more hearing it ringing forth the words of life. Mr. Spurgeon himself has never yet despaired of recovery, and it may be that the great Father intends to bring him out of this fiery ordeal, chastened and qualified for higher service still in the cause of suffering humanity. Let this, at all events, be our earnest prayer.

M. P. D.

' Boys flying kites haul in their white-winged birds :
You can't do that way when you're flying words.
" Careful with fire " is good advice, we know :
Careful with words is ten times doubly so.
Thoughts, unexpressed, may sometimes fall back dead,
But God Himself can't kill them when they're said.'

THERE IS A FOUNTAIN FILLED WITH BLOOD.

Hymn 328, Primitive Methodist Hymnal.

(Arranged for Evangelistic Services.)

Words by W. Cowper.　　　　　Music by Rev. W. L. Taylor.

THERE IS A FOUNTAIN FILLED WITH BLOOD.

Hymn 323, PRIMITIVE METHODIST HYMNAL.

Words by W. COWPER. *(Arranged for Evangelistic Services.)*

KEY A♭. *mf* Music by Rev. W. L. TAYLOR.

There is a foun-tain filled with blood, Drawn from Em-man-uel's veins; And
sin-ners plunged be-neath that flood, Lose all their guil-ty stains.
CHORUS. *ff*
The foun-tain of the Sa-viour's blood . .
The foun-tain of the Sa-viour's blood, The foun-tain of the Sa-viour's
The foun tain of the Sa-viour's blood . . .
. . . . . Is flow-ing full and free.
blood Is flow-ing full flow-ing full and free, Is flow-ing full and free.
. . . Is flow-ing full and free.
By faith I plunge in-to its flood,
By faith I plunge in-to its flood, By faith I plunge in-to its
By faith I plunge in-to its flood,
And know it cleans-eth me.
flood, And know it cleans-eth me, and know it cleans-eth me.
And know it cleans-eth me.

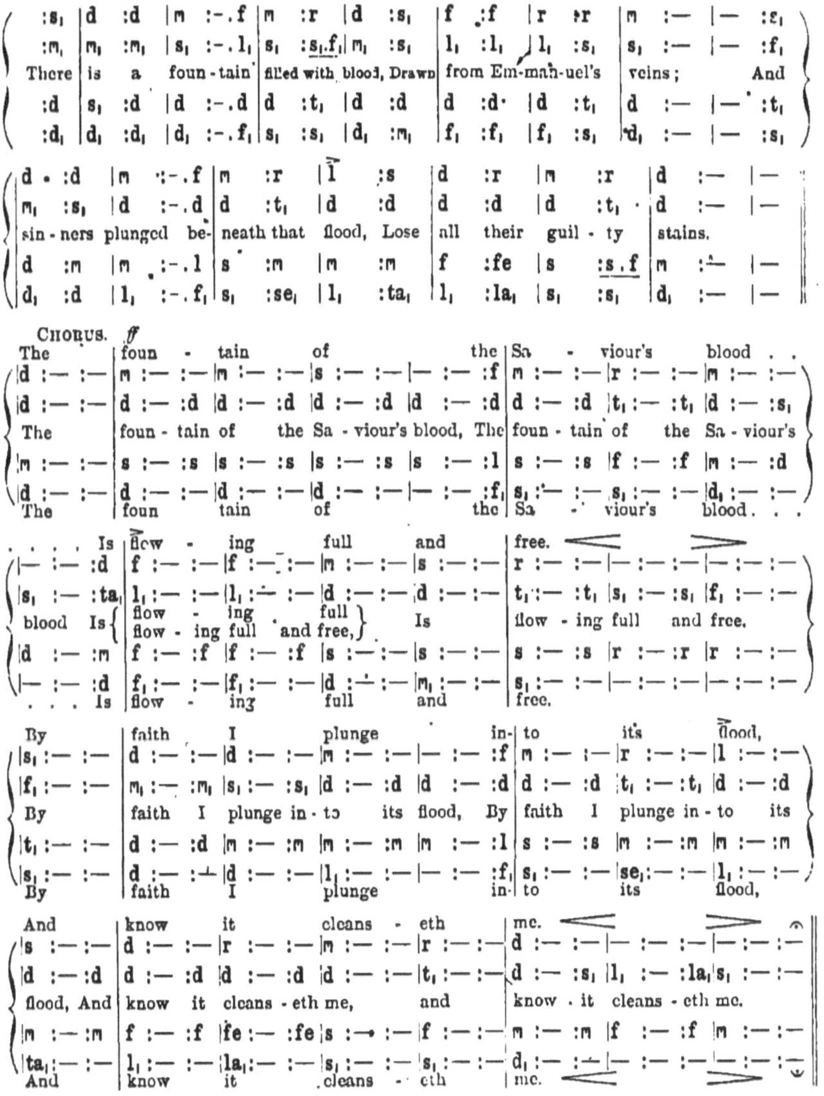

The Library.

HANDSOME centenary volume has just been issued by the Wesleyan Book Room, which I am sure our young readers will be glad to know and have an account of. It bears the title, *Wesley the Man, his Teaching and his Work*, and comprises the sermons and addresses delivered in City Road Chapel at the centenary commemoration of John Wesley's death last March. The value of the book consists in its catholicity—in the many testimonies it brings together from diverse men and diverse minds, representing many communions, concerning the character, genius, and influence of the great founder of Methodism. Here, for example, are Dr. Dale and Dr. Stoughton of the Congregationalists; Principal Rainey and Dr. Cairns speaking for the Presbyterians; Dr. Clifford representing the Baptists; and Archdeacon Farrar speaking in the name of the Church of England. Of course, all the sister and daughter sections of Methodism have their spokesmen, among whom not the least worthy and able is our own ex-President, the Rev. J. Hallam, whose address, though brief, is brimful of good feeling, good taste, and good sense. The Countess of Huntingdon's Connexion figures in the person of the Rev. J. B. Figgis, M.A., while Mr. J. Bevan Braithwaite speaks for the Society of Friends. Even the Unitarians bring their offering in the shape of an address signed by representatives of over two hundred Unitarian families, including the Earl of Carlisle, Dr. Martineau, Dr. Crosskey, the Rev. Stopford Brooke. 'Spontaneously and entirely of their own accord,' said Dr. Stephenson, 'that address was forthcoming.' Altogether, it was a remarkable series of gatherings which this books records, and there is not a single aspect of Wesley's many-sided activity which is not touched and treated here. Dr. Dale's sermon is on 'The Theology of John

Wesley.' Dr. Rainey deals with the same topic from his own special standpoint; while Dr. Clifford discourses on the 'Prophet of the Eighteenth Century.' The relations of Methodism to the masses, to education, to literature, and to missions are duly noted, while the 'Young People of Methodism' receive a full share of sympathetic attention. A very vigorous and characteristic address is that of Rev. Hugh Price Hughes on 'The Characteristics of Young Methodism.' He claims that young Methodism is very old-fashioned, thirsting after spiritual holiness, and loving the class-meeting and the prayer-meeting better than ever. And 'never again,' said he, 'will we consent to play the *rôle* of a poor relation of the Established Church. Young Methodists believe that the President of the Wesleyan Conference is as truly and eminently a minister of Christ as the Archbishop of Canterbury.' Young Methodism is democratic, and wants very much to mend the present world. 'We believe that the vision which John Wesley had was a vision not of heaven, but of earth, changed and purified, and blessed by the power of Jesus Christ, and that was the vision which St. John had in the Apocalypse. He saw the city of God coming down out of heaven. For my own part, I know very little about heaven. It is down here on earth that our sympathy ought to go forth, down here where there is a public-house at the corner of every street, where the pavements are crowded with scoundrels and their victims, and where it is so difficult to do right.' He told the following story to illustrate the tendency of the times as compared with the past :—'The first time my grandfather went to the Conference, a young man, not less than forty-five years of age, rose to address the Conference. Dr. Bunting looked at him with astonishment, and then said in a decisive tone, "Young man, sit down." And the young man did sit down. If your successor at the next Conference, sir, said that to me, I should sit down, because I am one of the most docile of mankind, but there would be a great deal of hubbub.' Mr. Watkinson, a very different sort of man, gave an equally characteristic address on Methodism and Literature. He dwelt on the essentially practical character of Methodist literature. 'Being always in such close touch with the life of the people and the facts of evangelization, it has been saved from many errors and heresies. Dr. Lardner, a theorist, wrote an able and conclusive book to prove the impossibility of a steamship crossing the Atlantic, and the first steamer that crossed from Liverpool to New York carried that book with it, and everybody except scientists believed that Dr. Lardner was refuted. Life, experience, fact, spoilt many a fine theory; and the fact that Methodism has been a working church has given its literature far more practical worth than speculative interest.' Mr. Watkinson is nothing without his ' story.' He is like Abraham Lincoln in that respect, as in some others. Here is one. ' An American was addressing a number of young men, when he said, " Look at me, gentlemen, and see how I have got on in life. When I first came to this country I was not worth sixpence, and now I owe 200,000 dollars."' There is a passage, a humorous passage, in Wesley's Journal, that reminds one of this anecdote :— ' Wednesday and Thursday I settled my temporal business. It is now about eighteen years since I began writing and printing books. And how much in that time have I gained by printing? Why, on summing up my accounts, I found that on March 1, 1756, I had gained, by printing and preaching together, a debt of £1,236.' A book like this should find a large constituency amongst our reading young Primitive Methodists.

The Bottom of the Sea.

THE Hydrographic Office of the U.S. Navy, from careful surveys by soundings and dredgings, has been able to present an approximately accurate description of the depths of the ocean, to map out the mountains and valleys, and to bring to the light the flora and fauna of the ocean world. A writer in the Boston *Transcript* gives this graphic account of a supposed walk on the bed of the Pacific Ocean :—

In starting to take a walk over the floor of the ocean perhaps it would be as much fun as any other plan to set out from San Francisco for a view of the Pacific's bed. For the first twenty-nine miles of the journey westward, you will proceed over a level plateau formed of detritus, which the river water has cast out through the Golden Gate for a thousand centuries. The depth of the sea for that distance is only about two hundred feet, but at the end of it the bottom drops suddenly to two and a half miles. To get to the foot of this tremendous hill is likely to be difficult, inasmuch as you must climb from a greater relative altitude, and by a much steeper incline, than that by which a traveller passes from the summit of the Sierra Nevada range to the valley of California below at Sacramento.

At the foot of the great declivity you will find a seemingly interminable plain, like a prairie. It is the beginning of the floor of the Pacific, which is for the most part so wonderfully level that you could drive over it with the utmost comfort in a light carriage, were the water all taken away. As you proceed westward, though the slope is so smooth and gradual that you do not notice it, the bottom descends at a slight incline, until, at five hundred miles from the land, the surface of the ocean is three miles and a quarter above your head. This is the normal depth of the vast Pacific plateau. You travel over it for another five hundred miles, when you come upon a gigantic mountain, which towers up from the ocean floor to the height of nearly three miles. Its existence has only been ascertained by soundings, because half a mile of sea water flows over it.

Beyond the mountain is the plain again. It is a dead level of shelly ooze, such as covers pretty much all of the ocean floor. The mixture. sometimes greenish and sometimes brownish, is partly detritus washed by rivers from the land, and partly shells of almost microscopic animals, called *foraminifera*, which fall upon the bottom in a gentle and continuous rain. All the chalk beds in the world are formed of such shells, and the very stones of which the Pyramids of Egypt were built are composed almost wholly of them.

There is a certain monotony about the aspect of things in these enormous depths. One may well be oppressed, too, by the absolute silence which reigns. Frightful storms may be raging on the surface, but here, three and a half miles beneath, all is as still as death, and not even the murmur of a wavelet reaches the ear. Everywhere, if you close your lantern, is the darkness of absolute black—a liquid darkness that makes itself felt by a pressure of two tons to the square inch. The water is so cold as to be very little above freezing point. On every side spreads a desert of interminable extent, frightful in its desolation, with not a blade or sprout of any sort—nothing, in fact, but the shelly ooze, into which your foot sinks somewhat as you tread. Perchance there are a few sea lilies in your path, but you know that they are animals and not of the vegetable nature, which they feebly counterfeit.

You might follow the same dead level, now and then coming across an isolated elevation, all the way across to Asia, 10,000 miles farther, if you liked.

Helps to Patience.

 WOMAN whose life had been long and chequered with many reverses said lately:—'Nothing has given me more courage to face every day's duties and troubles than a few words spoken to me, when I was a child, by my old father. He was the village doctor. I came into his office where he was compounding medicine one day, looking cross and ready to cry.

' "What is the matter, Mary?"

' "I'm tired. I've been making beds and washing dishes all day, and every day, and what good does it do? To-morrow the beds will be to make and the dishes to wash over again."

' "Look, my child," he said; "do you see these little things, of no value in themselves; but in one I put a deadly poison, in another a sweet perfume, in a third a healing medicine. Nobody cares for the vials; it is that which they carry that kills or cures.

Your daily work, the dishes washed or the floor swept are homely things, and count for nothing in themselves; but it is the anger, or the sweet patience, or zeal, or high thoughts that you put into them that shall last. These make your life." '

No strain is harder upon the young than to be forced to do work which they feel is beneath their faculties, yet no discipline is more helpful. 'The wise builder,' says Bolton, 'watches not the bricks which his journeyman lays, but the manner in which he lays them.'

The man who is half-hearted and lagging as a private soldier, will be half-hearted and lagging as a commander. Even in this world, he who uses his talents rightly as a servant is often given the control of many cities. 'They also serve,' said John Milton, 'who only stand and wait.'

We should remember, above all, that the greatest of all men spent thirty years of His earthly life waiting the appointed time to fulfil His mission.—*Youth's Companion.*

The Young Christian's Resolve.

 ' UST as I am,' Thine own to be,
    Friend of the young, who
      lovest me;
  To consecrate myself to Thee,
    O Jesus Christ, I come.

In the glad morning of my day,
  My life to give, my vows to pay,
With no reserve and no delay,
  With all my heart I come.

I would live ever in the light,
  I would work ever for the right.
I would *serve* Thee with *all my might*,
  Therefore to Thee I come.

'Just as I am,' *young, strong,* and *free,*
  To be the best that I can be,
For truth and righteousness and Thee,
  Lord of my *life,* I come.

And for Thy *sake* to *win renown,*
  And then to take my *victor's crown,*
And at Thy feet to cast it *down,*
  O *Master! Lord!* I come.

SPRINGTIME :

A Magazine for Our Young Men and Maidens.

Vol. VI. No. 11.] NOVEMBER, 1891. [Price Twopence.

A Bad Calculation.

By ROBERT HIND,

Author of ' Crosby Dalton: Local Preacher and Village Demagogue,' ' The Ruby Pendant,' &c.

CHAPTER XXI.

THE CONCERT.

'The purifying trouble grew and grew
Till silentness was more than I could bear.'
ROBERT BUCHANAN.

HE hall of Priory College was well filled on the night of the concert, and the students moved about briskly, looking after the comfort of the friends they had invited.

Rye Harland was on the programme for a piano solo. She had hoped for a duet with Arthur Brixton, and felt disappointed that he had declined to take any part in the entertainment. Something, she knew, must have happened; what it was she could not guess.

When the concert began, Arthur was sitting beside Isa Saunders and her father and mother. He did not look happy. A sense of misery was indeed his normal condition; but, just now, although he tried to comfort himself with the thought that he was beside one of the most beautiful and best-dressed young ladies in the assembly, he was more wretched than usual. It is not in human nature to be content to be an Ishmael, and Arthur felt himself at that moment to be truly a son of Hagar. Standing at the corner of the room to his right, close up to the platform, were a group of half-a-dozen students, who were regarded by the audience as of some importance just then. They were, in fact, the committee who had made the arrangements, and Arthur observed with some envy that Jack Benson was by far the most distinguished and handsome of the group. On the platform were some others, and he could not keep from his heart a sense of bitterness as he thought he might have been there, or in one of the ante-rooms, with his violin. But no, he was alone with his friends from Canongate, who he observed were not recognized by any in the hall save Jack Benson, who had come and shaken hands with them a few minutes before.

The performances of the musicians were not of the highest, but they were fairly good, and it was observable that the amateurs were more highly appreciated than the two or three professional singers who were present.

Immediately behind Arthur and his friends were a party of ladies in middle life and a student, the latter of whom answered the questions which the former kept asking incessantly. When Rye Harland took her seat at the piano, Arthur could not help hearing the remarks of his neighbours.

'Most decidedly good-looking. And who is she? I have not met her; and yet her features seem familiar.'

'Her name is Miss Harland, as you will see from the programme.'

'Not of Rockingham?'

'Yes. The Mount.'

'Are the people of the Mount recluses? I

know the house, but have never met the people in any gathering I have attended.'

'Perhaps that is because they are Dissenters,' the young man said with apparent *naïveté*.

In reality, however, he was only teasing his maiden aunt, who was a good Churchwoman of the most correct and narrow order.

'Dissenters are they? And yet she is not only handsome, but carries herself with quite a grand air. And she is decidedly distinguished besides.'

The young man could not act his *rôle* longer. A smile broke over his countenance as he said,

'All of which qualities should be the exclusive property of Church people, and are totally out of place when seen in the person of one of those wicked Dissenters. Is it not so, aunt?'

The lady did not smile, but looked angry. What she might have said remained unknown to Arthur, for by this time Rye had begun to play, and in listening to her music the audience were spell-bound. It was Mendelssohn's 'Capriccio' in E-Minor, so like the mad rush of cavalry in battle. The audience was thrilled, and although composed of people accustomed to control their feelings and to regard demonstrations as slightly vulgar, forgot itself, and cheered the fair performer right heartily.

'And I might have shared that applause, and helped to make it even louder and heartier than it is, although she is the star of the evening,' Arthur thought.

'How well Miss Harland acts,' Isa Saunders observed to him.

'I hardly understand.'

'Well, she would seem as though she was unconscious she had done well, and equally unconscious that she had made a better impression than any of the others.'

It was a spiteful speech, and one which Arthur should have rebuked, but he allowed it to pass.

Rye, it is true, was unhurt by it, and was hardly aware of the feelings of the audience. What she was most conscious of was that the music had touched her own soul.

Walking home that night with Jack Benson she said,

'Was Arthur Brixton present? I suppose he would be, but I had expected to see him in the ante-room. He was not one of those, who I presume were the committee, who thanked me and the others. I never saw the audience excepting in a vague, shadowy way.'

'Arthur Brixton again! what an infatuation she has for him!' Jack thought. To her he said, 'He was present.'

'Very likely he had some special duties. You should know what they were, and whether it was necessary on account of them to decline to play with me.'

'She is sorry he was not beside her. It is dreadful to think how a good and clever girl can be deceived, in one with whom she has been acquainted all her life too,' Jack thought again.

'You are not an attentive hearer to-night, cousin Jack.'

'Pardon. Arthur was not specially busy. Indeed, he sat with Mr. and Mrs. Saunders and Isa.'

'Is not this strange? I thought he was one of the committee, and would therefore be quite full-handed with work.'

Jack felt matters were getting warm for him. He had no desire to seek an advantage by telling tales. Indeed, there was just the element in the situation that made him shrink from touching it in any way. On the other hand, he was grieved beyond measure at what he regarded the delusion of his cousin. What was he to do? If the conversation continued on this line it was clear he would have to speak out, for, frank and open as he was, he could not prevaricate.

'He has not been on the committee lately. He resigned of his own accord.'

Rye said nothing for some time, and Jack hoped there the matter had ended for the present. He was mistaken, however. She was thinking and wondering.

'You did not tell me this, Jack,' she said at length; and poor Jack was stung with the tone of rebuke in her words.

Not receiving a reply, Rye continued,

'Arthur must have had a serious reason. He would like the work, and the position it gave him, and would not willingly resign. Do you know the reason ? '

The question was direct enough, and, Jack thought, exactly characteristic of Rye Harland. It demanded a direct answer. But still he would not tell all the truth yet, but only so much as was necessary.

'The reason was that he thought he had received less than fair treatment from some of the members of the committee.'

Could Jack have seen his cousin's face at that moment he would have observed the faintest flicker of a smile there. For Rye remembered that to feel aggrieved was characteristic of Arthur.

'Did you think so ? '

'At the time I did.'

'But not now ? '

'You are putting me through a catechism. If you must know, I think he received treatment as good as he deserved.'

'You will pardon me, I am sure. I am curious to know all about it. I have confidence in your judgment and am sorry on account of what I have heard. But you know our interest in Arthur, and how we desire him to do well. I cannot think he has done anything very wrong, but should like to know wherein he was to blame. If you can tell one who wants to be his friend you might tell me.'

Jack Benson would not yield even yet, painful as it was to deny his cousin any request, strong as was the temptation to tell all.

'You must excuse me at present; afterwards perhaps I will tell you the whole story.'

And Rye, who could not press her request, only felt more curious.

CHAPTER XXII.

A ONE-SIDED AFFAIR.

'A little glimmering
Is all we crave !
The lustre of a love
That hath no being.
The pale point of a little star above,
Flashing and fleeing
Contents our seeing.'

ROBERT BUCHANAN.

JACK BENSON did not feel comfortable. The turn affairs had taken was too perplexing to be quite agreeable to one of so open and straightforward a disposition   Although he saw clearly that should he choose to repeat to Rye the story told him by Frank Everton, even she, despite her kindness of heart and readiness to forgive a personal wrong, would once and for ever discard her old friend Arthur, he had no intention of being the tale-bearer himself.

No doubt it might be advantageous for himself to do this, seeing that in his mind it would dispose of the chief difficulty of gaining the prize in life he felt he desired above all others. For the eyes of love are jealous, and in all the interest Rye had manifested in Arthur, Jack could see nothing but so many proofs of her allegiance to her old lover, notwithstanding the barriers that had arisen between them. How easily he might turn her affection into repugnance, and set her fancy free ! But Jack was not inclined to act from a motive like that.

And yet he felt she ought to know. More than this, he was resolved that, rather than see her continue to worship at the shrine of so poor an idol, she should know, if the knowledge had to come to her even from his lips. For Jack was not one of those unhealthy-minded people who are prepared to make themselves into heroes and martyrs, and set at naught all truth and righteousness, for the sake of a false sentiment. He did not desire, he would never consent to buy an advantage for himself at Arthur's expense, but he certainly would not stand by and allow Rye to sacrifice herself to a delusion.

On another point his mind was made up. Arthur's conduct had freed him from any further obligation with regard to his promise to be his friend. From this time onward he should feel bound, out of respect to himself, to treat him with cool indifference. And should it be necessary, in his own justification, to give his reason for this to Rye, he should have no hesitation in doing so.

Thus far his course was clear, but after all, so long as Rye was in ignorance of all this, he could not be happy. Should Arthur call at the Mount, even ever so occasionally, it would be a torture to him, and it was the opposite of pleasant to have to pass with the coolest recognition one in whose company he had lately spent a good deal of his leisure. He felt it would have been better could he have told Arthur himself, but that young man was not at all likely to give him the opportunity. He was probably in ignorance of the cause of the change in his position in Jack's regard, and did not dream that his own conduct had anything to do with it, but at least he was not allowed to remain ignorant of the change itself. The consequence was that he grew more morbidly sensitive than ever, and at the same time began to cultivate a desperate cynicism not calculated to add to the beauty of his disposition. Everything that was happening at present was a disappointment to the hopes he had entertained of the effect likely to be produced upon his own position by entering the University. Comparing things now with what had been a few months previously, he found that instead of any improvement in social status having taken place, there had been retrogression. Hardly any one at the University knew him, and he was separated from the Harlands, through whom at least he had sometimes been able to meet on equal terms those who belonged to an altogether different world from his.

There remained to him still the Saunders family, and in his desperation and loneliness he was learning to forget, what had once impressed him very strongly, the different atmosphere in the grand house in Canongate from that which he was accustomed to find at the Mount. It was his one retreat now; and yet he never came away from the place without feeling rather miserable. He did not trust Isa as he had trusted Rye, and he was not quite sure that their show of friendliness was genuine.

Had the Saunders succeeded better in their own plans, this question would have been settled for Arthur, if not quite to his satisfaction, at least in such a manner as to place it beyond the possibility of doubt. But in spite of their show of wealth, the persistent efforts they had made to break down caste prejudice, their regular attendance at the parish church of St. Mary's, and what was perhaps their best weapon, the undeniable beauty of Isa, they continued after all these months to live alone among their neighbours.

Their own experience enabled them to understand Arthur's; and having some power of penetration, their chagrin was tempered by amusement at his defeat and consequent misery.

He, on the other hand, whilst fully aware of the fact that his Canongate friends had failed in their first efforts to cultivate the acquaintance of the Rockingham families, knew nothing of the number of those attempts and the sense of mortification felt because of their failure. For not only were Mr. and Mrs. Saunders adepts in the art of genteel dissimulation, but even Isa was sufficiently a woman of the world to think that it was not well to inform others, even by a look, that they were all angry with the Rockingham people and their exclusiveness. To Arthur, therefore, it seemed as though they were quite contented and happy.

To him, at least, they appeared always kind, and Isa, whenever he called, was ready to devote herself to his entertainment. Sometimes he wondered at this, and, but for a certain marked pride, would have said so. This very thought was in his mind one day, a little while after the new year, when he found himself alone with Isa in the Canongate house.

'You have had a fair trial of Rockingham now,' he said to her, 'and must have made up your mind whether you like it or not.'

Isa was on the alert in a moment. She thought he was seeking information which it would be better not to give him.

'I have never been other than happy, and like Rockingham very well.'

'But it must have been a great change from Highbridge,' Arthur remarked, naming the town where they had last resided.

'Of course there is a difference. And I like changes.'

'For which reason you would not mind much if you were soon to make another change?' he inquired.

'That, at least, has not yet been thought of. But why should I care even had my father made up his mind to do so?'

'You would not have many reasons to care. Wherever you go you say you are happy, and, considering all things, it would be strange if you were not. Still there are those who cling tenaciously to one place. Rockingham, few as its interests are to me, is a place to which some people have so strong an attachment that they cannot imagine they would be happy anywhere else.'

'Indeed! Are they friends of yours? I am sure I would like to meet with them to compare notes. It would be interesting to have a little friendly debate on the subject of "The relative advantages of life in a great commercial centre and an old historic city."'

'There would be a good deal to say on both sides, I imagine,' Arthur said.

'Could we arrange a day for the conflict, I wonder? But you have not said who my antagonist would be in the circumstances.'

Arthur had been thinking of Rye, and of an evening that seemed to be years in the past, although it was really only a few months ago, when they two had stood together on the Prebend's-bridge, and he had heard her talk quite eloquently of the beauties of 'the banks,' and how sad of heart she would feel if ever she had to leave the dear old place.

Isa Saunders had no such feelings. To her all places were loved alike, and none of them very deeply. Although Arthur had never felt like Rye on the subject, he had esteemed her patriotism highly, and did not admire Isa because of her easy impartial cosmopolitanism.

'You could not expect me to make arrangements for the combat. I have not received a commission from the two principals, although no doubt it would be delightful to be a spectator.'

Isa knew in her heart of whom Arthur had been speaking, and was not pleased that he should be thinking of Rye, still less that he should object to speak frankly about her. Wanting other more eligible friends, Miss Saunders was anxious to appropriate Arthur altogether to her own personal service. This had been her aim for some time past, and on the whole she was fairly satisfied with the results of her efforts. She did not know all the circumstances, but was confident that the engagement between Rye and Arthur was broken, and that he was not visiting much at the Mount.

'Keep your secret,' she said, laughing as she spoke, 'and pray, would it be betraying a secret if you were to tell me who in Rockingham would be more sorry than I, should we leave the old city?'

Arthur reflected for a moment, and then said quite frankly and sincerely,

'You have said you would be as happy anywhere as here, just as you were happy before you came. In fact you could leave without any feeling of regret, and at the same time you are quite happy to stay. I hope you will stay for some time, for I should feel sorry if you were not here.'

'He is growing pathetic,' Isa said to herself; 'how interesting!' Aloud she remarked, 'That is generous and kind of you, and hearing you speak in that way makes me feel inclined to alter my position. Yes, now that I see the matter differently,' she said musingly, 'I should be sorry, for one or two reasons, to leave Rockingham.'

Arthur looked at her intently, and he could not deny she was fair to behold. Her hair almost blue-black, her creamy complexion, her eyes large and black as the sloe, her strong, rounded, supple figure, perfect in contour and outline in every part, made her a lovely object to look upon. She bore his look well, dropping her eyelids just a little, it is true, but that, as she knew, only added to the beauty of the picture she made. And then he glanced round the room with its luxurious appointments, and thought how suitable and harmonious were the conditions amidst which this fair girl lived. All were so different from his own that, despite his natural self-control, he could not quite repress the sigh that rose in his breast.

'Are you not quite happy, then?' she asked.

'Perhaps not,' he answered quickly, not caring to be questioned on the point. 'But some day fortune may smile upon me.'

'I hope so, I am sure. It is so difficult to help our friends, is it not, especially when they choose to be reserved?'

'Does she really wish to be my friend?'

Arthur inwardly inquired. 'Does this grand lady value my friendship, and has she so far forgotten conventional ideas that she can regard me her equal?'

He was sitting on the ottoman in the centre of the room. She was standing at the window, occasionally looking out on the river-banks, and sometimes directing her eyes to her visitor. She knew she was beautiful, and at that moment had the impression she looked her best, with her well-fitting black dress relieved only by a pink ribbon fastened round her shapely throat.

Arthur rose from his place and went beside her. She smiled encouragement, and he took her hand, saying,

'If only you would be something more than my friend; if only you would be wholly mine!'

The beautiful hand was not withdrawn from his grasp, and a great wonder took possession of the young man's mind. Was he not to be repulsed? Was his suit proving successful?

'Let us sit together on the ottoman a minute. You have taken my breath away, and—and I hardly know what to say.'

'But you consent?—you have consented. I have your promise, is it not so?' Arthur inquired eagerly.

'My heart consents, but I have promised nothing yet. I dare not. We must be for a time as we have been, very fast friends, and then after two or three years, perhaps all will be as you wish.'

'And is that all you have to say to me?'

'What more can I say, Arthur. You must become clever and promising, and then I am sure my father will consent. Until then it would only be upsetting our plan, and putting out our hopes, to say anything further.'

'My poverty again!' Arthur wailed.

'Come, now, no useless morbid complaining. Work, and you will succeed, and all will come out right.'

Good advice, doubtless, Isa Saunders gave to Arthur, whatever might be her motive. And thus a second time Arthur Brixton, if not in form, in reality was engaged to the daughter of a wealthy man.

(*To be continued.*)

Vision of Mirza.

ADAPTED FROM ADDISON.

A VALE below stretched deep and wide,
   And through it flowed a silent tide,
     That issued from a misty fold,
   And into solemn darkness rolled.
Above on spacious arches stood
A shadowy bridge that spanned the flood;
   Its ends the rayless clouds enshroud.
Across it streams a broken crowd,
   Whom pitfalls hid within the gloom,
Untimely bring to fearful doom;
   And all, ere yet the bridge be crost,
Are in the deep abysm lost.
   A myriad voiceless birds on high
Seemed strangely checked, and hovering fly.
   While I the mystic scene surveyed,
My guide this explanation made:
   'The vale thou seest is misery's vale;
The stream is Time's eternal tale;
   That is the bridge of human life,
Those birds the passions of its strife.'
   He bade me then direct my gaze
To where the scene was wrapt in haze;
   Lo! as I looked, the clouds dispelled,
The river into ocean swelled,
   And, by a rock divided, showed
One part obscured in night's abode,
   The other, stretching far away
Aglow with islands bright and gay—
   Islands, where virtue reigns supreme,
Unknown to vice's boldest dream.
   Gazing upon this blissful sight,
I longed to share its pure delight;
   And as I looked, the genius said:
'Those are the mansions of the dead.
   The pathway to them lies between
The gates of death which thou hast seen.
   O, Mirza, doth not this repay
The storms, the struggles, on the way?
   Rewards not all this toil and strife,
To live hereafter such a life?'
   'Tell me,' I said at length, 'what means
The secret of those darker scenes?'
   I waited his reply in vain,
For he was gone; I turned again
   To view those wondrous isles; but they
Had vanished tokenless away.

ANNIE E. HIRST.

The Boyhood of Great Men.

NAPOLEON BONAPARTE.

HE great Napoleon was born at Ajaccio, in the island of Corsica, on August 15, 1769. The popular idea is that he was of humble extraction, and for this false impression Napoleon has partly himself to blame. He invariably discouraged any investigation into his pedigree. When the Duke of Feltré was despatched to represent Napoleon at the Court of Florence, the ambassador began to busy himself with inquiries into the emperor's antecedents, but his prying curiosity was rudely cut short by the message, 'I am the first of my family.' Similarly the Emperor of Austria, on the eve of his marriage with Napoleon's daughter, sought to enhance the dignity of the match by setting the heralds to work to trace the genealogy of the father of his bride up to the old Italian nobility. Napoleon only gave him the curt rejoinder that 'he would rather be the son of a peasant than descended from any of the petty tyrants of Italy.' Nevertheless, the blood of Italian nobles did flow in his veins. He was no upstart by birth. His mother came of a good family in Naples, whilst his father, Charles Bonaparte, could trace his ancestors in unbroken line for several centuries, and could claim kinship with some of the bluest blood of Italy. The Bonaparte family sprang originally from Tuscany, and many of its members had won an honourable fame. In the little state of Treviso some had held sovereign power, whilst in the republics of Florence and Bologna others as senators had guided the affairs of state. Some, abjuring the stormy path of politics, had climbed to eminence in the more peaceful garb of the priesthood. Others had trodden the flowery road of litera-

ture, and by treatises and histories had handed their names down to posterity. A Bonaparte is honourably associated with the foundation of the Chair of Jurisprudence in the University of Bologna. A man's worth is rightly determined by what he is himself rather than by what his father was; but if pride of ancestry be at all lawful, Napoleon could have been justifiably proud of his. He belonged to a younger branch of the family, which, owing to internal dissensions, had been driven from Florence in the 15th century, and had first settled at Sarzana and afterwards in Corsica. That island henceforth became their home, and here the Bonapartes grew and multiplied, whilst the elder branch, which had lingered on Italian soil, gradually disappeared.

Napoleon came into the world at a stormy time, when his island-home was rocked with wars and tumult. His father was by profession a lawyer. He had received his education at Rome, and afterwards at the University of Pisa, where he won the diploma of a 'Doctor of Laws.' After his return to his native land he married, and became advocate to the royal court of assize in Ajaccio. But troublous days were before him. In 1768 the independence of his little country was menaced by France. The patriot's spirit awoke within him, and, laying down his lawyer's brief, he girt on the sword. He had a wife as brave and high-spirited as himself. Together they shared the hardships of that brief campaign, and, when Ajaccio was seized by the enemy, they followed the Corsican army in its march over the mountains, and lived for a while, first at Corté in the heart of the island, and afterwards on the summit of Monte Rotundo. During a brief respite from hostilities permission was obtained to return to Ajaccio, and shortly afterwards Napoleon was born. It is probably to the patriotic spirit of his parents and to the eventful period of his birth that he owed that impatience at his country's subjugation which was for many years one of his most striking characteristics.

The war, as might have been expected, ended in favour of France. Charles Bonaparte, like other patriots, preferring exile to dependence, would have left his native shores had not the entreaties of friends and his love for his wife and children turned him from his purpose. Events proved the wisdom of his decision. France used her advantage with discretion, and removed much of the soreness arising from her conquest by retaining many of the native institutions. Leading Corsicans were appointed to posts of authority, not even those being excepted who had actively opposed the invader. Charles Bonaparte had a magistracy assigned to him, and became assessor to the supreme court of Ajaccio. This was a position of great influence in the island, and in the peaceful discharge of its duties and in the care of his increasing family the years passed quietly away.

It would seem, however, as though the mother was the central figure of that home. Napoleon never tires of singing her praises. She appears to have been a most remarkable woman, endowed with a strong will and great force of character. The task of training her children fell almost entirely upon her. Her husband was too fond of pleasure to bear his fitting share in the discipline of the household. If ever he interfered, it was to find some excuses for the youthful offenders, and so free them from punishment; but such interference came so rarely that, when it did come, it was always resented. 'Let them alone,' said his wife, 'it is not your business; it is I who must look after them;' and their management could not have been entrusted to better hands. Napoleon once very fittingly described her as having 'the head of a man placed on the body of a woman.' It was the character of her children that awoke her tenderest solicitude. She would not have a single weed growing in the fair garden of their hearts. She took great pains to discourage in them every low and ungenerous feeling, only suffering that which was exalted and noble to permanently root itself in their life. A lie she positively hated, and an act of disobedience was so provoking to her that it never failed to receive the chastisement it deserved. It was just such a mother as this that Napoleon needed.

As a child he was wilful and headstrong, and endowed with a perfect genius for getting into mischief. When disposed to be quarrel-some (and that not unfrequently happened), he would beat one and scratch another, and become the plague and terror of the home. He was afraid of nothing or nobody. His brother Joseph, in spite of his seniority, invariably got the worst of it in their childish encounters, and, before he could recover from the confusion caused by his defeat, the victor had gone to his mother, and had so ingeniously framed his complaint as to screen himself and throw the blame on his brother. There was probably abundant foundation for the prophecy that an uncle of these two boys made about their future, as he lay upon his death-bed. He had watched them from their infancy, and, when the lads came to bid him a last farewell, he said, ''Tis needless to think about Napoleon's fortune. He will make it for himself. Joseph, you are the eldest of the family, but Napoleon is the head of it.' Time proved how truly he had read their natures and predicted their destiny.

When Napoleon was five years of age his education began. He was sent to a school the mistress of which was a friend of the family, and where, as it happened, all the rest of the scholars were girls. He formed a childish liking for one of the little girls in his class, and might often have been seen after school, with his stockings down about his heels, walking along the street hand in hand with his favourite companion. The other scholars, prompt at anything that meant teasing or mischief, composed a little rhyme about them, and chanted it after them, whenever they were seen together. This was too much for the fiery temper of Napoleon. He seized sticks, stones, anything that came to hand, and rushed madly upon them. Luckily someone always came by and saved him, or the consequences might sometimes have been serious. It was somewhat prophetic of the man that, as a child, Napoleon never lingered to court his enemies, and was never frightened by numbers.

In the year 1779 a new page was opened in his life. His father had been appointed by the nobles of Corsica to represent them on an embassy to Paris. He set out, taking his two sons, Joseph and Napoleon, with him, and travelling through Italy on his way. The boys were delighted with the tour, nor was Napoleon less pleased when, instead of returning home, he was placed as a pupil in the military school of Brienne. He was fired by an ambition to distinguish himself, and flung himself at once heart and soul into his studies. He simply devoured every book that came in his way, and so speedily outstripped all competitors, that before a month was over he was the talk of the school, admired of some, and envied of others. The latter soon found ways to annoy the high-spirited Corsican. They stung him to the quick by casting a vile slander on his mother; they never suffered him to forget that he was poor, and consequently their inferior; they poured scorn upon that patriotic spirit which made him still resent the subjugation of his native island. Even the masters misjudged the boy's high-strung spirit, for, shortly after his arrival, one of the ushers ordered him to be clad in a coarse woollen dress, and to have his dinner on his knees at the door of the dining-room. It was a mark of degradation, and Napoleon felt it intensely. Serious vomiting and hysteria followed. The head-master, hearing of the incident, sharply rebuked the offending usher, whilst the mathematical teacher bitterly complained that his first mathematician should have been so thoughtlessly degraded. The iron entered deep into the boy's soul, and it was these humiliations, meted out to him by those who were his superiors in nothing but wealth, that burnt into him the maxim that talent was the true test of worth, and made him, during his imperial reign, shut the door on office-seekers whose only claims were rank and wealth, whilst he flung it wide open to those who presented the credentials of talent. At Brienne he seemed to move in a world of his own. He grew shy and retiring, and made but few friends. His favourite companions were his books. They never chafed or wearied him; and often, when the rest of the boys were merry at their sports, Napoleon might have been found in some quiet nook in the library poring over the pages of Plutarch or some volume of history. It was unwise of him, just at an age when fresh air and exercise

were so needful, to play the recluse so much. It was probably his abstinence from fitting recreation during his boyhood that stunted his growth, and gave him, as a man, that dwarfed appearance which won him the name of the ' little corporal.' Yet he could play sometimes, and when, one winter, the pupils constructed a regular fort in the snow, Napoleon was first among the foremost, and in the mimic attack and defence of the position displayed as much spirit and prudence as if the contest had been more tragic. Already his mind was filled with images of war, and it was a favourite practice of his, first at Brienne, and afterwards at the military school of Paris, to marshal imaginary armies, to conceive how certain positions might be kept or won, and arrange the whole machinery of war. Already in the arena of fancy he played the part of the conqueror, which he afterwards acted with such grim reality.

Napoleon stayed at Brienne till the end of the year 1784. His relations with his fellow-students improved but little, but he stood high in the esteem of his teachers. He could be very awkward with his equals, but his love of order and his respect for power restrained him from disobedience to those above him. Moreover, his diligence in the acquisition of knowledge won him their favour. His studies were ever of a practical kind. For art and the lighter branches of literature he had no relish whatever, but in history and mathematics his mind simply revelled. It was in the painstaking study of these that he laid the basis of that victorious generalship by which he afterwards led the armies of France from one triumph to another. His general proficiency gained him promotion from Brienne to the national military school at Paris. He remained there less than two years, but that was long enough to enable keen observers to detect in him unusual power and promise. ' Napoleon,' wrote his professor in history, ' is a Corsican by birth and character; he will do something great if circumstances favour him.' In August, 1795, he was examined by La Place, the great mathematician, and passed so creditably that he received an appointment as second lieutenant in a regiment of artillery.

He was transported with joy. To his youthful imagination it seemed as though human ambition could crave nothing more, unless it were to be a colonel, which, he thought, would be the very summit of human grandeur. It would have been well had his ambition always retained its youthful modesty. But, alas! it widened its horizon until not even the generalship of armies and imperial honours sufficed him. An emperor he would be, but over a wider realm than France; and so, followed by his legions, he led the way across the Pyrenees, and the snow-crowned Alps, and the frozen steppes of Russia, until a whole continent writhed under the scourge of war. We cannot marvel that such 'vaulting ambition overleaped itself;' ever greedy to get more, he, like the dog in the fable, finally lost all he had, and ended his days in disappointment and disgrace, a lonely exile on a distant island in the stormy bosom of the Atlantic.

A. Lewis Humphries, B.A.

Current Electricity.

The discovery of current electricity is due to a trivial circumstance. About 1780, a physician prescribed a dish of dressed frogs to Madame Galvani, who was at that time an invalid. Some of these, which had been skinned, lay on a table, when the accidental discharging of an electric machine near it caused a strong contraction of the muscles of the frogs, although they had not been touched by the spark.

The same effect was produced afterwards, when two dissimilar metals were placed in contact with a nerve and muscle respectively, and then brought in contact with each other. Galvani thought this action was due to the electricity generated by the frog's leg itself; but Volta, a professor of physics at Pavia, combatted this view, and ultimately proved that the electricity arose from the contact of the dissimilar metals.

How many great discoverers have died in ignorance of the worth and far-reaching importance of their discoveries, rendered famous as benefactors of the race by that which was to them, apparently, accidental and trivial! We say 'apparently' accidental, for we believe the world's education is controlled by God, to whom nothing is trivial; and that these discoveries, which have proved to be such important factors in the education of men, were given at the time they could best advance the purposes of God concerning men. Providence is always opportune. God's great gifts to man are never 'born out of due time.'

The first manipulators in current electricity little knew of the stupendous results that would be achieved by its aid. And although our bells are rung, rocks blasted, streets lighted, thoughts and voices conveyed hundreds of miles, &c., by its instrumentality, we cannot well conceive the many wondrous things yet to be achieved by it.

But to return to the subject. To prove that the electric current arose from the contact of two dissimilar metals, Volta constructed an apparatus which, in honour of the discoverer, has been called the Voltaic pile. It is made by placing a pair of discs of zinc and copper in contact, then laying on the copper disc a piece of cloth or flannel moistened with brine, then another pair of discs of zinc and copper, and so on, each pair being separated by the cloth. Such a pile, composed of a number of such discs, will produce a current of electricity when the top and bottom discs are connected with a wire. This instrument is seldom used now, in consequence of more convenient arrangements upon the same principle. We will now describe a more convenient arrangement, and one equally simple. Place in a glass jar separately two strips, one of zinc, the other of copper. Add some water in which is salt, vinegar, or better still, a little sulphuric acid. So long as the strips do not touch each other they are unaffected. But if connected by means of a copper wire a current of electricity is produced. When the current flows the zinc plate begins to waste away; its consumption furnishing the energy necessary to propel the current through the jar and connecting wire.

A few bubbles of hydrogen gas appear on the copper plate. The copper plate is called the positive pole, and the zinc the negative. The positive current only is usually considered, and this flows from the zinc plate to the copper plate in the liquid, and from the copper to the zinc outside the liquid, thus completing the circuit.

The amount of work done by a battery is in proportion to the zinc dissolved. Zinc, tin, lead, iron, copper, silver, gold, platinum, and carbon, may be used in making batteries. In this list zinc is positive to all the others, and any one of the list is positive to those that follow it, and negative to all that are before it. Besides sulphuric acid, nitric acid, bichromate of potassa, and sulphate of copper are exciting fluids.

There are many kinds of batteries—some, as the one described, consisting of a single fluid cell, others of two fluid cells. We have not space to refer to specific forms of battery, beyond stating that for simple experiments we have generally used one as described, or a Leclanché. The Leclanché is generally used for electric bells. Doubtless many of our readers are already familiar with it; unlike others, it retains its power without attention for months, if not years.

It has two fluid cells; the outer one of glass contains a zinc rod, and is charged with a solution of sal ammoniac; the inner one is of porous earthenware, and contains a carbon plate, and is filled up with a mixture of peroxide of manganese and broken gas-carbon.

As we only know of the presence of electricity by the effects it produces, we must briefly consider what those effects are. They are of four kinds, viz. :—Magnetic, Chemical, Healing, and Physiological.

(1.) *Magnetic.* The true connection between magnetism and electricity was not known till about 1819, although, previous to this, lightning had been known to magnetise knives and other objects of steel.

Professor Œrsted, of Copenhagen, discovered that if the connecting wire of a battery is brought parallel to a magnetic needle, the needle is deflected. If the current be flowing along the wire above the needle, in the direction from north to south, the north pole of the needle will turn eastwards. If it flows from south to north, the north pole will turn westwards. If the wire is below the needle, the motions will be reversed. Let us suppose that we have our battery at one end of the room, while the two wires are carried from the poles to the other end of the room, and are there joined together, so that the battery is now in action. Suspend a magnetic needle near the wire, at the end most remote from the battery, and this will be deflected. Disconnect the wire from one pole of the battery, and the magnetic needle will resume its ordinary position. This action would take place even if the wires connecting the poles were thousands of miles long before the circuit was completed. Telegraphy is but the application of the facts just detailed to some of the requirements of daily life. Again, when a current is passed through a copper wire twisted in the form of a helix, the coil acts exactly like a magnet. If a small bar of iron be placed within the helix, it will, if tested by iron filings, be found to have become a magnet. Disconnect the wire from one pole of the battery, and the magnetism of the iron disappears. Thus it is evident that if a wire carrying a current of electricity be wound round an iron bar, temporary magnetism is communicated to the bar. A bar of iron thus magnetised is called an electro magnet. An induced magnetic force can in this way be obtained sufficient to sustain a weight of hundreds of pounds. Not only can magnetism be induced by an electric current, but an electric current can be excited in a wire helix by the action of a permanent magnet.

(2.) *Chemical.* Besides the chemical action inside the cells of the battery, which always accompanies the production of a current, and to which we have already alluded, there are chemical actions produced outside the battery when the current is caused to pass through certain liquids.

In the year 1800, Carlisle and Nicholson discovered that an electric current could be passed through water, and that in passing through it decomposed a portion into its constituent gases. These gases appeared in bubbles at the ends of the wires which led the current into and out of the liquid ; bubbles of oxygen appearing on the point where the current entered the water, and hydrogen bubbles where it left.

Other liquids, particularly dilute acids and solutions of metallic salts, may be decomposed by an electric current.

(3.) *Heating.* If a thin platinum wire is placed between the wires from each pole of the battery, it becomes red hot. Hence there is no difficulty in exploding gunpowder, discharging guns, &c., with the electric current.

(4.) *Physiological.* Most of our readers will have experienced some of the physiological effects. When currents of electricity are passed through the limbs, the nerves are affected with sensations more or less painful, and the muscles undergo involuntary contractions. If we place a silver coin on the tongue and a steel pen under it, bringing the edges of them in contact, a certain taste is produced. The same taste is noticed if the two wires from a battery are placed in contact with the tongue. The eye, ear, and organs of smell are also affected when a current of electricity is passed through them. Indeed, each of these senses can be stimulated into activity by the current. Although man does not possess a special sense for the perception of electric forces, as he does for sound and light, it is very probable that some of the lower animals do.

Electric currents have proved very helpful aids in restoring persons rescued from drowning, the contraction of the muscles of the chest causing respiration. The following experiment shows the effect of feeble currents on cold-blooded animals. If a copper or silver coin be placed on a piece of sheet zinc and a snail made to crawl over the zinc, when it comes in contact with the copper it will suddenly pull in its horns and shrink its body. The bodies of sheep, oxen, and other animals are found to suffer spasmodic muscular contractions when the current is passed through them ; and one electrician, by sending a current through a newly-killed grasshopper, caused it to emit its familiar chirp. Dewar has shown that an electric current is set up in the optic nerve when light falls upon the retina of the eye.

In conclusion, we would advise our readers to be wary in buying some of the much-advertised sham electric appliances. We believe that the fancied good they have done is rather due to the flannel than the magnetism.

In some cases of paralysis and other affections, doubtless the nerves have been stimulated by electricity, although we have seen cases where positive injury has resulted from the unadvised application of electric currents.

For the explanation of certain technical terms used in this paper we will refer our readers to the former papers on magnetism and electricity which, by the kindness of the Editor, have appeared in previous numbers of *Springtime.* J. T. E.

Wholesome Fiction.

ANNIE SWAN (Mrs. Burnett Smith) is one of those writers we have pleasure in recommending to readers of wholesome fiction. Her appearance as a novelist is but comparatively recent, but her books are very numerous ; and we are glad to find them placed before the public at a price which will bring them within the reach of those who are without great command of cash. She does not belong to the sensational or 'fleshly' school of novelists. The reader of the highly-seasoned novel, or the merely worldly romance, will not find aught in her pages to suit his or her tooth. For Miss Swan always takes up her pen with a high moral and religious purpose, and aims at touching heart and conscience, as well as pleasing the intellect and fancy. She has written much, and still continues to pour forth from a seemingly exhaustless storehouse. This has its drawbacks, of course, and we do not wonder that there should be a good deal that is unequal and commonplace. Yet there is not one of her books which is not healthy in tone and replete with useful lessons for the formation of sound and honourable character. Her name stands deservedly at the head of the younger school of religious novelists, who are doing much, we are thankful to say, in combatting a class of novel that deals with religious subjects in a spirit of doubt, if not of flippant denial of what we account most dear to us in our beliefs, and of saving worth to human lives. We venture the opinion that as religious gift-books her works have a wider circulation than those of most of her compeers, both north and south of the Tweed.

Her chief strength lies in her scenes and characters of Scottish rural life. Her character delineation is never overdrawn, but simple and natural, and at the same time vivid and realistic. Considering that she writes so much, it is remarkable how varied and life-like are the pictures she can draw, and how well she manages to keep up the interest of her stories. We agree, on the whole, with the opinion that has been expressed that she is never very strong; but she is always charmingly fresh and engaging, and never morbid. It is sometimes brought as a charge against the class of writers, of which Annie Swan is a leading type, that their religious ideas are narrow and mawkish. Cant, or what is called 'goody-goodiness,' it is said, colours or rather discolours their pages, and gives a sickly and an impossible hue to the characters portrayed. Miss Swan is quite free from such blemishes, and generally treats religious phases with much delicacy and a certain human wholesomeness.

'Aldersyde' and 'Carlowrie' have been regarded as on the whole her best and most equal productions ; but as tastes and critics differ, we must leave our readers to judge for themselves. We may state that, to our mind, a good average specimen of her work is to be found in one of her latest volumes, 'Maitland of Laurieston.'

It is an interesting family tale, and some of the rural sketches are quite idyllic in their charm. Michael Maitland, the father, is a stern old Calvinist, strong and sober and good, but somewhat severe and outwardly harsh. His wife is a gentle, unselfish creature, and one of the finest characters in the book. John, one of the sons, revolts from his father's creed with its hard conceptions of God and its religious narrowness, and he becomes a sceptic. An important turn is given to the story when

Agnes and Willie Laurie—the children of a friend of Mrs. Maitland, who had married a gentlemanly scoundrel and died young — come to live with the Maitlands. Agnes is an attractive girl and an earnest Christian. In due course, in spite of his sceptical opinions, she marries John Maitland, and around these two the interest of the story mainly gathers to the close. John becomes Assistant Professor of Moral Philosophy in Edinburgh University, and more pronounced in his scepticism ; while Agnes is full of a faith which ennobles her life. Their united life is not happy, because of the difference in their beliefs, and we are reminded of the relations between Robert and Catherine in ' Robert Elsmere.' But in the end, John, partly by the discipline of sorrow and partly by the influence of his wife, is brought to the Christian faith ; and matters all round begin to brighten. Everybody indeed improves, and the story runs to a satisfactory ending. Even the worthless old Laurie reforms, and makes a happy marriage ; and Willie, the son, after making a runaway match with Maitland's daughter, settles down into a respectable farmer. A cheerful, hopeful spirit and strong faith in the better side of human nature pervade the book. Good hits are given at the silly vapourings of the Edinburgh students who call themselves Agnostics, and delight to air their crotchets because it gives them the credit of being deemed intellectual. Lessons of a salutary kind are not far to seek in the pages of the novel and in the *dénoûement* of the story. It is shown that religion may, by reason of a narrow creed, be presented in forbidding aspects in human character, and accordingly repel the youthful and impressionable mind. On the other hand, it is clear that honest doubt will generally, in the long run, come to the light ; but it is suicidal and irrational only to believe our doubts and to doubt our beliefs. Sorrow also is seen to be salutary and saving in its effects. The bitter aloe, it is said, is often planted by the Samoans beside the decaying bread-fruit tree to revitalise it and cause it to bear fruit ; so, in the discipline of life, our doubts and denials of truth may yield to the pressure of sorrow and make us fruitful in faith, and hope, and love. On the whole, as a set-off to 'Robert Elsmere,' with a happier and more consistent ending, we know of no work we can more heartily recommend to our youthful and intelligent readers. H. Y.

Reason and Instinct as they appear in Man and Animals.

PHILOSOPHICALLY considered there is little doubt that the earth is mother of all physical life. In it are found the spores of all animal being, and death is but the calling in of the circulation of life's properties for subsequent reissue. But all intellectual and moral life is the direct gift of God. The first question in this line of thought is, what are the characteristics which may differentiate reason and instinct, wherever they may be found? This will require an analysis and comparison of the qualities of reason as common to man and intelligent animals—if there be any difference between instinct and reason, as it is hard to demonstrate that instinct is not reason. The difference between them is more in quantity than in quality.

Instinct is perception acting spontaneously as a law unto itself; it is that perceptive power of the mind by which, independent of instruction or experience, animals and uneducated men can unerringly and spontaneously do whatever is necessary for the preservation of the individual or the continuation of the species. In reasoning the mind acts mediately through education and experience; but in instinct or intuition, which corresponds to it, it acts immediately. Closing the eyelid to shelter the eye in danger is called instinct, but is it not rather reason or perception acting immediately and in its sovereignty? Untaught perception is the source of instinct, as it is called; the moment perception calls to its aid the other mental attributes, and they become concurrent, it is reason.

Nest-building is classified as the work of instinct because there is seen in it no element of progress, for perception unaided cannot make progress. A somewhat eminent philosopher in one of the learned societies in London took the position, and maintained it with great probability, that birds do not build their nests by instinct, but that the young learn the art by observation while in them.

Reason differs from what is called instinct as previously described, but it must have in it the exercise of the will, without which there is no reason. Instinct is intelligent acting without the will; reasoning is the deduction of conclusions from premises. It will be the purpose of this argument to show that the faculty of drawing conclusions from premises belongs to animals as well as to man, but in a much lower degree. It is the superiority of this power which they possess, though in an inferior degree, that enables man to rule over them, just as it is the same reasoning power, in a higher degree, which enables man to rule over thousands of other men. In both man and beast reason dominates and conquers instinct.

The cravings for food in both man and beast are held in check by conscious fear of favour or punishment. Any intelligent animal can be educated to subordinate its instincts to reason. There are multitudes of examples of animals doing unusual and surprising things through the same motives which actuate their masters.

The late Dr. Young, formerly president of Centre College, was a great bird-hunter, and had an old dog as his constant companion in the recitation room, as well as in the field. He once said that at the end of the bird season game would become wild and rise out of range, and he did not succeed in bringing anything down until the dog, of his own motion, changed his tactics. Knowing the range of his master's gun, he took in the situation and met the exigency by going to the windward side. Detecting the birds just beyond game range, he would circle around with his head set outward from the game, and then, with his back to them, would hold up his paw, as much as to say, 'All right!' Here the instinct to go directly towards them, as he did through all the early season, changed into a kind of rational circumvention. By observation, comparison, and generalization he had come to the rational conclusion that the gun had a definite range beyond which birds could not be shot; also, that there had been a change in the birds which required of him a change of action so as to deceive them as to his purpose and keep them still. This is exactly the same process followed by the South American sportsman, who locates a partridge and commences riding in circles, nearer and nearer, the bird squatting closer to the earth as he approaches, hoping not to be seen, until it is struck dead with the handle of the hunter's whip.

An example is well authenticated of a dog whose master, a Scotch tippler, got ugly every afternoon. The Scotch terrier followed him everywhere, and was a great favourite. The master in the morning took two drinks, and went home to dinner stupid and ugly. One day, after he had taken four, he beat his dog cruelly. Ever after the dog went with him until he had taken the third glass, and would then go home, crawl under the barn, and nothing would induce him to come out until the next morning. Last summer we saw a water dog sent into the river after a rail. He first took it in the middle and swam with it to the only landing-place, which proved too narrow. He swam out again, turned the rail around and brought it endwise to his master. It was thrown back several times and he always brought it out by the end. His master had crippled a crow and flung it, while living, into the water, and commanded the dog to bring it out, which he did very tenderly. His master then cut off its head and threw the body again into the river and tried to make him go after it, but he could neither by coaxing nor threats be induced to do it. A friend living on the Gatineau River, Canada, is the owner of several collie dogs and a little house terrier. He vouches for the following: The little dog, attempting to follow a member of the family across a small brook which flowed into the river, fell off the log into the water. The stream was terrifically swift, and he was being borne rapidly into the river. A collie saw it and rushed about three hundred yards down the stream and entered it just in time to catch the terrier. What can that power of calculating the swiftness of the current be called? In a semi-agricultural paper, dealing with stock, called *Land and Water*, examples are given of the reasoning powers of cows. The door of a corn crib opened outward and a latch on the inside was lifted by the finger through a hole. A cow studied it out and thrust in the little end of her horn and opened it. After eating as much as she wanted she closed the door by pushing it with her horns. A watch was set for the thief, and she was discovered to be the guilty party.

Professor Cope has given an account of a monkey and its reasoning powers. He was kept in a cage, but always directed his attention to the hinges of the door. No matter how they were fixed, he would extract screws and nails and so open the door at the hinge side. A strap was then fastened around his waist, but he picked the threads from the lap on the buckle, and after he had loosed himself, being still in the cage, he utilized the strap to draw things from the floor to himself, displaying great accuracy of aim. Professor Cope says:—'No reasonable man could doubt that every one of these acts was prompted by reason, which, so far from being even aided by instinct, was acting in direct opposition to it. Instinct would have led him to force, but in this instance the same reason guided him that would guide a reasoning criminal in like circumstances. It was impossible for instinct to teach him that the hinges were the weak parts of the door, or the threads in the strap, nor did instinct teach him to use the strap as a lasso.'

General Sir Hope Grant has furnished the following incident occurring during the Sepoy war. After the Secunda Bagh had been taken in Cawnpore, Sir Hope Grant's nephew gave his horse to a Sikh soldier to hold. A magazine exploded, killing the holder and burning the horse frightfully. A soldier was told to shoot him, but missing his aim wounded him. The horse broke away, dashed through the lines of the enemy, and as straight as an arrow went five miles to the sick horse stables of the Ninth Lancers and presented himself for treatment at the right door.—*The Presbyterian.*

Sketches of the British Isles.
THE ISLE OF ANGLESEA.

In the years of the distant past the Isle of Anglesea was called 'Mona' by the Romans. The Anglo-Saxons gave it the name of 'Angle's Ey,' *i.e.* 'The Englishman's Island;' which has been modernised as Anglesea. In desolate moorland and pleasant valleys. There are indications that the island in the formative period of the earth's history was wave-washed, and the peculiar formation of the crust—as far as Anglesea is concerned—proves the assertion of De la Beche, that 'The dry land of the world is little else than the bottom of seas and lakes.' At intervals masses of lichen-covered dark rocks appear. Minerals are numerous; and comprise limestone, mica

shape, it resembles an irregular triangle, the base being opposite the shores of the mainland, and is separated therefrom by a narrow arm of the sea, called Menai Straits. The extreme length of the island is twenty-one miles, the breadth nineteen, and the total land area is slightly over three hundred square miles. The surface is an undulating table-land of slight elevation, intersected with stretches of schist, granite, marble, serpentine, soap-stone, and coal. The copper mines of Parys and Mona were opened in the year 1768; large quantities of lead ore containing a high percentage of silver have also been found. On the whole, the climate is mild, but foggy; during the months of summer it is exceedingly pleasant, but during the remainder of the year, owing to the severe blasts from the Atlantic, it is only adapted for the 'children of the storm,' whose constitutions are strong and healthy. The foliage and trees are stunted in growth and gnarled in their outline by the succession of severe gales.

Anglesea possesses a greater number and variety of remains of a prehistoric people than are to be found elsewhere in the Principality. The British antiquities consist of hill camps,

have also been exhumed. The British regarded Mona as a sacred island. Dryden described its historical associations : —

> ' In many an ancient wood,
> Whose often-twined tops great I'hœbus' fires withstood,
> The fearless British priests, under an aged oak,
> Taking a milk-white bull, unstrained with the yoke,
> And with an axe of gold from that Jove-sacred tree
> The mistletoe cut down : then with a bended knee
> On the unhewed altar laid, put to the hallowed fires.'

Britannia Tubular Bridge.

surrounded by an outer work of rough walls of stone, thrown together in a cyclopean style; village groups of rude huts; sepulchral mounds and cromlechs; perpendicular blocks of stone, respecting which archæologists are undecided in their opinions, whether they are memorials for the distinguished dead, or rude temples for Druidical worship. Many domestic articles, such as pieces of broken pottery, stone and bronze implements, and hunting weapons,

For information respecting the early history of the island annalists are greatly indebted to Tacitus. It appears that about a century after the landing of the Roman legionaries on British shores, Suetonius Paulinus, governor of the province, about the year A.D. 60, meditated an attack on Mona, which, owing to its peculiar position, was regarded as being one of the most formidable strongholds of the British. Tacitus, who writes with the flowing pen of a nineteenth-century newspaper ' war correspondent,' in his 'Annals' gives a very graphic description of the struggle. He says : ' Suetonius Paulinus prepared for an attack on Mona, an island inhabited by a sturdy race, and a home for fugitives, and got ready flat-bottomed boats, as the opposite shore was shallow and dangerous. Thus the infantry crossed ; the cavalry passed over by fording and swimming their horses through the deeper water.

' A serried but motley band, bristling with arms, was drawn up to defend their shore. Among the soldiers women ran to and fro, in black garb, and with streaming hair, waving torches like furies ; behind them stood the Druids with upraised hands calling down imprecations upon their assailants. The strangeness of the sight daunted the soldiers ; for a space they stood, as if paralysed, to be cut down. But soon aroused by their general, and goading on one another with reproaches for being frightened at a band of women and fanatics, they charge upon the foe, and, sweeping all before them, drive the vanquished into the flames which they had kindled. After the victory a military post is established in the conquered country, and the groves, sacred to cruel superstitions, are cut down ; for it was a part of their religion to sacrifice captives on their altars, and seek to know the will of their gods by examining the entrails of men.'

The struggle for British independence led by Queen Boadicea recalled Paulinus from Wales to the south of England. Agricola followed up the conquests of his predecessors, and Mona, about the year A.D. 76, was made subservient to the military authority of Imperial Rome. At the withdrawal of the Roman legions from Britain, Mona passed into the hands of chieftains, or Konnings, *i.e.*, ' Able Men,' of their own race. Although Mercians, Danes, and Irish in succession tried to take Anglesea, it retained its independency until and for some years following the Norman conquest. During the reign of Henry III., the weaknesses of government and the factious disturbances of the people of England enabled Llewelyn ap Jorweth to main-

tain his independency. The popular rhymes of the people declared :—

' Their Lord they will praise,
Their speech they shall keep,
Their land they shall lose,—
Except wild Wales.'

Another Llewelyn, the son of Gruffyd, who had been called the Lord of Snowdon, assumed the title of Prince of Wales. At the accession of Edward I., after repeated requests, the Welsh prince failed to appear before the king to do homage for his possessions. In 1277, Edward despatched a fleet from the Cinque Ports which completely reduced Anglesea. Llewelyn threw himself upon the mercy of the king, who magnanimously spared his life. David, the brother of Llewelyn, revolted in the year 1282, and the struggle was reopened. The English detachments constructed a temporary bridge over the Menai Straits, and after a prolonged contest, which lasted for several months, Anglesea was subdued. Llewelyn was killed in a skirmish on the banks of the Wye. David was taken prisoner and sentenced to a traitor's death. Strong castles were built, English laws and customs were introduced, and Anglesea, along with North Wales, became part and parcel of the English realm.

At the north-eastern extremity of Anglesea, and overlooking the Straits, is Beaumaris Castle, erected by Edward I., to protect the little port and town of Beaumaris, and also as a military stronghold to prevent rebellion on the part of the conquered people. Evidently, the site of the castle was selected on account of its proximity to the sea, with which it communicates by a canal. The style of architecture is exceedingly bald ; and the pile has not the striking, picturesque effect that is found in most of the Welsh castles. The outer walls are hexagonal in plan, are massive throughout, and at intervals are protected by circular towers of considerable strength. A second inner wall of defence is square in style. The main entrance consists of a gateway with a machicolated parapet, strengthened by two circular towers and a portcullis. On one side is an outwork—the gunner's wall—extending from one of the round towers, and crossing the

South Stack Rock Lighthouse.

meat, and was constructed to protect the supplies which would be brought by boats to the gates of the castle. The quadrangle is almost square, the greatest length being one hundred and ninety feet. Along the sides of this were built the principal rooms of the castle; an imposing room, called the great hall, was seventy feet long, and was lighted by five highly decorated windows. The chapel is in an excellent state of preservation, and is adorned with a groined roof and lancet windows. Extra precaution was taken in the defence of the castle, by the construction of a corridor built in the thickness of the internal walls, and traversing the whole length of the building. Historically considered, the incidents of the castle are uninteresting. At the Cromwellian period it was held by a Royalist of the name of Bulkeley, who submitted to General Mytton in command of the Parliamentarians. The castle was subsequently dismantled, and allowed to fall into ruins. Beaumaris, the capital of Anglesea, was formerly encircled by a wall, only a mere fragment of which remains. A house known as Hen Blas was the town residence of the Bulkeley family. Some remaining portions of the building date from the reign of Henry VIII. The church, throughout, is a heavy structure, and was erected about the same time as the castle. In contains some imposing monuments belonging to the Bulkeley family.

Another noteworthy feature of Anglesea is the mansion of Plas Newydd, the seat of the Marquis of Anglesea, finely situated among woodlands, and fronted with velvety lawns that stretch to the extreme edge of the Straits. Architects speak of the mansion as being an ugly specimen of a feeble semi-Gothic style. Her Majesty, when Princess Victoria, spent the summer months of 1832 at Plas Newydd, which had been previously visited by her royal uncle, George IV. The grounds contain an ancient cromlech, in an excellent state of preservation ; and also a tumulus, with a sepulchral chamber constructed of limestone slabs; it is seven feet long, one yard in width, and about three-quarters of a yard high. On the outskirts of the park is a tall, imposing column erected in memory of the first Marquis of Anglesea, who had command of the Light Cavalry at Waterloo ; who for a number of years after the memorable battle lived ' with one foot in the grave,' one of his legs having been dislocated on the plains by one of the last of the French cannon-shots.

Telford's Bridge, over the Menai Straits, although surpassed by more recent erections, is considered to be one of the greatest achievements of the engineering world. Before its erection communication between North Wales and Anglesea consisted of ferries which were exceedingly dangerous. It is computed that previous to 1842 as many as one hundred and eighty passengers, in as many years, had been unfortunately drowned. Telford selected a point where the Straits narrowed, and the cliffs on either side were both bold and rocky, permitting a roadway of considerable height, and securing reefs in the bed of the channel for solid foundations for the ends of the piers, which are one hundred and fifty feet high. These are connected with the shore by gracefully formed tapering archways. The main length of the suspended portion of the bridge is five hundred and seventy-nine feet ; and it is hung at a height of a hundred feet above high-water mark. The timber roadway rests on iron joists, attached to sixteen chains, coupled in fours, each being nearly the third of a mile long ; these for some distance are carried underground, and then safely fastened to the rocks. Over the piers, the chains are placed upon rollers, to permit expansion and contraction of the iron-work during climatic changes. Allowance has been made for the bridge to bear the weight of two thousand tons, while the bridge itself only amounts to about one-fifth of that weight. One hundred and twenty thousand pounds were spent on its construction.

At a contraction of the Straits, about three-quarters of a mile below the suspension bridge, is Robert Stephenson's wrought-iron Britannia Tubular Bridge, so-named after the Britannia Rock, on which the central pier is erected. The conception of the bridge was more daring than Telford's, but the bridge in itself is considered ungraceful. It was the original intention of Stephenson to bridge the Straits by two cast-iron arches ; these were condemned by the Admiralty as being unsuitable for shipping purposes : although the centre of the proposed arches was a hundred feet above sea level, their side springs were only fifty feet. After repeated experiments it was decided to build a tubular bridge. The central tower is built on the Britannia Rock, the basement being sixty-two feet long and fifty-two feet wide ; the height is two hundred and thirty feet ;

about three hundred thousand cubic feet of stone were employed in its construction. On either side are the land towers, and beyond these are the abutments, adorned with couchant lions carved in stone-work. The bridge consists of four spans, the two over the water being four hundred and sixty feet, and the two over the land two hundred and thirty feet. Each tube was constructed by the edge of the Straits, floated on pontoons, and by means of hydraulic presses was lifted to its proper position. Over two millions of iron rivets were used in the construction of the bridge, and the total cost was over half a million of money. An allowance of one foot is made for changes of temperature. The deflection of the tubes caused by a train passing over laden with two hundred tons of coal was only four-tenths of an inch; while it is computed that thirteen inches for deflection might be allowed with perfect safety.

The observations of Mr. E. Clarke are specially interesting. He says: 'A short spell of sunshine on the top of the tube raised it on one occasion nearly an inch in half-an-hour, with a load of two hundred tons at the centre, the top plates of the bridge being expanded by increase of temperature, while the lower plates remained at constant temperature by radiation to the water beneath them. In like manner, the tube was drawn sideways to the extent of an inch by the sun shining on one side, and it returned immediately to its normal position as clouds passed over the sun. The tubes sometimes move as much as two inches-and-a-half vertically or horizontally when the sun shines on them.' In March, 1850, the Britannia Bridge was formally opened by three powerful engines passing through it. A second experimental train, consisting of twenty-four waggons, with a weight of three hundred tons, was at slow speed drawn through the tubes, while the spectators stood breathless waiting for the result. As the train emerged at the opposite end, the valley of the Menai echoed the lusty cheers of the people and the reports of the cannon. The satisfactory completion of the bridge was a great relief to Mr. Stephenson, who says: 'Often at night I would lie tossing about, seeking sleep in vain. The tubes filled my head. I went to bed with them and got up with them. In the grey of the morning, when I looked across Gloucester-square, it seemed an immense distance across to the houses on the opposite side. It was nearly the same length as the span of my tubular bridge.'

On the western coast of Anglesea is the small island of Holyhead, or, as it was anciently termed, 'Holy Island.' It is separated from Anglesea by a narrow channel spanned by a causeway—arched in the centre for the tide to flow through; over the bridge runs the main thoroughfare, and the London and North-Western Railway. The island is about eight miles long, three and a half miles in breadth, and maintains a population of ten thousand, who are chiefly employed in ship-building, rope-making, and a variety of marine occupations. The greater part of the island is barren and rocky. Pen-Caer-Gybi, reaching an altitude of seven hundred feet, is the highest hill. On the slopes are numerous British and Roman remains, from which some interesting and valuable antiquarian curiosities have been obtained. The coast scenery is very impressive. On the north-east are two isolated masses of rock, called respectively the North and South Stack Rock; the latter has a lighthouse, towering to the height of nearly two hundred feet, and its bright, flashing light can be seen at a distance of twenty miles. The lighthouse is reached by a stairway of about four hundred steps cut in the face of the solid rock. The coast is perforated with numerous caverns, inhabited by a countless number of wild sea-fowls; their discordant shrieks and cries adding to the solitariness of the scene. On the north-west are a cluster of little islets called the Skerries, which proved to be valuable to their owner, who received from the Government the purchase money of 444,948l. for the dues connected therewith.

Holyhead town is of considerable antiquity; the streets are irregular, and the buildings have an old-time appearance. Holyhead is well known in travelling circles as being the terminus of the London and North-Western Railway, and the port for Dublin. Holyhead also forms a link in the mail and passenger traffic between England and America. The railway station is of an elegant character. The platforms are lit with electricity. A decorative plate records that the station improvements were commenced in 1875, and completed in 1880, and that they were inaugurated by the Prince of Wales. The station is built on land that, at an immense outlay of wealth, has been reclaimed from the sea, and connected therewith are fifteen miles of railway sidings. The marine accommodation consists of a sheltered harbour, comprising four hundred acres, protected by a break-water of solid masonry rising over thirty-eight feet above low water mark, and extending for over a mile and a half, thus affording a magnificent promenade. The Admiralty Pier has a main length of one thousand feet, and is adorned with a superb marble arch, commemorating the visit of King George IV. in the year 1821. Altogether the Government works and improvements cost nearly a million and a half of money, and twenty-six years were spent in completing them.

ALBERT A. BIRCHENOUGH.

The Site of Solomon's Temple.

R. H. A. HARPER, who writes under the auspices of the Palestine Exploration Fund, and who knows the Holy Land familiarly, has just published a cheaper edition of his valuable book, 'The Bible and Modern Discoveries,' in which he writes at some length on the site of Solomon's Temple; he notes Mr. Ferguson's different opinion, and says :—' It is proved, I think without doubt, that the "Dome of the Rock," or the Mosque of Omar, covers the true site of Solomon's Temple.' The whole plateau is an area of 1,500 feet from north to south, 1,900 feet from east to west, with a massive front wall of nearly 80 feet high. About the centre of this plateau is a four-sided paved platform rising sixteen feet, in the centre of which the sacred rock crops up. There is no question but that some of the remaining wall is on the site of, or actually is, a portion of the old wall of the outer court.

It is proved that the Holy City is built upon a series of rocky spurs, that in the early days the site of Jerusalem was a series of rocky slopes; therefore when we get to the rock, we see it just as it was before the city was built. The rock-levels examined by means of shafts and tunnels show that the ridge of rock at the north-east angle is 162 feet below the sacred rock; at the north-west angle, 150 feet below the rock. Now the Temple was not placed in a hole; it must be a conspicuous building in Jerusalem, —*the* building of the city. So it stood on this huge platform, which was raised by means of walls and arches, the spaces below being used as storerooms, with secret passages, underground cisterns to hold both spring and rain water—one cistern so large that it was called 'the underground sea.' This platform was raised and carried across to the highest point of the rock, which ridge of rock was the threshing-floor of Araunah the Jebusite, where the angel's foot was stayed. Going down for a foundation for this great wall the builders came to the black mould, which was cut away and the rock itself cut into so that the stones might have a secure position.

Low down at the very base of Sir Charles Warren's excavations, in a niche cut out of the rock, was found a Phœnician jar. Who put it there, and for what? After being there for more than 3,000 years, it is now at the office of the Palestine Exploration Fund. Hiram the Phœnician sent his masons to do the work—for, remember, the Jew was never a builder. Though no stone chippings were found in the black mould, fragments of potsherds were found, with Phœnician inscriptions on them, which were numerals, masons' special marks, and quarry signs. What do these marks prove? Why, that the Biblical accounts which tell us of the work of a Phœnician master-builder are absolutely correct. How justly the terms ' great stones,' ' costly stones' are used is seen in the fact that one stone at the south-east angle weighs 100 tons, and another at the opposite angle is thirty-eight feet long, and others proportionately large. Where were these stones prepared? In what is now called the Cotton Grotto, the entrance to which is near the Damascus Gate, huge stones lie scattered about—stones cut thousands of years ago. From these you can tell the size and shape of the tools these old workers used. The marks are quite fresh and remind you of the quarries at Assouan, in Egypt. You fancy it must be the dinner hour, and that the workmen will return ere long. Some stones still remain which are only partially cut away. From the mass of stone chippings it is quite plain that the stones were prepared and 'dressed' here. The absence of stone chips near the foundation-stones, and their presence here, prove to the very hilt the truth of the Bible statement. And those letters and marks in red paint are instructions where to lay each stone; so that the sound of 'no tool was heard,' because each stone was dressed in the quarry.

It was imperative that the Temple be erected over the threshing-floor of Araunah, and in the East threshing-floors are always, and were always, at the highest point of the ridge, to catch the wind to blow away the chaff. They could not cut down the ridge, for to this day scarce a tool has touched it, so the huge walls and arches must be built up to provide an area large enough for the Temple and Temple Courts. More than this,—the spot is sacred because it was the hill on which Abraham erected the altar for the offering of Isaac. Here then, on this very spot, was built the altar of burnt-offering.   E. H. G.

A Man is What He is When Alone.

 NE of the most interesting revelations of childhood, foretelling the trend of the future, is to shut it up in a room by itself and observe what it will do to amuse itself. Matured manhood and womanhood must be submitted to the same test. What will they do in the isolated hours of life when God shuts them up unto their own companionship? How will they comfort themselves if they are compelled to tread the

wine-press of sorrow alone? Will the ingenuities of the soul come forth then and beget new sources of occupation and comfort? In 1 Cor. xvi. the Apostle Paul was in Ephesus alone, and it reveals what he did in his solitary hours. The Apostle Paul was, at the time of the writing of this part of the Epistle, in the greatest and wickedest city, without a welcome smile. It must be of interest to know what a man of his cast of mind and culture would do in his enforced loneliness. Many, we know—we ourselves might be among the number—would mope in half despair and fall into a soul-dishonouring *ennui*. Some would complain and say, 'It is always our luck to "miss connections," and have to lie over aimlessly and uselessly in unpleasant places.' The railroads would be abused, the hotels would be denounced; and perhaps some would in these classes of trial rave at Providence; others would rise into higher moral altitudes and fall back in similar loneliness on the blessed soul-poising conviction that all these trials are from God and will in some way be for the best. Such people get strong on their solitary trials, which toughen every fibre of their being. They grow wise, as the chronic invalid learns to handle pain so that it does not strike so vitally or hard as it does in the life of the inexperienced. Such subsidize their foes and gain over them the sublimest victories of their lives.

The Apostle was a master in his philosophy; there was not much that was in the form of what would be called reverse from which he did not get a revenue. His history of perils and persecutions, his foes and victories, reads like a romance. He got so much immortality out of his trials that he has never, so far as the world knows, been even buried. Tradition tells us of his martyrdom and points to the place, but even tradition is dumb as to his burial. The fact is that a man who could get so much of immortality out of adversity will never find a grave deep enough to bury him, for the world will be forever reanimating him. It is not an incredible thing that God should raise the dead, but it is that men should do it.

The Apostle has left facts about his isolation in this strange city enough to show us that the only policy which brings victories is to put petty torments under our feet. The glints of light incidentally thrown from this event reveal all that is needed to show us a true philosophy of life. These disjointed sentences, each perfect in its kind, give insight into the secret of the Apostle's force and of the character it projected from itself. These chips off the great general themes of the epistle, like dust from the wheel that polishes the diamond, are still radiant with the light of the central gem. Christian isolation in trial is not a species of torment, but a time of spiritual upbuilding. It makes the man both architect and builder. He observes each flaw in his own life, for he has nothing to divert him from the duty of self-inspection. Society develops character outwardly, but loneliness in life's struggles builds inwardly. Strong natures have been lonely natures; in the battles they have had neither help from without nor cheer. Such characters will know more of both depraved and saved human nature; one will be as the dark banks of mists against which the glories of the sun will display the richest colours. Such men will ever have before them two ideals—one of what human nature is, and the other of what it can be and ought to be. In segregation of spiritual life the Christian discovers that a man is not undone or even hindered by trials to his faith. The Apostle discovered in Ephesus that he had many enemies. He had no friends and many foes. Well, if a man's enemies are outside of himself he can slay them even with the jawbone of an ass, if he carries a steady head and a devout heart. None of these things move a great man.

There is no way of so thoroughly discerning the true inwardness of a man as in the disposition he makes of his enemies and what he gets out of them. If they can do no more than sting him into unusual activity he is rising by them as an eagle rises higher by the violence of the storm. The moral power of a man may be measured by the enmities he arouses, as you may know the strength of the current by opposing it. Resistance will raise hostilities in the stupidest natures. Flints, the dullest, most lifeless substances in nature, will draw

fire if they are brought in contact with steel. But enemies and enmities to the spiritually poised, open doors of opportunity for victories. What great man in any mission of life does not owe his success as much to his enemies as to himself? They gave him opportunities to show his inward strength—they called out his reserved force. No great man's friends do half so much for him as his foes. A rising young man was assaulted by a contemptible village paper, and some of his unwise friends advised personal castigation. He said, 'No, that would spoil all my prospects. If I let him alone he will defame me into Congress yet.' It was only a prophecy of what occurred. —*The Presbyterian.*

<hr>

Current Topics.

ATHLETICS.

W are now in the midst of the football season. The popularity to which this game has suddenly risen is very surprising. It is an ancient pastime, but it is only recently that it has taken any real hold upon public affection. The ardour with which it is followed has produced a remarkable change in the young life of this country. Previously, when the weather became too cold for cricket, boating and other summer games, the athletic season was supposed to have closed. There might be during the winter a little skating, a little snowballing, or an occasional 'paper-chase,' but there was little else. Now, however, the winter is the most exciting time of all; for this is the season for football. And in spite of the weather it attracts far greater crowds and excites a far deeper interest than any other game.

Whether this is a good or a bad thing I am not prepared to say. To be frank, I am not sufficiently familiar with football to pronounce judgment upon it. I once ventured the opinion that it was not so scientific a game as cricket, and was for that very reason more popular with certain classes. But I shall not commit that rashness again. To do so would be simply to invite discomfiture. The footballer is prepared to defend his game with all the spirit with which he plays it. This is sufficient to make any discreet person very cautious in challenging him to conflict. And it must be admitted that, so far as morality is concerned, he has justice on his side. There is no real difference between the moral character of football and any other athletic game. In all essential particulars they are all on the same footing, and if you allow certain of them you cannot condemn others. We may have our likes and dislikes, and there may be games beneficial to one boy and injurious to another, but a game is not to be condemned because it does not suit everybody.

Are athletic sports desirable at all? Physically, there can be no doubt about their advantage. A great authority upon the subject tells us that 'next to food and sleep, which are the great restoratives of physical power, athletics may claim to have the largest share in the recreation of human life. The man of business and the student alike find in them that variety and change from the regular work of life which refreshes and re-invigorates both mind and body. Each able-bodied individual,' he says, will, if he be wise, 'provide for himself both exercise and recreation in a way suitable to his age and power (and occupation as well), with a view to pre-serving for himself a sound mind in a sound body.'

Athletics, too, may be a benefit morally as well as physically. They may at any rate keep us out of the mischief which Satan always finds for 'idle hands' to do. Then the preparation they require must be a fine thing for enabling a youth to gain a mastery over himself. Paul knew something about this, and he exhorts the Christians to follow the example of the athletes of that time in 'keep-ing their body under,' in order that they might win a grander prize. In all wholesome athletic

games the players must be trained in patience and endurance, and in a thousand ways, too, the generous rivalry which they excite oper-ates to the curbing of hasty tempers and selfish inclinations in the individuals who take part in them. The necessary demand for fair-ness in a game is in itself a condemnation of meanness and trickery in the individual, and tends to foster a chivalrous and generous element. There are indeed games which appear to excite evil passions in the players, but per-haps these are for this very reason a better means of discipline. For in all well-conducted games, it is accounted 'bad form' for the player to give extravagant expression to his feelings, and any ebullition of ill-temper would be ruthlessly put down. The player, therefore, if he does not wish to be disgraced, is compelled to keep himself well in hand.

Athletics have, however, their dangers. This cannot be forgotten. There is the danger of allowing these pursuits to engross too much of our time and attention. They should be regarded strictly as a recreation, for as soon as ever they begin to interfere with our studies, our business, or our worship, then they become an evil. What has tended more than anything else, however, to destroy the benefit of athletics is the practice of gambling. When, like a huge monster, it stalks into a field, it seems at once to change the whole aspect of the game. Every healthful, joyous feeling is somehow extinguished, and the brutal, selfish dispositions are brought into play. This has brought many a pleasing pastime into dis-repute, and has been the cause of untold mischief to the individuals who have given way to its indulgence. There, too, is the danger of falling into evil companionship in connection with athletic games. In these pursuits young people are brought very close together, and strong friendships are often the result. How important that these friendships should be helpful. And does not this all show the need of churches taking some interest in the amusements of their young people? A bishop, writing on this subject, maintains that the clergyman who ministers only to the souls of the young is 'guilty of heresy.' 'Cricket and football,' he says, 'without religion will give not a little purity; religion without games will do much; but where the two join hands, you guard and raise the whole man.'

The passion for outdoor games is one of the peculiarities of the Anglo-Saxon race. It is one of the things that make the English a puzzle to the people of other nations. An Oriental traveller was once taken to watch a game of cricket, and he was polite enough to express himself as highly entertained by the agility of the players. He was, however, thrown into a state of utter bewilderment on being told that many of those taking part in the game were rich men. 'Why,' he asked, 'did they not pay some poor people to do it for them?' The idea that it was in the doing of it that the chief pleasure lay never seemed to dawn upon him.

The important question of 'training' has recently been discussed in one of the magazines by Sir Morell Mackenzie. He defines it as 'the higher education of the body, whereby not only the muscles (which supply the movements) but the great vital motors which govern them—especially the heart and lungs—are developed to the highest obtainable perfection, and drilled to harmonious co-operation with each other.' A well-trained athlete in fact is one who has not only acquired skill in some particular exercise, but is in the enjoyment of perfect health. A complete system of training, therefore, must include not only appropriate muscular exercise but the regulation of the diet and a strictly disciplined manner of living. Sir Morell has a good deal to say about diet, but he confesses that the proper food for each individual may be best determined by the answers to the questions—Do you like it? and Does it agree with you? He gives the following as the regimen of the young Oxford oarsmen when training for the great University boat-race, viz. :—'On getting up at 7.15 a.m. they take a biscuit and a glass of milk, then they go for a gentle walk for a mile. Break-

fast at 8 30 consists of tea or cocoa (two cups at most), sole or some other kind of fish, chop with a poached egg on it, and some green food. No marmalade is allowed till two weeks before the race. At luncheon they have cold meat with one glass of beer. At dinner the *menu* includes fish, chicken, turkey or joint (always some kind of fresh meat), milk pudding and stewed fruit (rhubarb by preference); two glasses of beer are allowed, and after dinner one orange and a glass of port may be taken. At 10 p.m. they go to bed.' To many of us such a diet would be simply ruinous, but as it is in keeping with their previous mode of life these young men apparently thrive upon it.

Sir Morell Mackenzie himself has not a great deal to say in its approval. He quotes Dr. Parke, who tells us of the generations of splendid men who, in former times, were reared in the North of England and in Scotland upon oatmeal and milk, and also of 'the Roman gladiator trained on barley, and the Roman soldier in campaigns where meat could not be got, carrying corn, which he ground in hand mills, and then boiled in water and made a kind of strong vegetable soup, something like old English furmenty. On this food he marched and conquered as no other race has done.' Upon this, Sir Morell remarks, 'I do not think the young Englishmen, especially of the class which supplies University oarsmen, would care to train on barley.' Probably not; but this scarcely settles the question as to which kind of food is best for the promotion of health and strength.

In the opinion of many people these young men would be better without their allowance of beer and wine. This, however, is not the opinion of Dr. Mortimer Granville, a fashionable doctor in the West-end of London. This gentleman is so convinced that the spread of teetotalism in this country is destroying the moral, mental, and physical health of the people, that he has written to the *Times* on the subject. 'There is,' he says, 'less stamina in the life of the average Englishman now than there was forty years ago. He may live a little longer, but he is not so well able to resist the invading germs of disease, or to recover from the debilitating effects of such an invasion, as he was when good wine and sound ale formed integral parts of his daily diet.' Dr. Granville thinks the time has come when all who think as he does should ' show the courage of their convictions.' And certainly the letter he has written is much more indicative of his courage than his wisdom. It would scarcely be polite to express all the thoughts that such an effusion suggests, but two remarks may be made. In the first place, his long letter does not contain a single proof that the stamina of Englishmen is declining; and secondly, the statement contradicts itself. For if we have not the same powers of resisting disease as our fathers had, how is it that we live longer ?

' Oh that mine adversary would write a book ! ' We have reason to be grateful to Dr. Granville for his letter, for it not only shows the folly of attempting to defend alcohol, but it has been the means of bringing out some facts well worth knowing. Dr. Collins points out that the Registrar-General assures us in his 52nd annual report that the death rates for the last three years are by far the lowest as yet recorded since civil registration began in 1838 ; and that whereas the death rate from fever in England was 1,246 per million in 1847-50, in recent years it had been under 200 per million. These facts cannot be disputed, but they do not show that there is ' less stamina in the life of the average Englishman ' of to-day than formerly, or that he is less able to ' recover from the debilitating effects ' of disease. Another writer, Dr. Ridge, gives us his opinion upon the subject in these words —' Wherever two bodies of people can be fairly compared, one abstaining and the other not, the advantage lies with the abstainers. For strength, endurance, and every kind of vigour for work or play, other things being equal, the abstainer wins. Alcohol is a drag on the nation, and the only people that need dread its departure are the doctors.'

Dr. A. Carpenter makes a weighty contribution to the controversy. After stating what had led to his own abstinence, and testifying to the improvement of his health in consequence, he tells us of the beneficial effects it has had upon his patients, and then proceeds :— ' Further inquiry into the treatment of all diseases among all classes of the community has satisfied me that those who wish to enjoy perfect health had better avoid the daily use of alcohol, and that there are very few forms of disease in which its use is really beneficial.' Such facts and testimonies as these cannot be set aside by the special pleading of any number of fashionable West-end physicians.

Alcohol is an insidious poison, and no one who has considered its effects upon the system would ever hope to keep the body in a vigorous state of health by its means. And Sir Andrew Clark warns us that this subtle destroyer may be doing its work upon a man who not only looks but feels well. ' It upsets the stomach, the stomach upsets the other organs, and by-and-bye, under this fair and genial and jovial outside, the constitution is being sapped, and suddenly, some fine day, this hale, hearty man . . . tumbles down in a fit.' That, he says, is how alcohol taken in excess saps the constitution. Even if there were no moral considerations to be taken into account, there is surely sufficient here to confirm any prudent man in his temperance principles.

M. P. D.

Here is a whole sermon in a sentence by Hannah More :—' He who cannot find time to consult his Bible will one day find that he has time to be sick; he who has no time to pray must find time to die; he who can find no time to reflect is most likely to find time to sin ; he who cannot find time for repentance will find an eternity in which repentance will be of no avail; he who cannot find time to work for others may find an eternity in which to suffer for himself.

TO THEE, O LOVING SAVIOUR.

TO THEE, O LOVING SAVIOUR.

J. P. T.   R. J. DRING.

KEY A.

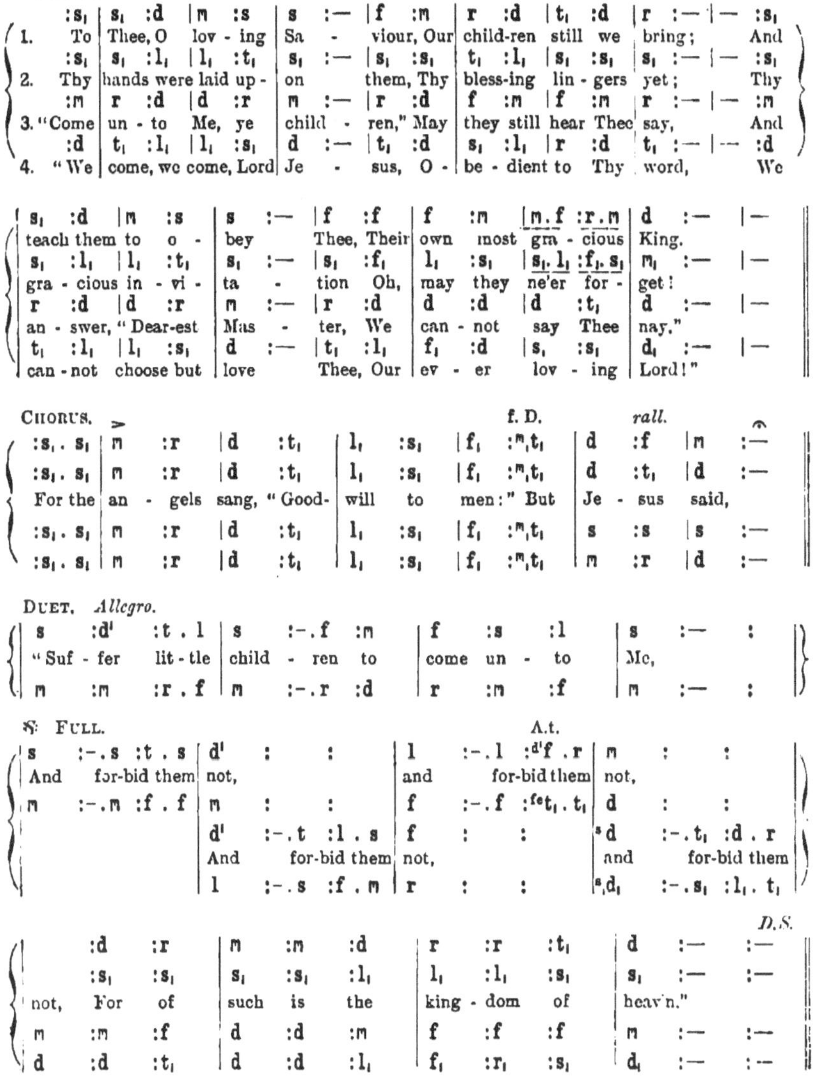

1. To Thee, O lov-ing Sa - viour, Our child-ren still we bring; And
2. Thy hands were laid up-on them, Thy bless-ing lin - gers yet; Thy
3. "Come un - to Me, ye child - ren," May they still hear Thee say, And
4. "We come, we come, Lord Je - sus, O - be - dient to Thy word, We

teach them to o - bey Thee, Their own most gra - cious King.
gra - cious in - vi - ta - tion Oh, may they ne'er for - get!
an - swer, "Dear-est Mas - ter, We can - not say Thee nay."
can - not choose but love Thee, Our ev - er lov - ing Lord!"

CHORUS.   f. D.   rall.

For the an - gels sang, "Good- will to men:" But Je - sus said,

DUET. *Allegro.*

"Suf - fer lit - tle child - ren to come un - to Me,

S. FULL.   A.t.

And for-bid them not, and for-bid them not,

And for-bid them not, and for-bid them

D.S.

not, For of such is the king - dom of heav'n."

The Young People's Page.

TO THE EDITOR OF *Springtime.*

SIR,—G. W. B. is anxious to understand the two following passages, 2 Kings ii. 11, and John iii. 13, which appear to be contradictory.   Yours truly,
A BELIEVER.

The apparent contradiction between these two portions of Scripture lies in the statement that 'Elijah went up by a whirlwind into heaven,' and that 'no man hath ascended into heaven, but He that descended out of heaven.' Now if the term heaven means the same thing in both texts they cannot be reconciled; but if the heaven into which it is said Elijah went up is not the heaven of which our Lord speaks, then the difficulty vanishes. There are several words in the Old Testament Scriptures which are used to indicate what is variously meant by the English word heaven. The most common is *shamayim*, and this is the word used in 2 Kings ii. 11. It is a noun in the dual number. And this is supposed by some commentators to imply the existence of a lower and an upper heaven, or of a physical and spiritual heaven, as in the phrase ' the heaven and the heaven of heavens.' This diversity of meaning is referred to in the following quotation from Lampe: ' Generatim cœlum est symbolum rerum omnium supra nos et extra conspectum nostrum in altum evectarum.' Generally heaven is a symbol of every thing stretching away into heights above and beyond our sight. The original idea represented by the root *shamah* is generally conceived to be height; and this is radically the meaning of our English word heaven—what is heaved up, the uplifted expanse in which fowl fly, where the clouds are formed, and upwards to the immense regions which contain innumerable stars; so *shamayim* is synonymous with our English sky. Perhaps a very literal rendering of the text in the Hamiltonian style may be somewhat helpful. ' And it shall be (came to pass) they walking to walk and talked, and behold a chariot of fire and horses of fire, and parted between both, and shall ascend (ascended) Elijah in a storm towards the sky.' It is not here said that Elijah ascended in a fiery chariot drawn by fiery steeds, and thus rode in the midst of flaming fire right into heaven; that would have been as grandly absurd as to suppose that from physical laws, or sensation consciousness, thought and moral faculties would have their origin. The statement substantially is this—as they continued walking, they talked, and a chariot and horses of fire appeared, and parted them, and then being separated, Elijah was caught up and borne towards the sky in a storm of wind, and thus he went heavenwards, not *into* but *towards* heaven. The same expression occurs in the following passages. ' They mount up to the heaven' (Psalm cvii. 26); ' Though Babylon should mount up to heaven' (Jeremiah li. 53). But manifestly neither the mariners referred to by the Psalmist nor the Babylon spoken of by the prophet were conceived of as possibly entering the state of eternal blessedness; that Elijah entered that state cannot be doubted, but that is implied rather than expressed in the text, and many things necessarily connected with this wonderful event are not named.

Were we to join the affirmation in Kings with the negation in John, we should have what in rhetoric is called an antanaclasis, that is, a figure of speech which consists in repeating the same word in a different sense, as, ' gold is gold,' ' the hero was not a hero,' ' learn some *craft* when young, that when old you may live without *craft*.' Thus ' Elijah went up by a whirlwind into heaven,' but ' no man hath ascended up to heaven,' &c. Accepting both statements as true, we must attach one meaning to the term heaven in the first clause, and another to it in the second. If this can be sustained, we get rid of the apparent contradiction. In the conversation recorded by John our Lord calls the attention of Nicodemus to his spiritual obtuseness: ' Art thou the teacher of Israel, and understandest not these things?' — the things which had been the subject of their conversation, namely, the new birth, and the kingdom of God, and especially the new birth as a condition of entering that kingdom ; and 'these things' are described as earthly, not because there is anything carnal in their nature, for there is nothing on earth more spiritual, but because they belong to the sphere of time; the new birth takes place on earth ; the regenerating operations of the Holy Spirit will not be experienced in eternity, they are limited to the earth, to this world, to the present probationary state. These 'earthly things' are placed in antithesis with 'heavenly things,' and they are so designated because they belong to a higher region of thought than any earthly thing. These heavenly things into which the mind of Christ entered in this conversation are so transcendental that no living man while on earth has throughout all the ages ever reached their heights ; neither Moses nor Elijah is an exception. There is, however, One who had done this, for He dwelt in the bosom of the Father before the foundation of the world. In Him are hid all the treasures of wisdom and knowledge. He is the effulgence of His Father's glory and the very image of His substance. He knows the Father, even as the Father knows Him. They are One. He dwelt in all past ages in the supernal heights of eternal truth, and knows all within the infinite extent of divine consciousness. No man has reached this elevation. 'No man hath seen God at any time ; the only begotten Son, which is in the bosom of the Father, He hath declared Him.'

This is the heaven of which Christ spoke. It is His own home, in which He dwelt before He appeared on earth, and even while He was on earth, and where He dwells for ever. This heaven is infinitely different from the sky towards which Elijah was borne. So we conclude that the heaven of the first text is altogether different from that of the second, and that consequently there is no contradiction between them.

In the dark cloud of a great sorrow the beautiful bow of God's promise is often seen, if we look up.—*Chaplin.*

Festive Religion.

CAN religion feast and dance ? Can it tell jolly stories and eat big dinners, as well as fast and pray ? Can it drive a tandem or ride a bicycle, or sail a yacht, as well as walk to the house of God in solemn company ? Can it play the fiddle at a wedding as well as the organ at a funeral ? Can it fire off torpedoes and rockets as well as teach in the Sunday-school ? In short, can it keep holiday with feast and song, as well as Good Friday with penance and sacrament ?

The religion of penance and fasting is good ; it was the religion of John the Baptist. But it is a one-sided religion, a religion not for every man, not for every day. It is not a religion for the complete man. In fact, the penance, and the fasting, and the praying, and the sacrament, are not the religion, but the forms of religion, and helps to religion ; expressions, perhaps, of religion, but the religion is behind them—in the heart, if anywhere, not in the visible show. Jesus prayed by Himself, and He attended the Sabbath services of His people, and He went, when He could, to the regular annual passover at Jerusalem ; but we do not hear of His fasting or of His making much of any religious forms. Indeed, we hear more of His partaking of social feasts. His critics complained that He came eating and drinking, with no show of religious service. When invited to a feast He went. His first miracle was to provide wine for the happiest and merriest of all feasts—the wedding feast of Cana, the invitation to which He accepted and brought His disciples with Him.

We may well understand that God meant us to be happy. For that reason He made all things beautiful. For that reason He put us in households—and ordained all the joys of wedded and family life. It is not the only existing Christian duty to save souls, but it is also a duty to make people happy in common, prosaic ways as we go along. Christians have a special right in whatever is beautiful and happy. If any one can honestly laugh, and shout, and sing, and dance, it is one who has done his duty to his God, and is trying to live a life that will please Him. If any one has a right in a festival, and in all its joys, if any one can '*eat the fat and drink the sweet,*' and make a feast for household and friends, it is one who loves his neighbour as himself, because he has first loved God with all his heart.

But the 'waste of time and money?' That was the voice of Judas Iscariot. The man who enters heartily into the joys of his fellow-men is not one that will shut his purse to their wants. He will be no miser. Let the Christian be one not to be feared for his austerity, but one to be loved for his happy good-fellowship. Remember Jesus, how the poor loved Him for His friendliness, for His approachableness, for His sympathy with human joys. The most holy of all men, the only One absolutely sinless, was warmly, broadly human, not a particle ascetic, a man of feasts rather than fasts. So let our children learn from our example that all the jollities of holiday times are for them, and that all the abandonment of innocent sport and pleasure can be enjoyed by them and sanctified for the spiritual and physical good, and the mental refreshment and growth of those who, with all their young affections, are trying to be children and servants of the blessed Master.   DR. PARKHURST.

The Spoiled Daughter.

IT is not best to love children so well that we make everybody else hate them; and it is a great pity to spoil good material by lack of proper training and bringing up.

A writer in the *Ladies' Home Journal* has some sensible words on this subject:

'I never see a petted, pampered girl, who is yielded to in every whim by the servants and parents, that I do not sigh with and for the man who will some day be her husband. It is the worshipped daughter, who has been taught that her whims and wishes are supreme in a household, who makes marriage a failure all her life. She has had her way in things great and small, and when she desired dresses, pleasures, or journeys which were beyond the family purse, she carried the day with tears or sulks, or posing as a martyr. The parents sacrificed and suffered for her sake, hoping finally to see her well married. They carefully hide her faults from suitors who seek her hand, and she is ever ready with smiles and allurements to win the hearts of men; and the average man is as blind to the faults of a pretty girl as a newly-hatched bird is blind to the worms upon the trees about him. He thinks her little pettish ways are mere girlish moods, but when she becomes his wife and reveals her selfish and cruel nature he is grieved and hurt to think fate has been so unkind to him.'

Young men will do well to think twice before they link their destinies with those of the spoiled daughters of silly and indulgent parents.

Things that Never Die.

THE pure, the bright, the beautiful,
   That stirred our hearts in youth,
The impulse of a wordless prayer,
   The dream of love and truth,
The longing after something lost,
   The Spirit's yearning cry,
The striving after better hopes—
   These things shall never die.

The timid hand stretched forth to aid
   The brother in his need,
The kindly word in grief's dark hour
   That proves a friend indeed,
The plea for mercy, softly breathed,
   When Justice threatens nigh;
The sorrowings of a contrite heart—
   These things shall never die.

Let nothing pass, for every hand
   Must find some work to do;
Lose not a chance to waken love,
   Be firm, and just, and true;
So shall a light that cannot fade
   Beam on thee from on high,
And angels' voices say to thee,
   'These things can never die.'

SPRINGTIME:

A Magazine for Our Young Men and Maidens.

VOL. VI. No. 12.]   DECEMBER, 1891.   [PRICE TWOPENCE.

A Bad Calculation.

BY ROBERT HIND,

Author of ' Crosby Dalton : Local Preacher and Village Demagogue,' ' The Ruby Pendant,' &c.

CHAPTER XXIII.

FORSAKEN AND ALONE.

'Hard are thy ways when that one thing is sought,
  Found, touched, and proven nought.
Far off it is a mighty magic, strong
    To lead a life along.
But, lo! it shooteth thitherward, and now
Droppeth, a rayless stone, upon the sod.—
    The world is lost.'

ROBERT BUCHANAN.

ou must be something of a prophet.'

Isa Saunders was the speaker, and her words were addressed to Arthur Brixton, on the day after he had made the proposal which, conditionally, she had half accepted.

'With respect to what, may I ask ?' Arthur inquired.

'We are to leave Rockingham.'

Arthur was startled, and did not hide his surprise.

'You are surprised,' the young lady continued ; 'and so am I. All kinds of astonishing things do happen, and therefore, if that were possible, we should always be expecting the unexpected. I was sufficiently in the dark not to expect this.'

'You go soon ? '

'Almost immediately. You know we are birds of passage, and never settle long in one place.'

'And where will you settle next ? '

'Not so far away. We go to Highbridge. Father must have tired rather suddenly of catching the train every morning, and, after his work was over, finding himself all these miles from home. So we learned last night he had actually taken a house, and we shall leave this at once.'

Arthur tried to console himself with the thought that Isa's affections were his, and, go where they might, he would always have the right to claim her as his friend, and some day more than his friend. And yet her manner of speaking about it made him uncertain even on this point. He was serious and depressed ; she, on the contrary, appeared quite light-hearted, and spoke of the matter even flippantly.

In truth she was as tired of Rockingham as her father and all the rest of them unquestionably were, although none of them had cared to confess it even to each other.

'Why have you come to this conclusion so suddenly ?' Mrs. Saunders had asked, when she and her husband were alone.

His manner of speaking to his wife when he had not on his ' company' airs was not the most gentle and polite.

'Suddenly! You should know me better than that by this time. I don't do these things suddenly. And you should have no difficulty in answering your question yourself.'

Mrs. Saunders did not grow angry or turn pale. She had become accustomed to these tempers of her husband. Of course they did not increase her respect for him, but she bore them with a kind of cynical good-nature.

'I might answer my own question, no doubt, but I wanted you to answer it.'

'Very well. I hate Rockingham.'

He spoke loudly and with a brutal plainness.

'And yet Rockingham is a lovely place. I am not romantic myself, and so cannot go into raptures about it like some people I have heard. But even I can see that it is a delightful old city in many respects.'

'And its people equally so.'

'At least they are select,' she remarked, with just the slightest emphasis on the last word.

'I agree with you. They are too select for us, and, seeing you are resolved to humiliate me by compelling me to say what you know is in my mind, let me get it over at once. I am sick of this struggle to break down prejudice. We are making no headway, and may as well acknowledge defeat. We have not much of a circle in Highbridge. They are afraid of our company even there—at least, those whom one would like best to call friends, —but Highbridge is not so exclusive as Rockingham.'

Isa had felt their lonely position as much as her elders. To her the antiquated old city was a place of exile. She could not see its beauty, and, being poverty-stricken in mind, with no resources within herself, she could not be happy without a good deal of visiting, and constant parties and pic-nics. From this kind of life she had been almost completely shut out at Rockingham. At Highbridge she thought all would be changed, and hence her pleasure at the prospect.

In two weeks from that time the house in Canongate was tenantless. With the departure of Mr. Saunders and his family, well-nigh the last bit of sunshine had gone out of Arthur Brixton's life.

A glimmering still remained.

'You will come every week to visit us? We shall all be glad to see you,' Isa said to him.

But the first time he called she had gone out, and would not be home till late. Mr. Saunders was at home, and was amiable in a patronising way, but Arthur felt unhappy as he returned home. He did not repeat his visit for two or three weeks. This time Isa was at home to welcome him, but there were other friends there, and of a class he had not met with before. He tried to talk with them, but found it impossible. And in his difficulty he remembered Jack Benson, and thought of all the times he had been in his company. Had Jack been present he would have conversed with him quite easily, because Jack had an intelligent and active mind. But these young men chatted about the 'Browns' of 'the Crescent,' and the 'Joneses' of 'the Square,' of the party that was held last week at the former place, and the one to be held next week at the latter. Arthur knew nothing of these things, and could not say one word about them.

Once or twice he tried to speak of a subject which they might find common ground for all, but the young men to whom he spoke answered him with vacant monosyllables. What was he to do?

'Who are these young men?' he inquired of Isa, in the only five minutes she gave him.

'They are young men of Highbridge. I cannot tell you much about them. Their fathers are friends of my father—merchants, I suppose, of some kind.'

'And rich?'

'I suppose so. But why should you ask such a question?'

'I was thinking their fathers must be different from them, or they would not be merchants.'

'Don't be severe, Arthur,' the young lady said, and turned away to devote her attention to some one else.

Two days after he received a little note from her, expressing her regret that he should find the company of her friends so irksome, and, fearing she had already made too great a demand upon his valuable time, begging to release him from his promise to call upon them in Highbridge.

The letter was freezingly polite, but it did

not surprise him. In his present state of mind hardly anything would have surprised him. He understood it quite well, and knew that his friendship was no longer wanted. The circumstance gave him an insight into the character of those whom he had admired and in some degree envied. He thought of Isa, fair and false, playing with his infatuation; of her new lover, some silly young man of her own class; and of the vain, foolish life she would live. And although he felt sore at heart, he was not sorry that an end had been brought to the delusion under which he had laboured.

With Arthur Brixton it was a time of crisis. He might, he thought, pursue the course upon which he had entered, not without some success in the end. But he could not shut out of his mind thoughts of what might have been had he cultivated a more contented spirit, and been true to the religious principles in which he had been trained. There were in him some repugnant feelings as he contrasted, with the light recent events had cast upon them, the difference between Isa Saunders and Rye Harland. It was not simply that he felt his circumstances would have been better to-day; there was regret also that he had not shown himself to be more worthy and heroic, more manly and less self-seeking. He might change, and as far as possible bring himself back into the old groove. 'Should he?' was the question he asked himself during the next few days—with what result we shall see.

CHAPTER XXIV.

THE CLOUDS DISPERSED.

'So my doubting days are ended,
  And the labour of life seems clear;
And life hums deeply around me,
  Just like the murmur here;
And quickens the sense of living,
  And shapes me for peace and storm,--
And dims my eye with gladness
  When it glides into colour and form.'
ROBERT BUCHANAN.

ON the following Sabbath evening, as Rye Harland, along with the other members of the family at the Mount, reached the gate in front of the Methodist chapel to which they were going for divine service, they met Arthur Brixton with his father and mother, who were on a similar errand. For months past Arthur had not been there, and his father and mother had been as much astonished as delighted when that evening he joined them. Rye had noticed his absence, and now, still friendly in her heart towards him, quite eagerly held out her hand.

'You never come to the Mount now,' she exclaimed in her gladness, forgetting in her pity for him that his visits had not yielded much pleasure.

Arthur excused himself for his lack in duty, but said he would call soon.

'I noticed you two young men did not shake hands, but simply bowed in a coldly polite fashion,' she said to Jack Benson that night after the service. 'There has not been any difference, I hope?'

'How anxious you are for us to be friends. Arthur, I am sure, does not care for my company.'

'You speak with great confidence. He has not Canongate to go to now, and I invited him specially to come to the Mount sometimes. Were you not glad to see him at chapel?'

'You compel me to be frank. I was not particularly glad. I might have been, perhaps, had I known everything, but as I know nothing of what has induced him to come after all these months of absence, I cannot pretend to feel unduly elated about it.'

'It is not like you to be ill-natured, Jack. I suspect Arthur has made some mistake,— committed a sin against a rule in that peculiar code of honour which young men sometimes put in the place of the ten commandments. You said you might tell me what it is some day. You must choose the day yourself, for of course I cannot ask you again.'

'I will tell you after he calls upon you.'

When Arthur came, his friends noticed his bearing was quiet even for him, and his face, sad as ever, had in it an expression more soft and subdued than he was accustomed to wear. In the course of the evening Rye and he were alone in the dining-room.

'We were glad you were at the chapel on Sunday evening,' she said. And then, as there was an uncomfortable pause, she added,—

'You must not think we are very much against you for going into the Church of England. You had a right to judge for yourself. Of course we were disappointed, but we hope you will get on well, and live a good and useful life. And even though you are to be a clergyman, it must be nice in the meantime for your father and mother to have you with them at chapel.'

'I do not think I shall be a clergyman. Indeed, I have made up my mind that I won't.'

Rye opened her eyes, but did not know exactly what to say.

'I have not found the change quite what I expected it would be, and events have happened lately which have opened my eyes. I see things differently now from what I did when I so foolishly opposed your wishes and the wishes of Mr. Harland; and I hope God has forgiven me.'

Had Rye looked for this she could not have held back her feelings, but, coming as it did quite unexpectedly, a great tenderness for her old lover took possession of her heart. Still she did not speak, but waited and listened.

'I shall try, of course, to complete my university course. And as I have just lately realized a great love for the work of the ministry, I shall offer myself to my father's church. You see I hardly dare just yet call it "our church."'

What more was said at that time need not be related. The story soon came to Jack's ears, and his heart was generous enough to be glad. Still, mingled with his pleasure was a feeling of anxiety. He would settle it once and for ever. If Rye really loved Arthur still, what had just taken place would reveal it to her own heart at least, and he was sure that to her heart she would be true. He desired this, for, much as he now knew he loved her, he would not think of trying to win her hand if her affections belonged to another. With her softened feelings towards Arthur, and the new position in which he had put himself, there was not much danger of her falling into that error.

He did not attempt gradually to lead up to

the matter in his heart, but in an open manner told her his feelings, and asked her if she could return them. What could she say? She had admired him when first her eyes fell upon him at the railway-station. Often she remembered, in the days when she was engaged to Arthur, she had wished he had been more like Jack Benson. Still later Jack had endeared himself to her by his kindness to Arthur, at a time when that young man, she was bound to admit, was not conducting himself in the best possible manner. And so she gave to the young Australian her heart and hand.

'Now you will tell me why you have changed towards Arthur?' she said.

And Jack, with a hesitating tongue, told her the story he had heard from Frank Everton. When he had finished, she said,

'That was Arthur as we have known him lately. But it is not the Arthur that I knew long ago, and not the Arthur that is to-day.'

'What curious opinions you entertain! I should have believed, but for you, that I have never heard of any other Arthur Brixton save one.'

'You have never understood him. Indeed, I am not sure I have, although I know more about him than you. He has his faults, and one of them, for a little while, took him under its power, and led him astray on many things. But he is clever, and not without some goodness. For a few months he has been the slave of a notion. It was a poor notion, but he was too good at bottom not to find out his mistake ere long, and conquer in the end. The end has come already, much sooner than I expected, and he will be a better man for what he has suffered than he could have been without it.'

Jack listened to all this in not the best frame of mind.

'I almost wish I had been the slave of a poor notion,' he said.

'Why?'

'Then I might find a defender who would excuse it, and discover in me some good qualities of which I am not conscious.'

'It appears to me,' Rye observed, with a

laughing twinkle in her eye, 'that your wish is going to be gratified.'

'How so?'

'Are you not becoming the slave of a poor notion, sir?'

She had read his jealous thought, and he felt ashamed of it. But this, instead of leading him to deny it, only paved the way to confession.

'And if I am, is there no reason? I loved you when I believed you belonged to another, and after that engagement was broken my mouth was stopped because I was made to think, by your solicitude for him, your heart was still his. And now, after you have made me happy, the cup of joy is mingled with some unpleasant ingredient, because you must needs chant the praises of your old lover. Perhaps it is very foolish on my part, but it is very human too.'

'What can I do,' she asked archly, 'to help you out of your difficulty?'

'You can tell me that in no circumstances would you consent to give your hand to Arthur Brixton, and that you have ceased to love him in that way.'

'To your first statement I agree; to the second I cannot.'

To say he was startled will only convey a very inadequate notion of the impression produced on him by Rye's words. He could not understand the situation, for she was not in the least agitated—indeed her face wore an expression betokening an unusual gaiety.

'You have not ceased to love him in that way?' he repeated.

'No.'

He had laid his hand on her arm, but when she had spoken that monosyllable it dropped, and a look of unutterable pain passed over his face.'

'Forgive me!' she exclaimed. 'You misunderstand me. I *never have* loved him "in that way." I thought I did, but I was mistaken, and so you see I cannot cease doing what I have never done.'

'I am more than satisfied,' he said hurriedly. 'But what an agony you put me into, and how foolish I have been!'

They talked for an hour or more of those things which are so full of interest to lovers, and so devoid of meaning to all the rest of the world. It was a sweet and pleasant hour to both of them—an hour in which the great world outside themselves was lost sight of.

'I had a letter from Australia to-day,' Jack observed, by-and-bye. 'I hope,' he added, 'you will like Australia.'

Rye turned pale, and replied, catching her breath as she spoke—

'Oh yes, I shall like it.'

'But not so well as Rockingham. You told me once there was no place in all the world like Rockingham.'

He spoke lightly, but she felt serious, and there was no joy in her tone as she answered,

'I think so still. I shall always think so. But I can love other places a great deal. Still I shall feel it very keenly when I have to say farewell to it. Going to Australia is different from going to some other part of England. In the latter case one could visit it sometimes and think of the Mount as home.'

'And yet you will go with me to Australia?'

'Yes, I will go.'

'What will you say when I tell you there is no need?'

'What do you mean?'

'Just this. My father, in the letter I had to-day, informs me he has made up his mind to sell out and return to England. And he is going to live in or near Rockingham. The place must be enchanted, for it seems that he regards it with much the same feelings as you.'

'That is just delightful! You cannot imagine what a load has gone from my mind. I love Rockingham, but you know there are those in Rockingham I love more dearly than the old city, with all its beauty and grand associations. When you asked that question just now, that cost me so much to answer, I was not thinking of Rockingham, but of father and mother.'

'To have taken you sixteen thousand miles from them would have been very cruel indeed.'

'And now you will be a Methodist minister in England, and perhaps, some day, of this very city of Rockingham. How delightful! And in a few months your father and mother will be here, and will be buying "Bellemont," or "Western Lodge," or some of the big houses about the place. But I shan't be afraid of him, because he was my father's friend, and because, sir, he is your father.'

We may leave our two friends in their enjoyment of a pleasant prospect. It was all realized in time. As for Arthur Brixton, he, like his friend Jack Benson (and they are true friends), in time became an able minister of the Methodist denomination. Always, however, there is a soberness and reserve in his bearing which prevent him from being as popular as the open-minded, sunny-natured Mr. Benson; and in his bachelorhood sadly does he think of a youthful infatuation that lost him one of the finest women in England.

THE END.

A New Year's Eve.

NCE more, 'A NEW YEAR'S EVE!'
    My strain began
    With sober thoughts—with such
       it well may end :
For when, O when should these come home
    to man,
    With such a season if they may not
       blend ?
My gentle reader, let an unknown friend
    Remind thee of the ceaseless lapse of time !
Nor will his serious tone thine ear offend,
    If love may plead his pardon for the crime
Of blending solemn truth with minstrel's
       simple rhyme.

Christ died for ALL. But in that general debt
    He bled to cancel—dost not thou partake ?
Is *thine*, too, blotted out ? O do not set
    Upon a doubtful issue such a stake !
Each faculty of soul and sense awake ;
    Trust not a *general* truth which may be
       vain
To thee ; but rather, for thy Saviour's sake,
    And for thine own, some evidence attain :
For thee indeed He died—for thee hath risen
       again.

Are thy looks white with many long-past
    years ?
    One more is dawning : which thy last may
       be.
Art thou in middle age, by worldly fears
    And hopes surrounded ? Set thy spirit
       free,
More awful fears, more glorious hopes to
    see.
    Art thou in blooming youth ? Thyself
       engage
To serve and honour HIM who unto thee
    Would be a Guide and Guard through
       life's first stage,
Wisdom in manhood's strength, and green-
       ness in old age.

              BERNARD BARTON.

Christmas Gossip.

HRISTMAS ! Who does not love the very name ? Christmas, uniter of the parted, the reconciler of disputes, the generous helper of the poor, the indulgent friend of childhood. Christmas, associated from our earliest years with pleasures and gifts. A festive season, all the more welcome from the fact of its coming at the very dreariest and most dead season of the year. Nor does it take off from the real significance and sacredness of Christmas to be told that in the northern countries of Europe, at least, this Christian festival is engrafted on a heathen one.

Whether the tradition of our Lord's having been born at this season be true or not, certain it is that our pagan forefathers had, long before the introduction of Christianity, a festival they called Yule (the name by which Christmas is still designated in Sweden and Denmark), which was kept during the last days of December, and to which the early missionaries did not put a stop, as by so doing they would have lost their hold upon their converts. Wisely they determined to regulate these festivities and to connect them with Christian associations, just as the missionaries in the South Sea Islands at the present day endeavour to regulate and control the pantomimic dances and similar amusements of the natives, feeling that to put them down would be impossible, owing to the deep root they have taken in the popular heart. But the festival of Christmas has for so many ages been associated all over Christendom with the birth of our Redeemer, that even though its origin *may* have been partly pagan, it ever brings to us a reminder of the cradle of Bethlehem, and is, therefore, to all intents and purposes a Christian festival. Would that it were always more Christianly observed; that there were more sobriety, less excess, more done to brighten the lives of the poor at this season, even than there is. But there has been a wonderful improvement in this respect of late years.

In England there are few traces of the old pagan element in the observance of Christmas. In some parts of the country, indeed, the log burned on the Christmas hearth is called the *Yule* log (or clog, or block), but the name has otherwise died out. Some trace the word Yule to the worship of the sun, and identify it with Welsh *haul*, Latin *sol*, etc., but that seems to be a far-fetched origin, and we feel more disposed to agree with those who connect it with *wheel*, because it comes just at the *turn* of the year.

In Germany the observance of Christmas bears many traces of the old worship of Thor, and of Odin or Woden—though few of those who keep up the ancient rites are probably aware of their being relics of paganism. Just about a fortnight before Christmas Day a mysterious personage, called in different localities ' Pelz Nickel ' (Furry Nicholas), ' Kuecht Ruprecht' (Servant Rupert), and ' The Christmas Man ' pays a visit to the children.

' " Pelz Nickel," ' says William Howitt in his work on Germany, ' is a man disguised in a fur cap, carrying a rod, having a capacious sack, pouch, or bag, a large chain thrown round him. . . . and sometimes a number of little bells about him. . . . His name of *Servant* Rupert is most likely derived from the idea that he is the servant of the Christ-child, who sends him to prepare for His own arrival on Christmas Eve. He is, in fact, some servant or dependent of the family, who engage him to undertake this office, and furnish him with the necessary information. The children above eight or nine years of age are let into the secret. . . . The younger children, as the time draws on, are often reminded that Christmas is coming, and that according as they are good or naughty he will reward them. . . . This has a strong effect upon the children—they have a notion that Pelz Nickel, or the Christ-child, has his eyes upon them when they are not aware.'

' About St. Nicholas's Day '* (Furry Nicholas has been supposed to be St. Nicholas, the patron-saint of children) ' all is expectation, and scarcely is tea over ere there comes a ring at the door-bell. The door opens, and in stalks the strange figure of Pelz Nickel.' He questions the children as to their lessons, and perhaps asks to see the school-books, but still more does he examine them as to their conduct, startling them by his, to them, incomprehensible knowledge as to what they have done that is wrong, threatening them with punishment or promising rewards, as the case may be, and ending the performance by throwing from his bag nuts, apples, and cakes upon the floor, during the general scramble for which he disappears.

This mysterious personage, though the idea is made use of for the purpose of inciting small children to be good, and though he is identified to a certain extent with St. Nicholas, the patron-saint of childhood, seems really to mean Odin, who was especially worshipped at Yuletide, and concerning whose appearance on earth and interference with the concerns of mortals at this particular season there are innumerable legends in North Germany. A good many of these stories confuse the idea of Odin with that of that hero of popular legend, the ' Wild Huntsman ';† but the huntsman possesses many of the attributes of the old god. Odin appears

---

* December 9th.

† A wicked, profane man who hunted on Sundays and other sacred days instead of going to church, and was punished by having, according to the legend, to continue hunting after death.

again in many of the old masques and dramas in Germany, under the title of Schimmel-Reiter (Rider of the pied horse), which evidently refers to Odin's horse in the ancient mythology. But there is no mythology, only Christian tradition, in the idea of the Christ-kindchen, the Child-Christ, who is supposed to come down from heaven and present to the children the treasures of the Christmas tree. In some parts of Germany a young person—curiously enough, most frequently a girl—is actually dressed up to represent Christ-kindchen, and stands beside the Christmas tree, with a gilt crown and wings and long veil ornamented with gold. To the English mind there is something repulsively irreverent, not to say profane, in this. We do not, however, find that it appears in that light to the Germans—probably long usage, dating from unenlightened, half barbarous ages, has accustomed them to the idea. The Christmas tree is regarded by some antiquarians as a pagan idea, a relic of the Eastern tree-worship, brought from the far East by the first ancestors of the German races. It is now, we believe, universal throughout Denmark, Sweden, and Norway, and to a certain extent universal throughout Germany, the only exception in the latter country being, that in the Roman Catholic districts, as in other Continental countries, instead of a tree laden with fruit, lights, and gifts, a representation is made in miniature, sometimes small and rude, sometimes costly and on a large scale, of the manger at Bethlehem, with the accompani·ment of the Saviour's cradle, the oxen, the asses, and figures to represent the Virgin Mary, Joseph, and the shepherds. The Christmas tree seems to be considered in Germany somewhat as an accompaniment of Protestantism. It has been introduced, as we all know, largely into English Christmas festivities of late years, to the great delectation of the juveniles, and it is a great improvement upon the jovial and somewhat vulgar old English celebration of Christmas with its sirloins of beef and kissing under the mistletoe bough. Our popular personification of 'Father Christmas,' as a jolly red-faced man with a long white beard, is perhaps taken from some old farce or comedy, and has nothing in common with Pelz Nickel,

the Christmas Man, etc., beings whose existence is really believed in by German children.

Of course, in connection with such a season, popular superstition and credulity have been busy, and many are the legends of Christmastide. One of these superstitions held in various localities is that on Christmas Eve no evil spirit is able to do harm, and that at twelve o'clock on that night oxen kneel down in their stalls. Mrs. Jameson tells us, in her ' Sacred and Legendary Art, that there was an ancient legend of the ox and the ass in the stable at Bethlehem accompanying the Holy Family in their flight into Egypt. Oxen seem to figure especially in Christmas legends.* Here is one : In a village in the north of Germany, called Neckitz, it was the custom to usher in Christmas by ringing the church bells. ' After a time, however, the inhabitants of the village grew lazy, careless, and irreverent, and the bells no longer sounded out at the holy season. But once again at midnight on Christmas Eve the well-known sound arose from the churchtower. The sexton ran in great excitement to the pastor, and the two men went to the top of the tower together, to see who it was that was ringing, and saw, to their extreme astonishment, a milk-white bull pulling the bell-rope. A rope ladder was procured, and the mysterious animal came quietly down from the belfry, descending the steps of the ladder gently and carefully. But directly after it had come down it disappeared.'†

Our own custom of decorating churches and houses at Christmas is said, like the Christmas tree, to have had a pagan origin. Antiquarians derive it from the custom of the ancient Romans to decorate their houses for their festival of the Saturnalia, which, like our Christmas, took place in December.

Strutt, in his amusing work, ' Sports and Pastimes of the People of England,' traces the ' Lord of Misrule,' that marked feature in the old English Christmas pastimes, also to the Saturnalia. He says : ' It is said of the English that formerly they were remarkable

---

* Perhaps eating beef at Christmas has some connection with this.

† ' Legends, Traditions, and Superstitions of Mecklenburgh,' by Carl Bartsch.

for the manner in which they celebrated the festival of Christmas, at which season they admitted a variety of sports and pastimes not practised in other countries. The mock prince, or Lord of Misrule, whose reign extended through the greater part of the holidays, is particularly remarked by foreign writers as a personage rarely to be met with out of England.' This Lord of Misrule was an officer appointed to superintend the Christmas revels in royal palaces and the houses of the nobility: he had a number of men under him, who were all attired gaily in green, yellow, and other light colours, and otherwise fantastically got up. A Puritan writer says:

'As though they were not gaudy enough, they bedecke themselves with scarffes, ribbons, and laces, hanged all over with gold ringes, pretious stones, and other jewels. This done, they tie aboute either legge twentie or fourtie belles, with riche handkerchiefes in their handes, and sometimes laide across their shoulders and neckes.'

Several other mock dignitaries were elected to preside over Christmas sports (though some were confined to particular localities), as the King of Christmas, the King of the Bean, and the Bishop of Fools, which latter functionary, while satirizing the mummeries of the Church of Rome, doubtless did and said much that was profane and irreverent respecting things really sacred. The King of the Bean is described thus by Strutt:—

'We read that some time back it was a common Christmas gambol, in both universities and other places, to give the name of king or queen to that person whose extraordinary good luck it was to hit upon that part of a divided cake which was honoured above the others by having a bean in it. The reader' (Strutt goes on to say) 'will readily trace the vestige of this custom, though somewhat differently managed, and without the bean, in the present method of " drawing," as it is called, for king and queen on Twelfth Day.'

In Scotland and other localities the bean is still baked in twelfth cakes and birthday ones, with a coin to indicate the finder will be rich, and a thimble to show that anyone cutting that slice will, if a female, remain unmarried.

All these grotesque dignities—Lord of Misrule, Bishop of Fools, King of the Bean, etc.—Strutt considers to be derived from the old Saturnalia, or feasts of Saturn, when the masters waited upon their servants, who were honoured with mock titles, and permitted to assume the state and deportment of their lords.

'The Mirror,' an old magazine of between sixty and seventy years ago, gives a curious description of some Christmas customs still existing at that date, particularly in Yorkshire, and with them we may close our desultory 'gossip.' Perhaps some of the customs alluded to still exist in remote country places. 'In the north they have yet their "fools' plough," and in Cornwall their "goose-dancers."'* The latter still exhibit an old hunch-backed man called "The King of Christmas," and sometimes "The Father." The wassail-bowl was regularly carried from door to door in Cornwall forty or fifty years ago, and even now a measure of flip, ale, porter, and sugar, or some such beverage, is handed round while the Yule log is burning. The first intimation of Christmas in Yorkshire is by what are there called "*the vessel-cup singers*," generally poor old women who, about three weeks before Christmas, go from house to house with a waxen or a wooden doll, fantastically dressed, and sometimes adorned with an orange, or a fine rosy-tinged apple. With this in their hands they sing or chant an old carol, of which the following homely stanza forms a part—

> " God bless the master of this house,
>   The mistress also,
>   And all the little children,
>   That round the table go."

'The image of the child is, no doubt, intended to represent the infant Saviour. The "vessel-cup" is probably the remains of the wassail-bowl.' The writer goes on to speak of the housewife putting a scratch in the dough of her pastry to denote the manger. Time and space fail us, or we might just glance at the modes of celebrating Christmas in some other lands, such as France, Italy, and Spain, all of them being picturesque and characteristic. The representation of the Saviour's manger-bed is a highly elaborate affair in Rome.

JESSIE YOUNG.

* Probably '*guise-dancers*,' i.e., *disguised dancers*.

Sketches of the British Isles.

SANDOWN AND SHANKLIN.

N the south-eastern coast of the Isle of Wight, between the chalk headlands of Culver cliffs and the steep sandy promontory of Dunnose point, is the spacious expanse of Sandown Bay; specially characterized for its invigorating sea-breezes, and the evenness of its salubrious climate. On the shores of the centre of the extensive curving inland sea is the attractive watering-place of Sandown. Within the memory of the present generation, where Sandown is built, there was only an unpretentious village. Its rapid development is traceable to the opening of the railway from Ryde. The sea-front is occupied with long terraces of comfortable houses, and pretty detached villas, with their verandahs almost reaching to the water's edge. The favourite promenades are the substantial iron-work pier and the esplanade, bounded on either side by the sea-wall, and a covered arcade. The pier or landing-place is protected by the Barrack Battery, which has replaced an antiquated fort, that was built during Cromwellian times. Sandown Castle, erected as one of the coast defence-works during the reign of Henry VIII., has entirely disappeared. The business part of the town is well supplied with a number of excellent shops. The sands afford a delightful recreation ground for both young and old. During the last century Sandown was the favourite marine residence of the notorious John Wilkes. At Sandown, the Emperor and Empress of Germany spent the summer of 1874. Amongst the favourite resorts of Sandown are the ancient church and Elizabethan manor-house of Yanerland; and also the higher ranges of Whitcliffe Downs, where a lofty column has been erected in memory of the second Earl of

Yarborough, and also as a recognition of his services as the founder and first Commodore of the Royal Yacht Squadron. Northwards of Sandown is the unsophisticated sea-board village of Bembridge with its interesting glade, called the Ducie Avenue, oyster fisheries, and celebrated Golf Links. Further still, is the antiquated village of St. Helens, with its ancient houses clustered around the green. About the year 1155 a Cluniac Priory was founded, probably from which the village derives its name. The revenues were confiscated during the reign of Henry VI., and devoted to the erection of the famous college of Eton. A much-frequented walk from Sandown is to the hamlet of Morton, where, in 1880, through the merest accident, excavations were subsequently made, which resulted in unearthing the remains of a Roman Villa, that evidently belonged to some person of considerable wealth and social importance. The discovery is one of the most valuable of antiquarian lore that has been made. The buildings comprise an entrance-court and twelve rooms; one of which is a chamber of considerable extent, with a handsome mosaic-work flooring. Another building on the east contains a hypocaust. The articles that have been found comprise pottery, household utensils, and coins, the more recent being those of the reign of Constans, 350 A.D.

Two miles to the south of Sandown, and on much higher ground, is its noted rival, Shanklin. It is no longer 'small and scattery,' as it was locally described nearly forty years ago, but a compact 'townlet,' with an enterprising governing Local Board. The town may be divided into three distinct groups—commercial, residential, and pleasure-seeking. Its High-street is well supplied with commodious shops, and from this business thoroughfare numerous branching road-ways lead to the shore. The residential portion consists of stately mansions built in their own grounds, on the summits of the cliffs. The boarding houses for visitors are built beneath the sheltering cliffs, and face the sea-shore. The great source of unrivalled attraction at Shanklin is the fairy-like glen, or as it is termed Shanklin Chine, which may be fittingly described as the 'gem' of all the noted beauties of the Isle of Wight. This popular ravine, which gradually slopes to the sea, is about a quarter of a mile long, and terminates at the mouth with an inner depth of two hundred feet. The chasm has been formed by the action of the dripping water, which has worn away the brown sand-stone face-work of rock, and strikingly illustrates the declaration of Scripture, 'That the waters wear the stones.' At an angle of the road leading from Shanklin to the upper entrance of the Chine, is a miniature drinking-fountain,

analysis of its iron-charged and chemical constituents. On the immediate right is the first or principal fall of the crystal stream, which gains a depth of over forty feet. During the months of summer the water-fall is often disappointing, owing to the limited supply of water issuing from the rocks. However, the luxuriant herbage, many-tinted mosses, variegated ivies, graceful ferns, leafy trees, with the back-ground of the Chine, consisting of richly coloured crags, makes a picture that the student of nature is enraptured with. The

SANDOWN.

protected by a rock-work of stone slabs, and bearing an invitation to the weary traveller, written in the year 1868 by Longfellow, the American bard:—

> 'O traveller, stay thy weary feet,
> Drink of this fountain, pure and sweet:
> It flows for rich and poor the same.
> Then go thy way, remembering still
> The wayside well beneath the hill,
> The cup of water in His name.'

The entrance lodge to the Chine is at the extreme end of a shady lane. Within the gates and on the left hand side is a chalybeate spring; and the visitor is favoured with an

labyrinthian paths of the Chine wind amidst a profuse growth of underwood. This fairy-like region is furnished with rustic seats, and at intervals the cascade is crossed by rural and fantastic bridges of wood-work, from whence the visitor may look upwards to the sky-line, and the streaks of golden sunshine; or downwards upon the beauties in the bewildering depths below. At one or two points, where the Chine widens, delightful views are gained of the expansive waters of Sandown Bay. Some persons prefer exploring this natural botanical museum by entering the

Chine from the lower entrance, when they are delighted with what the wits call ' an ascending scale of beauty.' Adjoining the Chine is a refreshment bar and resting-room, well supplied with the leading newspapers and monthlies.

A tragic event is associated with the history of the Chine. During the French War of 1545 a detachment of French soldiers, under the command of Chevalier d'Eulx, ventured on shore to obtain supplies of fresh water from the cascade of the Chine. Owing to the smallness of the stream, the work of serving the ships with water was exceedingly monotonous. The Chevalier, who had been appointed with a few companies of soldiers to protect the watering parties, had not the slightest apprehension of danger, and accordingly wandered inland, where he was trapped in an ambuscade ; and, as the historians say, the Chevalier, ' after defending himself like a hero, was killed, and most of his followers.'

Within easy walking distance of Shanklin are many interesting localities and choice bits of island scenery. The walk along the shore to Luccombe Chine is both interesting and profitable. Luccombe is about a mile distant from Shanklin, in a southerly direction. The pedestrian, while inhaling the ozone-charged breezes, may employ his leisure in gathering the fossils for the enrichment of his cabinet, belonging to the Lower Greensand, or scientifically speaking the Neocamian formation ; or if he have an aptitude for sketching he can find many beautiful scenes for his ' brush and canvas,' and if he should care for neither, he can still derive pleasure from the sights of land and ocean. The higher road to Luccombe over the lofty chalk cliffs rivals the path along the shore. Magnificent views of wide-stretched sea-scapes are obtained, and the inland panorama of far-reaching downs is equally interesting.

Luccombe consists of a wide declivity in the hills, with grassy banks and slopes stretching downwards to the sea, where are the rude dwellings of the fishermen. The Chine is a narrow winding descent, with a murmuring streamlet flowing amidst a lavish profusion of old Dame Nature's beautiful flowers and foliage. About two miles inland, and equi-distant from Shanklin and Luccombe, amid undulating farm lands, is Appuldurcombe House, an imposing eighteenth century residence belonging to the Worsleys—one of the historic families belonging to the Isle of Wight. The fine park encircling the hall contains many fine natural beauties. On the adjoining downs is an imposing granite obelisk, perpetuating the name and memory of Sir Robert Worsley, the founder of the present mansion.

> ' Any man that walks the mead,
>   In bud, or blade, or bloom may find,
> According as his humours lead,
>   A meaning suited to his mind.'

On the Sunday afternoon of March 24, 1878, Her Majesty's training-ship *Eurydice* was lost in the waters of Sandown Bay, and within only two to three miles distance from the shores of Shanklin. The vessel had a displacement of nine hundred and twenty-one tons, carried four guns, and had a crew of over three hundred efficient second-class seamen, who had nearly completed their period of training. She was returning from Bermuda, and was only two hours' sail from harbour. When passing Dunnose, with open ports and full sail flying, she was caught in a sudden squall. She heeled over, and the waters rushed across her decks and through her open portways. She righted herself, and was struck a second time, and immediately foundered. Only two of the crew escaped. Several pathetic incidents of the catastrophe are related. In one street in Southsea more than one half of the houses were darkened with the signs of mourning for the loss of husbands or sons. They were near the white cliffs of England, and were full of expectation. One of the officers was anticipating rejoining his wife to whom he had been married shortly before the outward voyage. On board were also five prisoners, one of whom was in irons, and these along with the happier ones perished beneath the waves. Shortly afterwards, the unfortunate vessel was raised and beached near the Culver Cliffs, and was subsequently broken up.

ALBERT A. BIRCHENOUGH.

Our Domestic Pets.

THE RABBIT.

HE rabbit is one of those few animals in England known in the wild and also in the domesticated condition. In large books that deal with things in general, such as the Encyclopædia, the subject is often considered with that of the hare, which in many respects differs from the rabbit. It is not within the province of a brief article to deal with those differences. It is manifest that there is a difference between the wild rabbit and the domesticated. The wild rabbit weighs from two to three pounds, and its skin consists of thick hair of a dark grey. The domesticated rabbit has a fine skin of almost every variety of colour, and is sometimes fed up to fourteen pounds. The wild rabbit burrows in the ground, and makes an underground path stretching a long way, making for itself a road through an estate with which it becomes thoroughly acquainted. It knows all the windings of the road, so that if it should be hunted by a dog it knows the ground and the various turns it may take with advantage. The path which it makes for itself is too narrow for a dog to travel any distance in, and hence when it is desired to force the rabbit out from its hiding the ferret is generally employed, a creature that is in some respects like the dog, but much thinner and sharper. It is also very keen and eager in its pursuit of the rabbit. In large estates of land which gentlemen rent for sport, there is made what is called a rabbit warren, that is, an arrangement so that the paths of rabbits may be guarded, tracked, and pursued, so that when rabbits are wanted they can be driven out of their holes, and started on a race which sportsmen may be able to follow with the dog and gun. The greyhound is the dog that is chiefly employed in the hunting of the rabbit, and

for this purpose there is a well-known sport, too commonly established in England, called greyhound coursing, in which the best greyhounds for sport and skill are tested according to their speed and skill in overtaking the rabbit and killing it. It is a brutal sport, and a disgrace to our civilization that men should assemble to witness the destruction of anything so innocent as the rabbit, and that they should call it pleasure. Very far have men carried their love for this sport. They not only have encouraged their breed of rabbits for sport, but farms were let subject to the provision that the farmer should not kill any, even though they should become so numerous and active as to overrun his farm and destroy his crops. The farmer must leave them untouched that they might all be reserved for the sport of the sportsman. The effect of such an arrangement was to render many farms unremunerative, and to dishearten the farmer in his enterprise and work. This evil has been frustrated and overcome by that valuable measure of Parliament, called the Hares and Rabbits Bill, according to which the farmer has a legal right to kill all rabbits he may find on his own land. In more than one of our colonies the problem is to know what to do with the rabbits, they are so numerous and so destructive. They are not so much the game of sportsmen alone, because anyone has a right to kill them, in order that they may be got rid of quick enough. The flesh of the rabbit is good for human food, and is especially commended to those who find it difficult to digest fat. In England considerable attention is given to the breeding of the domestic rabbit. The children and grandchildren of the Queen have been encouraged to have their rabbits and to attend to them. In poor families they are kept as the only kind of flesh they may have the chance to eat, whilst in better families it is thought well to encourage the children to keep them because the keeping has a beneficial influence upon the children, rabbits being so gentle and innocent that children seldom think of becoming unkind to them. The keeping also makes the children responsible for the life of something in particular, and it cultivates in them unselfishness, attention, and kindness to animals. To meet the taste in the keeping of rabbits there are held all over the country rabbit shows, at which the choicest rabbits take prizes. A large trade is done in rabbits, wild and domestic. It is estimated that the number annually brought to the market cannot be less than ten millions, which at a shilling each represents a total expenditure of 841,733*l.* It is stated on authority that a pair of females will produce in the course of a year more flesh than a couple af ewes. Besides the flesh there is the trade in skins. These skins are chiefly used in the manufacture of felt hats. France heads the list, supplying the largest number of the skins of domestic rabbits. England and Belgium come next. The skin of the French rabbit is supposed to be the finest, and hence Paris is the great centre of the preparation of the skins. As the demand for rabbits is gradually increasing many are turning their attention to rabbit farming, and to men of small capital it may turn out to be a desirable thing to invest in this way.

Our Mission in Central Africa.

HE accompanying illustrations furnish some idea of the mode of travelling in Africa, and the manner in which travellers may sometimes have to bury their dead. Some of their paths are so narrow, and the fences so high, that they can only travel on foot and in single file with their loads upon their heads. In other parts of the country they have to travel over the most rugged roads imaginable, in jolting wagons, drawn by bullocks, or else along the rivers in native canoes.

The last-mentioned, as our readers are aware, were the methods of travelling by which our new mission party reached the Barotse Country—that is, both by wagons and by canoes.

As we look upon the illustration of the funeral procession, we are reminded how many brave travellers, explorers, and missionaries in Africa face the greatest perils, and often succumb to hostile foes, fevers, and death. Every great missionary society has its honoured roll of illustrious dead.

Some of the most heroic men and women are sleeping in African graves till they shall be awakened by the resurrection trumpet. We are reminded of our own missionary annals of mortality on the West Coast of Africa. Surely every missionary, as he traverses the dark continent, may very emphatically adopt what Gilfillan calls the most poetic verse in our language—

> 'Art is long, and life is fleeting,
> And our hearts, though stout and brave,
> Still like muffled drums are beating
> Funeral marches to the grave.'

No one can fully realize the hardships and perils through which our missionaries have passed in their journey to the Barotse Country. No one can too fully appreciate or too gratefully recognize the all-gracious and beneficent Providence that has watched over them. But the dangers of the journey are past; its hardships and perils have been bravely encountered.

What deep emotions of thankfulness would well up from the hearts of our missionaries, like the sparkling waters of a fountain, at their first sight of the far-famed Zambesi! But who can imagine what Mr. Buckenham felt when he first stood before the sovereign of the country? There he is before the Barotse king, pleading for permission to go into the darkest portion of His Majesty's territory. What thoughts he has of home! What ejaculations of prayer rise from his beating heart! What a sacred fire glows in his bosom for the salvation of souls! What a deep disappointment he feels, as the king wishes him to wait till the chiefs of the country have been consulted, occasioning a delay of several months. There are no railways, telegraphs, or postal union there. Three letters have just been received from Mr. Buckenham, full of the deepest interest, mixed, it is true, with reports of unexpected trials and losses, but full of faith, and hope, and trust in God.

The first letter, dated April 8 of this year, speaks of early and heavy rains, of both

SHAW'S MODE OF MARCHING.

Mr. Ward and Mr. Baldwin having had fever, and of inability to procure drivers—Mr. Ward and himself having had to drive the wagons as best they could. Then the bullocks were seized with disease, and died one after another. Having four swollen rivers to cross, wagon-travelling had to be abandoned. He tells, then, of a most trying and disastrous journey of twenty-five days up the river in a canoe. Twice during the time he was taken ill, once with ague, which reduced him so low that he could only walk a few yards at a time. During these illnesses he had but little support. On February 17, his canoe was caught in one of the rapids and overturned, throwing his things into the water, some of which were recovered, but others destroyed. Owing to the heavy rains, the rivers were full and the valleys covered with water, so that they had for days to cross over parts of the country where cattle are wont to graze. In some places the cattle were wading in water, and men tending them in canoes. The villages in the Barotse Valley are built on mounds, like the villages on the Nile in Egypt. What do our readers think of missionary life? Is it not much easier to give and collect for missions than it would be to go and face such difficulties as those to which we have referred?

In his return journey of ten days to Shesheka, Mr. Buckenham's canoe was upset by a hippopotamus, involving the loss of his photo apparatus, value £15; but he himself escaped with a few bruises. That heavenly Father who numbers the hairs of our heads, observes the falling of a sparrow, and feeds the young ravens when they cry, kindly watched over and preserved him.

What faith in God, and what moral heroism must Mrs. Buckenham require to be thus left for weeks, and even months, in such a strange land, and having the constant apprehension that her husband was passing along such perilous journeys during his absence from her. Mr. Buckenham is a man of a thousand. He has already opened our mission field in South Africa. He has braved the fever of Western Africa, and left his first dear wife to slumber beneath the spreading foliage of the Cameroons. He has now left his two daughters in England, because it was not safe to take

them, and has plunged into the thickest gloom of the dark continent itself. Are not he and his devoted wife and noble colleagues worthy of our deepest sympathy and our untiring support?

The third letter is dated May 4, the chief feature of which is an earnest appeal for the prayers of the people who have sent him forth into this distant land. Shall his request be denied, or receive even a feeble response? Is there not a God in heaven who is delighted both to hear and answer prayer? Are we not doing His will by sending His Gospel to the oppressed sons of Ham? What are difficulties? The mountain shall become a plain before the great Captain of our salvation. He may permit our faith and patience to be tried, as He did the Syro-Phœnician woman's. But a great and effectual door shall be opened up along all the banks of the Zambesi. The land of Mashukulombwe shall resound with the triumphs of the cross. What is wanted, then, to accomplish all this, and even more than we can ask or think? Prayer, united, believing prayer. Oh, is there a single Primitive Methodist who will enter into his closet, and shut his door, and yet forget to pray for the Zambesi Mission? J. ASHWORTH.

IF sin were not so deceitful, it would not be so delightful. Like an angler, it shows the bait, but conceals the hook. Now it represents its present painted beauty, but casts a covering over its future obliquity. Wickedness is certainly like a river which begins in a quiet spring, but ends in a tumultuous sea. Every being produces its own likeness. 'Do men gather grapes of thorns, or figs of thistles?' The grapes of tranquillity cannot grow upon the thorns of impiety. A good way to have conscience untormented is to have it undefiled. He who made you clean within will also keep you calm within.

'How many a man from love of pelf,
 To stuff his coffers, starves himself;
Labours, accumulates, and spares,
 To lay up ruin for his heirs;
Grudges the poor their scanty dole;
Saves everything, except his soul;
Always anxious, always vexed;
Loses this world and the next.'

BURYING OUR DEAD.

Bible Teaching on Systematic Giving.

ILLUSTRATIVE INSTANCES.

MONGST the earliest instances of generosity on a large scale, and for strictly religious objects, were the gifts of the people of Israel for the erection of the tabernacle in the wilderness. The people had left the land of Egypt, and were in process of being formed into a great nation. And amongst the most important institutions of their incipient national life were those of public worship and religious instruction. There was thus given to them by Divine revelation the moral law, in the Ten Commandments; and the ceremonial law which regulated and enforced all the details of devotion and sacrifice. And for the more efficient observance of these great duties and privileges specific times and places were appointed where they should be attended to. Hence the erection of the tabernacle. The structure, though movable, was of the costliest material. The pattern of it was revealed to Moses in the mount. God would have His people present to Him the *best* they had, and could give. And yet it was left to the voluntary gifts of the congregation. 'Whosoever is of a willing heart, let him bring it, an offering unto the Lord.' The whole people were invited to share in the work; but the spirit of the giver must be sincere and willing. The people took time for reflection, counsel, and prayer. And mark the result. 'They came, every one whose heart stirred him up, and every one whose spirit made him willing, and they brought the Lord's offering to the work of the tabernacle of the congregation.' The gifts were contributed both by 'men and women.'

Each section brought its share. The poor joined with the rich, and made the offering a truly national and acceptable one. It is noteworthy, too, that this outburst of sanctified generosity occurred in the wilderness, where the people were absolutely dependent on the providence of God for daily food, and where they could do nothing either to increase their resources or supply their wants. Neither agriculture nor commerce was open to them. Temptation would doubtless be strong to retain what they had, and yet they offered willingly unto the Lord. There was thus an ample supply for the work in hand; the tabernacle was built according to plan and arrangement; and for hundreds of years was a centre of religious light and blessing—the visible dwelling-place of Jehovah—to the nation at large. God invited His people to provide by their gifts a place for the worship of His name; and He has thus left a great object lesson for the instruction of subsequent ages on the duty and privilege of maintaining the public worship of His name.

The erection of the Temple was another illustration, five hundred years later, of generosity in the cause of God. When the national life had solidified, and orderly government had been established, when the resources of the people had greatly increased by successful industry and commerce, and when it became necessary to centralize the religious ideas, exercises, and forces of the nation's life, the Temple at Jerusalem was projected by the devout and poetic King David. He was not allowed, however, to carry out this dearly-cherished object. He was a military man, and had been engaged in many wars and much bloodshed. And while his military successes had given peace and prosperity to the nation, the work of building a House for the Lord better befitted the more peaceful times of Solomon's reign. The generous-hearted David made preparations on the greatest scale. If not permitted to complete the structure, there was no prohibition debarring him from doing all that was possible to help the work; and as he desired that the house should be "exceeding magnifical, of fame and of glory throughout all countries,' his preparatory gifts were of the most lavish description. The contributions of the people, too, inspired by the noble example of the aged king, were on a truly magnificent scale. It has been calculated that the joint contributions of king and people for this one object amounted to thirty million pounds of our money. What a splendid example of large-hearted generosity is here furnished! The method pursued is full of instruction. David called together ' the princes of Israel,' and all the men of rank and wealth in the nation, and invited their co-operation. And they readily responded, and ' offered willingly.' The effect of so worthy an example in high places could not fail to stimulate the generosity of the rest of the nation. 'The people rejoiced.' The poorest had their part as well as the richest; and they do not seem to have ever thought that the larger gifts of the wealthy afforded any excuse for the absence of the smaller gifts of the poor. The work was a common one, and all shared the duty and the privilege of carrying it out.

These gifts were distinctly and emphatically religious. They were inspired by piety and love to God. The spirit of prayer and consecration pervaded and sanctified the whole proceedings. At the commencement and at the close "David blessed the Lord before all the congregation." Our giving should ever thus be allied to our worship. It should be part of our religion—the expression of our love and loyalty to God, in the maintenance of His Church, and in philanthropic service to His needy creatures about us.

The widow's mite, recorded in the New Testament, is full of interest and instruction. Christ had been watching the rich cast, of their abundance, into the Lord's treasury, ' And there came a certain poor widow, and she threw in two mites, which make a farthing.' The larger contributions of the rich, if given in a proper spirit, would be approved; but Christ makes no reference to them, except for purposes of comparison. He fixes our attention on the small gift of the poor widow, and affirms it to be the largest gift there presented. Why! ' They all did cast in of their abundance, but she of her want did cast in all that she had,

even her living. Two things determine the worth of our gifts to God's cause—the motive which prompts them, and the reserve store left after the gift has been offered. The large offerings of the rich were taken from larger resources, and may have occassioned no inconvenience at all; the ' mites ' of the widow were her all, and left her, apparently, in want of the necessaries of life. The spirit of devotion and self-sacrifice which inspired the gift imparted to the widow's farthing a dignity and worth to which the larger gifts of the wealthy could lay no claim.

PRECEPTS.

There are many readers of the Scriptures who have but the faintest conception of the amplitude of Biblical teaching on this important question. Perhaps none fully realize to what an extent we have there, line upon line, and precept upon precept, on this matter, but those who have specially studied the subject, and grouped together the divine commands concerning it. Our limits of space only admit of a few examples being given, but they illustrate very much more of a similar and equally emphatic character. ' Honour the Lord with thy substance, and with the first-fruits of all thine increase; so shall thy barns be filled with plenty and thy presses burst out with new wine.'

Here we are expressly commanded to honour the Lord with our material resources. The contribution is not an optional one—one we can give or withhold at our own pleasure; it is a definite precept, and cannot be ignored without specific neglect of duty. We are thus called to give something to Christian and philanthropic work, but how much? We must give in a way that will honour God, in a way that will harmonise with our religious profession, and be consistent both with the amount at our command and our indebtedness to God for every temporal and spiritual good. A small and niggardly gift can never honour the Lord, when a large and generous one is possible to us. The widow's ' mite ' was her all, and was a noble gift; but many plead her example for a small contribution, who are neither widows nor in poverty, and whose ample reserve stores should put to the blush so inadequate an offering. This question then should be asked and answered, 'Will this gift honour God?' Will He, who sees both the motive and the amount, and knows fully all the circumstances, commend it?' Surely a frank and faithful consideration of this question would revolutionize much of our giving! And then, the proportion is on 'all thine increase.' Whatever is added to our income must make its due proportion—the first-fruits—to the sum of our beneficence. God would thus bring us into close and constant contact with Himself; first, by calling on us to recognize His unfailing bounty, and, at the same time, by doing good to the needy creatures about us.

And what a benediction is promised to those who obey this precept: 'So shall thy barns be filled with plenty, and thy presses burst out with new wine.' Not only is a Christian duty observed, the name of God honoured, and religious institutions maintained by such an honouring of God with our substance, but our substance itself is increased. In an infinite variety of ways God can fulfil His own promises, and thousands of His faithful children have proved their literal fulfilment.

The precept just considered related to personal life, but the principle implied belongs equally to the collective life of a church or nation. The prophet Malachi asks, 'Will a man rob God?' and he answers his own question as he speaks in God's name: 'Yet ye have robbed Me. But ye say, Wherein have we robbed Thee? In tithes and offering. Ye are cursed with a curse, for ye have robbed Me, even this whole nation.' Israel had backsliden from God. She had become negligent of His worship and claims. And one of the evidences and results of this declension and decay was the withholding of the tithes—or tenth part of income—from the service of God. Such an omission was a robbery of God. How few regard covetousness in its true light—a robbery of God; and yet such is the inspired description of Malachi. But the prophet does not leave the matter there. He sternly condemns the offence, but he points out also the means and conditions of amendment. 'Bring ye all the tithes into the storehouse, that there may be meat in Mine

house, and prove Me now herewith, saith the Lord of hosts, if I will not open you the windows of heaven and pour you out a blessing that there shall not be room enough to receive it.' The one condition of again enjoying the smile of God is to correct what is wrong. The most niggardly giver may share the benediction of the liberal giver 'if he will abandon his niggardliness and become liberal; *but on that condition only.* God wants to forgive those even who have robbed Him; but only on condition that the robbery ceases and honest recognition of His claims is made. Given that condition of bringing all the tithes into the storehouse, and there is no blessing which the individual or the church needs but may be shared in largest measure.

Dew.

EVERYONE will remember the beautiful references to 'dew' in the Bible. Job speaking of his earlier prosperity and happiness tells us that 'the dew lay all night upon his branch.' The Psalmist finely compares brotherly love and unity to the dew that came down upon the slopes of Hermon and upon the mountains of Zion. The 'Proverbs' liken the king's favour to 'dew upon the grass,' and Hosea, the much-tried and tender-hearted prophet, caps all these references in his lovely verses—'I will be as the dew unto Israel: he shall grow as the lily, and cast forth his roots as Lebanon. His branches shall spread, and his beauty shall be as the olive-tree, and his smell as Lebanon.' In the droughty East the dew must be a special blessing.

But what is dew? The most curious guesses have been made as to its origin and nature. In the Middle Ages the alchemists regarded it as an exudation from the stars. Others, as Pliny, thought it a sort of fine rain thrown down from the higher regions of the air; while others again, like Nardius of Florence, held it to be an emanation distilled from the ground. It was thought, too, that if it fell from the heavens the moon caused the fine particles to rush together into drops. Eighty years ago only did any part of the real secret of the dew become known, and within the last

a physician of London, whose experiments began in the year 1784. His opinion then was that dew was the parent and not the off-

five years new and unexpected light has been thrown on the subject.

The first scientist who penetrated to the core of the mystery was Dr. Charles William Wells,

spring of cold. But by a series of experiments he reached the conclusion set forth in his 'Essay on Dew,' published in 1814, of which work Sir John Herschell says—'It is one of the most beautiful specimens we can call to mind of inductive experimental inquiry lying within moderate compass.' Something very like an accident set him first on the right track. He was staying on a certain occasion in the country, and observed that a thermometer which he had placed on the grass when the latter was wet with dew indicated a temperature eight degrees lower than another instrument suspended two feet above the ground. He then devised a number of simple experiments in order to trace out the relation between this fact of cold and the deposition of dew. He took a lump of common cotton-wool, and first weighed it out into little parcels of ten grains each. After 'teasing' and loosening out the fibres until each parcel assumed the appearance of a flat round flock, exactly two inches in diameter, he exposed these flocks in different ways to the atmosphere for a whole night, and on weighing them next morning, easily ascertained, of course, the amount of moisture which they had collected during the night. His first experiment was as follows:— He set up, upon slender wooden props, a painted board, one inch thick, and on the *top* of this board fixed one of his flocks, while *beneath* it he attached another. Next morning he found that the flock looking up to the sky had gained 14 grains in weight, while the flock which looked downwards only gained 4 grains. Varying the conditions he next arranged two exactly similar flocks of wool upon the grass a little distance apart, sheltering one from the sky by a pent-house of cardboard, but leaving the other without any covering at all. After a whole night's exposure, the latter flock had increased in weight 16 grains, while the protected one gained only 2 grains. But, he asked, might not the uncovered wool owe its increase of weight to rain? To test this he placed a circular cylinder of baked clay, 12 inches in diameter and *open at the top*, round one flock of wool, and then exposed another close by upon the open grass. That rain was not the cause of the increase of weight was proved by the fact that the first flock received only 8 grains of moisture, while the exposed one received 16 grains. Still further, Dr. Wells found that upon *grass*

the wool collected 16 grains, while upon *grave* only 9 grains were received. Comparing the temperatures of the grass and the gravel he discovered that two and a half hours after sunset the gravel was sixteen degrees warmer than the grass. Cold, then, was evidently the *cause* of the heavier deposit of dew. Clearly the cotton-wool acted like the grass, in radiating off its heat into space, and in then condensing upon itself the moisture held in suspension in the air above it. The pasteboard pent-house and the cylinder of baked clay had prevented the heat from escaping from the wool to some extent, and hence the smaller amount of moisture deposited in the wool when so protected. Dew, then, concluded Dr. Wells, is just ' the . moisture abstracted from the air by the rapid cooling of the bodies with which that air is in contact.' It forms best on clear nights when there are no clouds to act as the paste-board and the baked clay in preventing radiation.

So the question of dew rested until about four or five years ago—Dr. Wells' conclusion being universally and undoubtingly accepted. But at the time just mentioned a most original and painstaking observer, Mr. John Aitken, F.R.S., of Falkirk, saw reason to doubt the adequacy of Dr. Wells' explanation (the latter was right, but only so far). First of all, Mr. Aitken has proved that what is called ' dew ' on vegetation is often only an exudation from the plant itself. 'He selected a small turf, placed over it a glass receiver, and left it till drops were excreted. Removing the receiver he selected a blade having a drop attached to it. He dried this blade, and inserted its tip into a small glass receiver, so as to isolate it from the damp air of the larger receiver. The open end of the small receiver was closed by means of a very thin plate of metal cemented to it. In the centre of this plate was pierced a small opening to admit the top of the blade; but the opening was then carefully made air-tight by means of an india-rubber solution. After a time, though this blade was thoroughly isolated, he saw that a drop was formed on the tip, of the same size as the drops formed on the blades under the large receiver. He, of course, was entitled to conclude that the drops on the outside blades as well as on the isolated blade were really exuded by the plant, and not extracted from the air.' When, then, Shakespeare makes some one say—

> ' I must go seek some dew-drops here,
> And hang a pearl in every cowslip's ear,'

he is miscalling that ' dew,' which is really derived from the cowslip's own moisture. It is from within not from without. The difference between the true and the false dew on grass can be easily detected. You will always find the former lying evenly all over the blades; while the latter as uniformly collects in drops near the tips of the blades.

But in another important respect Mr. Aitken has corrected the old doctrine of the dew. He has shown that there is a dew which rises from the ground, as well as a dew which is deposited from the atmosphere. Noticing the fact that, a little below the surface the ground is warmer than the air above it, and surmising that moisture from the earth passing upwards into the cooler air must condense as dew on a surface cool enough, he set to work to test his surmise in the following way :—He made some trays of tinplate, three inches deep and about a foot square, and after sunset placed them upside down on the grass. ' At eleven o'clock at night he examined the trays and found that there was always more moisture on the grass *inside* the trays than outside, that there was always a deposit of dew inside the trays, and that there was often a deposit outside the trays ; but the deposit outside was always less than on the inside, and sometimes there was no deposit outside when there was one inside.' In confirmation of this conclusion it will be found, in nature, that the *under-*surfaces of the large leaves of plants are often heavily wetted, while the upper surfaces remain dry.

Another set of experiments undertaken by Mr. Aitken is described as follows :—' He prepared a shallow pan six inches square and quarter inch deep, and placed in it a slightly smaller piece of turf, which he cut out of the lawn. The pan and the turf were then carefully weighed in an open shed with a balance sensitive enough to turn with one quarter grain. The turf was cut at sunset when dew was forming. After being weighed, the pan and turf were placed in the open cut in the lawn where the turf had been cut out. They were left from 5.15 p.m. to 10.15 p.m. on October 7th, and then weighed, when it was found that the loss of moisture was 24 grains out of 3,500 grains. Numerous experiments were made with similar results. This decisive test showed clearly that the soil loses weight, and that vapour really rises from the ground even while dew is forming ; therefore the dew then found on the grass must have been formed out of the vapour rising from the ground at the time. The dew on the grass was, in fact, formed by the cold grass trapping the vapour as it rose from the ground, the blades acting as a kind of condenser.'

Dew and hoar-frost (which is simply *frozen dew*) form, too, on the *under*-sides of clods and small stones—another proof that dew rises as well as falls. Mr. Aitken advises experimenters to test this by taking two slates and placing them on gravel or even a hard part of the road. On dewy nights it will be found that while the upper surfaces of the slates, and the road all around are quite dry, the under-sides of the slates drip with wet. Dr. McPherson tells us that once when walking about in the neighbourhood of Hexham, with an acute observer trained to farming, he remarked that the farmer ought to remove the extraordinary quantity of small stones which must obstruct the growth of the grain. ' No,' said his companion, ' these stones collect moisture from the ground ; the soil is thin, with a gravelly subsoil, and unless the greatest possible amount of moisture is collected (which can only be done by allowing these stones to remain) there would be a very deficient crop. They must not then be removed.' The moral of this story of the true theory of dew is a very plain and a very practical one. It is this : Never, *on any subject*, tie yourself down to any fixed opinion. Always look out for more light, and be ready to welcome it whencesoever it comes. There is no human dogma which will not bear revising. 'Prove all things; hold fast that which is good.'

SPRINGTIME.

THE ANGELS' SONG.

(*Christmas Carol.*)

Music and Words by Rev. W. L. TAYLOR.

THE ANGELS' SONG.
(*Christmas Carol.*)

Key D.

f Joyfully.   Music and Words by Rev. W. L. Taylor.

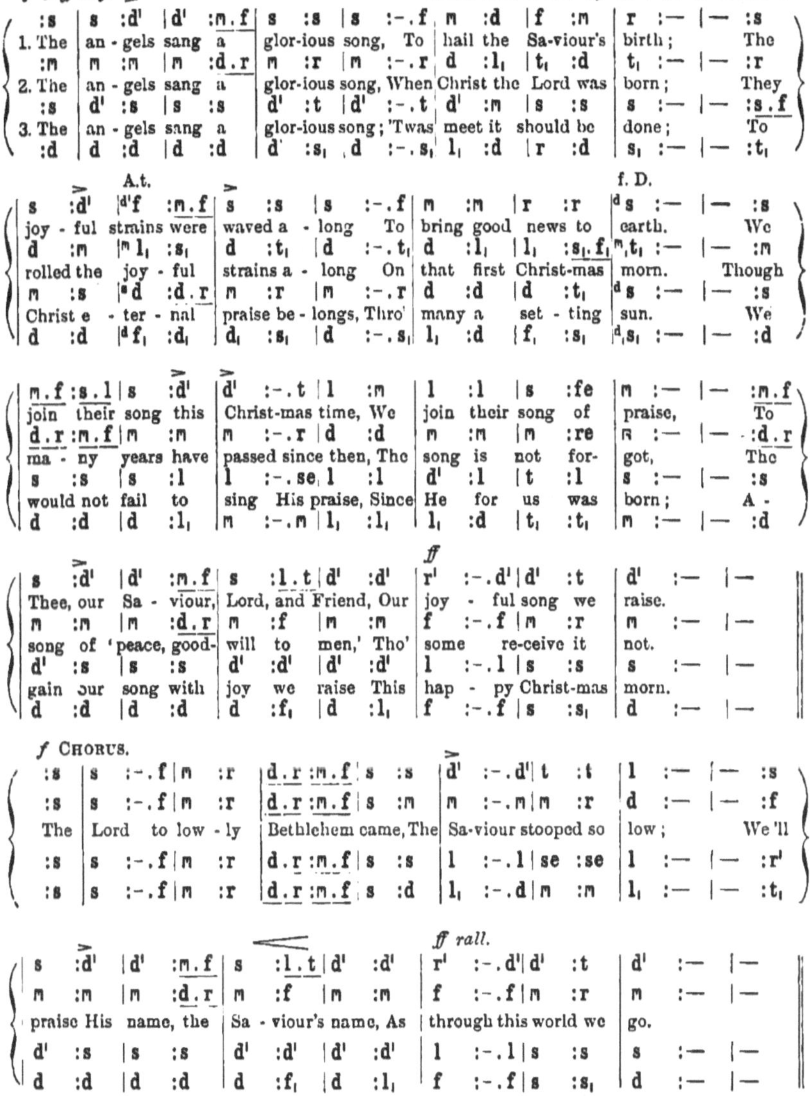

```
:s  | s  :d' |d' :m.f | s  :s  |s  :-.f | m  :d  |f  :m  | r  :— |— :s  )
1. The | an - gels sang a | glor-ious song, To | hail the  Sa-viour's | birth ;        The
:m  | m  :m  |m  :d.r | m  :r  |m  :-.r | d  :l, |t, :d  | t, :— |— :r
2. The | an - gels sang a | glor-ious song, When Christ the  Lord was | born ;        They
:s  | d' :s  |s  :s   | d' :t  |d' :-.t | d' :m  |s  :s  | s  :— |— :s.f )
3. The | an - gels sang a | glor-ious song; 'Twas meet it  should be | done ;        To
:d  | d  :d  |d  :d   | d' :s, ,d :-.s, |l, :d  |r  :d  | s, :— |— :t,
```

```
    A.t.                                        f. D.
s  :d' |d'f :m.f | s  :s  |s  :-.f | m  :m  |r  :r  |d s :— |— :s  )
joy - ful  strains were | waved a - long  To | bring good  news to | earth.        We
d  :m  |m l, :s, | d  :t, |d  :-.t, | d  :l, |l, :s, f, m,t, :— |— :m )
rolled the  joy - ful | strains a - long  On | that  first Christ-mas | morn.        Though
m  :s  |s d :d.r | m  :r  |m  :-.r | d  :d  |d  :t, |d s :— |— :s
Christ e - ter - nal | praise be - longs, Thro' | many a   set - ting | sun.        We
d  :d  |d f, :d, | d, :s, |d  :-.s, | l, :d  |f, :s, |d,s, :— |— :d  )
```

```
m.f :s.l |s  :d' | d' :-.t |l  :m  | l  :l  |s  :fe | m  :— |— :m.f )
join their song this | Christ-mas time, We | join their song of | praise,        To
d.r :m.f |m  :m  | m  :-.r |d  :d  | m  :m  |m  :re | m  :— |— :d.r
ma - ny  years have | passed since then, The | song is  not for- | got,        The
s  :s  |s  :l   | l  :-.se |l  :l  | d' :l  |t  :l  | s  :— |— :s  )
would not fail  to | sing  His praise, Since | He  for  us  was | born ;        A -
d  :d  |d  :l,  | m  :-.m |l, :l, | l, :d  |t, :t, | m  :— |— :d
```

```
s  :d' |d' :m.f | s  :l.t |d' :d' | r' :-.d'|d' :t  | d' :— |—     ||
Thee, our  Sa - viour, | Lord, and Friend, Our | joy - ful song we | raise.
m  :m  |m  :d.r | m  :f  |m  :m  | f  :-.f |m  :r  | m  :— |—
song of 'peace, good- | will  to  men,' Tho' | some  re-ceive it | not.
d' :s  |s  :s   | d' :d' |d' :d' | l  :-.l |s  :s  | s  :— |—
gain our  song with | joy  we  raise This | hap - py Christ-mas | morn.
d  :d  |d  :d   | d  :f, |d  :l, | f  :-.f |s  :s, | d  :— |—
```

f CHORUS.

```
:s  | s  :-.f |m  :r  | d.r :m.f |s  :s  | d' :-.d'|t  :t  | l  :— |— :s  )
:s  | s  :-.f |m  :r  | d.r :m.f |s  :m  | m  :-.m|m  :r  | d  :— |— :f
The | Lord  to low - ly | Bethlehem came, The | Sa-viour stooped so | low ;        We 'll )
:s  | s  :-.f |m  :r  | d.r :m.f |s  :s  | l  :-.l |se :se | l  :— |— :r'
:s  | s  :-.f |m  :r  | d.r :m.f |s  :d  | l, :-.d |m  :m  | l, :— |— :t,
```

ff rall.

```
s  :d' |d' :m.f | s  :l.t |d' :d' | r' :-.d'|d' :t  | d' :— |—     ||
m  :m  |m  :d.r | m  :f  |m  :m  | f  :-.f |m  :r  | m  :— |—
praise His  name, the | Sa - viour's name, As | through this world we | go.
d' :s  |s  :s   | d' :d' |d' :d' | l  :-.l |s  :s  | s  :— |—
d  :d  |d  :d   | d  :f, |d  :l, | f  :-.f |s  :s, | d  :— |—
```

Current Topics.

VILLAGE INDUSTRIES.

NATION,' said John Bright, 'dwells in its cottages.' But what is to become of a nation whose cottages are going to ruins, and whose villages and small towns are becoming depopulated? This is the state of things we are having to face in England, and every year the question is becoming more serious. Look at the case of Rome. It was only after her people had given up the healthy occupations of the country, and had crowded within her city walls, that that mighty empire was obliged to surrender her proud supremacy to a stronger nation. Everybody feels that something must be done by the English nation to check the rush of people now going on from the country to the towns, or it may be she will have to encounter similar disaster. But what must be done? Politicians have their rival plans, and these proposals will have a great deal to do with deciding the next election. It may be taken for granted that the next Parliament will be pledged to do something substantial for the villages. In June, we indicated how much the establishment of village home rule might do for rural life, not only by quickening its pulse, but by augmenting its resources. But Parliament cannot do everything. The people in the country must rely upon themselves, and if they would only set about it, they might make a much better struggle against the attractions of the town.

———

The landowners might do a great deal. And if they could but read the signs of the times, they would set about doing it at once. They must make a better use of their estates, or they will not be suffered to retain them. In a small country like this, with a rapidly increasing population, it is simple folly to suppose that large tracts of land can be allowed to lie in waste in order that a few wealthy men may have the privilege of shooting deer. The descendants of the people who were banished from the hills and straths of Scotland to make room for the landlord's game will have to be invited back to the lands of their fathers. And plenty of employment might be found for them. The moors and the mountains will not grow corn to profit, but they will grow trees. Some years ago, a French expert was employed by the Government to investigate this matter, and he reported that north of a line drawn from Perth to Greenock, six million acres of the waste lands of Scotland were suitable for the growth of valuable timber. The labour entailed in planting and attending to even a moderate part of this acreage would afford employment for thousands. But would it pay? Not at once, but in course of time such an enterprize would yield a splendid return. The forests of America are rapidly becoming exhausted, and the people who plant now may rest assured that they or their sons will find an excellent market for their produce. It is pleasing to know that some of the great landowners are showing themselves alive to their opportunities. A late Earl of Seafield planted no fewer than sixty million trees in the valley of the Spey, and the growing woods, beside affording employment to an army of foresters, are beginning to render habitable many tracts of country once only fit for grouse and deer. The question of arboriculture is, in fact, being heartily taken up all over the country. A Society for promoting it has recently been formed, with an energetic Primitive Methodis for its secretary, and it promises to do excellent service.

———

The cultivation of fruit and flowers is another mine of wealth lying within the reach of the villagers. Since Mr. Gladstone drew attention to this subject much has been done, but the fact that last year we spent 8,000,000*l.* in foreign fruit shows that there is still room for improvement. And if the farm labourer had his allotment and was instructed in their cultivation, there is no doubt that for hardy fruits he would soon become a successful com-

petitor with the foreigner. This business could easily be made very profitable. In 1890, though it was a poor fruit year, Lord Sudeley made upon his fruit farm of 500 acres a profit of 10,000*l.* This is scarcely credible, but I give the statement upon excellent authority. Many of the villagers in the vicinity of large towns make a nice sum every year by the cultivation of flowers, but this delightful occupation might be greatly extended if the labourers only had a little direction and help in the work. It has been pointed out, too, that much more might be made of the nut and bramble-berry harvest. We all know what a delicious fruit the bramble-berry is, but the only people who seem to know about its market value are the people from the back slums of the large towns. And the presence of these people in their woods and fields sends both farmer and gamekeeper almost wild. And to prevent the depredations which they sometimes make the bushes are not unfrequently destroyed. But why cannot the labourers' children, under proper conditions, have permission to gather the fruit and thus eke out the family income?

Other methods of making a living are often suggested to the country labourer. He may have the choice of bee-keeping, rabbit-rearing, poultry-growing, or any number of other small industries, which, when well-managed, sometimes yield a capital return. At one time, however, most of the villages had a special trade. One would be noted for its nail-making, another for its lead-smelting, another for its weaving, and so on. Then in every village you had shoemakers and tailors, blacksmiths and cabinet-makers, all engaged in meeting a constant demand for the products of their different handicrafts. Now every one of these industries has been affected by the competition of the factories in the towns. Some of them have been totally destroyed, and many a once prosperous manufacturing village is now lying in ruins. A very good illustration of the disastrous effects of modern competition may be witnessed amongst the crofter villages of the Scottish Highlands. At one time the crofter produced food directly for the consumption of his own family. He then could easily secure enough fish, and grow sufficient corn and potatoes for the needs of his household, whilst his wife spun the wool of his sheep into comfortable clothing, and a few weeks' labour on the landlord's estate could easily be spared by way of rent. But when coin currency was substituted for payment in kind, then the unfortunate crofter discovered that he had surrendered his position of semi-independence amongst the hills, and had entered upon an unequal struggle for existence with the capitalist. His fish must now be turned into money, in order to enable his family to purchase the necessaries of life at the store. But, hampered by his distance from market, and in competition with the steam-trawlers, and the expensively fitted boats of the fishing companies, he finds that his individual labour yields but a meagre return. The result is poverty, hunger, discontent, sometimes relieved by emigration.

The competition of the factory system has produced similar effects all over the country. And much as we may admire the achievements of modern industry, we cannot lose sight of its ill effects upon ourselves. By changing our occupation it has done much to modify our characters. Machinery does more than manufacture our clothes, and our furniture; it modifies ourselves. It is making us a very different people from what we were a generation or two ago. For one thing it seems to be destroying our individuality. We are becoming all alike. Where are the eccentrics who used to give such a picturesque appearance to our streets, and imparted such piquancy to the life of our villages? They have nearly all disappeared. Eccentricity is too expensive nowadays. A man who is not prepared to eat, dress, and live as other people do must be prepared for both expense and annoyance. For instance, at present we all wear hats with very small brims, but here is one whose spirit refuses to brook the ruthless dominance of fashion. He wants a hat with a more expansive border. But where is he to get it? 'These have all gone out,' the shopman tells him, at the same time modestly suggesting that the new styles would be much more becoming for

his customer. The customer thinks differently, however, and he wants to know why he cannot have one made to suit him. Then he finds that the 'hatter' to whom he appeals is very likely no 'hatter' at all, but only a dealer in the articles turned out by the wholesale manufacturer. And if this troublesome customer still persists in having his fancy, then he must wait until a special order has been despatched, for which, of course, a special price must be paid. This is the case with many things besides hats, and as in these days we must have things cheap, we mostly submit to take what the factory owner and the shopkeeper find it convenient to supply. These autocrats, indeed, profess to consult the tastes of the people, but in fact they treat the unfortunate public pretty much as a miller treats the stream which he diverts into his own channel and compels to drive his own mill.

This state of things is sure to come to an end. Man is too fond of liberty to allow it to slip away from him without a struggle, and as civilization advances the demand for the beautiful and the picturesque is sure to become more imperative. There are not wanting signs that this re-action is already taking place. Here and there people are beginning to show a preference for hand-made goods. The shawls of Shetland, the tweeds woven in the hand-looms, and the hose knitted by patient Highland fingers are found to possess qualities of comfort and durability far surpassing the wholesale productions of the steam factory. The enquiry for these articles, indeed, is becoming so great that the manufacturers are beginning to produce colourable imitations of them. We shall never get back to the industrial methods of the Middle Ages. Machinery, indeed, has become essential to our earthly life, and no one who knows anything of its vast possibilities would wish to deprive mankind of its help in the battle of life. But it cannot be allowed to check the development of artistic feeling, nor deprive mankind of the pleasures of manual skill, not to speak of the satisfaction of knowing that we can 'fend for ourselves,' whatever happens to the machinery.

Some years ago an organization, entitled the Home Arts and Industries Association, was started with the object of instructing artisans' children and others in such simple arts as might both form a healthy amusement for leisure hours and assist the family income to some extent in case of necessity. This laudable attempt, it seems, has had quite an unlooked-for success. With head-quarters at the Royal Albert Hall, London, the institution has now branches in all parts of the kingdom. What do my young readers, especially in country villages, say about taking advantage of its help? Every one ought to become the master of some handicraft. The practice of some mechanical art is not only a fine training, but a pleasing relaxation. The dark nights are upon us, and if the young people would learn some simple art in which they could take a pride, their cheerful toil would banish the dulness from many a cottage kitchen. That such little industries can be made profitable is beyond all question. By making toys during the winter, when no other work is to be had, the peasant families of Leipsic and Nuremberg can earn from twelve to eighteen shillings a week. Grants of money have recently been made to our County Councils for the promotion of technical education. When village councils are formed, with powers to carry out the details of this and other matters, we may surely hope that our English peasantry will be helped to regain some of the mechanical skill that made their villages so prosperous in the days gone by, but which modern commercial developments have tended to discourage.　　M. P. D.

Being perplexed, I say,
　Lord, make it right;
Night is as day to Thee,
　Darkness is light.
　I am afraid to touch
Things that involve so much;
　My trembling hand may shake,
· My skill-less hand may break;
　Thine can make no mistake.

www.ingramcontent.com/pod-product-compliance
Lightning Source LLC
Chambersburg PA
CBHW021537110726
47902CB00004B/910